THE
HOLMES REPORT
Vol.I

THE SIAM QUESTION

THE SIAM QUESTION

Timothy Francis Sheil

CAMDEN HOUSE PUBLISHING LIMITED

First Edition/First Impression. Printed and bound in Thailand. Design by Camden House. Published by Camden House Publishing Limited, 54 Kestrel Ave., London SE24 OEB.

THE HOLMES REPORT
1891 -1894
Vol. I

THE SIAM QUESTION

A Narrative of the Exploits
of
Sherlock Holmes
during the years
1891-1894
at
Tibet, Siam
& London

Written for the Foreign Office
at the request of

Mycroft Holmes - Advisor to the Prime Minister

by

Dr. John H. Watson, M.D.

Based in good part on the Journals
of
M. Francois le Villard

To Remain Under Seal for One Hundred Years
Anno Domini 1899
LONDON

Dedicated to

Jonathan Somerville Price
&
Victoria Ada Louise Sheil

CONTENTS

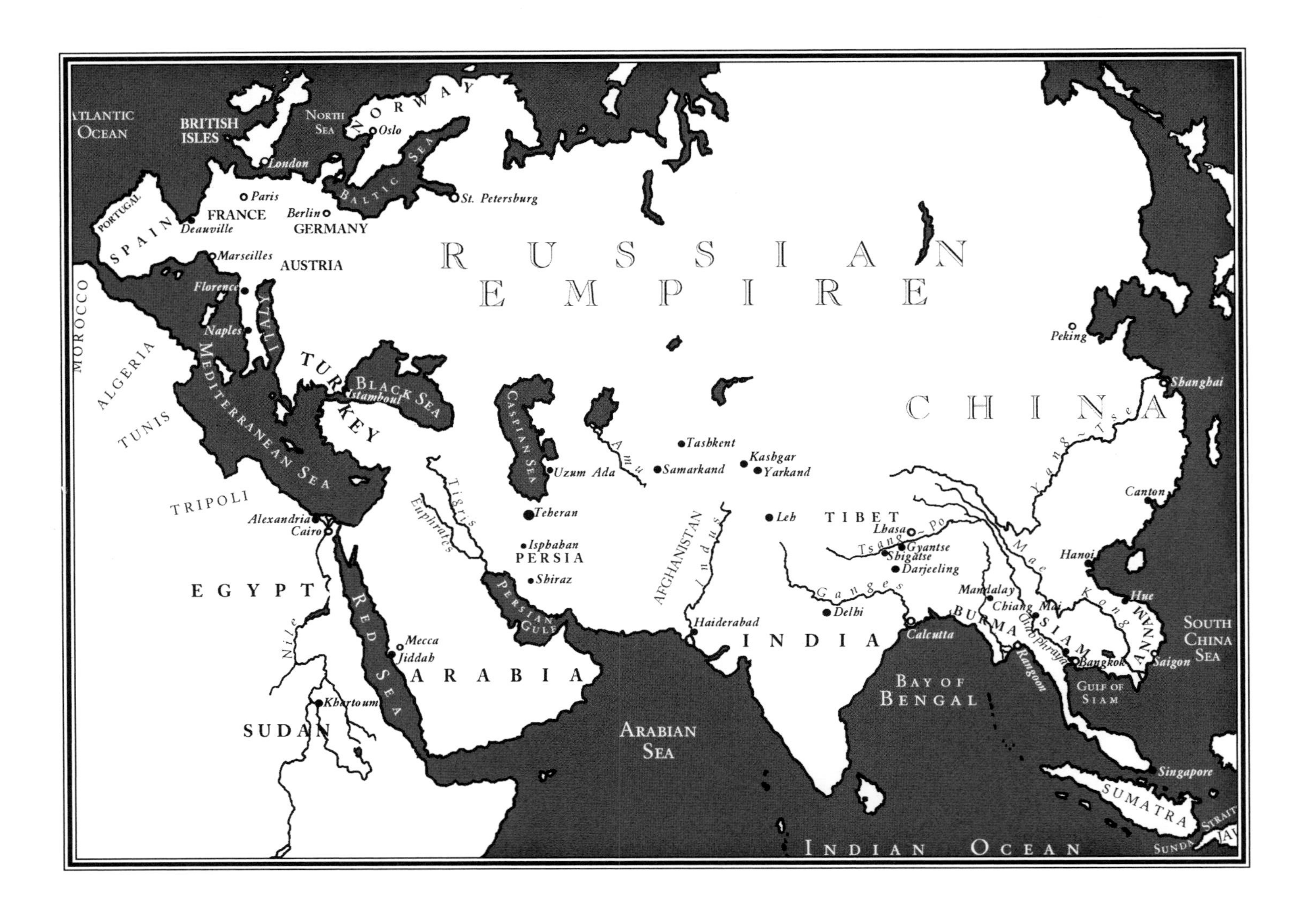
ATLANTIC OCEAN
BRITISH ISLES
NORTH SEA
NORWAY
Oslo
London
BALTIC SEA
St. Petersburg
Paris
FRANCE
Berlin
GERMANY
PORTUGAL
SPAIN
Deauville
Marseilles
AUSTRIA
RUSSIAN EMPIRE
MOROCCO
ALGERIA
TUNIS
Florence
Naples
ITALY
MEDITERRANEAN SEA
TURKEY
BLACK SEA
Istamboul
CASPIAN SEA
Peking
Shanghai
CHINA
Yang-tse
Tashkent
Kashgar
Samarkand
Yarkand
Uzum Ada
Amu
Canton
TRIPOLI
Alexandria
Cairo
Tigris
Euphrates
Teheran
Leh
TIBET
Lhasa
Tsang Po
Gyantse
Shigatse
Darjeeling
Isphahan
PERSIA
Shiraz
AFGHANISTAN
Indus
Ganges
Delhi
Hanoi
Mae Kong
Hue
ANNAM
Mandalay
Chiang Mai
EGYPT
PERSIAN GULF
Haiderabad
Calcutta
BURMA
SIAM
Chaophraya
SOUTH CHINA SEA
Nile
Mecca
Jiddah
RED SEA
ARABIA
INDIA
Rangoon
Bangkok
Saigon
BAY OF BENGAL
GULF OF SIAM
Khartoum
SUDAN
ARABIAN SEA
Singapore
SUMATRA
INDIAN OCEAN
SUNDA STRAIT

Prologue

IN OTHER CASE-BOOKS that I have the honour of having penned, I have introduced the figure of Mr. Mycroft Holmes - elder brother to Sherlock Holmes, my friend and erstwhile room-mate - who has of necessity been dealt with rather sparingly in such accounts as have been published. There is, as I recollect, a perfectly adequate description of Mycroft Holmes - by his brother - in the Report that follows below. Let it suffice for the purposes of this preface to repeat Holmes's remark that, at times, Mycroft '*is* the government'!

In another one of those cases (*The Adventure of the Bruce-Partington Plans* - written, but not as yet published, for reasons which will be explained in a few moments) I recorded that Mycroft Holmes made a passing reference to 'the present state of Siam'. Thus it seems appropriate that in this, the first Volume of the recently completed Holmes Report, much of the subject matter is concerned with the 'state of Siam'.

The present volume has been reviewed and revised since first presented, in Final Draft form, to the gentleman who commissioned the Report in the first place - Mr. Mycroft Holmes. Such revisions as there are, have been made solely to ensure the accuracy, and occasionally, the clarity of the original account.

The Report that follows has been written, as Mycroft acknowledges, for a small readership indeed. (I was present, upon one occasion following the completion of the first draft of this Volume, when Mycroft requested that the Holmes Report be sealed for a period of thirty years, as recommended by Her Majesty. A civil service mandarin then stated his reasons, specious but couched in the usual impenetrable phrasing, insisting that it be classified F.O.C.P. - Foreign Office Confidential Print - and sealed for a hundred years. His arguments carried the day.)

Those who are familiar with the original Volume I of the Holmes Report are, no doubt, aware that at the time of writing in 1894, the two 'missing volumes' of Francois le Villard's Journals had not as yet been located. Thus the account of the entire three-year period of Sherlock Holmes's absence lacked the 'middle years'. Those missing notebooks recorded events which occurred between Holmes' and le Villard's arrival in early 1892 (after their long journey across the Roof of Asia) at the Persian shore of the Caspian Sea - and their departure over a year later from Port Suakin in the Sudan, bound for Siam.

After consultation with Mycroft Holmes, I have decided that events as recorded in those recently recovered Journals will *not* be included in the revision of this present Report, which will shortly be reprinted as *'The Siam Question' ~ Volume I of the Holmes Report* (with the abovementioned corrections and revisions).

The entire account of Sherlock Holmes's protracted absence from London between early 1891 and the spring of 1894 - and his activities on behalf of the Crown during that period- is to be completed by the addition of *'The Egypt Question' ~ Volume II of the Holmes Report.'* Volume II also includes an account of those significant events in Northern Africa and Europe that have so recently developed, in good part, from the original Journey to Khartoum undertaken by Sherlock Holmes and Francois le Villard - including the humble role played by your Narrator.

(This second Volume is at the Government printers, for proof-corrections, as I write these notes.)

I have on several occasions asked Holmes if I might not publish some of this material for my, or rather, his, devoted readership. His invariable reply has been that the time is not yet right! Since his return from his long journey, four years ago, the situation has remained rather at odds and evens. Scotland Yard was, of course, aware that Holmes was back in London, and active again at his old profession. The criminal fraternity - the Underworld - knew immediately, and the newspapermen not long after that. However, throughout those most fruitful years of his career to date, Mycroft managed to prevail upon publishers and editors - and Holmes upon Scotland Yard - to refrain from crediting Holmes with any of his numerous successes.

The unfortunate sufferers of all this reticence have been my readers. I have, for example, recently completed for Holmes's approval a short account of his remarkable return from the dead - as I thought it at the time. In that much expurgated rendering, which I have entitled *The Adventure of the Empty House,* I have refrained from making any but a passing reference to the long years of absence, and have omitted several matters entirely. Regardless, Holmes continues to withhold his approval, saying that it may be some years yet before he is again prepared to submit his affairs to public scrutiny.

I have asked my old companion whether he regards my previously published accounts as having contributed to the debacle of the Moriarty Gang swoop. He vigorously denies that that is the case, or has ever been so, and insists that that, if he has bound me with these restrictions it is for reasons of personal security and the need for a certain degree of public anonymity.

Mycroft Holmes assures me, however, that before long these restrictions will be somewhat eased, at least so far as Holmes's domestic investigations are concerned. For myself, that day can not come too soon!

John H. Watson M.D.
London
January 10th 1899

PART ONE

THE GREAT GAME

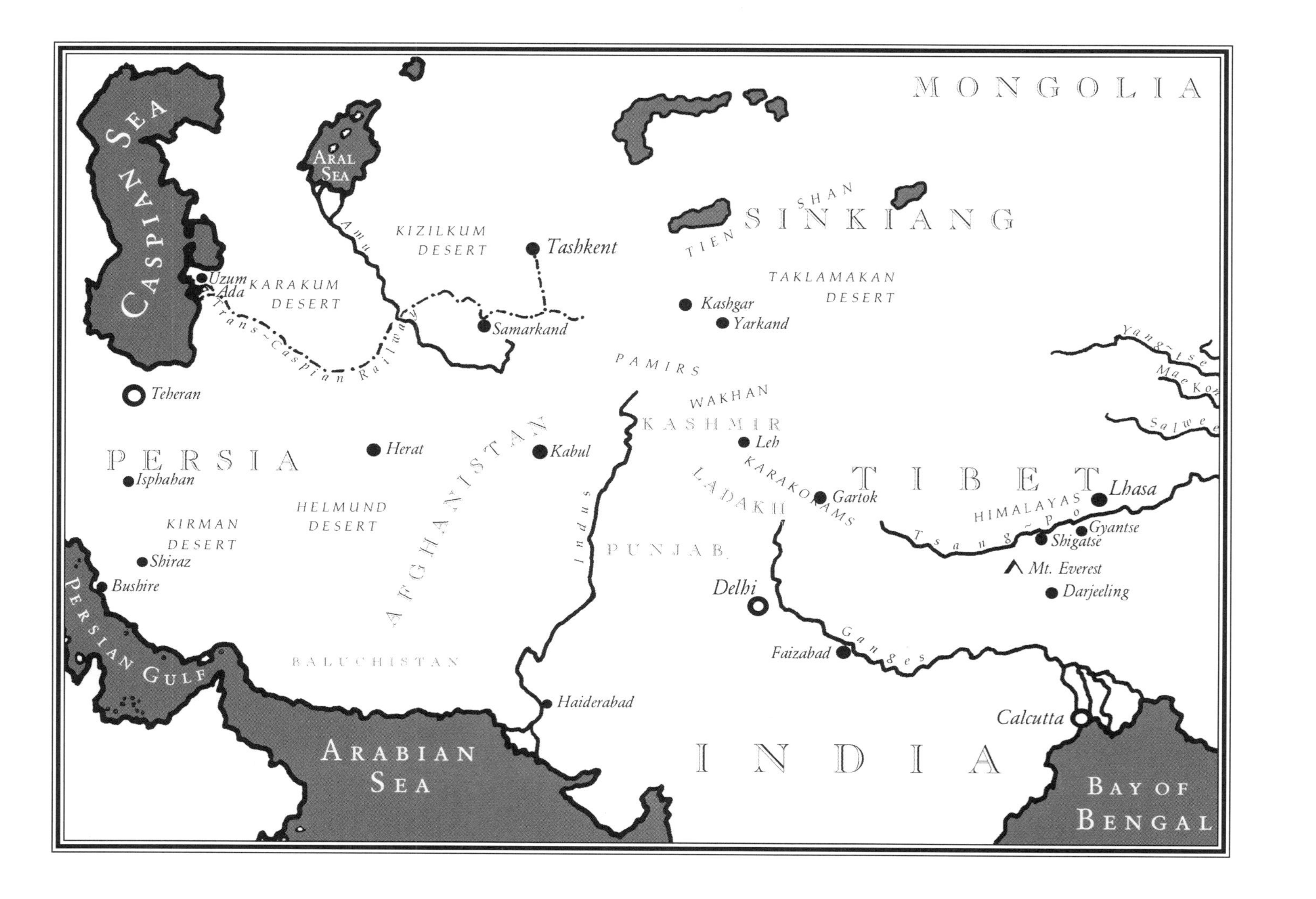
MONGOLIA
CASPIAN SEA
ARAL SEA
SINKIANG
TIEN SHAN
KIZILKUM DESERT
Tashkent
Amu
KARAKUM DESERT
Uzum Ada
Trans-Caspian Railway
Samarkand
TAKLAMAKAN DESERT
Kashgar
Yarkand
PAMIRS
Teheran
WAKHAN
KASHMIR
Leh
Yang-tse
Mae Kon
Salwee
PERSIA
Herat
AFGHANISTAN
Kabul
TIBET
Lhasa
Isphahan
HELMUND DESERT
KARAKORAMS
LADAKH
Gartok
HIMALAYAS
Tsang-Po
Gyantse
Shigatse
KIRMAN DESERT
Shiraz
Indus
PUNJAB
Mt. Everest
Darjeeling
Bushire
Delhi
PERSIAN GULF
Faizabad
Ganges
BALUCHISTAN
Haiderabad
Calcutta
ARABIAN SEA
INDIA
BAY OF BENGAL

DAY ONE

APRIL 6TH 1894

CHAPTER I

"EXCELLENT TIMING, Watson!" cried Sherlock Holmes. He stood at the open doorway of 221B Baker Street, brandishing a buff-coloured envelope which had been slit open, and a sheet of foolscap with a few lines penned upon it in an even hand. "This was handed to Mrs. Hudson just a few minutes ago."

As he spoke I noticed that he looked, not at me, but at the rapidly diminishing figure of an uniformed commissionaire whom I had just moments before passed. Following his gaze, I noticed a rather shabbily-attired youth emerge from a storefront doorway where he had been sheltering from the chill wind which had, if anything, increased in its violence since the previous night. He made as if to follow the commissionaire, but glanced at Holmes as he did so. Holmes made an almost imperceptible gesture and the youth casually lounged back into his shelter.

"As you see, we have our forces in place. Wiggins and the street arabs are my eyes and ears, but that messenger will have been hired through the Corps of Commissionaires by some nondescript fellow merely earning a few shillings. Certainly nothing is to be learned there."

So saying, he turned and greeted me with an effusive, "Good morning, Watson. Come inside and let us examine this together, as I only glanced at it before rushing to the front door. It's from Moriarty."

At this remarkable utterance I was rendered momentarily speechless!

My years with Holmes should have prepared me for anything, especially since his amazing resurrection following an apparent plunge into the watery chasm of the Reichenbach Falls. But Holmes himself had only the previous evening assured me that he had overmatched his opponent, and had witnessed Professor Moriarty tumble into the turbulent spray, dashing himself to destruction on the craggy boulders far below as he fell to his certain death – three years previously. And now, Moriarty has sent him a message!

This was too much to absorb, following as it did upon those incredible newspaper headlines which I had only briefly perused as I strode up Baker Street, and I looked with some exasperation at the retreating back of Holmes as he started up the stairs.

Despite the excitement and late hours of the previous night's events, I had risen earlier than usual, and so adjusted my rounds that I had finished with my last patient shortly after ten o'clock. I then proceeded to those rooms at

Baker Street where Holmes and I had shared so many adventures, but as I passed the newsstand at the corner the bold legend on a billboard had leaped to my attention.

SCANDAL AT
SCOTLAND YARD
CAPTURE, ESCAPE
OF ADAIR CASE
MURDERER

Purchasing my *Daily Chronicle* I scanned the headlines as I hurried to 221B to get full details from Holmes, whom I expected to find in a state of near apoplexy. After the failed attempt on his life the previous evening by the murderer of the Honourable Ronald Adair, Colonel Sebastian Moran, which had led to Moran's capture, the last we had seen of Professor Moriarty's chief-of-staff as Lestrade led him away in cuffs was his lean, snarling face cursing Holmes.

Perhaps Holmes was unaware of Moran's escape, which I could scarcely credit, but I could not otherwise reconcile this news with his air of insouciance. When I thought of the bullet hole drilled with such accuracy through his wax likeness by Moran's air gun I was surprised to note, as I followed him into our old apartments, that he had not closed the shutters.

Bleak morning light from the large bow-windows was rendered more cheerful by the logs blazing in the fireplace, and this morning I noticed that Mrs. Hudson had indeed preserved our old apartments exactly as Holmes had left them three years before. Even the small damage caused at that time by Professor Moriarty's henchmen setting fire to the place had been meticulously repaired, and the room restored to its previous character exactly.

"My dear Holmes," I expostulated, "can it be possible? I should never have believed that we should be back here together in these rooms, seemingly so little changed since those days – and now Professor Moriarty, back from the dead as well! Surely this cannot be so!"

"No, Watson, indeed I saw him perish, and no amount of luck or ingenuity will ever return the late Professor to his evil and ambitious ways. This," said Holmes, indicating the letter in his hand, "is a message from his brother, *Colonel* James Moriarty, and I suppose we had better see what he has to say. I see from your newspaper that you are aware that Lestrade has misplaced his man. I expect him and Gregson to arrive at any moment; I imagine he has his work cut out for him right now explaining this little incident to the press, let alone the Commissioner."

With this he motioned me towards my old basket-chair by the fire, and with a wave of the amber stem of his pipe indicated the cigars and tantalus in their accustomed locations. Accepting the chair and declining the latter, it still being morning, I made myself comfortable with my paper while Holmes, having first ascertained that I had already eaten, went in search of Mrs. Hudson to request a late breakfast.

The headlines were as bold as the billboard. The accompanying story left little doubt that, with senior police officers like Lestrade at large, the community was in imminent danger of violence and chaos at the hands of the criminal elements, which so clearly had the upper hand in London at least.

As to the details, the events were only hours old at press time, and the reporter had managed to glean only that the Adair Murderer had been identified and dramatically apprehended by Inspector Lestrade, acting on a tip-off, and had been dispatched under heavy guard to Scotland Yard for questioning. The suspect was held in a solitary holding-cell for almost an hour, when a signed order arrived transferring him to the lock-up at Tower Bridge. With remarkable speed he was rattled across London and signed in to the overnight cells there, preparatory to being committed for trial at the morning assizes. In the same cell was a South African, being held on suspicion of stealing the Ardmore sapphires. Kemper, for that was his name, was of similar build and swarthy complexion to Moran, and was released in the early hours of the morning, as there were insufficient grounds for holding him. Only hours later, when Lestrade and Gregson went to question Moran at the Yard, was the transfer discovered. Making all haste to Tower Bridge police station, they were at first relieved to find that Moran was still in custody, and then most distressed to discover that in fact he had been released as Kemper, and Kemper was still in his cell, protesting his innocence of the entire affair.

This was the full extent of known details, but the reporter left little doubt but that this could have taken place only with the active assistance of corrupt public officials in high places. He finished by again casting aspersions on the competence, if not the ethics, of the police detectives involved.

Holmes had returned and settled himself at table to await his breakfast, and I read aloud to him some of the highlights of the news report, in which he seemed but little interested. At the same time, his intent reading of the letter from Colonel Moriarty elicited a series of exclamations and muttered comments. He read it several times in quick succession, and then chuckled to himself as he leaned over to pass it to me.

"An interesting study for you, Doctor, but further danger for all of us, I fear, before this matter is settled, let alone understood."

Putting aside the *Chronicle*, I read what the brother of Sherlock Holmes's late archenemy had written.

'Sherlock Holmes, Esq.,

I write, sir, in order to warn you.

My brother warned you, and then you had the good fortune that he slipped at Reichenbach Falls. I vowed then that I should exact revenge for his death. However, certain of my brother's former associates have now asked that I put aside that desire, and contact you, in the capacity of an intermediary, to propose an accommodation.

My personal animus has faded somewhat, and I must accord expediency its due. I have other more important matters to attend to just for now, and will be leaving England again shortly. By now, you will have evidence of the far-reaching powers his associates wield, still. You may have thwarted them this time, and escaped death by doing so, but they slip away unscathed.'

At that moment, Mrs. Hudson bustled into the room, backwards, protecting a tray laden with oatmeal and milk, eggs and bacon, kippers, toast and marmalade, coffee for Holmes and tea for myself. Placing it on the sideboard while she quickly set a place for Holmes, Mrs. Hudson apologised for the slow arrival of breakfast, saying "If I'd only known, Mr. Holmes, I should have got some help in, but with you gone away so long!" She fussed around, serving Holmes while he flicked through his *'Daily Gazette'*. I noticed that his habit of turning from the headlines directly to the obituaries and the agonies was unaltered.

"And a very good-morning to you, Doctor. Here's your tea, nice and strong as I knows you like," said Mrs. Hudson, as she set a cup and saucer on the low table beside my chair. With this she left us, and as Holmes attended to his meal I returned my attention to Moriarty's letter.

'Please do not, however, take my personal forbearance to mean that you may pursue them without paying the penalty. I am not my brother, and we have no personal grudges to hold one against the other, other than the matter of my brother's death. This, as I have said, I am prepared to set aside for now.

'In the three years that have passed since his death, I am informed that you have raised various unwelcome ghosts, harassed their people, thwarted their schemes, and in general made of yourself a major obstacle to their prosperity and plans for the future.

'I know that you have already amassed a small fortune from your previous

cases on behalf of various kings and captains of industry. Surely after three years of absence and hardship, with neither financial reward nor clear victory in sight regarding this matter, you must be tempted to cease and desist from all this, and retire to your chemical researches. You have my word as a soldier that, should you agree to this, your life will be held safe from harm.

'But I must warn you, as I have been asked to do, that should you continue to harry them as you have done, your life and the lives of any of your colleagues who assist you to block them shall be forfeit. Upon this certainty you have their word, and I assure you, none of my regrets.'

'Colonel John Moriarty'

Finishing this missive for the third time, I found I had been so engrossed that my tea had become undrinkably tepid. I set it aside.

"Surely, Holmes," said I, "you can have the man for this letter. He explicitly threatens yourself and others, and gives his reasons."

"Not a threat, Watson. A warning! If I choose to accept their amnesty, they carry on, and he must be hopeful for some reason that I will do so. If I decline, and attempt to charge Moriarty over these threats, I should have the devil of a time in court for a nominal victory, and would additionally present them with a ready-made target. Either way, he is safe."

"My dear Holmes! Seriously! What *have* you really been up to these past three years? Last night you made no reference to this resurgent organisation which has so clearly outlived Moriarty - Professor Moriarty, that is to say."

"That is so. Last night I thought we had trapped the last serious antagonist remaining in London, and that that particular chapter was closed. For several years now they have concentrated their activities in Europe and further afield, as Britain was made too hot for them at the time of Professor Moriarty's death and thereafter. However, not long after you left for your rooms last night, I received an urgent message from Mycroft which made it immediately clear that bigger fish were circling in the depths of London's underworld and, not to put too fine a point upon it, we threw Moran back as bait."

"Threw him back! It says here that Moran escaped by subterfuge, due to his luck in being billeted with a chap of similar appearance who was on his way out."

"Precisely what we want the public to believe. When it became evident that powerful men were concerning themselves over the arrest of Moran, and that within minutes of his arrest a strategy was being implemented to secure his transfer to Tower Bridge, Mycroft agreed that our best counter was to allow them to think their plan had worked. We decided to release Moran, and arrange to have him followed by the Irregulars. If the general public knew of the eminence of some of those whom we must suspect of being involved in his release, there would be a change of government by nightfall, which would accomplish nothing. But we can't act upon suspicion, even if we ourselves knew the guilty party."

"But Holmes, really! Moran is a multiple murderer, and you have assisted his escape. Surely you must realise he will kill again."

"It is a risk, I acknowledge that – but the consequences of not destroying them all are so profoundly far-reaching that I must take that burden on my conscience. Hopefully he will lead us to the heart of their cabal, and we can remove Moran and his paymasters all at once."

"Then you will not take up Moriarty's offer of an amnesty? You are still determined to pursue this investigation, even at such a risk to your life?" I asked, knowing even as I asked what the reply would be.

Holmes stood and walked to the leather wingback chair beside the fire, tamped his smouldering pipe with his thumb, and re-lit it from a taper he had held in the flames. Taking several deep draughts upon it, he sat down, settled back in his armchair, and gazed for a while into the dancing flames as though he saw I know not what ghosts there. A long and companionable silence ensued, which was at last broken by Holmes, speaking with a quiet but clear voice.

"No, Watson, of course I shan't," Holmes dismissed the thought.

"How many times in the past three years I have missed your companionship and good common sense, and your essential decency. Indeed, Watson, I owe you many a long explanation! And a full accounting you shall have, for it is a most remarkable tale, of a journey never yet made by Europeans, nor, I dare say, by any other; a tale of intrigue and danger, of exotic places and seemingly-omniscient villains. By any reckoning, our efforts to investigate their activities and to thwart their conspiracies must be accounted successful – for the first time they are evidently becoming seriously concerned, as their master strategy, whatever it is, must have been compromised by their recent string of reversals. The hardships and sacrifices involved have been worth the results, of this I am certain."

With this, he seized the poker and gave the fire a stir, causing streams of sparks to leap up the flue, then tapped his pipe out on the grate, speaking as if to himself, staring distantly into the flames.

"And yet – to my eternal sorrow, our involvement in all of this resulted in a burden which neither time nor distance can ever lift from my soul. The guilt for this I shall never seek to avoid."

What on earth had Holmes to feel guilty about? Unbidden thoughts crossed my mind, causing me to remember that the case against Professor Moriarty was never conclusively proven, and that there were many - particularly at Scotland Yard - who had stopped just short of accusing Holmes of unwarranted persecution of a harmless retired mathematical coach to the Army. Was this guilt-laden reference a sign that Holmes had indeed lost track of reality? Was he now living his life in a waking dream where his inimitable deductive powers were being marshalled to the destruction of blameless citizens and shadowy conspiracies, and where he held himself responsible for events that had happened half a world away?

None of this, however, would explain away the homicidal Colonel Sebastian Moran, or the air-gun bullet, or the threatening letter received that very morning from Colonel Moriarty. These were real, of that there could be no doubt, and I banished the previous uncharitable thoughts from my mind, and resolved that I would let Holmes reveal his adventures of the past years at his own pleasure. In the meantime, for my own amusement I should attempt to piece together what was clearly a complex and consequential investigation, basing my case on whatever Holmes saw fit to reveal, purely to see if I were able to do so. Frankly, I expected little success at this endeavour, and thought I should never have the temerity to voice my theories as they developed - however valid they seemed.

I could have had no way of knowing that before the day was done I should be commissioned to compile a complete report on Sherlock Holmes's activities on behalf of the Empire during those three long years when he was away from his beloved London.

CHAPTER II

MY REVERIE WAS rudely interrupted by an ungodly row emanating from the region of our doorstep - and apparently headed our way, as Mrs. Hudson had no other tenants at that time. I glanced at Holmes, who had just finished with his coffee and was preparing his post-breakfast pipe. Sensing my gaze upon him, Holmes looked up at me somewhat quizzically, and then broke into a smile of understanding.

"Very well, Watson; it *has* been a long time. Let us see! That he is the glazier's assistant you will have already deduced, as the sounds of glass off-cuts chinking around in a tool-kit, combined with the bullet-hole in the pane, must surely indicate that Mrs. Hudson has sent young Billy for assistance in that department."

Nodding sagely, I murmured my assent to this, although it had not in fact occurred to me to make that assumption. "And what else?"

The maid had answered the knock at the street door and, after a minute or two, had admitted the workman. Then had come a loud crashing noise, which is what first alerted us that something unusual was afoot, followed by an uneven but rapid ascent, with snatches of a vaguely familiar whistled tune audible amongst the din. The noises from the staircase sounded to my ear to be nothing more distinctive than would be made by any man with a heavy tool-kit hurrying up stairs, save that his pace did slow a little as he ascended to our landing.

Eyes narrowed so that only a little grey was visible, Holmes casually said, "As usual, I can't tell a lot. But, very briefly, our glazier is just past his prime, tall, with a noticeable disability to his left foot. He is left-handed, although his tool-kit is carried in his right hand. He has a slight squint, and a thin face, and yet he would be generally accounted handsome enough. He is a bachelor. His complexion is likely to be swarthy, although I may be wrong on that. But either he or his parents *are* Italian. Will that do to be going on with?" Holmes enquired of me.

"Certainly," I replied.

The clatter finished off with a brisk tattoo at our hall door.

"Come!" said Sherlock Holmes; the door opened smartly and in stepped, not to my surprise, a personable-looking man in his late-twenties, carrying a wooden tool chest in his right hand. He was tall and slender, but of an athletic thinness rather than that of ill health. His fingers were unadorned by wedding bands. His colouring was indeed Mediterranean, yet his nationality was not evident, except that he spoke the English common to workmen from the East End of London.

"221B. Window needs replacing?" enquired he, thumbing a small and grubby notebook.

Holmes motioned towards the shattered pane with his pipe-stem. "As you see."

As the young man crossed the sitting room, it was obvious to a medical eye that he suffered from a slight clubfoot, causing just a hitch to one side as he walked. He placed his kit on the window-seat, and examined the broken crystal.

"This here's from a pistol shot!" exclaimed he, and whistled in appreciation of the unusual.

Turning around, his gaze found the mark where the soft-nosed air gun round had flattened itself against the sturdy oak panelling. Sighting down along the line of fire, he examined the view outside, correctly directing his attention across the street to that downstairs window in Camden House. Then, swivelling his head around again, he noticed the position of the rocking chair, which last evening had been replaced by the small table carrying the wax bust of Holmes.

"Lucky no one was sitting there, they'd have been shot!" he exclaimed.

At this, Holmes and I glanced at each other, and then at the wax-bust covered by a cloth, still in the corner of the sitting room where Mrs. Hudson had left it last night.

"Lucky indeed," remarked Holmes, with a chuckle.

The glazier carried on with his measuring, scribing and tapping, producing a crystal ready to be installed, but I noticed that at all times, until he had finished and gone, he worked from the side of the window enclosure. I can't say that I blamed him. As he left, I requested a signed receipt and added a small gratuity in addition to settling the bill.

On a page torn from his grimy book he wrote out a receipt on behalf of his firm, and signed it 'Pietro Rubino.' He wrote, as he had worked, using his left hand.

It was by now a pleasure to watch Holmes's effortless deductive processes in action once again. Any scepticism I may once have entertained about his talents - I had once called him a charlatan for just such a demonstration as this - had long been replaced by the healthiest respect. I did not ask for an explanation of the thought processes and connections, which had come so naturally to him, and neither did he volunteer any such accounting. This 'staircase game' had become almost a standing joke between us in years gone by. Holmes had eventually remarked, with not a little acerbity, that, "if I was so damnably curious as to our visitors, even before they arrived", then I should simply train myself to observe more closely, "for you see and hear everything as I do." With that I had had to be satisfied.

But that was then; it had indeed been a long time, and Holmes had clearly enjoyed, just for this once, repeating one of the more memorable of those little rituals which had characterised our bachelor establishment.

"You mentioned young Billy, is he still here?" I enquired. "'Not so young' Billy, I should imagine by now; I must say I'm surprised to find him still situated as page to Mrs. Hudson's establishment."

"Perhaps you would be surprised - Billy is still just a lad. He was tall for his age, and mature beyond his years. Anyway, he is indeed still here, and I for one am thankful; with both Mrs. H. and Billy around, the appalling standard of the maids - which I must say has deteriorated if anything - is far less distressing."

So saying, Holmes rose from his armchair and, reaching down a thick volume from his shelf of reference books, leafed through its pages to the 'M's'. He immediately closed it and continued in a business-like manner, "I thought not - we had no record of Colonel Moriarty prior to my departure, so he was either not involved in his brother's conspiracies at that time, or was exceedingly clever to escape detection."

"Perhaps he was out of the country at the time," said I.

"Indeed, that is most likely. We do know that he was here writing to the papers in his brother's defence less than a year ago."

"At the time of his letters, I did some little researches of my own," said I, "and found that he was apparently a much-decorated officer, at least in his younger days, with no official record of criminality attached to his name - certainly no indication of involvement in his brother's schemes."

"I should be surprised otherwise - after all, MacDonald still believes there's a possibility that the professor himself was an upright citizen," replied Holmes. "However, this is not the first indication I have had of the colonel's involvement in these affairs. I note that he served at various times in India, Persia and the Sudan - precisely those regions I have recently frequented - and in each of those places events occurred which caused me the chill, eerie sensation that the ghost of the late professor had a hand in directing things."

"You mean, Colonel Moriarty was responsible - how could you tell?"

"Quite frankly, I had no evidence at all. I attributed the sensations to the fact that Professor Moriarty had long commanded senior staff of exceptional calibre - men such as Moran - and at the time I suspected that if anybody, somehow Moran was involved. But there was a certain process of thought, the constant reassessment of a situation, with alterations to tactics even as events unfolded, such that whenever we seemed certain to have our quarry, it would slip away leaving us with further mysteries rather than answers. These were all trademarks of my previous encounters with the professor. The personal and idiosyncratic stamp of Moriarty seemed to be too clearly evident for it to be Moran or another. On reflection, this indication of Colonel Moriarty's central involvement comes as no great surprise. "Either way, it's clear that we require further information concerning our fine colonel. See if young Billy is around, please Watson; I shall require a commissionaire to take a message to Mycroft." He had seized paper and pen as I went in search of Billy, and when I had informed the maid as to Holmes's requirements and returned to our sitting room, his message was in a sealed envelope on the table.

I pondered whether this was the right time to seek answers to a question which certain of Holmes's remarks had raised in my mind, but decided to wait until the message had been sent on its way to Mycroft. I sat again to continue with my *Chronicle*, as Holmes was clearly engaged in deep thought, pacing the length of the room in front of the broad windows.

Several minutes passed thus, before a confident knock at the door announced the arrival of Billy, our former page. He was certainly taller, and it was clear that Mrs. Hudson provided well, for a better nourished page would be difficult to find in London. Introducing myself anew, for Billy had been sent away the previous day for his own protection as soon as Holmes had arrived back at 221B, I was unreasonably pleased that he recalled several small kindnesses I had done him as a lad, and thanked me for them most graciously. Then, receiving the envelope and his instructions from Holmes, he hurried off to the office of the Corps of Commissionaires.

I had no chance to put my question to Holmes, however, for no sooner had Billy's footsteps faded away into the sounds of Baker Street than the official-sounding tones of Inspector Lestrade announced his presence at our street door. Within moments, Lestrade and Inspector Gregson both burst into our sitting room, and would have immediately begun addressing Holmes had he not raised his palm in their direction to quieten them, at the same time indicating two chairs.

"Good morning, officers. As you see," said he, indicating the headline of my newspaper, "we are discussing the unfortunate events of last night, or should I say, this morning." Clearly then, Holmes was not going to confess his role in the matter, and I intended to follow his lead.

"Unfortunate my eye," blustered Lestrade, "it was . . ."

"Completely beyond our control," interrupted Gregson, somewhat less excitably, "we had him banged away well and proper, and it being almost dawn we thought . . ."

"And why shouldn't we, I'd like to know. We had our man fair and square." Lestrade was indignant, then remembered the actual course of last night's events. "All due credit to your good self, of course, Mr. Holmes," somewhat apologetically, and then he was away again. "Laughing-stock of the whole Yard we are, and as for Commissioner MacDonald - blister paint, it would. Anyone would think we turned that rascal Moran out into the streets ourselves, the way some people . . ."

Holmes interrupted this tirade, turning abruptly away from the window and towards them, saying, "Gentlemen, calm yourselves. It is quite clear that powerful forces are at play here; rest assured that I at least understand that you are not to be held responsible. We will recapture the elusive Colonel Moran, it only remains to be seen how and when."

"But meanwhile, our reputations . . ."

"Are waiting to be made illustrious by the heroic and brilliant recapture of the villain!" interjected Holmes, clearly losing patience with Lestrade's self pity, which I privately thought a little much, considering his direct responsibility for the detectives' plight. "Practically now, what measures have you taken?"

Gregson spoke, elbows on knees, as he leaned forward. "The usual - railway stations and ports have been alerted; our informers are out in the underworld; description circulated to all officers on the beat - but let's face it, a criminal as cunning as Moran could be well out of the country by now, and us none the wiser."

"I think not," said Holmes. "He will prevail upon his masters to allow him another chance to destroy me, and they will agree to it. They have little choice, for my destruction is the only sure way to evade their own."

"Exactly who are these mysterious 'masters' of whom you speak, Mr. Holmes?" enquired Lestrade suspiciously. "You wouldn't be withholding information material to a criminal matter, now would you, sir?"

"Of course not, Lestrade," dissembled Holmes. "Their identity and motives are as much a mystery to me as they are to the Yard. This I will say, however. They exist, their intentions are definitely not good, and I shall have them all sooner or later - or rather, *we* shall, gentlemen, for in this affair my name must remain unmentioned."

"Mister 'Olmes, Mister 'Olmes, if you please, sir," came a cry from our landing, accompanied by a sharp knocking.

Holmes rapidly crossed the room and unceremoniously flung open the door to reveal the same shabbily dressed youth from the street, who looked with contempt at the police officers, and waited for Holmes to speak.

Lestrade got in first, however, "Well now, if it isn't our little villain Wiggins? I've several matters to take up with you, me young lad, now that we're all here - you've been spotted, you know, helping those longshoremen 'lose' some of their cargo, you and your disreputable little gang of thieves - and now's as good a time as any." Lestrade moved towards the door, but Holmes turned towards him, saying, "I think not, my dear Lestrade. I suggest, rather, that an amnesty in that direction would be a capital idea, at least for now, as I have some urgent matters to discuss with Wiggins, not necessarily unconnected with your little problem. If Wiggins and his Baker Street Irregulars, as I prefer to call them, have proven invaluable to my investigations in the past, it is precisely because of their ready entree into the haunts of our London criminals. I do suggest to you that to lose these advantages in order to recover a few bales of broadcloth is not the best way to resuscitate your reputations."

"Now, if we can agree as to that, gentlemen, I must send Wiggins here on a mission, and then I am due elsewhere."

Lestrade looked for a moment as though he would combust spontaneously, so red did his face become, as he fought to control his emotions.

Inspector Gregson, obviously fearing a Lestrade explosion, spoke quietly in his stead.

"It's a pleasure to have you back in London, Mr. Holmes, and we're grateful for the chance to nab Moran in the first place, don't think otherwise. But the law is the law, and you'll be well advised that things are different now that Commissioner MacDonald is in charge. Your old ways will soon enough get you into trouble without my help if you carry on as before, flouting police procedure and acting outside the law, however honourable your motives," and with those words he ushered Lestrade safely past Wiggins.

"We also have our methods, and will proceed with them. I trust that, in return for this little 'amnesty', as you term it, you will inform the Yard immediately you have any information. We want Moran, and we'll have him, mark my words. Good day, Holmes! Good day, Doctor!"

Wiggins watched them descend, no expression on his face, and then followed Holmes back into the sitting room.

Holmes stood with his back to the flames, then spoke to Wiggins. "He's right, of course. There is a distinct difference between a rascal, which is what you used to be, and a rogue, which if Lestrade is correct, is what you risk becoming. You, especially, have the wits to see an opportunity, and the hustle to take advantage of it before others do. That opportunity does not necessarily have to be criminal in nature, and I suggest that you seriously consider whether the game is worth the candle before you find anything else falling off a dray. Lestrade may sometimes appear slow on the uptake, but he is persistent, and you're on his patch."

To all this Wiggins made no response whatsoever, merely waiting until Holmes had finished, then announcing "Knows where 'e is, though, doesn't us. Say as yer will, Wiggins and 'is Baker Street Hirregulars knows where 'e is, your Colonel Moran, and Mister bloody 'igh-and-mighty copper doesn't."

Holmes immediately abandoned his uncharacteristically avuncular pose, and demanded all details from Wiggins.

Holmes's unspoken trust in the loyalty and capability of this ragtag band of street urchins was, to an outsider, inconceivable. Even I - who had seen them so many times in action and witnessed the results - found it difficult to believe. Holmes had prevailed upon some of the highest authorities in the realm to release a killer such as Moran, against his own personal assurance of Moran's recapture, with no other resources at his disposal than a band of street arabs, the eldest only just sixteen.

Although he had elected to guard over Baker Street himself, against the unlikely chance that Moran would immediately return for his promised vengeance, Wiggins had set his three most trusted and resourceful lieutenants to the task of tracking Moran from the moment of his release from the Tower Bridge cells.

Moran had been called for by two men, dressed like swells, who had hustled him into a coach-and-four, and driven off at breakneck speed after loudly giving directions for Stepney, with one of the Irregulars clinging to the postillion. This left the other two to notice that Moran had actually exited the other side of the coach as soon as the door was closed. Swirled up in a cape against the bitter wind, he had casually strolled around the corner as the coach had thundered away into the breaking dawn. Walking slowly and seeming to have no concerns other than to avoid slipping on the icy cobblestones, Moran had nevertheless kept a watchful eye on his surroundings. First on foot, thence by several trains and buses, Wiggins's Irregulars had stayed on his trail.

By leapfrogging each other's position, and by well-timed addition or removal of various caps and other garments, these two trackers had managed to track one of the great hunters of the East to his lair. Colonel Sebastian Moran finally disappeared into the service entrance of a sailor's rest-home, at the corner of a riverside lane in Greenwich.

This establishment was well-known to the lads, as they had run errands for the ill-tempered proprietor on occasion, and had been grateful more than once for a bowl of soup and a crust from the fat old cook when the old skinflint had paid them out short. The decrepit building had two entrances, one on each street frontage, but as they could both be observed from the one vantage point one Irregular was left on guard while the other had hurried to make his report to Wiggins. The third was presumably finding his way back from wherever the coach had finally come to a halt, and would then be sent to reinforce the watcher.

Such was the intelligence delivered unto Holmes by his young assistants, and for all his nonchalance, it was evident that he had been awaiting this information with some anxiety and was most relieved that his gamble had, so far, paid good odds.

Holmes commended Wiggins for work well done, paid him sufficient for himself and lieutenants, and sent him on his way with instructions regarding surveillance of the Sailor's Home, and further trailing if Moran should emerge. Holmes particularly enjoined him to be aware of any attempt at escape in disguise by Moran, and distractions created by outsiders. Wiggins acknowledged these terse instructions by tipping forefinger to cap, pocketed the coins in his waistcoat, and was soon out in the street.

Moving to the window I watched as he returned to his post, this time in a different doorway, and held a brief conference with a smaller lad. A few coins changed hands, and the other boy dashed off around the corner with as much speed as the slick footing allowed.

"At last," I thought to myself, "I have Holmes's undivided attention," and was wording my question to put to him when yet another interruption forestalled me. This time it was the return of Billy, who had stopped at the same news-stand as myself, and had bought a later edition of the *Daily Telegraph*, which he presented to Holmes, saying "I thought I should get this, judging by the headlines."

Holmes unfolded the paper, scanned the heads, and whistled softly through his teeth as he skimmed the details. "Quite rightly too, Billy. Very sharp of you." So saying, he handed a coin to Billy, who quietly let himself out.

I moved around beside Holmes and read:

VICIOUS MURDERS -YARD BAFFLED
AS RIVERSIDE SLASHER CLAIMS TWO

Clearly there was a mystery to be solved here, but we were still in the midst of the Moran escape case, and I could not imagine Holmes allowing any distraction from that investigation, given that not only his career but also his life was in the balance.

Nevertheless, Holmes seemed highly pleased at the news story, and when he laid the newspaper down, I retrieved it and read the story behind the headlines.

"Further mysteries!" remarked Holmes, almost to himself.

Reading the news story, sensational though it certainly was, provided me with no further insights into the matter at hand. I wondered just exactly what Holmes had seen in this new report, when all I could see was the tale of the discovery of two most gruesomely mutilated bodies in the Thames that very morning - and I had still not had the chance to put my question to Holmes.

CHAPTER III

"THEY'LL HAVE sent the bodies to Whitechapel mortuary, no doubt," exclaimed Holmes. "Hurry, Watson, I want to inspect those cadavers before Lestrade has an opportunity to order some foolish procedure which will accomplish nothing further than to obliterate any real clues. I trust my access to the morgue will be as it was; nevertheless, your medical credentials may well prove valuable - that is, of course, if you have no other pressing engagements."

"My time is my own at present," I replied, "and I can think of nothing more congenial than to assist you, if indeed I can be of any assistance at all."

I should not have spoken so forthrightly had I known the horror we were on our way to investigate.

"Splendid!" cried Holmes. "Just like old times, indeed. Swiftly now, your coat and hat, for we may visit the riverside as well. We have no time to spare if we are to beat Lestrade."

Holmes rapidly dashed off another note for Mycroft, as we had not yet had his reply, and was just handing it to Mrs. Hudson in the hallway when the commissionaire hurried up with a message. Tearing it open and reading the few lines, Holmes dismissed the messenger with thanks, and said with evident relief, "Excellent! Mycroft is meeting with the Prime Minister and cabinet until three o'clock, and will receive us at four at his club. No need, therefore, for this reply," and so saying he retrieved the message from Mrs. H., and we set forth on my first investigation with Holmes in over three years.

Hailing a growler, we leapt in and Holmes gave his directions to the cabby, promising an extra shilling for a speedy arrival. This had its effect, and we were soon dashing through small lanes and mews, of the existence of which I had no knowledge, as short cuts between the major thoroughfares. Pulling up outside the morgue at Whitechapel, our cab was still slowing to a halt when an official conveyance rounded the corner and drew up directly behind us, horses snorting cloudlets of mist into the chill air. First Gregson exited the vehicle, followed by Lestrade and two uniformed constables of immense size.

"They're already dead, I believe," said Holmes mildly to Gregson. "I doubt you'll need the reinforcements.

Gregson smiled a little at that, but Lestrade was still smarting from their last exchange, and merely scowled

"I see there's to be little change from before. Wherever we go on our police business," said he, emphasising the possessives, "it seems we are destined to have to deal with the unofficial forces as well. Obviously, Holmes, your influence in high places is unimpaired, so I suppose we must co-operate." With that he strode into the mortuary entrance.

"Why, thank you, I'm sure. Most gracious of you," said Holmes to no one in particular, and we followed Lestrade.

The mortuary attendant, seeing the officers with us, made no difficulties; soon enough we were inside. The morgue was a depressing place, not surprisingly, with utilitarian white tiling on all surfaces up to eye-level, and in the examination room, heavy deal benches topped with zinc sheeting, with drains letting out into a channel running the length of the room. To one side, in the dim shadows beyond the reach of the gas lamps, were several tiers of seating; clearly the room was used for demonstrations at times. The attendant indicated the two benches farthest from the entrance, around which, even in this charnel house, a temporary screen had been erected to shield the unwary from the horror that lay there.

"As if there's not enough to deal with," complained Lestrade, as we walked the length of the chamber, past other benches with their patient occupants. "First this accursed Moran, and now when our only priority is to recapture him, along comes some maniac getting his thrills by dismantling people indiscriminately."

"On what grounds do you make that assessment, Lestrade?" enquired Holmes, a thoughtful expression informing his aquiline features.

"This is not the first." Again, Gregson answered for Lestrade. "Two other bodies abused in the same fashion have been fished out by river-police from the Thames Division over the past week." With this he looked at the two large constables, who were from that division, and told us they had delivered those bodies from Woolwich to the nearest police wharf for collection by the mortuary van, before going on to report directly to Scotland Yard

"We managed to keep those out of the papers, on strict instructions from the Home Office. The Ripper affair at Whitechapel is still too fresh in the memory of the public, and what with suffragettes, Bolsheviks, anti-vivisectionists, and what have you causing no end of public disturbances right now, the last thing the government needs, or so we are informed, is another bout of general hysterics. Thus, the hush on this affair."

Lestrade added, "Unfortunately, these last two were found by the public, and the press got wind of it as soon as we did - damned vultures - so now we'll have two major scandals on our hands."

"The lot of a policeman is rarely a happy one, my dear Lestrade," commiserated Holmes, as we reached the sheltering screens.

Even my medical training, and my recollections of the horrors of the battlefields at Afghanistan, did little to prepare me for the wanton savagery and brutality of the injuries visited upon these two murdered souls. Even the most cursory inspection was sufficient to conclude that the same evil hand had been at work on both victims.

At that moment we were joined by a youngish man, with inappropriate moustaches for his facial shape, wearing thick-glassed spectacles, which gave him a perpetual air of wide-eyed wonder.

"Mr. Holmes; our Medical Examiner, Doctor Stevenage; he also did for the last two," Gregson made the introductions. "And this is Doctor Watson."

Introductions thus dispensed with, we all turned to the gruesome exhibits. The most noticeable difference between the two was colour. One cadaver was that of a middle-aged European, the other was an Asiatic of some type, with naturally dark pigmentation and a noticeable scar running from cheekbone to jawbone. The features of both were grotesquely disfigured and distorted, with black and swollen tongues protruding obscenely from their gaping mouths. Clearly rats and other vermin had been feasting on the European, for the whole left side of his face had been gnawed away to the cheekbone. Ligature marks were visible around both necks, so both had obviously been strangled. But this had not been sufficient for our fiend. All four eyes had been stabbed clear through, and the ocular fluids had drained away, leaving deflated sacs in the sockets. All this was visible from where we stood. Stevenage was the first to speak.

"They were found naked, as before, and although it seems that strangulation was the cause of death - there being no water in the lungs of the previous victims, and I expect no difference when I get these two opened up - severe violence was subsequently visited upon their corpses." He moved towards the benches. "If you'll just come here for a moment, I'll show you."

"Exactly the same injuries to both victims, as you see," he continued, demonstrating as he spoke. "Strangulation by a thin cord, broken neck, spinal column snapped in the region of the lower vertebrae;" he indicated these areas, then lifted the arm of the dead Asiatic, who had been still a young man when sudden death overtook him. The wound was bluish-purple turned white at the edges, where water exposure had begun its dissolving action. "Deep penetration knife wounds, from the armpits up through the throat; stab wounds right through both eyeballs, apparently from a different, smaller blade than the other wounds. And finally, as if all that were not enough," he said, rather dryly I thought, "he did this!"

Stevenage reached for the white cloth covering each of the bodies' loins, and gently removed both. "He has pounded their genitals with some kind of blunt instrument, it seems to me."

"Most observant, Stevenage," said Holmes. "What can you tell us about time and place of death, if anything?"

"As you say, 'if anything!'" rejoined the medical examiner. "Morbidity tells us little, as both bodies have been immersed naked in freezing water, most likely since shortly after their death."

"Yes, I see what you mean," remarked Holmes. "And complete absence of pooling of the blood is consistent with their having been tumbled about during those critical hours when lividity sets in. An educated guess?" he queried raising an eyebrow towards Stevenage.

"Without any commitment, my estimate would be in the region of eight to ten hours in the water."

"And they were fished out at . . .?" This time he cocked an eyebrow towards the constables.

"Noon, sir, or near enough," replied one of those stalwarts. "Both within ten minutes of each other, and less than a hundred paces apart they were, all caught up in the pilings by the Woolwich Ferry. Spotted by the flower sellers on the walk, and the constable on the beat signalled us in a few minutes later."

"Which puts time of death at around two to four in the morning," said Holmes to himself. "May I?" he asked Lestrade, moving to inspect the bodies more closely.

"I suppose it can do no harm, though what else you need to see is beyond me. It is clearly the work of some depraved fiend, who will sooner or later get caught in the act of his grisly trade; or else, like that damned Ripper, simply cease his campaign of terror one fine day, so that we never can find him out." Obviously an unfortunate topic for Lestrade to dwell upon! Holmes had lifted the head of the Asiatic and rotated it gently.

"In the previous cases, was the neck also broken *backwards*, as it were?" he enquired of Stevenage.

"Now that you ask, yes."

"And this bruising at both wrists and ankles?"

"Again, yes, but I assumed this was the result of being carried to the river's edge for disposal. My report at the time indicated the possibility of an accomplice to the crime, but the consistency of the wounds and mutilations indicates one murderer. I think he would be both tall enough that the victim would be looking upwards at him, thus exposing his neck to the cord - and strong enough to strangle a large man cleanly. You see, there are no other contusions around the neck area. It is also likely that the victims knew the killer well, for he must have been close up, and unsuspected, in order to kill like this. All this is in my report," concluded Stevenage.

"Signs of 'interference' with any of the victims?" asked Holmes.

"Other than the mutilation, none that we could detect. Have to check these two, but as I said, this is an exceptionally consistent killer, even more so than our friend Jack – and I had the dubious privilege of seeing his handiwork at the time; sort of my internship, you might call it."

"Have you finished your external examination?" asked Holmes. "May I examine for a moment before you commence?"

By this time Stevenage had donned a heavy apron, and was wielding a scalpel; he stepped back and allowed Holmes to examine the bodies minutely. At times searching for the articulation of bones beneath the flesh, then examining the wounds closely with his large glass, Holmes finally scrutinised the ligature marks around both necks. With a tweezers he removed a minute hair or fibre from the proud flesh around the welt of the European corpse, and folded it into a small paper in his pocket book.

"Thank you, Stevenage. Your examination has been most thorough, and essentially you have it right. I suspect that some of your conclusions will require a little revision as the case unfolds, but I must congratulate you on your powers of observation. Clearly, you have chosen the wrong profession."

Holmes uttered this with a completely straight face, but I fancy Lestrade flushed rather redder than before, and turned to leave.

Holmes consulted his pocket-watch, saying to me, "And we must be on our way as well, Watson. I doubt we will learn much from the location where the bodies were found; in any case, it is an area with which I am very familiar. Of far greater interest are the questions, 'Where were they tipped into the river, and where killed? Why two, and how were they killed by the same man so closely together that the killing of one should surely have alerted the other?'"

As we emerged from the gloom of the mortuary, Holmes said cheerfully, "Well, things are looking up, don't you think?" and set off in the direction of

Pall Mall. "We must take a cab if we are to keep our appointment with Mycroft, but we have time to walk a little first. Ah, London! – How I have missed its grimy streets and essentially English villainy."

With this, the first and greatest consulting detective in Europe strode off, leaving me to struggle with my umbrella, which had been turned inside out by the whipping wind. I hurried after him, wondering yet again what he had seen in that clinical chamber of horror, where all I had seen was the cruelty and devastation of which man is capable.

CHAPTER IV

"FINALLY," I thought, "here is my opportunity; before anything else interrupts, I shall have my answer."

We had walked as far as Stepney Market before Holmes hailed a cab, and now we were sitting privately in as much comfort as a London cab allows I was determined to have my satisfaction.

"Holmes," I ventured, "I have noticed that, today, whenever you have made reference to your travels and adventures in Asia, you have used the plural. 'We; our; us', and so forth. As I know you are unlikely to affect the royal 'we'; is it unreasonable to ask . . . That is to say, well, had you a companion on those travels?"

If I were to be absolutely honest with myself, there was perhaps just a small streak of personal jealousy niggling at my less honourable characteristics. Until now, *I* had enjoyed being Holmes's companion in many of his investigations, and had been personally involved in many of the adventures resulting therefrom.

Underlying this, however, was that very fact – that in my role as unofficial biographer to Holmes, I felt obliged to account for those 'missing years', and I had not been present during any of that period. I knew well that, for all his energy when once on a scent, Holmes was entirely hopeless when it came to rendering an account of his own adventures, even though most of our 'cases' required mere days, or perhaps weeks, to bring to a conclusion. How, then, could I expect any coherent and comprehensive report of his three years of wandering?

But if there had been a companion! Perhaps he had taken notes, kept records - anything! I had speculated idly on just this matter for the last half day, and had hardly dared to expect the reply which Holmes, looking straight ahead the while, addressed to me.

"My most dear Watson, how can you think so ill of me! It is as well, given your wounds, that you were not with me on some of the more demanding of our adventures, but I never once forgot my Boswell. The answer, Watson, is that not only did I have a companion in adventure, but that he was with me, with only a few short interludes, virtually the entire period I was gone."

This was excellent news indeed, but Holmes continued. "There is more. I, also, required a record of the entire journey, as we were acting at all times on behalf of the Foreign Office - specifically, at the request of Mycroft. Ironically, we were also acting on behalf of the *Quai d'Orsay*.

"I suppose, "said Holmes with a mischievous half-smile, "that as I already have Mycroft's consent, I had better stop torturing you, and let you know in confidence that my fellow adventurer was specifically enjoined to keep a journal of notes covering all of our travels. Furthermore, he is already known to you as the French translator of some of my monographs on crime and detection."

At this I turned to Holmes. "Francois le Villard!" I cried out. "Surely not?" scarcely daring to believe my good fortune.

Several years younger than Holmes, le Villard had been a rising young detective in the French detective service. In addition to translating some of his works, le Villard maintained an irregular correspondence with Holmes, and had consulted him on at least two occasions since Holmes had extended his practice to the Continent some years before. Praise from Holmes was ever high praise indeed, and I recalled his comment that le Villard possessed two of the three qualities most necessary to the ideal detective: the power of observation and that of deduction, and was wanting only in experience, which would come in time.

I reflected that, having spent three years on the road with Holmes, le Villard would no longer lack for experience.

"It is so," said Holmes simply. "You will also be gratified to know that le Villard carried one or two volumes of our cases when we set out, and only parted with them when we had to decide on books or food in our packs. But keep a journal he did, or rather, a series of them. Two of the first three volumes he sent back to his home from Persia, and again from Khartoum, for safekeeping at his mother's place in Marseilles. The first and the most recent of the four volumes, dealing with our adventures at Tibet and at Siam, are locked in my chest at Baker Street, and as soon as I get the opportunity to unpack, you shall have them. They should keep you occupied until le Villard arrives, when he will no doubt arrange to deliver the remaining volumes to you."

"Le Villard is coming to London - why, that's wonderful." I was already planning my interviews with him. "When, may I ask?"

"Mycroft received word from Malta yesterday - Le Villard is travelling aboard the clipper ship *'White Bird'* arriving from Singapore within the week, in company with Prince Phichai, the Siamese special envoy. Mycroft's counterpart at the *Quai d'Orsay* will cross the Channel immediately he receives Mycroft's telegram, and will attend our first little conclave. Now, here we are at Mycroft's club; you must be patient a little longer, but your patience will be amply rewarded, I assure you."

We debouched from the cab in front of the stately edifice of the Diogenes Club, that unique institution of which Sherlock Holmes's elder brother Mycroft was a founding member. Dedicated to the principle of remaining the club of choice for the most unclubable gentlemen in London, the Diogenes eschewed talking or indeed, any communication, within the premises, on pain of expulsion for a third offence. This rule was relaxed only in the Stranger's Room, and after Holmes had presented his card to the concierge, we were shown to this island in a sea of silence to await Mycroft's arrival.

Only a minute or two had elapsed before Mycroft appeared at the glass-paned door leading from the club proper. He was a tall man; at least as stout as when I had last seen him, and still retained the aura of supreme intelligence that had so impressed me at our previous encounter. Waiting until the door was firmly closed behind him, he and Sherlock Holmes contemplated each other for a brief moment. Mycroft crossed to where Holmes stood.

"Welcome home, Sherlock - it is indeed wonderful to have you back, safe and sound." Mycroft strove to remain unemotional, but it was clear that he was immensely relieved at the safe return of his younger brother.

Holmes made no attempt to conceal his pleasure at seeing Mycroft again. Clasping Mycroft's extended hand firmly between both of his, Holmes said simply, "Mycroft, believe me, the pleasure is all mine. I have lost count of the number of times it seemed certain we should never return. Were it not for your strategic assistance at times, le Villard and myself should have perished many times over."

Mycroft summoned refreshments, and we repaired to a grouping of lounge-chairs in a corner. Holmes lit a cigarette, and relaxed into the depths of his chair. "Splendid!" he remarked. "And now, Mycroft, to the business at hand, much as I should enjoy a good loll in your lounge-chair." He leaned forward, elbows on knees, saying, "I do think the first order of business should be to acquaint the good Doctor with at least the basics of our campaign, as it began and as it developed in time."

"Precisely," replied Mycroft. "My apologies for avoiding you during Sherlock's absence, Watson, but we both felt that for the sake of yourself and your late wife, it was wisest to keep you well insulated from these scoundrels. Please allow me also to express my sadness at the untimely demise of your Mary, before going on to happier things."

"Thank you, Mycroft. I have had time to learn to accept the unacceptable. What I am having trouble with right now is coming to terms with the return of your brother; it still seems utterly fantastic."

Holmes spoke, "The way things are going, I'd better watch my step, or I'll have survived the rigours of the East only to succumb in London, on my own doorstep as it were."

"And exactly how *are* things going, Sherlock?" enquired Mycroft, "if Doctor Watson will allow us a minute or two to cover the ground, before I return to the main purpose of this meeting. You will understand, Doctor, that Sherlock and I have been in constant communication since his arrival, but only by telegraph and messenger. This is our first chance to talk at length."

"Of course," I replied, rising, "shall I leave you in private?"

"Not at all, quite the contrary, as you shall soon see. From henceforth, Doctor; if you accept the commission I shall shortly propose to you, it will be imperative that you remain cognisant of the many aspects of our far-flung investigation. Now, Sherlock - report."

Holmes extinguished his cigarette in an ashtray, and proceeded to do just that - report. I must confess that I, who had known Holmes for so long, had never yet seen this humble side of Holmes.

"As to Moran, our little venture has paid handsome dividends. He has gone to ground in Greenwich, and the Irregulars have him under close surveillance. I doubt he will make any move before dark, but we have plans to cover that contingency. I shall turn my attention to that matter as soon as we take our leave of you. This will certainly be of interest," said Holmes, handing Mycroft the envelope containing Colonel Moriarty's note.

While Mycroft read the note, Holmes lit another cigarette.

"Continue!" commanded Mycroft, as he read the letter a second time.

"Very well. The failure to assassinate me last night, compounded by allowing us to turn the tables and seize the hunter, has no doubt caused heads to roll, but they will certainly not give up. This is proven by the resources employed to free Moran, at the risk of compromising some of their highly-placed minions."

They then carried on a conversation regarding the possible candidates amongst the officials involved, which caused me to reflect that, if the commission Mycroft had spoken of were to involve keeping up with these two, I should withdraw my candidacy or risk my sanity. As much was left unsaid as was spoken aloud - and we had been only a few minutes with Mycroft.

Turning back to me, Mycroft continued, "I ordered Colonel Moriarty watched, at the time of his letters to the press, but it seems he spends most of his time abroad. No great surprises there; at least now we have flushed him out. We do know that it was Colonel Moriarty who obtained the air gun from von Herder, and who provided the information as to your reappearance in London. I shall send a messenger around to your rooms this evening with a copy of my most recent dossier on Colonel Moriarty. You'll need to know some of it; I had the good fortune to unearth an old Indian Army colleague of his, who provided a great deal of insight into his character.

"Finally, Sherlock, once Le Villard and Prince Phichai have landed, I shall notify you as to the time of our appointment to review the situation at Siam. I expect this to take place as soon as M. de Benoist can get over here and the Prime Minister has a free hour.

"And now, Doctor, as I have a most pressing engagement, let us discuss your commission. Much has happened since last we met; not the least of which is that I have made the time to read all of your previous accounts of Sherlock's cases. I have also discovered that I am not alone in my appreciation of those most instructive and entertaining reports; indeed the distinguished personage on whom I shall shortly be calling has on several occasions made it evident that she is also your most distinguished reader."

I acknowledged this compliment with some embarrassment, and Mycroft continued.

"This, as it eventuates, is most convenient. Her Majesty has been informed of Sherlock's return, and in broad terms, was kept informed of his activities during his absence. Immediately she learnt that he had penetrated to Lhasa, and had spent some time there with the chief lamas, I was commanded to arrange for a full report of his travels to be compiled. When I suggested that I could think of none better suited to this task than Doctor Watson, her delight was clearly apparent, and she remarked that for once she could look forward to her official reading, as she was sorely tried just now, and in need of some amusement.

"In brief, then, should you choose to accept this assignment, you will be officially retained by the Foreign Office to compile what will be termed *The*

Holmes Report, covering the entire period of Sherlock's absence. You will report to me; the entire account is to be regarded as strictly confidential, and you will be required to sign the usual papers. The report will be printed and bound in a very limited number of copies, which will be circulated only as necessary within the appropriate departments of the government. Following review and amendment where required, a copy will be made available to the *Quai*. All copies, once read, will be collected and archived under seal for some considerable time, so this will not be one of your best-sellers, I'm afraid, Doctor Watson. Potential international complications may well develop from some of the situations involved here, with complications reaching into the highest levels of governments, major and minor. The royal houses of several nations have been involved, as you will discover. Nevertheless, what your readership lacks in numbers, it makes up in distinction, and that must be your consolation. For myself, I would not have this report from any other pen, and I look forward to reading it.

"I have already arranged for a generous stipend to allow you to concentrate on the task. Your primary source materials will be the journals kept by le Villard. At Sherlock's request he was seconded from the French police to this expedition, which was fully funded by the British government. The initial aims of the expedition were certain to be of mutual interest to both governments however, as both have compelling reasons to fear Russian expansion across Central Asia, and our quid pro quo for le Villard's involvement was the sharing of intelligence in that direction.

"Obviously, you will interview Sherlock, and le Villard while he is here, on any further clarifications you may need, and, where possible, I shall provide the background from the point of view of the Foreign Office. Should you require information from any other government department, I shall arrange for that - you may contact me at my office, or through Sherlock - and you may work either at Whitehall, where I can easily make a private room available, or at a place of your own choice.

"Well, Doctor, what do you say to that?" concluded Mycroft.

"Quite simply, I understand and accept the conditions, and I accept. So far as I am concerned, have the papers prepared for my signature, and I shall be ready to start at once. As to place of work, I should think Baker Street the ideal location; that is, if Holmes has no objections. I should then be able to pester him for those small details without which any report is incomplete."

"My dear Watson, of course you are welcome; in fact, I was going to suggest that, as you are once again on your own, and your old bedroom upstairs is still vacant, why not move back in at 221B?"

"Thank you, Holmes - I think that, for a while yet, I should prefer to remain where I am, as it is convenient to my current practice. Some time in the future I may well take you up on that offer if it stands. However, there is much to be said for my moving back in temporarily, at least until I have a clear grasp of the material, if that is all right with you?"

"Done!" said he, and rose to make our farewells, but Mycroft said, "I shall see you out, as I must be on my way as well."

Gathering our street apparel at the cloakroom, Mycroft addressed Holmes again.

"You will keep me posted on all developments, of course. Now, Sherlock, I must leave for the Palace to persuade Her Majesty that we don't have another Ripper loose in the streets. You know the rumours that flew about at that time; she wishes to avoid a repetition. The cabinet, including the Prime Minister, were unanimous in deputising to myself that unenviable task, therefore go I must."

We parted at the foot of the steps.

I had known some little of Mycroft before this, and had suspected more. That he held a high and confidential position in the government was clear. That Holmes considered Mycroft to have the keener intellect of the two brothers; that he lived a life of absolute regularity, so far as humanly possible - dividing his time between his rooms and his club at Pall Mall, and his offices at Whitehall; all this I knew. But I must confess my surprise at discovering the levels at which Mycroft really operated.

As we waited for a cab, I remonstrated mildly with Holmes. "It is abundantly clear, Holmes, that you have not yet fully apprised me of Mycroft's true status - as far as I was aware, he held some small office in the government!"

"Officially, that is correct. I did not know you so well in those days. One has to be discreet when one talks of high matters of state. You are right in thinking that he is under the British government. You would also be right in a sense if you said that occasionally he *is* the British government."

"My dear Holmes!" was all I could think to reply to this outrageous remark, as we climbed into a cab and were driven away towards Baker Street.

"I thought I might surprise you. Mycroft draws four hundred and fifty pounds a year, remains a subordinate, has no ambitions of any kind, will receive neither honour nor title, but remains the most indispensable man in the country."

"But how?"

"Well, his position is unique. He has made it for himself. There has never been anything like it before, nor will there ever be again. He has the tidiest and most orderly brain, with the greatest capacity for storing facts, of any man living. The same great powers that I have turned to the detection of crime he has used for this particular business. The conclusions of every department are passed to him, and he is the central exchange, the clearing-house, which makes out the balance. All other men are specialists, but his specialism is omniscience. We will suppose that a minister needs information as to a point which involves the Navy, India, Canada and the bimetallic question; he could get his separate advices from various departments upon each, but only Mycroft can focus them all, and say offhand how each factor would affect the other. They began by using him as a short cut, a convenience; now he has made himself an essential. In that great brain of his everything is pigeonholed and can be handed out in an instant. Again and again his word has decided the national policy. He lives in it. He thinks of nothing else save when, as an intellectual exercise, he unbends if I call upon him and ask him to advise me on one of my little problems."

"Quite amazing! An admirably concise portrait, I might add, more's the pity?"

"Why so?" asked Holmes.

"Well, as I am constrained to secrecy regarding this whole affair, I shall be unable to use it."

"Yes, I see what you mean. Tell me, you have already written of Mycroft, have you not?"

"Indeed; in connection with the matter of Kratides, the Greek interpreter; why do you ask?"

"In spite of his official reticence, Mycroft has his small vanities as well, and I recall his pleasure at his inclusion in your narrative. So long as his role in this present matter is not made public, I see no reason why you should not include the description I have just provided in your preamble to some other adventure in which he plays a role, some affair which takes place entirely on British soil. There will be others, you know - in addition to helping me out when I am stuck on some aspect of a case, Mycroft has occasion at times to call for my assistance in his more delicate affairs of state. Besides, it is merely a portrait, and can as well be included in some other adventure as in this - call it artist's licence; your select group of readers will surely approve."

Grey dusk was settling on London and the lamplighters were about their business as we arrived at home, as I still thought of 221B Baker Street in my own mind.

"So many questions;" I mused, "at least now I am assured of some answers."

As Holmes and I went inside I noticed Wiggins sidling back into his watcher's doorway.

"No messages as yet, Mrs. H.?" enquired Holmes as she opened the door to us.

"No indeed, sir," replied Mrs Hudson. "Will you have your dinner in now, and Doctor Watson – I've made enough, just in case?"

"Oh! I think let us enjoy a pipe before the fire for a half-hour or so; then I think some of your most excellent cooking would be extremely well received. You will stay, Watson?"

"Nothing could please me more; and thank you Mrs. Hudson, most thoughtful of you."

Once we were comfortably disposed, with tobacco and spirits to hand, and the fire crackling in the grate, Holmes remarked that it was high time he began his account of the three years which were to be the subject of *The Holmes Report*.

CHAPTER V

HOLMES MADE himself comfortable in the wing-backed leather armchair, firelight casting his keen profile into silhouette. He had chosen his old straight stemmed briar, and was enjoying the ritual of lighting up. I reflected that this was a man consciously learning to settle back into some form of domesticity after years spent in the barren wilds and steaming climes of Asia, frequently not knowing where he should rest on the morrow.

How different, and tame, it must all seem!

"Last night I told you of my narrow escape from death at the hands of Professor Moriarty. Also, that I escaped from the immediate area of the Reichenbach Falls under cover of darkness, and then made my way over the mountains to Florence, at which place I felt confident enough of my anonymity to risk contact with Mycroft. We have time at present. Let me fill in those gaps, which the urgency of last night's events precluded.

"Mycroft, who had believed me dead in the week that passed until then, took train immediately to see me – and you must know what pain that caused Mycroft, who abhors public transportation. We agreed that it was most unwise for me to attempt to return to my practice, at least until Moran and the others who escaped the dragnet were captured and convicted; also that the fiction of my demise should be allowed to stand. Within days, news of my death was common knowledge, as we intended."

"All the same, Holmes, I should have appreciated just a line or a word from you, if only a line . . ."

Holmes interrupted me, not unkindly. "That, above all, was my most profound regret, for I knew you should blame yourself endlessly for leaving me there at the falls. I should have given almost anything to ease your mind as to that. I say 'almost anything' because had you maintained your connection with me at that time, I should not have been able to ensure that yourself and your Mary would avoid becoming involved. These are men who will stop at nothing, and stoop to anything, to ensure the success of their evil designs. Take that also as a warning for the present time; we are still in extreme danger, even as we sit here, and were Mary still with us I should not agree to your involvement at all, even as historian. Therefore, do be on your guard!"

This was quite like old times, and for a moment it seemed as though the great hiatus in his London career had never occurred at all.

Holmes continued, puffing away. "If I could not return to London, the question arose as to just what I should do with myself – how could I employ my talents when all of Europe thought I was dead. Mycroft, of course, had the answer all planned out. It only remained for me to agree, and Mycroft, being seven years older than myself, knew exactly how to make his plan appealing to me."

"I shall ask Mycroft to give you a run-down on the political and economic aspects of the 'Great Game', as the continual tug-of-war for influence in Central Asia is known. On the one hand, Britain striving to protect its influence in India and now Burma; on the other, Russia threatening to sweep down the steppes to block the way to the interior of China and establish themselves along the northern marches of the Indian territories.

"As it turned out, le Villard and I stumbled into something at Lhasa which resulted in our hasty departure, and led us on across the roof of Asia. To Samarkand and beyond, then down through Persia and briefly to Mecca, and finally to Siam, we followed the hidden trails of conspiracies that threatened the interests of the British Empire in half a dozen of its spheres of influence. Unravelling the skeins of those tangles of leads and dead-ends required the next two years of our lives, and has now brought me full circle, back to London . . . and, it seems, to another Moriarty!

"I also found, as we journeyed far afield, that what I had taken – at the time leading up to Reichenbach – for the whole conspiracy, was in fact not more than the British and European chapters thereof, so to speak. That Professor Moriarty *was* the overall leader is certain, but his demise and the breaking up of his London gang caused but little inconvenience to the plotters overseas, as we have seen. Now they carry on, both here and abroad, under new leadership - increasing their influence in subtle ways, and secretly planning for something momentous, we know not what. But I shall have them, Watson, mark my words!"

Holmes had spoken with increasing intensity as he hinted for the first time at the nature of his chosen prey, and I sensed once again the suppressed rage that I had noticed before. I felt certain that Holmes would track these villains down, at whatever price to himself, and see that just retribution - as he understood it - was exacted.

"But back to the 'Great Game'! Mycroft had come into possession of certain unofficial communications between Lhasa and St. Petersburg that were the cause of great concern to the Foreign Office. The long and short of it is that he wanted me to proceed to Darjeeling for training, by a retired *pundit* from the Great Trigonometrical Survey, to fit me for a journey in disguise to Lhasa - the Forbidden City. This, as I soon learnt, was no light undertaking. No European had penetrated to Lhasa for almost a century; those who tried were either turned back, or killed if they got too close to Lhasa, and any Tibetan found to have aided an interloper in any way was most gruesomely murdered, as were his family. The ramparts of the highest mountains in the world shield them effectively, as does their isolation on a vast and lonely plateau on the roof of the world. Even Indians are not allowed to enter, although there are several border tribes permitted to cross into Tibet, though not so far as Lhasa. To attempt to penetrate to their capital, I should need the most convincing of disguises, for the lamas are extremely suspicious of all travellers, and as their lives depended on it, the entire population seemed to consider themselves detectives. Additionally, so I was briefed, the country is garrisoned by Chinese Mohommedans who are even more xenophobic about Tibet, as they must answer to Peking, which is controlled by the Manchu Emperors for whom these regions are their hereditary and mystical homelands.

"This seemed an impossible task, and so of course I accepted the challenge, as Mycroft knew I should. Mycroft carried a dossier covering the basics of my training, which should begin immediately I boarded ship. Native speakers of the appropriate dialects of Hindi, Pushtu and Tibetan had been arranged to provide intensive language tuition - also Persian so that I could pass as a Persian, which was a disguise more suited to my features and physical characteristics. It was the mention of Persian which interested me so, for I was loath to undertake such a venture alone, and yet most reluctant to entrust my security and perhaps my life to another. I recalled that my younger friend and sometime colleague, Francois le Villard, had spent several years in the French possessions in North Africa and the Middle East. There he had attained near fluency in Persian and several other Arabic tongues, and was proficient in Pushtu as well. Le Villard also kept himself in excellent physical condition, and had considerable mountaineering experience dating back to his youth in the French Alps.

"When I enquired of Mycroft whether there was any reason why I should not ask le Villard to accompany me, Mycroft approved immediately, as he already knew of him in connection with those cases about which le Villard had consulted me over the previous years. France, it seems, was as concerned about their Indochinese possessions as we about India; in fact, the intercepted Russian communication was provided to him personally by de Benoist, his counterpart at the *Quai d'Orsay*. Mycroft then began pulling his strings, with the result that le Villard, whom I had seen only several months previously at Nimes, was relieved of all duties in Paris and within two days had joined us at Florence.

"There we made arrangements for our journey, which at that time we thought would occupy less than one year, including our training. Outfitting took very little time, as we would carry little, and most of that would be purchased locally at Darjeeling, or supplied by our *pundit*."

Holmes' pipe was smoked out and cooling by now; he tapped it out on the fire-guard, and proceeded to recharge it with tobacco from his pouch. I dared not interrupt, for I was already fascinated, and wanted to hear all of it.

That, however, was to be as far as we got, as Mrs. Hudson wheeled in a trolley with our meal under covers, and with the assistance of the maid, set out our supper. Neither of us had taken lunch, and so before long we were relaxing with port and a Havana cigar apiece.

We received two further visitors that evening. Firstly, a messenger arrived from Mycroft, bearing the dossier on Colonel Moriarty in a manila envelope displaying the seal of the Foreign Office. Almost immediately, the bell rang again, and the maid showed in Wiggins.

"No activity 'ereabouts, Mr. 'Olmes, but before I takes off and leaves Jem on guard, I'll just report on 'ow it is with Colonel Moran at present."

Taking a scrap of paper from his vest pocket, he consulted it at arm's length.

"Been in 'is room all day, top floor, rear left, only comin' out to visit the lav'. All 'is meals is taken up to 'is room, and the maids 'ave been told to stay out. No visitors to the room, but round dusk a blighter shows up with two pigeons in covered cages; 'ear 'em cooin', we could. They was delivered to the 'allway outside the Colonel's room, and when our Ellie peeked ten minutes later, the birds 'ad gone, cages an' all.

"Then, about 'alf an hour later, 'is winder opens and out flies one o' the little beauties, and Jem as seen it swears there was somethin' strapped to its leg. Another 'alf hour or so, and back flies a different bird, only this one flies straight to the coop on the roof. Now our Mr. Moran's room 'as a door givin' on to that roof, so Jem shimmies up a tree for a look, an' sure enough, out comes the Colonel and removes somethin' from the bird. So it looks like 'e's got chums someplace, Mr. 'Olmes!"

"Thank you, Wiggins. Nothing further? Very well, here are your instructions. It seems as though he is settled for the evening, but to be certain you must maintain your watch on the place. Knock me up immediately if he moves, and for heavens sake, don't lose him.

"He still has one of the pigeons that were delivered. I deduce that the first was used to establish contact, and prepare for his removal to a safer place on the morrow. I suspect they need the evening to prepare for this, and that final instructions will be sent, most likely tomorrow morning. The second of Moran's birds will be used to confirm that Moran has received the escape plan, and that the coast is still clear. It remains only to intercept that message, and with luck we shall be able to follow Moran to the lair of his superiors, or even arrive there before him. At that time we must decide whether to move in and seize them, or to carry on tracking them."

He made no reference to a method for intercepting a message attached to a high-flying bird, and the more I considered the problem the more difficult it seemed. Firearms would bring it to ground, but then Moran would be alerted and the element of surprise forfeit. An accurate marksman with a slingshot may be able to bring a bird to ground without killing it, but of this he could not be certain. There was always the possibility that Holmes was planning to infiltrate one of the Irregulars up to the roof, but then came the risk that at the slightest noise Moran would open his door and discover the intruder. I considered several further schemes, each less likely to succeed than the one preceding it, until finally I gave it up.

Holmes obviously had his plan ready to hand, for he paid no further attention to the matter, other than to advise me to prepare for an early start the next morning. And with that he rose, assured that I would be comfortable, and bade me a good night.

The manila envelope containing Mycroft's dossier on Colonel Moriarty remained where he had left it on the sideboard, seal still intact. Holmes's chest, containing le Villard's journals, rested on the floor beside his chemical workbench, still locked. It had been a long day for myself, even longer for Holmes, and I thought he was quite right to put off both matters until we had rested well. I went up to bed.

DAY TWO

APRIL 7TH 1894

CHAPTER VI

HOLMES STOOD AT the hearth, where kindling had just been lit under the morning fire. He had upended the ashtray on the mantelpiece, and was busily scraping amongst yesterday's debris.

"Ah! I see you still favour plugs and dottles as your before-breakfast pipe-mixture," said I, entering the sitting room.

"We'll have time only for tea and toast, which I've already ordered," said Holmes in reply, lighting his foul-smelling pipe with satisfaction. "Billy has been sent for a cab; we have just enough time to stop at your rooms and pack up your things. He can bring them back here while we carry on." Drinking down my tea, I remembered that bird hunting was to be our occupation this morning, specifically, pigeon-hunting.

Baker Street was wreathed in early-morning fog, an occasional lumiere still glowing against the pale wintry light of a London dawn as we clattered away towards my rooms at Kensington. Holmes remained silent as we passed through the awakening streets, and even after I had packed a Gladstone bag with my belongings and sent it back to Baker Street in the care of Billy, and we were again rattling along, he remained silent. Evidently Holmes had informed the cabby as to our destination while I had been in my apartments, and it was not until we approached the lower quarter of Lambeth, and I was remembering having passed this way before, that he shook off those thoughts with which he had been preoccupied.

"Yes, Watson, we have a challenge for old Sherman," said he, as we turned in to Pinchin Lane and came to a halt in front of No. 3. The last time I had been here had been to collect Toby the drag-hound, at the time of the case of *The Sign of Four*. On that occasion Old Sherman had at first greeted my midnight knock-up by threatening to dump a viper on my head from the second-floor window, until I mentioned the name 'Sherlock Holmes'.

Sherman himself appeared just then at his door, braces loose around his thighs and traces of lather on his scraggly chin, a straight razor in hand.

"Mr. Sherlock, well I'll be," he cried, recognising Holmes. "Toby again?"

"Good morning to you, Sherman. No, not this time. May we come in?"

The old naturalist and bird-stuffer – for that was his profession – waved us inside, where the now-familiar rows of caged animals of all descriptions lined both sides of the narrow rooms leading through to the back of the building.

"My apologies for the uncivil timing of our call, but it is imperative that we get an early start if we are to have a chance of success," said Holmes. The old naturalist waved this away, saying that when your trade was in live animals you must rise well before the sun, and that he had already mucked out and fed his charges before attending to his own belated toilet.

"So, 'oo will it be this time, Mr. Sherlock?" enquired Sherman as he turned and led us to cage No. 7 on the left, where old Toby lay quietly, seemingly uninterested in visitors. "Good thing it weren't Toby as you wanted, Mr. Sherlock. Gettin' on, is our old Toby. Sense of smell's goin' as well, hain't been out draggin' in a while now, but I takes 'im for walks down by riverside and lets 'im snuffle 'round a bit fer old times sake."

"Yourself, Sherman, is who; if you are free for the morning, for I think that is all that will be required. And my Lady Gwendolyn, if she has not also succumbed to advancing years. "

"Ah, Lady Gwendolyn is it. Don't worry yerself about neither matter, Mr. Sherlock. Lady Gwendolyn's in the prime o' life, and as fer meself, if it's a week yer needs, well, yer only 'as ter say so."

We proceeded through the house, passing an assortment of animals, including a chimp which Sherman informed us used to be one of the finest jewel-thieves in London - so long as no food was closer to hand - until his former master and trainer was sent away for the thefts. A small crocodile, which he had bought young from a lascar off a ship, now lazed around in the back yard.

"Not much trouble with intruders now," said Sherman as we crossed the rear courtyard to the large cage set against the rear wall. "And how's me Lady today?" he enquired of the occupant, as he reached for a large glove of thick leather, and slipped the latch on the cage door.

Personally, I was glad to leave the crocodile behind, however tame, and before long our cab had deposited us all, Holmes and myself, Sherman and Lady Gwendolyn, in a small riverside park-area across from Greenwich Observatory. We had a clear view of the top floor of the Sailor's Retreat, whilst we were somewhat shielded from view by the foliage should Moran venture onto his rooftop terrace. The area was deserted at this hour, and our only companions were the wheeling gulls whose thin mewing drifted to us across the water along with that distinctive smell of Thames riverside.

Holmes lit a pipe, looking around as though expecting someone - who shortly enough appeared in the form of Wiggins. A brief conversation followed, which I did not hear as I was assisting Sherman with the cage. Wiggins disappeared back into the narrow alley from which he had emerged, and Holmes strolled back to us, puffing nonchalantly on his pipe as though he were taking the river air, rather than on the trail of an escaped killer.

"So far, so good. Moran is still in his room, no birds in or out since last evening. We are in time, for I feel certain they will send a message to move him as soon as arrangements can be made - then, I think, we will have sport for Lady Gwendolyn." Saying this, Holmes placed himself squarely before the large cage, which we had placed on the broad coping of the park wall under the canopy of an old oak.

He stood, arms akimbo, intently studying the peregrine falcon, which bird equally intently fixed its glare on Holmes, and for a moment the two hunters remained with gazes locked. "Trained to hunt and trap, you say, not to kill."

"Mewed right in me own back courtyard, was Lady Gwendolyn," said Sherman, as he reached into the cage with gloved hand and hooded the fierce vulpine head before removing the falcon from its cage. "She earns 'er mice by trapping birds for me ter sell or stuff, so she's trained to bring 'er catch back to me alive. Now then, Mr. Sherlock, what's yer job?"

"Our quarry is in that top floor room," said Holmes, indicating Colonel Moran's eyrie with his stick, "and has already sent and received messages by carrier-pigeon. We know he has colleagues elsewhere in London, probably nearby, and that he is most likely expecting another message the same way." Holmes indicated the direction of flight of yesterday's birds.

"Obviously this safe-house has been prepared well in advance against just this kind of situation, and on the off-chance that the fugitive may have been followed, or that a messenger may be intercepted, a bird-loft was installed and maintained, with a door to that room. Ingenious and seemingly fool-proof! Birds are delivered - perfectly normal; messages are delivered direct by air; no compromise or diversion is considered possible. I am hopeful they will not think it necessary to cipher their messages.

"We should, with a little luck, be able to pluck the message out of the air, read it and replace it, and then send it on its way undamaged. If Moran sends a reply it will surely come swiftly, and we may intercept it in the same way. We are sufficiently distant, I hope, but perhaps not. Much depends on what Moran does, whether he lingers to watch his bird or darts back inside."

Sherman winked knowingly at Holmes. "Ah, so we're *followin'*, are we? Well, my Lady Gwendolyn will snatch them pigeons clean out o' the sky, and deliver 'em 'ere with nary a feather ruffled. Nothin' simpler, 'ey, me beauty."

We stamped around under our tree in a vain attempt to keep warm, and kept an alert eye for any speck which may prove to be a bird, especially if moving in a straight line, as though with a purpose. Pigeons not being exactly rare in London, Holmes had brought a powerful telescope along, and with this he inspected those few birds that flew into our field of vision, ignoring the ever-circling gulls.

I have always thought the riverside to be most entertaining, with the constant variety of craft plying back and forth across the stream, or else dropping down the Thames bound for far-flung ports of the Empire and beyond, and returning therefrom laden with hard-won spoils. I found it difficult, therefore, to concentrate my vision on a patch of empty sky, especially when the deep and haunting sound of a ship's horn carried through the lingering fog over the water, tempting me to guess at her cargo and destination.

I must confess I was aroused from just such a reverie by Holmes's imperative cry to Sherman. "Look sharp, man! There it is, low over the warehouses and heading our way. I can clearly see a container through the glass." Squinting through his blue-tinted glasses in the direction indicated by Holmes's telescope, Sherman replied by removing the hood from the falcon and thrusting her into the air in the general direction of the carrier pigeon. "Hunt, me beauty!" he commanded.

With a loud and powerful sound the peregrine rose swiftly into the air until well above the unsuspecting pigeon, then folded wings to body and dropped like a rock. Just above her prey, wings spread, she swooped into a shallow dive and seized the pigeon in outstretched talons, then spiralled down to where Sherman stood with his gauntleted forearm raised. The falcon seemed to hover briefly, wings flapping backwards, while she deposited the pigeon – alive and unharmed – into a canvas sack held by her master. Then she settled onto his glove, to be rewarded with a live mouse from a small bag, then hooded again. Old Sherman had murmured softly all the while, just as though she could hear and understand, encouraging her along, and although there seemed no affection involved, withal it was the most astonishing display of rapport between man and creature.

More importantly, in a canvas sack we had both carrier pigeon and message. Sherman placed Lady Gwendolyn back in her cage, and removed the pigeon from the canvas sack. A small metal container with a screw closure was attached to its leg, and from this Holmes removed a folded sheet of thin paper.

"Quickly, Watson. Jot this down, then we'll send this bird on its way."

Holmes read out a succession of words, which, although English, made no sense as a message. I furiously scribbled them down.

"Got that? Very well then," and he meticulously refolded the paper exactly as it had been, inserted it in the container, and handed this to Sherman, who reattached it to the pigeon. Holmes thought for a moment, then said, "Release the bird!"

The pigeon flew around a little uncertainly, then regained its bearings and homed in on its loft, disappearing into the coop on the roof-terrace of the Sailor's Retreat. Holmes motioned to us to conceal ourselves, which was easy thanks to the foliage, and used his spyglass. Almost immediately the roof doorway opened and a figure cautiously emerged, quickly crossed to the coop, and a minute or so later went back inside.

"Well, gentlemen, the first part of our campaign has worked flawlessly, though I still have not understood the message. Perhaps there will be a reply." He glanced at his pocket-watch, saying, "We will allow an hour, though I suspect it will be sooner if at all," then settled back unobtrusively against the bole of a large tree, and continued his vigil.

Sherman and I were discussing the merits of Toby's latest whelps as prospective drag-hounds some five minutes later when the figure re-appeared at the roof-top doorway. "It's Moran alright," said Holmes, tele-scope trained on a figure moving on the roof. Then, urgently, "Get back! Under cover quickly, he has a spy-glass as well. It's well that we chose this nook; I don't think he has spotted anything. Now he's releasing his second bird, with container. Are you ready, Sherman? Prepare yourself, though we may not be able to do this if he remains outside with his glass." Holmes was clearly exasperated as the pigeon slowly circled to get its bearings, then head-ed in our direction. "Confound it, man. Go back inside – Ah! Yes! That's right! Thank you, Colonel."

Turning to Sherman, who had prepared Lady Gwendolyn again for the hunt, he cried, "After that bird! Don't let it escape!" and Sherman once more thrust his falcon into the air. Once again she performed flawlessly the task for which she had been trained, and before long the pigeon was winging the ori-ginal of Colonel Moran's reply back to his shadowy friends. Meanwhile, my friend Sherlock Holmes had copies of both messages scrawled in my phys-icians' handwriting, to lead us, or so we hoped, to Moran and his villainous paymasters.

The morning was well upon us by this time. Holmes thanked old Sherman for his assistance, and thrust a generous payment upon him over Sherman's protest, adding that an extra mouse or two for Lady Gwendolyn would be most appropriate and well deserved. "People are starting to appear in some numbers and there are probably ordinances of some kind against hawking in a public area, so we should make ourselves scarce," said Holmes. He put Lady Gwendolyn and Sherman in one cab and sent them off, and hailed an-other to return us to Baker Street to examine our booty.

"If only every stratagem worked as smoothly as that, Watson!" remarked Holmes as we shed our coats and hats and went up to our sitting room. The fire still glowed in the grate, so I tipped more coals from the scuttle, tossed in a log or two, and gave a vigorous stir with the heavy brass poker, then stood warming my hands while Holmes, at the table, puzzled over the messages.

"Although not encrypted, thankfully, they appear to be using a private language. What are we to make of this?" Holmes chuckled as he handed me the first message, which I had written in block capitals.

'THIS NIGHT
PALACE
END
DRESS
DOG AND PONY
EIGHT'

He handed me the second slip of paper. "And of Moran's reply?"

'DONE
DURBAR'

I read the first, then the second, then both again. As when I had first scribbled them, both raised images in the mind, images of Queen Victoria surrounded by teams of dog carts and pony carts in the first case, and of a grand gathering of the Raja's and nabobs of Empire in the second. But neither made sense to me as a message to or from our fugitive Colonel Sebastian Moran. I said as much, causing Holmes to chuckle yet again.

"Although neither message would mean a thing to anyone who chanced upon it, when you once know the context it is mere child's play."

He retrieved both messages from my hand, and examined the first.

"*'THIS NIGHT'* is clear at least; *'PALACE'* we shall leave just for now; *'END'* implies the finish of some event; and *'DRESS'*, to a gentleman, means evening clothes – dress shirt, overcoat and topper. Put all those together and we have an instruction to Moran to come to meet our respondent at some palace or other, at the close of some event, and to dress for the occasion. Now we know that Moran was wearing evening clothes when captured, and we may reason that a crowded event would provide discreet cover for a rendezvous with a fugitive. But to return to *'PALACE'* – at which royal palace could such a fugitive appear at short notice without attracting attention?"

As this was clearly a rhetorical question, to which I had no answer anyway, I remained silent as he continued.

"Hand me one of those dailies, will you please?" and when I had done so

Holmes flicked through the pages until he found what he wanted. "Just as I thought. Other than Henry Wood's new Queen's Hall Orchestra, the only permanent orchestra in London is at Crystal Palace, and I suggest that it is *there*, at the close of tonight's performance, that our rendezvous will take place - excellent cover for a man in evening clothes, surrounded by similarly dressed swells. I expect Crystal Palace was chosen also because they have all made a party to there on some previous occasion, so that Moran would instantly understand."

"What then of *'DOG AND PONY'* and *'EIGHT'*?" I asked.

"Clearly you have not spent as much time with the criminal classes as either myself or Moran. In their argot a dog-and-pony show is put on for the benefit of a mark, so that the mark sees what the operator wants him to see. In this case I think we may expect some form of diversionary tactic at the Sailor's Home at eight o'clock tonight, to allow Moran to slip away in time to reach Crystal Palace. He would have several hours before the concert finishes - yes, it all fits!"

"And Moran's reply?"

"*'DONE'* and *'DURBAR'*. Ah! There is the payoff for the dogged sleuthhound, for unless I am mistaken, we have *two* ex-Indian Army officers communicating here; Moran is confirming that he will come, and requesting or demanding that all major figures involved in this conspiracy convene a meeting. Exactly as Mycroft hoped they would!"

"I must go out again, to interview Irene Adler's former dresser at Covent Garden. Will you forsake this blaze for the dubious delights of detection?" asked Holmes, as he went to the doorway of our sitting room to discuss some matter with Mrs. Hudson.

"Why Crystal Palace?" I asked myself as we drove along to the theatre. As every schoolchild knows, Crystal Palace was originally erected between Queen's Drive and Rotten Row in Hyde Park to house Prince Albert's Great Exhibition of 1851 - that first great showcase of the Empire and its achievements. Exotic objects from the fringes of civilisation, gleaming steam locomotives, working steam mills and fierce *papier-mâché* masks, totem poles and model bridges were all tumbled together from every corner of the farflung British Empire, and from a score of other countries as well. Proceeds from the Great Exhibition had established our Victoria and Albert, Natural History and Science Museums, and as every university student knows, Exhibition Scholarships.

Relocated the following year to Sydenham, Crystal Palace was now a well-established London landmark with its regular concerts and exhibitions, and a popular destination for families at weekends. But I could see no obvious reason why the conspirators had chosen such a distant rendezvous, and such a public one at that.

Even more intriguing, why interview Irene Adler's former dresser? I experienced a thrill of recognition at this, for this was a reference to the only woman to whom Holmes accorded equal respect - indeed, she had several times outwitted him. And yet, like so many events in these overwhelming few hours since Holmes first reappeared in my rooms, this was yet another mystery to be resolved. To the best of my knowledge, Irene Adler had perished in a boating accident on Lake Como, several months after fleeing London with Godfrey Norton at the conclusion of the case I have written up elsewhere as *A Scandal in Bohemia*. Holmes had been in London for some months both before and after the accident was reported, first in the Italian papers, and then throughout Europe and the Americas. Irene Adler, after all, was a woman of some renown, amongst other accomplishments having sung contralto at La Scala, and been prima donna at the Imperial Opera at Warsaw, before her retirement at an early age to London.

CHAPTER VII

WE ALIGHTED from our cab just around the corner from the entrance to the Royal Opera House at Covent Garden, where the matinee crowd was already queuing alongside the theatre wall for the cheaper seats. An old veteran of the Afghan campaigns was scraping away at his battered fiddle, open violin-case at his feet containing three or four small coins; his pitiable renderings of a tune popular twenty years before largely ignored by passers-by. Holmes reached into his vest pocket for some coins and bent over to place them in the instrument case. Exactly as he stooped, there came a familiar hissing, whizzing noise from across the broad street, and a loud report as a large chip of stone was blasted out of the wall, precisely where Holmes had been standing not one second before. A flattened slug of soft metal dropped at our feet, as Holmes scanned the opposite side of the street looking for the marksman, for both of us had recognised the distinctive sound of von Herder's air-gun.

The queued people adjacent started at the report and the flying stone chips, but were uncertain as to the cause; those a little further away seemed to have noticed nothing, and Holmes did not alarm them unnecessarily. Using his handkerchief he picked up the slug and placed it in his waistcoat pocket. Moving quickly away from the crowd, we entered the lobby of the famous theatre, the only stage in London to have been graced by Irene Adler before her retirement from a distinguished operatic career. I was only too happy to get off the street. I had read the report of the autopsy on the Hon. Ronald Adair, and realised just how close Holmes had come to the same violent extinction.

"So they have more than one weapon from von Herder - well, Lady Fortune has saved my life this time, and it's as well to know what we're up against. They won't try again here, but we must remain vigilant in public and private places both." With that he approached the uniformed doorman, presented his card, and enquired after the theatre manager's office. Several minutes with that worthy were sufficient to find out that Mischa, for that was the name of the dresser we had come to see, had left the theatre several years previously. He had come into some money and purchased an old building with the intention of refurbishing it for rental to other theatre people. He dropped in from time to time to see old acquaintances, but not for some time now.

The theatre manager then gave us Mischa's address, commenting that this was the second time today he had been asked the same questions, the first time by an uniformed police officer. I could see that Holmes was most curious about this official visit, but made no further queries.

Outside on the pavement the crowds had thickened, but the old fiddler had earned not one copper since we went inside. Holmes bade me hold his stick and coat, and slipped into a barred exit doorway, emerging several seconds later with dishevelled hair, disordered collar and cuffs, and scuffed shoes. Stepping over to the old fellow, Holmes discreetly slipped him a half-crown 'for the brief loan of your instrument', quickly re-tuned the strings and launched into a lively jig. This caught the attention of some of the waiting theatregoers, and when he followed on with a medley of popular favourites, coins began to sprinkle, and then rain into the battered violin-case. Holmes ability as an actor was such that he was taken at face value as a busker, for he looked almost as disreputable as the original. For several minutes Holmes entertained those patrons of the theatre, then finished up with a few brisk bars from God Save the Queen. He handed the fiddle back to the bewildered old fellow, bade him a good evening, and we walked away leaving him counting a large pile of copper and silver coins.

"The very least I could do, as I should now be dead were it not for his atrocious fiddling. You have never seen me as a busker, have you Watson. It is, I assure you, a most excellent guise when it is necessary to hang about on streets and corners for long periods. I have used the ploy successfully on many an occasion, and have even earned quite tidy sums while I was about it. Certainly it would be a safer occupation than consulting detective appears to be. This is the third time I have been shot at with an airgun, if you count the shots at my wax likeness. And that event certainly confirmed the deadly accuracy of the weapon. On the other occasion, quite frankly I was simply lucky. I cannot count on being so lucky a fourth time." He hailed a passing cab.

Our next destination was N°. 48 Islington High Road, in a seedy neighbourhood that had once been elegant. The buildings were of handsome proportions, laid out with some spaciousness, but the large houses were now divided into a multitude of small flats. Houses on either side of N°. 48, as far as could be seen, had gardens that were both overgrown and wild, or bare and muddy earth.

N°. 48, in contrast, was carefully tended and planted out most attractively following what appeared to be the architects' original intentions. The building was, like its neighbours, subdivided into small apartments, but again this had been done without undue violence to the original.

The entrance was under a portico at the side, down a short pathway lined with oleanders, rather than at the street front. Asking the jarvey to wait for us, Holmes and I rang at the polished brass bell-pull. Altogether, I thought, our Mischa has created an appealing residence for those of an artistic temperament, and judging by the cards in brass slots, his building was fully tenanted. According to the engraved brass plate, the basement flat was the *Office and Residence of M. M. Roborovsky, Building Proprietor and Manager*.

Alongside the entrance portico was a private stair with a black-painted door at the bottom. On a duplicate brass plate was the same legend, but repeated rings at the bell remained unanswered. Holmes sent me in search of a maid, while he continued ringing, muttering that he hoped we were not too late.

Locating the housekeeper in the main hallway, I convinced her to return with me. She became concerned, because she had been in sight of the entrance for the past hour, seeing to the parlour spring cleaning, and she had not seen M. Mischa depart.

"Besides, 'e never left without informin' either meself or Gilbert the yardman, an' 'e haint done neither because Gilbert 'as been 'elpin' me. Bit of a worry, that is. 'E was all right an hour ago when that policeman came to see 'im. And then that slip of a girl was down there just after, as well. But they both left. 'E never would let me 'ave a key to 'is flat, neither, but she 'as one alright."

At this Holmes cried, "Madam, send immediately for a doctor and find a policeman - a real policeman, for that was no genuine bobby you saw. And send Gilbert to us, we may need extra strength. Watson, help me to break down this door, and pray we are not too late." With that we threw ourselves bodily at the stout door, but it was not until Gilbert had arrived with reinforcement in the form of a large constable that we were able to force an entry, as all windows were barred against intruders.

When the door finally gave way we all tumbled in a heap in the hallway. Holmes instantly leaped to his feet, shouting, "Search every room, quickly!" Almost immediately came a cry from a room to the left, which Gilbert had entered. Rushing in to this office, which it clearly was, we all came to a halt, transfixed by the hideous sight behind the desk. Half-seated in the chair and arched over the back of it was a still-slender figure, elegantly clad and coifed. But the clothing had been torn open at the throat, the hair stood wildly in places as though violently raked through by those clutching fingers, and the thin frame was grotesquely distorted. He had vomited his whisky onto his waistcoat, and from his nose had flowed blood of a darkening cherry red colour. I had no doubt that Mischa, one-time dresser to Irene Adler, was quite dead. By this time, a general alert had been raised, with whistles blowing and curious onlookers gathering.

"I suggest we close the door until the Yard arrives, if it will still close," remarked Holmes to the constable. This was acted upon, and Holmes then introduced us, which seemed to satisfy the officer. Closer inspection of the corpse showed an unnaturally pink complexion; Holmes sniffed at the dead man's lips. "Symptoms appear to be those of acute cyanide poisoning," he said, confirming my own suspicions, "but there is no almond odour." A sniff at the glass of whisky close to the clawed hand corroborated this, and indicated that this was not the source of the toxin, if any. The whisky bottle also appeared to be unadulterated. There were no other glasses on the desk, which was uncluttered but disordered by the man's convulsions. The room itself had been thoroughly searched, and the small safe on the floor behind the desk was empty, door ajar.

We remained without further disturbing the body, other than to confirm death, until a knock on the door announced the arrival of Inspector Athelney Jones and his associates. Holmes and he were well acquainted, so there was no difficulty in relating our tale, leading up us to knocking at Mischa's door. The police surgeon, whom I knew quite well, inspected the corpse more closely than we had done, being official. He came to the conclusion that the victim had seemingly suffered a cardiac seizure, which caused death, but that the unnatural pinkness of the body gave sufficient cause for concern to order an autopsy. He reported as much to Jones, who took it all down rapidly in his shorthand, then added a few jottings of his own and put his notebook away.

"Care to take a look around, Mr. Holmes?" invited Jones, and they both carefully inspected the corpse, the glasses, the desk, and the room in general, Holmes in particular not missing any surface or space.

"Anything?" asked Jones when they had finished.

"The salient points? I suspect poisoning, specifically cyanide. No evidence of the poison or its container! Physically there seems to have been no coercion, if poison it was, but we don't know whether M. Roborovsky poisoned himself, or was poisoned unawares by either the false constable, or by the girl. He apparently was in the habit of answering his own door, as it gave directly onto stairs up to the front pathway. He also was forced to open his safe, or the keys were taken from his body, so it would appear that either valuables or documents were taken."

Holmes paused in his slow pacing, as though deciding whether or not to continue. He carried on. "Ever had a cyanide case before, Inspector?"

"Can't say as I have, Mr. Holmes. Why do you ask?"

"Cyanide in acute dosages can cause almost instantaneous death, but a healthy victim can stay alive for anywhere from minutes to hours. Clearly this was a massive dose, but either before or after being poisoned Mischa had time to scrawl several words with a theatrical grease pencil on the *underside* of his desk drawer," said Holmes. With a tug at the drawer-pull he released the tray from its slides, emptied the few contents onto the blotter-pad, and held the drawer up to the gilt-framed mirror mounted over the fireplace.

"The only difficulty is that, in writing upside down as it were, a man's natural writing is mirror-reversed."

The unintelligible scrawls on the base of the tray, when reflected in the glass resolved themselves into the crudely formed words *'Isobel. Dangerous. Warn '*, with the last word seeming to tail off into nothingness.

"What do you make of that, Jones?"

"Why, several possibilities, I'd say. If it turns out that the young lady who just left is this 'Isobel', it could mean that she's the poisoner, and that someone needs to be warned – but whom? Alternately," reasoned Athelney Jones, who was by no means a fool, "you seem to think the fellow in policeman's garb was the killer, and that fits with the message just as well. Mister ... the victim here, must have reason to think this Isobel is also in danger, and tries to warn her like this," he said, pointing at the shaky scrawl that had been all the dead man's last thoughts.

"We will check the movements of all constables assigned to this part of the city. Just why do you suspect the policeman – he may have been visiting for some legitimate reason?"

"Let's just say that my intuition tells me that the girl is innocent, and if so then the 'policeman' is not."

"Are you sure that's all? This is a matter for the Yard now, and you'd best step gingerly around Chief Inspector MacDonald or cover your ears, let me tell you. 'By the book or it's your stripes' is the way of it in the force these days."

"MacDonald and myself are old hunting colleagues, Inspector, from the days when he held your rank. We rub along together, though we haven't always seen eye-to-eye on everything."

A loud knocking at the door was followed by the irruption of Inspectors Lestrade and Gregson into the murder scene.

"First on the scene again, Holmes!" The half-joking tone sounded somewhat forced.

"In this case there was little option, my dear Lestrade, as we found the body and raised the alarm. But your point is noted. And now, as we have already given full details to Inspector Jones, with your permission, we are expected at Whitehall after our lunch."

Leaving the police to their routine, we mounted the stairs to depart only to find that, our cabby having fled during the commotion, we were obliged to walk to the High Street to hail another. Holmes seemed inordinately interested in the shrubs and flowerbeds lining the front path, and as we turned onto the public footpath, he gripped my arm.

"Just a moment, Watson." He stooped and peered under the fringing leaves. Spreading his handkerchief on the cobbled path, he extracted a small tweezers from his watch pocket and delicately picked up several small thin curved glass fragments, which he placed on the clean cloth and gently folded away. This was placed in the inner breast pocket of his overcoat. "Keep any onlookers away, please, Watson. There's a footprint there as well." Holmes then sought out the constable standing guard at the portico, and sent him to please ask Inspector Jones if he could step outside, and gave his name. Only a moment passed before Jones, followed by Lestrade and Gregson, stamped up the stairs and along the path.

"Found something else, Mr. Holmes?"

Parting the leaves again, Holmes said, "I think these glass fragments may have something to do with our poisoning. I have removed two pieces which, with your permission, I shall take with me for immediate analysis." Jones nodded his assent to this. "I also commend to your attention, with some reservations, the imprint of the shoe which appears to have crushed it. Gilbert the yardman has evidently watered here recently, and the earth is soft."

Holmes stood and brushed his fingertips together. "I caution you, however, that the obvious may not necessarily be the truth." With that, Holmes bade the detectives a terse farewell yet again, and we walked away towards the High Street.

We had walked some way before Holmes spoke; "Tell me Watson, was there not something strange about the pictures on the wall in Mischa's study?"

Like the rest of the building, Mischa's apartments had been decorated in discreet good taste. I had noticed that the walls, especially in his study, were covered all over with the sort of professional photographs with which theatre people commonly decorate their personal spaces.

"Nothing remarkable, mostly photographs of Mischa posed with various major or minor luminary of the footlights, many of them signed. But I noticed none with whom we have had any business."

"Did this not strike you as odd; not a single photograph nor any memento of Irene Adler, formerly his favourite?"

I flagged down a passing growler and we were soon back in front of a cheerful blaze at Baker Street, or I was, for Holmes had immediately gone to his chemical apparatus and was absorbed in an analysis of the residue he had scraped from the glass fragments. I had barely thawed before he called to me.

"It was fortunate that my first surmise proved correct, as there was material sufficient only for the one test. You will note the shapes of the two glass fragments. This one is from a cylindrical section, whereas the other is from a spheroid. The glass is very thin, probably blown like laboratory retorts. The total amount of crushed glass was not large, indicating a small vessel or device."

He indicated several stained slips of reactive paper, each one of a different colour, and said, "Both fragments carried a thin residue of hydrocyanic acid – prussic acid to the layman. I think we are looking at fragments of an atomiser such as artists use to spray size and lacquer onto canvases. Charged with a small amount of prussic acid and stoppered with rubber plugs, our murderer would only have to remove the plugs and pocket them and his weapon would be ready. Simply blowing through the atomiser would spray the poison in the victim's face. This causes instant constriction of the blood vessels and prevents absorption of oxygen, with the result appearing much the same as cardiac arrest. Rapid post-mortem relaxation wipes out the evidence before an autopsy can reveal it, and you have a 'near-as-possible' natural death."

"Why leave the blower behind, then?"

"Normally, being so thin, it would crush to dust - but the earth was soft there, and it only shattered. Also, this method of murder is not without risk to the killer, who must be either desperate, or very cool. Inadvertent swallowing or breathing of the acid or its fumes would kill him as effectively as the intended victim. Once used, it would still be dangerous to handle - especially if it broke - and best disposed of as soon as possible."

Holmes dashed off a telegram to Athelney Jones at Scotland Yard, describing his results, saying, "Now more than ever it is essential that we find Miss Isobel, for I fear her hours are numbered otherwise." This he placed on the table. He then occupied himself in unstrapping and unlocking his trunk, which he had lifted onto his chemical workbench.

This trunk was scarred and gouged all over from rough usage, and looked as though attempts had been made to force it open. It was of stout construction, however, and the locks and straps were robust. He took from it a cloth package, which he unwrapped. Holmes handed me two small leather-bound notebooks.

"Francois le Villard's first Journal, covering our travels and adventures in Tibet, and his latest, written at Siam during the year up till my arrival three months ago in Montpellier. I must dash off again, if that young lady is not to become the next statistic, but I should return within the hour. I have made a special request to Mrs. Hudson in the matter of our luncheon, and should hate to disappoint her. I think you would be well advised to postpone opening those journals until later, for perhaps a quick reading of Mycroft's dossier on Colonel Moriarty will cast the events of the past into a new perspective. That, anyway, is my immediate plan upon my return."

Holmes had gathered his hat and coat and was gone before I could even reply. His energy when on a case was clearly undiminished and I could only marvel at the range of murders in which he was involved after only a few days back in London. How they all fitted together was something I thought about briefly, but I gave it up until I had more information. For the present, I had no idea. I only knew that wherever Holmes went, excitement and sudden death were his constant companions. I don't think of myself as overly imaginative, but I was tempted to cross the room and close the shutters.

When a log cracked loudly in the grate I will confess my first thought was of gunshots. I was instantly wide awake and sitting upright, for I must have dozed off. Vague recollections of uneasy dreams came to me, but I shook them off by telling myself that the horrors of the world of Sherlock Holmes were no figments of a fevered imagination, they were dangerous and real.

I occupied myself until Holmes returned with less consequential thoughts, in trying to reason backwards and work out how Holmes had so swiftly pictured the glazier's assistant of the day before. The first thing was to walk out onto the landing outside the sitting-room door, and look down the familiar stairs to fix them, the front door, and the ground floor hall in my mind. This done, I sat and recalled the events, and tried to reconcile them with Holmes's deductions.

That the glazier's assistant was tall, and just past his prime could be deduced from the mere eight or so strides with which he mounted the seventeen stairs, and the marked slowing of the tempo as he rose. That he favoured his left foot was, I thought, based on the 'strong' sound coming first on the first stair, which creaked. The man had obviously crashed his tool-kit into the newel-post at the foot of our stairs, which would mean it was carried in the right hand and that our man was short-sighted but did not wear spectacles, hence the squint. Only a thin man would have even tried to dash through the space between the aspidistra and the newel-post carrying a large tool-kit. All this was relatively easy.

A little more thought, still reasoning backwards, resolved the question of his appearance - the amount of time the young maid, who generally gave short shrift to our callers, had kept our man at the door. She was a flirty-looking type of slavey, and knowing he'd been sent for, still detained him at the doorway for several minutes. There you have your Prince Charming! But try as I may, I could not account for Holmes's prediction as to his colouring and patrimony, which really were the same puzzle, for someone of Italian blood will likely have a swarthy complexion.

I had reached just this point when Holmes himself mounted the stairs and came in, and said, "Well, for now I can do no more. In addition to watching Moran, I have the Irregulars on Miss Isobel's trail as well, for she seems to have taken flight."

He selected a pipe from his rack, and picked up the envelope containing Mycroft's dossier on Colonel Moriarty. Opening it, he prepared to read it out to me. First, however, he informed me of the results of his search for Isobel Aster.

"She was born Isobel Ada Blood, in the East End, and has now legally taken her stage name, Isobel Aster. I now know that she was Mischa's closest confidante when he was at Covent Garden, but left at the same time as he. It was put about that she had found a wealthy mentor amongst the stage-door

Lotharios, as happens, and had forsaken the stage, but none seemed to know who it was – she seems to have been cagey about that, always meeting him elsewhere. Quite amazing what a chatty new stagehand can promote, if only he knows the argot. I found her room, nearby the theatre; she cleaned it out this morning and has vanished. Lestrade is also looking for her; I think he means to arrest her for poisoning Mischa. Frankly, I have more faith in Wiggins's researches amongst the jarveys and chophouses of the district. If she has travelled or had a meal recently around here, I shall know about it!"

"The usual shilling-a-day with a guinea to the finder?" I asked.

"Of course."

"Have you a minute free just now?"

"At least until lunchtime."

"Then how in the name of the Lord did you know he was Italian?"

"Who? Oh, I see! You're still dwelling on our young glazier. Actually, that was the easiest part! He was whistling a piece from a Donizetti opera that every Italian knows from childhood on, but is for some reason little known outside Italy. You see . . . no mystery about any of it! Are you ready now for Colonel Moriarty?"

I consoled myself that if I had not got it all, I had at least worked out the meat of it, and how could I be expected to know this Italian music anyway? Music hall, now that's more my line!

CHAPTER VIII

HOLMES STRETCHED out on the sofa with his pipe, and said, "If it's not too much to ask, perhaps *you* could read Mycroft's report aloud, while I recover my energies a little."

Breaking the wax seal I extracted half a dozen sheets of paper.

"Very well. Cover note from Mycroft to the effect that since this was compiled, Colonel Moriarty is reported as having remained mostly at his lakeside villa at Lago di Como, Italy. Current whereabouts thought to be London somewhere. Maintains apartment at Brighton, but rarely stays there."

"Fine! Carry on!"

"'Born James Thomas Moriarty, in 1850 at Calcutta, India. Father was William James Moriarty, of a good Anglo-Irish family with a long tradition of service in the Indian Army, bought his commission in the Indian Army in 1832, served honourably, twice decorated. Returned to England on leave in 1846, and married a pastor's daughter from Aldershot; apparently felt she married beneath herself, and as a result was not popular in India, but stayed with her husband, and bore him two sons, James Thomas in 1850, and Jonathan James three years later.'

"'In 1857 Lieutenant-Colonel Moriarty was stationed at Cawnpore, right in the heart of the Indian Mutiny, and saw his loyal sepoys rise up and slaughter every Briton in sight. His wife was back in England at this time, as her younger son was sickly, and she insisted he needed an English climate. Moriarty was apparently a brave and competent soldier, but while away from his compound one day early in the Mutiny his loyal servants were all murdered and his eldest son, then aged 7, was kidnapped. Moriarty helped suppress the Mutiny, and although he lashed more than forty mutineers across the mouth of a cannon and blew them away, he was one of those officers instrumental in co-opting their leaders and ultimately quelling the uprising. In the late days of the Mutiny, Moriarty was on patrol with an adjutant to an outlying village. When they failed to return a party was sent to search; both of them were found half-eaten by cannibalistic Aghorias, who were hunted down and brought to trial.'

"'When informed of the gruesome end of her husband, and the disappearance and presumed death of her elder son, Mrs. Moriarty settled in her native district, and took to calling her younger son by his second name, James, in memory of his elder brother. Four years later, in 1862, a roving patrol rounded up a gang of dacoits that had been preying on travellers around Allahabad. With them was a wild, fair skinned, English boy around twelve years of age, who had been with this family almost as long as he could remember, but was able to tell them his name. A search of the records of the Mutiny soon cleared up his identity, and the boy was sent on the next ship back to his mother in England.'

"'By this time the widow had remarried, to a local magistrate, who apparently did not welcome the wild youth with open arms. He was sent to various schools, from all of which he was expelled or removed, and as soon as he reached the age, signed up in his father's old regiment so as to get back to India. His school records indicated an exceptional intelligence which he was

unwilling to exercise in the classroom, athletic prowess above average, and natural leadership capabilities which earned him a loyal following amongst his more rebellious peers and the continual disapproval of prefects and masters. By all accounts he worshipped his brilliant younger brother, who in turn encouraged his own dreams of returning to India.'"

Holmes shifted on the sofa, puffing thoughtfully on his pipe. "Certainly had an adventurous upbringing, hadn't he!" he remarked. "No mention where Mycroft found all this history? No? . . . Well, it's of little importance. Proceed!"

I turned to the second sheet, and read on.

"'The Indian Army appears to have suited the young Moriarty very well. He was back amongst the Indians, for whom he retained a great affection. He professed to his fellow officers that he even forgave the Aghorias who had eaten his father, for they were simply following their age-old Indian ways. His uniform became wilder and more exotic as the years passed, with sabre and spurs, a length of turban wound around his pith helmet, and moustaches the envy of any Pathan warrior. His daring and unorthodox exploits soon won him promotions and a reputation. Before long his band of wild young officers and sepoys was being sent to trouble spots wherever needed, and when ceremony was required, none provided the arrogant swagger to match the splendour of caparisoned elephants in procession quite so splendidly as Moriarty's Horse.'

"'This was not an unusual situation in those days, but even the frontier had its limits and eventually Moriarty overstepped them, directly disobeying an order from Calcutta. He was given the choice of voluntary retirement or a commission closer to Calcutta, and chose the latter. And that, gentlemen, is how Colonel James Moriarty, Indian Army, came to be posted to the First Bangalore Pioneers, along with a certain Colonel Sebastian Moran.'

"'As we know, Moran was drummed out of the regiment soon after – irregularities with the mess fund was the cover story – and Moriarty resigned at the same time. There is no official record of their occupations thereafter, and no unofficial record for some years either.'"

"Ah! At last," exclaimed Holmes, "we come to the interesting part."

"There is little more," I warned him, as I continued reading to him.

"'As you are aware, the younger brother, Jonathan James, became a distinguished mathematician, and ultimately, Professor Moriarty, of mathematical and criminal distinction. Our best information, based on your own researches into the Moriarty

gang, is that the Professor at first recruited Moran as his Chief of Staff, with his own elder brother Colonel Moriarty as his Chief of Communications and Security, at the time when both left the Indian Army. In these positions they seem to have worked well together, for the organisation flourished, as you know. Moran, however, has always had a weakness for high-stakes card games, which created serious problems more than once, with the result that Moran was removed as Chief of Staff, and used thereafter only for occasional high-profile assassinations where his marksmanship and hunting skills made him indispensable. There is no conclusive evidence, but the consensus of our investigators is that the Professor made his brother Chief of Staff, and that after the Professor died at the Reichenbach Falls, Colonel Moriarty effectively took control of the whole criminal organisation his brilliant but twisted brother had created.'"

"Mycroft has indeed been busy, Watson. This report confirms my own suspicions, but I have been in no position to investigate for myself. I prevailed upon Mycroft, who has long been one of the few to believe in the existence and power of Moriarty's gang, to continue my lines of enquiry. Is that all?"

"No, shall I continue?"

"Please do."

"'Following the death of Professor Moriarty, and the vigorous prosecution of their gang in England, their criminal activities in Britain virtually ceased. Their continental activities, however, seem to have flourished, and there was evidence they had accepted commissions even farther afield even before we received your confirmation from Persia two years ago. Since that time a close watch has been kept on Moran, and on Colonel Moriarty. Moran has played cards, and cheated at cards, at clubs all over London, barely escaping charges on occasion; but somehow he has always managed to make good his losses. Periodically disappears entirely from London for weeks or months at a time, we suspect he is carrying out the occasional killing for the gang. Has proven impossible to trail, as he was a skilled hunter himself, but of late has become careless when drunk.'

"'As to Colonel Moriarty, to all appearances he is a recluse at his villa in Italy, neither visiting nor receiving visits from neighbours. His only visitors are his doctor and a lawyer from Torino, both quite frequently, but we can't question them without compelling reason. Maintains a small staff who have been with him for years now, none of them from the town of Como, and the only view we have of him is when he sits on the loggia in the late afternoons with his manservant reading to him. Currently sports a full beard. Runs a carriage-and-four, and a small steam launch which berths at the boathouse at the foot of his estate, but is never seen to use either himself. The launch is used frequently at night, but the local carabinieri have checked and found

only domestic activities involved, visits around the lake by staff, fishing and so forth.'

"'*The one truly remarkable fact is that we have been unable to locate a likeness of the Colonel, even where one should be, and the most recent description we have of the man is more than ten years old. In conclusion, your Colonel Moriarty may be what he appears to be. He would not be the first eccentric recluse who amassed, while stationed at India, riches sufficient to support his present establishment. However, we must now consider the possibility that he has in fact taken over from his brother, and that we know little more detail about their structure and activities than we did four years ago.*'"

I replaced the papers in the envelope, and waited for Holmes to comment.

"The connection between Moran and both Moriarty's, at least, is now clearly established, and the background on their early years is most interesting, but it's far short of the complete picture, in particular the recent details. I have more to add, but it will make no sense until you have progressed further with the journals. Thank you, Watson."

Holmes stood, and walked to the door.

"And now for our luncheon, following which I must deliver you up to Mycroft, then proceed to make my arrangements for this evening's entertainment at Crystal Palace."

The much-heralded luncheon arrived, and to my mild surprise turned out to consist of cold cuts with chutney, a loaf fresh from Mrs. Hudson's oven sliced and thickly spread with salted butter, red apples and a Stilton to finish, with porter ale to drink.

"Such simple fare, and yet there have been times when I'd have given a year's earnings for just such a repast," remarked Holmes as he finished his beer.

"And now, let us be off! Mycroft will be back at his desk. I have a few small matters to discuss with him, and then I shall leave you both. This evening's events may well prove crucial, and we will need an early start – that is, if you care to come along?"

"By all means, Holmes! I've arranged for young Stinson to take over my few patients for a while; they seem to approve of his treatment and his manner."

Holmes strode through the corridors of Whitehall, clearly familiar with the way to Mycroft's offices. A larger room – with framed maps affixed to all the walls, an immense wooden map-cabinet with shallow drawers, and a conference table for six – adjoined a smaller room in which was a roll-top desk, its pigeon-holes stuffed with documents folded lengthways and tied with tape, like barristers' briefs. Through the open door leading from the map room I could see clerks and typists at their work, before Mycroft entered and closed it behind himself.

"Sherlock, Doctor! Good afternoon! Please, come into my study. You have had an interesting morning, I believe. I have just been informed. Lestrade is busily turning the theatre district upside down looking for this Isobel girl. Has this poisoning some connection with our affair, Sherlock?"

"I fear that it was my enquiries as to the victim's whereabouts which led directly to his death."

"Why should that follow?"

"I think he knew something about criminal connections in the past between Godfrey Norton and that mysterious and powerful figure whose shadow kept reappearing in our affairs whilst abroad. Someone who is in league with the Moriarty gang, and has been for years, working indirectly through unsuspecting bureaucrats and functionaries to subvert justice in certain matters put before Parliament and the courts. Amongst other things, I detect his hand in the release of Moran, but I expect your official enquiries will come to nothing, or to evidence showing an unfortunate administrative error. A reprimand here, even a dismissal there; we know they pay well for silence, and kill if necessary."

"And the reason for this morning's murder?"

Holmes gave a succinct account of our morning's activities. He began with the trapping of messages to and from Moran and his deductions therefrom; then the shooting at Covent Garden, and lastly, the poisoning at Islington.

"Is it mere coincidence that M. Roborovsky was able to retire and purchase such a building at the time of Norton's hasty departure from England; dressers are not paid so well? So long as no one raked up the past, he was allowed to live and paid for his silence. But I have returned to England, and I was in contact with Irene Adler at Siam. Several attempts on my life have failed since then, including Moran's. Last night I enquired at the address last given to Irene Adler by Mischa. There I was informed that he had moved, and should ask at the theatre manager's office in the morning. I have no doubt that landlord was well paid to give the message, and to notify someone - quickly too - that a Mr. Sherlock Holmes had been making enquiries. That is the only reasonable explanation for the sniper at the Covent Garden, for how else could they have known I should be there. By sheer good fortune, once again they failed to eliminate the detective, so their next step was to destroy the evidence - in this case, Mischa."

"And you think this same mysterious gentleman will appear tonight at Crystal Palace?"

"I am hopeful. We no longer know who is involved in the Moriarty gang;

how many, or what positions they hold, but the fact that an air-gun was used in this morning's attempt clearly links the Moriarty gang to the affair of Godfrey Norton and his shadowy associate. If my deductions concerning tonight's *DURBAR* are correct, and if our man is, as I suspect, one of the powers in the Moriarty gang, then yes, I think he will be there. After all, they have taken what they believe to be foolproof precautions in arranging the meeting, and where better to allay suspicion than at a crowded event full of similarly dressed people.

"From your perspective, Mycroft, I think you must consider the possibility that the Moriarty gang is seeking political influence at high levels, and until their man is flushed out, we must be careful whom we entrust with details of our investigations."

"What will be your next step?"

"I'm curious about the knowledge which proved fatal to Mischa; I shall follow up on that. First priority, however, is to locate Isobel Aster before the law does. If Moran can be sprung from behind bars, it should not be difficult to silence a young songbird once caged. I must get to her first. I don't know her role in all this, but I get the feeling that what she knows adds up to her death-warrant. I must find her before she, too, is silenced."

"What exactly did Miss Adler tell you that is so dangerous to this man?"

"She told me what she knew, but knew no names. Irene Adler felt certain, however, that Mischa had made it his business to find out, for he had hinted as much. I got the distinct impression that, at the time, Miss Adler was none too pleased at the suggestion that Godfrey Norton may have had reasons other than elopement for giving up a promising career and disappearing abroad. Wishing to hear no ill of her fiancé, she dismissed the matter as malicious backstage gossip, but looking back on the incident with the bitter hindsight of disillusionment, she was not so sure that he had not been telling the truth. All she remembered Mischa saying was that Godfrey Norton had been involved in some form of legal chicanery, which had enriched his mysterious associate, at the cost of the deaths of at least four others. The matter had attracted some attention, which had been hushed up with money, but it was thought wise that Norton should leave the country for some time. "

"And they are still killing to protect this man, is that it?"

"How else to explain the seemingly meaningless murder of Mischa Roborovsky?"

"Then you had best get it sorted out as soon as you can, hadn't you, Sherlock? We most certainly don't want any more murders, and above all we must avert a political scandal at this delicate time, with the streets ready to erupt over all these murders. *Finem respice!*" said Mycroft, standing. "Now, good hunting, and leave me with the doctor here; we have much ground to cover."

Holmes, who had already gathered his things, took his leave of us, saying that he should return to Baker Street at six.

Mycroft settled his vast bulk in his chair, and spun around to look out his tall paned windows.

"You're a medical man, Watson, and you've seen combat at close quarters. Tell me, what was your opinion - as a medical man - of Sherlock's mental state during those last weeks leading up to Reichenbach?" He swivelled back to look directly at me, his grey eyes - strangely unfamiliar in that jowly face - so reminiscent of Holmes, huge yet delicate hands resting on the leather armrests. It was always disconcerting to be with Mycroft, whose gross features were informed by the same keen, thrusting bone structure as Holmes's.

I thought for a moment before replying. "Frankly, I was most concerned. At first I felt that the gravest threat was the physical, with three attacks upon his life in the course of a single day, and the ever-present threat of attack by air gun. As we fled across Europe, however, Holmes's seeming acceptance of the near-inevitability of his own death in a clash with Professor Moriarty became obvious, as though he were actively seeking such an end. I tried to reason with him that no one villain, however powerful, was worth the loss of his powers for good, but he was, I thought, unhealthily obsessed with Professor Moriarty. And so it seemed to me during those three sad years when I thought he had actually made that deal with the devil himself, and sacrificed his own life to rid the world of a criminal genius."

Mycroft removed his *pince-nez* and polished them on his cravat. "My own thoughts to a nicety. Sherlock spent that last day with me in my rooms before leaving for the Continent with you. I too was most concerned, and remonstrated with him. He would not listen - Moriarty must be destroyed, was all he thought of - and it was all I could do to persuade him to leave London at once while Patterson made the swoop on the gang. So it was with great relief that, playing at coachman, I dropped you at Victoria Station to depart with him for Europe. When I was informed that only part of the gang had been seized, and that the Professor had last been seen at Paris two days after your departure, my fears returned. So it came as no great surprise when I was informed by the Swiss ambassador of Sherlock's and Moriarty's deaths."

Recalling that painful time, I said, "I did call upon you at your club when I returned, after completing some brief formalities with the Swiss police, but was informed you had left the country with no return scheduled."

"I was aware of that, Doctor. The English press printed the story on May

7th, and a steady stream of condolences poured in, though our relation was not such common knowledge. Then a week later I received, in one of the happiest and most satisfying moments of my life, a ciphered telegraph message from Sherlock. It was from Florence, and I left to join him there, after first making some arrangements, which included calling upon the Ambassador of Norway. In accord with Sherlock's wishes I informed no-one, not even the Prime Minister when he expressed his condolences as I informed him I must travel to Meiringen."

He stopped abruptly. "I say, this is thirsty work. You'll join me in a Scotch?" he asked.

"Good, could you perhaps . . ?" as he indicated the decanter, siphon and glasses on his credenza. I rose and made two drinks, as Mycroft continued.

"I was several days in preparation, and would be several more *en route.* I telegraphed a date to Sherlock, so he amused himself with a journey to Cremona, where he tells me he visited the workshops of Amati and Stradivarius. When I arrived he was back at Florence, somewhat relaxed by this diversion."

"Surely with Moriarty dead he could have returned to his life as before?" said I, handing Mycroft a cut-glass tumbler.

"My own researches, after Sherlock's departure and the various police raids on the gang, convinced me of two things. Firstly, that Moriarty had very capable and vicious lieutenants who had also escaped the dragnet, and secondly that they could not have done so without collusion at high level within our police department, as we have recently seen with the 'escape' of Colonel Moran. For Sherlock to return to that situation was tantamount to suicide, and I was determined that he should not do so." Mycroft sipped appreciatively at the tawny liquid.

"Where were we . . ? Right! So what *should* he do? I had already made my plans on this score prior to leaving London. The one thing I determined was that he should on no account become entangled and obsessed with the rest of the gang as he had with Moriarty. My game, Doctor, is political advantage. The stakes are frequently very high but the adversaries are rarely personal, as must be the case in a game where today's adversaries are tomorrow's allies. Not so with Sherlock! Crime is crime, and rarely is it 'right'. Villains are villains, and usually remain so until stopped. It is a world of right and wrong, and can lead the zealous investigator to assume the role of crusader for the forces of right and decency. I am afraid this happened to Sherlock during the course of his campaign against Professor Moriarty."

Taking another decent drink of his whisky, Mycroft continued; "Sherlock's obsession with Moriarty was neither misguided nor malicious, as some have implied, but developed into an obsession with matching and mastering one of Europe's cleverest and most dangerously ambitious criminals. But when he talked seriously of his willingness to sacrifice his own life to achieve this end, I knew that he was on dangerous ground, as much from himself as from his foe. I had hopes it was a personal contest between the two of them, and that with the Professor dead Sherlock would soon return to his more normal nature, but I was prepared to take no chances."

"I determined that I should do my utmost to get him, for a while at least, away from the world of sordid criminal intrigues and their associations. Yet knowing Sherlock's need for stimulation and excitement, and his need to have a reason to exert himself, I determined to arrange something which would keep him occupied and stimulated both mentally and physically, which would tax his skills and his ingenuity. After some thought, during which I considered and rejected several options, I finally settled on a trip in disguise to Lhasa."

"After all, if he was to be 'dead' for a year or two he should be entirely out of the common way - not so easy for a publicly recognised figure. I always knew he would return to his previous occupation - it is in his very nature to be a detective - but I hoped he would do so with a more mature perspective on involving his own emotions in the success of a campaign."

Our glasses were empty by this time, and at Mycroft's insistence I re-charged them. "I have dwelt too long, however, on the why of it? What of the reason for penetrating to Lhasa, and how to achieve this when no other had been able, despite various attempts?"

He levered himself out of his chair, saying, "Bring your drink in here, Doctor. The maps are not only of great assistance in explaining 'the Great Game' - for that is the arena into which I was sending my brother - as you will see they are in some ways the start of the story. Please take a seat on that side of the table. I shall try to keep this as succinct as possible."

With this Mycroft seized a pointer from a rack, and on one of the maps indicated an area I knew only too well - Afghanistan.

"Sherlock tells me he has mentioned some of this already; forgive me if I repeat anything."

Chapter IX

"And so you will understand," said Mycroft, "our reasons for having a reliable report on Russian activities in the region."

For the past hour-and-a-half Mycroft had given a most impressive confirmation of Holmes's assessment of his elder brother. He had started with a brief but comprehensive history of recent expansion of the Raj to include Afghanistan, Sikkim and Assam, marked in red on his maps. Russia's expansion was plotted in blue, much of it in the forbidding and unknown regions of Central Asia, where their border marches with those of China's northern provinces. A railway built by the Russians from the eastern shore of the Caspian Sea across the arid desert to Samarkand and Tashkent had opened vast regions to their influence. Prejevalsky, the famed Russian explorer, had tried on several celebrated expeditions to achieve his lifelong dream and penetrate to Lhasa, on one occasion reaching a point only a week's march from the fabled mountain capital of Tibet. Other expeditions had achieved varying success.

"Less than ten years ago the Russians conquered Merv, only seventy miles from the Persian border with Afghanistan. Then in '85 Russian troops fired on the Afghanis at Panjdeh, and we had a declaration of war ready, just in case. Our agent, the explorer Ney Elias, had warned the government of a new Russian threat from the east. The Baroghil Pass through the Pamirs was thought vulnerable to an army with artillery. Any Russian advance on the Raj has always been considered as sweeping down through the north-western approaches, so this new threat caused great alarm.

"Carey and Dalgliesh were sent off to the Karakorum, which the Russians had always regarded as their area. Then, early in '86 the Tibetans invaded Sikkim, thus directly confronting the Indian Government. As you'll be aware from the newspapers, Tibet has become, like Afghanistan, an area where British and Russian interests are in conflict.

"Many regard this threat as unrealistic, but the Transcaspian Railway is a thousand miles long, and extends Russia's sphere of influence enormously. Using boats and trains, the Russians could move armies and materiel from Moscow to the very borders of Afghanistan in days. In contrast, our forces would require weeks simply to reach the frontiers of the Raj. Should the Russians determine upon doing so, we may be aware of their movements but unable to counteract until too late. Prejevalsky and others have continually advised St. Petersburg that a small force of determined and well-armed Russians could readily seize control of Tibet, which is nominally under the suzerainty of Peking. The Russians appear to have little respect for Chinese military might anyway. Confronted by a *fait accompli* in Tibet, with Russian troops on our very borders, and their rail link able to reinforce and supply them in the north-west, we should have the Russian bear at the throat of the Raj. An attack from Tibet could be real, or a feint intended to stretch our defences in the Hindu Kush.

"There was an equally plausible threat, and finally the reason why Sherlock went to Lhasa. With the Tibetans considered to be anti-British following their invasion of Sikkim, the possibility existed that the Russians might arm them with modern weapons, which would constitute a major threat to the government of British India. There had already been rumours of caravans of Russian weapons escorted by Cossacks crossing the high passes headed for Lhasa, escorted by camels bearing swivel-mounted machine-guns.

"We have long known that the tutor to the *Dalai Lama* was in fact a Russian-born monk, an educated Mongol named Lama Dorjieff, who had arrived at Lhasa in the mid-'80s and was then at the powerful Drepung monastery in Lhasa. Lama Dorjieff, who retains Russian citizenship, was reported in the Indian press to have linked up with Prejevalsky in his 1884 expedition to Tibet, and is thought to be a Russian intelligence agent. True or not, we do know that he encouraged the Tibetans to instigate discussions with Russia, ostensibly to balance the British threat."

I thought of the battles which could ensue if British India and Russia came into real conflict over Tibet and Afghanistan, and this train of thought led me to reflect on the horror of wars, including the campaign of Afghanistan in which I had myself served.

"I was wounded myself at the battle of Maiwand, and was lucky to survive. As we sit here and discuss these campaigns and conquests, British victories and defeats, it all seems as though there were some purpose; at the time, it was all too easy to lose sight of anything but the carnage all around, the horrifically wounded with no hope of medical attention. I felt so often that it was a strange fate which sent a lad from his village or town to die mangled on a bleak mountainside in Afghanistan, or to any of these other red-coloured patches on your map."

Mycroft finished the last of his whisky, then replied.

"It is a heavy burden on those who decide when and where to send those armies and navies. Not always! I know many will point to incompetent military leaders, and self-serving politicians, and the misguided and tragic campaigns upon which they seem so frequently to have embarked. My role is to provide advice, and often it is the only advice to hand and is thus acted upon, but I am spared public responsibility. I give no battle orders, command no fleets. I reap neither glory from victories, nor opprobrium from defeats. There will be no equestrian memorials, no streets renamed in my honour; neither will I be vilified in the public press. But it seems, Doctor Watson, that whatever advice I give, whether it be to retreat or advance, or to do nothing at all, someone will suffer, and someone gain."

"And what of those hundreds and thousands of young men who will never return, do they never torment your nights."

"The Empire as we know it, in this last decade of the century, has grown out of the sacrifices of those young men. We are not a nation of natural warriors, Doctor; ours was essentially an agricultural society, and a nation of traders, transformed by our lead in industrialisation. With our harnessing of steam power and development of the railways and steamships came progress in a hundred fields, but manufactures require markets, and raw materials. This, Watson, is what really caused the proliferation of red on the map - the expansion of trade. It is a commonplace these days that 'trade follows the flag'. Fact of the matter is, in most cases it has been the flag following the requirements of trade. Which is where British mastery of the seas comes in."

Mycroft pointed at Gibraltar, Malta, Cyprus; all red, at Simonstown in the Cape Province of South Africa, the Falkland Islands in the South Atlantic, and half a dozen other lonely dots of red scattered around the oceans. "All to protect our trade routes. Besides our manufactures shipped all over the world, there's wool from Australia, tea from China, nitrates from Chile, furs from Canada, timber from Burma. Hundreds of commodities from dozens of islands, coasts, mountains, lakes and plains, jungles and rivers."

He sat in his chair opposite me, and gazed out as the late afternoon light faded behind London's skyline. "Wherever a trader finds a market, or a commodity of value at home, sooner or later we will be called upon to uphold our rights, to enforce respect for our sovereign, to forestall encroachment by other nations. But whatever the stated reason, at bottom will always be found the driving force of trade."

"Now the fever of Empire has gripped our people, and has become the national obsession. The man in overalls, the charlady, the clerk, the manager, the mill-owner - sometimes it seems they have all become imperialists, and see no end to British conquests by land and by sea."

"Even catastrophic defeats and hopeless leadership are transmuted by this fierce public sentiment. Thus the tragic and unnecessary annihilation of the Kabul Army at Jalalabad, with only one man returning of the thousands who set forth, becomes Lady Butler's celebrated painting, and hangs on every schoolroom wall. Or that suicidal madman 'Chinese' Gordon causes an international incident at Khartoum and costs the lives of thousands in order to make himself a martyr at the hands of the *Mahdi*. Very poignant, and the picture of *that* moment hangs alongside Lady Butler's in the classrooms, providing inspiration for the next generation."

A framed picture of General Gordon, the hero of the Chinese wars of 1860, the general who put an end to slavery in Egypt, occupied an honoured place on my wall, and I was not a little taken aback to hear him spoken of in so cavalier a fashion. "I must say, Mycroft, you surprise me. As one of those at the very centre of this imperial enterprise you appear remarkably cynical about it all."

"I suppose it must seem so. It may seem a remarkable thing to say," said he, sweeping his pointer over the red dots and areas scattered across the map, "but the Empire as we know it has reached its apotheosis. There is little support at the highest levels for new expansion, and many question the costs of Empire and the benefits we derive therefrom. But possibly the surest knell for the whole business is that many of our most progressive thinkers are publicly questioning our rights as a nation to subject other peoples to our will. Others worry, and rightly so, that we are bequeathing to future generations not a legacy but an embarrassing burden. There is little Foreign Office support, in spite of the public fervour, for further imperial adventures. Our most recent territorial acquisitions have been largely forced upon us. King Thebaw, for example, warring on the eastern frontiers of India, forced our hand in '86, and with some official reluctance we annexed Northern Burma. But there will be an end to seeking new lands to conquer, and finally we will be glad to return much that we have acquired to the native inhabitants, cherishing always the notion that we have been a civilising influence."

"You don't believe we have?" asked I.

"Frankly, if we have it has been by accident in most cases, or as the result of the prodding of zealous reformers; rarely has it been government initiative."

"And what of the other colonial powers?" I asked, curious.

"Well, of course, as with any evidently successful venture, our Empire has been the cause of envy and resentment. Russia has long sought a Central Asian empire. The French have an ardent colonialist lobby pushing their expansionist policy, as you will see. The Prussians and the Dutch have further colonial ambitions. As with our government, there are often level-headed pragmatists in the ministries; colonial administrators and local business interests, however, so frequently create situations where national interests must be seen to be upheld, and the government is dragged into yet another colonial adventure.

"We'll look at that question again; it is of importance to our understanding. Today I particularly wanted to cover the beginnings of Sherlock's travels, so if you can be patient and bear with me, a more coherent picture will emerge. Sherlock has already briefed me verbally on all points of direct importance to the governments involved, but you are the first apart from Sherlock to read the journals kept by le Villard. From what Sherlock has already told me, there is complication enough in it all without adding confusion. So, let us return to Florence, and my arrival there to meet up with Sherlock.

"He was staying at an elegant old pile by the main railway station, so he walked across to greet me. He was the insistent Italian tout from the hotel, to any onlooker, and in fact it took a short moment for me to realise it, so effective was his simple disguise. I had employed several subterfuges of my own device, both in England and again at Paris, to ensure that I was not followed. Soon we were sharing an aperitif on the terrace of the hotel. My train had arrived in the late afternoon, and now the local inhabitants were taking the summer evening air. Nevertheless, I had urgent matters to attend to in London, and so wasted no time in arranging matters with Sherlock. I had brought with me a dossier prepared for his reading, outlining the task at hand. He read it through once only, quickly, then closed it. His only response, after a few seconds, was to ask if his old French colleague and protege le Villard could accompany him. I had anticipated this, and de Benoist had already cleared it with le Villard's superiors.

"So the matter was settled as easily as that. I suspect that a week or so of idleness, and his predilection for the *outré*, made the adventure instantly appealing. Le Villard was summonsed to the *Quai d'Orsay*, and given a ticket to Florence and sealed orders, but no idea as to his actual destination. Nor did he know who awaited him at Florence, for like the rest of Europe he believed Sherlock dead. Once he had recovered from the shock of finding him alive and well, he seemed delighted to go to Lhasa, even after the dangers and hardships were explained. His sealed package contained, when opened, travel documents in his own name, but listing his occupation as naturalist and biologist, and with a personal documents file which was entirely fabricated by the *Quai* – no names or addresses to lead back to his real family."

"You clearly regarded this as a dangerous assignment, Mycroft. Rather a strange way to keep your brother out of harm's way in Europe, I should have thought," I remarked.

"I agree; but you know Sherlock as well as I, perhaps better of late. You know he will always seek excitement and challenge. There was risk, but Sherlock is the most resourceful man I have ever known, and I felt he was the equal of any threat he may encounter - with one exception; his own obsession with the Moriarty gang. Fortunately time has vindicated my plan, as he has returned to us safely."

I had felt there was a ruthless streak in Mycroft ever since the death of the Greek, Kratides, which I had thought avoidable. Not for the first time, I wondered at the self-possession of this man who could send his brother into certain danger, in order to save him from another sort of danger. Mycroft was evidently one of those enviable creatures who are able to make decisions, then live with the outcome with no regrets. I decided that this was probably an essential element in the character of a man upon whose advice armies and navies were deployed and committed to battle, who dealt with international issues as routinely as I took temperatures and prescribed pills. Perhaps he simply understood Sherlock more completely than I. Whatever the reason, I began to glimpse the strength of the unspoken bonds which tied these two brilliant but different brothers.

"As to Sherlock's documentation, that had been the cause of the delay in my departure from London. With the co-operation of the Norwegian Ambassador at London, I had with me a complete set of travel and personal documents for one Doctor Olaf Sigerson, Norwegian archaeologist, lecturer and explorer, now Professor of Archaeology at the University of Oslo. His training in languages had been arranged for, both aboard ship to Calcutta, and at Darjeeling upon arrival. Fortunately, Sherlock has always had a gift for languages. We arranged tuition to brush up his rather rough Norwegian and he had to make a new start with the Persian, Pushtu and Tibetan dialects he would need. Le Villard was already fluent in Persian, and conversant with Pushtu, but would take the lessons anyway. A basic tropical wardrobe was all that remained for them to acquire and they were ready for departure, with the exception of financial arrangements. I handed Sherlock some written details for him to memorise, which would enable him to receive funds at any major city, and emergency funding at the British consular sections of certain of our embassies. Le Villard had an initial sum from the *Quai*, but as the 'expedition' was to be funded by our government, he had to depend on Sherlock's funds - not entirely satisfactory, but considered essential to maintain secrecy."

Mycroft stood, adjusted his somewhat rumpled attire, and moved towards the door.

"I'm afraid that's all we'll have time for today. I suggest you look into le Villard's journals, and when you think another briefing is in order, simply call upon me here or at my club."

As I exited his office door he said, "Do come back when you get stuck. We have much more ground to cover yet, for Sherlock was always on the move, rarely more than a few months at any one place, much of the time being spent simply getting from one place to another. No railway to Tibet, as yet!"

I thanked him, and walked out of the building, and out onto the middle of Westminster Bridge for a while, my mind still reeling a little from the whirlwind political education I had been receiving. It was very clear that writing this report was to be no easy task, but at least I had made a start in my preparation. What was also clear was that, whilst the 'Siam Question' may mean, to Mycroft Holmes, the political situation there, with all its ramifications, to Sherlock Holmes it meant something else - something more personal.

There being ample time before Holmes's return to Baker Street at six, I decided to walk back and enjoy the weather, which had improved considerably during the afternoon. I turned and retraced my steps across the bridge, passing just as the cracked bell of Big Ben tolled the hour overhead. Others had the same idea, and as there is nothing more enjoyable than an unhurried stroll through the streets of London of a spring evening, for an hour I forgot entirely about politics, conspiracies and murders. I arrived at Baker Street feeling quite exhilarated from the brisk exercise and the crisp air, which gave just the first hint of summer days to come.

Hanging up my hat and my coat, which I had been carrying over my arm, I was surprised to see Holmes's homburg and overcoat already on the hooks in the hallway. He was stretched out on the sofa in the sitting room, fast asleep. I closed the door quietly, fixed a scotch and soda, and sat in my old chair by the dying embers of the fire. I had taken some brief notes during Mycroft's discourse, and now spent a half-hour filling in details from memory. That completed, I simply relaxed with eyes closed, and marvelled at the changes in my life since Holmes returned from the dead.

The next moment, it seemed, Holmes was gently shaking my sleeve.

"Oh dear! Must have dozed off!" said I rather foolishly, as one does when newly woken.

"Never mind, Watson, it will serve us well to be rested and alert this evening. We don't know what we're getting involved in here, and should be prepared for any eventuality. Did you pack your revolver?"

"I certainly did, and I thought these may come in handy as well. As you say, one never knows.

I pulled out of my as-yet-unpacked luggage my old Webley service revolver and a box of cartridges, a set of brass knuckles, and a cosh. All of these had seen service at some time during the course of one or another adventure with Holmes

Holmes laughed out loud at my armoury, saying "A less doctor-like collection of implements I cannot imagine, Watson! For my part, I have my own revolver and several pair of regulation cuffs. Tonight we should only be trailing and watching, so we must be careful not to arouse the suspicion of the uniformed forces or we shall find ourselves making some embarrassing explanations. Nevertheless, in this instance we're justified in thus arming ourselves."

"Now, I must go to join Wiggins and observe the situation at the Sailor's Home. I calculate that Moran, once clear of the safe house, will take a roundabout route to Crystal Palace to make certain he's not followed. We, on the other hand, can go directly from Victoria; we have no need to follow, as we know his destination, if my deductions are correct. Wait for me therefore under the clock at Victoria Station at eight-thirty; I doubt I'll be much later. As we've had no supper we can sample the dubious delights of British railway cuisine, then take train for Crystal Palace."

Taking revolver and cuffs from his desk drawer and putting them in his coat pockets, he left.

With several hours to pass, and the prospect of an exciting evening ahead, I found it difficult to simply relax. I picked half-heartedly at the cold cuts remaining on the sideboard, and took a small glass of wine with it. That done, I took out kit and cleaned my Webley once again. As with all revolvers, there was no safety, so I left the cartridges in their box for now. The evening was turning chilly again, so I closed some of the windows and restored the fire to a healthy blaze, and was still restless.

Picking up the journals of Francois le Villard from the side-table where I had left them, I examined them closely for the first time. Both notebooks were identical, with pages of fine cotton-pulp paper in Crown Octavo size, and were covered with supple dark brown leather, stitched around three sides. They were of sturdy construction, with sewn signatures and decorative headstitching. Le Villard had chosen carefully when he selected these particular books for his journals. As a result, although they had evidently seen rough usage at times, both volumes were intact, with minimal staining and discoloration of the pages. He had had the foresight to use a waterproof ink. Thus the writing and sketching was still clear and legible, even though both volumes had clearly been soaked at some point.

I turned to the first entry, which proved to be an introductory preface. To my surprise, I found that it was addressed:

'To The Attention of John H. Watson, M.D., London, England,
Dated the 2nd day of November, 1893,
Bangkok, Siam.'

This was a mere five months past, and Holmes had been three months in France. Thus, it was clear that this was not so much a preface as a postscript, added after the completion of the journal.

'Dear Doctor Watson,' I read,

'By the time you read this you will be aware of the nature of the contents of these Journals, and thus it should come as no surprise to you that it is I, Francois le Villard, who commends them to your attention. I imagine you will have been given these two Journals by M. Holmes himself, or perhaps by his brother M. Mycroft Holmes. It was at the specific request of these two gentlemen that I began keeping these, the records of our travels. Of the nature and reasons for our journeys we shall soon treat, but at the first I should like to say that it was a great honour to me to be asked to accompany M. Sherlock Holmes on his journeys, which were undertaken on behalf of both our governments. It was an equal honour, to my mind, to be requested to keep a record of our journeys in such a form that Dr. Watson could subsequently work them up into a full report. It is for this reason that these Journals are in English, and I must apologise for any errors of usage.

I, who have worked closely with M. Holmes on several matters of grave importance to the Republic, have always been the greatest admirer of your accounts of his English cases. I have often wished I were free to do justice to his formidable triumphs on French soil, and elsewhere in Europe. However, as all the cases in which I was involved were matters of state this was, I regret, never possible. I have had to content myself with translating into French several of his monographs on various aspects of detection.

As my chosen 'occupation' and role in the expeditions of Dr. Sigerson was 'naturalist', you will perceive that my notes are rich in botanical and zoological details. This was deliberate, so that, upon a casual inspection, my Journals would appear as the collection of field-notes of a naturalist. You will no doubt wish to edit these items for your report, or even eliminate them entirely, although I, who admit to having written them, think them of considerable interest.

I should also point out that this Notebook – Vol. I of these Journals – predates three further Volumes, which cover the following periods:

June 1891 to July 1892

(Vol. II ~ covering our travels from Tibet to Persia),
August 1892 to March 1893
(Vol. III ~ which recorded our experiences at Mecca, Egypt and the Sudan) and lastly,
April 1893 to November 1893
(Vol. IV ~ recording our past year at Siam)

Vol. IV is included with this one. The other two Journals (Vols. II & III) were posted back from Aden more than one year ago as I write, and due to the circumstances at the time, were sent to an address in France known only to myself. In the event that something unfortunate should happen to me, instructions were sent separately for the package to be sent on in that case, unopened, to M. Mycroft Holmes.

When I have finished these few lines I shall hand both Vol. I and the last volume – Vol. IV – of these Journals to Holmes, who makes ready to depart for Singapore, where he will take ship for Marseilles in twelve days from now. His steamer to Singapore will depart upon the tide, for the bar is passable at present. I must hasten to complete these preliminaries, for tonight is that night known to the Siamese as Loy Kratong, and the steamer will require longer than usual to reach the bar. Most of the population is gathered at the riverside all along the riverbanks, and in thousands of small craft afloat on the river. There they will celebrate by each sending their wishes out to sea on a small float decorated with banana leaves, bearing lit joss-sticks and candles. Already the river is dotted with tiny floating lanterns, and the night air is filled with the music traditional to this ceremony, which appears to be held purely for the enjoyment of the Siamese participants, and seems to be neither a religious nor a royal occasion.

I can think of no more appropriate moment for Holmes to take his farewells of Siam, where we have spent so enjoyable and exciting a time, despite a certain tragic death. The joy of the occasion is also appropriate. Although only a very few of the most highly-placed Siamese are aware of it, their enjoyment of this night's festivities as a free people, rather than as the subjects of a great colonial power, are in some small measure due to the brilliant deductive reasoning, and courageous actions, of Sherlock Holmes.

Holmes has, without giving offence, refused the extravagant gifts sent by the Siamese, on the grounds that we were not acting in a private capacity. Fortunately, I was not obliged to forego the treasure I found here at Siam. My beloved Malee agreed to become my wife only two weeks ago, subject to her mother's approval, and I am only sorry that Holmes will not be here as my best man.

Finally, as I really must seal this for Holmes, it is my intention to bring my wife to France for a wedding in my home village, at which time I shall forward to you all the remaining volumes of my Journals. When that will be I have not yet decided, as Holmes has left some further small matters for me to investigate, but I shall not delay long.

Until that time, Doctor Watson, it remains only for me to wish you well, and to hope that my humble efforts at recording our remarkable journey, and Holmes's successes, meet with your approval.

Francois le Villard
Bangkok, Siam

Chapter X

Le Villard's preamble, or rather postscript, was followed by a title page, lettered by hand in small, neat block capitals, saying:

HERE BEGINS VOLUME I
of
THE JOURNALS of M. F. Le VILLARD,
NATURALIST TO THE EXPEDITIONS OF
Dr. OLAF SIGERSON (F. R. G. S.)

and immediately below the heading, with no space wasted, began his Journals.

24th May 1891
Paris, France
I was assigned to the Homicide Department at the *Quai d'Orfevres*, with the rank of Inspector, and had just solved the Didier Falcone murder case, which had the entire department puzzled as to how a man could commit a murder

six months after his own death. None doubted that he had murdered his former business partner, for he had stated in his will that he would do so, and had even given the month of the murder. The victim had not taken the threat seriously, until it was too late. The details of the solution to that mystery have been written up at length in the French press. I also made it the principal subject of a paper on detection, which I presented at the police college only the week before I received orders transferring my services to the Foreign Office of the French Republic.

Accompanying my transfer papers was a railway ticket to Florence, and an advice that I would be met at the Grand Terminal there; I knew nothing further.. The only times I had been similarly transferred in the past had been at the request of M. Sherlock Holmes, but he was now dead, and I could not even hazard a guess, as the train steamed across the border and into Italy, as to what awaited me at Florence. It was a distinct pleasure to leave Paris and its seamier underbelly and take train across Europe in summer. I dozed fitfully, read, and attempted to work at my translations. But my thoughts returned again and again to the mystery of my summons to Venice.

27th May 1891
Florence, Italy
As it was, not even my wildest imaginings would have included the amazing reality, that it was indeed my old patron and friend, Sherlock Holmes, thin but healthy, and most certainly alive, who stood before me in his suite at the hotel. M. Mycroft had stood on the platform as the train pulled in to the station. I immediately recognised his enormous figure, and as I had only an overnight bag, we were soon with Holmes. Over a meal and some red wine I caught up on details of Holmes's escape from death, and soon we came to discussion of the reasons for my summons to Florence.

Here le Villard's account substantially repeated the briefing I had already received from Mycroft, up to their leaving Italy.

The first thing I noticed was that Holmes was clearly *not* to be referred to throughout the journals as 'Dr. Olaf Sigerson'. This meant that the books had been kept somewhere secure and private at all times, otherwise they should have been scrupulously consistent with their covering story, in the event that they were too closely inspected by the authorities at any place. Obviously, were le Villard to refrain from describing Holmes's exploits in some detail, the report should be of no value to Mycroft, and those exploits were hardly likely to be those of an explorer and archaeologist. The fraudulent cover pages, together with the copious botanical and zoological notes and numerous sketches, were to be 'window dressing', as it were, whilst the body of the journal was in fact a straightforward account of their travels.

For this I was most grateful, as it would greatly simplify the task of editing, and I made a mental note to thank le Villard, as it must have increased the risk of exposure if the journals had fallen into the wrong hands. I read on,

3rd June 1891
Naples, Italy
We departed from Florence by train to board a coastal steamer to Naples, where we transferred to a passenger ship of the Cunard line, bound for Calcutta. Mycroft left us at Naples, to return to London via Paris, where he would be met by M. de Benoist, his counterpart in the French government. Mycroft had arranged that Holmes should pay a courtesy call, as Sigerson, to the British High Commissioner when we arrived at Calcutta, where further instructions would await us.

Also, at Naples came aboard our two language tutors, with whom we were to pass so many hours of shipboard instruction. Mycroft had arranged their employment, and their arrival at shipside ready to depart for India. They were to share a cabin in steerage. Mycroft had already given us a briefing on the backgrounds of the two men.

One was a Persian from Isphahan, named Nasir, who taught us his native Persian and Pushtu. I had some proficiency in both tongues, having served a two-year posting in our Persian consular office, ostensibly as a liaison officer, actually as an intelligence agent for our government. In fact, I was quite fluent in Persian, but I took all the lessons with Holmes anyway.

The other was a *pundit*, one of that small number of Indian spies, employed by the Great Trigonometrical Survey - now the Survey of India - to map those areas of Central Asia where Europeans were forbidden to trespass on pain of death. The entire area of India had finally, after seventy years, been mapped in detail, but knowledge of the 'forbidden areas' of Central Asia beyond the range of the observation towers built along the marches of the northern borders was scanty and inaccurate. For thirty years now the brave and resourceful *pundits* had met that need. They had been taught the 'measured stride' to calculate distances with remarkable accuracy; the use of compass and sextant, and how to conceal them in prayer wheel or staff-head; how to use a bowl of mercury as an artificial horizon; and dozens of other ploys and subterfuges to enable them to travel far and wide in regions where discovery would mean certain torture and death.

Sarat Chandra Das was, according to Mycroft, different from all the other *munshis* and *pundits*. Unlike most of them, he was not from one of the various regions bordering on Tibet, but was a native of coastal Bengal. He also worked for the government of India, rather than the Survey, as did most of the other *pundits.* After studies at Calcutta, he was appointed head of the Bhutia Boarding School at Darjeeling, to educate Sikkimese boys. After reading of Markham's journeys he determined to visit Tibet, and learnt fluent Tibetan. Das and his Tibetan language tutor Ugyen Gyatso had successfully crossed into Tibet.

Disguised as a Tibetan lama, Das had gone initially to Tashilhunpo Monastery, the spiritual capital of Tibet. There he had befriended the Prime Minister of Tibet, and taught him some English. He had an audience with the *Panchen Lama,* whose monastery it was. The *Panchen Lama* was regarded as being second in the land after the *Dalai Lama.* Several years later he returned with a printing press for the Prime Minister, and through him arranged a trip to Lhasa, where he met the boy *Dalai Lama.* Following his own journeys, Das had assisted the Survey in various ways. In 1888 and 1889 he had coached the Japanese monk Kawaguchi for his clandestine trip to Lhasa.

"A most charming gentleman, and a recognised scholar in the field as well," concluded Mycroft.

Das was returning from receiving his inscribed gold watch from the Royal Geographical Society in London, and was returning to live at Darjeeling, even though the Chief Lamas of Lhasa had put a price on his head which many would be happy to collect. He feared poisoning, he said, as this was the most likely form of murder. With poison, even your best friend could do away with you, and mourn at your funeral on the way to collect his payment. Although he had been asked to remain in England with his retired former mentor, Das said that he could never leave the foothills and peaks of the Himalayas when he was so near the end of his natural days anyway. Das taught us Tibetan, some Sanskrit and Hindi and, most importantly, the Bhotia dialect of that tribe of traders whose presence in Tibet was quite normal. No mention was made of our planned journey at this time.

Our fellow passengers were given the story of an expedition to the remote North Western provinces of British India, which would explain our schooling to any inquisitive person. Holmes spoke excellent Norwegian, which he had picked up several years previously when employed on behalf of the royal family, a case which occupied the best part of his time for almost a year. Posing as a Norwegian professor thus presented no problems for him, and we were accepted without reservation as Dr. Olaf Sigerson of Oslo University, explorer, and his assistant and naturalist, Francois le Villard. My talents at quick sketching, so useful to a detective, were of great value in my role, and I made sure that my work was observed by the more inquisitive of our shipmates.

Each morning before the sun rose, regardless of weather, Holmes and I made our way to the deserted games deck, where we spent an hour in the practice of that Oriental art of defence which Holmes calls *baritsu*. His proficiency at this martial art was the deciding factor in the final confrontation with Professor Moriarty, according to Holmes. Although I had been a schoolboy boxing champion, and later competed at Greek wrestling at the *Lycée de Chambery*, I was more than willing to learn the subtleties and feints so essential to positioning your opponent to his disadvantage, and the techniques of gathering power for the lightning-fast final blow.

Otherwise Holmes kept to his cabin, except at meals, as befitted a professor, whilst I passed my spare time making the acquaintance of such young and single ladies as I could find aboard, as befitted an assistant. The cuisine was tolerable, the wine less so, but the memory of several of those shipboard nights, with the gay dances and entertainments of an evening, and the lingering for quiet moments on the decks afterwards, remains with me.

In this way we passed the time as our ship steamed through the Suez Canal, with coaling stops at Port Suez and Aden, and at Colombo in Ceylon, before reaching Calcutta.

8th July 1891
Calcutta, India
Our ship steamed through the shoals at the mouth of the Ganges Delta; the low white city of Calcutta stretched elegantly along the bank of the Hooghly River. Tall masts on the south bank marked the wharves, with the city straggling away into the heat haze; the mass of a large fort contrasted with the green expanse of a botanical garden and the grand, white, classical buildings of the government of India.

We intended to remain only a short while at Calcutta. Once we had settled into a reasonable hotel, we washed up and took a brief stroll about the crowded streets, but it was too hot to go far. We contented ourselves with a gin-and-tonic on the terrace, some excellent curry and *pillau*, and an early night.

The next morning, while the streets were still cool, we took a gharrie to Government House, where Holmes sent his card and his compliments in to the High Commissioner. Almost immediately we were shown into a magnificent panelled study, with a vast desk and large, comfortable chairs. Enormous original oils decorated the walls, depicting events of great moment in the history of the Empire. In contrast to all this splendour, a small and somewhat rumpled man emerged from behind the desk, and crossed the marble floor to greet Holmes.

"Welcome to India, Mr. Holmes. Sir Charles Mortimer, but you must call me Charlie. Mycroft telegraphed that you were coming on the next P&O liner. We were at the House together, you know."

"Thank you, Sir Charles," replied Holmes, "It's nice to have a solid footing once again. Please allow me to introduce my colleague, Francois le Villard, who will accompany me on my little mission."

"How do you do, sir? You'll have your work cut out for you keeping up with young Sherlock here. You'll forgive my familiarity, I hope, Mr. Holmes, but the last time I saw you, your attire included short pants and a rather disreputable straw boater."

"Quite alright, Sir Charles, amongst ourselves, but I do hope . . ."

"Oh! Don't you worry about that Mr. Holmes. Mycroft impressed upon me the importance of your presence remaining secret, from everyone, even the Viceroy. Mycroft and I have good reason to trust in one another."

"Much appreciated, Sir Charles. Mycroft sends his warmest regards. He also said that you would have a message for me?"

Sir Charles unlocked a shallow drawer, then held out a telegraph reception form, which was covered all over with groupings of numbers arranged in rows and columns. "Hope you have the cipher for this; it arrived last week along with my cover telegraph from Mycroft in our standard current cipher. Nobody has had a crack at this, though. I was notified as soon as it came in, and I've had it locked in my desk ever since."

"I have the cipher with me, Sir Charles. It will require some time to decode this; may I return tomorrow to send a reply?"

"Of course, of course! Any time at all! Just ask for me - at my secretary's desk. Now, Mycroft asked me to organise several things for you, concerning your trip to Darjeeling and beyond. I've arranged for Captain Faunce to be at your disposal for as long as you need. Faunce is with the Intelligence Branch of the Army Quartermaster General's Department; he's our expert on clandestine crossings into Bhutan and Tibet. He will know you as Professor Sigerson. Shall I set up a meeting tomorrow? Three o'clock, then. Now, is there anything else I can do for you? No? Well, you have only to ask. Glad to help, and it's been a pleasure, Mr. Holmes. M. Le Villard." He rang for an aide to see us out.

We returned to our hotel, and after checking that our belongings had not been inspected during our absence, Holmes sat at the low table and spread his papers. Several hours passed before he spoke again.

"Very well, le Villard, my friend. We have a clear text . . . and an extended itinerary for our journey. Once we have reached Lhasa, and have made contact with Mycroft's agent there, we are to travel with him along the old trade road to Ladakh, then make our way to Samarkand, and thence down to the sea at Persia."

Holmes unfolded several of the excellent maps given him by Mycroft in Italy. Printed on very fine waterproof vellum, each folded up to a very small size; his complete set of maps required less volume than a single one of the five excellent leather-bound notebooks I had purchased at Florence when informed of the purpose of our journey. Overlapped to provide a continuous chart of our projected journey, the maps covered the top of the low table.

"What do think, le Villard?"

"I think that both Mycroft and de Benoist should be committed to an institution, is my first reaction," I replied, after carefully inspecting the planned route. "Much of the journey is to be through territories forbidden to outsiders, and most of the remainder has barely been charted. As an experienced alpinist I'd like to point out that most of this journey is to be at elevations higher than the tallest peak in Europe. Some of these passes are estimated at sixteen and seventeen, even nineteen thousand feet. It can be done, I suppose, with a fair amount of hardship. There are at least local trade paths or roads for most of the distance, according to this legend. Superb maps, I must say, Holmes."

"Yes. Not surprisingly, Mycroft's map cabinets contain probably the world's most comprehensive and accurate maps of the globe, in many cases surpassing in detail those published by the Royal Geographical Society."

"Why the extended journey? Surely that means that any report we make from Lhasa will be greatly delayed in reaching Europe."

"Not exactly; his agent at Lhasa will send our ciphered report back down to Darjeeling with a messenger, or with our returning guide. It seems that since we departed Europe there have been more serious rumours of Russian activities in various places along our route. Apparently, none of these reports is regarded as reliable, originating as they all do from rumours gleaned in bazaars and at intriguing courts. But the reports came from such a wide area, and were sufficiently credible, that it was decided at the highest levels that a trusted observer must be sent to make an accurate report.

"Spies sent in from the European side have seen tantalising glimpses of military activity, but the scope is impossible to tell, as the Russians are masters at concealing their military plans behind a facade of trade. Since Count Gorchakov declared in 1864 that the Russians would advance no further into Central Asia, Tashkent and Kokand have been captured and Khiva here," Holmes indicated the Khanates with his finger, "and Bokhara here, have become vassal states of Russia."

Holmes sat back from the maps. "Mycroft briefed me on all of this before you arrived at Florence. I am quite an authority now on all the countries between China and Persia. China constitutes the logical limit to Russian expansion to the East, and Persia, which has traditionally been the feared invasion route to India, provides the gateway to the passes of the Hindu Kush. The conquerors of India have come that way since history began.

"Less than a decade ago, in 1884, St. Petersburg sent missions to Chitral and Hunza, the first open Russian approach to an Indian state. They also annexed Merv, which puts Russian power less than a hundred miles from the border between Persia and Afghanistan."

"And now there are these reports from Lhasa!"

"Exactly. So the big question across Europe right now concerns Russian intentions towards British India. The Great Game!" remarked Holmes.

"How does our French government come to be involved in all this?" I asked.

"Simple. Many of the most recent and disturbing reports concerning the Russian threat have come to Mycroft from de Benoist, who receives them from the intelligence services operated by your mendicant and missionary orders; Benedictines, Capuchins, Franciscans and Jesuits, who are active wherever they are tolerated. There are those at the Russian court who dismiss the Chinese as militarily weak, and the British in India as complacent and vulnerable. Not surprisingly, given relations between France and Russia over the past century, France has no desire to see St. Petersburg invade either British India, with all its riches and trade, or China, which has the same, or both."

"So de Benoist informs Mycroft, and the Foreign Office ups the ante by sending Sherlock Holmes to investigate," I said.

"And the *Quai d'Orsay* sees the bid by sending Francois le Villard along for the ride," laughed Holmes. "I see you comprehend perfectly."

Holmes folded away his maps, and said, "This is all very well, le Villard. But there is something I must say! When we began this venture, it was to be a quick trip into Tibet and back. With all the training, not more than nine months or so! You're a younger man than I, and this promises to be a fine adventure. I felt certain you would not refuse. This new journey, however, will be a very different affair. It will take the best part of two years, in all likelihood. That is a long time to spend away from civilisation, tramping and climbing on frozen mountains at the end of the world. I would fully understand if you chose to return directly from Lhasa, as agreed."

I let Holmes finish speaking while I considered what he had said. It was true that two years is a long time. That the journey would be cold and arduous in the extreme I had no doubt. But, it was also true that I was young, single and healthy, and that this promised to be an adventure to remember until I was old and grey. If we survived to remember anything!

"Holmes," I said, "how can I possibly let pass the only chance I may ever have to be indispensable to you. I am your superior in very few things, but two of them are alpine climbing, and mastery of Persian. You need me, and therefore I will go."

10th July 1891
Calcutta, India
At three in the afternoon, after a day spent in making a few local purchases for our journey, we returned to Government House, and asked for Sir Charles. Holmes first arranged the dispatch of a ciphered telegraph message, I presumed to Mycroft, and then returned to Sir Charles's office, where I had remained. Captain Faunce was introduced to us, and was briefed on our requirements. Sir Charles, pleading other engagements, sent us off with the Captain to his offices at the rear of the building. The door to Faunce's office carried the simple legend 'PURCHASING'.

"So, you want to get to Lhasa!" said Faunce. "So do a lot of other people." He sat, and indicated worn wooden armchairs for us.

"Right now, Prince Henri of Orleans and his party are attempting an approach from the East. Reports have reached us of a female American missionary, who has just been turned back, only days from Lhasa. But you know, Professor, we've never been able to get a non-Asiatic into Lhasa, and it's not for want of trying. Western Tibet, away from Lhasa, yes. But their intelligence system is very efficient, and their spies are usually aware of an approach long before it gets near their capital."

"Are you saying that it's not possible, Captain Faunce?" asked Holmes.

"No, Professor, I've always believed it to be possible. And you may be ideally qualified for the method I have in mind. You see, I believe that the element of surprise is the key. Firstly, it is absolutely necessary to avoid gossip and rumour in the bazaar at Darjeeling, or Dehra Dun or wherever you set out from."

"Is it necessary to go to Darjeeling at all?" I enquired.

"You'll need an experienced guide, one who has travelled the route before and knows where the border posts and checkpoints are, because the only way to get you two to Lhasa is to avoid them entirely."

"And is that possible?" asked Holmes.

"I have a lot of experience in this area, Professor, including several crossings into Tibet. It's possible, but in my opinion only for a small party travelling light, and able to traverse difficult terrain. You would need to move quickly, as food will become a problem. Living off the land will be necessary where possible. The greatest difficulty will be passing the border posts, and crossing the Tsangpo River. You can, with difficulty, skirt all of the checkpoints but one, but the river is impossible to cross except by the iron chain bridge at Chaksam. You won't be able to use the ferry, and you will need all your ingenuity to get past that obstacle."

"Do you have any large scale maps or directions to these areas?"

"Yes we do. Quite accurate as well, thanks to our *pundits*."

"Excellent."

"Your disguise will not withstand close scrutiny, and at the slightest suspicion you will be held for investigation. These guards know that their life depends on keeping out all intruders, and that even the highest lama in the land is subject to death and disgrace for failure in this respect. Once you have reached the Tsangpo, you must travel only at night, and avoid all habitation. Your only chance to enter Lhasa is to sneak in at dead of night. I believe you have a contact in the Mahommedan quarter there; our agents have compiled an extremely accurate map of Lhasa, which should be of some help."

Holmes thought for a moment, then said, "My instructions were to follow your guidance, so what else do we need to do?"

"You have already made the acquaintance of Sarat Chandra Das. Have you discussed your journey with him?"

"Not at all, only language instruction so far."

"Very well. We will leave tomorrow for Darjeeling. There we will meet again with Das, but it must be in secret, as Tibetan spies closely watch him. He will bring along another of the native explorers, Kintup, who will be your guide. He has been to Lhasa before. However this is different, as he bluffed his way past the border posts, rather than skirting them."

"A reliable guide?" asked Holmes.

"Professor, the *pundits* are a remarkable group of men, and if an Englishman had made just one of the journeys these men have, he would be inundated with medals and awards. Kintup may be illiterate, but he is amongst the very best of that select group, in my opinion."

"Fine. And as to training?"

"You'll need toughening up. Your cover story is that your health is poor, and a course of mountain exercise and fresh air has been recommended. I have arranged for some strenuous climbs in the area around Darjeeling, which M. Le Villard can also explain away as pursuing his botanical researches. Couple of weeks of that should do. Meanwhile, Das and Kintup can give you a great deal of sound advice regarding possible complications, and how to avoid them. Remember, they've been through this before – their advice is worth heeding."

"How do we arrange that, with all the spies around?" I asked.

"Chandra Das is the Principal of the Bhutia Boarding School at Darjeeling. Kintup is a tailor in town. You must never be seen even talking to either of them. I can set up discreet meetings with both of them, without attracting attention. Any equipment or supplies you require will be prepared at Silliguri, where the railway from Calcutta terminates. When it is time to go, you will leave Darjeeling with tickets to Calcutta, with all of your luggage and specimens. Better put it about that you are leaving India, your recuperation and researches complete. You will be watched until Silliguri, and onto the Calcutta train, so you should travel several stations down the line. It will be safe to return to Silliguri the next day. Kintup and myself will await you there, and that will be your starting point. After that you will be on your own."

"When will that be?" asked Holmes.

"You'll want to get over the Himalayas proper well before the winter snows close the passes, as you'll not be travelling on the paths. I think three weeks local climbing and a week for instruction should do it. Let us set a tentative departure date for 12th August. You should make sure to get plenty of sun, it will help your disguise while it lasts."

"I take it you will return to Calcutta once we are settled at Darjeeling?"

"Not exactly Calcutta, Professor Sigerson, but close by. I shall keep in touch with the High Commissioner at Darjeeling by telegraph, so we can communicate in that way if necessary. Don't forget that much of the government will also be in Darjeeling right now. Makes it more difficult for their spies to keep tabs on everyone. Soon the weather will turn cooler, and the place will be almost deserted. That is when you must be on your guard against the inadvertent remark, or the too obvious question. Not only at the bazaar! This applies equally to the Anglos at Darjeeling, and especially to their servants. Your lives will depend upon your success in keeping your journey entirely secret."

12th July 1891
Darjeeling, India
Silliguri was a fourteen hour rail journey from Calcutta, and from there the extension of the track brought us to Darjeeling, the hill station sanatorium for the Government of India at Calcutta. Only recently ceded by Sikkim to the British for this purpose, Darjeeling had already developed from virgin wilderness into a clean and elegant village, set in forested highlands, with sweeping views over the steaming, unhealthy *terai* below. As I looked

around, I was reminded of the small Alpine towns where I had done much of my youthful climbing. Steep pitched roofs on villas set in spacious lawns and gardens; a charming street running though the centre of town, along the wooded ridge, with tea rooms and restaurants, a playhouse, the post office and police station, all so familiar and comforting to the European eye. Layered down the slopes were the houses and shanties of the various classes of Indians, the merchants, servants, porters and so forth, all essential to the comfort of their British masters. All around, the stupendous snow-tipped peaks of the Himalayas towered overhead. The crisp air and icy, crystal clear streams were a welcome and refreshing respite for us, coming as we were from our ocean voyage through the tropics, followed immediately by the late summer heat of Calcutta.

We were soon settled, as Professor Sigerson and assistant, in our own bungalow, which had a steeply pitched roof set low on its half-timbered stone walls, a flagged path winding through a well-tended front garden, and flowers at every windowsill. Our rooms were most comfortable, with stone fireplaces and wood-panelled walls; polished brass lamps placed all around promised adequate light for night work. The sitting room gave directly onto a wooden balcony, providing excellent views over the valleys below, with the massive granite peak of Kanchenjunga blocking half the sky to the North.

Captain Faunce introduced us to our Hindu servant, then left us to visit the British High Commission, carrying with him Professor Sigerson's letters of introduction. The Professor himself, it was explained, was still recuperating from the long trip, and felt too unwell after the train journey to come himself. In this way the British at Darjeeling were made aware of our arrival, and of the supposed reasons for our coming there.

That evening, at the invitation of the High Commissioner at Darjeeling, we went with the Captain to the Playhouse. A cast of officers and civil servants and their wives had put up a creditable performance of *The Pirates of Penzance*, to the great amusement of the rest of the European populace. Here we were introduced to the High Commissioner and his family, and spent some time fielding questions regarding our previous researches. Holmes gave quite a performance himself, as a man brought to the brink of physical collapse by the rigours of exploration in Africa, and now forced to interrupt his journey to Oceania in order to repair his health.

Shortly after midnight Captain Faunce, who had earlier left us to walk home by ourselves, appeared at our villa with two Asiatic gentlemen, one of whom was our old friend Chandra Das. The other was Kintup. Introductions all round, followed by Captain Faunce saying, "Let us get down to business, gentlemen; I must leave before dawn. You needn't worry about the servant.

He's my man, and sees and hears nothing. Damn fine cook as well."

We discussed, with the aid of Holmes's excellent maps, the route we would take, the difficulties of the various passes, and the disposition of Tibetan observation posts. Seasonal weather, snow conditions, population and availability of food were all considered. Decisions were made as to clothing and equipment, keeping in mind our need to move fast to escape detection. Firearms and ammunition requirements were finalised with the Captain, who would arrange for all the necessary goods to be procured, and would bring them himself to Silliguri. Hollow staffs for concealment of funds in gold bullion form, and woven baskets with hidden compartments were considered and rejected; the common Tibetan guards were by now aware of these old tricks of the Survey. Our strategy, as far as Lhasa at least, was to avoid contact rather than to rely on subterfuge.

Arrangements were made for late night meetings with Chandra Das later in our stay. It was considered too risky to meet again with Kintup, as he would be going with us. We would see him next outside Silliguri, near where the road from Darjeeling links up with the old trade pathway to Lhasa. Word had already been given out in Darjeeling that Kintup had been summoned to Dehra Dun, the headquarters of the Survey of India, to assist with a report on his previous journey, and would be gone some time.

17th July 1891
Darjeeling, India
Das's final words upon leaving had been a warning that we should avoid contact with a certain M. Nicolae Chevron, a Roumanian Theosophist, who had arrived at Darjeeling some months before. This man was one amongst those wealthy 'pilgrims' who were convinced that behind the Himalayas were caves sheltering the wise 'mahatmas', guardians of the secret knowledge that was lost to the Western world when Atlantis sank into the waves. M. Chevron had spent his time at Darjeeling explaining his beliefs to anyone who would listen, and his money on preparing for a journey to Lhasa and beyond. Every Tibetan spy in the bazaar knew of his plans, said Das. He had been warned off at first, then finally had been forbidden by the High Commissioner to make any attempt to cross into Tibet from Darjeeling. Apparently, he intended to ignore these officious restrictions. We were, of course, curious about this theosophical adventurer. Several days later we found ourselves seated in the wicker armchairs on the terrace of the main hotel of Darjeeling, savouring the late afternoon views from this imperial belvedere, when we were greeted by a trim, slight European of middle height. His most conspicuous feature was a magnificent waxed moustache,

with the ends twirled up into points. His pomaded hair receded dramatically at the temples. Both his hair and his moustaches were coal-black, and he was dressed in a rather flamboyant style for Darjeeling.

"Good morning, Professor," said he to Holmes, and nodded a greeting in my direction. "I have heard of your researches in Africa, and felt I simply must introduce myself to a fellow explorer. M. Nicolae Chevron at your service, sirs." He clicked his heels, and bowed slightly. "May I join you?"

As we seemed to have little alternative, Holmes and I both rose, and politely shook hands with the Roumanian we had been warned to avoid. We all sat again, and more drinks were soon ordered. Chevron laid his book on the table; I noted the title lettered on the spine: 'The Voice of the Silence' by Helene Blavatsky.

"It is a pleasure to meet you, sir," said Holmes, "however, I fear our talk must be brief, as I have a dinner engagement this evening, and must finish some writing before going on. But tell me, M. Chevron, are you exploring in these regions at all?"

"Indeed yes!" exclaimed Chevron. "Or rather, I soon will be. I shall depart very shortly for Lhasa in Tibet. My small expedition is almost fully prepared. I expect it will be a difficult journey, but I have the finest Alpine equipment from London, and I have employed several most experienced guides."

"But I have heard that it is a virtual impossibility for a European to get to Lhasa," remarked Holmes. "You seem most confident of success."

The Roumanian picked up his book, and said, "Have you heard of Madame Blavatsky, Professor?"

"Of course. Actually, I had several discussions with her when she was in London. A most remarkable woman indeed!"

"Ah! Then you will know of the Masters, who dwell high in the Himalayas," exclaimed Chevron, with a sweeping gesture up towards the lofty peaks of those mountains. "I first met Madame Blavatsky when she was with Countess Wachtmeister at Wurzburg. Four years ago, in London, I was made a member of the Inner Group of her students. I spent time with her whenever I was in London, and just before she died, I told her I wished to meet with the Masters in Tibet. She gave me a message for her Master, Koot Hoomi. When I asked how I should find the Masters, Madame said that I should simply set out for Lhasa, and the way would become clear. Shortly after I left to come here, Madame passed on."

"That must have been very recently, as she died only months ago," said Holmes. "Around the 7th or 8th of May, wasn't it? I noted the date because a very dear friend of mine was reported dead in the same week, and their obituaries appeared on the same day."

"Exactly, Professor; it was the 8th. In fact, I took the entire affair as a message that I had been chosen to carry on her great teachings." M. Chevron sat back in his wicker chair. "I left London as soon as I had made some purchases, and sailed for India. I have the greatest confidence that all obstacles will fall away, and that someday I will return, when I have absorbed the Wisdom of the Ancients, to take up Madame's work."

"Oh dear!" exclaimed Holmes, looking at his pocket watch, "I fear we must leave you, M. Chevron. We are also leaving Darjeeling soon, but in the other direction. Our interests lie in the myriad isles of Oceania. It has been most interesting talking with you, and I'm sure M. Le Villard joins me in wishing you success. Good evening sir."

We settled the bill and walked back to our bungalow. "Unfortunate, Holmes, that we have been seen publicly with that fool," I remarked.

"Oh, I don't think it will cause any comment. I suspect that our friend has had the same conversation with anyone who will listen; we are just two of many, in this case, and there is safety in numbers."

"What chance do you give him, Holmes? Can he do it, do you think?" I asked.

"He will be turned back at the first border checkpoint in Tibet, and politely but firmly sent back here. Some of his money will stay with the local guides and porters, who will make better use of it than he, and M. Chevron will thrill groups of young Theosophists for years to come with the tale of his daring expedition to Tibet. Frankly, my only concern is to ensure that we are not following the same paths as he. I must check with Das; he is certain to know."

28th July 1891
Darjeeling, India
Captain Faunce had organised a guide for us, to take us on innocent but physically demanding climbs in the hills surrounding Darjeeling. Holmes gradually 'recovered' his health as we roamed further afield and included rock climbing in our walks. I took my notebook, and made field sketches of botanical specimens, collecting flowers and leaves as I went.

In between our 'nature rambles' we acted as naturally as possible: taking tea in the teashop at eleven each morning, reading the Calcutta newspapers, and *The Times* when it arrived. We visited the bazaar and bought a few curios, and strolled around the village in the late afternoons, chatting aimlessly with new-found friends.

We even visited the Playhouse again, when the play changed, and afterwards were introduced by the High Commissioner to his houseguests, Brigadier-General Sir Edmund Wrothesly, now retired, and his charming wife. A lively discussion ensued regarding the merits of Darjeeling as compared to Simla and Poona, the other famous hill stations of India, where thanks to the convenience of the telegraph and the railways, most government business was conducted throughout the summer months. The Brigadier-General's wife was rather scathing about loose morals at Simla and Poona, remarking that with modern transportation, there was no good reason why an officer should not marry early, and bring his wife to India with him. Other than that, she thought all three places were most charming and refined, compared to the squalor of Calcutta, where they had been obliged to spend three weeks before arriving at Darjeeling. Morals were even looser in the heat of the plains, she thought. Her husband changed the subject rather hastily, as there were several unaccompanied officers in the party, some of whom seemed a little discomfited by the subject.

Soon the Brigadier-General was boring the assembly with tales of his last command, in Egypt, and his part in Gordon's first journey up the Nile to the Sudan. "Even then," commented his wife, "I went as far as Abu Simbel with them, and there I awaited his return." The old soldier acknowledged defeat, and he and his wife bade the party farewell. They strolled away up the moonlit street towards their lodgings at the High Commission, her hand on his forearm, her head resting lightly on his shoulder. As someone commented, rather caustically, "The Very Picture of Connubial Bliss."

5th August 1891
Darjeeling, India
Sarat Chandra Das came for his third and last visit before our departure. Holmes and he had gone over every aspect of the journey again and again, and had also covered various aspects of our onward journey from Lhasa, within the areas he knew. Each time he came we spent some time on languages. This time he said that although our languages were adequate in a pinch, we should try as much as possible to use the language of a stranger, wherever we were, but a stranger with a plausible excuse for being wherever we were. This was sound advice, which we came to follow throughout our travels.

We had talked about adding a fourth to our small party, but as Das could not recommend anyone qualified, we decided to travel with a party of only three. This had its advantages in mobility and speed, and ability to hide. The disadvantage was mainly that of food. We would be weeks in the freezing wastes of the Himalayas, and unable to seek food from the few habitations we passed. There was a limit to how much provisions and ammunition we could carry. Das thought that a good shot could live off the land even well above the snow line, and there was always one last resort. We could send Kintup into some isolated village as a lost wayfarer, and hope to disappear into the surrounding mountains before any word was passed to the Tibetan border guards. With less than a week left in Darjeeling before our departure, we took our leave of Das, memorised messages for several monks he wanted to be remembered to at Tashilhunpo, should the chance arise, and watched as he slipped into the silent darkness outside our bungalow door.

6th August 1891
Darjeeling, India
After almost three weeks at Darjeeling Holmes and I were both in excellent physical condition, and spent much of our time out in the woods and on the rock-faces, preparing for our journey under the guise of exercise and recuperation. I made numerous botanical sketches, and made a point of letting them be seen. I also sent away several crates of botanical samples to the University of Oslo, Norway, marked: 'To await the return of Professor Olaf Sigerson'.

Holmes played the part of the Professor so convincingly, he was asked by the British Ladies Committee of Darjeeling to present a speech to the community about his work. This he 'reluctantly' declined, citing his health and the press of time.

"Doesn't do to push my luck too far with this disguise. Not amongst the British, anyway," he said to me, laughing at the irony of it all.

CHAPTER XI

8th August 1891
Darjeeling, India
HOLMES WAS IN a quandary. We were sitting in our favourite tea shop, reading the papers, as we did each morning when in town. He had been reading in the Calcutta press the rather lurid accounts of the mysterious deaths of a number of Army officers at various locations. The two most recent

cases had occurred at Calcutta, and bore close similarities to deaths at several other places around India. All the victims were Officers in the Indian Army, and all held the same rank, Captain, or higher. All had been poisoned with massive doses of an unidentifiable poison, which killed them outright, but in a most peaceful way. All were found as if slumbering, usually relaxed in an easy chair on the terrace, or before the fire.

Their wives back in England had all received, within days of their deaths, a card of condolence, always the same cheap pink heart-shaped card, with crude lettering expressing regret at the untimely death of their husband, always worded the same way. The horrible thing, which first attracted the attention of the police, was that the cards were postmarked from India, bearing dates up to two weeks before the death occurred. The examining doctors had diagnosed the first two known cases, at Simla and at Agra, as massive heart attacks, until the arrival of the pink cards alarmed their families in England.

After the sixth of these mysterious deaths had splashed the headlines for several days, Holmes looked at me one morning over the local Darjeeling newssheet, and cried, "Of course, that's it! It should have been obvious who was doing it, and how. But how do I act upon it, before another unfortunate officer becomes the next victim of the Pink Ticket Murderer."

"You know who this murderer is, then?" I asked. "How can that be, when we have hardly set foot in India, other than here?"

"You also know the murderer, le Villard. The question is how to seize the killer, and stop the murders, without giving away that we are detectives? There is no proof; it may take weeks to prove circumstantially, and yet the whole sorry matter is as clear as can be."

"Perhaps you could have a word with the High Commissioner, and he could take some restraining action."

"That would be excellent advice, le Villard, if the murderer was not his own houseguest."

"Sir Edmund Wrothesly? Are you serious, Holmes? He seems to be just another retired soldier, living on his memories and his family money."

"Not the Brigadier-General, le Villard. His wife, the Lady Wrothesly, is our Pink Ticket Murderer. But convincing the High Commissioner that that is the case will not be easy," said Holmes.

"Try convincing me," said I, "as I still cannot see your reasoning myself."

"Very well. You will recall when we met the Wrotheslys at the Playhouse how vocal she was on the subject of officers staying for years in India while their wives stayed at home in England. 'Loose morals', I believe she called it. You will also recall that she mentioned that she and her husband had recently stayed at Poona, and at Agra, and at Simla, and more recently at Calcutta. These are all locations of these murders.

"That alone would be coincidence enough, and I've no doubt that an investigation will show they were in those places at the right times. But there is more. All the victims died of a massive dose of a poison that killed quickly, quietly, and apparently painlessly. Now you know, le Villard, that almost all poisons capable of killing outright cause great pain and trauma, usually causing a ghastly appearance in the corpse. One of the very few toxins that qualify is that one selected, after much trial and error on her slaves, by Cleopatra - the venom of the asp. The asp, as you should know, is a small snake of the cobra family, and is found, not in India, but in Africa. I also recall that its venom is much in demand amongst poisoners in Egypt to this day.

"You remember where our couple were posted last - Egypt and the Sudan. I suspect we will find a similar pattern of murders in Cairo and Alexandria, stopping mysteriously at the time when the Wrotheslys left for India. She has a stock of asp venom somewhere in her reticule, I'll warrant, and is murdering soldiers here in India now."

"But what suddenly makes you so certain, Holmes?" I asked, picking up the newspaper which had started his chain of deductions. I read again the details, by now familiar, of the crimes and what was known about them.

"The colour of the cards sent by the murderer, my friend. Pink! Why always pink? There was something about the phrase 'pink card' which rang familiar. It took a few moments to recall the discussion with Lady Wrothesly, when she had become mildly exercised about the 'loose morals' of those officers who stayed here for years on a 'pink ticket'. At the time I paid no attention to it, but I remember Doctor Watson using the phrase when we discussed his experiences in Afghanistan. It's an old Army term for tacit permission, from the wife, for a soldier to take a native mistress when stationed for long periods overseas.

"Any one of the above could be ascribed to coincidence. But combine her animus towards soldiers with 'pink tickets'; their recent arrival from Egypt, and the nature of the poison used; and the parallels between towns they have visited and locations of murders. There you have a chain of deduction solid enough that I am fearful of the lives of the officers here, and yet weak enough that it will not stand the burden of official examination. As I say, I am in a quandary."

"It's more than likely that she poisons her victims just before leaving a town," said I, "and I overheard in the tea shop today that they will depart within the week."

"Exactly, le Villard. We have no time to waste."

Early next morning, the 9th of August, Holmes sent away several ciphered telegraph messages to London, and the following morning was informed by a servant that there were several replies for him at the High Commission. I went myself to collect them, brought them back to the bungalow, and waited while Holmes decoded them. Both were short messages from Mycroft. The first confirmed that a series of unsolved poisonings in Egypt, complete with the familiar pink cards, had suddenly stopped at the same time as our suspects had left Africa. The second message was a précis of Lady Wrothesly's record of confinement for 'hysteria' when her husband was at Aldershot, early in his Army career, and was informed of his first overseas posting.

This still left unresolved the problem of arresting the murderess without becoming involved ourselves. The High Commissioner was not aware of our real identities, and Holmes wanted to keep things that way, with our departure only days away. We discussed various options, and discarded them for one reason or another. Finally Holmes said, "The only way we can be certain she commits no more murders is to remove the poison. I think we need to visit the High Commissioner's residence one last time, and while you create a diversion, I shall search their belongings."

Half an hour later we were seated with the High Commissioner in his study when I was seized with severe stomach cramps, which sent Holmes looking for help while the Commissioner made me comfortable on the window seat. The suspects were seated in the garden having afternoon tea with the Commissioner's wife and several other village notables. I noticed through the tall glass-paned doors that Lady Wrothesly did not have her reticule with her, her hands holding only a lace-trimmed handkerchief and an inhaler of pierced silver metal.

Holmes was gone only five or six minutes, which he explained by pretending he had become lost for a moment, and gave me a quick wink indicating success. My cramps eased miraculously, and we soon sent a final telegraph message, this time to Captain Faunce, coded with the simple cipher we had agreed upon. We left without confronting the Wrotheslys, and returned to our bungalow.

"I have it, le Villard. I'm sure this is it," said Holmes, holding out a glass phial containing a viscous pale yellow liquid. "Be careful how you handle it. You will notice that, although labelled as an expensive French perfume, the liquid has no odour at all. I checked all the other vials, and all contained their scent as labelled, so I'm hopeful that this is her only supply."

Holmes cleared a space on the table, and carefully unstoppered the phial. I sniffed at it cautiously, and it was indeed scentless.

"Could you please rinse out that small medicine bottle," he requested. "I shall send a sample of this to Faunce in her own vial; he'll know what to do with it when he receives my telegraph."

"And what about the balance of the poison?" I asked of Holmes. "From what you say, there is still sufficient there to kill a troop of soldiers."

"That thought had occurred to me, le Villard. Given where we are going, and the antagonism we may well encounter, this small bottle may prove worth keeping."

I knew that Holmes had a deep knowledge of poisons, and of the poisoner's arts, yet this action of his surprised me. I suddenly realised that Holmes took the threats we were facing most seriously, and that not only the geographical challenges were of concern. It also occurred to me that perhaps Holmes saw the poison of serene and painless death as an escape of absolute last resort. I did not want to dwell on the vast number of ways we could come to that situation, and so put the matter from my mind.

11th August 1891
Darjeeling, India

The Wrotheslys left the High Commission early the next morning, after a hysterical search for missing 'valuables' by her Ladyship. Packing hastily, they made for the railway station, and set out on the next train for Calcutta, where they were met by Faunce and the Indian police and detained for questioning, according to the next morning's *Calcutta Clarion*, in connection with the so-called Pink Ticket Murders.

After hours of interrogation, Sir Edmund broke down, and confessed that he had suspected for some time that his wife was the culprit, but hadn't the nerve to say anything, in case she turned on him. Clearly terrified of his wife's hysteria, he had allowed her to decide where and when they went next, and went along with her public charade of mutual devotion. Confronted with her husband's confession, Lady Wrothesly had changed her tune entirely. She boasted of the number of 'cads' she had tricked into killing themselves, for she never actually administered the poison herself. Wherever she went she had soon established a reputation for making the most delicious lemon cordial, which, mixed with soda from the gasogene, made a cool and welcome drink for visitors calling at their residence of the moment. Lady Wrothesly had frequently made a parting gift to visitors of a small bottle of her cordial. Unaccompanied married officers over the rank of Captain were, it seems, likely to receive a bottle laced with asp toxin, and the next time they made a cool drink, died peacefully where they sat. All this she proudly confessed, and was subsequently charged with fourteen self-confessed counts of murder by poisoning. Sir Edmund was charged as an accessory in the crimes, which were all the scandal throughout India and colonial Africa for months afterwards. The small phial containing the remaining toxin was shown to the murderer, and she willingly identified it as hers. Analysis of the liquid took some time, but was finally shown to be asp toxin in pure form, with a few drops sufficing to kill a man.

The one thing *The Calcutta Clarion* did not clarify was the nature of the 'information received' that had led to the arrests in the first place.

12th August 1891
Silliguri, India

Kintup had left Darjeeling almost two weeks previously, ostensibly to make his way to Dehra Dun. In actuality, he was with Captain Faunce somewhere outside Calcutta, preparing our equipment. We had said our farewells to Das, and were fit and healthy. Our supplies, firearms and ammunition should all be ready as agreed, and our preparation was as complete as could be, given the minimal equipment we would carry.

Holmes and I packed our gear, said our goodbyes - as the Professor and his assistant - to those acquaintances we had picked up during our short stay, and left Darjeeling on the morning train, with tickets for Calcutta. As planned, we alighted at the third station down the line, and stopped overnight at a small guest house.

The next day we waited until evening for a local train to return us to Silliguri. If I were going to withdraw, this would be my last opportunity. I confess I did consider it, however briefly. We made our way to a certain small guest house, as instructed by Captain Faunce, and took a room for the evening. Later that night there was a soft knock at the door. I opened it to admit Faunce, alone. Kintup was staying elsewhere, and would meet us on the morrow. After a brief discussion about the Wrothesly case, as he called it, we turned in on the thin mattresses, Faunce sleeping on the floor. "Quite used to it," said he, "besides, this will be your last night of comfort for a long time. Might as well savour it, my lads. Tomorrow it begins."

He laughed as he blew out the lamp. "Wish I was going with you, is the truth. Always had my heart set on being the first into Lhasa! Funny old world, isn't it?"

Chapter XII

I had become so engrossed in the Journals that I had forgotten the time entirely. Fortunately I had also neglected the fire, which finally collapsed into its own embers in a shower of sparks, and roused me from my reading. The clock on the mantel chimed eight, and I was obliged to hustle along in order to reach Victoria Station by half-past. I found Holmes already seated at a table in the Dining Room, a pot of coffee in front of him and his forefinger hooked through the handle of a thick white china cup. An open newspaper was spread in front of him; a pile of disordered news-sheets indicated that he had arrived some little time before.

"'Evening, Holmes, sorry I'm late," I apologised, a little breathless from hurrying.

"Good evening, Watson. As you see, the business at Greenwich was quickly done with, and I arrived here early. A reasonably convincing scenario, which would have fooled the locals! Luckily for us, we were only watching. At around five minutes to eight a half-dozen or so drunken soldiers came staggering past the Sailor's Home, coincidentally at the same time as a squad of tars emerged from the Slug and Lettuce next door. The usual hurly-burly, until the whistles started blowing. Then, as they all took to their heels, Moran slipped in amongst the sailors, wearing similar attire, and carrying a duffel bag - which no doubt contains his evening dress. All I needed was confirmation with my own eyes that Moran had moved out at eight. I had that much right, and so was confident that the rest would also be correct. Thus, while Colonel Moran ducks and dodges around to elude any pursuers, we may relax here, confident that we shall pick up his trail. And now to survey the gastronomic landscape as offered by the inimitable British railway café!"

Holmes summoned a waiter, ordered two steak-and-kidney specials, and then gathered his dailies together.

"These will provide us some diversion on the journey. Lestrade and his cohorts are still taking quite a beating over losing Moran; I can almost find it in myself to sympathise with him. At least this should keep him occupied. He doesn't appear to have changed while I've been away. A good press has him in raptures, while a bad press drives him to distraction. For now let us devote our attention to steak-and-kidney pie, and hope it is the gravest threat we face this evening."

We finished our meal, paid the bill, and boarded the next train for Crystal

Palace Station.

At that hour of the night Crystal Palace was mostly in darkness. Only the concert-hall was still ablaze with electric lights. The vast glass and iron structure more nearly resembled a cathedral stretching away into the darkness, an impression reinforced by the cruciform layout of the building. Our interest lay in the well-dressed crowd of concert-goers just then emerging from the hall into the foyer. Holmes and myself had arrived some thirty minutes prior to the end of the programme, when few patrons were about. He had chosen a small table for two in a dimly lit corner of the bar and lounge area on the mezzanine floor, which afforded us a clear view of the entire public area without being ourselves visible.

It was clear that Holmes was becoming a little restless. There had been no sign of Colonel Moran, and the crowd would soon disperse, either to their homes or to seek further entertainment at Stepney or Whitechapel.

"Surely I've not misunderstood the message! What else could it mean?" said Holmes, to himself rather than to me. I could well understand his concern; after all, Moran had been allowed free against Holmes's word that he would be recaptured, along with his superiors in the gang. I had faith, however, that he had not reasoned incorrectly, and was about to say as much, when Holmes gripped my arm.

"Don't turn around! He's just arrived - by the column at the far end. He's scouting for enemy forces. Making no attempt at disguise or subterfuge either. Hasn't even shaved his moustaches, which is the first thing I should have done in his situation. He has changed back into his evening clothes, at the railway restrooms, I should imagine - I've always found that a useful dodge myself. I suppose he feels quite safe here - he knows that he'll be looked for at all the ports, but why should anyone expect him to attend a concert in London's outer suburbs?"

I had loaded my revolver in the privacy of the hansom on the way from the station. I felt the heavy bulge it made in the pocket of my overcoat, needlessly reassuring myself that it was still there; cosh and knuckles were in the other pocket. "Any sign of others?" I asked, fixing my gaze on the tablecloth.

Holmes's only reply was to say, "Let's drink our whisky. Appear normal and we'll remain unnoticed. *Someone* will come. The question is, what will they do then?"

"And what will *we* do then?" I countered.

"I've not deployed the Irregulars here," said Holmes, "as I need all their resources concentrated on locating Isobel Aster. So we're on our own, Watson. Are you still up to the game?"

I looked at him and saw that, in spite of his discreet but intent surveillance of Moran, there was an amused curl at the corners of his mouth.

"I'm not sure I could handle this alone if spotted," he said. "Moran's nerves must be rubbed fairly raw by now, so do be alert, Watson. He is certain to be armed, and we don't know how many of their gang are here, or where disposed."

And so we remained, sipping at our drinks, Holmes occasionally consulting his pocket watch as though awaiting someone, while the concert crowd dwindled. A good few made straight for the bar, providing us extra cover, but none approached Moran as he leafed through a concert programme near the entrance.

Then, just as I was becoming seriously worried that soon Holmes and I would be left exposed, alone in the lounge, he said, "That was it! No contact, just a quiet nod and a wink in reply, and now Moran is on the move, following the messenger at a distance."

We had already paid our bill in anticipation, so when Moran had cast one last glance over his shoulder, and Holmes said, "Right, Watson, let's see where he leads us, and to whom!" I rose and followed him down the curving stairs and into the main lobby. Colonel Moran's black cape and top-hat were just disappearing into a narrow corridor leading from the far side of the lobby and running down the side of the main hall, and we had to fairly sprint across the lobby to make sure not to lose sight of him for long.

"I hope they've not posted lookouts in the foyer, or we're done for," I said. Holmes paid no attention, intent on following Moran without overrunning the man. But when we reached the corner, we saw that the corridor ran the full length of the hall, and that Moran and his escort were already out of sight. As we approached the first of four or five openings set in the left side of the carpeted corridor, Holmes motioned me to slow down, and cautiously looked around the corner. Clearly he saw nothing of interest there, as he carried on, inspecting the next three openings in the same way.

"All of them are service entrances or lead to props rooms," he whispered into my ear. "Our goal must be through this last door," for this last opening had a pair of swinging doors made of polished mahogany wood set across it. He slipped his hand into his coat pocket and gripped his revolver, ready to fire instantly if required. Naturally I followed suit.

Holmes edged one of the doors open a little, then slipped through it, and I followed. We were now in a narrower yet more luxurious passage, with linen-fold panelling in more mahogany, which seemed as though it must lead to manager's offices or boardrooms, or the like. In fact, as we walked on our toes along the thick carpeting, it became clear from the sounds of cutlery chinking on bone china and the muted murmur of conversation that we were approaching a dining room.

Opposite to the dining room doors was the counter of waiters' serving station, with a small pantry leading off behind it, the door of which was made of polished wood louvers set in a frame. Holmes motioned me inside this small space, little larger than a closet, followed me in, then half closed the door so that we should not be visible to anyone passing. Standing on his toes and looking through the topmost louvers, Holmes whispered that he was able to see the dining room doors up to chest height.

We stayed there several minutes in silence, unable to make anything of the conversation through the closed doors, until a waiter in a crisp white coat appeared wheeling a loaded trolley, which he pushed through the doors into the dining room. One of the doors remained just a little ajar when it swung back, and we were able to make out conversation. Colonel Moran's voice was familiar from our previous encounter: some of the other voices carried to us clearly, while at times several other voices could be distinguished, but not understood.

"I did precisely what I should have. The fault lies entirely with your team of watchers. I myself saw Holmes enter his house." Obviously, Moran was loudly defending himself in the matter of his failure to assassinate Holmes. "He didn't come out the front door, not even in disguise. Parker here can testify to that. So it must have been those bumbling fools who were assigned the rear exit. I'll flay the hides from their bodies for this, see if I don't."

An unintelligible response came, to which Moran replied, "Just as well. Save me the trouble! But I'm the one who got nabbed, and thanks to Holmes, the Yard will make that Adair case stick, now that he has given them one of the airguns. Damned inconvenient! I shan't be able to play cards in London ever again. I swear it on the ace of spades, I'll get Holmes in my sights again, just once – the real Holmes this time – and I shan't miss my target this time either."

I heard Holmes's almost silent laughter at this. It was obvious, however, that Moran's gambling habits, with their consequent debts and murder, were under fire. He defended himself vigorously.

"At one point, please recall, I was myself Chief of Staff of this organisation, and your superior. I was not removed from that position, I *asked* the Professor to replace me. I never was cut out for running an organisation. I am a hunter; that is what I do, and that is what I love. Big game, up close and on its own terms! Dangerous animals – or men, often the most dangerous prey of all! As my chosen relaxation from these risky occupations, I play at cards for high stakes, or visit the casino."

Another single, muffled sentence was followed by Moran's sharp reply.

"This I have always done, and the Professor understood that my chief value was as an assassin, not an administrator. In his wisdom, he approved, and appointed you to my old position. But, should you feel that I have become more of a liability than I am worth, you have only to say so. The world is shrinking, but is still a big place in which a clever man may lose himself. I am a survivor, at the end."

A further muffled voice followed Moran's, but different in tone from the first. There was something familiar about it, but I could not think just what at that moment. Whatever it said it clearly mollified Colonel Moran, who replied, "Very well, you make the arrangements, I'll go with Parker and wait, but not at his crib. The police will know about that. I know a place. Where and when do we communicate again?" This was followed by a longer passage from the familiar-sounding voice – unfortunately, still unintelligible for some reason.

At that moment one of the doors opened wide, and the waiter emerged with his trolley full of dishes, and headed off towards the kitchen. Holmes seized the opportunity seemingly without forethought. Slipping out of our pantry hide, he donned a waiter's white coat, which was hanging on a hook there, and threw a folded napkin across his left forearm. "Your pocket comb, Watson," he whispered urgently, "and your reading glasses." Half a minute later, hair centre-parted, bespectacled, stooping and with buck-teeth, an unrecognisable Holmes stepped across the corridor and into the dining room.

I was in some apprehension of the return of the bona fide waiter, but Holmes slipped back through the door within less than a minute, laden with stacked dishes. These he tucked inside the pantry door, out of sight, then took off the waiter's coat and replaced it on the coat hook; then he rejoined me in the pantry. The sounds of a toast, and what seemed to be a general oath-taking ceremony, with calls and responses, came muffled through the doors. A bell rang in a distant kitchen. Leaning over, Holmes whispered, "There's a screened table at the back of the room, with three men seated behind it, evidently the men whose identity we seek. Parker was there, and I recognised some of the others, but our targets remain unidentified. I didn't want to remain longer in case our waiter friend returned."

Which is what the waiter did just at that moment, putting on his white coat and pushing his trolley into the dining room once more. Within minutes a half dozen men had exited the dining room and left in the direction we had come, down the panelled passage, and we heard the noise of their subdued conversation until it was abruptly cut by the closure of the swing doors at the entrance.

Holmes whispered again. "The leaders will wait until the troops are clear, or they would not have had the screen. Unfortunately, unless they are extremely short, the angle of these louvers will prevent us seeing their faces. Nothing we can do now, we dare not risk moving."

There came the sound of voices approaching the dining room doors from the other side. We could see the door opening, and the four pairs of legs that came through it. I could tell by the voice that one of them was Colonel Moran; the other three all appeared to be wearing overcoats in grey or black, dark or evening dress trousers, black shoes or boots, and all carried sticks of some sort. We had but a moment to notice these few details, as they turned out of the door and down the passage, following in the footsteps of their underlings.

Just as I was wondering how we should be able to follow them and gain a better view, a shouted alarm was raised and the door burst open. The waiter darted into the passage, all decorum forgotten, with an ugly revolver in his hand.

"Make a break for it, Watson. He's one of the gang," whispered Holmes. "Now!" he shouted loudly, as he pushed the pantry door open into the face of the surprised waiter, who reeled back against the wall. He was raising his revolver to fire at Holmes when I stepped out from behind the door, which had hidden me from his view, and laid my brass knuckles perfectly on the angle of his jaw. He went down like a felled tree, for he was a bigger and stronger man than the usual waiter. Holmes looked at me in some surprise. He had his revolver out by now, but said only, "He's well out of it. Run for it, this way!" and he dashed off in the opposite direction to all the gang, further down the passage.

While this *fracas* was underway, the gang leaders had clearly heard the commotion. As we turned a corner out of the passageway I saw Colonel Moran come charging back through the mahogany doors, and now he too had a revolver in hand. The waiter had recovered from my blow, and was struggling to his feet, unfortunately still armed. I heard orders being shouted beyond the double doors, followed by the sound of running feet. No doubt the troops were being called back for the chase.

The passage made a right turn some twenty yards from the dining room, and we found ourselves in an enormous kitchen area, with huge cauldrons suspended over gas ranges the size of a small buggy, and great copper pots and pans hung on hooks. We burst in on the skeleton staff, which was still there, cleaning and tidying for the next morning. Holmes and I ran at full speed straight through the kitchen and out of the servery doors to the restaurant beyond. Heavy footsteps pounded after us. The crack of a revolver and the ricochet of a bullet striking metal just behind us meant we had close pursuit.

Although the restaurant had obviously finished serving for the evening, there were still waiters trying to move along a few scattered groups of late diners. Alerted by the shots, they were all looking as Holmes and I hurtled through the room, revolvers in hand, pursued at some distance by Moran and his cohorts. More shots rang out as we ran out of the restaurant, to find ourselves on a gallery running along one wall of the cavernous central nave of the Great Hall. Only the gallery was lit, the Exhibition area having closed hours before. I followed Holmes as he headed for the stairs leading down from the gallery, but that escape was suddenly blocked. At the foot of the broad staircase appeared two running men with revolvers. Clearly they knew the layout of the building.

Spinning round, the tails of his coat flying out behind him, Holmes darted back across the gallery, past the open restaurant doors. I stayed as close behind him as I could. A volley of rounds came through the opening, and whistled by into the vast empty space of the deserted hall. We were past by then, and I followed Holmes as he climbed a long and narrow ladder, which rose steeply from a corner of the gallery to a service gangway running the full length of the building, tucked in just under the eaves. More shots rang out as we headed down the steel gangway, the sound of our boots reverberating in the cavernous void. The noise made as our pursuers climbed the stairs after us, and the sound of the armed men running along the main floor, filled me with trepidation. The space was vast, but open, and our silhouettes would be starkly outlined against the moonlit glass roof arching away over us.

At that very moment, a large panel of glass almost directly over our head shattered, showering us with shards of broken glass. I felt several sharp pricks, but we kept on running as fast as the narrowness of the steel footway allowed. Loud revolver shots fired from the ground floor continued as we ran headlong, panes of glass exploding above, until we reached the transept of the building. Far below we could see the fountain pool, stilled now.

Suddenly, throughout the vast space came a symphony of strange mechanical whirrings, followed by a medley of chiming, striking, ringing, and other assorted noises, as all the clocks in Crystal Palace raggedly struck the hour of midnight. Enormous four-faced suspended clocks, grandfather clocks, Chinese clocks, Swiss clocks with cuckoo calls - a thousand timepieces from the corners of the globe sounded a ragged celebration of yet another midnight in London. I could only hope it was not to be our requiem symphony.

Certainly it was loud enough, mingled with the ringing of steel-tipped shoes on metal, the crash of revolver shots, and set to the smashing, tinkling accompaniment of great sheets of glass sundering overhead and falling silently, until shattering to fragments on the floor and darkened exhibits far below us.

"Here, Watson, this way! This central area is roofed with wood – no silhouettes – the men below can't see which of the three arms we take." With this he took a right hand turn in the gangway, which led us into one of the shorter arms of the 'cross.' I ran after him, needing no encouragement.

The shots from below ceased, but the swift pounding of feet on the upper walkway meant our pursuers would soon see which way we had gone. We dashed onwards, towards the end of the wing. Just as I was feeling we were trapped like captive birds, Holmes gripped my arm and said, "Through here . . . I was expecting just this. I knew there must be access to the roof from somewhere up here." He turned the handle on the steel framed glass door, but it was evidently locked, and would not open.

"Stand back," cried Holmes, as he aimed his revolver at the lock, shielded his face with his coat sleeve and blasted the lock clean out of the door into the night sky. He pushed the doorframe open, and as shots blasted out anew from the central nave, smashing more glass out of the end of the gallery beyond us, we clambered up a short steel ladder to yet another service gangway, this time on the very outside of the roof. Our dark outlines were once again visible against the glass, as more shots came from the floor directly below us, but not so distant that the rounds lost their force. Glass sheets erupted into silvery fountains of shards all around us, marking our progress as we ran to the end of the wing.

We halted at the very end of the wing, breathless and sweating from our exertions. "They've brought in a repeating rifle, Watson – more accurate and more powerful. So far I've counted eight rounds, which means he'll have eight to ten more rounds in the magazine. He'll not reload now, and risk missing a shot while we're trapped here."

He looked around the corner, along the short end of the arm of the cross. "It must be here somewhere, Watson!" shouted Holmes over the din. "This building was an engineering showpiece; they have allowed for cleaning all this glass, as you can see. The question is, how is the exterior cleaned?"

There had been no way for us to create an obstruction to pursuit onto the roof, and as we stood there a shout from the broken door told us we had been followed up the ladder. Holmes shouted against the wind, "Keep them pinned down . . . I see something in the darkness up there which may be our salvation."

He cautiously edged along the dark walkway, for it was narrow and on the very edge of the building, with only a low handrail for protection. The bright moon cast his shadow onto the glass, and more rifle shots cracked from below. Broken glass flew around Holmes, but he had time to reach shelter behind an enormous steel beam just as the sniper got his range. Meanwhile, I pulled out my revolver and fired at the dark shapes emerging onto the roof; they ducked back inside, and I kept them pinned there until I heard Holmes cry out, "Watson, I've found it! Up here, man, if you want to see the morning. But you'll need some cover. That rifle still has at least four rounds left."

He darted back out of his shelter, and made as if to run back the way he had just come. Then, almost immediately, he darted back behind his steel beam. The ruse worked wonderfully, however, for the rifleman emptied his magazine into the glass. I loosed off two more rounds, and went after Holmes.

He was already aboard a gondola-like service platform, which was suspended by cables from curved overhead stanchions and hung over the side of the building. A winch at each end of the platform provided for raising and lowering the platform, and Holmes shouted, "As fast as we can, but we must keep in unison or we shall tip up," and began lowering his end by turning the crank. I quickly matched his efforts, and we descended in jerks and starts.

"Do you see, Watson! I believe our masterminds are making good their escape." Without breaking his rotation of the crank, he pointed to the driveway below us, which wound through the gardens alongside Crystal Palace. Some distance along it a coach-and-four was waiting, alongside a handsome brougham. Two of our well-dressed gentlemen clambered in, and the two carriages flew away down the gravelled road and out of sight around the front corner of the building. "Our birds don't want to be around when this destruction is investigated," said Holmes, and indeed we could hear distant whistles blown urgently.

We must have made a superb target from inside, but although a half dozen panes exploded nearby, we were not hit. The glazed exterior wall at that end of the hall was partly blocked by exhibits, or booths, as the shots ceased when we neared the ground, although shouts and a volley of rounds came from our frustrated pursuers overhead.

Our gondola touched the ground and we leapt out, Holmes saying, "Quickly, into the gardens, we must conceal ourselves now from the law as well as our hunters." We crashed through garden beds until well hidden. Halting to catch our breath, we looked back and saw our pursuers hurtle from a doorway, guns in hand, searching for traces of us. We had made quite a swathe through the gardens, and I was hoping they would not be able to follow the obvious trail. Several uniformed policemen rounded the corner just at that moment – spotting three armed men, they gave chase, blowing loudly at their whistles for reinforcements, and were soon lost from view in the darkness. Lanterns and shouts soon followed in that direction, but none searched near our little grove.

Holmes and I breathed deeply, and he whispered, "Squat down, and remain still. They'll leave soon, and we can get away from here before reinforcements arrive."

"Well," said I, "it was certainly an exciting chase, quite like old times, and one which I am most thankful to have survived. But it seems we've lost Moran again, and have gained precious little further knowledge as to whom he was dining with."

"Ah, Watson. It is not quite so bad as all that. Although I saw only the lower half of our villains, those details which *were* visible were most instructive."

We had seen the same men from the same limited viewpoint, yet had I been asked to describe any of them I simply could not have done so. But so used had I become to Holmes's awesome powers of observation that I was not surprised at his statement.

"We know Moran is planning something, and is with Parker now. We know that their current Chief of Staff was present, although we have no evidence that it was Colonel Moriarty. And I learnt something else here tonight which I had not expected, but which in retrospect is not as surprising as it might at first seem." When I pressed him further on the matter he only replied, "It is too soon to be certain, and I prefer to keep my own counsel in this particular. Besides, it is time we made some distance between ourselves and this mayhem."

I looked at Holmes, and noticed that he was bleeding from several small cuts to his face and hands; I touched my own face and felt the warm stickiness of blood, and smelt the iron-rich smell of it on my fingers as I held them up. Black in the moonlight, thin streaks of blood marbled the pale skin of my hands.

"Yes, Doctor; we are neither of us in a fit state to be seen, especially by any constables and with these weapons in our pockets. I suggest that we clean ourselves up as best we can at that ornamental fountain further into the park there, then, keeping our cover under the woods, make our way down the hill into Sydenham, where, as I recall, a medical colleague of yours maintains his practice."

DAY THREE

APRIL 8TH 1894

CHAPTER XIII

HOLMES AND I WERE stamping our feet to keep out the damp cold, but with little success. A few constables were keeping order by restricting entry to police and press only. We stood apart from the small knot of Scotland Yard detectives gathered in front of the main entrance to Crystal Palace. Inspector Lestrade was there, along with Tobias Gregson. And Chief Inspector Athelney Jones stood to one side conferring with a small group of newspaper reporters; all of them asking questions at the same time.

"Was this the work of anarchists?" asked one; another favoured the Irish republicans, yet another thought it may be student vandals from the College nearby, unable to resist the temptation of smashing all that glass. The Chief Inspector diplomatically informed them that the culprits were known, and that arrests were expected shortly. Being seasoned campaigners, this was greeted by the reporters with sceptical groans. Jones smiled wryly, and said, "You'll be allowed inside shortly, and can sketch or take photographs if you wish. We'll let you know as soon as we have anything further to report." With that, he left the group and walked across the driveway to talk with a tall, clean-shaven, hard-faced man sporting stiff collars and cravat, and wearing a bowler hat, who stood by himself at the open door of his carriage.

"You recognise Commissioner MacDonald, don't you Watson?" said Holmes quietly. "He has risen fast in the force since the days when he was an Inspector working on the Moriarty gang investigation. He and Patterson managed to get many of the gang, including several of their key members. Not one would tell them a thing - either misguided loyalty, or more likely fear of retribution - and the evidence was insufficient to seize either the Professor or his most senior lieutenants. But in fact the publicity and the arrests - and there were many - made his a household name, with the results as you see."

"What became of Inspector Patterson, then?" I enquired.

"Ah! Yes. Patterson was held responsible, indirectly, for the failure to secure the evidence against the Professor."

"But surely, Holmes - you told me you left the evidence against Moriarty for him in your pigeonholes - I informed Inspector Patterson myself, as you had requested of me."

"As I did. The blue envelope was indeed found there, as it was supposed to be, with *'Moriarty'* written on it by me . . . but it had been tampered with. Mycroft followed up on this later, at my request; it was found that the crucial documentary proofs of Professor Moriarty's guilt, for murders and other serious criminal matters, had been removed. Although there was never any conclusive proof, it got about that Patterson must have removed the most important evidence, as he was the one to retrieve the envelope. He was not publicly disciplined in the matter, but his rise in the force was blocked from that day forth, and he soon applied for transfer to a regional force to escape the talk."

"I have often wondered what went wrong," said I. "You seemed so confident of getting them all."

"Indeed," replied Holmes. "I should like a few words with Inspector Patterson myself some day - no one could credit the work and risk invested in piecing together that evidence. You will recall that our rooms were partially burnt on the evening of our departure for the continent. Someone was in there, and when they left they set the place afire. I suspect the fire was lit, not to destroy all the evidence, but to make it seem as though an *unsuccessful* attempt had been made to do so. Thus, the remaining documents would prove embarrassingly short of conclusive proof, and it would seem to many, as was no doubt intended, that my accusations against Professor Moriarty were the result of obsession with my delusion that he was a great criminal mastermind.

"It was said at the trials that all the minor crimes which were successfully prosecuted were in fact unrelated crimes. The major crimes - murders, robberies, forgery, blackmail - were largely unproven, and many could not be prosecuted, as the evidence was no longer sufficient. It was never conclusively decided whether or not a conspiracy had ever existed, and Colonel Moriarty's letters to the papers defending his late brother's memory were no doubt intended to reinforce that impression."

It was early on the morning following the events at Crystal Palace, and we had slept in Sydenham town itself. Holmes and I had knocked up Smithers, my M.D. friend, who had been a fellow medical student. Like myself, he had found general practice congenial to his habits. We had kept in contact, casually, ever since. Once he realised who was ringing his doorbell, and I had introduced Holmes, he ushered us in and had soon attended to our wounds, which fortunately were all superficial. Covered all over with tincture and plasters, we had then shared a glass of Smithers' excellent brandy around the embers of the fire in his sitting room.

"May we ask your discretion as to our visit this evening, Doctor Smithers?" enquired Holmes of our host; "We have no desire to be arrested for vandalism in the morning."

I answered for him. "He'll do, Holmes! I'll vouch for him. We were at

Medical School together. Smithers has at one time or another met each of my wives, and never has a word escaped him about our rather disreputable days, or nights rather, when we were there, eh! Smithers."

"Can't remember 'em myself," said Smithers, with a distinct twinkle in his eye. "Married, you know! Off to see the mother tonight though, so we can have another brandy before we retire." Smithers and I caught up on old times for a while: then, when Holmes suggested we sleep at an hotel, Smithers would have none of it. We had bedded down comfortably, myself on the sofa, Holmes on the broad window seat. Almost as soon as we closed our eyes, it seemed our host was waking us with cups of steaming coffee and fresh rolls, along with a crock of butter and small pots each of honey and marmalade. He also had his morning newspaper, which carried a 'Stop Press' box in the top corner headed *'Midnight Orgy of Destruction at Crystal Palace'*, giving some very basic details of the events.

Smithers handed it to Holmes, saying, "Now I can understand your desire for discretion. I take it that I can't be had for harbouring Vandals or Visigoths."

"You may rest your conscience as to that; and thank you most kindly for your hospitality." Holmes perused the paper as we breakfasted. "We had best get over there, Watson. There are several things I should like to investigate in daylight. However, we should not arrive too early, or we may arouse suspicion. It must seem that we have come out from London this morning, in response to this report. Doctor Smithers, as a last imposition upon your hospitality, could you spare a few pounds of plaster, such as you commonly use for setting broken limbs, and a length of gauze bandage?"

So we had walked to the railway station, and had hired a dog-cart to deliver us, along with a horde of newsmen in their own carts, up the hill to Crystal Palace.

"Come, Watson. Let us reintroduce ourselves to the much-feared Commissioner MacDonald. I've not had the opportunity since my return." We walked across the gravel to the commissioner's carriage, where MacDonald and Jones were still in discussion.

"I hope I'm not interrupting anything, MacDonald. We decided to come out to investigate this sacrilegious desecration when we read the papers."

MacDonald turned, and it seemed he was highly pleased to see Holmes again.

"Somehow I never could believe you really were dead, Holmes. More lives than a cat, it seems. Good to have you back." Seizing Holmes's hand he shook it vigorously. His broad Scots accent and his quiet demeanour gave him an air of rectitude and authority which made it seem unsurprising that he had risen to the top as a police detective. "I've heard of your return, of course, but I only returned myself from Scotland yesterday evening. You will remember Chief Inspector Jones, of course?"

Jones shook hands with both of us, and said, "Whatever has happened to you both; you look most peculiar with those plasters all over." We had removed all but the most necessary, but still had a half dozen or so each, covering the deeper cuts we had sustained, and tincture on others less serious.

"Oh! As to that," laughed Holmes, "Watson was assisting last night at one of my chemical experiments; we had a slight - and unexpected - explosion, which shattered a glass retort in our faces whilst we were manipulating the apparatus. The liquid was neither boiling nor corrosive, fortunately, and we suffered only the slight damages you see."

I thought Jones looked a little askance at this ingenuous explanation, but he accepted it well enough, and continued, "Have you any news as to Colonel Moran's whereabouts, Holmes? No? Well, we'd certainly like him back under lock and key. The press is all over us about this, and I can let you know this much, we have received information in the past twenty four hours about several other gambling debts which Moran may have settled in similar fashion. People have come forward, and some unsolved murder cases are being reopened."

"I've been meaning to ask, as it was I whom Moran was trying to kill; just how was his escape managed?" Holmes addressed this query directly to MacDonald, his grey eyes fixed on the Scotsman's impassive face.

"Still not sure," replied MacDonald. "It's clear there was bribery at the police cells level, but there are several possible candidates, and they're all denying their involvement, saying it was simply confusion. As to evidence regarding how he was transferred in the first place, it seems the official documents concerned have been pilfered by tearing pages from registers and by theft from files in my own outer offices. Needless to say, a full investigation is already underway, and an oversight committee comprised of senior officers has been appointed to report to the Home Office.

"Nevertheless, it is difficult to see how we can proceed without these stolen documents. There is no agreement, even, amongst those who saw the release documents before they were removed - different clerks and officers remember different authorising names on them. They may even have been clever forgeries in the first place. Whatever the case, it was a most daring and audacious undertaking, which unfortunately seems to have caught us all flat footed. For now we must try to unravel the mystery and ensure that it can never be repeated. And when it *is* unravelled, heads will most certainly roll."

I thought the Police Department had selected well when they named Alec MacDonald as Commissioner of Police. Spoken of in MacDonald's quiet Scots accent, the whole affair seemed as though it was a most unfortunate occurrence – the investigation was well in hand, and the public could be reassured of the fundamental solidity of the metropolitan police forces.

"I for one will sleep more easily once he is behind bars again," said Holmes. I remembered Moran's threats of the previous night, when he was unaware that we could overhear his every word, and I felt the cold chill of certainty that he meant to carry out the threats he had made.

"As will we all, Holmes, as will we all. Well, I must get back to the Yard," said MacDonald, as he stepped up into his carriage. "Blast these vandals. Moran on the loose, a crazed killer down by the riverside, and I have to come out here and show my face or the papers will say we don't care. I will take Jones back in with me, and leave Lestrade and Gregson here. Technically, this should be a matter for the local police, but Crystal Palace was Prince Albert's pride and joy, and Her Majesty wants to know who has smashed up his legacy." His coachman whipped the horses into motion, and the carriage crunched away down the gravelled driveway.

"Come along, Watson. Let us make our escape before Lestrade attaches himself to us. I have a little something to do which I should prefer him not to see. Let us stroll this way, as though inspecting the damaged exterior."

We walked off without haste, down the side of the building, where there was little activity, most of the police constables and newsmen being inside the building at that moment. The damage done was quite spectacular. Through great, jagged holes in the glass walls we could see that entire glass roof panels were gone, and a sullen sky was threatening to rain through the gaping voids.

Holmes stopped and searched around on the ground, in the general area where the two carriages had rested the night before. He cast around for several minutes, occasionally using his magnifying lens to examine some minute detail on the muddy soil alongside the narrow roadway.

"I think this will do, Watson," said he. "Now, we shall need a container of some kind." He looked around, until his glance came to rest on a stack of unused earthen pots, stacked upside down, in a small nurseryman's shelter. "Could I trouble you to fill one of those with water from the pond. This will be a little crude, but should be effective nonetheless."

I fetched the pot of water. Holmes took from his coat the packet of plaster-of-Paris, and the gauze bandage. Using a stick made from a stripped branch, Holmes stirred powder into the water until a thick consistency was obtained, then immediately poured the mixture into the depression left by a shoe, stopping once it overflowed. Taking the length of gauze bandage from his pocket, he folded it into several layers, and let it gently sink into the wet plaster.

That done he washed and dried his hands, and sat on a garden bench to smoke his pipe while the plaster in the cast set up. This took only a few minutes, and by the time he had finished his pipe, the cast was quite rigid enough to lift from the footprint. At first glance, the cast was that of a large man's shoe, square-toed, and showed clear marks of steel toe and heel caps, recently renewed. The leather sole was more deeply scored than these caps, I noticed, and pointed this out to Holmes.

"There are further clues, if we use the lens," he said. "But quite frankly, they aren't necessary. All I really require is the outline." Taking out a sharp folding knife, Holmes scraped and shaved the cast as close to the outline as possible, then simply cut the whole cast neatly in two, wrapped the pieces in his and my handkerchiefs, and put the whole thing in the two pockets of his overcoat. "And now, let us pay a visit to Lestrade before taking train back to London."

We retraced our steps to the main entrance, and asked for Lestrade. Following directions, we soon found ourselves in the main hall, with shattered glass lying everywhere, but little else damaged. Lestrade was questioning the manager of the entire building, one Alfred Stein, who could shed no light at all on the destruction. As usual, once the main exhibition hall had closed, his specific duties done, he had gone home. What was known, from questioning late night patrons in the restaurant, was that shots were first heard coming from the area of a private dining room in the back of the concert hall. Several witnesses had followed after the armed men as they chased two others through the restaurant and out to the gallery, and had witnessed the chase through the roof, and some of the spectacular destruction. Others had alerted local police, but all the miscreants had escaped into the wooded park all around, blasting an exit through locked glass doors. The concert hall, with its various restaurants and bars, was managed separately under licence; the manager seemed to have fled the scene in panic when the havoc began, and had not been seen since. But he was a Frenchman, and was always excessively wary of figures of authority, even fire inspectors, so that did not necessarily signify. Mr. Stein could shed no light on the occupants of the private dining room the previous evening, but did say that it was not usually available to the public, being intended for private functions arranged by the management.

Holmes walked further, down to the junction of the nave and the transept, then turned right, into the gallery into which we had fled. Casting his gaze around the fragmented glass laying everywhere, Holmes finally found that which he was evidently seeking - he stooped and picked up a shiny brass cartridge case, then inspected the markings on the case-head.

"If I'm not wrong, this was fired from a Winchester 1886 repeating rifle, chambered for these U.S. Government-issued .45-70 cartridges. It's available to the public; thousands have been sold, mostly in America, but many in Europe as well. All we can say is that these men know their weapons, and take care to have the finest available arms as and when they need them. This comes as no surprise." Holmes slipped the spent shell into his pocket, no doubt to add to the growing collection of bullets fired at him by the Moriarty gang. And no doubt it would at sometime join the others in his locked steel dispatch box, along with so many other mementoes of his cases, always assuming the next bullet did not find it's target. That there would be further bullets - or other deadly devices - aimed at Holmes seemed exceedingly likely.

We took our leave of Lestrade and Gregson, as they stood by the central fountain, dwarfed by acres of glass roofing, and tried to make sense of the seemingly mindless destruction. Swarms of workmen in overalls had begun the task of cleaning up smashed glass, which lay all about, while others worked overhead to sling tarpaulins in case of rain.

Holmes and I returned downhill through the park to the railway station, savouring the brisk morning air as we walked. Dew still lay in patches on the grass under trees, and hung in silvered beads on spider's webs amongst the leaves; birds called to each other as they darted busily through the branches, swooping down to pluck earthworms from the freshly tilled soil of the flowerbeds. I reflected on the contrast between this scene of bucolic charm and the murderous mayhem we had been involved in the previous night, only a few steps distant. Holmes merely whistled quietly to himself, as though he had neither a care nor a thought to distract him, and otherwise was entirely silent until we were seated in our railway carriage and headed for London.

Chapter XIV

Mrs. Hudson greeted us at the front door. "Mr. Mycroft is upstairs, sir. I left 'im in your sittin' room, with the papers and a cup o' tea. I told 'im as I didn't know what time you would be in; an' 'e said 'e'd wait for a bit. 'E seemed to think you'd not be long." She said this with the satisfied air of someone proved right, and went back in to her apartments on the ground floor.

Mycroft sat in the rocking chair; the newspaper was still folded alongside his teacup on the side table. He raised his bulk slightly, and nodded at us in greeting.

"Well, Sherlock, clearly you have not lost your talent for drama."

He tapped the newspaper, which was a late morning edition, and indicated the bold headlines splashed across the top, with several columns of the front page devoted to the destruction at Crystal Palace.

"I'm happy to see you have suffered no severe injuries. I trust you had some success in your endeavours; I don't like to think about the repair bill that your villains have left us. Her Majesty is absolutely livid. I saw a personal note to the Prime Minister not an hour ago, furiously underlined in many places. Her Highness is *most* displeased, and feels *strongly* that this *wanton* destruction is intended as a *personal* affront to herself, and to the memory of her dear Albert. It must be the *highest* priority of the police to apprehend the perpetrators of this outrage, and see that *severe* punishment is meted out to them. This kind of behaviour simply will *not* be tolerated. Or words to that effect."

"Yes, the damage was somewhat excessive. Glass houses, you know! Watson and I were lucky to escape with our lives. Fortunately we were *outside* the glass before they could deploy their Remington, and the angle of the moon cast our shadows obliquely, with the result that our shadows were shot through and through. I have little doubt that had Moran himself been behind that repeating rifle we should both be dead.

"However, I learnt quite a lot about our adversaries, and there are several promising leads that I shall follow up immediately. As to Colonel Moran, he was there, and none too happy about the foul-ups leading to his arrest. They were having a cosy private dinner, and I suspect they've used that private dining room for their regular meetings. Ideal cover for a group of gentlemen, and some not so reputable men as well, to get together on a regular basis without arousing suspicion. The manager of the concert hall has fled the scene, and I doubt he'll be back. Either a member of the gang, or in their pay."

"And Moran himself! We must get him back in custody soon, or the lid will blow off this whole affair," said Mycroft quietly.

"One of the leads I mentioned. He's going to ground with Parker, but at a place of his own choosing. What he may not have considered is that Parker is addicted to his pipe of opium, and when the urge comes upon him, he will go to one of several places for his pipe. I shall have all of them watched by the Irregulars, and Parker will lead us back to the Colonel wherever he may be."

"I think its high time we got him back, Sherlock. Questions are being asked privately about the identity of those who arranged things so that his 'release' could take place, and I expect that soon the matter will be raised in the House. We certainly don't want our highly-placed quarry, whoever he is, becoming alarmed by the pressure and doing a bunk before we can lay our hands on him. Even more importantly, I took personal responsibility in this affair, and if the Opposition get wind of my involvement, I may end up branded as the villain myself. I'm supposed to remain politically neutral, you know."

"I need just a little more time, Mycroft. Can you stand the heat another two days, or three at the most?" replied Holmes.

"At the absolute outside, Sherlock. You have three days, or I may be forced to go public with the government's role in this. At this critical moment, that could bring down the government, and I should be most unpopular indeed."

"Thank you, Mycroft. I appreciate your position."

"Meanwhile, I have a report from Scotland Yard on the other 'Slash and Strangle' victims; we asked to be kept fully informed, as the public mood is ugly enough, and we want to avoid panic as well if we can." Mycroft passed to Holmes a file folder marked 'CONFIDENTIAL'.

"This will save me a visit to the Yard. Very thoughtful of you, Mycroft! Many thanks."

"Well, I shall leave you to develop your leads. Back to Whitehall, where I shall try to get the Army and the Navy to actually *talk* to each other. Do you know that there are no official channels for direct communication between the two services? All contact is through civilian liaison offices. Absurd! And in this modern world, with the rapid development of the technology of warfare, it's potentially catastrophic. But can I get either service to agree to talk directly with the other? Two years I've worked towards this end, Sherlock, and I must say it still looks as hopeless as when I began."

I had sent for a cab, which had now arrived at the street door. Mycroft nodded goodbye to Holmes. I walked him downstairs, and as he donned his coat and gloves he spoke to me. "Do you remember, three years ago; you took a cab to Victoria Station, to catch the Continental Express with Sherlock?"

"Very clearly. Holmes told me the day he returned that you were in fact my cab driver."

"Does that surprise you? I get out more than Sherlock gives me credit for, Doctor. You know, I enjoyed driving that cab so much that after you got down I took a couple of turns around Hyde Park. I am a bulky man these days and regular sporting activities are out of the question, but I so relished the movement and sense of control over my own direction that I soon took to driving around late at night, when I could go somewhat faster. The local mews have now become used to the sight of me, and several nights each month I drive myself around London, finishing up with a hot toddy at any pub that appeals to me. Perhaps some night, when this situation is resolved, you would care to join me?"

"By all means, Mycroft. Thank you for the invitation. And yes, you do surprise me."

Mycroft left, and I returned to our sitting room. Holmes had stretched out on the sofa, and as I entered he said, "Please be so kind as to rouse me in an hour, Watson. I have things to attend to, but we had little rest last night and it may be some while before I sleep again." He loosened his necktie, closed his eyes, and within seconds was asleep.

In order not to fall asleep myself, I busied myself with unpacking and placing my few personal possessions about my bedroom, as I had not had any chance to do so, and soon the hour had elapsed. I woke Holmes, who went upstairs to wash up, and returned in fresh attire.

"I feel like a new man, Watson. I recommend the same treatment for you after I leave. I've no idea how long I'll be gone, so let us just look into this first," said he, as he opened the file folder left by Mycroft.

Inside were a police report, a coroner's examination report and several grainy photographic prints, taken at the morgue using flash lighting. First Holmes looked at the prints, examined them closely under his large lens, and then handed them to me. He began to read aloud the more important parts of the two reports.

"The coroners report first, as you're looking at the prints:

'Two corpses – both of them Indians, by their general physiognomy – from where difficult to say, as they were found unclothed. Both exhibit identical injuries – strangulation, broken neck, smashed vertebrae, knife wounds under the armpits, stabbed eyeballs . . .' It's all the same, Watson . . . *smashed genitals!'"*

"What kind of fiend *is* this, Holmes? What deep-seated hatred could he have had for these people, to have abused them so completely *after* killing them."

"Unless I am mistaken, Watson, we are looking for more than one killer. Furthermore, I suspect that *these* victims were unknown to their killers until only days, or even hours, before they unsuspectingly went to their deaths; and that what relations there were between them were of the most amicable and friendly sort."

"Then what was the motive?" I asked.

"In this case, I think it may be robbery only. In the case of the previous two victims, I suspect that punishment was the prime motive, and that an example was made. To whom? Well, that is one of the things we must discover. Perhaps the police report throws a little light on matters."

"Perhaps it was prepared by Lestrade!" said I.

"Don't think I am too hard on Lestrade, Watson. By and large, he's as competent as any at the Yard, and he's straight as well. He is just so easy to bait, and at times I simply can't resist the temptation."

He picked up the report. "As it turns out, I don't recognise the officer's name. Must expect that, I suppose, after three years away. Very well."

Holmes read the report aloud, as before. The two victims had been identified several days after their bodies were found. Their hotel had reported them missing, and that their rooms had been ransacked. Travel documents showed that they were Indians, but resident at Persia, where they apparently conducted a profitable trade in gemstones and jewellery. They were frequent visitors to London, coming once or even twice each year to Rotterdam and London, and they always stayed at the Golden Peacock Hotel. This was a small but comfortable hotel, catering exclusively to Eastern clientele. They were valued customers, frequently entertaining and doing business with their clients over mint tea or coffee in the lobby lounge. Their clients had been primarily Asiatics or Arabs of some description, but from time to time there were *feringhi* amongst them, according to the Arab desk clerk.

On the last night they were seen in the hotel they were entertaining a group of four or five fellow Indians, and the waiter attested to the general friendly atmosphere amongst the group. Questioned further, the staff had noticed no other unusual customers, except for two Englishmen, who had taken an interest in the Indian jewellers, to the extent of asking the front desk for their names. They claimed they wished to sell these two gentlemen some insurance, as they had heard that the Indians were wealthy travellers. When told that it would not be possible to divulge guests' names, but that an introduction could be arranged when the Indian guests were free, the Englishmen had said they could wait until another occasion. Leaving a card - which, upon later police investigation, proved to carry a false name and address - they left the hotel without attempting to speak with any of the Indians.

Shortly thereafter the Indian guests departed, and half an hour later the two Indian jewellers from Persia also left. They informed the front desk that they would be dining at an Indian restaurant, and when given the Englishmen's card, had laughed and given it back, saying that they had travelled for years, and had no need of insurance. They then left the hotel, and were not seen again.

The Persian manager of the Golden Peacock, who had spoken frequently with these two gentlemen over the years, said they always travelled together, and he had the impression that the relation between them was more that of teacher and pupil than friends. What he could confirm was that they had had in their possession a collection of fine coloured gemstones, the sale of which they were hoping to negotiate. The manager had urged them to secure their jewels in a deposit box, or a bank, but they had paid no heed.

A description of the Englishmen was pieced together by talking further with the staff, with the assistance of the hotel manager, who translated for those whose English was poor. The only point which distinguished this description from that of a thousand other Englishmen seemed to be that the taller of the two had amused himself while waiting by playing upon a strange musical instrument, which was held between the teeth and plucked in some way.

No more was known of the whereabouts or activities of the victims before the discovery of their corpses except that they had in fact eaten their meal - at an Indian restaurant - according to the autopsy report.

"Not terribly helpful, Watson, except for one item. Parker plays the jew's harp; it's a habit which may cost him dear one day. And that description fit him like a bespoke glove."

CHAPTER XV

I MADE MYSELF comfortable in the wicker armchair, and once again picked up the first volume of Francois le Villard's journals. It was now three in the afternoon. Holmes had not yet returned. I had followed his excellent advice as to rest and refreshment, and felt quite rejuvenated. The skies remained clear, a fresh breeze blew in through the open bow windows, and all in all things were so tranquil I felt it necessary to remind myself that, wherever he may have gone, danger still awaited Holmes.

As I opened the Journal I noted once again the musty odour that rose from the pages, that compound of mildewed leather mixed with once-damp paper. I picked up the second volume. Both volumes smelled the same; I reasoned that they had been kept together until given to Holmes. This time, I leafed rapidly through the pages. Le Villard's precise handwriting remained consistent throughout, hardly varying from the first entry to the last. His hand was neat, small, and elegant, and with the tiny sketches in ink which adorn many of the pages, the journals were in and of themselves objects of some charm.

It was clear, even from the little I had previously read, that le Villard possessed a considerable descriptive talent, and much of his writing was devoted to portraying the diverse places through which he and Holmes travelled. His descriptions of the flora and fauna, and especially of the peoples of these regions, were succinct yet perceptive. I was greatly pleased at all this, as this material could be edited to provide a realistic and colourful backdrop to the hard facts of *'The Holmes Report'*, as I now thought of the work I had been engaged to write.

It was a great temptation to dip into the journals at various places; however I was determined to resist, and to allow the adventures to unfold in the order of their occurrence. Therefore, it was to the page bookmarked - with a portrait photograph of *'H.M. King Chulalongkorn of Siam'*, according to the legend printed across the bottom - that I turned, to continue reading, where I had left off the previous day, of the travels of Francois le Villard and Sherlock Holmes.

CHAPTER XVI

12th August 1891
Silliguri, India

FAUNCE WOKE us well before dawn; we had settled our accounts the evening before, and slipped out of the town before sunrise. As the sun lit the peaks of the Himalayas we stepped into a small hut just off the main trade path between India and Tibet. Here we found Das and Kintup, with all our gear neatly stowed on two shaggy ponies tethered in the muddy courtyard.

"Good morning, Professor," said Das. "We must hurry and get you away from here. Put these on."

He handed us the garments worn by men of the *Bahrashri* tribe, welcomed as traders in Tibet. The morning was sufficiently cold that we could turn up our collars and pull down our fur hats.

Faunce pointed at the ancient rifles leaning against a wall of the hut. "Three Enfields, and cartridge belts to match. Standard issue in these hills; nobody will look twice. However, once you reach the border, you'll find a couple of nice surprises under that lot. Just break up the wooden pack frame when you ditch the ponies, eh!

"All your other equipment is packed ready for an Alpine-style assault, as we agreed. Kintup will make sure you have no problems while you're in British territory; he's been told what to say. Just this side of the border you will go 'over the hill', and after that, until you reach Lhasa, the fewer people who see you the better."

Das said goodbye to Kintup, and then to us. It was clear that he wanted us gone so that he could slip away unnoticed. Faunce threw us both a mock salute; we took no offence – it was typical of his sardonic way of handling all situations. Then he was gone, and Das with him.

"Better we go, sir," said Kintup, his voice issuing low but resonant from his barrel chest. His weathered features and thick-set physique marked him as a man very familiar with the mountains. "Traders get an early start from here; better try to pass Cleft of the Winds before dark, sir."

Although illiterate, after years of guiding sportsmen and explorers Kintup spoke reasonable English, and of course excellent Tibetan; our Tibetan was workable, so thankfully we had little problem in basic communication with each other. That first day we made our way across the *terai* towards the gorge of the Tista River, coming eventually to forests of tall and shady Sal-trees. Emerging at Sivok we understood why the gorge was named the Cleft of the Winds.

"All day good air blows down to *terai* from the mountains. All night, sick air blows from *terai* back up the mountains. Not good camping here, sir. Better we go on."

A terrific blast of mist and wind blew down through the narrow defile cut by the Tista, and we hurried on to avoid the malarial air when the wind turned, pausing only long enough to purchase some walnuts and oranges brought down for hillmen encamped there for the winter. Wild beasts of every description could be heard, and sometimes seen, in the dense growth all around. "Tiger country," said Kintup. We carried on through the most spectacular riverine gorges I had ever seen. From time to time we passed a group of Tibetan traders, with their laden ponies and huge mastiffs. Kintup would say a few words to these picturesquely dressed hillmen, and pass on.

The road was an old trade track, widened by the Army several years before in the campaign to drive the Tibetans out of the Jelep Pass area. Winding along high above the valley floor, frequently cut into the solid rock, it is made hazardous by sudden landslips; and where it hugs the river's edge it threatens at times to crumble into the turbulent stream. We soon passed the Government Cinchona plantations at Riang, where grows the raw material for the tons of quinine needed to combat malaria throughout India, and crossed the river at Tista Bridge. I knew that a French Catholic missionary, Father Desgodins, had his chapel in the forest near here, but even had we had the time, it would have been unwise to contact him. Nevertheless, I regretted that I could not meet, as the last European we encountered, a fellow countryman.

Passing the junction of the Tista with the Rangit, we came after several marches to Rangpo in Native Sikkim. From here, the way dwindled to a bridle-track that would lead at last to the Jelep Pass, beyond which, at its frontier with Sikkim, lay the first walled border post blocking the path to Tibet.

After Rongli we began our ascent, climbing more than ten thousand feet within fifteen miles or so. In a single day we passed from the bamboos, figs and cinnamon of the semi-tropical *terai*, up through forests of elm and oak, and groves of ash, maple and chestnut, at last climbing into pine forest white with snow. Even after our rigorous training at Darjeeling we were at first frequently breathless. Kintup, although unaffected, waited patiently each time while we regained our wind and strength. Finally, at Lingtu, the path levelled off and, muffled up with all our clothing against the biting winds, we soon reached Gnatong, set amongst black pines at the edge of an ancient glacier. On this alpine plain, at twelve thousand feet above sea-level, were the dilapidated barracks built for the Connaught Rangers some years before, with its magnificent views of Kanchenjunga and, further off, Mount Everest. The furthest outpost of Indian government power . . . now abandoned to the icy winds!

Here at Gnatong we were to abandon our sturdy pack-ponies and leave the well-travelled paths between India and Tibet, at least when near any settlements. We knew that the Tibetans had an efficient system of express couriers throughout their country, riding or running in stages with urgent news. From here on we would have to avoid being seen, even by travellers bound down the mountain to India.

We rested as well as we could in the freezing barracks, and on the 18th of August prepared to cross clandestinely into hostile Tibet.

CHAPTER XVII

18th August 1891
Gnatong, Sikkim, India

WE ROSE BEFORE dawn, and by the time the sun was up were well away from the main path. We would have to use the main crossing at Jelep Pass, but had agreed that we should remain out of sight until the last moment, in case a caravan of traders should come down from the pass. Once hidden from the path we unloaded our ponies, fed them well, then sent them back down to graze by the glacial lake.

Prying apart the wooden pack-frames, we found, broken down and packed in thin greased felt, two carbines, along with a modest supply of cartridges.

"Ah! Faunce, you have indeed surprised me," cried Holmes. "Wherever he got hold of these, I'm grateful. Are you familiar with the Mauser, le Villard?"

"Not up close," I replied. "Our standard issue was the Lebel. I take it you approve, Holmes?"

"Indeed," he replied, as he carefully assembled the weapons, demonstrating the process to Kintup and I. "Bolt-action, automatic cam-cocking, in-line magazine, elastic extractors, ejectors, manual safety; chambered in 7.62 mm, and the cartridges are smokeless. That feature alone is worth the freight, in these bare mountains. Not a lot of cartridges, though! We must make our shots count when hunting. In fact, we should use the Enfields for hunting until our .303 ammunition runs out."

A further surprise awaited us when we unpacked the sealed packages at the bottom of each wicker pannier: four in all. Altogether, they yielded a powerful Webley revolver, a Remington double-barrelled over-under derringer, a dark lantern, three sets of smoked-glass snow goggles, and other small but essential items for our journey. One packet contained prismatic compass, small sextant and artificial horizon, boiling point thermometer, an aluminium telescope and two precision chronometers, all of the smallest and most durable construction possible, thanks to Faunce's years of experience in outfitting the *pundits*. The heaviest item was ammunition for the various firearms, but distributed amongst the three of us, it was manageable.

Food supplies consisted of sacks of *tsampa*, the ground barley meal that the Tibetans mix to a gruel with water, augmented by a stock of strips of dried mutton, some dried apricots and grapes, and a mixture of nuts. Water would be no problem, whether from stream or melted ice. Shelter was provided in the form of a beehive-shaped collapsible frame with light canvas cover, just large enough for three. This design would present minimum resistance to the howling winds, and its natural colour and shape would blend with the landscape. Finally, there were some small bundles of cut and dried kindling, for starting fires, which we could augment with fallen wood or dried yak-dung. Kintup, of course, had his stock of ingredients for making tea with rancid yak-butter, the staple of all hillmen.

We looked like a band of the most fearsome brigands, slung about with bandoliers and rifles, as we made a quick meal, then set off at a forced march for the Jelep Pass, ten miles distant. Our intention was to cross the ridge just before dusk on the second day, and quickly descend into the valley before we froze to death. Progress was slower than if we had stayed on the path, which we glimpsed below us from time to time, but we were in good shape, and there were few travellers to worry about anyway.

We passed the night of 19th August at the tree line, half way to the pass, then pressed on the next day, until within sight of the pass. Holmes used the telescope to inspect well ahead of us as we rejoined the pathway, climbing all the while. By now we were nearing the saddle-shaped ridge between two granite masses that was the Jelep Pass. I had climbed the highest peaks in Europe. They were as nothing compared to this fearsome alpine barrier, which, at over fourteen thousand feet, was dwarfed by peaks almost as high again. In compete solitude, with daylight fading, we crossed the knife-blade of the pass. The remorseless wind sliced cleanly through all our clothes and furs, and drove the breath from our straining lungs.

Thankfully, we were soon out of the worst of the wind, and slithered down the loose shale towards a pine-filled ravine, where shone the lights of a lonely monastery, the sole sign of life. The towering peak of Chumolhari loomed over us as night fell, and we made camp in a sheltered ravine, alongside a small lake of green ice. The next morning we descended almost to the floor of the valley, thankful for the cover of the silver firs, as there were hillmen on the tracks passing in both directions. Once we saw a small party of Chinese soldiers, marching out from their encampment at the first fortified wall protecting the frontiers of Tibet.

As we approached this fortified block wall, our spyglass revealed that the gate was open, but was manned by sentries. Fortunately, this barrier was easily skirted, as the surrounding ridges are not high. We waited until nightfall, then set off under the light of the half moon. Several hours before dawn, well past the frontier, we found a cave and slept until woken by the bright sun. Well rested, and out of sight of the paths, we made good time across the alpine meadows of the Chumbi valley.

Here, nestled between the jagged peaks, lies the village of Rinchengang. Two and three storey wooden chalets cluster in narrow lanes. With their wide eaves, steep roofs and brightly painted walls, they looked most charming. Wild flowers added their colour to the scene, as did groups of red-robed monks walking unhurriedly, holding their alms bowls. Holmes and I made camp in a secluded grove away from the village, and as the sun went down, Kintup slipped into the village. He had a trusted friend here who could advise him of conditions ahead of us, especially the movements of the roving patrols of Tibetan and Chinese soldiers who guard the frontier.

Kintup returned several hours after dark, bearing some fresh fruit and cooked mutton, along with some unleavened bread. He also brought the news that there were no unusual movements of frontier guards, and that the party we had seen going down the valley was the only patrol known. This was welcome news, although we should still have to remain hidden and travel across pathless country, for any peasant would inform against us. It meant, however, that if this should happen, we would have much more time to escape from the area of search. I noted also that Kintup seemed very pleased with himself, presumably because he had secured fresh food. We found another cave for the night, and Holmes and I shared the food – Kintup had eaten in the village.

Next morning we made our way up a most beautiful alpine valley, with the river running clear and cold between willows. We remained under cover of the birch and pine further from the stream, until we passed the even more charming village of Chema, where the gorge widened again. Soon we passed the gilt roofs of the summer house of the Raja of Sikkim, which Faunce had warned us to avoid, as it was here that the Raja had intrigued with the Tibetans against the British, and may still be garrisoned. It seemed deserted, however, except for a few retainers lazing around, and a few sentries with enormous mastiffs, so we made only a small detour, and then set out in the direction of the fortified town of Phari.

24th August 1891
Phari, Tibet
Phari lies at the edge of the great plain of Tibet, guarding the Chumbi valley approaches to the Forbidden City. We had marched as far and fast as we could, but the valley ascended steeply and, with our heavy packs, we were frequently forced to halt to catch our breath. Bypassing Chumbi village under cover of darkness, we made our way up paths cut into a huge ancient landslip, coming at last to the moonlit plain, spreading peacefully before us. We found shelter in this delightful meadow, and rose to the sound of rushing water and birdsong. Kintup fished for speckled trout, and we risked a fire to cook them. Much as we wished to boil water to wash, we had decided against washing or shaving - at least until we reached Lhasa - lest our disguise become the more readily apparent. Until now, on the very few occasions when we had encountered wayfarers off the beaten paths, Kintup had spoken with them while Holmes and I remained a little way off, twirling prayer wheels and seemingly lost in meditation. Our weapons, other than Kintup's Enfield, were concealed in our rolled blankets, which we had carefully prepared so that we could have our carbines out in an instant if required.

Through the telescope we saw scattered hillmen, and as there were several monasteries clinging to the mountain crags high above us, we rested in a thickly wooded copse for that day in order to regain our strength. We could not afford to linger, and the next day climbed up out of this enchanting valley into the barren and wild landscape above the tree line. Here, at almost fourteen thousand feet, our long and arduous climb was almost over. The wind was bitterly cold, and we moved fast, if only to keep warm, as we descended into the plain of Phari. The great peak of Chumolhari loomed only a dozen miles ahead of us, with the fort of Phari visible some four miles off, situated on a low hill, its massive sloping walls appearing impregnable. We knew that the Tibetans had stored enormous quantities of bullets and gunpowder here, and maintained a powerful garrison, answerable directly to Lhasa, to command their trade route from India. Even through the telescope we could make out very little, as we dared not approach close enough across the bare plain, but stayed hidden in the rocky foothills as we skirted the fort.

We decided against Kintup venturing into the town of Phari, although fresh food would have been welcome. He had a friend here also, a Bhotia who could be trusted. So far we had climbed up into Tibet without causing alarm, and here, with the garrison at hand, was not the place to be discovered and identified as interlopers. Besides, the stench that the wind carried in our direction from the mean sod huts huddled around the fort provided reason enough to avoid the town.

Now we faced the final climb, crossing the ridge of the Himalayas at Tang Pass, then on to Tuna. One day, walking fast, should do it.

26th August 1891
Tang Pass, Tibet
We crossed at dawn on the 26th, after an uncomfortable night in our tent, exposed to the howling wind. The *Tang La,* at just over fifteen thousand feet, is the highest point of ascent on the road to Lhasa. From here, the great plateau of Tibet stretched away to the distance. We had finally crossed the Himalayas.

28th August 1891
Guru, Tibet
As soon as possible after crossing the pass, which we did several miles away from the usual path, we made for the shelter of the surrounding hills, and pressed on past Tuna, and the great Rham Lake. Now that we were out of the defiles and gorges that so often defined our path during the ascent, it was possible to stay further from roads and paths. Kintup knew that ahead of us, at Guru, we should find the second of the Tibetan block-walls, with the heights above it fortified and garrisoned. A wide detour, over rocky and mountainous terrain, enabled us to bypass this obstacle. Our next destination was Gyantse, eighty miles distant.

2nd September 1891
Kangamar, Tibet
The path descended again into cultivated fields alongside the stream flowing from the lake, and we flanked the path as near as we dared. Soon we were able to fish and hunt, as winter had not yet set in. We made good time in this

fashion, passing through a great variety of gorges, river valleys, and arid plains, as we bypassed the villages of Chalu, Shamda, and Kangamar.

It was not long after passing Kangamar that our luck turned. As we hurried at dawn through a chasm that we could not bypass, we ran headlong into a patrol of Chinese soldiers. Somewhere along the way, we had aroused suspicion, and this news had been communicated rapidly along the paths while we toiled across rough country. We were expected. It seemed as though here, with not even the chance to unpack our weapons, our adventure was over. We could only hope that we would be sent back to India, and not executed summarily. The *Tung-ling* – the Chinese commander – was most courteous, and we were not interfered with in any way.

With Kintup translating, we were given to understand that we were to be sent, unharmed, under a small escort, to the Fort at Gyantse. There we would await the arrival of the Chinese *Amban*, who was expected from Lhasa within the week. The *Amban*, we knew, was one of the two most senior Chinese officials posted by the Celestial Emperor to administer the affairs of Tibet. Kintup assured us we would be untouched until he arrived, but that he expected we would be executed as spies once he arrived. Even our packs were left rolled, which greatly surprised us, but Kintup's rifle was taken from him.

Under close escort, we were marched, carrying our own packs, into the great mediaeval-looking fort of Gyantse, looking rather like Mont St. Michel without the ocean. A patrol of Tibetan cavalry passed us, coming from the fort. Dressed mostly in tunics of crude grey homespun with coloured collars, with shaved heads and pigtails, matchlocks and sometimes bows slung across their backs, spears in hand, these Tibetan soldiers presented an archaic yet fearsome appearance. A few of them, especially the officers, wore chain-mail armour and cuirasses, and their horses were similarly armoured.

At Gyantse Fort we were taken through the vast and busy central court-yard, where every Tibetan turned to stare at us, to a large room, deep within the fort, where we waited under guard. It was tempting to try to shoot our way out of there, while we still had our weapons concealed, but we decided against it. There were simply too many of them, and we did not know the layout of our prison. Perhaps later their vigilance would lapse!

Alas, after several hours a more senior Tibetan official appeared. Kintup identified him as the *De-pon*, or Civil Governor for Gyantse, under the Chinese *Ambans*. According to Kintup, this *De-pon* had a reputation for ruthless cruelty, even by Tibetan standards, and the only thing saving us – for now – was the imminent arrival of the *Amban* himself. The *De-pon* clearly wanted to ransack our belongings, but the Chinese commander insisted that we be left alone, so he contented himself with inspecting Holmes and myself closely, then cursed loudly, issued shouted orders to the Tibetan guards, and swept from the room.

We were escorted down a narrow stone staircase, through a barred gate, and pushed into a foetid chamber with walls of stone blocks. The front wall had stout wooden bars across the front, with an iron-framed door set in the centre. By the time we were locked in, the sun had long set, and the only illumination came from a feeble butter-lamp in the outer chamber. Here a guard was posted, and it was here that our equipment was stacked against a wall, still untouched. Obviously, said Kintup, the *Amban* was held in awe by the Tibetans, who would normally have stolen everything and then fought over it amongst themselves.

"We must get out of this place, Mr. Sigerson," pleaded Kintup, beside himself with worry. "They will surely kill us, this close to Lhasa. And now they say the *Amban* will be here within two days. Whatever are we to do?"

"Patience, Kintup. We have more than twenty-four hours until then. There must be some way out of this predicament. Meantime, we should rest ourselves so that, if an opportunity arises, we will be fresh and able to take best advantage of it. These wooden benches will do for two; I shall sit and ponder a little, while you sleep. In a few hours, we can change around. Good night, gentlemen."

Exhausted as we were, sleep soon overtook us, in spite of our fears. I woke as the first dim rays of sunlight filtered in from a small window set high in the wall of the corridor outside our cell.

"Holmes, you did not wake us," I cried out, seeing him seated cross-legged in the corner. Kintup sat up suddenly at the noise of my exclamation.

"There was no need, my dear le Villard. I see our way out of this, if we just play our cards right. I shall need Kintup's co-operation, a thespian's sense of timing, and a good deal of luck."

"What have we to do, then? How can I help?" I asked.

"The first thing is to keep your reaction under control, and casually take a look at the contents of the chamber opposite to ours."

I did as he said. Turning slowly to look into the room which had been in pitch darkness the night before, it was all I could do not to scream out in horror at the sight before me, visible across the narrow corridor, through wooden bars exactly like ours. Stacked in rows, which had tumbled into disarray in places, were human heads. Decapitated, and obviously desiccated by the cold dry air of the mountains, a hundred heads were grinning at us with a hundred ghastly dried mouths, and staring from two hundred vacant eye-sockets at every corner of this storehouse for the *De-*

pon's harvest of death. Many of these dried heads retained their hair, adding to the gruesome unreality of the tableau.

Even Kintup, who was hardened to the cruelties of life in Tibet, was visibly shocked, and drew back to the farthest corner of our cell, muttering mantras to ward off evil spirits. Once I had recovered my wits, I began to wonder how these lifeless heads could possibly assist us to escape with our heads still attached. I turned to Holmes, and raised my brows in query.

"Make another slow survey, le Villard, and look at the newest additions, not far inside the door. What do you see?"

I peered through the dust motes dancing in the narrow shaft of light, and inspected the heads more closely. Suddenly I saw what Holmes had noticed. One of the heads stared straight at us, vacant eyes under receding black hair; grinning rictus of smile showing under a wide, waxed moustache, the features still clearly European.

"Nicolae Chevron," I exclaimed through my teeth. "By all that's holy! He can only have been here a month ahead of us. Perhaps his fate has something to do with our being left alone. Maybe the *De-pon* overstepped his authority that time."

"I think maybe his guides lead him here, and take money," said Kintup. "I cannot see any of their heads with his." He had now overcome his fears, and was looking at the heads with us, as though there was nothing unusual about the occupants of the opposite cell. The warder, who had been changed during the night, paid us little attention.

"Kintup, see if we can arrange some food or drink, and it is most important that the guard comes into the cell. If so, we make no move. We only want them to see that we accept our imprisonment, but want our food."

I still could not see clearly what Holmes intended to do, but did not interrupt. Kintup spoke in Tibetan to the guard, who listened without reaction. Kintup spoke again. This time the guard looked a little alarmed, and disappeared for a minute, returning with a superior officer. This man also looked worried, then turned and left. We heard shouting as he disappeared from view.

"What did you say, exactly, Kintup? You both spoke so quickly."

"I told him that the Chief Spy, as he calls you, suffered from a disease which would certainly kill him, if he was not given some food soon. I also said that we should most certainly be killed anyway, but that if the Chief Spy died before the *Amban* arrived, then his poor head would most surely join those over there. He is not so very clever, this fellow, but he suspected my story was untruthful. However, he did not want to take a chance at all; I hope his officer feels the very same way."

'Indeed!" said Holmes. We waited over an hour before anything happened. By this time, Holmes had taken to one of the benches, and looked quite believably ill. He had hollowed his cheeks and eyes with just a little grime, expertly applied, and moaned very faintly as he rolled his head.

The officer returned, with a servant or slave carrying a crude tray upon which were several rough bowls. These contained *tsampa,* and some form of mutton stew cooked in rancid yak-butter. There was sufficient for three, and Tibetan tea as well. Obviously, Kintup's ploy had worked. Even better, the guards had to unlock the door to place the food inside. They watched as we ate. Kintup downed his portion quite happily. Holmes and myself had some trouble getting the food down, but we forced ourselves, as this was clearly part of the plan.

Holmes then asked Kintup to have the dishes removed. This caused some difficulty, but was done at last. By this time, Kintup and the guard were on speaking terms.

"Find out what time he goes off duty, Kintup," said Holmes. "We need him here for our gambit."

"I have already asked him that, Mr. Sigerson. He and the first guard have been put on extra duty, sir. He will stay until the gate to the fort is closed for the night, and then sleep in the guard chamber outside."

"Not ideal, but it will have to do. Very well! Except for a little preparation, there is nothing to do but wait."

The day carried on in this way. Twice more Kintup demanded food, and Holmes appeared more ill each time. Both times the food was brought, and each time our gaoler appeared more worried about being punished for something. We all took care never to appear anxious to escape, and this seemed to puzzle and worry him the more.

The sun set, and our ray of light faded and died. The lamp was lit, and threw an angled light into our cell. We waited two hours more, as best we were able to judge, and then Holmes began to moan most piteously, and rolled on his rough bunk, clutching his stomach. The guard came to the bars when called by Kintup, who said that the Chief Spy was certain he would die that night in his cell, and had some important information, which he would give only to the *De-pon*. After much consultation with the other guard and the officer, they decided to drag Holmes to the *De-pon*'s chambers, at which Holmes promptly fainted quite away. After more consultation they locked us in once more, then hurried off.

"Quickly, le Villard. Help me. We'll need some of this *tsampa* paste, and a lock of Kintup's hair. And, we'll need this!" With a flourish, he produced a tiny, razor sharp knife from the folds of his coat lining. "A little more grime, and a dab of fresh blood!"

Several minutes later there was a loud commotion in the passage leading down to the guard chamber. The *De-pon* swept into the guard chamber, his flat visage twisted into a mask of fury. He screamed at us, and we feigned ignorance. Holmes remained slumped on the bench, his face turned to the wall, moaning loudly. The *De-pon* shrieked at him, but he appeared not to hear. This was too much for the terrified *De-pon*, who shouted for the cell-door to be unlocked, and rushed inside, followed by the guards, now four in number, armed with wicked knives and old muskets. Kintup and I stayed back, against the walls at the sides.

The *De-pon* made to seize Holmes by the shoulder, but just before he could do so, Holmes sprang to his feet with a hideous, blood-chilling scream from deep in his throat. The *De-pon* screamed even more hideously, and sank to his knees in abject terror. The guards looked at Holmes, and followed their *De-pon*'s lead, one even fainting from sheer fright.

"Quickly," shouted Holmes. "Outside, and lock the door! The keyring is still in the lock!" He gathered their muskets and tossed them outside the cell.

We did as he said, while the Tibetans cowered in the corner, shielding their faces from the horror that was Holmes. We snatched up our packs, and removed from them our carbines and the revolver. Holmes slipped the derringer into his sleeve.

"I think I shall leave myself as I am," cried Holmes. "It was even more effective than I had hoped. Perhaps it will help us yet. They may have shut the gate by now. We must bring the *De-pon* with us. Kintup, get him out of there. Just him!"

The *De-pon*, however, refused to move, so terrified was he! I looked at Holmes. He did look ghastly, that I had to concede. Using his sharp knife he had shaved his hairline at the temples back even further than usual, and had scraped off most of his beard, leaving only his moustache. To this he had glued, using a paste made of *tsampa* from the food tray, a magnificent set of black moustaches, fashioned from the black lock cut from Kintup's hair, stiffened with *tsampa* mixed with black grime. More grime hollowed his cheeks, and his eyes glowed fiercely in pools of dark shadow. A thin line of blood trickled from each corner of his mouth and pooled with the blood welling from the crimson slash across his throat.

"We can't waste any more time," cried Holmes. "I shall have to reveal my tricks, after all. Train the guns on him."

With his moustaches plucked away, and a few wipes of his sleeve, Holmes's more normal appearance returned sufficiently that the terrified *De-pon* began to realise that he had been duped. He started to scream for help, but two rifles pointed at his head and cocked soon stopped that.

"Get him out of there," repeated Holmes.

This time the *De-pon* moved, though reluctantly.

"Tell him, Kintup, that he has two choices. One is that we kill him right here and now. The other is that he assists us to get away from here, and I would suggest that he takes to the hills himself, lest he join his victims here as punishment for letting us escape."

"But how do we get past all the guards, and the gatekeepers?" asked Kintup.

"Just tell him to be quick about it, or I'll save Lhasa the trouble!"

The *De-pon* understood this, now that his terror had receded. His cunning mind was clearly looking for a way out of this trap; he cautiously emerged from the small cell, with his tongue poked out in supplication. I locked the door behind him, although the guards all seemed still too terrified to move. Holmes slipped the derringer from his sleeve, and showed it to the *De-pon*, who appeared amused at the tiny pistol.

"Put the rifles under cover, while I show our hero here what this toy can do. Sorry about this, fellows, but it's the surest way to get his attention."

Holmes raised the derringer and took dead aim at one of those severed heads, at the top of the heap. He squeezed the trigger, and the dried head disintegrated against the wall behind it. He then showed the *De-pon* the other bullet, still chambered.

"I think that he got my message," said Holmes. "Now, let's get away from here."

He dug his pistol into the ribs of the Governor, and said, in Tibetan, "If you help us, you may escape to kill yourself honourably, or to flee for your life. There is nothing here for you now but dishonour and death. What is it to be?"

The *De-pon*, now visibly cowed, muttered something into his fur collar.

"He says he will go quietly, and will help," said Kintup, "if we will promise to take him two marches away from here, to a place he knows where he can hide."

"That we cannot do, but we will make sure he is well away from here, and release him where he cannot know which direction we have taken. We will give him supplies and a knife. Then he is on his own. Explain, quickly!" This was done.

"He accepts."

"About time," I shouted. "Now, shoulder packs, and let's move. This is making me very nervous."

Pushing the *De-pon* ahead of us, we locked the door to the cells, and mounted to the ground level.

"He says he has a secret escape passage from his suite, and that is the only way to avoid all the guards at the gate," said Kintup.

"Ah! Very convenient, but hardly surprising, given his hobbies," said Holmes. "I imagine all these forts are riddled with tunnels. Nice of him to tell us about it though, I must say."

Our little entourage received puzzled looks from the few Tibetan soldiers and functionaries we passed in the passageways on the way to the *De-pon*'s rooms; nevertheless, we arrived without incident. The only aide in his rooms was ordered out, and the door barred behind him. The *De-pon* went to a small chest behind a screen, and went to open it. Three rifles pointed at him, but he only removed a leather sack, which he stuffed inside his tunic.

Crossing to a carved panel on the wall, one of several, he swung it inwards after releasing a catch. He reached for a lamp from a sconce on the wall; but Holmes halted him with a signal.

"Le Villard, you know where the dark lantern is stowed?" he asked.

I had already unstrapped that bundle, and soon had the lantern lit.

"Ready!"

"You first, Governor! If I have to shoot you in the back, I don't want to hit anyone else."

But the *De-pon* had clearly decided that he must cast his lot with us, and gave no further trouble. I sealed the heavy wooden panel behind us with a stout bar provided to thwart pursuit.

The passage dipped sharply under the walls of the ancient fortress, then levelled out for a distance of several hundred feet, before rising gently and coming to a dead end at a mud-brick wall.

"He says we must break this down. It is sealed, but not strongly built."

So it proved, and we soon had it crumbled away sufficiently for us to pass through into a mud floored hut, with the only door barred from the inside. Here the *De-pon* removed his tunic, and his felt hat with its opaque blue button insignia of rank, and cast them heedlessly on the ground. A dusty peasant's robe hung on a wooden peg; this he slung around his squat shoulders, covered his head with the hood, and unbarred the door. I extinguished the lantern, and we all slipped out into the darkness. The hut was on the perimeter of the village, and we were not noticed as we walked calmly away into the deserted plain surrounding the fort. Unchallenged, we soon gained the low foothills, and by dawn were far away. During the night we had walked long distances along shallow streams before emerging far off, to confuse trackers, if any. But trackers need a trail to start with, and we hoped the *De-pon*'s secret passage would remain hidden for some time. His mysterious disappearance would set the whole country to searching, so we had to come up with a suitable plan of action, and quickly.

As soon as we were well away from the Gyantse fort, I asked Holmes why he had been so certain of the *De-pon*'s reaction to his charade.

"Very simply, le Villard, even the most sophisticated of assassins harbours a secret dread of his murdered victims returning to haunt him. I was sure he killed most, if not all, of the unfortunates in his trophy room, and I had the advantage of having met Chevron, so I was able to mimic his appearance, with a little impromptu makeup. The final touch was the slash across the neck, and the only way to make it appear convincing was to make a shallow cut, exactly where he severed head from neck. The blood oozed convincingly - you know how one bleeds from shaving nicks - and the spectre was complete. The real trick was to get him there in the first place, as he was to be our ticket out of the fort. The secret passage was pure bonus, but I should have guessed at it."

6th September 1891
Tashilhunpo Monastery
Shigatse, Tibet

Away from the *De-pon*, Holmes consulted his maps and compass. He considered various options, but return to India was not amongst them.

"We will head for Shigatse, le Villard. Firstly, we will be expected to either return to India; or else to carry on to Lhasa. Secondly, I have an introduction from Faunce to the Regent of the *Panchen Lama* at the Tashilhunpo Monastery. We may be able to shelter there for a while. According to Faunce, the government exchanged letters with this Regent in 1884. The fanatic monks from Lhasa blocked any progress in that direction. Nevertheless, this Regent is thought to be far more open to Western influences than the Regent of the *Dalai Lama*.

"The risk is that this is where Das stayed for a while during his last trip to Tibet. Unfortunately, the *Panchen Lama* of that time has died, and Das's friend the Prime Minister was disgraced and killed for assisting him. We may not be welcomed, but I think it is a risk we must take if we are to continue on to Lhasa."

"What about the *De-pon*?" I asked.

"We will take him further, before letting him go. He'll get no mercy for turning us in, not now."

We returned to Kintup and the Governor, heaved our packs on our backs, and set out on the fifty-mile overland journey to Shigatse. This took us three days and nights of hard walking, marching parallel to the trade road alongside the Nyang River, in the foothills of the tall mountain range to our left.

Fortunately, we encountered only a few hillmen on our way, and a display of the concealed derringer kept the De-pon quiet. After the first day we tried to send the De-pon away, as agreed, but he refused to leave, and trailed along behind us. Holmes then sent Kintup to bring him back to us, on strict understandings of co-operation or death.

At the outer limits of the town of Shigatse we halted to shelter in a cave for the night, and as I watched the setting sun flashing from the golden spires of the great monastery, I wondered what sort of reception awaited us there. Later, by the flickering light of several dried slips of willow branch, which Kintup had brought with him, I worked on my Journal. When I was finished I prepared them for burial at the city outskirts, as was my usual practice in case of search or suspicion. In the morning Holmes gave the letter of introduction to Kintup, along with a metal font from a printing press for the capital letter 'D' – to signify 'Das'. Armed only with an Enfield, and carrying only Tibetan goods, Kintup was to enter the town at dawn, seek out the secretary to the *Panchen Lama* at the Tashilhunpo Monastery, and present his token and letter.

This he did faithfully, and with little incident, but it could have cost him his life . . . and ours with it. After handing his letter over, he was seated with tea to wait, but almost instantly summonsed inside the inner sanctum, where he found himself in the presence of the Regent himself. Brief introductions were made, and then the questions began. Had he shown these letters to any other? Had he been seen with these British near to Shigatse? The whole countryside was in an uproar over the escape of the British from Gyantse and the disappearance of the Governor, who was thought to have fled in disgrace. Having answered these questions to their satisfaction, Kintup was then sent back to arrange for us to slip into the monastery late that night, by a certain side door, where the secretary would await us all. We followed instructions, and arrived at the side door without incident. The secretary awaited us in the deep shadow of the alcove.

We mounted hundreds of stairs, then passed down a long passage with neither doors nor windows, and entered a small chamber, which seemed to be a study. A Tibetan monk, in the simplest of robes, sat cross-legged on a small dais.

Thus, late at night on the 6th of September, we had our first meeting with the Regent to the *Panchen Lama*. He was a lean man of fifty or so years, with a broad forehead and prominent eyes, dressed in the yellow robe of his sect. He fingered a rosary of simple wooden beads as he spoke, although the solid gold images around him were worth a fortune.

Communication with the Regent proved rather difficult. Speaking slowly and almost inaudibly in Tibetan to his secretary, who repeated his words to Kintup, who then translated into English, he asked who had sent the letters. Holmes admitted to this, and was told that had any other than this trusted secretary seen them, he should have no choice but to have us seized as spies. As it was, we had been fortunate. He then informed us that Das's friend, the Prime Minister, had been disgraced and murdered for letting Das visit Lhasa, and the Governors at Gyantse and Dongtse were still imprisoned for life for helping him. The printing press had been cast into a chasm, and the then *Panchen Lama* himself had only escaped punishment because he had remained distant from Das, allowing the Prime Minister to maintain contact.

"But the truth is, he supported him, and was most saddened at his death. The teacher Das is well known to Lhasa as a British spy, and you should not even mention his name. However, I still feel, as I did then, that the Lamas at Lhasa make a grave mistake by their policy of exclusion of all Western influence. The Chinese do nothing but exact their tribute and enforce their edicts, yet I hear tales of great progress in the areas of Bengal and Sikkim, just across our borders in British India."

"That is most gratifying to hear," replied Holmes. "But perhaps I may presume to ask what is to become of us, given the situation."

The Regent looked in the direction of the *De-pon*. "This rogue I know well from my visits to Gyantse. Tibet is a harsh and cruel country, and I know that many of our ways are thought by the British to be barbarous. This man, however, relishes the cruelty and pain he is able, by virtue of his office, to inflict upon others. His life is already forfeit if he is found, but as you have chosen to risk your lives rather than kill him, as he would most certainly have done to you, I shall ask what you expect should be done with him."

"He has already lost all his power and position." Holmes thought for a moment. "I should like to think that he could never return to his cruel behaviour. And that he had some reason to repent his actions, if only to acknowledge the brutal death of the harmless and unfortunate M. Chevron, which averted our own."

The *De-pon*, understanding that his future was being discussed, reached into his tunic, and brought forth the leather sack he had taken from his office. Opening it, he poured out onto the floor a quantity of gold coins and nuggets. He offered them towards the secretary, asking to be hidden at the monastery.

"Put your gold away, beast," the Regent rebuked him. This was not translated, but we had enough Tibetan to understand. "You will need it where you are going. There are hermitages in the caves in the hills across the river from Dongtse, where misguided zealots voluntarily lock themselves away from the world in lightless cells, receiving a little food with gloved hand through a hole in the locked door. I regard this as useless self-punishment, and discourage the practise, but at last I have found a worthy occupant."

He turned to the *De-pon*, and said, "Tomorrow at dawn you will be taken to this hermitage. There you will enter one of the cells and be locked in, by your own choice. The only key will be brought here to me. No man will know the identity of the occupant, and you will never tell anyone. The head attendant there is an indolent and greedy monk, who has long ago undergone the six-month and three-year initiations in the cells, and after ten years, wisely delays the final and permanent penance. He will take your gold, until it is gone, but he can never release you. You have my word that your name will disappear with you. Now, begone, and spend your dark years contemplating your victims' cruel deaths."

The secretary had noted all that was said, and without speaking led the *De-pon* from the chamber. He returned several minutes later, and no further mention was ever made of the murderous former governor of Gyantse fort.

This unpleasantness behind us, the Regent offered us tea. Then he said that he would decide the following morning what must be done with us, made arrangements for us to remain the night in his private quarters, and retired for the night.

The chiming of temple bells and the sonorous chanting of the monks at their morning devotions woke us, well before dawn. Our room on the roof of the temple had a balcony, from which we could see the distant junction of the Nyang River with the broad waters of the Tsangpo. The enormous monastery, with its thousands of monks, was already well astir. Before long, our door was unlocked, and the secretary entered, followed by a deaf mute monk bearing a tray of food.

"This fellow will take care of you while you are here. He understands simple commands, and is devoted to our Lama. You must remain here for the day, and this evening we will move you to a small compound used for spiritual retreats by visiting dignitaries. It is entirely private, and your presence there will cause no comment. It is unsafe for you to venture out of the monastery until the hunt has been abandoned. Please stay out of sight. The *Panchen Lama* has been informed of your arrival, and has asked that you meet with him tomorrow evening, to discuss your future plans." With those words, he left us alone for the day. After our arduous climb up to Tibet, and our adventures at Gyantse, a day of complete rest was welcome indeed, but by evening we were all becoming restless.

Holmes passed the day, with Kintup's assistance, in cleaning and checking our weapons and instruments, while I brought my journal up to date. We were moved, very late that evening, to the private compound, and slept immediately on the nearest couches. Next morning we awoke to find ourselves in a charming cottage, all of finely carved wood, with a roof of golden tile. Set in its own walled garden, large enough for several spreading shade trees and an ornamental pool teeming with white and golden carp, the cottage had an adjoining chapel for the devotions of its more usual occupants.

At least we could move about in the fresh air, and get a little exercise. The deaf mute monk, who appeared to have no name, came with us, and saw to our water and food supplies. These were meagre, as befits monks in retreat, but we supplemented them with rations from our stores.

Here, chained in a small hutch behind the cottage, and being cared for after a fashion by our monk servant, we found a young male mastiff dog. He howled piteously, or else growled low in his throat, and would not let us approach. When he tried to walk, it was obvious that his right front paw was very badly infected, and was not being treated in any way. The swelling, with yellow fluid oozing from it, was visible from some distance. With nothing else to do, I began to think of relieving the poor animal's misery. We had sulphur and various tinctures; but how were we to approach a hostile animal that is the size of a small pony, and can easily pull down and savage a fully-grown billy mountain goat, or a buck gazelle on the run?

At my request, Kintup sent our man for a bowl of the mastiff's normal food, which turned out to be *tsampa* mixed with a little dried yak meat. I laced this with a dose of soporific sufficient to knock out three men, and fed it to the great hound, which wolfed it all down in two or three great gulps then returned to whining. Slowly the enormous bulk of the young mastiff relaxed until it slumped, unconscious, in the doorway to its hutch.

With Kintup's help, we tied the dog down as best we could, then Holmes used his sharp knife to lance the swelling. He drained it, and washed the wound, using boiled water and clean cloths, swabbed with neat alcohol, then applied sulphur powder to the open wound. We bound the massive paw tightly with fresh clean cloths, and lashed it in such a way that he could not walk when he awoke.

The mastiff accepted his dressings well, when he awoke several hours later. Clearly he was much less distressed by pain, and drifted in and out of sleep for most of the day. His whining ceased almost entirely, and the deaf mute monk was beside himself with joy. In the early evening we repeated the process, but put far less of the sleeping draught in his food. Later that evening, the secretary announced the arrival of the Regent and the *Panchen*

Lama. The first thing that happened, even before introductions were made, was that the deaf mute grasped the hand of the second highest monk in the land, and almost dragged him around to see the great hound. The mastiff was dozing peacefully with head rested on his bandaged paw. The monk's beaming smile and rosy cheeks were so innocently joyful that the young *Panchen Lama* took no offence at being thus handled, and asked the secretary who had treated the animal.

On being informed that we had all helped, he smiled slightly, and said in halting English, "Thank you, very good doing this. We talk more, please."

After formal introductions, the Regent explained that, following his contacts with the British, some ten years earlier, he had secretly brought in a Persian who knew both English and Tibetan, to tutor the boy Lama in English. He had thus learned a little English, but was unable to speak with anyone now that the Persian had left. The secretary had learned only a few words, and continued to translate through Kintup, as before.

Inside the cottage, with the *Panchen Lama* seated on a raised divan and his Regent at his side, whilst we sat cross-legged on the floor, we had the first of many private discussions with the head lama of Tashilhunpo Monastery, the great spiritual centre of Tibet.

17th September 1891
Tashilhunpo Monastery
Shigatse, Tibet

After ten days at Shigatse, Holmes was eager to move on to Lhasa. His contact in the Mahommedan Quarter would soon be leaving for Ladakh. If we were to escape from Tibet, and accomplish our goals, it was essential that we get to Lhasa quickly. The days here passed uneventfully, though we were told that the search was still in progress in the Chumbi valley, where we were assumed to have fled, headed for safety in India. I made my gymnasium each morning, and Holmes and I practised our *baritsu* daily, to the amusement of Kintup and the monk. As we did whenever we had the chance, we worked at improving our various languages.

The mastiff's paw was fully healed. After the second day, we stopped the sleeping draught, and the hound allowed us to dress his wound with no more than the odd whimper. As soon as he was able, he took to following me around the compound, remaining one or two paces behind me, and dropping in a heap at my feet whenever I sat down, his huge head resting against my ankles.

"You appear to have made a devotee, le Villard, although I hope he remembers that we all helped him," said Holmes in jest. "I shouldn't like him at my throat in anger."

Most evenings, once evensong prayers had been said throughout the monastery, the *Panchen Lama* would come to converse with Holmes. He was still a youth, having not yet reached his majority of eighteen years, and had the curiosity usual at this age. Our discussions were conducted in a mixture of English, Tibetan and Persian, with the help of the secretary, and ranged across a variety of topics. Mahommedan, Christian and Buddhist philosophy, European warfare and weapons, recent advances in science and medicine, the modern telegraph and the advent of steam travel by land and sea, and a hundred other things. Where I thought it helpful, I added some quick sketches to the conversation, to assist the Lama in understanding things of which he had never heard, but about which he had the liveliest curiosity.

Holmes also brought out all our weapons and instruments, explaining and demonstrating their use as best he could. The Lama was intrigued, examining each item minutely, and asked to be taught how to use the sextant and compass.

For his part, Holmes asked about Russian influence at Lhasa, and was told by the Regent that Lama Dorjieff, the Russian-born Mongolian monk, was now at Lhasa, where he was the favoured tutor to the *Dalai Lama*. The Regent distrusted the man, regarding him as a Russian spy who was twisting ancient Tibetan legends around to try to legitimise a rapprochement with Russia, while supporting the exclusion of all other Europeans, as now. But the *Dalai Lama*, or his regent, was traditionally the political power in the land, and the *Panchen Lama* had no influence in these matters, however he may feel.

One evening, Holmes enquired of the Lama whether, as spiritual leader of the Tibetans, he could tell us anything of the immortal Mahatmas in their hidden Himalayan caves, or of the ancient Atlantean philosophies supposedly preserved here when the ocean floor was upthrust to form the Himalayas aeons ago. The Regent answered.

"I know of wise men who have chosen to withdraw from the society of men, in order to contemplate in freedom, but to my knowledge they sooner or later pass the way of all flesh, and are cast into the pits to be gnawed clean by vultures and pariah dogs. I know of no Immortals, in truth, though I could point out many that make that claim. They will surely pay for their presumption in their next reincarnation. As for wisdom from libraries at the floor of the ocean, I can scarcely comprehend the question."

18th September 1891
Tashilhunpo Monastery
Shigatse, Tibet
The Regent came today to inform us that the *Panchen Lama* had finally arranged for our passage to Lhasa. The patrols in this direction had stopped searching for the British spies, and he felt we could travel safely now, provided we followed instructions exactly. Holmes and I were to travel disguised as *bahrashri* pilgrims, travelling for safety with a party of pilgrims proceeding from the monastery to the Great Cathedral at Lhasa, while Kintup would assume the position of Tibetan servant to the two wealthy pilgrims. The Regent provided us with a dark brown liquid with which to stain our hands, faces and necks, saying that otherwise our disguises were worthless. The party would leave before dawn on the morrow; so we packed all our gear inconspicuously in our rolls and leather sacks, Holmes and I painted ourselves liberally with the brown solution, stored the remainder in my pack, and had our evening meal.

After prayers, the *Panchen Lama* called on us for the last time. Smiling at our strangely altered appearance, he gave us some instructions for our journey, then blessed us briefly in Tibetan. Before he left us, Holmes asked the Regent to please present our spare chronometer to the *Panchen Lama,* in token of our gratitude, saying that we should need the rest of the equipment for our journey, or else we should leave it all. The Lama was greatly pleased at this, and after some thought, spoke quietly to us all.

"It has been a most interesting experience for me to have spent this time with men from a world so different from Tibet. I should like to send a gift with you, but I know you need no extra weight. I fear gold would mean nothing, and we have no marvels such as these to give you in return. But there is, happily, a solution. In Tibet, it is great merit to give and to receive a dog, as it is a dishonour to sell or offer to buy one. I give you, as your companion in your travels, the dog you have healed.

"I have noticed that he follows your friend here, the one who draws pictures, everywhere he goes." He turned to me. "And that you have a name for him, is that not so?"

Rather sheepishly, I admitted that I did call him by name, as it seemed that neither he nor the young monk had one.

"And what, may I ask, is that name?" he enquired, a gentle smile on his lips.

"I meant no offence, sir, but I call him 'Tashi', as he comes from the Tashi monastery," said I, "but we can easily change that."

"He seems to answer to the name. You may use it, with my blessing, as a gift with the animal. And now, I must leave you to rest, as you will be awoken in the middle of the night."

The *Panchen Lama* retired, and left us wondering how we should deal with Tashi, when we were fugitives in Tibet. Nevertheless, the thought of that enormous hound at our side in any affair was somehow a great comfort. However we managed it, I was pleased that we should not have to leave the young mastiff behind.

19th September 1891
Tashilhunpo Monastery
Shigatse, Tibet
As we were to be part of the caravan of pilgrims headed for Lhasa before the worst of winter, we assembled at four in the morning in the great courtyard of the monastery. Bells chimed softly, muffled by the morning mist, calling the faithful to prayer; yellow and red-robed monks moved, silently and slowly in single file, down the innumerable stairs and ramparts; pungent smoke from cooking fires and incense pots curled upwards into the darkness. The asses and ponies snorted in the cold air as we marched out through the massive iron-studded wooden gates of Tashilhunpo Monastery, home of the *Panchen Lama,* bound at last for the Forbidden City of Tibet.

CHAPTER XVIII

29th September 1891
Lhasa, Tibet
OUR CARAVAN moved slowly, but was the best possible disguise for our presence. With a pass from the *Panchen Lama,* and an escort of forty monks, our varied group of pilgrims attracted no attention. Holmes and I kept to ourselves, the picture of hooded devotees, as we twirled our prayer wheels, indifferent to all those who tried to speak with us. Kintup and Tashi remained close by at all times, and kept others at a distance. This was not unusual behaviour for pilgrims, and went unremarked. The monks had their

instructions to leave us alone.

We had some worries as we passed again through Gyantse on the fourth morning, but the caravan pressed on to spend that night at Gabzhi. From there, we travelled down the valley of the Ralung River, scattered with houses banded in broad vertical stripes of blue and white and red. Climbing up the open moor, we crossed the *Kharol La* in a freezing blast of wind, and descended from that pass down to the fort of Nagartse, striped like the houses of the valley, with beyond it the vast inland sea of Yamdok Lake.

From there, we marched on past Palte fort to the Kamba Pass where, at an elevation of over sixteen thousand feet, we crossed into Central Tibet. Looking back from the broad ridge of the pass, we could see the vast lake; to the front, the valley of the Tsangpo lay four thousand feet below us. Four miles further, and we came down to the river at Chak-sam. This was the location of the old Chinese iron suspension-bridge, which Faunce had warned we should have to cross. The power of the rushing torrent was soon apparent, when two Tibetans set out to cross the stream in a frail wood-framed leather coracle. They were soon tossed about, until their craft capsized, tipping the unfortunate occupants into the raging waters to be swiftly swept out of sight downstream.

Travelling in the protection of the pilgrimage, however, we crossed in comparative comfort and safety on the ferryboat. This box-like vessel, made of massive walnut planks, had at the prow a beam of wood carved like a horse's head; we realised how appropriate this was as the ferry headed out into the current, with twenty ponies and asses, a dozen monks and pilgrims, and our stores aboard. As soon as we left the calm water in the lee of the bank the swift current seized the heavy craft, and tossed it about like a leaping stallion, hurtling us all downstream at a fearsome rate, until finally lines were secured to stanchions set in the opposite bank. We disembarked, and the ferry was towed and poled upstream to take passengers back across, when the whole cumbersome process began again. While we waited for the rest of our party to cross the Tsangpo, Kintup and Tashi played at fishing in the shallows, and caught several fine large carp. Afterwards, Kintup told us tales of his explorations further downstream, when he was exploring in disguise for the Survey; his aim had been to prove, once and for all, that the Tsangpo was in fact the same river as the Brahmaputra. His explorations had taken him almost to the lands of the cannibalistic Abors, who apparently followed the quaint custom of eating the bride's mother as the main course of the wedding feast.

We then set out on the last stage of our journey to Lhasa, through groves of poplar and alder, past apricot and walnut orchards ripe with autumn fruit, admiring the fine old willows along the banks of the river as we passed by.

This was the main trade and pilgrimage route into the city of Lhasa, along the northern bank of the mighty Kyi River, which joined the Tsangpo some few miles downstream from the ferry. This river valley led at first through fertile country, but soon narrowed to a gorge where only one at a time could traverse the path hewn into the face of granite cliffs, with the river rushing past below. We found out here that Tashi was as sure-footed as any mountain goat.

The trail passed through the desert heat of a vast sandy valley, then along a series of rocky defiles, with their precipitous, narrow paths, past numerous rock-carvings and inscriptions invoking the Tibetan divinities, until finally, several marches from the ferry, we caught our first glimpse of Lhasa. From a rocky bluff high above the clear waters of the Kyi we could see a golden temple roof flashing in the bright sun. Several miles later the view of Lhasa itself opened before us, the crimson palace of the *Dalai Lama* with its roof of gold visible from miles away.

A few hours later we were, at last, in the centre of Lhasa itself, having passed through streets thronged with Tibetans, Chinese soldiers, Nepalese and Mahommedan traders, and Asiatics of all types. Most of them, other than the monks, carried weapons of some kind. Finally, our party of pilgrims turned into the narrow entrance of a caravansery belonging to the Tashil-hunpo Monastery. Kintup unloaded our packs from the ponies, and we were shown into the small suite of chambers on the upper floor, overlooking the courtyard, that had been arranged for us at the order of the *Panchen Lama*. Tashi insisted on staying with us, and we were in no position to dispute his will. He was enormous, and still growing.

30th September 1891
Lhasa, Tibet

We ventured forth next morning, in our guise of *bahrashri* pilgrims, to explore the town of Lhasa. Holmes had several places to visit, and wished to know something of the locale before going. He had previously mentioned the Mahommedan he was expecting to arrive at Lhasa. Now he confided that we would also call, discreetly, upon the Nepalese Consul, and if possible, upon a senior aide to the Chinese *Amban*, who had once worked as a British spy under Gordon in China, many years ago. In some way or other, I understood, these contacts were all agents in Mycroft Holmes's vast network.

I suppose one does not sit at the centre of a web of international political intrigue for years without developing a wide range of informers, agents and outright spies. Given the extent of the British Empire, so much larger than our French possessions, it should not have surprised me that even here, in the forbidden capital of the most reclusive country on the face of the globe, Mycroft had agents of a sort in place.

The first thing we did was to join the endless parade of the devout in walking clockwise three times around the road that ringed the city proper. The entire city was not large, being some two and a half miles in circumference, and was dominated by the twin hills of the Potala, and of the Medical University. Leaving our caravansery, we walked by side streets, passing the Nepalese consulate, to the cemetery at the corner of the circular road. Joining the pilgrims, we came immediately upon the beggar's town, made of yak bones and gazelle horns, covered with skins straight from the nearby slaughterhouse. Following this was the butcher's quarter, outside the city walls, and then the slaughterhouses.

We completed only half of a full circuit, turning away to pass again under Potala Hill with the *Dalai Lama*'s palace towering so magnificently above us. We walked on down this main thoroughfare, which was, like all roads in Lhasa, unpaved and undrained. The main buildings and better houses were of stone, and the lesser dwellings of mud brick. The houses were all of two or three storeys, brilliant with fresh whitewash, with a band of dull maroon picking out the eaves. Square canvas shades at the windows of many of the better buildings reminded me of parts of Italy. Perhaps they were the legacy of Italian missionaries who had dwelt here so long ago, before Tibet closed its borders to the rest of the world. With asters and marigolds blooming in pots at the windows, and caged songbirds hanging in open doorways, these dwellings had an air both charming and decorative. A glance within any of these sparkling exteriors, however, soon revealed the filth and disorder that prevailed in the houses of all Tibetans.

Passing our place of lodging, we strolled casually around the immediate area, where we soon located the Mahommedan magistrates building, the shops of the *newaris* from Nepal, and nearby, a small Mahommedan trading store, with dried fruits, nuts and saffron displayed in cloth sacks around the entrance. This was the store where, later, we would meet with Mycroft's man.

Holmes's map of Lhasa, provided by Das, was remarkably accurate. We made our way, using this guide, past the horse and grass market to a Mahommedan Chinese eating house, where we made a passable lunch. Our meal done with, we finally explored the Chinese quarter, located along the ditch that provided the town latrine. Passing the Chinese theatre, we came upon the traditional single-storey Chinese houses, then past the town pigsties to the barracks of the Chinese garrison. We halted when the compound of the Chinese *Ambans* came into view, and retraced our steps to our lodgings.

The late autumn weather was most delightful; bright blue skies, with clear air, free of the dust so prevalent at Gyantse and on the plains through which we had passed. Scattered around Lhasa are numerous finely wooded parks and gardens, with shrines where offerings are constantly replenished. At every turn are temples, their porches protected from evil spirits by stuffed mastiffs hung, high up under the eaves, at each of the four corners.

Tucked away in a shoulder of the great ranges of the Himalayas, Lhasa is somewhat sheltered from the bitter extremes of the surrounding bleak tablelands and looming peaks. We took advantage of this fine weather to spend some time at the various shrines, twirling our prayer wheels like the pious pilgrims all around us. Holmes's disguise was a little more extravagant than my own. With his full beard parted at the centre and curled outwards, extravagant moustaches to match, and a turban of sorts wound loosely around his head, he appeared to be just another prosperous pilgrim. I wore less costly robes, humbler beard and moustaches, and a cap. My precious Journals I kept tucked in my sash, in specially sewn pockets, their shape concealed by the rough folds of coarse fabric.

7th October 1891
Lhasa, Tibet

After a week in Lhasa we became familiar with the small city. With Tashi we visited the leather and harness market, where I had a strong harness made, with thick straps inset with heavy brass rings, so that Tashi could carry his own food as we travelled. We also took some exercise by walking in the parks and woods outside the city walls. By this time, Holmes was sure that we were not being followed around, as had been the case for the first few days after our arrival. This was normal, and we acted the part of pilgrims at all times.

Now Holmes felt we could make contact with the Mahommedan visitor. Accordingly, we took a stroll in the Mahommedan quarter, stopping to make small purchases here and there, and finally called at the shop where we were to make ourselves known. Our small party of three was inconspicuous in the crowded street, full of the bustle and noise of any Eastern bazaar, so when Holmes spoke with the elderly proprietor, and minutes later we were invited inside to take some mint tea, nobody paid the least attention.

We were led through a clean, whitewashed room, with rugs on the polished floor, and down several steps to a small courtyard with a covered well and a shade tree. Here, seated on the bare swept earth, we were introduced to Mohamed Abdul Beg. He was tall and lean, a man of the broad steppes, with the weather-beaten features and slow movements born of years spent in the barren wilderness of Central Asia. Several of his tribesmen, heavily armed with muskets and short curved swords, sat in a loose circle around him, drinking tea and smoking foul-smelling tobacco from a large hookah. Through an archway we saw more of his tribesmen, with half a dozen of their Bactrian camels tethered to a rail.

Once we had drunk the obligatory tea, and made the customary small talk in Persian, Mohamed Abdul Beg informed us that he had been sent from Kashgar to Lhasa five months previously at the behest of his father, the hereditary *Atalik* of Kashgar. His people, he explained, were regular traders with the Tibetans, their *kafilas* sometimes numbering forty camels, bringing goods from Kashgar and Turkistan to Lhasa, and returning home with Tibetan furs, saffron and other goods for sale at the markets at Ladakh and Yarkand, before returning to Kashgar.

He and his people had been at Lhasa for over a month already, camped out at the sports ground for *kashmiri* merchants, outside the city. Mohamed Abdul Beg himself was lodging with their tribe's agent, the merchant. They had decided to remain at Lhasa for the worst months of winter, then set out on the long journey back to Ladakh and Kashgar early in the spring, before the rivers became swollen and unfordable. Mohamed Abdul Beg had no message for us, other than that his father had ordered that he escort us safely back to Kashgar. He did, however, have a wax-sealed letter, sent on by his father, addressed to Professor Olaf Sigerson, no address given. This he gave to Holmes, who tucked it away without opening it.

"I thank you very much," said Holmes, slipping the letter inside his robe. "There remains only to discuss the details of our journey, as it would be better if we kept our distance until your departure. We will leave Lhasa in the direction of Gyantse, then double back in the night, meeting with you at a place of your choosing."

"So be it," replied the *kashgari*. "Let us meet, on the night of the 13th day of your month of February, at the small grove of pines a half-day's march along the road to the monastery at Sera. Until then, may your gods be with you."

We left the dried fruit merchant's store, having spent no more time there than required for a sociable cup of tea, and carried on with our desultory shopping in the nearby shops and at the bazaar, before returning to our lodgings.

"Well, fellows, it seems we will spend the winter here at Lhasa," remarked Holmes, once we were back in our chambers. "I suppose it's preferable to being stuck halfway across a frozen desert, but I would prefer to move on as soon as we can. This place is too small for my liking. Now, I must decipher this message. It is from Mycroft, of course."

While I continued with braiding strong, coarse yak-hair twine into thick and supple alpinists' rope, Holmes spent the next hour transposing the rows and columns of figures into plain text. When finished, he handed the result to me. I read:

'Dearest Brother,

As you have arrived at Lhasa, and received this message, I presume you and le Villard are proceeding with the expedition as planned. I await your news from Lhasa: please forward as urgently as possible. Large issues must be decided, and this information is crucial to the process. I have received information regarding recent arrival at Lhasa of one Tserenpil, also known as Bogdanovich. Like Lama Dorjieff, he is a Mongol Buryat. Please investigate.

Once you have concluded your investigations at Lhasa, you should travel to Kashgar, in Chinese Turkistan, in the caravan of Mohamed Abdul Beg. He is the eldest son of an old friend of mine, the hereditary Atalik of Kashgar. His people are the dominant tribe for hundreds of miles around. The Chinese retook the region in 1877, when they defeated the last ruling Atalik, Yakub Beg. Although pledging allegiance to the Chinese, Kashgar is increasingly under threat of attack by the Russians, and if that should happen, the entire region would fall into the Russian sphere. Control of that region will mean Russia owns the gateway to all of western Central Asia, and will soon have that vast area under its hegemony. We would as soon prevent that from happening.

As Britain cannot be seen to be interfering in these regions without causing an international incident, I have suggested that, as Mahommedans, they seek the support of Mecca to counter the threat, and perhaps drive the Chinese out. Accordingly, the Atalik must make the Hajj pilgrimage to Mecca this coming year, so that he may meet with the mullahs and sheiks while there.

All this has been agreed, but St. Petersburg knew of these plans almost as soon as they were made. We know that an attempt will be made, by agents whose employment can never be traced back to the Russians, to ensure that the Atalik never reaches his appointed contacts at Mecca.

If you can ensure that the Atalik arrives safely at Mecca, you will have done us a great service. Although not in power in his own lands, he is the only hereditary ruler sufficiently respected to forge an effective resistance, should the Russians move in force. It would take the Chinese a long time to reinforce their position, if they chose to fight.

Your trip to Kashgar will take some time, the distances being what they are. The good news is that, by the time you have made this journey, I expect that London will be safe for your return.

So, make a safe return to London, where we will arrange for your resurrection. My regards to le Villard! And de Benoist's to you both!

Mycroft.'

18th October 1891
Tibet, Lhasa
Holmes tried my patience more than somewhat during this period of inactivity. Remembering some of Doctor Watson's earlier tales, I had prepared myself for his black moods when I accepted the invitation to join him. I decided simply to take his own advice to Watson, and leave him be until his mood passed.

His ill will was rarely directed at Kintup, or myself. Rather, it seemed closer akin to self-loathing. In more fanciful moments I imagined that he had substituted the goals of Britain's rivalry with Russia in Central Asia for the battle of wits between himself and Professor Moriarty in the arena of crime, detection, and retribution. That, by involving himself in the Great Game, he was somehow exorcising the ghosts of his Pyrrhic victory over Moriarty!

Only once did he open up, and mention the Professor Moriarty affair specifically.

"How could we have failed?" he had brooded, more to himself than to me. "I had produced evidence sufficient to convict them all - leaders included - several times over. Professor Moriarty, I knew, was already committed to an appearance to defend his most recent mathematical paper at the Society, so he should have been ready to hand in London.

"If you only knew the amount of time and energy expended on this one case, le Villard . . . it's true it would have been the jewel in the crown of my career, but that's beside the point. The point is, my friend, I failed - miserably, in what should have been a triumph, and I still can not understand why. I go over it again and again in my mind. That the Professor also failed, and lost his life doing so, is of little comfort." He had then resorted to a moody silence.

My usual response was to take a long walk with Tashi, and occasionally Kintup, out into the surrounding valleys, as far as the snow and cold would allow. We moved briskly, to keep warm, and I found it a pleasantly exhausting way to pass otherwise idle days.

When he came out of this particular mood, which had already lasted three days, Holmes sent Kintup out, with a note, to the residence of the Nepalese

Consul, the result being that a meeting was arranged, ostensibly to discuss trade, at the consulate building. Accordingly, late in the afternoon, Holmes and I walked the short distance to the consulate, and paid our respects to the genial elderly Nepalese who had represented Nepal for two decades and more.

Following the usual pleasantries, conducted with his staff present, we were invited to his inner room, and were made comfortable on mats on the floor. He made certain nobody was listening, then spoke to us in halting English.

"Welcome to Lhasa, sir. I have words from Kathmandu to expect some British. We must talk our business quickly; suspicion is so very easy here at Lhasa. I know you are looking for information about the Russian man Dorjieff. Before he was only teacher of *Dalai Lama*. Now he makes an arsenal for Tibet, some Indian men making rifles, near Lhasa. There is a new Russian to help Dorjieff make guns for Tibetan soldiers. They use a water-machine at Kyi River, upstream one day. Name is Bogdanovich, or Tserenpil. We hear the Regent and *Dalai Lama* like the Russian King very much, listen to everything Dorjieff says."

"Very interesting, indeed; ties in with Mycroft's information as well. Exactly how do we get to this arsenal?" enquired Holmes.

"Summer time use the river, now the ice starts. You take the road, soldiers will stop you. You must go across country, no road. Then you can find the arsenal, near to the river. Many soldiers to arrest you there, too."

"Where exactly does Dorjieff stay when he's in Lhasa?"

"At Potala Palace or Drepung Monastery."

"And the other Russian, Bogdanovich?"

"Before he stayed at Drepung. Now we think he is boss at the arsenal, or else gone back to Russian country. Not so sure."

"We must leave. Is there anything else you can report?" asked Holmes, rising to his feet.

"The *Amban* who went to Gyantse, he came back with the very same Chinese soldier who arrested you the first time. Maybe they think you come to Lhasa after all!"

We took our polite departure from the Consul in his public front room, loudly discussing the possibilities of the *pashm* shawl-wool trade. From that time on, we avoided Chinese officers as much as possible when we walked about Lhasa, and stayed away from the market places, sending Kintup and Tashi to shop for our supplies.

27th October 1891
Lhasa, Tibet
The last of Mycroft's agents in Lhasa was the senior aide to the *Amban*, who had spied for Gordon so long ago. In view of the information from the Consul, we were nervous about making any approach to this man, once Kintup had identified him. We found that Kintup had a facility for making friends, in particular friends of the female kind. At first, this caused us great concern, but we soon found that he was most discreet about our cover story, and that his behaviour was considered quite usual for a servant.

In this way, Kintup found out many snips of information that helped us. One such was that the aide we wished to meet was lodged inside the *Amban*'s walled compound, where we certainly could not go. This officer, however, had a weakness for the Chinese theatre. Several nights a week he attended, as the theatre was close by the compound and barracks, and afterwards usually walked to the Chinese restaurant by the market. Kintup had noticed that each afternoon he went on tours of inspection on behalf of the *Ambans*, and was not accountable for his time during this period. One evening, as the Chinese left the restaurant to return home, Kintup managed to slip him a message. Holmes had requested to meet with him near the parade ground of the Chinese troops, in the afternoon of the next day.

28th October 1891
Lhasa, Tibet
We had almost given up on the Chinese aide when he finally appeared, alone, at the edge of the parade ground across from where we had made our picnic under the shade trees. He was dressed, as were all Chinese officials, in pale blue silk frock coat and collar, with a jacket of dark blue silk over it, and black velvet boots. His pigtail hung from the back of his shaved head, on which he wore the usual black Chinese felt hat with brim upturned. Acting the part of hospitable *bahrashri*s, we invited him to share tea and sweetmeats with us, which he accepted with grace.

We squatted thus for no more than a polite ten minutes, but that was sufficient. He had forgotten most of the little English he learned, but had spent several years at the Chinese legation at Paris, which was where de Benoist and Mycroft had used his services. We conversed in French, which Holmes of course speaks like a Parisian.

He told us that the Chinese, too, were very concerned about the Russians, fearing for their northern borders. The government at Peking was aware of Colonel Przhevalsky's report to the effect that a small but determined force of Russian-led Cossacks could even sack Peking. They knew of the existing

Tibetan arsenal at Lhasa, but were excluded from the new arsenal upriver. The power of the *Ambans* was diminishing, and disrespect was no longer uncommon from the Tibetans. Lately the *Ambans* had confined themselves to *appearing* to enforce Chinese rule, even sending false reports back to Peking confirming this, and to collecting bribes from Tibetans seeking higher positions in the priest-ruled government. In daily matters, their authority was still evident, but in high affairs of state, it was the Russian Lama Dorjieff who was consulted every time.

We paid this gentleman handsomely for the risk he had taken, and he soon left us to continue our leisurely picnic.

22nd November 1891
Lhasa, Tibet
Holmes decided that it was time we had a look at the arsenal. I was glad that at last we had a firm goal. The past four weeks had been spent in making 'pilgrimages' to monasteries around Lhasa, especially to the east of the city, or else learning our languages in the privacy of our roof-top rooms. On several occasions Holmes had retreated into one of his brown studies, becoming uncommunicative in the extreme, and seemingly desirous of nothing but peace and quiet in which to indulge his fit of melancholy, or whatever it was that caused his withdrawals from our society, even when in our midst.

I thought back to the dreadful fear I had experienced upon waking early one morning, on a traverse across a sheer rock wall crossing the frozen Himalayan peaks. We had come the previous night to a wide area in the otherwise narrow pathway, which I realised was because a huge flat rock was embedded in the cliff face, jutting out like an enormous ledge. I'd had one of my not-infrequent *nuits blanches,* and was late in waking. Kintup had gone on ahead to scout the path, and Holmes was unaware I had arisen. I pulled back the tent-flaps, and it was all I could do to refrain from screaming out at Holmes. He was standing at the very edge of the flat rock, arms outspread, and was jumping vigorously up and down, as though performing his morning gymnasium in the centre of a field. A single misstep and he would surely have plummeted to his death. I was too terrified to call to him, not wishing to alarm him, and inadvertently cause just that which I most feared. So I remained silent, watching in amazement as Sherlock Holmes heedlessly risked his life on the very edge of a precipice.

After a few moments he ceased jumping about, and sat down with his legs dangling over the yawning void. I closed the tent-flap, made a few noises as though moving about, and loudly opened the tent again. Holmes heard me, and glanced around as he lit his pipe from a phosphor-match. Squinting against the morning light, I crossed over to where he sat, and joined him in contemplating the stupendous vista spread at our feet. Below us huge lammergeyer vultures soared and spiralled on the wind rushing up the face of the mountain. I glanced at my companion, but could glean no insight there into the reason for his risky athletics. Whether he was still feeling oppressed by his failure to bag the Moriarty gang in its entirety, and was defying fate to dash him from his precarious foothold - or whether he was doing a jig of celebration at finding himself unfettered and alive on the very roof of the world, surrounded only by the most magnificent peaks to be found on our globe - I was unable to divine.

I made no mention of having witnessed this extraordinary display, and we had continued along our way. His bouts of melancholy were soon passed by, and Kintup and I had both learned to recognise when our silence or absence would be advisable, until his good humour returned, and he was again the ever-fascinating Holmes of old.

Our Nepalese friend had given us instructions to follow to the location of the arsenal. We set off, therefore, in the opposite direction, towards the Drepung monastery, and several miles out of town struck off from the road towards the river. According to our maps, we were about seven miles from the river, and some fifteen miles from the location of the arsenal. Taking a direct line would bring us slowly nearer to the river, and we headed off across the barren, hilly country. Our excuse, should we be intercepted, was that we had lost our way while searching for ancient cave shrines.

As we neared the river, the terrain changed to wooded hills with thick undergrowth, and then to large granite cliffs and boulders bordering the broad stream. By the time we had drawn near to the arsenal evening was upon us, and soon we took advantage of the bright moonlight to approach as close as we dared on this occasion. There were a number of Tibetan soldiers posted around the perimeters. Evidently, they had few curious visitors to keep them alert, for none seemed vigilant in the least. Numerous smaller outbuildings, most likely storehouses for the factory and lodgings for the workers, surrounded the arsenal building. There was no barrier around the compound, but there were three guardhouses, one on each of the trails leading to it.

It seemed that the workers had finished work for the day, as lamps were lit one by one in the smaller buildings, and the smells of stew cooking wafted to us. We circled around until we were upstream of the low stone building. From here, we could see a large water wheel set in a stone-banked sluice. It turned smoothly as the river water rushed by in the main stream. Kintup stole down to the water's edge, and tested the temperature.

"Very soon ice, Mr. Sigerson. Wheel can't turn." We noted a jetty at the river's edge, where no doubt they loaded finished rifles for shipment to Lhasa. Holmes handed me the telescope, which I used to inspect the whole area carefully. Suddenly a splash of yellow lit the snow as a door opened. A barrel-chested Mongol, dressed in rather unusual monk's garb, came out of the building, followed by three turbaned Indians. They carried on an animated conversation, but we could make out none of it at that distance. They disappeared into the largest of the huts, and closed the door behind them. Tibetans, in small groups, came out from the same door and dispersed to their various huts, the day's work done.

There was little more to learn without approaching closer. We decided against it, at this time, and made our way back to the road we had set out on, making camp as soon as we reached it. Next morning, we carried on to the monastery as planned, stayed for a day and a night, then returned to Lhasa.

11th December 1891
Lhasa, Tibet
Kintup was in the market last week, purchasing fresh vegetables for the evening's stew. Turning around, he came face to face with the Chinese commander from Gyantse. He returned to our lodgings in quite a state, certain that we should soon all be arrested again. We convinced him that nobody had followed him, or else we would all be in the garrison buildings right now, under heavy guard. After that he arranged for one of the other servants to shop for us, and would not venture out into the streets of Lhasa in daylight hours, until he found out that the Chinese had returned to the Chumbi valley. Heavy snow fell every day, and built to thick ledges on the flat roofs of all the buildings. Only the gold spires on the roofs of the Grand Cathedral and the *Dalai Lama*'s palace stood out against the ocean of white, dazzling when the snow stopped falling and the winter sun shone through.

24th December 1891
Lhasa, Tibet
Christmas Eve! Holmes surprised us by producing a very passable plum pudding, filled with the dried fruits and nuts so plentiful in the market, and sprinkled with shredded dried orange rinds. He sent Kintup out - he had recovered his nerve when he saw that Holmes and I were moving freely around the town in our disguise - to fetch a small pine tree, complete with tiny perfect pinecones. He had purchased gifts of sweetmeats and nuts, and some small examples of the silver and turquoise jewellery of the Lhasa hill-

men; these he had taken to the Chinese stores, to have them gift-wrapped in their extravagant fashion.

There were gifts enough for all. These we soon attached to the tree, which we decorated with coloured threads and ribbons from the bazaar and topped with a tiny star cut from a thin sheet of hammered gold. Surrounded by a host of small butter-lamps flickering in our dark room, the tree was a nostalgic reminder of childhood Christmas. Our room had a stone hearth for the fire, with a hole piercing the roof as the only chimney. Smoke trapped in the room over many long winters had japanned the whitewashed ceilings a rich hue of brown, against which the bright fire blazed away, adding to the festive appearance.

After our evening stew, we opened a bottle of the fiery local brandy, and toasted each other quite merrily, until suddenly the bottle was empty.

25th December 1891
Lhasa, Tibet
Christmas Day! As we had little else to do, we enjoyed unwrapping our small gifts to each other, then played at cards until lunchtime. Tashi received a leather collar inset with a small turquoise, carved with his name in Tibetan script.

Kintup had arranged for a fowl to be roasted, and had prepared vegetables to go with it. With it, we drank several bottles of Bulldog Stout, purchased for five shillings the bottle at the stall which sold European stores, and finished with the plum pudding, doused liberally with brandy and set ablaze.

"As long as I can remember, le Villard, I have not celebrated Christmas. It seems there was never the time in London, as I was always involved in this case or that. Somehow it seems right that here, miles from the nearest Christian, we should celebrate in good cheer."

With that, he proposed a toast to the Queen Empress Victoria. We lounged around the hearth after our heavy meal, grateful for the change in our daily routine, and I confess we all dozed off, waking to the warmth from the glowing embers. The butter-lamps still flickered, and it seemed no one was in a hurry to go anywhere or do anything.

Later in the afternoon we took Tashi to a secluded bend of the frozen river, where I tried to teach him to skate around on his paws, without notable success, but with a great deal of loud encouragement from Holmes and Kintup on the shore. We returned fresh-faced from the brisk weather to enjoy cold cuts from the fowl, washed down with more of the brandy.

In this fashion Holmes and I – the first Europeans to visit Lhasa in almost a century – passed the Christmas of 1891, with Kintup and Tashi as our companions.

7th January 1892
Lhasa, Tibet
We decided that now, when all the rivers and streams were frozen solid, and the snow lay thick on the countryside, was the ideal time to return to have a closer look at the arsenal. The Nepalese Consul had told us that the factory closed for the winter months, and the workers returned to their homes until work started again in the spring.

Retracing our path through the snowy countryside, Holmes, Kintup and I came to the same vantage point as before, overlooking the snow-clad buildings. The arsenal looked to be completely deserted, and the huts were unoccupied, judging by the absence of chimney smoke. A token watch was maintained at the main guardhouse, but the other two were empty. The water wheel was still, its sluice drained of water to prevent damage to the blades from expanding ice.

Keeping the main building between the guardhouse and ourselves, we crept up to the rear wall of the arsenal. The few windows were shuttered against the weather. Set in the wall halfway down the side of the building was a low wooden door, with a massive iron lock of ancient design. Holmes soon had that open, and we slipped inside. We waited a moment, but it seemed there was no one in the entire building.

Looking around, we saw, ranged down one side of the building, a row of lathes of English manufacture, and a collection of other machine tools for cutting, boring, shaping and finishing steel. Each of these machines was linked by pulleys, gears and belts to a steel shaft which ran the entire length of the building, and was in turn driven by a set of enormous brass-bound wooden gears. The propulsion gear was driven directly by the extended axle of the water wheel, projecting through the stone wall.

Wooden crates were stacked in tall rows against the opposite walls, with some still not sealed. Using our dark lantern, Holmes inspected the finished rifles packed inside one of them.

"Copies of the old Martini. Not badly made, either, given the primitive conditions."

He inspected the cartridges, which were also made here.

"Spirally-twisted brass plate! Should give quite a range!"

We also found several crates stacked to one side, with Cyrillic lettering stencilled on the sides. We carefully prised open one of these, and found that they contained Russian-made rifles stamped with the Imperial Arms. A row of small rooms lined the narrow end of the building, empty now, but obviously the crude offices of the managers. Not wanting to visibly disturb anything, Holmes merely looked at the order books, which we could not read, and picked through some of the loose papers.

"Ah ha!" he cried, holding up a sheaf of receipts made out in English. "They've smuggled much of this up from Calcutta. Faunce will be pleased at that, I'm sure."

He jotted down a few names and addresses from the heads of these documents.

"Now, le Villard, what are we to do with this factory? If we do any obvious damage, we will raise the alert while we are still at Lhasa. We don't want to risk returning later, but it would be a very good thing to put this place out of action. It would take a long time to replace all this," he said, sweeping his arm wide to indicate the banks of machines.

"Come with me!" I said. "I have an idea."

I was carrying in my pack several alpinists' pitons. We went to the main gears, and, with the aid of the dark lantern, soon found what I was looking for.

"If we drive one of these pitons through that shaft just here, where no one can see, it won't be able to turn. When the sluice is filled and the current allowed to flow, the gears will tear this whole assembly apart, and with luck, the water-wheel will destroy itself."

Holmes agreed, and soon we had found a heavy mallet and driven the piton into the wooden shaft until the head was level with the wood. We worried at first about the noise, and kept the Mauser rifles at the ready, but no one came.

"Now, these lathes. The heaviest part is the bed, but there is not much we can do there." Holmes pointed at the machined strips of oiled steel attached to the cast-iron bed. "These slides, however, are another matter. If we move the tool-chuck down a little, a few good blows with this cold chisel will soon disable the machine. With the tool-chuck back in place, the damage may not be discovered till they start the wheels. By then, we will be far from Lhasa."

This, too, was soon done. I was sorry we could not be there to see the results of our efforts, when the Russian monk returned with his Indian artisans, and released the rushing spring waters into the sluice. There would be no weapons made here for some time to come. We had made certain of that.

Replacing all the tools exactly as we had found them, we let ourselves out, and locked the door behind us. Before long, we were on our way back to Lhasa.

18th January 1892
Lhasa, Tibet
There was, of course, no way we could meet the *Dalai Lama*, and risk exposure as spies. However, as the snow fell lightly, we heard the clangour of bells announcing a royal progress. We watched as the grand procession slowly passed by, and managed to glimpse his palanquin as it was borne past on the shoulders of four sturdy Tibetans, with its curtains drawn back. The *Dalai Lama* was a fresh-faced youth of seventeen or eighteen, with the fair complexion and rosy cheeks typical of the Tibetans. He sat quite still, looking directly in front of him, appearing grave beyond his years.

It was common knowledge that few *Dalai Lama*s reached their majority at eighteen, most being poisoned by their regents before attaining that age. It was easy to see why this youth should lend a ready ear to the lama from Russia, who promised such a different future.

12th February 1892
Lhasa, Tibet
We had spent four months here at Lhasa, and in two days we would leave, to meet with Mohamed Abdul Beg on the road to Sera Monastery. Holmes was glad to be on the move, and even the dog sensed the excitement, as we carefully packed away our weapons, and prepared our stores for the long journey to Kashgar.

Soon the river would thaw, and the Tibetan arsenal would commence operations again. We wanted to be well on our way before then. Someone could remember the two journeys we took in that direction. Kintup was to travel some distance with us, then make his way separately back to India, using a different Pass from the Jelep. We thanked him warmly, for he had been a cheerful and willing member of our little band, and we would miss his ready smile. Tashi would miss his romping in the snow when we took walks around Lhasa. As a 'pilgrim', I could not join in.

13th February 1892
Lhasa, Tibet
All of the day was spent in preparing for our departure, ostensibly to make further pilgrimages before returning to our homelands. I packed food for the dog, and strapped it onto Tashi's harness. We had already done this many times, so that he would be ready for the journey. He made no fuss, and I removed it again. Everything else was prepared for loading on our few ponies. We had no farewells to make, although I noticed that Kintup slipped away in the early evening.

Holmes and I had completed a final review of our preparations when we heard the stamp and rattle of mounted soldiers in the courtyard below. Heavy footsteps thudded up the wooden stairs leading to our rooms, and a fist pounded at the door. Holmes and I looked at each other, then at the bedding rolls where our rifles were tucked away.

The loud banging at our door was followed by shouts and kicks, until Holmes opened it, to reveal the Chinese aide to the *Amban*; the same one we had met with at the Parade Ground – Mycroft's agent. He made a great show of aggressive shouting and abuse, for the benefit of his men, but a discreet look at Holmes showed that he was shamming. He made his men wait outside, and had a conversation in hushed tones with Holmes, making it appear that he was collecting a sum of money in return for leniency. Holmes understood, and slipped him some coins to distribute to his men. I overheard most of their conversation; enough to understand that we should depart Lhasa immediately, and in the direction of India at first.

Our friend's superior had, fortunately, called him in to inform the visitors that it was necessary that they come to visit the *Amban* personally before leaving Lhasa, as he had heard they were planning to do. Our Chinese friend would report that we had just left before his arrival, and as the *Ambans* at Lhasa had become corrupt and lazy, the deception was unlikely to be found out.

Holmes asked the reason for the summons, and was told it was the routine, whenever a party left Lhasa, for the *Amban* and some of his cronies amongst the Palace officials at the Potala to extricate one last sum of money from them. In this case, however, the Chinese was certain that on such close examination our disguises would certainly be inadequate, so we had to flee immediately.

CHAPTER XIX

AS THE FOLLOWING two pages had been roughly torn out – according to the next Journal heading – this tantalising passage was the last entry until 1st

May, 1892, when Holmes and le Villard were at Lake Manasarowar. There were a few entries on the reverse of the previous page, and then the narrative was broken in mid-sentence. I had not noticed the few missing pages when I flicked through the Journals before, so I inspected both volumes more closely. I found no further lacunae. Holmes had said nothing about this, nor had le Villard mentioned it in his cover note to me. I glanced at the clock, and saw that it was almost time for dinner. I decided to take up the tale again later, after my meal. In the meantime, perhaps Holmes could shed some light on this mystery of the missing pages. I put both Journals carefully aside, and went in search of Mrs. Hudson to see about some dinner.

From the landing outside our sitting-room door I could detect various tantalising aromas drifting up from the region of Mrs. Hudson's kitchen at the lower rear of the house. That worthy woman had not changed at all, in one respect at least, during Holmes's absence. She would still brook no intrusion into her kitchen, saying that she had cooked in her own way for far too long to change now. Protests, compliments; nothing could shake her resolve, and she would smile sweetly as she barred the way.

According to Holmes, the only exception she had ever made was when Mycroft had come to dine, one evening years before, when I had been settled happily with my beloved Mary. Holmes claimed to have been struck speechless when Mycroft - after first complimenting Mrs. Hudson on her veal pie - had made a suggestion to improve the pastry, and had been invited into the forbidden regions to demonstrate. Several hours later, covered in flour, a beaming Mycroft had been ushered to the front door with a freshly baked minced-fruit pie, and an invitation to return whenever he wished to trade recipes. Since then, Mycroft's pastry had become a standard casing for her most excellent pies, and Holmes had had to admit that his elder brother possessed a not-inconsiderable charm. Neither Holmes nor myself had been invited to take such liberties.

From the aroma, I divined that one of Mrs. Hudson's delicious roast chicken dinners was being prepared, and forgave her stubbornness entirely. I had barely finished my dinner when a messenger arrived with a telegraph message from Holmes, informing me that he would not be returning that night, and not to concern myself at his prolonged absence. This, I thought, was a change from the Holmes of old, who would have given little consideration to easing the concerns of others, concentrating solely on the hunt of the moment. I thought it a change for the better.

After a glass of port, I enjoyed a smoke in front of the fire, which I had coaxed back to crackling life while the maid set out my dinner things, and thought of the remarkable Journals I was reading. My chief regret was that I would not be able to share these adventures with that legion of avid readers of all my humble accounts of Holmes's private investigations. Nevertheless, I could hardly wait to resume reading le Villard's account of their escape from being unmasked as British spies in Lhasa. Afterwards I passed an half-hour musing on various matters, not the least of which was wondering just where Holmes's investigations could have taken him for the night. I knew he was still urgently attempting to find both Isobel Aster and Godfrey Norton, and to track the whereabouts of Parker and, thereby, Colonel Sebastian Moran.

I gave up speculating, realising that he could be anywhere in London, or even further afield. Picking up the now-familiar Journal, I went upstairs and washed up. I then retired to my bed with the leather-covered notebook, to rejoin Holmes and le Villard in their hurried flight from Lhasa. The first thing that I noticed was that the next entry in the Journal was dated some six weeks after the last, and a little reading ahead provided no ready explanation.

CHAPTER XX

1st April 1892
Lake Manasarowar, Tibet

MOST DAYS FOLLOWED each other without significant event, continuing along the well travelled road, which ran for the most part alongside the banks of the Tsangpo River, in the valley formed by the two main ranges of the Himalayas. The only halt was for a night and day at Tradom Monastery. The weather had steadily improved, with the snowline receding, but with the rivers not yet in full spate. Our *kafila* had travelled at a fast clip, as those not mounted on two-humped Bactrian camels rode swift and sturdy ponies from Turkistan. We routinely covered twenty and more miles each day, despite the two heavy loads so carefully lashed to each beast. Holmes and I usually rode alongside Mohamed Abdul Beg, who rarely spoke, to us or to others. Tashi padded along at a steady pace, keeping up with some difficulty. If he wasn't so big, perhaps he could ride, but he hated the camels anyway.

The most dangerous event of our journey thus far began seven days ago.

We had passed by the road leading across the Pass to Mustang, the centre for trade between Lhasa, Nepal and India, and famous for the superb ponies to be found at the horse market there. The scouts noticed that our caravan was being followed at a distance by a large band of nomads from the East, notorious for their raids on traders travelling from Ladakh to Lhasa and back. The nomads outnumbered us by three to one, and although our *kashgaris* were heavily armed, so were the nomads. What caused us particular alarm was the sight of laden camels remaining far in the distance, too far even for Holmes's telescope to penetrate the heat haze. We'd heard rumours of bands of raiders farther north riding camels carrying swivel-mounted machine-guns.

For two days and nights they trailed us, sometimes behind, sometimes from one flank or the other. For hours they would disappear from view, but always returned, waiting for a place where we should be most vulnerable.

"I think its high time we pulled out the Mausers, le Villard," said Holmes, when it became clear that they intended to attack.

Until now we had used only the Enfields, on the few occasions when we had hunted for the pot. The sight of the superb Mauser carbines caused exclamations of respect amongst the *kashgaris*, who were excellent marksmen with their primitive rifles. We kept them at the ready from then on. We marched on each night until we found a readily defensible position, and set up a system of watches around our camp. The *kashgaris* were used to this, having made the journey before, but I noticed that even they seemed concerned by the size of the horde following us.

On the third morning we awoke and found that the nomads had all departed in the night. Scouts sent to the surrounding ridges reported none in sight, and their tracks headed away across the plains. Hopes were voiced that we had been spared as too difficult a prey, being armed and mobile. We continued, still wary but a little relieved.

"Oh, dear!" sighed Holmes, as we rounded a bend in a narrow defile, a little later, to find a large force of mounted nomads blocking the way forward through the pass. As we turned to look to our rear, another phalanx of horsemen swept over the ridge and down the rocky slopes to block our escape back along the valley floor. The swift Tsangpo at one side of the road was too deep to ford, and the slopes of the defile too steep for our animals to climb. We seemed to be trapped, and I could see why the nomads had waited until here to attack us.

All the *kashgaris* had their rifles loaded and at the ready, but they would be no match for the superior numbers of the nomads.

"We have a great advantage in range and firepower, le Villard, and I hope that will turn the tide in our favour." Holmes spoke quietly, for my hearing only. "But we are not here as conquistadors, I think. Our task is simply to get through these rascals as quickly as possible. Nevertheless, I find it difficult to shoot at the horses, which are but innocent beasts. Aim for the men's shoulders. They need them to ride and to shoot."

Holmes then turned to Mohamed Abdul Beg.

"Our only chance is to break through their barricade. Carry on at the same speed, and do not break ranks. Le Villard and I will open fire at 1200 paces, and again at 900 paces. If that is ineffective, at 500 paces, we all charge straight at the centre, firing all weapons."

The *Atalik*'s son gave orders to his men, and the *kafila* bunched more tightly together, camels in front of the ponies. The nomads behind us began to close the distance from our rearguard, and to spread up the side of the valley to block a dash in that direction. We kept on at our steady pace, until we judged our range correct. Le Villard and I urged our camels out twenty paces in front of the others, then stopped, in order to have a steadier aim.

"Open fire!" commanded Holmes. We aimed carefully, not wasting our shots. At first, the nomads seemed surprised that their fellows were dropping from the saddles alongside them. Carrying steadily on, we approached closer to the line of robbers, now in some disarray. We held our fire until we were at 900 paces, and opened fire again, this time with more deadly accuracy. Almost all of those few brave horsemen who broke into a headlong charge at us were stopped even before their weapons were in range. Two or three managed to penetrate the deadly hail of cartridges, and loosed off shots before being blasted by our *kashgaris*' rifles firing in concert. One of our camel-riders toppled to the ground, dead instantly from a bullet through the brain, another was wounded in the arm, and two ponies were hit, tumbling their riders under the hoofs of the racing horses behind.

I wheeled to the rear, and began to fire at the column of riders surging up from behind. By this time, our *kashgaris* had opened fire with their ancient weapons, which at these ranges were loud rather than deadly. Holmes carried on firing at the barricade of horsemen, which finally, under the hail of fire from his Mauser carbine, broke and fled to save their lives. No other of their cavalry had even come within useful range for their rifles, yet thirty or more riders were on the ground already, and more falling every minute.

In utter panic, the remaining robbers in front of us broke and fled out of the defile where they had hoped to trap us. Our caravan increased speed, and Holmes joined me in picking off the more adventurous of the robbers to our rear, as always, shooting to wound. With two of our high-velocity carbines firing at them, these brigands soon realised that, as we were no longer trapped to the front, they risked dying for a lost cause, and broke off their pursuit. The last we saw of them was their remaining armed riders rounding up loose horses, and with less diligence, attending to their wounded.

We kept a fast pace for some time after that, to make pursuit more difficult, but we had no more incidents until before reaching Lake Manasarowar, half-way between Lhasa and the *ladakhi* capital at Leh. Here, with the peak of the sacred Mt. Kailas reflected in the perfectly still waters of the lake, our caravan rested for a day and a night. Holmes and I, as had been our custom through-out, had kept to ourselves. Until now, none of the camel drivers or horsemen had spoken with us, and any necessary communication was with Mohamed Abdul Beg or his assistant.

Now, one of the men approached us directly. Another of the camel riders was in great pain; the one who had been wounded in the forearm during the battle with the nomad robbers. His own people had treated him since then, but it was clear he was suffering from serious blood infection, and that his wound would soon turn gangrenous. The infection had progressed to the point that the man was delirious.

Holmes and I spoke with Mohamed Abdul Beg, asking permission to look at the man's wound. This granted, we boiled some cotton cloths, and set them to dry in the blazing sun. More water was boiled, and the wound was washed, revealing a bone-deep gash where the rough bullet had torn away a mass of flesh. The entire wound was suppurating, and Holmes said, "I had no idea he was so badly hurt. The pain must have been unendurable, and yet we haven't heard a word from him since then. Quite remarkable."

We set to work, swabbing and cleaning, but Holmes soon said, "This wound must be cauterised, or he'll not survive. As it is, his arm will be use-less."

This was conveyed to Mohamed Abdul Beg, who simply said, "This is one of my younger brothers. If you say you must administer brandy, so be it. As good Mahommedans, we will look the other way. He has always been my bravest fighter, and for both reasons I should hate to lose him. But if that is God's will, so be it!"

That settled, Holmes took one of our two bottles of Lhasa brandy from his pack, and poured a liberal dose into a small tin cup. The wounded man dra-nk it in one gulp, collapsed in a fit of coughing as the fiery liquid burned his throat, and was soon in an alcoholic daze. Meanwhile, a short, broad sword had been heated to red heat in the flames, and a small iron pot of oil brought to the boil.

Holmes explained to Mohamed Abdul Beg that he must remove the man's lower forearm, or the infection would spread and kill him. After considerable discussion, it was agreed that, as it was his left hand, this would be permitted.

Holmes exclaimed to me, "Le Villard, I am not a surgeon! This may be a dangerous interference, as we may be blamed if he should die after we have treated him. What do you think?"

"He will surely die otherwise. I don't see that we have any choice but to try, and to trust in our antiseptics and sulphur drugs. Besides, I overheard them discussing this quietly amongst themselves, and my Persian is better than is yours. They expect him to die anyway. It is usual."

"Very well. Let's get on with it then!"

The keenest blade in the tribe belonged to Mohamed Abdul Beg's personal guard, and he was adjudged the finest swordsman as well. With four of his tribesmen holding him down, the wounded man's forearm was stretched on a block of wood and severed cleanly with one swift stroke of the blade. Holmes applied the heated short sword to the bleeding stump. The man screamed in pain, then fainted away, mercifully for us. We immersed the end of his severed arm in the boiling oil for several seconds.

When the unfortunate man recovered consciousness, Holmes dosed him with laudanum and sedatives, and he lapsed into unconsciousness again. The next morning we cleaned the blistered stump with antiseptics, applied sulphur powder, and wrapped the wound in clean bandages. Though suffering greatly, his feverishness had subsided, and he was lucid.

7th April 1892
Valley of the Tsangpo, Tibet
Here, in the absolute solitude of this Himalayan valley, we left the valley of the Tsangpo, and struck off across the barren plateau towards the headwaters of the Indus. Soon we would cross the border, leaving Tibet, and enter the ancient homeland of the *ladakhi*s. Our caravan maintained pace; we had crossed Tibet from East to West in a matter of 53 days. Had we been travelling alone, not only should we have faced a great deal more difficulty in dealing with the occasional Tibetan patrol which we encountered, but the journey would have required twice the time or more. Despite the wild beauty of the Central Asian vastness, by now both Holmes and I felt that a little civilisation would be a welcome thing.

On our long journey through Tibet we noted no Russian forces as such, and no evidence of preparations for wholesale invasion of India, either across the Baroghil Pass in the Pamirs, or elsewhere. However, we had verified the presence and influence of the Russian monk Dorjieff at Lhasa, and found concrete evidence of Russian arms, and of Russian involvement in arming the Tibetans. Besides putting the Lhasa arsenal out of commission, hopefully for a long time, I had little doubt that this eyewitness evidence, when presented by Mycroft to the War Office, would give much additional weight to the arguments of those who advocate a British advance on Lhasa to enforce a treaty. France always benefits when Russia is contained, therefore I had no reservations about the benefits obtained by our risk and effort.

Holmes also seemed pleased with the results. His 'brown studies', and the bitter cynicism with which he responded on the few occasions when I would attempt to draw him out of these depressions. had become less and less frequent, and of shorter duration when they did come over him. As usual, I simply let him alone until he emerged, usually at his most helpful and buoyant, from these strange periods of withdrawal from the world around him. Perhaps it was the sheer magnificence of the Himalayan world through which we travelled, the majesty of the loftiest peaks in the world. Whatever the reason, at last he seemed to have let go of his obsession with the Moriarty gang, about which Mycroft had said a private word or two to me, before he left Naples.

Holmes's few recent references to those events implied that it was simply another of his many criminal investigations, albeit of longer duration and of broader scope than any other in his vast experience. I had heard little mention of the gang or its leader since leaving Lhasa. I must say, though, that it is easy to put events into perspective when viewed from the remote distances of the Roof of the World. It remains to be seen whether Holmes can retain this objectivity upon his return to London.

The wounded camel rider – the younger brother of Mohamed Abdul Beg - recovered well. We treated his wound twice daily – a concept seemingly unknown to these stoic men of the Himalayas, who accept wounds and their consequences with Mahommedan fatalism – and ensured that he kept the limb strapped to his chest. As one who had fully expected to die, he seemed to regard Holmes as a magician, a healer of unknown powers. Before long it became evident that the rest of his tribesmen felt the same awe, and we were both treated with the utmost of respect from then on. Even Mohamed Abdul Beg, who always retained his slightly arrogant dignity, thanked Holmes profusely, and presented us both with small curved daggers – apparently a great honour for one not of their own kind.

20th April 1892
Leh, Ladakh
Leh was a substantial town, the capital of the *ladakhis*, so of course the city's markets corresponded in size. All the trade between Central Asia and Nepal

passes through here, and Leh seemed prosperous. Although prayer wheels were still much in evidence, Asiatic traders of many kinds bustled their way through the crowded streets, some leading heavily laden camels or asses. The markets smelled of spices and leather, horses and hay, and the usual Asiatic odours. The women and men both wore an abundance of beads and jewellery of ivory and gold.

Here the *kashgaris* sold their furs and much of their Tibetan trade-goods, and purchased *ladakhi* goods for sale at Kashgar. News awaited Mohamed Abdul Beg that his father was anxious to leave for his pilgrimage to Mecca, our caravan being somewhat overdue. An express courier was sent off to Kashgar, informing him of our imminent arrival. We departed immediately from Leh, taking the road leading over the Karakorum Pass to Yarkand and Kashgar.

27th May 1892
Yarkand, Chinese Turkistan
Thankful for the summer weather, our caravan crossed the forbidding Karakorum Passes, after first passing rapidly through Shahidula and Rudok. According to the men, this territory is notorious for bands of robbers. Holmes and I had approached the desert oasis city of Yarkand with some trepidation. Many years before, one of the Survey's *pundits* reported that every unknown traveller coming from Lhasa was stopped outside the town walls, and their likeness expertly sketched. This sketch was then sent off for verification by Chinese authorities. We feared that the sabotage of the arsenal at Lhasa might have been blamed on us, and the Chinese governor at Yangtse alerted by the *Ambans* at Lhasa. Tibetan couriers, we knew, thought nothing of riding five hundred miles with a message tucked inside their sewn-up vest, and could have moved much faster than we had done.

Our fears were unfounded. Things had clearly changed a little since then, and a few Europeans had penetrated to Yarkand recently. As part of Mohamed Abdul Beg's annual *kafila* to Lhasa, we were scarcely glanced at as we passed the guard post set in the thick walls of the city. By this time our patina of dust and dirt had made us virtually indistinguishable from the *kashgaris*, whose garb we had adopted since leaving Lhasa. Tashi was looking little the worse for his long journey. Lean and lithe, he could now lope along now for endless hours, keeping pace with the camels and ponies. I had cropped his winter coat to keep him cool, and my camel carried his food pack.

We passed through Yarkand without delaying, and, travelling along the fringe of the great Gobi Desert, made for Kashgar.

3rd June 1892
Kashgar, Chinese Turkistan
Our *kafila* arrived at Kashgar very late in the evening, passing by the silent walls of the ancient city several miles from the new town. The only sound breaking the stillness was the tinkling of the bells on our camels, and the occasional sneeze of one of the beasts. The advance scout had gone ahead to announce our approach, so the gate was still manned, and we passed through at dead of night.

After a fitful night spent in makeshift guest quarters inside the Yangi-shahr fort, Holmes and I were moved in the morning to more comfortable rooms in this, the former palace of the *Atalik*. This was not a terribly grand affair, as Kashgar is not an ancient capital. The *Atalik*, although retaining his titles and lands, had not been ruler here since the Emir Yakub Beg, his father, had been defeated by invading Chinese, some fifteen years earlier. He had been informed of our arrival, we were told, but an important matter had kept him occupied. I first went to see that Tashi was being well cared for, but I need not have worried. The camel riders had taken a liking to him, and he was being pampered in a corner of the courtyard.

I returned to find that Mohamed Abdul Beg was in our room with Holmes, discussing the *Atalik*'s difficulty. It seemed that a nobly born young lady of a neighbouring tribe had been promised to the *Atalik*'s eldest son in marriage, and her arrival had been planned to coincide with our return from Lhasa. Before she had reached the safety of Kashgar, however, her small party of *kashgari* guards was overwhelmed by a band of slavers, headed for the slave marts at Faizabad, and very happy to add the young lady and her maids-in-waiting to their string. The younger men were taken as well, and the older men murdered.

The *Atalik* was furious, apparently, because he had provided the escort. Therefore, her kidnapping was his responsibility, and would cost him a great deal of embarrassment, not to mention cash reparations. His pilgrimage to Mecca would have to be postponed while he waited for his men to report the whereabouts of the slavers.

However, we were given a sealed envelope that had arrived only two days before by courier from Leh, and also the trunk from Mycroft, which had been promised in Mycroft's last ciphered message.

Holmes spent a little time deciphering the message from Mycroft. It was soon done. Holmes handed his version to me. It was dated at London three weeks previously, and, according to the *Atalik*, had been sent by telegraph to Rawalpindi, then hand carried to Kashgar.

'Dear Sherlock,

Further to last message. Assassination attempt planned at Aden or Jiddah, to prevent arrival of Atalik at Mecca. According to our latest information Russia has hired assassin, now tentatively identified as a Colonel Moran. Subject seen in conference with Russian intelligence agent stationed at Istamboul. Has been sent to Persia, to link with Persian who knows Atalik well. Moran and Persian to travel to Mecca as pilgrims. Persian may approach Atalik initially. My man is houseboy to Russian agent at Istamboul. Information considered very reliable. No information on identity of Persian.

Possible contact Persia is Moran's father. Former Consul to Persia, retired and divorced English wife, returned to live at Isphahan. Lives small villa, large carob tree in courtyard, white wall, green wrought-iron gate, at end of lane leading from left side of market near central mosque. Lives alone, except two houseboys and maid. Be warned, he presents a deceptively mild-mannered appearance, but is ruthless and clever. I have dealt with him before.

Suggest you send Atalik and party by usual pilgrim route, and make all speed to Persia. Kashgar to Tashkent is nine days march, from there take Transcaspian Railway to Caspian Sea. At Tashkent, present yourself as Professor Sigerson to Russian authorities. Royal Geographical Society ready to vouch for your bona fide explorations from Tibet (not Lhasa) to Tashkent. Ditto Norwegian Royal Geographical Society. Cover letter from R.G.S. attached; present at Tashkent. Bank draft in Swiss francs at Tashkent branch, Bank Novozcdev, transferred from Imperial Bank of Persia and credited to Professor Sigerson. Present papers for payment.

Russians have spy in Atalik's household or court. Message will be sent to Istamboul to announce departure of Atalik for Mecca. Sender of message will be the spy.

Contact me by telegraph, using coded plain language, when you reach Tashkent.

Regards to you both,

Mycroft.'

In a separate envelope was the promised letter for the authorities at Tashkent, signed and sealed by dignitaries of the R.G.S.

We were finally taken to meet the *Atalik* in the afternoon, in his audience hall. Only three or four advisers, his son, and ourselves were present. The

Atalik was of medium stature, inclined to corpulence, but was clearly, like his son, a man of the high mountain country. He was dressed in simple robes, but they were of quality cloth. He sat on a bear's skin spread over a low divan, legs crossed. The *Atalik* seemed to register a slight shock of recognition when he saw Holmes walk into the room, and studied his features intently.

Once the lengthy polite greetings were over with, and tea had been offered and drunk, Holmes suggested that we discuss his journey to Mecca. The *Atalik* dismissed all of his advisers, including his son.

"Please bar that door, Mr. Holmes," said the *Atalik* in excellent Oxford English. "Yes, I speak English, although it's a trifle rusty, I fear. And, although I am to know you as Professor Sigerson, I know you must be the younger brother – the detective. Am I not correct, sir?"

Holmes turned to me.

"So much for the disguise, le Villard. We may as well wear toppers and spats, it seems." He turned back to the *Atalik*.

"Forgive my rudeness, sir. Clearly, it would be pointless to deny it, but pray tell, how do you come to know my identity when I have passed through half of British India without being caught out?"

The *Atalik* smiled broadly, showing teeth filled with gold.

"No great mystery, Mister Holmes. Your brother Mycroft, who has sent you here, was posted to the British Consulate at Teheran, in the time when my father was still the ruler here at Kashgar. Mycroft supported my father in a dispute at the court at Teheran when his caravan was passing through there, returning from a trading venture to Turkey. Your brother was a young man then, and was speaking out of turn, for the British embassy was only barely tolerated by the Persians. But the Shah had admired his spirit before, and listened to him."

The *Atalik* offered us more coffee, which he poured himself. We drank, and enjoyed the pistachio nut and honey pastries, before he continued his tale. It was clear that all this was news to Sherlock, and that he was fascinated by this account of Mycroft's younger years, spent overseas learning his way around the world of political rivalry.

"Please, carry on!" said Holmes.

"My father stood to lose his caravan, his wealth, and his hereditary position, if the charges were proved. He would also forfeit his wife, who was at the centre of the dispute. She happened to be my father's favourite wife, and is my mother. The problem was that there had been treachery in our own family, yet family honour demanded that nothing be said. In his desperation, he took a most unusual step. He consulted the young *feringhi* at the British

Consulate, who had a reputation at Teheran as a man of justice, and had somehow gained the respectful ear of the Shah. Your brother was not only clever enough to see the truth, but was also astute enough to find evidence proving it. All of this would have remained worthless, except that young Mycroft Holmes was also wise enough to present his findings to the Shah in such a way that justice prevailed.

"My father's opponent, who had amassed great power and riches at court, was sentenced by the Shah to what at first seemed a mild punishment. It was, however, cleverly designed to destroy the man more completely than sharpened steel or silken noose. Every day, one of his powers was removed, one of his entitlements, one of his privileges. Inexorably, little by little, his influence waned, and his debts rose, and he could do nothing to halt the slide. When he tried to run away one day, he was prevented by force, and installed back in his palatial quarters, now unlit and with no servants. By the time my father returned, two years later, his opponent had gone quite mad, and was roaming the streets of Teheran begging for scraps of food. My father found him, and saw that he was taken care of in the poorer quarter of town. He lives there still, an old and broken man now, destroyed by his own greed and dishonour, with no memory of his former life.

"My father, the Emir, wondered how it was that a man as young as your brother should possess such wisdom and judgement, and decided that it must be due to his schooling at Oxford. I was being schooled in Teheran at the time, but my father badgered the British until it was agreed that if I could pass two years of schooling at a decent public school with credit, then I should be admitted to Oxford. As the son of a potential ally, I expect they made allowances. Nevertheless, I was sent off, passed my two years with flying colours, to everyone's great surprise including my own, and went up to Oxford.

"It was while I was at Oxford that Mycroft was finally brought back to London permanently, and he became my mentor at college. You were two years behind my class, and at Cambridge, so we never met, but Mycroft talked about you constantly. After hearing his tales of your clever solutions to various mysteries, it was no surprise when your fame as a detective came to my notice, years later.

"As it was, all of my schooling came to nought. The Chinese attacked Kashgar again, and my father was defeated. He died shortly thereafter, and I am now the hereditary occupant of a powerless throne. My people are Mahommedans, and they chafe under the rule of these Chinese. I know, as my father found to his bitter disappointment, that few of the British are as honourable as is your brother, and that in a crisis, they will sit back and plead that diplomatic niceties prevent their interference. The Russians are no better, and we fear them more than the Chinese. It seems as though they are preparing, at some time or other, to overrun Kashgar, and Yarkand, and all of Turkistan. There has been substantial military activity at Tashkent and Samarkand, and the Chinese garrison here is undermanned. For this reason, I have decided to take Mycroft's advice, to ask at Mecca for the gold that I will need to mount a resistance with some chance of success. I shall also ask their blessing, which will comfort my warriors.

"You have been most patient. I hope you will understand now why I recognised you immediately, especially as you have been sent by Mycroft. You are thinner than he was, but not so much older than he was then. The family resemblance is quite unmistakable. No one else at Kashgar knows of your identity, or will do so."

The *Atalik* settled back after this lengthy account, and lit his water pipe, inhaling deeply and blowing out a thick plume of tobacco smoke. He offered the mouthpiece to Holmes, who took it and inhaled likewise. Holmes was an inveterate pipe-smoker at any time, and had used a variety of small pipes of local manufacture throughout our journey through Tibet, so the thick smoke of the hookah did not affect him. For myself, while I enjoy a fine cigar after a meal, I knew that the pungent smoke billowing from the pipe would likely knock me out, if I accepted. I declined, as politely as I could.

"Now, sir," said Holmes after a polite interval, "perhaps we can discuss your trip to Mecca, and your troubles here which prevent your leaving?"

"Certainly. My son Mohamed, who escorted you here from Lhasa, was to marry this girl, as his first wife. She comes from the tribe now known to the English as the White Huns, of Sogdiana, where the women have long been regarded, even by the Persians, as the most comely of women. They trace their descent back to Bokhara and Samarkand, to the *turkiman* soldiers left behind so long ago by Ginghiz Khan and his Golden Horde, who brought their women with them as they passed through. This whole region was once theirs, but the Uzbeks came, and drove their leader Baber to India. There, he founded the Moghul dynasty. Of those that remained, some submitted to the Uzbeks, and the rest fled into the wild, and became the White Huns. I have seen this maiden, and she is a beauty, even for them.

"My son is determined to marry her, and no other, and I wish it also, in light of the coming conflict. The marriage will also forge bonds of tradition between our peoples, and many neighbouring peoples also. Besides, I have our honour to consider. If I allow the kidnappers of my son's bride-to-be to escape with her, my authority over these regions will be finished, and all our chances of autonomy will be dashed forever."

"When did this occur?" I asked.

"The evening before last. Our guards were making their camp for the night when the slavers struck. Before they knew it, it was all over. One of the older guards was mortally wounded and left for dead, but survived until morning, when a patrol found the camp. He was able to tell them that the slavers were heading for Faizabad, where slaves have been traded for thousands of years. There were about a dozen fighters, mounted on horses, and they were driving about forty slaves on foot, before coming upon our party camped by the road."

"Was there any indication of the road they would take to Faizabad?" asked Holmes, as he cleared a space amongst the coffee cups and plates on the low table, took from inside his skin coat one of his thin vellum maps, and spread it before us all.

"Oh! Excellent!" cried the *Atalik*. It was difficult now to think of him as an Asiatic warlord, while we shared his coffee and delicacies as he talked in the gentlemanly English tones learnt at Oxford. "Oh! A decent map. Let me see, where are we?"

And he leant forward just like a curious schoolboy, while we discussed the possible routes that would be taken by the slavers. Finally, Holmes pointed at the map, saying, "It seems that, if they are in a hurry to sell their wares and return to their lands before winter, they will take one of these three ways. Now, whichever route they take, they must still cross the Pamirs by this pass, or else take a very long detour. With slaves walking determining their pace, it seems to me that if a fast-moving troop was to be sent to here, they could be intercepted."

"Agreed," replied the *Atalik*, "except that we must seek permission from the local rulers to send armed patrols there, or risk alarming the locals and causing panic and resistance. There is no time for that."

"Would your son, with some of his most trusted riders, be prepared to risk such a venture," asked Holmes.

"He too has seen his future bride. He says little, and has shown no interest in education. He loves his desert, and the life of the *kafila* is congenial to him. However, for this bride my son would ride his camel to Peking and fight the Emperor himself. His men will follow him, anywhere, at anytime, without question. You would need to take ponies, rather than camels, as the track is hazardous."

"Then I suggest that you have him prepare for departure before dawn with provisions for a week or more. Le Villard and I will go with them. With our superior firepower we will have the kidnappers at a disadvantage, if we can find them. We will try to get ahead of them, and surprise them without battle.

The sooner we get your daughter-in-law to Kashgar, the sooner le Villard and I can get on to Tashkent."

Holmes reached into his coat pocket again, and brought out his version of Mycroft's message.

"As your English is so good, it will save a deal of explanation if you read this for yourself, sir." He handed it to the *Atalik,* who read it through, then said, "Very well, sir! There is risk in every direction, it seems. Unfortunately, there is now just as much risk in inactivity, which has been our refuge of late. When you return with my daughter-in-law, I will be ready to leave. We will go by the usual roads across to Ladakh, then head east to Rawalpindi." He pointed at Holmes's map. "From there it is a short journey to the Indus River, which will take us to the sea at Haiderabad. I have taken the journey before, and it can be pleasant. Knowing that I shall be safe until Arabia, I shall enjoy the journey. Steamers leave regularly from there for Aden and Jiddah, specially for the pilgrimage."

"I suggest that you remain at Haiderabad, then, until le Villard and I have been to Persia," said Holmes, "We can telegraph to you, at the Indus River Steamer Company offices there, and we will arrive at Aden before you do." Holmes folded his map and put it away. "Is that all agreed?" asked Holmes.

"Certainly!" replied the *Atalik.*

"Then we should sleep early, and leave betimes, le Villard."

We politely took our leave and returned to our rooms, after checking that Tashi was settled. He would come on with us. By now, Tashi was a veteran campaigner, having crossed Tibet with us, hunting game and wild birds as we went; he had even acquitted himself well in our battle with the robbers at the Tsangpo River, harrying fallen nomads like wild game for the pot. Few of them had argued with this enormous beast, carrying a leather pack, which seemed only to want them to stay still until collected by his masters. The one or two men who had tried to run were suddenly confronted with the most terrifyingly savage animal from their nightmares, all sinew, muscle, fangs, and slathering jowls. I was glad he was coming with us in our pursuit of the stolen princess and her kidnappers. The kidnappers may not be so pleased, I thought to myself.

DAY FOUR

APRIL 9TH 1894

CHAPTER XXI

ONCE AGAIN, the thread of the tale had been interrupted, this time by my own weariness. The pages I had last read had described the small party's departure from Kashgar the next morning, leaving towards Yarkand, then heading east at Yangi Hissar. Le Villard had briefly noted their decision to use the pass across the Pamirs, which was the more difficult route, but faster. Here, I had put down the Journal, turned out the lamp, and slept.

When I came down to the sitting room, it was to find Holmes seated in front of the remains of his breakfast, with his newspaper spread in front of him. He greeted me cheerfully enough, but offered no explanation as to his activities the previous night. The years had taught me that if there were no significant results from a particular course of enquiry as yet, Holmes was unlikely to discuss the topic at all. I rather thought, then, that his efforts had so far produced no results. But I had also learnt that, even when he had achieved something, he would at times make no mention of it. This was, generally, either because he was uncertain as to its value, or because he somehow felt that discussing a current line of enquiry would rob it of energy and thus jeopardise his chances of success.

I poured myself a cup of tea and glanced at the headlines. No mention of any of Holmes's cases, other than a piece low on the front page about a Royal Commission being formed to examine the procedures for release of prisoners from Her Majesty's gaols. As I ate a light breakfast. I remarked to Holmes that there seemed little progress in these various matters. I hoped that perhaps he would enlighten me as to his activities and results, but he calmly sipped at his third cup of tea, and went through the obituaries and the agony columns with meticulous care, having barely glanced at the news and other features contained within his Daily Gazette.

When Holmes had finished with his newspaper, I ventured to ask him about the six-week gap in le Villard's account following their departure from Lhasa, and about the two missing pages.

"Ah! I see that the small mysteries as well as the larger interest you still, Doctor. In this case, there is a ready explanation for both. Firstly, the matter of the six-week gap, as you term it. Quite simply, le Villard was taken ill, and was frequently barely able to remain astride his camel. We lashed him on, in the end. After a week or so he recovered, but felt too weakened to risk writing his Journals until his health was restored. I concurred, as there was little to report anyway.

"As to the missing pages – following the visit from our Chinese friend, le Villard and I were anxious to leave as soon as we could, and hide out in the countryside until our appointment the next night with Mohamed Abdul Beg and his *kafila.* The only problem was that Kintup had slipped out earlier, and had not yet returned. I was becoming rather concerned, as I suspected he had gone to the compound of the Nepalese Consul, where he had become most friendly with the not-unattractive daughter of the cook. I feared that he would stay out a long while yet, it being his last night in Lhasa as well, as tomorrow he would return to Darjeeling – by a different pass – and carry our report back for Mycroft.

"Just as I was becoming truly concerned, and making plans in case he failed to return soon, Tashi growled softly, and then we heard the familiar sound of Kintup's felt-soled boots mounting the stairs. He was flushed from running, and his ruddy cheeks glowed pink in the lamplight. Reaching inside his tunic, he handed me a sealed envelope, saying that it had just arrived from Khatmandu, and he was urgently instructed by the consul to hand-deliver it to the travellers he had so recently met. Knowing of Kintup's nightly visits to his household, he had had him brought to his office. At first Kintup thought he was to be punished for romancing the cook's daughter, but soon realised the truth, and put off his last dalliance to rush back to us.

"While le Villard and Kintup finalised all our preparations for departure, I quickly decoded the message. Within twenty minutes I was done, as it was a brief message. If you look in the back end papers of the Journal you will find a paper pocket, and inserted therein, you will find the plain text of that message. It is a record of the sorts of courtesies extended to their opponents by the real players on both sides of the Great Game!

"As all my own stock of paper had been packed away already, the first deciphered plain-text was written by me on one of those two missing sheets of paper. I then destroyed it immediately so that it would not be kept with the original, which I adjudged the safer version for le Villard to retain. I deciphered it again for you while I was at Montpellier, from the ciphered original, which I left with le Villard at the time.

"On the second of the missing sheets I wrote out a brief ciphered report for Mycroft, covering our exploits at the armoury, and the situation regarding the Russians at Lhasa. This I gave to Kintup, with instructions to give it immediately to Captain Faunce when he returned to Darjeeling.

"Then, while the Chinese and his men watched slyly from around their corner, we made our quiet departure from the caravansery belonging to the Tashilhunpo Monastery, where we had passed our long winter in Lhasa, and slipped out of the town into the frozen white landscape. We were on the road once again.

"The next night we circled around and met up with the *kafila,* said a sad goodbye to our ever-faithful and friendly Kintup, and bade him farewell as he trudged away, a lonely figure, into that vast whiteness. Le Villard and I, who knew of the strengths of Kintup and his race, could not help wondering if he would be able, alone and unaided, to make his way back to India when the winter snows had yet to thaw on the high passes. As you know, Watson, he did indeed make it, and it was with some pride that I received a telegraph message from him when we arrived at Persia, saying that our trip together to Lhasa had been the most enjoyable of all his forays into forbidden Tibet.

"I should also mention the message from Sarat Chandra Das, as le Villard and I both had had occasion to remember him with gratitude. In those frozen Himalayas there is little room for error, and mistakes can easily prove fatal. Again and again, the gentle advice of Das had been our best guide in times of trouble, and rarely was it found wanting. Even on subjects of which he had not spoken, at times when le Villard, Kintup and I were debating a course of action, one or other of us was likely to say what he thought Das would do in that situation."

When Holmes had left I turned to the back of the Journal, and found the page slipped into a pocket folded and glued onto the end paper. I removed it and read, in Holmes's spidery handwriting, Mycroft's message sent via Nepal to Holmes in Lhasa.

'My dearest Sherlock,

There is one other matter to bear in mind as you traverse Central Asia. As you know, I try to maintain my personal contacts with my counterparts in the various countries, large and small, with which Britain has dealings of any kind. These contacts are maintained regardless of prevailing political alignments and animosities, and, where possible, we try to assist each other in the difficult balancing act required of us.

I have been asked by my counterpart at St. Petersburg to alert any agents I may have deployed in the field in Central Asia to the presence of one of his trusted lieutenants, a certain Captain Alexei Dolghurokov. He had been sent to clandestinely explore the border areas between Russia and the Chinese Empire, travelling in disguise, on camelback. Captain Dolghurokov has the reputation of being a superb linguist, well versed in the ways of the region, and a most resourceful officer in a difficult situation. We've dealt with him before. His father is well-connected at St. Petersburg, but this time, it seems as though he may be in more trouble than even he can handle.

Part of his mission was to contact a certain local chieftain thought to be sympathetic to the Russians rather than the Chinese, if they had to have an overlord. Apparently he was on his way when he and his party disappeared, and no trace of his movements seemed possible. Then, two things happened to alter matters.

Firstly, news reached Russian agents at Tashkent that Captain Dolghurokov had probably been abducted. Certain of his possessions had turned up in the market at a small village near where he disappeared, and rewards had produced the man who'd brought them to market. He in turn told that he'd traded the goods for two sheep, a block of dates and some bags of grain, with two nomads. He'd never seen the men before.

Secondly, for various political reasons, it is now imperative that Captain Dolghurokov not contact the tribe he set out to visit. Captain Dolghurokov has escaped from similar situations before, so it is a possibility that must be considered. Should he succeed, a series of events could follow which could bring Persia, the Ottoman Empire and even China into the conflict, and would make it difficult to prevent Russia and Britain from declaring hostilities. At this time, neither side wishes to do so, and for excellent reasons. Both our Empires are stretched far beyond our real ability to control the territories encompassed, and the last thing we need is another Crimean fiasco. So it is in our interests as much as it is the Russians' to divert the Captain from reaching his goal in the Pamirs. Should you have the good fortune to be able to communicate with him, your message will be authenticated as coming from St. Petersburg if you use the words 'Winter Palace' in Russian or English, as the Captain's English is excellent. You should do anything you can to assist him in his predicament, as he is both a gentleman and a brave officer.

I realise that this is sketchy information at best, and that Asia is no small place, but you may hear something of interest in connection with this matter.

Having read this, I pondered a moment on the strange and contradictory nature of Mycroft's world, forever changing as he strove to keep abreast of it all. His was a world where enormous effort and expense was laid out to secure the allegiance of tiny principalities and remote tribes, only to abandon them in favour of their erstwhile opponents. It was a world of ever-shifting loyalties and fragile alliances, where at times appearances mattered as much as reality. It seemed rather akin to an enormously complex board game, but one where the rules were not in the least immutable, and the principal players, by and large, were either open to manipulation, or expendable.

But, by now I recognised another world, underlying the shifting political surface of his milieu. This was the world of his colleagues, and his counterparts within other governments; of his informants and agents scattered in even the most unlikely corners of the world; of his discreet access to the shadowy reality behind world events. A remarkable man, I decided.

Holmes had not mentioned his plans when he left - other than to remark that if he couldn't get a cab immediately he would miss his train. I reached again for le Villard's Journal, determined to finish the first volume at this sitting.

Chapter XXII

11th June 1892
The Pamirs, Chinese Turkistan

FOR THE PREVIOUS three days, our party had climbed and descended several mountain ranges in succession in our approach to the Pamirs proper. Nevertheless, these were high ridges indeed, with freezing winds that stuck flesh to metal instantly. The ground was blinding white at times, sometimes from snow, usually from the alkali soil in the valleys, and we were forced to wear snow-goggles. The *kashgaris* fashioned their own from woven horsehair, so I made a pair for Tashi. He soon got used to them, and was clearly more comfortable.

We had travelled by a different, more direct route than our quarry, and so had no idea where we were, relative to the slavers. Perhaps they were moving slowly, but by now, reasoned Holmes, the slavers would have been told whom they had kidnapped, and would try to put as many miles between themselves and Kashgaria as possible. He consulted his maps yet again, and called to Mohamed Abdul Beg.

"Tashkurgan, where they are almost certainly headed, is almost directly across from where we are now, but the road winds around the range up to the easy pass. Is there a way across those peaks there, and down the other side to Tashkurgan? We could save two days. They will have crossed much further north, here, and couldn't be closer than here," and he pointed at a spot some distance from the marked position of Tashkurgan. "We would have them for sure, then. With the element of surprise, possibly the hostages can be rescued without losing any of our people."

Mohamed Abdul Beg left us, and consulted with his men. A few minutes later, after much discussion and gesticulation towards the range, he returned. As always, we spoke in Persian.

"Two of them have travelled this way before, and they know there is a pathway used by the sheepherders to reach their flocks from Tashkurgan. These are their summer grazing grounds. This path is not for horses, so we must carry our packs. The horses can be hobbled, and most of the supplies can be left here, and collected on our return. We'll leave two men to guard them, and the other two of my men can come with us. We'll leave at first light, and try to cross in one day. The dog can stay with my men."

"Tashi comes with me," I said. "He climbs like a goat, and with his harness and yak-hair ropes, I can portage him anywhere we can climb, so long as the pitons hold out. He's big, but still weighs less than a burly mountaineer."

No one argued, so that was settled, and next morning we set out. The climb became steep almost immediately, and soon we were breathlessly clawing our way up a narrow track cut into the sheer granite walls. It was, in fact, a pathway, but at places the only progress was by stepping from one iron spike driven into the granite to the next, with a sheer drop below our feet. At these places, and there were several, we divided into two groups, to portage Tashi across in his special harness. The *kashgaris* clearly thought we were insane to do so, but helped without complaint. Tashi was the best of dogs, staying still while in the air, then clambering onto solid ground at the other side. After the first time, I think he enjoyed the experience.

The rock path was icy, and at places melted ice formed slides across the path, which we had to chip away with our picks. Progress was slower than we had hoped, and by late afternoon it became clear that we should have to spend the night on the mountain. Finding a sheltered place behind some huge fallen boulders, we lit a fire of yak-dung and made tea and a stew of *tsampa* with mutton and vegetable, the snow falling lightly around us. The night was extremely cold, but with Tashi between Holmes and myself, throwing off heat like a furnace, we suffered through until dawn. The *kashgaris* were more used to the extreme cold, but even they sheltered behind rocks when we crossed the ridge early the next morning. Holmes used his telescope to survey Tashkurgan, which was visible a half-day's march away once we were out of the mountains.

"They'll come down that road, and just beyond the bend there I see an ideal place for an ambush. The problem is, we are too few. I think a stratagem is required here. They won't think their pursuers are ahead of them. How can we use that to our advantage?" Holmes continued muttering to himself. "I think we must set up an innocent-looking camp which will entice them to investigate us. With our weapons concealed, and their strength in numbers, there should come a moment when they drop their guard. At a signal, we get the advantage of them. I have the derringer, and le Villard has a Webley; these we can secrete in our cloaks. Mohamed Abdul Beg and his men can carry their rifles openly, but not in a threatening manner. We must appear as though we have just completed a good bit of business in Faizabad, and are returning to Ladakh via Yarkand."

We agreed to this, and made our way, as quickly as we could, down from the ridge to the place Holmes had selected, and here we set up our small camp. By nightfall there was still no sign of the slavers, and we wondered if they had passed already, or even taken another route altogether. We thought both unlikely, but decided to investigate at Tashkurgan before wasting any more time. We did not enter the town, except for Mohamed Abdul Beg. He slipped in through the gates just as dusk fell, and spent the night at a caravansery for pilgrims. Here, and at the markets, posing as a potential buyer, he asked for news of the slavers. They were obviously known, and their arrival expected, as they apparently passed this way each year with slaves from the Chinese regions far to the east, always headed for Faizabad. In the morning, Mohamed Abdul Beg made some small purchases at the market, then as soon as the city gates opened, he hurried back with his news, and we settled down to wait.

At mid-morning Holmes, perched on a rocky outcrop above our rude camp with his spyglass, shouted down to us to prepare ourselves, as the slavers would pass by within thirty minutes. We boiled water and made tea, and set out food for our morning meal. Tashi was tied to the trunk of a stunted tree, using the yak-hair rope. I used an old sailor's knot that released with a single tug on the free tail of the rope - perhaps we would need his strength and ferocity.

The sounds of the approaching slavers and their captives reached us well before the lead guards came into view.

"The leader is in the middle of the front rank, on the black. Keep your eyes on him, and look for small signals."

But that was unnecessary. As soon as he saw us, he wheeled his mount in our direction. The two horsemen flanking him came with him. We saw that there were eight or so other mounted slavers, driving around forty slaves on foot as though they were animals. The slavers appeared rough and violent, and their captives were almost all in poor shape, having marched hundreds of miles already to reach here. In the normal course of events, they would march hundreds more, only to be sold into lifelong captivity. The entire column had halted now, and some of the slaves cast envious glances our way.

The slaver's leader looked first at our rifles, and decided they posed no threat. He looked at Tashi, and it was clear that he saw a valuable dog, worth a good sum at Faizabad. Men who had such a fine animal must have other wealth, and to sit unprotected like this, well, they must be fools as well. We could see his cunning greed as he took in the details of our few packs and small canvas shelter.

Mohamed Abdul Beg spoke first.

"May we have the honour of offering tea and our poor hospitality to you and your lieutenants?" he asked humbly. "I see that you have much responsibility, and must have travelled far. Perhaps a little refreshment before you pass on?"

"That would be most welcome," replied the leader, who looked even rougher and more violent than did his men. "To start with," he added, ominously. He and his lieutenants dismounted, and approached our small fire. Our carbines were hidden under the mats we sat upon, but we had agreed that we should have all the slavers together, if possible, before showing our hand.

"Perhaps your men would care for some tea also?" said Mohamed Abdul Beg, speaking in Persian. "Your slaves will not run far, hobbled and tied as they are. And we have some small treats that we bought just yesterday at Tashkurgan. We would be most honoured to share these with our fellow travellers." He struck just the right fearful note, of outnumbered men hoping to avert trouble with a little generosity. His voice quavered a little, and his hand trembled as he indicated our meal and delicacies.

"Why not! I see you have enough for us, though there may be little left for you," replied the leader, also in Persian, and he laughed loudly as he ordered his men to dismount. Soon all the men were seated in a loose circle around the fire, and weapons were laid carelessly to one side as they drank and ate. Mohamed Abdul Beg could not restrain his curiosity; his eyes kept straying to the hobbled slaves, searching no doubt for his betrothed. We had not seen her in the string, but perhaps she was on the far side.

I said quietly to Holmes, "If we are to do anything, it had better be soon." Unfortunately, just then, one of the maids-in-waiting remembered her mistress's suitor from his visit the previous year. She began screaming hysterically and pointing in his direction. The slaver's leader, seeing this, became instantly alert, and gave a curt command. Every weapon was suddenly pointed at us, tea and pastries forgotten for now. We were made to stand, hands raised, and our camp was searched, which took but a few moments.

We had lost our element of surprise, I thought, thanks to that desperate cry for help. Our *kashgaris'* rifles were taken from them. The mats were lifted, and the carbines discovered. A search of our persons discovered the revolvers, and our cache of instruments. My Journals were inspected and tossed aside. Our two packs containing food supplies were opened, but otherwise left untouched.

This added a new element to the situation; the leader now looked at us more closely, and realised that Mohamed Abdul Beg was a *kashgari.* He shouted orders, and two of his men went across to the string of slaves, and unlocked the princess from Sogdiana. She was roughly pushed across the rocky earth, stumbling several times because of the hobbles on her ankles. When she stood before us, though her hands and knees were bleeding, and her clothes in tatters and shreds, I realised why Mohamed Abdul Beg was so ready to brave anything for her.

Her skin was still pale, though burned by the sun. With her long, oval face, slightly almond-shaped eyes, and straight, fine nose, she seemed to have stepped from an ancient frieze. She was not tall, but her figure had the flawless proportions a classical sculptor would have matched to such a face. Her hair was of a deep shade of red, and her eyes of clear blue. I had no idea that such creatures existed in these inhospitable mountains. Then I remembered that the *Atalik* had said the White Huns were descendants of Ginghiz Khan's warriors and their women, left here after his death like driftwood marking the previous high tide. Except Ginghiz Khan never returned, and his people were abandoned all across Central Asia, scattered remnants of that heroic conqueror's dream of world domination.

We had heard of these peoples during our travels, and, in various places, had come across nobles who claimed direct descent from Ginghiz Khan, and even from Alexander himself. In all cases, these claimants had appeared no different from the indigenous peoples of the region, and their tales we regarded as self-serving fantasies. They were frequently honoured for their heritage, and had passed on the tale to generations of their descendants, until it came to be believed as fact. This was different.

I looked across at her maids-in-waiting, still in the string of slaves, but looking our way. Though not so striking as the princess, it was clear that her beauty was no exception amongst her people. To a lesser degree, they had the features that so distinguished their mistress. Pale skin, aquiline features, blue or green eyes. The slavers must have counted their blessings when they came upon the bridal party, for these women would fetch excellent prices at Faizabad. Having never been married, their value would be far higher than usual. I looked for Mohamed Abdul Beg's men amongst the slaves, and noted four wearing the remains of their Kashgar guards' clothing. They were all mere youths, and wisely were not looking at their chief. I suppose our situation did not inspire confidence.

The princess was brought face to face with Mohamed Abdul Beg. Neither said a word, but it was clear that she was proud that he had come to rescue her. She held her head high, and looked at the horizon. She did not reply to the leader's questions, even when struck with the back of his hand. Blood trickled from her cut lips, but still she would acknowledge nothing. After ten minutes of this, the leader tired of her obstinacy, and struck her such a fearful blow that she collapsed, unconscious, at his feet. Her maids screamed out, and slavers ran across and beat them as well until they were silent. Mohamed Abdul Beg stood, motionless. Holmes said, quietly, when he had a chance, "Be patient! In their arrogance, they will do something foolish. Until then, bide your time."

The day dragged on, and the slavers showed no signs of moving on. Their leader appeared to have a streak of malicious villainy, and seemed to be plotting something. From our weapons and instruments, it was clear that we were no itinerant wayfarers. Perhaps he thought he could trade us back to our people, whoever they were. That, after all, was his business.

The afternoon shadows lengthened to evening, and the slavers decided to make camp there for the night. The fire was built up, and the slavers made several of the women prepare a meal of *tsampa* and unleavened scones for the slaves. We were still herded together in our shelter, with the slavers in a half-circle on the other side of the fire. The leader went for a walk into the desert as the sun set, to prostrate himself towards Mecca. All his men did the same where they sat, but two kept their guns trained on us throughout. We made a little conversation amongst ourselves, until the guards were accustomed to the murmur.

"Their own language is difficult for me to understand fully," said Mohamed Abdul Beg, "but they have decided to steal all your goods, and the dog. Their leader is not sure about us. He will leave us here under guard, while they go on to Tashkurgan. There, he will make enquiries, and if he can sell you two, he will send men back here for you, and will do so. If no one returns by tomorrow evening his men will kill us here, and catch up with the band on the road to Faizabad. I and my two men will be killed anyway, as they suspect who I am, and dare not leave me alive."

The leader had returned from his prayers, and saw us talking. Speaking in Persian, he ordered us separated, and clubbed us with his rifle butt for good measure, or just for pleasure. Mohamed Abdul Beg was tied to the same tree stump as Tashi, and the leader said, "First, we eat. Then, for entertainment, we shall see how long it takes for the Kashgar hero to roast at the fire. Perhaps that will loosen the tongue of the girl. I want to know how we can return to her valley. These are not true Mahommedans; look at their hair and eyes. They are infidels, and the Koran allows us to enslave them for the benefit of their souls. It is better to be a Mahommedan proselyte than to be an infidel king. And think of the riches to be had if we brought a whole string of these beauties to Faizabad."

The slavers prepared to eat their meal, but then decided to use our supplies rather than theirs. Our food supplies were spilled from the sacks onto the ground in front of the fire. Amongst the small sacks of *tsampa* and *jimpa* we had brought with us from Tibet, which we hoarded for our journeys, and never used if we could eat from the local produce, there were the two bottles of Tibetan brandy. One was still full, the other half emptied, following the operation on the arm of the *Atalik*'s younger son.

One of the slavers picked up the opened bottle, uncorked it, and sniffed at the open neck of the bottle. He wrinkled his nose at the alcoholic fumes. The leader snatched the bottle from his hands, and sniffed in his turn.

'Ah! Whisky!," he cried. "I suspected that you two were infidels, and now it is proven. Good Mahommedans do not use alcoholic spirits," he declared, his voice louder now. He broke into a high, maniacal laugh, which echoed from the rocky walls of the defile, so that it seemed there were several of him. "But perhaps, we are not always good Mahommedans, not today. Tomorrow we will make penance. Tonight, we will enjoy your spirits, and the slow burning of this *kashgari* rubbish." He raised the bottle to his lips, and drank. The unopened bottle he tucked inside his cloak.

Tibetan brandy is distilled from their barley beer, and although there seemed but little drunkenness amongst the Tibetans, it is a highly potent spirit. The slaver was not used to it, and coughing and spluttering, turned crimson in the face for a few moments. He soon recovered, and took another drink, then handed the bottle to his lieutenant. The bottle was passed around all the men several times, each taking a small drink before passing the bottle on. It was clear that many had never drunk spirits before, and soon they were behaving just like foolish schoolboys on a day out, pushing and slapping at each other, and laughing at the smallest thing.

Their meal finished, the leader gave some instructions, and Mohamed Abdul Beg was dragged over to the fire, which had been built to a blazing pyre with dry wood gathered from around the camp. His shirt was stripped from his back, and he was tied by a rope around the neck. The rope passed through the flames, and into the hands of the slavers' leader. It began to char a little, but was a stout rope. When the rope had burned through a little, and looked as though it would soon part, the slaver pulled the rope a yard or so, and a fresh section of the rope began to char, then burn. Mohamed Abdul Beg was also dragged a yard closer to the flames.

The slaver spoke to the princess from time to time, in a tongue we could not understand, but clearly she was refusing his demands, for he became further angered, and edged Mohamed Abdul Beg even closer to the flames. His skin had long since reddened, and blisters had formed across his chest. His beard and eyebrows were singed and smoking, and beads of sweat trickled from his forehead. Still, he said not a word. His men looked on silently, hands tied behind their backs.

"Holmes! We must do something. He will be roasted soon." I spoke as softly as I could, but was heard, and received another blow from a rifle butt to silence me. By this time, the other slavers were enjoying the vicious spectacle provided by their leader, and were drunkenly cheering every time he tugged the rope, now only inches at a time, to extend the torture. By now Mohamed Abdul Beg was in serious pain, and would soon faint away into the fire.

"Our rescue is already at hand," said Holmes, enigmatically. I could see no one or nothing that could rescue us from this predicament, and wondered what he was talking about. "The question is, are we morally justified in doing nothing about it. I admit, I can think of no other way out, and yet my conscience protests that we must seek one." I had no idea what Holmes was talking about. It seemed such nonsense, especially at that time, and with Mohamed Abdul Beg inching closer to the fire every minute, it seemed as though Holmes rather than he had become unhinged.

The slaver shouted again at the princess, who remained silent. He slapped her again, then raised the brandy bottle to drink. It was empty, and with a shout of disgust, he hurled it at the nearest rock, where it shattered. Tashi, by this time, was howling loudly, and strained at his rope, eager to attack the tormentors of his masters. One of the slavers raised a rifle to shoot him. The leader struck the barrel down, and the bullet ploughed into the sandy soil at Tashi's feet. Clearly, even though drunk, the leader did not want to lose a valuable dog. He told the man to shoot only if the dog broke free, as none dared to tie another rope to him.

The leader shouted another order, and the princess was brought to him. He caressed her face with his coarse hands, and looked drunkenly at her, still beautiful despite her filthy clothes and the dried blood on her chin. Taking the second, unopened, brandy bottle from his cloak, he uncorked it and raised it to drink, but then seemed to be distracted by the beautiful face of his captive, so near his open lips.

Holmes shouted, "No! There must be another . . ," and leaped at the head of the lead slaver. One of the lieutenants struck him a terrible blow to the temple with his rifle butt, and Holmes collapsed in an unconscious heap at my feet. At first I thought he had been killed, but slowly his shallow breathing returned. The leader stood, rather unsteadily, and delivered himself of two sharp kicks to Holmes's midriff. Leering at the princess, he uncorked the brandy, and took a deep drink, belched loudly, then drank again. He passed the bottle to his lieutenants, who drank in turn, then it was passed around the rest of the men. When they had all drunk, the bottle was passed back to the leader.

He did not take it, even when spoken to. It seemed the brandy had sent him to sleep. If so, thought I, perhaps soon we should have our chance to escape. At least Mohamed Abdul Beg was no longer being dragged slowly into the fire. The man with the bottle then handed it to one of the lieutenants, but he too was asleep. So too was the next lieutenant. Fear suddenly flared in the man's eyes, and he let the bottle slip from his hands to smash on the ground. I followed his gaze around the circle of slavers. One by one, it seemed, the slavers were dropping off to sleep. Incredulous, the last man to drink shook a lieutenant, who slumped to the ground, then his chief, who did the same. But no man ever slept with his eyes wide open, as both of his leaders seemed to be. He shook others by the shoulders, but they all slumped over, dead, if they hadn't already done so. Just as he realised that what had befallen them would soon be his fate as well, and turned to shoot at Holmes's prostrate body, Tashi's rope snapped. Luckily the man was dead before he reached the ground, because what Tashi did to his face was too terrible to contemplate. Dimly sensing what had happened, I used all the authority I could summons, and shouted at Tashi to stop. I did not want my faithful mastiff to die the same swift death as the slavers.

For a moment, all was absolutely still, a tableau of death and violence, of victims and their dead tormentors. The sudden reversal of roles took everyone by surprise. The princess, looking at the corpse of the lead slaver, leaned down, and spit three times in his open mouth, then cursed him. She untied her champion, and began to inspect the burns he had suffered, which caused him to make a noise for the first time since his torture began. Then he fainted away from pain, his head cradled in her lap, her tears falling onto his blistered chest. Holmes was still unconscious, but was breathing easily. I made him comfortable, and went to make sure that all the slavers were dead. They were – as swiftly, silently and painlessly as men had ever died.

I gathered together all our rifles and possessions, and repacked them ready for travel. The string of slaves had lain down to sleep, still tied together, on the bare ground, covered with the few shared furs provided by the slavers. By now, some had realised that things were changed, and soon there was a clamour from them to be released. I could not do this with Holmes and Mohamed Abdul Beg still unconscious, but I took the princess over to explain that we should soon set them free to return to their homes. Several complained, but the princess spoke to them, and they were quieted.

We returned to the dying fire, and I threw some more wood on the blaze. I untied the two *kashgaris'* hands, and they went to the assistance of their master. With the princess's help, I rifled the cloaks and packs of the chief slaver and his lieutenants, finding a considerable sum in silver and gold coins. This I put aside to divide amongst the slavers' victims on the morrow, and we dragged the bodies well away from the camp, for fear of attracting wild animals during what was left of the night.

Holmes regained consciousness twenty minutes later, and by that time Mohamed Abdul Beg was awake as well. After a short rest, Holmes was able to rise, although he looked very ill. Mohamed Abdul Beg was badly burnt, but seemed not to notice the pain in his delight that his betrothed was rescued. His skin would be forever scarred, but would heal. He asked again and again what had happened, as he had witnessed nothing of the deaths of the slavers. I was unsure, and Holmes made no response. I did not want to question him right then. He looked slowly around at the dead slavers, then down at the ground for a moment.

"What's done is done, le Villard. I suppose it is for the best, and a rough justice was served upon them; I would like to think they died by their own hand. So be it."

"I thought we'd stay here until dawn," I said, "then take their horses back to where we left ours."

"Fine. But there is something I must do before anything else. Will you assist me. Le Villard, as I am still groggy from the blow."

"Of course, Holmes," I replied, "but perhaps you should rest awhile first?"

"I'll be fine, once I start moving around. Just help me over to the slave lines, and keep your pistol handy, just in case."

I did as he asked, and within moments we were slowly making our way down the rows of manacled, dishevelled prisoners. Holmes paid no attention to women or girls, or to the few elderly men. Clearly he had an objective, as once or twice he examined a slave more closely, or asked a few innocent questions, before passing on. We had almost come to the last of the captives when I sensed Holmes's interest roused.

He had stopped before a hunched figure, huddled into the few rags it owned. The man was probably around forty or so, his heavy beard and hair matted with dirt. He cowered away from us, and turned away when spoken to in Persian. I expected Holmes to pass by, as he had with the others, but he spoke again - in English - softly and slowly.

"It is cold tonight - almost as cold as the Winter Palace, I imagine."

The captive reared back as though struck, then looked closely at Holmes through his matted hair.

"But not half so beautiful, my friend. Who are you, if I may ask?"

"I shall be more than happy to oblige you, Captain Dolghurokov, as soon as we have released your shackles. But firstly, please allow me to present to you my esteemed colleague. M. Francois le Villard . . . Captain Alexei Dolghurokov of the Russian Imperial Army. I have a message for you, Captain!"

"I shall listen to your message with interest - whatever it is. So long as it is in a civilised language."

Holmes then delivered his oral message from St. Petersburg, to the immense gratitude of the Russian officer. Captain Dolghurokov knew that Holmes - by finding him first - had certainly saved his life, and the honour of the Tsar as well. He thanked Holmes profusely, and promised to reward us upon his return to Russia - which Holmes gracefully declined.

"You certainly picked a dramatic way to deliver your message, sir! Now, may I know who addresses me?"

"Professor Olaf Sigerson, of the University of Oslo, Captain. And my assistant, M. Francois le Villard! We have come from India via Nepal - in the interests of science, you understand."

"But, of course!" replied the Russian officer, as I supervised the striking of his shackles. "Why else would you be wandering around here in one of the most desolate places on earth? And with messages from St. Petersburg!"

I detected a hint of humour behind the man's remarks, and glanced up from my task. A slight smile played at the corners of his chapped lips, but then . . . he'd just been rescued from slavery, and a certain death. I, too, would smile at that, I thought.

12th June 1892
The Pamirs, Chinese Turkistan
Dawn slowly lightened the sky, and the captives woke, restless for release. Once Holmes and Mohamed Abdul Beg were up and about - though neither

looked well – we walked to where the string of captives were staked to the ground. Mohamed Abdul Beg spoke in Persian, which is the lingua franca of the region.

"You have all suffered greatly, and were destined to a life of servile captivity. By the beneficence of God, you have been spared that fate, and you are all freed again. The gold and silver of the slavers will be divided up amongst you, so that you may return to your former homes. Any amongst you who wish to return with myself and my bride to Kashgar will be provided with employment, as free men and women, so long as your loyalty is pledged to my father, the *Atalik*."

"But how did they die so?" asked one of the captives.

"This I cannot answer," he replied, "but of one thing I am certain. Their punishment was just. My father has always told me that we must free the slaves in our service. This I have always resisted, as it is the way of our forefathers. But I have seen my betrothed hobbled and chained for no reason other than the greed and cruelty of her fellow men. Henceforth, I shall stand with my father against his advisers. Let them say his education has softened him. I now see his strength, in desiring this change, and saying so. Many will be unhappy, and they are powerful men, but together we may prevail. I make this my marriage vow. Now, prepare yourselves for your journeys, wherever they may take you, and may God go with you! You are free again! Men, strike off these chains!"

He turned to the four *kashgari* escorts who had been captured by the slavers.

"As for you, I fear that in my joy I shall be too lenient. I shall let my father decide your fate. Now, begone, and assist your elder guardsmen to prepare for the journey."

Captain Dolghurokov sat to one side, saying nothing. The night before, once he had overcome his astonishment at being rescued so unexpectedly, he had entered into lively discussion with us. It was difficult for me to credit the fact, but the Russian claimed he had deliberately arranged to be captured by the slavers, as being the safest and surest disguise in which to cross the dangerous territory between him and his destination in the Pamirs. The hardships, he claimed, were bearable, and he had no doubt that he could easily escape from his new master once sold at the Faizabad slave-mart.

"But Professor Sigerson – how did you know it was I, in amongst these human chattels of the slavers?"

"Simple, Captain Dolghurokov. You did exactly as I should have done. When we received news of the presence of these slavers – and from discreet enquiries amongst our companions I ascertained that this was the only slave-caravan to pass regularly, every year, from that direction. I consulted my maps, and noted that you had disappeared at a place and time where the slaver's caravan was known to pass. Then I noted your planned destination, and saw that it was not far off the slavers' ultimate destination.

"I took advantage of the fact that they'd captured the *Atalik*'s prospective daughter-in-law to give chase. Our trap almost backfired on us, as you no doubt observed, but I felt certain that, amongst the captives, we should find an intrepid Russian officer. You would not meet my eyes, sir, because you knew that yours were not the eyes of an Asiatic slave."

Later that day, when we were away from the others, I asked the question which had preyed on my mind all night.

"Was that what I think, Holmes? Asp toxin?"

"Of course," he replied. "What else kills in that fashion?"

"But how . . ?" I began, but Holmes interrupted me, not unkindly.

"Some day, le Villard, I shall explain it all. But not now! It is sufficient that we are alive, and Captain Dolghurokov and the captives rescued."

16th June 1892
Kashgar, Chinese Turkistan

We left the vultures to deal with the dead slavers, and headed back by the slavers' route, as the captives were too weak to cross the ridge. A few opted to continue to Tashkurgan, and some to live their lives at Kashgar, but most captives simply wished to return to their homes. We escorted them back to Yangi Hissar, and from there they made their own way. Our party turned north to Kashgar, and was greeted with jubilation. Preparations were begun immediately for the wedding celebrations, which should have taken place the month before. The *Atalik* was most thankful.

Captain Dolghurokov was not present, having remained in our chambers, and it was only because the *Atalik* was a civilised fellow that he was not dealt with severely. That he was a Russian spy had been impossible for us to conceal, but Holmes had insisted, as one gentleman to another, on providing safe passage to Tashkent for the Russian.

"My son has told me several times of the events at Tashkurgan, and it is still no clearer to my mind just exactly what happened. I shall leave it at that, unless you wish to enlighten me. However, it is only fair to tell you that, as far as our men are concerned, you are a most fearful magician, who can strike all his enemies dead at a blow."

"It is a reputation I shall be glad to leave here when we depart in the morning," replied Holmes. "We must leave immediately for Tashkent, if you could spare us an escort. And you, sir, must prepare to depart for

Haiderabad."

"And so I shall, just as soon as my son is married." He winked slyly at us. "I told you she was beautiful, did I not? I look forward to the grandchildren I shall soon be blessed with, and I have you both to thank for it. Your escort will be ready for you in the morning; you may leave when you desire, but I do wish you would stay for the celebrations."

"Much as we would like to, sir, it would be most unwise. There are those who are plotting your death, and we must hurry to make up time. As it is, we may have missed them in Persia. We will leave at dawn. Now, before we retire, I think we will take our leave of your son and his brave wife."

CHAPTER XXIII

27th June 1892
Tashkent, Russian Protectorate of Bokhara

NINE DAYS MORE on camel-back. I suppose it is better than walking. Finally it was over. Holmes, Captain Dolghurokov and I arrived at Tashkent, which was already a prosperous small city, with wide paved avenues and solid buildings of three and four storeys, made of cut stone. Tashkent boasts several hotels, banks and a telegraph office, besides the all-important railway station.

Our papers were received with a great deal of excitement. We appeared out of the Central Asian vastness, looking – and I daresay smelling – little different from our *kashgari* escorts. We had dealt with several levels of minor officialdom before we found a Russian officer who took us seriously. Captain Dolghurokov remained quietly in the background at this stage. Finally we presented our letters of introduction to the Governor's office, and at last had them accredited. The Captain slipped away, once we were inside the Governor's mansion, without a further word of thanks.

We were released, and found ourselves to be the talk of the town; the Norwegian explorer and his assistant who had almost penetrated to Lhasa reaching as far as Shigatse. Only then did we realise what an obsession the world, and the Tsarevich in particular, had with this remote and mysterious Asian capital. The local news reporter took our photographs with our *kashgari* warriors, all of us on our camels. Then the *kashgaris* turned their camels towards the vast emptiness, and were soon lost in the haze of the desert sands beyond the city gates.

We used some of our gold coins to reserve a suite at the Tashkent Grand Hotel, bought a few basic items of wardrobe, and went in search of an establishment offering Turkish baths. After several hours there, somewhat relieved of our travel weariness, we dressed in European clothing for the first time in over a year, and returned to our hotel suite, where we slept for the best part of a day.

When we had woken and dressed, we went to the bank and collected the funds deposited for us by Mycroft's agent, then returned to the clothiers, where we bought an appropriate wardrobe for our further travels. By the time we returned to our hotel, there was a small crowd in the lobby, and a deputation including the mayor of the town and the town council. They wanted more photographs, of them standing alongside the intrepid explorers. Holmes went along with the clamour for our exclusive story, as being the most credible behaviour. "Let us get it over with as soon as possible, then slip away."

By the next morning, congratulatory telegrams had arrived from half a dozen geographical societies, several royals, a host of journalists, and Mycroft. Our exploits were hailed by the West as rivalling those of the great explorers of Darkest Africa. The Eastern Europeans proclaimed ours the equal of the great journeys of Przhevalsky and the Hungarian Count Szechenyi, and their journeys to Saitu – the 'City of Sands' – and beyond into the wastelands between Tibet and the Great Wall of China. I thought of the dozens of native *pundits* who had made such hazardous journeys, but whose exploits remained secret, their names unknown, in the interests of security of the Empire.

It was altogether too much! We gladly bought tickets on the next train leaving Tashkent for Uzum Ada, on the eastern shore of the Caspian Sea. The sudden thought of fresh caviar with sour cream crossed my mind, and I was impatient to leave.

Mycroft's telegram, signed 'm', simply said, 'congratulations professor sigerson stop splendid results stop all agreed explorations to proceed stop further instructions at sponsors representative teheran.'

The others offered everything from enormous sums for the exclusive story, from the American newspapers, to enquiries from the families of missing explorers. Holmes issued a standard response, and said that the detailed account of our expedition must wait until publication, which would be in a scholarly journal, rather than an American tabloid. That evening we were guests at a dinner held in our honour by the mayor. I doubted the Russians would have feted us so had they known of our sabotage of the Arsenal at Lhasa, but that news had obviously failed to reach Tashkent.

Only hours later that situation had changed. We heard a commotion at the city gates an hour after they had been locked for the night, and heard that, against all custom, a rider from Tibet had been admitted to Tashkent.

An hour or so later our hotel door burst open and a squad of uniformed Russian troops followed a gaudily dressed Colonel into our spacious room. Holmes protested in his passable Russian, but to no avail. The officer informed us that we were to be held under house arrest for the sabotage of vital Russian military installations, spying for Britain, and illegal entry to Russian Tashkent. Instructions from the Russian consul at Constantinople were awaited, but the officer let us know that his preference was for summary execution, and let the explanations come later. He seemed to think he'd not have long to wait before being given a free hand with us, but that if it did not arrive, a convenient accident - in the course of an unsuccessful escape attempt - had already been arranged.

Our possessions were not searched - I presume pending instructions - but two armed guards were stationed outside our door, and two more on the terrace outside our first-floor windows. More soldiers were posted around the town square onto which our hotel fronted, and as the moon was full we were able to see shadows cast by men moving around on the hotel's roof. Escape seemed to be impossible.

"Obviously they've just received word of our efforts at Lhasa. The thaw must have come just after our departure, and their new armoury is obviously destroyed. We have that consolation at least. But - how do we get ourselves out of this? I don't much like the look of our gaoler, and I believe him when he says he's arranged an accident for us."

"Nice timing on the part of Captain Dolghurokov," I remarked. "First he disappears, and within hours we're under house-arrest. A fine way to show his appreciation, don't you think, Holmes?"

"The Captain may know nothing about this, le Villard. However, I agree that the timing is suspicious. There appears to be little we can do right now, and there are too many people still abroad to make any attempt for freedom now. Besides, even if we do escape, we are still stranded in Russian Tashkent, thousands of miles from the nearest friendly hand."

"What do you propose that we do, then, Holmes?"

"Well, as you are standing already, do you think you could hand me down my new tobacco pouch and pipe. It would be a crime indeed to forego such uncommon luxury simply because a rabid Russian officer is threatening to execute us tonight, don't you think?"

I did as asked, wondering as I did so whether Holmes had a plan simmering in his cunning brain, or whether he was simply displaying bravado in a difficult situation. I sent down for a meal for the two of us, which was permitted by our captors. Clearly, our recent status as heroes - and the uncertainty of the charges against us - meant that we were to be accorded the basic civilities until further orders arrived. Or until our unfortunate 'escape attempt'.

Just as the town seemed to be settling down for the night, I noticed a large number of soldiers being deployed around the town square, and that our guards on the terrace had been withdrawn. I mentioned this to Holmes, who rose from his chair and opened the door to the corridor.

"Those guards are gone as well!" he said. "Looks like we're being invited to make a break for it."

"So? What then?" I asked.

"The Colonel would only be doing this if he was worried about not receiving official permission to execute us. So I think we'll not give him the satisfaction. Another pipe is in order, I think."

So saying, Holmes resumed his seat, calmly re-packed his pipe, and lit up. By this time, it was past ten in the o'clock. I confess that I was becoming concerned at our predicament. At half-past there came the sounds of hoofs and harnesses from the far corner of the square, and I went out onto our terrace to investigate. As I stood, Holmes rose as well, took his lightweight telescope from his pack, and suggested that I light a cigar while standing in the doorway.

"In that way," he said, "I shall be able to rest my glass on your shoulder, and remain concealed in the darkness. I should like to know what is going on down there."

Accordingly, I took a fine Turkish cigar, which I had purchased just that day when Holmes and I had visited the tobacconists' shop in the hotel lobby, and made a show of trimming and lighting it as I lounged across the doorway, with my coat open. Concealed behind me, Holmes surveyed the square from corner to corner, including the visible rooftops, before homing in on the far corner from whence came the noises of a troop of mounted horse.

"Snipers posted on every roof-top that I can see, but no overtly visible guards. Our Colonel is tucked away in the shadows of the portico to that Emporium over there. Around the corner is a troop of Cossacks, formed up for action. Snipers posted on every rooftop that I can see, but no overtly visible guards. Around the corner is a troop of Cossacks, formed up for action. It seems as though their officer is in conference with the Colonel; he has his back to us, and seems rather exercised about something or other. Move across just a little, please, le Villard."

Holmes shifted the telescope to my other shoulder, and when he had re-adjusted his view I heard him exclaim, "Ah! So it's you, is it, Captain Alexei Dolghurokov?"

Holmes was silent for a long minute or two, before lowering his eyeglass. I saw the dark mass of the distant troop of Cossacks wheel and turn, with a muffled stamping and snorting, and disappear from view behind the Emporium.

"Very interesting, le Villard. It seems as though the Colonel's patience is exhausted. I think we may expect visitors at any moment. Well, as we have already packed our things away, I propose to enjoy one last pipe before Fate arrives."

But I noticed that, although Holmes charged and lit his pipe once again, he did not resume his seat, stayed away from the windows and doors, and instructed me to do the same. I was most concerned by now, and said that if we were to be executed anyway, why not at least try to make a break for it. We had, after all, escaped from many a tight spot before this.

Holmes's only reply was to smile enigmatically, and offer me a light for my cigar, which I had allowed to go out. He said only the one word.

"Patience!"

Then he resumed his thoughtful pacing of the dark side of our chamber. This went on for several nerve-wracking minutes, until broken by the sound of spurred boots marching in unison up the stairs and turning towards our room. The marching ceased at our door, and was followed by an officious-sounding knock.

Holmes sat down again, and asked if I would be so good as to see to it. I looked at my companion of the past year and more, and marvelled at his coolness. Surrounded by Russian soldiers and far from help of any kind, with our *kashgaris* long departed back into their desert, there was a certain dignity to not allowing ourselves to be shot down like slinking dogs. The rapping at the door was repeated, with more urgency, and a shouted command in Russian. I unlatched the door and opened it, prepared to greet the Colonel and his men, only to find myself face-to-face with a smiling Captain Dolghurokov and a half-dozen or so heavily armed Cossack troops.

"If Professor Sigerson will receive me, I have a favour to return. May I?"

Without stirring, Holmes replied, "Of course, Captain. Do come in; I've been expecting you."

The Captain gave orders in Russian to his men, four of whom took up positions on either side of the door, and two on the terrace outside the windows.

"I have more men guarding the stairs and the front and rear entrances, Professor. I hope we shall have no need of them."

"I notice that the Colonel's men are still in the square, Captain," said Holmes. "I thought he promised to remove them!"

"How could you possibly have known that, Professor?" the Captain exclaimed. "We were hundreds of paces from here, and in shadow.

"Indeed, you were. Let it be a lesson for the future, Captain."

Holmes produced the collapsed telescope from his coat pocket, and smiled. "I understand Russian, and I read lips."

Comprehension dawned on the Russian officer at the same time as I realised why Holmes had been so calm at the sound of the troops at our door. The Captain laughed out loud, then spoke to Holmes.

"Colonel Gerinovsky is the nominal commander of the troops here at Tashkent. He loathes it here, so he's ambitious to make his mark and get back nearer to the corridors of power. You have almost provided him just such an opportunity. It seems that a messenger arrived from Tibet, carrying news of the sabotage of the armoury at Lhasa. The establishment of the armoury was the responsibility of a monk known to us as Bogdanovich, who reported to Colonel Gerinovsky. The loss of the armoury will be a severe blow to his reputation, but if he can report that he has caught the saboteurs – who were, unfortunately, killed while attempting to flee – then his career may actually be enhanced by the capture of two British agents in Russian territory.

"All of this he proposed to me, out there in the square. I was back with my troops at the barracks when I heard of the arrival of the messenger, and the calling-out of troops to the square. These men, and the others below, have been with me for years, through hells of various sorts.

"I know that Colonel Gerinovsky has not the authority to order a summary execution, but technically he is the commanding officer, and he wants your deaths to be a *fait accompli* before the morning dispatches arrive."

"What is the situation, then, Captain?" I asked.

"Something of a stand-off, I think," he answered, tugging at his moustaches. "May I take a seat?"

"Of course, Captain." Holmes indicated the sofa, and asked if the Captain would like a drink. We had purchased a bottle of Scotch whisky earlier, and had ordered a siphon and tumblers with our evening meal.

"A drink is an excellent idea, gentlemen, but I insist we drink vodka.

Excuse me a moment."

He crossed to the door, opened it, and gave orders to his men, then returned to sit alone on the sofa. I heard one pair of footsteps go away down the corridor, only to return within the minute. The Captain crossed one leg over the other, placed his revolvers in front of him on the low table, and smiled broadly at us.

"How nice to have the opportunity to repay you so swiftly," he remarked, and laughed out loud again. A light rapping at the door he answered with a command. The door opened, and a waiter pushed a trolley into the room It was loaded high with several bottles of vodka, a bucket of ice, *blinis* and sour cream, a host of pickled fish and vegetables, white dumplings in a thick stew, black and white breads, winter apples. The sight of all the food made me realise how hungry I was.

We needed little urging from the Captain to pour healthy shares of liquor into our tumblers, and load our plates high.

"We will be here until morning, my friends," said he, "so I see no reason why we should not enjoy the company of fellow-adventurers while we may. A toast, gentlemen!

"To the *'Bolshaya Igra'*, gentlemen . . . the Great Game – and long may it live!"

Holmes raised his glass to clink against first the Captain's glass, then ours.

"'The Great Game!'" we all intoned, then set to our food with relish.

Perhaps we were not destined to die that night after all. Things were certainly very much improved, anyway, I thought. Several glasses of vodka later, Holmes ventured to ask about plans for the morning.

"Well, my friends, we will have to see how Colonel Gerinovsky feels about me then. Right now I imagine he is not pleased with me. You see, he has advocated an extreme forward policy in Central Asia, and this Lhasa idea was his bid for glory. He knows of the Tsar's fascination with Lhasa, and rightly calculated that a big success there would catapult him to fame and fortune – as indeed it would. But now, thanks to two saboteurs, his plan is in tatters – and he would like to pin the blame on you two fellows who have just conveniently arrived from that direction.

"Now, you may well be the saboteurs, but he has no proof of it. If you are dead, no proof will be required. Alive, accountability must be observed, and he knows it. After all, you are both famous explorers, are you not. Therefore, in order to avoid an ugly international incident, I have placed you under my protection until I can escort you by tomorrow's train to the Caspian. By the time we arrive there, instructions from St. Petersburg should have arrived. At least, that is what I told him."

"So we are safe for the night, at least?" I asked.

"The Colonel is a desperate man, and there is no love lost between us. A lot depends on whether his men will attack Russian troops on his command. Somehow I doubt it. I'm gambling they won't; here's hoping I'm right."

He raised his glass to toast that excellent sentiment, and we gladly joined him.

Some little while later the Captain suggested that, as all the food and most of the vodka had been consumed, Holmes and I should try to rest a little, while he remained alert. To my surprise, Holmes concurred, and we lay down in the darkened room as the Captain, still on the sofa, poured himself another glass.

Before I knew it I was shaken awake by Holmes to a room lit by grey morning light tinged with pink and orange as the sun rose above the city walls. The Captain was in the open doorway, talking to his men, and the two Cossacks from the terrace were lifting our baggage to carry it downstairs.

I dashed cold water onto my face from a blue-and-white porcelain jug over a matching basin, and towelled myself dry. Glancing out of the window I noted that no troops were visible in the square, even in the shadows.

I followed Holmes and Captain Dolghurokov along the corridor and down the curved stairs to the reception lobby, where more of the Captain's loyal Cossacks were posted. As the last of us stepped off the stairs, the double-doors from the Ballroom burst open. A phalanx of troops led by Colonel Gerinovsky divided into two columns, which rushed along both walls of the lobby, meeting at the main entrance, and effectively surrounding our contingent. Now I knew why there were no troops in the square!

The Colonel barked orders to his troops, who moved to seize Holmes and myself. Captain Dolghurokov approached the Colonel as though to speak with him, but instead swiftly drew his service revolver and placed its muzzle against the Colonel's temple. He spoke rapidly and forcefully in Russian, first to the Colonel, then to his troops. As he did so, he reached into an inner pocket of his tunic, and pulled forth a document bearing the Russian Imperial seal. This he held aloft briefly as he spoke, and then thrust in front of Colonel Gerinovsky for him to read.

The Colonel seemed to shrink inside his uniform. His face flushed bright red, and he turned on his heel and marched to the entrance door. He spoke softly with his second-in-command, who obviously ordered his troops back to barracks, and marched off alone across the square.

"What on earth was that all about, Holmes?" I whispered.

"I think I'll let the Captain tell us, le Villard."

Not for the first time during that long night, I felt I could gladly smother

Holmes for his reticence. I knew his Russian to be fluent, but he if chose not to enlighten me, there seemed little I could do about it.

An hour later, to the flash of news cameras, we boarded the train, and for the first time since leaving India, travelled in a wheeled conveyance.

30th June 1892
Uzum Ada, Turkmenia
The temperature soared as our train made its way across the shingle plains and sandy dunes. From Bokhara we crossed the Oxus by a rackety bridge into Turkmenia. As we rattled across, looking down at the river, Holmes quoted a few lines that I remembered from an anthology, read as a child in the library of my English-born grandmother:

'Oxus, forgetting the bright speed he had,
in his high mountain cradle in Pamere.'

"I've always wanted to cross the Oxus, Captain. It sounded so remote and mythical. Now that it is called the Amu, it seems just another stream."

The Captain laughed again, but made no reply.

We carried on towards the Caspian, with few interruptions save frequent stops when the Cossacks swept sand from the tracks. At one point I caught the Captain alone, and asked him how he had engineered our escape that final morning, in the hotel lobby.

"Has the Professor not told you? I am surprised. However, as you ask, I did two things I have never done before. Firstly, I lied to my fellow-officer, when I told him that I had very clear evidence, which I was not at liberty to divulge to him, that you had indeed come from Nepal, as you have claimed. Secondly, I showed him my *laissez-passer* from the Tsar himself. You see, my father commanded the Royal Guard until recently, and the Tsar looks upon me as his favourite adventurer. I had left the document in my quarters here before heading off to the Pamirs. That, my friend, is why I left you both as soon as we arrived here. I suspected some trouble of this sort, and wanted the document in hand before any confrontation."

"Thankfully, it worked," I remarked, and again expressed our gratitude for the risks he was taking on our behalf.

"As I said, M le Villard, I am merely repaying one gentleman's favour with another."

On the evening of the 29th our train pulled in to the terminus at Uzum Ada, and we gazed at the sparkling beauty of the vast Caspian, so refreshing after our year in the deserts and mountains. Captain Dolghurokov arranged for us to stay overnight at an inn, and next morning arranged passage for us on a small steam launch bound for the Persian shore at the southern end of the inland sea.

He and his Cossacks bid us farewell as our vessel pulled away from the pier. Our overnight celebrity was left behind us at Tashkent, and we became once again two European explorers, now on our way to research the ancient civilisations of Persia.

CHAPTER XXIV

THE NIGHT had become distinctly chilly, the more so as I had neglected to tend the fire properly. But I had indeed finished the first of the two Journals of Francois le Villard, with only a brief break for my supper. Even that simple meal I had asked Mrs. Hudson to bring on a tray, so that I should not have to move from my armchair.

My mind was still full of images of Holmes and le Villard in high Asia - and, for some reason, of Samarkand. I'd always wanted to see fabled Samarkand, and, for a fleeting moment, sorely regretted that it had not been I whom Holmes had chosen as his companion in these adventures. The moment soon passed. I reflected that, with Holmes back in London, there would surely be cases aplenty to investigate with my erstwhile companion. And my accounts of those cases would not, I hoped, suffer those restrictions on publication placed upon this present Report.

Closing the small leather-covered book, I stood and stretched the stiffness from my limbs, then crossed to the bookshelves. I exchanged le Villard's first Journal for its companion, set that later Journal on the small table beside my usual chair, and - after setting the brass screen across the fireplace - went up to bed.

PART TWO

The Siam Question

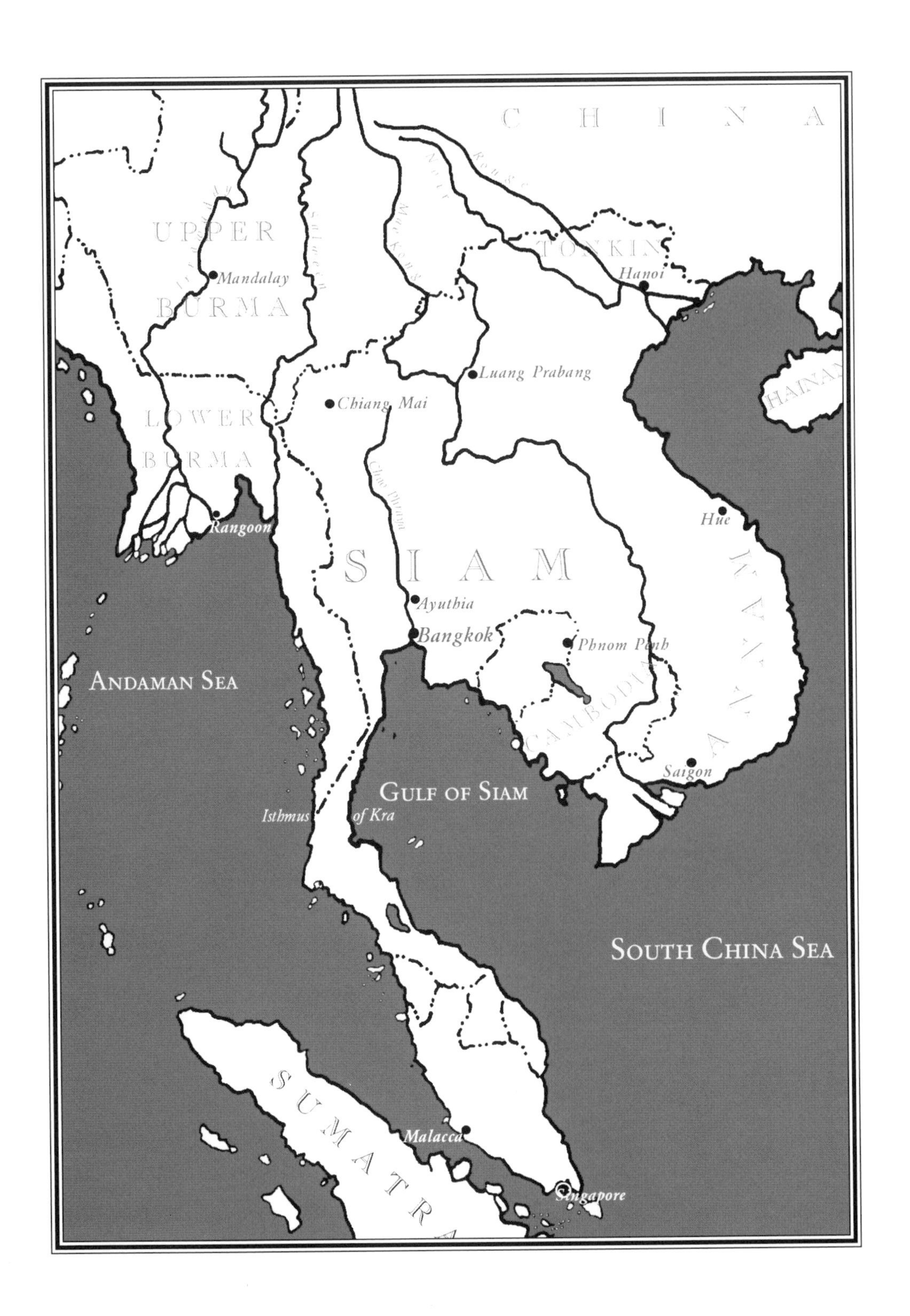

CHINA
UPPER BURMA
Mandalay
LOWER BURMA
Rangoon
TONKIN
Hanoi
Luang Prabang
Chiang Mai
SIAM
Ayuthia
Bangkok
Phnom Penh
CAMBODIA
Hue
ANNAM
Saigon
ANDAMAN SEA
GULF OF SIAM
Isthmus of Kra
SOUTH CHINA SEA
Malacca
Singapore

DAY FIVE

APRIL 10TH 1894

CHAPTER XXV

HOLMES HAD ALREADY left the house by the time I awoke. He hadn't mentioned his intended destination the previous evening and I had refrained from asking. Three years away from London clearly hadn't changed his habit of reticence until certain of the results of his investigations.

Mrs. Hudson came herself and cleared away Holmes's plate and cup when I called down for my breakfast, and returned minutes later with my tea and a rack of fresh toast. I decided to take advantage of the morning's quiet period to return to my practice at Kensington and check with Stinson, in case any of my patients had suffered unforeseen complications.

An hour there was sufficient to set my mind at ease. Afterwards I walked aimlessly for some distance, purely for the exercise. The weather was cool, the sky cloudless. I took a pleasant stroll along the Broad Walk through Kensington Gardens, and read my newspaper while I lunched at an open-air cafe facing the Round Pond. Exiting opposite the Albert Hall, I hailed a hansom to take me back to 221B Baker Street, where the second of Francois le Villard's fascinating Journals awaited my perusal.

I was well aware that the next volume did not follow on directly from the first; there were two other volumes between the two Holmes had handed me. I suppose I should have waited until le Villard arrived. I could then arrange it with him to secure the missing two volumes, which apparently dealt with the exploits of Holmes and le Villard between their arrival at Persia and their departure less than a year later from the port of Suakin on the Red Sea coast of Egypt.

However, as I gathered from his first Journal that le Villard had sent those volumes to France somewhere for safekeeping, and having no firm date for his arrival at London, I decided that I would carry on reading the second volume in my possession. I justified this to myself by reasoning that Holmes's elder brother Mycroft had already commissioned my report on Holmes's activities during his absence from London, but I confess that my curiosity was the determining factor.

The first Journal had revealed new dimensions to Holmes's character, resources that had never been called upon in facing the challenges we had faced in London and, occasionally, on the Continent. I had also been fascinated by the occasional glimpses of Mycroft as a Foreign Office field man - a young man seemingly very different from the self-effacing civil servant he had become. Perhaps not so different, I reflected! Now so set in his ways in the physical sense, Mycroft's brilliant mind continued to rove across the vast panorama of world politics, making sense of the incomprehensible for the decision makers of the day.

By the time I arrived back at our old rooms it was already mid-afternoon. I sat in my old chair, and reached for the other volume of le Villard's Journals.

CHAPTER XXVI

30th May 1893
Si Chang Island, Siam

THE *MAHA CHAKKRI*, royal yacht of the King of Siam, lay at anchor in the middle of the bay, her hull a gleaming white set against the blue of the deeper water where she was obliged to moor. A gaily-decorated steam-launch put off from her companionway, and soon delivered a small party to the jetty in front of the King's Summer Palace. Coconut palms fringed the sweeping curve of the white sand beach, and the turquoise sea lapped gently against the grey boulders of the headland, one of which I shared with an English doctor.

"The women of the Royal Household will certainly be enjoying this!" remarked the physician, with whom I had made an acquaintance during the steamer crossing to this island in the Gulf of Siam.

I surveyed the scene spread before us. Directly ashore from the royal yacht was the Royal Palace, and in front of it, the King's pavilion, hastily erected for the occasion, but impressive nonetheless, with its layers of gently curved roofs and spires supported on slender tapered columns of teak wood. Woven and embroidered gold draperies hung at the window apertures, and multiple-tiered umbrellas at the entrance proclaimed its royal purpose. Brightly caparisoned elephants were tethered nearby; their long tusks garlanded with flowers woven in intricate patterns.

The King was inside his pavilion, preparing to receive in audience some of the consular representatives who were assembled in the roped-off enclosure in front of the building. More Europeans were gathered some little distance away, including wives and children, waiting to catch a rare glimpse of the Siamese monarch and his retinue. All around, sheltered from the scorching sunlight by the coconut palms, were the Siamese residents of this island. I have been told that King Chulalongkorn, like his father before him, encourages his subjects to look upon him when he travels in public. But amidst this varied mass of people, the one element conspicuous by its absence was the women of the Siamese court. Puzzled by the doctor's remark, I asked him the reason for his comment.

"Right now, M. Le Villard," replied the doctor, "bathing and frolicking in the sea on the other side of this island, protected from the eyes of commoners by a guard of women, are the King's favourite wives and their attendants, not to mention the Royal children. I am glad for them, for they are birds in a gilded cage when at court at Bangkok. Thousands of them! All jammed together in a gorgeous private world, but unable to leave it except on these rare outings on the royal yachts, or else when they voyage up river to the royal palaces there. They will soon return to the Palace and be taunted by those left behind for the darkness of their skin, and be told they look like the common people. But they know it is sheer envy, and wouldn't change places for the world."

"How is it you are so familiar with all this, Doctor?" I asked.

"Ah! Yes! You see, M. Le Villard, in addition to my medical practice for the Europeans here, I am personal physician attending the King's principal Queen. In that capacity I am the only male - other than His Majesty - allowed into the Inside Palace, as his *harem* is known.

"And you, sir? What brings you to Siam, and to *Koh* Si Chang?" he asked.

"I have the honour of being naturalist in the employ of Professor Olaf Sigerson. He is an explorer and archaeologist. Perhaps you have heard . . ?"

"Indeed yes! How interesting that must be. I have read accounts of his recent expeditions. I should very much like to meet him. Is he here at Siam with you?"

"We're on our way to investigate his theories regarding the tribes of Oceania, which he suspects may have migrated from these regions. The Professor was taken with the fever at Singapore. Once the crisis had passed I left him there to recuperate while I journeyed to Annam - to Saigon - where we had some researches to carry out. I am here to meet up with him again. He is expected today at the latest, so you may well have your chance."

From the enclosure by the royal pavilion came the strident noise of a brass band playing a European martial tune, and the consular corps formed itself into a semblance of order. Reluctantly leaving the breezy shade of our rocky seat, the doctor and I joined the throng. The band finished its rendition, and the blowing of conch-shell trumpets heralded the appearance of the King. He soon emerged from his pavilion, accompanied by several of his ministers. All were dressed in European-style uniform, with sashes and epaulettes setting off the bright colours of their tunics. The King was a slight figure, in his mid-forties I should guess, and he seemed quite comfortable as he received his guests, though the doctor said he had been frequently unwell lately.

"Personally, I suspect that the ceaseless pressure from the French is wearing him down. But then, you're French yourself, aren't you? I do hope I haven't given offence."

"Not at all. I may be French, but a less political animal you are scarce likely to encounter. I devote myself to the timeless study of plants and animals, and leave these transitory affairs to those who have the taste for them. The Professor cares even less who governs what. Only let him follow his researches where they lead him, and he is perfectly content."

I was aware that others may query the doctor as to our reasons for arriving at Siam, and saw no harm in establishing our credentials as scientific types, merely passing through, with one eye in the history books and the other applied to a microscope. The good doctor carried on, seeming to accept my declaration of political disinterest at face value.

"The gentleman next to him is Prince Ranawongse, who is the King's younger brother, and his minister for foreign affairs. He absorbs much of the day-to-day abuse from the French consul, Pavie."

He discreetly indicated a bearded fellow in frock-coat and cravat, who was engaged in muted discussion with several other soberly dressed Europeans as they awaited their turn to be presented to His Majesty.

"The gentlemen with Pavie are the cream of our consular corps, such as it is," remarked the doctor. "The Chevalier de Keun is the Dutch consul; next to him is the English resident minister, Captain Jones, and French, who is consul at our British legation - little love lost there, I can tell you. Then you have Boyd, Vice-Consul General for the Americans, and next to him are the German consul and the Italian resident minister."

Obviously, many of the principal figures of concern to Holmes and I were present. Equally clearly, the doctor was well informed as to affairs at Bangkok, so I took advantage of his familiarity to acquaint myself with the names and positions attached to each face.

"And those fellows in uniform, who may they be?"

"The closest to the King is the General Adviser to the Government of Siam, Rolin. Next is Commodore du Plessis de Richelieu. He is actually in charge of the naval defences, although not officially. But he's a great friend of the King, and is well respected by the nobles. Talking with him is Captain Bush, the harbour-master at Bangkok."

"Who are the civilians in the next row?" I asked. "They seem rather a mixed bag."

"And so they are. The tall, distinguished-looking chap is Lord Coledale, the railway and shipping tycoon. Sailed here from Brindisi in his steam-yacht, I hear." He pointed at an elegant vessel anchored at the near end of the bay. Even at this distance the white topsides, with varnished brightwork and polished brass, marked the yacht as the private vessel of an extremely wealthy man. I guessed that she was well over 500 tons deadweight, with comfortable accommodations for extended ocean voyaging.

"Hoping to do some business in the railway line, I believe - excuse the feeble pun - and reporting to the House on business and political developments in Siam as well. Then, next to him you have Campbell, who has made a mess of *his* railway concession here. Talking with both of them is Thorne. He edits the *Bangkok Times*, which is the semi-official rag. There is another, the *Siam Free Press*, which is the work of that weaselly little Irishman you see scurrying around with his notebook, over there. Very pro-French, and not popular, but he's got the advertising columns, which keep him in business."

The doctor and I continued our desultory examination of the assemblage as the Royal audience progressed, with the King taking a keen interest in his guests as they came forward in turn. Finally, the last dignitaries were presented, the conch-horns sounded again, and the King retired to the inner chambers of his pavilion, accompanied by his nobles. I noticed that his General Adviser, Rolin, was the only European to enter the pavilion with the royal party.

We had only just entered the marquee where refreshments were served when a loud commotion arose at the seashore. New arrivals at the tent informed us that a steamer was approaching the island, and was generally assumed to be the French gun-boat, which had been expected. I noticed that Pavie, the French resident, wore a smug look as he hurried out to watch the approach of the steamer. We finished our glasses of champagne, and then we too headed for the shoreline, now crowded with Siamese and Europeans both. The Siamese were fearful, and the Europeans held differing views, depending on their allegiance.

It was indeed a surprise to all, and especially to Pavie, when the ship was identified as a British gun-boat, the *Pallas*, arriving from Singapore. The only one not surprised was myself, as I had been expecting her arrival at any time. The ship's cutter approached the jetty, and her commander came ashore, accompanied by several of his officers. With them was a rather nondescript civilian, in high collar and coat despite the heat.

As they strode along the jetty, I recognised - trailing a little behind as he walked with the aid of a stick - the tall, stooped figure of Sherlock Holmes, in the persona of Professor Sigerson. At his heels, and on a leash for appearance sake, was my mastiff, Tashi. It seemed as though a month billeted in the police kennels at Singapore had done him no harm.

I turned to my companion. "There, dear sir, is the Professor himself. If you will excuse me, I must go to meet him. Perhaps we will meet later in the day."

"Quite an entrance, I must say," remarked the doctor. "Certainly beats the filthy coaster that delivered me to Bangkok."

I hastened to the jetty and called loudly to Professor Sigerson, so that all may hear. Holmes looked up, and gave an absent smile and a wave in my direction. Soon we were standing side by side, but not before Tashi had leaped all over me and given my face a decent bath. Holmes still looked haggard but was vastly improved since I had left him at Singapore, satisfied that the poison he had been given shortly after our arrival from Ceylon had left no permanent damage. His recovery had been slow, he informed me, but he was now in reasonably good health, though still easily fatigued. I was briefly introduced to the commander of the *Pallas* before Holmes and I made our excuses and slipped away to a quiet place where we could speak without being overheard.

"Is Rolin here?" was his first question. I answered that he was currently *en suite* with His Majesty, and had been for almost two hours. "It is imperative that we speak with him, urgently. Can this be arranged discreetly?"

I thought for a moment and decided that we could safely ask the doctor to carry a message to him from an ailing friend. I told Holmes as much.

"Very well. Let us use the time until then to review your progress at Saigon. Firstly, did you meet with de Lanessan?"

"Indeed. He is very much from the same mould as the French colonialists at Egypt. To him Britain will always be *perfide Albion!* A great exponent of forward policies, and willing to sacrifice any number of lives, French, British or native, to achieve imperial glory for France. I mentioned our explorations in Tibet, and our near-crossing the trail of Prince Henri d'Orleans. He opened up after that. After all, I am a Frenchman, and appeared willing to succumb to the blandishments of the French Naval chiefs at Saigon. Clearly, they perceived the value of having a French spy along on all of Professor Sigerson's explorations - especially in Siam and Greater Indochina, as they all term the region in anticipation.

"De Lanessan expounded at some length on his plans for the Greater Indochinese Empire - French, of course - which is to include Cochin China,

Annam, Laos, Cambodia, and lastly . . . Siam! I heard about plans to cut a canal across the Kra Isthmus between the Andaman Sea and the Gulf of Siam, and to construct a rail link from Annam to Yunnan to open up the Chinese trade for the benefit of France. As governor-general at Saigon, and with the advantage of being on the spot, his conviction of his right to decide French policy is self-evident. I can see why de Benoist and the *Quai* are concerned at his adventurism. All I can say is that, *this* far from Paris, he is even more inclined to take policy into his own hands than those gentlemen had feared. In short, he means to take Siam by fair means or foul, and present the *Quai d'Orsay* with a *fait-accompli*."

"Did he reveal anything of the strategy by which he means to accomplish this?"

"Not in so many words, but it was clear that Pavie has been instructed to raise as many complaints as he can to the Siamese, and to create the basis for dispute wherever possible."

"And is Pavie doing so?"

"He is, and scarcely a day passes that the consul does not catalogue yet another Siamese insult to French pride, or complain of the undue preference shown to the British. The situation on the Mekong River, of course, provides an inexhaustible source of conflict, and Pavie uses it to good effect."

"How did you manage to get so close to de Lanessan?" asked Holmes at last.

"Simplicity itself. I introduced myself as the emissary of the eminent - *and* Francophile - explorer, Professor Sigerson, and enquired about making a journey of exploration to the headwaters of the Red River, then travelling westwards as far as possible towards the marches of Burma. All expenses to be borne by the expedition, of course. De Lanessan is determined that France should acquire an overseas empire to match that of Queen Victoria, and that the Greater Indochinese region should become a major part of it. Our expedition is approved in principle, by the way."

"Very well," said Holmes. "And now, as I think I see our man coming out from the King's pavilion, is there anything else from Saigon that I should know about?"

The General Adviser was indeed descending the stairs from the pavilion, hand on the hilt of his ceremonial sword, and looking decidedly uncomfortable in his full regalia.

"Only that the Navy is still very much a power in the colony, and its officers are firmly committed to colonial expansion. The Admiral and the governor-general seem equally determined to acquire Siam."

Holmes spoke briefly with the commander of the *Pallas*, arranging for his baggage to be offloaded at the bar at the mouth of the Chao Phraya River. From there it would be carried by launch to our accommodations at the new Oriental Hotel, which had everywhere been recommended to us as the finest hostelry at Bangkok. We then went in search of the doctor, having first assured ourselves that Rolin was comfortably seated in the refreshment marquee, enjoying a glass of champagne chilled with ice ferried ashore from the royal yacht.

"And as you see, Doctor Smith, I am not as yet fully recovered from my fever, and wish to conserve the little strength I have." Holmes spoke with the shortness of breath and harshness of throat that were the legacies of his poisoning. "My assistant, M. Le Villard, has not been introduced to M. Rolin, and I should be most grateful, as you know him personally, if you would deliver to him a message from an old friend."

We sat at the end of the beach, in the farthest of the marquees that had been erected for the King's guests. The doctor smiled, and happily agreed to deliver the message, and to return with a reply. Holmes rapidly penned a brief message on a page torn from his notebook, folded it once, and handed it to the doctor. We sat and enjoyed the sea breeze until he returned some ten minutes later, with the message that the General Adviser was strolling in the gardens with M. Pavie, and would gladly join his old friend Professor Sigerson as soon as he was free. He then excused himself, saying that he should enquire after his medical charge, the Queen of Siam.

Holmes and I sat and discussed various matters, catching up with each others' doings since we parted at Singapore, some three weeks previously. Tashi, well-trained in obedience, lay across my feet, though it was obvious that he would have preferred chasing the sea birds perched on the boulders.

"I had some interesting discussions with some of the leading traders and merchants of Singapore," began Holmes. "To a man, they are only waiting for the French to seize part of Siam, so that they can pressure the Colonial Office and the War Office to seize the rest. Siam has few real friends at Singapore, even though they already control almost all trade with Siam.

"Also, another attempt was made on my life, not long after you sailed for Saigon. Proof ample, as if we needed it, that my poisoning was no accident. Clearly, someone must have discovered either the nature of our mission, or worse, my identity, and therefore, the continued existence of Sherlock Holmes. I know we upset a few people during our time in Egypt and the Sudan; or perhaps it started back in Persia, but I never felt that my true identity had been discovered.

"This time I was dozing in my bed at Raffles Hotel, almost asleep, when I heard the sound of someone slowly forcing open the jalousies. I rolled off the bed and placed the bolster under the sheets, bent at the middle. In the half light, with bars of shade confusing the contours, the assassin fell for the ruse. From my vantage point under the bed I saw a reed extend through the jalousies, and heard rather than saw the flight of the lethal dart. It struck the dense kapok-stuffed bolster with a satisfyingly solid thud, and remained embedded in it. The reed immediately withdrew, and I heard soft footsteps steal away down the terrace upon which my room opened. I was too weak still to pursue the assassin, and dared not raise an alarm with all the attendant public attention. I had Mycroft's man at Singapore bring me some reagent chemicals, and analysed the poison on the dart. I had to send for a comparative sample to confirm my results. No asp toxin this time! The dart was grooved, and smeared liberally with the venom of the *krait* . . . possibly the deadliest of Asian reptiles. Having read of its effects, I was at pains to keep the jalousies latched thereafter, and made sure that only picked nursing-staff attended my room. Discreet enquiries revealed that an Indian had been seen ascending the stairs to the terrace at that time, but as Singapore is home to thousands of Indians, this lead was of no use."

We lapsed into our accustomed friendly silence, both of us happy to be alive, with the added bonus of a tropical afternoon spent by the sea, with the promise of a lavish feast at evening. Soon enough, a figure detached itself from the throng surrounding the marquee where the gala feast was to be served, and approached our quiet resting place by the sea. Polished boots crunching in the sand, M. Auguste Rolin - General Adviser to the court of King Chulalongkorn - introduced himself to us.

He was quite a tall man, clearly enjoyed his food, and seemed most uncomfortable in his starched uniform, continually tugging at it.

"My new uniforms are on the way from Paris, but this outfit may well send me mad before then." He loosened his high collar a little, and sat in a canework chair beside us. "Is that beast hound or horseflesh?" he asked, pointing at Tashi. He glanced around to assure himself that we would not be overheard.

"Welcome to Siam, Mr. Holmes. Mycroft telegraphed, using a cipher of course, that you would soon arrive. I have mentioned this to nobody other than Prince Ranawongse, as Mycroft instructed. You are aware, I take it, that it was Mycroft who recommended to the Prince that the Siamese government engage my services. As a recognised expert in international jurisprudence, I have dealt with Mycroft on several occasions prior to this. I imagine it seemed a natural recommendation to make."

"He said as much in my last message from him," replied Holmes. "What is more important now, however, is this matter of death threats. I believe there has been a recent attempt on your life?"

"Indeed there has. For some time I have been feeling unwell, whereas I have always enjoyed robust health. I felt progressively weaker and weaker, over a period of about a month, then one evening I suffered the most terrible stomach cramps. I thought that perhaps the evening meal had been contaminated with botulism, so I sent a portion of each foodstuff to Doctor Smith at the hospital, and asked him to take a look at it. Contaminated it was, but not with botulism. The food was found to be laced with a moderate dosage of arsenic - not enough to kill outright, but sufficient to render me ill for several days. I took the doctor into my confidence about the death threats, and swore him to silence.

"His conclusion was that my meals had probably been poisoned for the month since I had first fallen ill. The dosage was being steadily increased, so that when death finally came, it should seem the result of a chronic malady, and be accounted as death by natural causes. The doctor thought that the poisoner had misjudged his dosage that evening, causing the severe crisis that alarmed me so.

"I immediately dismissed all of my household staff, and replaced them. A trusted cook and assistant from the doctor's own staff was made responsible for preparation of all meals. Finally, I sent my family back home to Belgium immediately."

"What of the threats?" asked Holmes. "Have you been able to retain any evidence?"

"Regrettably, no. You see, nothing was written or spoken. The first instance was finding a cockerel dangling from my front gate, with its throat newly cut. I thought that perhaps some careless servant had left it there, though why I could not imagine. The next was when my wife's pet spaniel suffered the same fate. Now we thought we must have, somehow, upset someone in the neighbourhood of our villa. The last, and unmistakable, threat came just before the illness began, and took place far from my villa. I was returning from the Prince's palace very late one night, when a stray dog, still alive but with its throat freshly cut, was tossed into my carriage. The unfortunate creature expired immediately, but I was left covered in gore, and very much shaken."

"Not surprisingly," remarked Holmes. "So, no evidence, other than that our enemy is possessed of a diabolical sense of the macabre, and will not hesitate to kill when it suits his purpose. Very well, sir. I think you had best return to your colleagues, and we can arrange to meet again more privately, but soon. But just before you go, may I enquire as to the subject of your discussion with M. Pavie?"

"Of course. He revealed, with a little prodding and encouragement, that the governor-general at Saigon desires a French protectorate over Siam, and was sounding my response to that. Clearly, the arrival of a second British vessel has alarmed him, and his judgement may have slipped a little. I doubt that he came here today with the intention of discussing this matter with me. As to meeting again, I shall send a carriage to your hotel tomorrow morning at eleven. In the evening I must attend the Ball, and later go to the Prince's house or the Foreign Ministry. Both the King and the Prince work through the night and sleep during the day, unless important ceremonies or matters of state decree otherwise. I have no choice but to conform my hours to theirs. Admittedly, it is cooler at night, but I feel they carry matters a little to excess in turning night into day."

He shook hands with both of us, and hurried back to the marquee, adjusting his collar and tunic as he walked.

"More poisoning!" remarked Holmes. "Is it the same hand behind both campaigns? Whatever, we must remain alert at all times, and assume that someone knows who and what we are."

Just then an enormous brass gong was struck repeatedly, the note ascending and descending before dying away. The King's guests were summoned to the marquee, where a lavish banquet had been laid out for our enjoyment, to be followed by an entertainment. Rolin had quietly arranged our invitations several days before, when Mycroft informed him that Holmes was to arrive on the *Pallas*.

CHAPTER XXVII

31st May 1893
Bangkok, Siam

LATE AT NIGHT the small steamer *Gladys* disembarked many of the King's foreign guests at the Oriental Hotel jetty. The staff saw us to our rooms, and made sure we had all the items required for a comfortable nights' sleep - or at least as comfortable as was possible in the sweltering heat of Bangkok.

Unlike Singapore, the Siamese had not introduced the *punkah*, and the air was still and humid. Our muslin nets kept the mosquitoes at bay, but their musical humming made us aware that they were there, awaiting the least lifting of the fine gauze. After a month's separation, Tashi would not let me leave him in the kitchen courtyard, and we finally settled for tying his leash to the veranda post on the terrace outside our bedroom doors.

His low growling, as the servant boys slipped into our rooms with tea, waked us. The doors were impossible to lock, or even barricade effectively. Rather disturbing, in view of the attempts on Holmes's life, but my previous room at the Bangkok Hotel had been no more secure. We should have to rig some form of alarm to warn of intruders near the bed. Tashi was altogether too trusting to rely upon as a sentinel, though anyone who threatened either Holmes or myself could expect to find himself pinned to the ground, with those awesome fangs at his throat.

After bathing, using a dipper to scoop cool water from an enormous earthenware jar, I knocked at the door to Holmes's room, and we went down to breakfast. We decided on the small, sand-floored terrace, where cane-work tables with comfortable matching chairs were already filling with hotel guests and Bangkok residents come to enjoy a proper English breakfast. Through an arched doorway we could see a long bar, which apparently dispensed libations at all hours. Imbibers, some in seamen's attire, occupied several stools.

As we ate, rather lightly after the feast of the previous evening, Holmes read out snippets from the *Bangkok Times*. This has become a habit, on those infrequent occasions when we are in a city or town large enough to boast a daily newspaper. I rather approve of the practice, as I am one of those who either reads every word in a tabloid or none at all. With Holmes reading the news, I have the advantage of judicious selections of important news, as well as the odd strange tale.

There was little that we hadn't already learned of from the General Adviser; a good deal of reporting about the air of panic caused by the arrival of French warships in the heart of the city.

At precisely eleven o'clock, a handsome carriage drawn by two fine horse pulled up under the portico of the Oriental Hotel, and the driver asked for Professor Sigerson and party. We were soon jostling our way along the New Road, occasionally crossing humped bridges spanning the canals of Bangkok. Tashi caused a great deal of comment, sitting up in our carriage as we made our way through swarms of Chinese, Siamese, Hindoo, Lascar, and every other type of Asiatic, for Bangkok is a most cosmopolitan city. None had ever seen a hound even half his size, as the pariah dogs of Siam are but poor excuses for a dog, forever cringing from the expected kick.

The view along the canals from the middle of these raised bridges is most interesting. Some are quite broad, and crowded with small craft of all kinds. Half the commerce of Bangkok is seemingly conducted from these varied skiffs and boats. On these floating stalls can be seen foodstuffs of all kinds, pots and pans, cottons and sarongs, cheap jewellery and trinkets, charms and amulets, and all manner of other goods, mingled in with floating barber shops, dye-houses, itinerant musicians, fortune-tellers, rice-wine sellers, etc.. The water of these large canals was inevitably covered with the detritus of trade and humanity, and looked decidedly suspect.

From time to time we crossed a smaller canal, where the water was far cleaner. Here there was little traffic, and broad canopies of bamboos and rain-trees met overhead, creating tranquil green colonnades, with here and there a peaked thatch roof or a jetty with decorated pavilion, from which naked brown children leaped and dived into the cool waters of the canal.

After some time our carriage turned from the road onto a smaller lane, which ran parallel to one of these smaller canals. A few more minutes of driving and we halted in front of a spacious villa in the European style. A Hindoo doorman greeted us, and showed us into a comfortable study, where I sat in a cane-work armchair while Holmes briefly inspected the library. Mostly legal volumes, with the occasional section devoted to literature or popular novels, as far as I could tell from where I sat. Tashi remained outside, lolling in the shade of the carriage.

Rolin soon joined us, and after greeting us warmly, rang the small hand-bell that rested on the black lacquered table at his elbow. Almost immediately the door opened, and two Siamese maids, clearly sisters, came into the room, bowing and nodding as he ordered whisky for us all, with soda. They returned a moment later, bowing as they passed in front of us, then kneeling at our sides as they expertly poured whisky and siphoned soda for each of us. That done, the maids bowed their way out of the room backwards. Moments later they returned with trays of freshly cut pineapple, and those delicious purple-skinned fruits, cleverly cut to reveal snow-white segments.

Hospitality thus dealt with, Rolin, like any good lawyer, came straight to business: in this case, the threat to his life, and why he believed it was directly connected to the threat to an independent Siam.

"I think I shall first outline the most recent developments here at Siam," began the General Adviser. "You'll need to know something of the background. I suppose I should start with the negotiations to settle Siam's border with the French on the Mae Kong River. It is now abundantly clear to me that the French do not want the matter settled. They prefer it remain unresolved as an excuse for intervention in the future. In early March I met with Pavie at the Oriental Hotel. He brought to my attention a message from Develle, the French Foreign Minister, giving him instructions to claim the left bank of the Mae Kong for France. I immediately responded in the *Bangkok Times,* as some of the press reports from Paris showed me that the French public, and their current Cabinet, were being deliberately and cynically inflamed over the Siam Question.

"A few days later Pavie officially notified me of his instructions to claim the left bank as the border, the first we really knew of France's true intentions. Captain Jones was as incensed as I was, and at that time we both thought the British would step in to prevent French adventurism. We were both proved wrong, and have had our knuckles rapped for it. Two days later the *Lutin* arrived unannounced at Bangkok, but I advised the Siamese to remain diplomatic and greet the French as guests, even though she is a warship. I even attended a *diner* with the French captain and officers, and arranged for them to be seated in front of the King at a public ceremony. The next day we learned that the *Lutin* would remain at Siam pending further instructions. Throughout the rest of March the French created numerous disputes over legal claims by French *protégés* against Siamese in the border areas. The King allocated budget to build forts in the disputed areas, from his own purse.

"By the middle of April His Majesty, myself and the Prince were discussing how to counter a French attack on Bangkok. The Siamese were determined to resist. I counselled them to do so without unnecessary provocation. Rumours flew around Bangkok, especially regarding the intentions of the French warships. I wanted to balance the threat with ships from other countries; I talked with the German consul and the American diplomat Eaton, in order to gauge their support for Siamese resistance. Despite his poor health, His Majesty even attended the Foreign Affairs Ball, which was considered most unusual.

"Many of the foreign community had their suitcases packed. I wrote again to the *Bangkok Times* to scotch some of the wilder rumours. I'm sure these originated from the offices of the *Siam Free Press,* though they're more careful these days what they print. In the middle of April a British gun-boat arrived, but that didn't halt the disputes on the Mae Kong. One report had it that a French resident told Siamese officials that France was claiming the whole of the river, under an agreement with Siam. Pavie then claimed the island of Samit, as well as demanding delimitation of the frontier, and the immediate settlement of several outstanding disputes.

"I strongly suspect that behind all this agitation is the Governor General at Saigon. De Lanessan wants to force Siam to retaliate with force, thus providing the pretext he needs to take military action and declare Siam a French protectorate. At the end of last month we received messages from Lord Rosebery advising Siam not to expect too much of Britain, and that they should transfer negotiations to Paris. I suppose in that way he meant to escape the influence of the *colons* at Saigon. Early this month there was more fighting on the border, and on Khone Island; then Stung Treng was occupied. Later Captain Jones's sources at Saigon informed him there were European officers amongst the casualties there, and the French thought they may at last have their pretext.

"The next day, after seeing my wife off to Brussels, there was a Council of Ministers. Lord Rosebery had telegraphed that an approach to the Russians to mediate might succeed. The British Ambassador at Paris agreed, so long as the Americans, who had already been asked to mediate, were notified and approved. I drafted messages to Paris, Washington and St. Petersburg, and sent them off. The next morning I was informed that the Siamese had captured a Captain Thoreaux, the French commander at the battles on the Mae Kong. Now the French *really* thought they had a pretext. The protests and demands increased in frequency and belligerence.

"I visited Jones, who showed me some reassuring messages from England. Then I sent off a dispatch to Reuters giving the true version of the incident, in which the French advanced into Siamese territory and their Annamite troops fired first. I also stated that Siam had no desire for war, and intended to continue negotiating. Apparently there has been great public agitation at Paris regarding this affair.

"Recently Jones has been pessimistic about British support, and we heard that the Americans have declined to mediate. Just last week it was found that the French had brought in a cannon without declaring it, which caused a row, and now the Siamese have it from somewhere that the British will refuse entry of arms from Tavoy in Burma if the French blockade Bangkok. Now the King talks of breaking with England, and I have to talk him out of it. Most depressing all round, really. Just last week I lunched privately with Pavie. He regards war as inevitable. I told him I am not an agent of the British, and that even were I to counsel surrender of the left bank the Siamese would fight regardless. I stressed that my intention was to avoid providing the British with a pretext to demand, in their turn, a large part of Siam. He seemed unconvinced. I suggested guarantees of neutrality, but he paid no attention.

"Recently the *Siam Free Press* has taken to publishing false reports of my activities, making it seem as though I have advised submission to French demands, in an attempt to discredit me with the Siamese. I was forced to demand a retraction, and may yet prosecute. I have already told you of Pavie's proposals yesterday at Si Chang Island about declaring Siam a French protectorate.

"And that, I believe, brings us up to date. Well, gentlemen, I hope you will join me for lunch. Then I think I must rest a little. Tonight there is a Ball at your hotel, and I am expected to provide music on the piano while Fusco's orchestra takes a break. I shall see you there if you attend, though I retire early when I have the opportunity, assuming my presence is not required at the Foreign Ministry."

After a rather undistinguished meal we returned to rest at our hotel, refusing the sight-seeing tours offered by the Indian guides and rickashaw boys at the hotel entrance. Tashi was once again tied to the railing outside our room, where he was content to wait whenever we left, knowing we would return. The room-boys were not happy at first, being fearful of so large a dog, but they soon befriended him and tried to feed him sweetmeats. We always found these uneaten when we returned. The first step in his training had been never to accept food from a stranger or from anyone whom I had not previously approved. This I would do by having them offer food, and I would command Tashi in Tibetan to eat. After that he could accept food from them.

"In the normal run of things attending a Ball is not my idea of time well-spent," said Holmes, as we descended to the main floor of the hostelry. "In this instance, however, we have the opportunity to meet many of the foreign community at close quarters. As small as the European community is here at Bangkok, it is likely that someone here this evening is involved in the plot against Rolin."

We crossed the foyer and entered the Ballroom, which was lit by the new electric lamps of which the management was so proud. The room was decorated in the Italianate style so popular at Bangkok these days, and was already crowded with foreigners - many of whom we had seen at Si Chang island - and their wives. All the *grande monde* of Bangkok! A number of Siamese notables were present, their colourful uniforms vying with the more extravagantly dressed of the Europeans, but none of their womenfolk attended. Officers from the various foreign ships then in port, smartly turned out in starched tropical whites, congregated in clusters around the bar servery where whiskies and strong potions were dispensed. Everywhere there were Siamese servants in traditional Siamese pantaloons and white monkey-jackets, bowing low as they offered around trays filled with glasses of champagne and beer, or *canapés*.

It was a colourful scene, and the room was filled with lively conversation. Our friend Doctor Smith greeted us first, then immediately collared a passing servant. Champagne in hand, we surveyed the scene. Amongst the Siamese was the Prince, talking with Rolin by the tall windows overlooking the river. With them were several other Siamese nobles, all in European dress, but once again, none of their women were present.

Pavie was there; deep in conversation with the commander of one of the French warships that Rolin had informed us were anchored at the French legation only a few hundred yards upstream. I noticed that several of the diplomatic corps were also gathered together in conclave, while their wives chatted amongst themselves. Despite the festive appearance of the gathering there was a perceptible tension in the room, with occasional raised voices betraying the serious nature of some of the conversations taking place. I was reminded that this was a city that anticipated trouble in one form or another in the days to come.

Perhaps sensing that distraction was required Rolin moved to the grand piano on the band-stand and proceeded to play some popular melodies. He played well and the atmosphere lightened perceptibly. Diplomats returned to their wives, the sailors quietened, and polite, meaningless conversation could be heard on all sides. Champagne flowed and good humour prevailed. After several tunes from the piano a small orchestra of Siamese musicians took the band-stand and tuned their instruments. The master-of-ceremonies made a short speech, introducing first the Siamese royals present, to much applause, and then the principal foreign dignitaries. The band struck up a lively waltz, and the dance floor was soon crowded with couples. I noticed that the band-master was the proprietor of the Bangkok Hotel, where I had stayed for the few days I had spent at Bangkok after arriving from Saigon.

I had passed those days quite happily in exploring streets and markets and some of the many temples of this remarkable capital city of Siam. At the central assembly grounds known as the Pramane I had spent lazy hours lying under a rain-tree, admiring the spectacle of thousands of kites aloft on the gusting north-east monsoon winds prevalent during this season. I bought myself a small kite for a couple of *satang,* and sent it aloft. Soon I had my own circle of curious Siamese, so I had also practised my Siamese among the people there. Here it was that I had found that to a Frenchman, who sings his words anyway, the tonal differences that convey meaning came with ease. My thoughts returned from these recollections to the present moment. The Ball, swirling and noisy, was becoming more animated by the moment.

Soon the more gregarious naval officers were cutting in on couples and the occasion was in full swing. Holmes remained to one side chatting aimlessly with the doctor while I made a point of introducing myself to one of the very few young, single women there. A most attractive young lady of Denmark, whose father, as I soon found out, was a leading teak-wood forester in the northern states. She danced divinely, but regrettably, all too soon a lieutenant from the *Pallas* cut me out.

As I rejoined Holmes and the doctor, a ripple of whispers spread across the room, originating from the entrance to the Ballroom. Heads turned, dancers hesitated, and conversation ceased. Only the orchestra continued unabated, now playing a lively waltz. A party led by Lord Coledale was at the door. With him were the captain and officers of his yacht, splendidly uniformed, and several men and women who had formed his party at Si Chang island. Lord Coledale himself was immaculate in evening clothes, his silver-topped ebony stick held nonchalantly in spotlessly white-gloved hands. A monocle flashed in one eye, reflecting the electric lamplight.

For all this, the focus of all attention was not the English lord; rather it was the woman next to him, entering on the arm of a well-dressed Englishman who, though still handsome, was showing signs of the dissipation brought on by excess. She had left behind the fresh bloom of youth, but in its place was a mature and radiant beauty. Her cheekbones were high and her face oval. Her nose was perfection, and her figure was still that of the girl she had once been. In repose, her mouth was serene yet sultry, but it was when she turned to Lord Coledale and smiled that her face simply dazzled the eye. Their party moved into the room, and the noise resumed, as the guests returned to their dancing or conversation.

When I turned back to ask Holmes what were our plans for the morrow, I was astounded to see, for the first and only time, a look of astonished amazement on his normally inexpressive features. His gaze was fixed on the woman who had just entered, and he was muttering to himself.

CHAPTER XXVIII

AT THIS MOMENT, as the clock in the hallway struck eleven, I closed the leather-covered notebook and decided it was time to retire for the evening. Holmes had not yet returned, but that was not unusual for him when on a case. I was reaching to turn down the lamp by which I had been reading when I heard a cab pull to a halt at our door, and the doorbell rang.

I had no idea as to who could be calling at this hour: Holmes had his key, unless he had somehow lost it, and I was not expecting anyone. My first thoughts were of Holmes's warning that these were dangerous times, and that we should remain on guard against further violence. I glanced out of the corner of a darkened window at Camden House across the street, from whence Colonel Moran had fired at Holmes on the night of my friend's return.

All the windows were closed, and at the corner of the street I could see an uniformed constable pacing slowly back and forth, keeping an eye on the street. The cabbie waited patiently, and I noticed a mariner's duffel-bag strapped on the baggage rack at the rear. From my vantage point I was unable to see who was ringing at our door, and decided to go downstairs before Mrs. Hudson opened the front door.

As I came out onto our landing I saw that worthy lady emerging from her apartment by the foot of the stairs. I called softly to her that I thought it better that I should answer the door. Mrs. Hudson nodded and smiled as she went back into her hallway, closing the door behind her. Just to be on the safe side, I hurried back into our sitting room and slipped my revolver into the pocket of my dressing gown. At the foot of the stairs I paused as the bell rang again, then crossed to the front door and slipped the chain onto the latch. I opened the door a small distance, ready to slam it shut in an instant if necessary.

A complete stranger stood before me, his hand raised to ring again at the doorbell. He was swarthy of complexion, clean-shaven, with coal-black hair tied back in a sailor's pigtail. He was of middle height, but his physique was solidly muscled, and I noticed that his hand was callused and roughened, as though he had been pulling on strong ropes.

Just as our caller opened his mouth to address me it dawned upon me. Sun darkened skin, rough hands . . . and the stance of a seaman! Calling at Holmes's door in the middle of the night! I had been so engrossed in reading the Journals of Francois le Villard that I had forgotten that the man himself was expected to arrive at any moment.

"Good evening," said our visitor, in excellent English with more than a trace of a French accent. "Unless I am much mistaken, you must be Doctor Watson."

"I am indeed," I replied. "And you, sir, are M. Francois le Villard."

"And most honoured I am to make your acquaintance at last, Doctor. I take it Mr. Holmes is away at present?"

"He is," said I, hurrying to remove the door-chain and open the door wide to greet this most welcome of visitors. "And I can't tell you when he will return. But please, do come in. That's your bag on the rack, I take it? Let me fetch it for you."

"Not necessary, Doctor Watson," le Villard replied, and he returned to pay off his driver and collect his single bag. I stepped back into the hall, and ushered him in past me.

"I can't tell you how much pleasure it gives me to finally meet you in person, M. le Villard," I said as we shook hands vigorously. "In fact, I have just this moment put aside your Journal, and now here you are. Wonderful!"

"And I have, for many years, wished to meet the biographer of Sherlock Holmes face to face. And here *you* are!"

Soon we were comfortably seated before the fire in our sitting room. I stirred the embers and threw in a scuttle of washed coal, then went to the tantalus and busied myself pouring brandy for each of us. Le Villard's bag lay in the corner, and he had removed his coat. I had rarely met a man seemingly so at ease with himself and his surroundings. Then I reflected that, had he been otherwise, he would likely have been unable to remain with Holmes for the three long and arduous years they had travelled together.

Le Villard, in response to my query, informed me that the clipper *White Bird*, which had brought him to London, had berthed at eight o'clock that evening at the East India Docks wharf. At ten he had accompanied *Señor* Jose Felipe Azcevado Marques to the St. Pancras Hotel, where he had dined with the old gentleman before coming on to Baker Street.

"I wasn't quite sure what Holmes expected me to do, so I kept my kit with me," said he.

"You must stay the night here, le Villard," said I. "I don't know when he'll return, but I'm sure he will want to see you as soon as he possibly can. You'll find the sofa quite comfortable, and Mrs. Hudson provides an excellent breakfast."

We sipped our brandy after warming it on the hearth, and talked. I had a thousand questions to ask about their travels and adventures, but did not want to importune our guest so late at night, and so soon after his arrival. Also, I did not wish to trespass into Holmes's investigation. I contented myself with making general conversation about the miracle of Holmes's seeming return from the dead, London's weather, horse racing in France, and the game of *bezique* (which I had taken up recently following the death of Thurston, my former weekly rival at billiards). Le Villard, it seems, is an *aficionado,* and we soon agreed to play a few games when time allowed.

When Holmes had not returned at half past midnight I suggested that perhaps we should turn in.

"An excellent idea, Doctor Watson. I confess I am fatigued a little by the unaccustomed bustle of a big city."

I made le Villard comfortable with pillow and quilt, stoked the fire and placed the brass-framed fireguard in front of it, and retired to my bedroom upstairs. As I opened the leather-covered book once again, it occurred to me that I hadn't thought to ask about the missing volumes of those Journals, so suddenly come to life with the arrival at 221B of Holmes's other biographer.

CHAPTER XXIX

31st May 1893
Bangkok, Siam

"IT IS SHE! It could be no other. But she is dead! Drowned! Can this be so?" Holmes gripped my forearm in his vice-like fingers, and continued.

"But that is certainly Godfrey Norton, a little gone to seed, but unmistakably Norton. So it must be, le Villard, it *must* be her!"

Having already translated many of Doctor Watson's tales for Holmes's legion of French admirers, I was familiar with the name Godfrey Norton, and the events that took place during the investigation of *A Scandal in Bohemia*.

"Irene Adler, Holmes?" I asked, comprehending at last the reasons for his reaction to her appearance here at the Ball. "Do you mean that . . . that is Irene Adler?"

"I do indeed, le Villard. There could be no duplicate of that smile. Though how she comes to be here at Bangkok, alive, is entirely beyond me."

"Bear in mind, Holmes," I gently chided him, "that you are also dead, so far as the world is concerned. Two ghosts appearing at the same Ball is more than I can stand. I think I need whisky. Can I bring you one?" I turned towards the bar, and heard Holmes call after me.

"I think I shall need a double, my friend, if you would be so kind."

The Ball whirled around me as I carried whiskies back for Holmes and myself. The doctor had returned, and was speaking with Holmes as I came up to them.

"Oh! You mean Mrs. Norton. Lovely, isn't she? And such a splendid singing voice. More than he deserves, if you ask me."

"They live here, in Bangkok?" enquired Holmes.

"Not exactly, Professor Sigerson. Norton had a legal practice here for a year or so, but seems to have found Singapore a more rewarding trove to plunder. He has business here still, however, and comes to Siam two or three times each year, sometimes staying for a month or two. Mrs. Norton sometimes accompanies him, as she became close to some of her Siamese students when Norton was living here."

"Students?" Holmes raised a quizzical eyebrow.

"Mrs. Norton became bored doing nothing, and I suggested that she give lessons in music and singing to ladies of the court, and daughters of the nobility. It seems she was a singer of some renown before her marriage."

"Indeed she was, Doctor Smith."

"So you do know her, Professor, after all," asked the doctor, who was no fool.

"Yes, though by her professional name. It was long ago, however, prior to her marriage. You don't seem terribly impressed by her husband, if I may say so. Why is that?"

"It is fairly common knowledge that the reason for his departure from Siam had a lot to do with his, shall we say, unsatisfactory habits."

"Was Norton ever your patient, Doctor Smith?"

"Never, sir! Why do you ask?"

"Because I should hesitate to ask you to breach your confidential relationship with a patient, Doctor. And yet, she was once the most glorious, independent spirit ever raised up by womanhood. Would you tell me more of his 'unsatisfactory habits', Doctor, or is that asking too much?"

"Not at all, Professor. It is all too common knowledge. Simply put, few were willing to entrust their legal affairs to a lawyer, however handsome and persuasive, who was as likely to be found in one of the local opium dens or brothels as in his chambers. His abusive manner to his charming wife when in his cups did not sit so well either in a small community such as this. I believe that when at Singapore he behaves himself somewhat. I suppose it was clear even to him that he could not carry on forever as he was, or he would soon run out of congenial places to go. I suspect that half the reason for his retaining business in Siam is so that he has an excuse to come here, conclude his business, and go on a binge. Sad, especially for her."

"So you know her quite well?"

"She has been my patient on occasion, when his abuse has become physical. That must remain in confidence, Professor. As a doctor I should not speak of it, but as a man, well, frankly, it makes my blood boil to see such a lovely creature so ill-treated. I cannot understand, for the life of me, why she remains with him. But I have said too much," said the doctor, setting down his still full glass of champagne. "Forgive me, I think I may have had a little too much of this excellent champagne."

"On the contrary, Doctor Smith. Forgive me for asking. And thank you for being so frank."

I followed Holmes out onto the terrace overlooking the broad river, still dotted with craft large and small, even at this late hour, all but the smallest carrying a lantern of some kind.

"I must speak with her," said Holmes. "But I dare not risk her using my real name, with so many English speakers around. Norton has never seen me face to face, at least not as Sherlock Holmes, so that is not a problem."

"Perhaps I could arrange to dance with her, and ask her to meet you here? A chance encounter while taking the air, you see."

"That would be the best way, I agree. Use my real name. But warn her in advance not to show surprise, whatever you may say. Irene Adler is the coolest woman I ever knew. She will cause no difficulties. Oh! Do come back shortly after she comes here, just in case Norton should come looking for her. I should hate to compromise her, and set that brute off again."

I adore dancing, and I flatter myself that I am not unattractive to the opposite sex. Thus it was the most natural thing in the world that I should approach Mrs. Norton, and ask for a dance. She graciously accepted my hand, and we danced. She, too, danced divinely, and I could see why Holmes admired her so.

We had travelled together through many countries, usually far from civilisation as we know it, and female companionship had usually been the farthest thing from my own mind during those periods. But when we did reach a town or city, I was always only too happy to enjoy the company of young ladies, when chance crossed our paths for us.

Holmes, however, had always seemed either immune or indifferent to their charms. This had never seemed unusual. As Doctor Watson once remarked, 'He never spoke of the softer passions except with a gibe and a sneer'.

Somehow, this was different. I had rarely seen Holmes throw caution to the wind, as perhaps he had just done, and certainly never when there was a woman involved. As a man, I had to admit that his taste in women was superb. As a Frenchman, I could only admire his devotion to this one particular woman. As a reader of *A Scandal in Bohemia*, it had always seemed to me that Holmes must have been, in his own scientific way, in love somehow with Irene Adler. That he had been witness - albeit in disguise - to her marriage to Norton, accorded perfectly with his devotion to his art of detection and deduction.

But to my mind the give-away had always been her cabinet photograph, his chosen memento of that interesting case. According to Doctor Watson it still hung in the alcove of the sitting-room at 221B Baker Street, positioned so that when Holmes raised his head as he sat in his high-backed leather armchair, his gaze naturally fell upon her portrait.

"You dance very well, Miss Adler," I said softly.

She drew back a little as we danced on, and scrutinised my face.

"How is that you know my maiden name, sir? Very few here do."

Her American accent was a reminder of her origins in New Jersey, before she attained fame as a diva at opera houses from St. Petersburg to Manaus.

"We have never met, Miss Adler, but do not be alarmed. I have a message for you. By pure chance, Mr. Sherlock Holmes is here, at the Ball, tonight, and would like to speak briefly with you."

Shock registered briefly in her eyes, followed by a spark and twinkle.

"Surely you are in error, sir," she mocked. "Mr. Holmes died several years ago, as all the world knows."

"Indeed not, Miss Adler. He is no more dead than are you! If my memory doesn't fail me, you perished, along with a steamer full of tourists, on Lake Como several years ago."

"*Touché, M'sieur.*" She paused briefly, as we danced on. "It seems you know a great deal about my past. Is Sherlock Holmes really still alive?"

"He is indeed. You have my word upon it."

"May I ask the name of the bearer of this most incredible news?"

"You may, *madame*. Francois le Villard, Inspector of the *Police Judiciare*, Paris, at your service."

"Very well, M. Le Villard. Please tell me where Mr. Holmes is to be found?"

"I think you will find him on the terrace."

"Then I think I shall visit the powder room, following which I shall need a little fresh air on the terrace. I hope we will meet again, and thank you."

The music had finished moments before, and M. Rolin was back at the grand piano. Irene Adler, as I could only think of her, returned to her party, collected her reticule, and excused herself.

I went to the bar, and ordered another whisky-and-soda. Several minutes later, glass emptied, I strolled out onto the terrace. Silhouetted against the moonlit expanse of river were Holmes and Irene Adler, standing side by side separated by a decorous space, looking out over the river. I coughed discreetly as I approached them. Just before then, I overheard Miss Adler, or rather,

Mrs. Norton, say, "I assure you, Mr. Holmes, much as I appreciate your concern, you need not trouble yourself over this matter".

They turned to me, and that wonderful smile lit her face.

"You spoke the truth, M. Le Villard, though I confess I dared not believe it until I saw with my own eyes. We were once adversaries, of a sort, but that all seems so long ago. Matching wits with the great Sherlock Holmes was great fun, and I miss those days in London something fierce. But here we all are, and two of us are dead! How very droll!" Her laughter was like a rippling brook, or temple chimes in a soft breeze.

"Irene!" The stern, slightly slurred voice came from the arched doorway to the Ballroom.

"How dare you embarrass me when I am with Lord Coledale! You have no idea how much this may cost me. Come inside at once. Who is that you're flirting with, by the way?"

Godfrey Norton, somewhat the worse for drink, lurched towards us. He thrust out his hand towards Holmes.

"Godfrey Norton, Barrister-at-Law, sir. In case you should require legal service of any kind. Any kind at all! And who may you be, didn't quite catch the name. Mine's Godfrey Norton."

Without waiting for a reply, he turned to his wife.

" Come inside, my dear. Mustn't keep his lordship waiting,"

Seizing her elbow, Norton steered Irene Adler back into the ballroom. As they disappeared from view Irene Adler looked over her shoulder at us. It seemed as though she were pleading for forgiveness for her husband's atrocious manners. Holmes turned and looked once more at the river traffic.

"Life is full of the most surprising twists and turns of fate, le Villard. It never ceases to amaze."

He said no more, and several minutes later suggested we return to the Ball, and carry on looking for leads to our poisoners. The first person to speak with us, as we passed their party, was Godfrey Norton, who leapt to his feet, full of *faux bonhomie* and apologies.

"Professor Sigerson, please forgive my unintended rudeness, I had no idea it was you I was addressing. We are most pleased to welcome such an eminent explorer to Siam, where I have connections of every sort. Please accept my card, sir. And may I introduce my esteemed client, Lord Coledale . . . Mister Barnes, captain of His Lordship's yacht . . . Miss Darnley, and her companion, Mrs. FitzGerald . . . and Mr. Quiney, aide to His Lordship."

"Professor Sigerson!" said Lord Coledale. "Surely I've heard of you. Tibet, Turkistan, and so forth, right?"

"I admit that is true," said Holmes. "May I introduce my assistant, and naturalist, M. Francois le Villard. We travel in a deal less comfort than yourselves, in our line of work. I was at Si Chang Island yesterday, and couldn't help but admire your magnificent yacht."

"*Sirdar*. She's rather a beauty, ain't she? Perhaps, if you're here for a few days, you'll accept my invitation to come aboard. A few drinks, dinner, a hand or two at whist? And you must come as well, Norton, with your charmin' wife, of course. Shall we say the evenin' after next? Splendid! Now, how about some more of that vile champagne they're servin' here!"

All those in his party laughed at his wit, with the exception of Irene Adler, and his aide, Quiney.

Holmes accepted his invitation, made our excuses and farewells, and we went in search of the doctor. He had, however, left to attend at the Queen's Palace. The Prince and his Siamese had also departed and with him had gone the General Adviser. The orchestra was still in fine form, but Holmes was ready to leave, so we retired to our rooms, and to our beds.

As we passed out of the Ballroom a small fellow followed us out, hurried past us, and turned around to block our way. He was dressed in a checked suit that was too tight, with an imitation-gold watch chain across his grubby waistcoat. Small *pince-nez* perched on his thin nose, and his pale eyes flickered around curiously under bushy ginger-coloured eyebrows. I noticed a note-pad in his waistcoat pocket, and a sharpened pencil-stub tucked behind his left ear. 'A left-handed reporter', I thought to myself. This turned out to be correct. His speech was the Irish of working Dubliners.

'Tell me sir, haven't I seen you before somewhere? I'm certain of it, but can't place where or when."

"Well, I have been a public figure from time to time, sir, when not exploring. Perhaps you attended one of my lectures?"

"No, I should remember that. It's something else, something that seems odd, but . . ."

"I'm afraid you must excuse us. I have had a tiring day, and wish to retire. Perhaps it will come to you sometime later. Goodnight, sir."

Holmes attempted to pass, but the little Irishman held his ground a moment.

"My apologies, but the resemblance, the resemblance! My dear sir, you so closely *resemble* someone who is dead . . ."

"I shall overlook your unfortunate choice of phrasing. I assure you that, however dead I may look, I am Professor Olaf Sigerson, at your service, sir, and very much alive. And you, sir, are . . ?"

The man introduced himself as Lillie, of the *Siam Free Press,* before stepping aside to allow us to pass.

"A fair example of the breed, le Villard. Reporters are rarely charming, as I am sure you have noticed before now."

"But he seems to think he knows who you are."

"Let him check! Mycroft will have done a thorough job, and Lillie will find ample evidence of Professor Olaf Sigerson's existence and eminent reputation both."

Before retiring I fed Tashi with some cold-cuts I had rescued from the buffet supper. We hung small bells on the door to Holmes's room and scattered glass marbles on the floor between his bed and the doorway.

CHAPTER XXX

1st June 1893
Paknam, Siam

A HACKNEY ARRIVED just before seven o'clock, sent by Rolin. It seemed that Prince Svasti - another of the King's brothers - had roused him, with an invitation for him and his party to accompany the ministers to see the King at his fortifications at the mouth of the Chao Phraya River.

A special train was to depart on the newly opened railway line to Paknam at half past seven o'clock, and Holmes and I arrived at the railway station with only moments to spare. We had left Tashi in the care of one of the hotel staff, who was paid to keep him fed throughout the day. I introduced Tashi to the boy, and left his special dish, as he had been trained to eat only from that or from my hand.

Rolin had kept seats for us. We settled back to enjoy the scenery; the train steamed through rice-fields and coconut palm plantations that from time to time allowed a view of the river, and of Paknam.

At nine o'clock we arrived at Paknam, and transferred by the King's launch to the *Maha Chakkri*. From a distance - as we had seen her at Si Chang Island - she appeared to be a luxurious liner, graceful of line, with a sweeping sheer and an aggressive reversed stem. At closer quarters it was clear that she had a more serious purpose as well. Mounted on her decks in the bows and amidships were armoured installation positions for heavy guns, some of which were already in place, and she was obviously heavily built as befits a ship-of-war.

Our entire party was graciously received by the King, and settled down to an enormous Siamese breakfast. Rice *congee*, numerous curries and condiments, shark's fin, salt-preserved boiled eggs and every kind of tropical fruit were served. I had to admire the appetites of the Siamese princes.

Following breakfast we were taken by barge to a jetty on the West bank, then by a short Decauville railway track to the new fortifications commanding the mouth of the river. I noticed that the King placed Rolin at his side wherever they went, even on the barge and railcar.

The King's party inspected the seven brick towers, still awaiting their final casing of earthworks, each housing a heavy calibre Armstrong gun. These enormous cannon remain concealed until required, when they are raised hydraulically, aimed and fired, then sink slyly out of view after the shot. Three deafening shots were fired at a target in the river, delighting the King when a hit was made with the first shell. Several shells malfunctioned, but the King seemed highly diverted by it all nonetheless, inspecting every aspect of the installation.

Rolin found time to point out to us the locations where the Siamese had sunk old ships, filled with rocks and concrete, to create an underwater barrier to ships attempting to force the mouth of the river.

"A narrow channel is still open for navigation, and can be sealed with mines and more sunken ships on three days notice. Hopefully, matters will not come to that, but I fear the French at Saigon intend to provoke a conflict, whatever Siam does to conciliate them. Their *parti colon* lobby in the French government will support them, once it is done, and they mean to get away with it."

By two o'clock we were back aboard the *Maha Chakkri*, and Rolin was closeted with the King and his ministers in a salon on the main deck. The royal yacht departed for Bangkok, several hours of slow steaming away up the winding Chao Phraya. Holmes and I wandered about the yacht for a while, in company with an English lieutenant in the King's service.

"Most interesting commission I've ever 'ad," he said. "The designers, bless their souls, were told about the size of the King's family, and provided staterooms for a legion of 'em. But they could never 'ave imagined this," he said. "Seems everyone in the Palace wants to come on these jaunts, and this 'ere ship is packed like a steamer full o' day-trippers back 'ome. See them canvas screens there . . . No man is allowed forrard o' there, except 'is Majesty o' course. Only 'undreds and 'undreds of the royal women an' children. Same thing below! Makes runnin' a ship quite a challenge."

At half past five we were nearing the Palace jetty, when a servant came for us. We were shown into a small library, where Rolin was seated alongside Prince Ranawongse. Both rose as we entered. When Rolin introduced us to the Prince, he used Holmes's real name, as had been agreed.

"It is a pleasure to welcome you to Siam, Mr. Holmes," said the Prince. "At present I am the only one, other than our General Adviser, who knows you are here. I have not as yet informed His Majesty, who knows your reputation well from the Scandinavian royal families. It is my brother Svasti, however, who is your greatest local admirer. He has a complete collection of Doctor Watson's case histories, and was shocked at your 'demise'."

"Thank you, Prince Ranawongse. I had no idea my reputation extended so far afield. I think we must leave matters as they are - perhaps some day I can revert to my real character, but until we have a better idea who is threatening M. Rolin, it is better that all know me as Professor Sigerson."

Rolin spoke, saying that as we had berthed already, he had arranged that we would call on the Prince the following evening, at his Palace.

"Unfortunately, decisions had to be made concerning reinforcements to be sent to the Mekong. Also, the London Legation seems to be balking at dispatching the arms and ammunition we have requested, and that required discussion as well. I shall call for you at eight o'clock tomorrow evening then. I must accompany the Prince to the Ministry, so I shall leave you now. A carriage has been arranged to take you to the Oriental Hotel. Good evening, gentlemen."

He and the Prince left together. A few minutes later Holmes and I mounted to the main deck of the *Maha Chakkri* and caught our first sight of the King's Palace. The King's cortege was winding slowly out of sight around the base of the massive, crenellated walls, manned by hundreds of helmeted soldiers at the ramparts. The royal children slept peacefully in their litters as they were carried in procession to their Palace home, exhausted, after the days of revelry by the sea.

We, too, were tired, and were most pleased to find our carriage awaiting us shoreside. After a light meal in the hotel dining room, we retired to our rooms for the night.

2nd June 1893
Bangkok, Siam
Rolin called for us in a carriage sent by the Prince. Before long, after a most interesting drive through the lantern-lit city, we turned towards the river. The Prince's residence is impressive from the exterior, but it was clear that neither

he nor his household cared overly for housekeeping. The drawing room had the neglected air of a rarely-used parlour, with dust and cobwebs visible in the dim light. We passed directly through to the Prince's personal apartments, where we found him working on papers, seated cross-legged on cushions at a low table. He greeted us informally, and begged us to join him, indicating several low divans ranged around the polished teak-wood floor.

Tea was served in small porcelain cups, with small dishes of Siamese delicacies for us to pick at as we talked.

"Please excuse me for a few moments more, Mr. Holmes. I have an urgent telegraph message to compose to our London Legation. They seem not to recognise the urgency of our armaments situation, which Commodore de Richelieu informs me is somewhat desperate. White ants have eaten the wooden parts of all the new carbines stored in our armoury, the heat and humidity have rendered many of our cannon shells useless, and the list goes on . . ."

He sighed audibly.

"Oh, by the way, Mr. Holmes. This telegraph from your brother arrived at the Ministry this afternoon."

The Prince handed Holmes a sheet of paper covered with the familiar rows and blocks of letters characteristic of a ciphered message. Holmes thanked him, and folded the document into his pocketbook, as the Prince returned to his task. I could not help but notice the even, delicate handwriting, and the fluency of his composition, and was reminded that the Siamese princes had all been educated in Europe . . . but always in countries where the monarchy remained in place.

Prince Ranawongse, like his brothers Prince Damrong and Prince Svasti, had received the finest of British education allied to his traditional Siamese court upbringing. According to the good doctor, this had been distilled from high-Brahmin manners by successive *Khmer* dynasties, then brought to Siam after the conquest of the *Khmer* Kings, and accounted for the superb manners that characterised the entire Siamese royal family.

At that moment a servant entered and informed the Prince that our old friend Doctor Smith was outside, and wished a moment with the Prince. Our Siamese, though imperfect, allowed us to understand the conversation, though much of it was in the dialect reserved for use when addressing royalty. We had learnt some of this as well, our shipboard tutor being of royal lineage himself.

The doctor entered, and seemed pleased to meet us again. It seems he had been called to attend to one of the Princes' two principal wives.

"What news, Doctor? You may speak freely. Nothing serious I hope?"

"You may rest easy on that score, Prince Ranawongse. There is nothing wrong with her that would not be set to rights by a little less dedication to card-games, and a little more to rest. If you could limit her to, say, not more than twelve hours at a sitting, it would be most beneficial."

"There you have me, Doctor!" declared the Prince, with a smile. "For all my reputation as a diplomat, that is one agreement I have never been able to conclude to my satisfaction."

"Well, do what you can. If truth be told, I suspect that the complaint originates chiefly from pique at her losses last night, rather than from any real malady. But it is as well to call me, anyway. Forgive me, gentlemen, I am due at the Palace. The Queen is feeling out of sorts as well, and none of her ladies can cheer her up."

He left, and we sat again, as the Prince finished his letter, and set aside his pen.

"Do forgive my rudeness," he said, "But we have a crisis on our hands. The French have forced our hand at the Mae Kong River, and I am uncertain as to how His Majesty should respond. He is forever concerned for his beloved Lao subjects, and cannot abide the thought of abandoning them."

He turned to Rolin, who said, "As I have pointed out previously, Prince Ranawongse, the important thing is to stand firm against them, without provoking them."

"Very well. I shall consider that, and perhaps we can put it to His Majesty later tonight. You will drive to the Palace with me, and the carriage can send Mr. Holmes and M. le Villard back home when we have done with our discussions. As you know, the Legation at Paris has telegraphed that our ambassador has been called in by the Foreign Minister. They suspect it will be to announce the breaking off of diplomatic relations.

"Now . . . Mr. Holmes! About these death threats! Is there anything you can do to help us? We should hate to lose our General Adviser."

Holmes turned towards the General Adviser.

"Answers to a few questions may help. Firstly, do you have any enemies that you know of?"

"None," replied Rolin. "I have always been a jurist. I think the closest I have previously come to physical violence was when I was threatened with having my nose pulled at The Hague."

"And you, Prince? Can you suggest any reason other than the obvious?"

"I confess I dismissed the first incidents as a local problem, perhaps a disaffected neighbour. Even the worst of Siamese villains would balk at killing an animal merely to frighten someone, but Bangkok is home to many races, some of which have no aversion to shedding blood. The last incident, however, happened so far from there. I am now certain it is something far more serious. Beyond that, I can suggest nothing other than, as you say, the obvious. Someone is trying to scare M. Rolin into leaving Siam. The question is, who?"

"Very well. Let us examine the question, *'Cui bono?'*", said Holmes.

"Who benefits if M. Rolin is removed from the scene?" replied the Prince. "Clearly the French at Saigon, but isn't that a little too obvious. I know that the British at Singapore are covetous of Bangkok, and would like to control the trade here even more than they do. Then again, it could be some private individual - perhaps one of the many foreigners seeking concessions in Siam - whose interests are affected by M. Rolin's advice to our government. My last thoughts are, could it be a warning of vengeance from someone who felt that he had been ruined by decisions taken at his advice, in some country where he has previously been employed? Unlikely, but I suppose it should be considered as a possibility."

"I agree," said Holmes, "as in that case the intention is to carry out the threat, not merely to frighten off. As to the rest of your most astute observations, all had occurred to us, but perhaps there were elements of which we were unaware."

"But does not the attempted poisoning point to homicidal intentions," I asked.

"Perhaps not," replied Holmes. "It may have been another way to encourage an early resignation, this time on the grounds of ill-health. Tell me, Prince Ranawongse, are there any Siamese of your court, or some other faction, who could be the perpetrators? Forgive my asking, but it is necessary."

The Prince thought for a moment, and replied that he had considered the question in depth himself, many times, but that the method seemed so uncharacteristic of the Siamese that he doubted their involvement.

"M. Rolin has been employed by the King not only to deal with direct threats to his sovereignty, but more importantly, to implement the reforms which both our father, King Mongkut, and the King himself, have deemed crucial in order to, shall we say, 'self-colonise' Siam. We have seen over the years that the usual reason put forward for annexing a territory is the bestowing of civilisation upon the benighted heathens, who should therefore be grateful for surrendering their freedom. Our father, King Mongkut, used to agonise over whether it was better to swim up-river to consort with the French wolf, or downstream to join with the English crocodiles. Having spent his first forty years in the monkhood, he was the best-educated man in Siam by the time he was made King. He was wise enough to recognise that our sole chance of survival as a free country lay in implementing these reforms ourselves, and thus spilling the wind from the colonists' sails. This process inevitably causes distress to powerful established interests, and the King's power is perhaps less absolute than may seem apparent at first.

"As a result, there are indeed many powerful Siamese, and others with vested interests, who would like to see the back of M. Rolin. I find myself somewhere in the middle, for I hate to see our old ways disappearing. But if we are to avoid the fate of the Kings of Annam, Cochin-China, Cambodia, and the Burmans, I recognise that we must change, or be swept away like those forgotten royals.

"That said, we Siamese have, after all, so many ways of our own to achieve these ends . . . but quite differently, I assure you. Personally, I don't think the threats originate from that quarter. But do feel free to investigate any leads that seem promising. You will have my support in your efforts. I advise discretion, for all our sakes. And now, gentlemen, I invite you to join me in my meal, while we carry on our discussion."

He rang a bell, and immediately trays loaded with dishes were laid before us - the usual Siamese curries in abundance, and some we'd never yet encountered, with rice and the array of condiments we had come to expect. The Prince picked at a little of this and a little of that as we spoke, and expected us to do the same. There seemed no sense of urgency about the meal, and discussion ranged over many topics as we enjoyed the Prince's hospitality.

At one point, at around eleven o'clock, Holmes remarked upon a lovely fragrance which, of a sudden, came wafting through the open windows from the garden outside.

"Siam has many flowers which scent the evening air," said the Prince, smiling, "and they are so desirous of our attention that they do not compete. One after the other, throughout the night, they take their turn to open and release their fragrance, each different, and all delightful. We like to plant them outside the chambers we normally use at that particular time of the evening. These are all native to Siam; the *dok champi* have just opened and caught your notice. However, if you wait just a moment I have a distinct treat for you, from halfway round the globe."

He called to his servants, who soon brought in a tray bearing several enormous blossoms from the *victoria regis* lilies we had seen seemingly afloat on the moonlit surface of the ponds in the Palace grounds, with spreading pads upturned at the edges, and huge, exotic pink blooms.

"These lilies open at dusk, but as I am rarely here at that time the staff sew the petals together until I arrive."

With that, he seized a pair of silver scissors from the tray, and cut the threads binding the blooms. A different scent filled the chamber immediately, a scent so sweet it was almost cloying. The Prince leaned forward, holding one large blossom in both hands, and thrust his face deep into the soft pink petals of the lily, inhaling vast draughts of the heady scent with enormous enjoyment. He invited us to do the same, so Holmes and I followed his example. Never could I have conceived of the existence of an odour so affecting, so redolent of all the sweetness that this earth has to offer, a scent that all the *parfumiers* at Paris together could never imagine, let alone duplicate.

"Magnificent," cried Holmes. "The *victoria regis* at Kew pale in comparison."

"Yes, they seem to thrive here. I suppose it is because our climate is so like their native Amazonia," rejoined the Prince. He set down the blossom. "Now, where were we? What should we do to guard against this evil, Mr. Holmes?"

"We have only just arrived at Siam, Prince Ranawongse, and need to familiarise ourselves with the situation here. However, certain basic steps recommend themselves. Firstly, a discreet guard should be placed at the home of M. Rolin. Someone intelligent and trustworthy! Is there anyone you can recommend?"

The Prince spoke first. "Perhaps you could take that up with Mr. Sheriff, who is our Chief Inspector of Police. M. Rolin can arrange a meeting tomorrow."

"Secondly, I will need a list of all those concessions with which the General Adviser is involved. It matters not whether the matter is still at the proposal stage, is already agreed, or is subject to dispute or re-negotiation. A detailed report on each of the concessions, including as much personal information as possible regarding the principals, would also be most helpful."

"That I can readily provide," said Rolin. "I shall prepare all the reports tonight at the Ministry, and send a carriage for you when they are ready. The carriage will collect you tomorrow morning, then deliver you to the Chief Inspector, and you may retain the driver until you are finished your rounds, whatever they may be. Will that be satisfactory?"

"Certainly. Then, Your Highness, I should appreciate it if any suspicions occur to you concerning your own people. May I ask that, without giving offence?"

"As I said, you may expect my co-operation, wherever the trail may lead. And I shall give the matter further thought."

"Finally," added Holmes, "our best bet may be to lay a trap for the villains, though just exactly how is not yet obvious. There is little more we can do right now. We will wait at our hotel in the morning, then, until your man arrives."

"Wonderful," said the Prince. "And now, as it is almost midnight, I shall call on Svasti, and we will go on to the Ministry. I must get this message away. Good night, Mr. Homes, and M. Le Villard! It has been a pleasure meeting you both, and I shall rest easier knowing that you are interesting yourselves in our affairs."

CHAPTER XXXI

3rd June 1893
Bangkok, Siam

BEFORE RETIRING Holmes had deciphered the latest telegraph message from Mycroft. At breakfast he reviewed the message, and read aloud from the plain text.

'Dearest Brother,

By now you are at Siam, and will have met the Prince, and perhaps others of the Siamese court with whom I have maintained contact over the years.

I believe you may trust in the Prince; if not, I fear there is little we can do to help the Siamese, for he is devoted to his brother the King, and is the most astute of the Siamese I have dealt with.

His brother, Prince Damrong, is equally devoted to the King, and as Minister of the Interior is responsible for implementing the internal reforms that Rolin has recommended.

Prince Svasti I have also met. He appears to be the stormy petrel of the family, exceptionally able when he chooses to be, but somewhat mercurial in his enthusiasms. Beware his temper, for he is easily aroused, though as easily mollified, in my view.

These are the princes whom I have made it my business to know about, when they were at school and university here, and through my informants at Siam.

I suggest you contact Captain Jones, our Resident Minister at Bangkok. He is a tough old soldier, rather than a career diplomat, and can be blunt in his comments.

But he has, I believe, a genuine concern for the plight of the Siamese, and wishes to see them retain their independence as a neutral state. As this happens to be the desire of the Foreign Office as well, we keep him there as a balance to our diplomats, who are more likely to negotiate that freedom away. You need not reveal your identity, simply that Professor Sigerson, like himself, is one of my agents in the field. He may very well introduce you to another of my agents there, a Portuguese fellow. You may rely on him implicitly.

I have suggested to Rolin that he continue, and intensify, his excellent work in informing the general public, via the press, of the true situation prevailing at Siam. The Siam Question is in all the editorials of late, is provoking more discussion than ever before, and relations with France - and Europe - are delicately balanced. Rolin's previous articles in the Bangkok Times *have had a profound effect in counteracting the propaganda emanating from the parti colon faction at Paris. Until now, the public has taken their inflammatory and slanted campaign at face value at large, but no longer. Questions are now being asked in high places, and they are having a more difficult time of it.*

Finally, I have heard over lunch with de Benoist, who has it from his man at Singapore, that le Villard still keeps that mastiff. Why any sane man, especially one perpetually on the road, would saddle himself with a dog the size of a bear is beyond me. I thought only the English were so eccentric in that regard. Nevertheless, I wish them both well. I hope to have news for you shortly which will permit of your safe return to London, and eventually, to your public resurrection. Until then, do take care. Large issues are at stake here, with all their attendant danger for those who would interfere.

My best regards,

Mycroft'

"I do believe we should frame this message, le Villard. It is the first we have received from Mycroft that hasn't sent us off to someplace else. Speaking of which, our carriage should be here shortly. Let us wait in the lobby."

Less than half an hour later the carriage appeared. The driver handed a message to Holmes. It was from Rolin, apologising for the delay in preparing the reports we had asked for. He also explained that Chief Inspector Sheriff had a crisis on his hands in the Chinatown section, and the only way to be sure to see him was to go there. He had been informed of our intention, and would see us as soon as he had the chance.

Chinatown proved to be nearby, and our destination was the New Road, where it ran through their district. Our carriage overtook a new electric tram, its bell clanging to warn off the swarming mass of mostly Chinese pedestrians, and followed along the tram tracks that bisected the New Road. As we approached the Chinatown area a loud sound of Chinese fireworks rent the air, sounding very much like gunshots. Our carriage pulled to one side, and the driver refused to go further.

In our unpractised Siamese we asked him why, but he simply pointed across the intersection, where we could see a large body of uniformed Siamese army and police officers sheltering behind any solid object available. Standing in back of them were several European and Siamese officers, including a tall fellow in a leather-sashed tunic, holding a spotlessly white pith helmet in the crook of one arm. In the other he held a large service revolver at the ready.

Assuming this to be Chief Inspector Sheriff of the Siamese police force, we dashed across the intersection to join him. Just as we did so another volley of reports rattled off. As we gained the shelter of the buildings alongside the police detachment the tall man turned to us, saying, "That was a damn fool thing to do! Lucky you didn't get shot up. Been expecting you. Sheriff's the name. And you, I believe, are Professor Sigerson." He holstered his revolver, now that we were safely behind shelter, and shook hands with us.

"That is so," replied Holmes, "and this is my assistant, M. Francois le Villard. Quite a lively party you have going here! What's all the excitement about, if I may ask?"

"Take a look down there," replied Sheriff, pointing along the main road leading through Chinatown. On both sides of the street were crude barricades, formed of zinc sheets and furniture. Behind the barricades were hundreds of Chinese, armed with revolvers, knives, clubs, cane-knives, and other assorted weapons. Occasional shots rang out, and farther down the street we could see vicious hand-to-hand fighting between two groups of Chinese, though both sides were indistinguishable to my eyes. Most had shaved heads, with a long plaited queue. Many were tattooed.

"Been going on two days and nights now," spat Sheriff. "Twenty dead, over a hundred injured, first night alone. The biggest gang here, formerly under *Sia* Ang Yi, split into two factions. Battle is to decide who controls Chinatown. We've plenty of men. Not enough firepower to deal with 'em all at once. They're more concerned with obliterating each other anyway. So far we've only been a nuisance to 'em. Called in the army; even they're stumped. You see that road. Like a defile. Opposing ambuscades either side. Every time we make a move in that direction we're driven back. Short of artillery, it's difficult to see how we can get at 'em."

Just then, a furious exchange of gunfire came from the near end of the street. Two small bands of Chinese broke cover and met, slashing and kicking, in the middle of the roadway. The fighting was vicious, and serious. No quarter was given. Soon one Chinese was dead, his throat gaping and spurting arterial blood into the gutter, and at least four were seriously injured. Fighters who attempted to retreat behind their barricades before the order was given were beaten or fired upon until they returned to the fray. Innocent bypassers foolhardy enough to have ventured into the street during the skirmish were dealt the same treatment. Being unarmed, they were soon felled and bleeding in the roadway.

Holmes turned to me. "Well, le Villard. I suppose we can't expect the Chief Inspector to have time to attend to our little matter until this affair is sorted out." He turned to Sheriff, and asked, "Would you mind if I made a suggestion?"

"Not at all, sir! Any idea better than none! This being their patch, it's impossible to take them unawares from the rear. If we attack from both ends we run the serious risk of shooting our own men. Already failed at penetrating from this end only. They're stretched out too far down New Road."

"Exactly," said Holmes. "What you need is to deliver an effective force into the middle of the battle zone. That will divide the two camps into four. Your men can then fight their way out, rather than in. Any of their fighters exiting the battle area can be arrested by your police and army units at the ends of the street. You'll need to take plenty of ammunition with you."

Sheriff looked at Holmes a little askance, as though wondering whether to take him seriously or not. "How do we do that, Professor Sigerson? Unable to fight our way even a few yards into that death-trap."

"It would be risky, I agree. Tell me, Chief Inspector, what has happened to the tram we passed on our way here. I notice that the tracks continue the length of New Road, but it has not approached."

"Of course not! Too dangerous by half! Since this has been on, they stop well short of here. Take an old branch track around us."

"The tram-cars seemed solidly built, with fairly high sides. Several of those filled with armed men could build up speed well before the gangs knew what was coming. Your forces would be exactly where you want them before the gangs could do anything about it. Sufficient ammunition could be carried, and the cars would provide shelter of a sort."

Sheriff simply stared at Holmes for a moment, then turned and spoke in rapid Siamese to the senior of the local police and army officers. A brief discussion followed, questions were asked of others, and a decision was arrived at.

"We will have to get permission from the concessionaires, but they will be compensated. No problem there. I've called for volunteers to drive the trams. Four to hand. Cars should be here in a half-hour or so. Speed and surprise are essential, or the cars will be stopped in their tracks before we get through. Thanks, Professor. Should have come up with that ourselves.'

"Sometimes an outsider is better placed to see the obvious than those who live close to hand," replied Holmes. "If it helps to end this slaughter, it seems worth the risk."

"Meanwhile," said the Chief Inspector, "what can I do for you. I have a moment, at least listen to your problem. Doubt I'll have time to do much about anything for a while, though."

"Nothing quite so dramatic as this, I assure you," said Holmes. "If we could step over here for a moment, where we may speak privately?"

"Of course."

"That's better. You see, Chief Inspector, we have a second string to our bow, and I trust you will respect our confidence. Our purpose here is to protect the General Adviser from any, shall we say, misadventure that may befall him in these critical days for Siam. At the suggestion of the Minister of Foreign Affairs, we ask if you can recommend a truly trustworthy watchdog for him. Someone who can remain inconspicuous in his household, and is immune to bribery or coercion! Experience with weapons would be essential, I think, and a fair grasp of either English or French. Tall order at short notice, I realise, but the Prince seemed to think you could help us, if any could."

"Just a minute," said Sheriff, and turned to speak briefly with one of the European police officers. "Got just the man for you! Wanted to check where he is, that's all. He's around here somewhere. Sent for him already! Fits your requirements like a glove. *Goorkha* chap, about forty I should think. Ex-Indian army. Came here as batman to a retired Indian Army officer. Friend of mine from the frontier days. Poor fellow came here, fit as a fiddle. Been here only a month or so. Dinner one evening with us all at the club, hale and hearty. Next evening we attended his funeral. Cholera, you see."

"Anyway, your *Goorkha* was left here, at a loose end. We found things for him to do, and before long he found himself a delightful local lass. Likes it here now, quite happy to stay on. Ideal for you, I should think. Come and see me after this, and we'll sort it all out. Well, that was easy. Now for the tricky bit! Want to stay and watch the fun?"

Holmes and I looked at each other.

"As Wiggins would put it, 'Wouldn't miss it for quids!'" said Holmes.

"Nor would I."

"Very well," said Sheriff, smiling. "Rather unorthodox academics, if you ask me. Follow me, but do be careful. I should hate to have to explain any, ah! . . . misfortunes to the Palace. The tram-cars will assemble several hundred yards up the street, past the bend, with ammunition already aboard. As soon as we see the Chinese regrouping their forces, we'll march in new troops. Make it look as though they are reinforcements coming here. At the last moment, they'll leap aboard the trams; take off immediately. Take too long about it and the spying beggars will be waiting for us."

"Sounds like a workable plan," said Holmes.

We took a roundabout route to where the first of the tram-cars waited, grey wooden ammunition chests stacked in the middle of the aisle. The seats had been removed, and were being replaced in such a way as to close the window apertures. Soon the other three cars arrived, and were similarly fortified. Close behind was a troop of Siamese soldiers, armed with carbines and revolvers.

"Seems a pity to shoot up these cars," said Sheriff. "Brand new, they are, too . . . Danish. First in Asia. Don't even have electric trams back in Copenhagen, I hear. Well, let's get on with it! Looks like they're pulling back for now."

He gave a curt order, and Siamese soldiers leaped aboard three of the four trams now lined up. The first accelerated to maximum speed as fast as possible, followed closely by the two behind it. Bells clanging furiously the tram-cars sped round the bend and hurtled down the tracks towards the disputed stretch of roadway. From both sides of the street came urgent shouts, followed by a fusillade of shots aimed at the trams. The fire was returned with equal ferocity by the troops in their mobile barricades.

Surprise seemed to be on the side of the forces of law and order and two of the three cars soon came to a halt, as planned, beyond the dead centre of the fray. From them a withering hail of rifle bullets pinned the Chinese gangs behind their barricades. The driver of the third of the tram-cars was not so fortunate. Warned by the noisy approach of the first two cars, the Chinese marksmen were ready for the third. The driver took a round through the chest, and we saw him slump out of sight. His tram-car slowed to a halt, separated from the others by a good fifty yards, and directly in front of the main forces of the two gangs. The halt had been planned beyond that point, so as to beat the gangs back into the cordon waiting at this end of the street. A small force had been detailed to mop up stragglers escaping from the other end.

For over two hours the battle raged. At times it was difficult to see what was happening. Gun-powder smoke soon filled the air, and the reek of cordite wafted down New Road. Slowly, however, the army gained the upper hand, and we saw the two trams reversing in sporadic jerks back towards the third, herding gang members up the street. Troops had sealed all escape routes to the rear, we knew, and the action was intensifying as the gangs realised their plight, and threw everything they had against the tram-cars. At times small bands of them dashed out to attempt to seize the trams, but were beaten back by sheer firepower, with occasional hand-to-hand battle spilling out into the murderous street.

The less-dedicated gangsters, deciding to save their lives, were already streaming out of the battle, into the waiting arms of the police. But those who fought on were in no mood for surrender. The two gangs shouted back and forth during lulls between burst of gunfire. Soon it became clear that together they intended to attack the third tram before the other two could link up with it. Perhaps they thought they could use it to escape. Whatever the reason, large numbers of gang fighters suddenly converged on that solitary tram, ignoring the hail of rifle fire coming from it. By sheer weight of numbers they began to swarm around the car, trying to slash and shoot their way through the barricaded doors and windows.

Sheriff had just returned to where we stood after arranging procedures for arrest and detention of vast numbers of prisoners. He was clearly disturbed at the developing situation.

"If they don't get out of there, they'll be overrun within minutes," he shouted over the din.

"I think the driver is down," said Holmes. "Maybe nobody else knows how to drive it in reverse."

"These cars have self-linking mechanisms at each end," said Sheriff. "Maybe we can drive this fourth car down. Hook that one and drag it back out of harm's way.

He strode off towards the tram, only to return a moment later, cursing softly.

"Driver's done a bunk. Probably thought we'd send him into that hell. Can't say as I blame him. Couldn't order him to go anyway. Civilian, you see. No one else seems to know how the damn things work, or so they all say."

"If they're anything like London trams, *I* do," grinned Holmes, climbing aboard and heading for the driver's compartment at the end of the aisle.

"Had to pose as a tram driver for a week once. Waste of time, as I recall."

I followed, with Sheriff close behind.

"Not exactly what you came here for, Professor Sigerson," shouted Sheriff from behind.

"That, dear sir, is hardly an unusual experience for us. I don't see any difficulty here. If you could find us some side-arms, we'll be off."

Holmes familiarised himself with the controls, while I improved the barricading of the driver's cab, particularly the access from the main body of the tram. Sheriff was soon back with revolvers and, following him, a stocky Mongolian-featured *Goorkha* in the uniform of the Siamese police force, hefting a crate of ammunition.

"Found your man. He insists on coming with you. Introductions later. Love to come with you . . . must get over to the army brass, work out how to finish this off. Good luck. We'll send in covering fire from this end."

We shook hands with our new friend, who set about checking and arranging weapons and ammunition in a most workmanlike fashion. He looked up at us as he squatted at the opened crate, grinning broadly, eyes wrinkled with joy.

"Wouldn't miss this for anything," he said in excellent Indian English. "Just like old times. Never thought I'd see a decent fight again. Everything's ready here."

Holmes cranked up the throttle, and released the brake. The tram swiftly gathered speed as we charged around the bend and into the fray. Our strategy was to get in, hook the beleaguered tram-car, and get back out as quickly as possible. We had no trouble until we neared the stationary car, when we had to slow gradually. Chinese from both sides swarmed aboard. Our *Goorkha* friend and myself fired through gaps in the barricade, effectively keeping them at a distance, but our attention was soon diverted by cut-throats attacking from the more vulnerable front.

The car ground to a halt, brakes screeching loudly. Several Chinese leaped out of the way just before we collided with the other tram. The links meshed with a most satisfying clanking sound. Loud cheering resounded from the other tram-car when the trapped soldiers realised what was happening.

"Capital," cried Holmes. "Now let's get out of here."

He threw the drive mechanism into reverse, released the brakes, and eased out the throttle. The tram obstinately refused to move.

"The other tram-car must still be engaged in forward gear." He pointed up at the latched ventilation hatch set in the overhead. "Perhaps we can communicate with them without having to run the gauntlet along the roof-tops."

He reached up to the bell-rope, and rang out a strangely staccato pealing, which puzzled our Chinese attackers. Holmes continued ringing, while testing the throttle from moment to moment.

"Surely someone there understands Morse. These fellows will be through that barricade any moment now."

Indeed, our defences were in danger of being broken down. Our *Goorkha* and I continued firing through the slits, concentrating on those with firearms. Soon, however, the attackers' overwhelming numbers must tell, and we were now locked to the other tram-car, with no way of uncoupling from it.

The troops trapped in the other car were firing indiscriminately. Amid the deafening roar of sustained gunfire, we barely heard the answering bell from the driverless tram. Holmes stopped ringing his bell and we listened carefully. I made out the short message.

"Go!" I said. "They've done it, thank God."

Holmes slowly opened the throttle yet again. This time the tram, although sluggish with the doubled load, slowly gathered speed. Seeing the possibility of seizing an escape conveyance, even more of the Chinese leaped into the passenger compartment of our tram, or clung to the sides. With pistol butts and our friend's billy-club, our *Goorkha* and myself smashed many of these on the fingers or the head, and they fell away. At one point a Chinese forced a gap in the barrier protecting Holmes and was poised to slash his neck with a wicked looking cane-knife. Our *Goorkha* saw him first and shouted a warning.

"You would, would you?" cried Holmes as he stepped back, unsheathed the blade from his swordstick, and pinked the villain at his throat. The Chinese dropped away out of sight, clutching at his bleeding neck. Our little convoy steadily gained speed.

As we approached the military and police lines the Chinese in the passenger compartment realised it was too late to seize the tram. They jumped down and tried to escape. Few did, as the police had the street well sealed. They soon joined the hundreds of prisoners already taken, seated on the ground down a side street in manacled rows, with their shirts removed to eliminate the hazard of hidden knives or deadly home-made pistols.

Once safely around the corner Holmes slowed the trams to a halt, and the soldiers alighted, cheering. We were congratulated and our hands shaken again and again, until we could politely make a line for Sheriff's command post.

"Great stuff, Professor. Bit touch-and-go for a while, but it did the trick."

The battle raged on for two more hours, but finally the soldiers were able to alight from their carriages and drive the remaining Chinese into the police cordon.

At last the battle was over. Silence settled on that bloody stretch of New Road, broken only by the shouts of the police herding away their sullen prisoners.

"Ten more gangsters killed, twenty more seriously wounded, and eight hundred headed for the stockade. Not a bad days work! Got a good handful of *Sia* Ang Yi's top men, as well. Should keep 'em quiet for a while."

A commotion came from within a gaudy Chinese arched gateway, and a small deputation of well-dressed Chinese approached the Chief Inspector. A conversation in rapid Chinese followed - with much smiling and bowing - before the deputation retraced its steps and disappeared through the arch, back into Chinatown.

"Come to thank us for stopping the mayhem, and restoring order. Most grateful! A thousand thanks, etc.."

"You seem singularly unimpressed," observed Holmes.

"Damned hypocrite," rejoined Sheriff. "He's the one who ordered the split of the gang in the first place, and he knows I know it. Taking advantage of the current unrest over this French crisis, if you ask me. The Chinese merchants are in a panic. Donating more junks to sink at the mouth of the river. I'll get him one day! Slimy beggar! Controls half the gambling, opium dens and brothels in the city by now. Probably figures we've done his work for him here. Worried stiff about all this reform stuff, though. Now that this lot is over, he'll turn his attention to subverting all that, mark my words. Rolin will have a difficult job reforming his business, I'll tell you that much." Holmes and I exchanged glances.

"What is our illustrious Chinese gentleman's name?" enquired Holmes.

"His real name is never used. He is known to all as *Sia* Ah Foo or Godfather Ah Foo. I'd be extremely careful of crossing swords with *Sia* Ah Foo, Professor Sigerson. As you see, it's taken the army just to slow them down here. But the vice and illicit trade, the smuggling and gambling will all carry on, just the same. This was merely to decide who controls it all."

After arranging for our *Goorkha* candidate to meet us at Police Headquarters the next day we went in search of our carriage. To our astonishment it was exactly where we had left it, the driver squatting patiently in its shade. He climbed into the driver's seat when he saw us approaching, as though we had just returned from a trip to one of the temples. Turning the carriage he drove us slowly back up New Road to the Oriental Hotel, where Holmes and I drew lots for the first hot bath.

CHAPTER XXXII

3rd June 1893
Bangkok, Siam

AFTER A BRIEF REST, we repaired to the long bar for a well-deserved whisky-and-soda, then strolled down the path crossing the lawn to the hotel jetty. There we hired a gondola to take us the few hundred yards to where the *Sirdar* was moored, just upstream from the British Legation.

Well over a hundred feet in waterline length, she was a handsome vessel from any angle. Her gleaming white hull was tinged pink by the sun, setting behind the lofty spires of the Temple of Dawn across the river. The brightwork and brass of her superstructure gleamed, bespeaking constant polishing and varnishing. We were piped aboard by a sallow-faced youth togged out in tropical whites - as were all of the crewmen - and shown to the on-deck saloon where Lord Coledale and his party were enjoying cocktails.

Lord Coledale himself introduced us to those guests we had not met at the Oriental Ball. Several local teak-mill owners, Murray the railway concessionaire; a German named Bethge, who was the largest mining concessionaire; several others, some with their wives.

A bluff-looking fellow, British Army written all over him, was introduced to us as Captain Jones, the British Resident Officer. His plain features and direct manner seemed ill at ease in this luxurious setting, with its varnished wood panelling and gently cambered beams overhead, deep plush sofas lining the walls below large glazed ports giving superb views in all directions, and a magnificently-carved marble fireplace. All, no doubt, *à grands frais!* Through the open etched-glass and louver doors giving onto the fantail I glimpsed more of his lordship's guests. Amongst them was Godfrey Norton, together with Irene Adler and several young Siamese ladies dressed in European fashion.

Inside the saloon, introductions having been made all round, Lord Coledale suggested that we might enjoy a tour of the yacht, seeing Holmes had admired it so. He called to his aide, Quiney, and instructed him to show us anything we wished to see, but particularly the engine room, which was the most up-to-date available at any price. Quiney, who was a large and well-built fellow with a choleric expression partly concealed by a thick black beard, said, "Very well, my lord," with barely concealed ill grace.

"If you will please follow me," said Quiney, as he disappeared through a companionway and down into a lower saloon. We followed, and were shown the accommodations forward - away from the noise and smoke of the engines, you see - and the well-appointed dining saloon with gimballed table, and prints of thoroughbreds framed in pearwood fastened to the bulkheads. We examined the spacious and well-equipped galley, and descended further to inspect the spotless engine room, and declared ourselves suitably impressed. The surly Quiney said not one unnecessary word, as he pointed out this feature and that, clearly having conducted this tour time and again.

We looked into the wheelhouse, and finally the charthouse with its broad, shallow mahogany chart drawers. As Holmes ascended the few steps leading up to the saloon, close behind our guide, I noticed a bulge at Quiney's waistband, under his jacket. "Carries a weapon, even aboard ship in port," I thought.

The tinkling notes of a pianoforte issued from the saloon, soon joined by several excellent female voices singing in superb harmony. Irene Adler, or should I say Mrs. Norton, was playing and singing, and accompanying her in a duet was the most beautiful Siamese girl I had yet seen. They were singing one of the most charming and affecting of French songs of unrequited love.

The two *chanteuses* effortlessly sang the difficult harmonies, with their shiftng minor keys, and there wasn't a noise to be heard until the song was finished. Everyone applauded, and more than politely, with the sole exception of Quiney. Lord Coledale's aide surveyed the scene haughtily, then disappeared below, I presumed to chivvy the galley staff, or perhaps to kick the ship's cat. Mrs. Norton and the Siamese girl, whom I took to be one of her voice pupils, softly began an Elizabethan ballad, which was as sweet and pure as wild honey. This was followed by a bravura piece from a minor Italian opera, which I had long forgotten, and they finished with a rousing tune from the Spanish *tarantella.*

I glanced at Holmes during the performance, and saw that, besides appreciating the music, his gaze slipped from time to time to rest on Godfrey Norton's impassive visage. Shortly before the last notes died away, and before the applause started once again, Norton stepped out onto the fantail. With a gesture of disgust, he flung his half-glassful of single-malt whisky over the railing into the dark waters, set the cut-crystal tumbler precariously on the teakwood rail, and disappeared, somewhat uncertainly, down the after gangplank to the pier.

The musical interlude finished with, Lord Coledale's guests mingled again, and Holmes and I found ourselves in conversation with Doctor Smith, whom we had greeted upon our arrival.

"Simply marvellous what Mrs. Norton has taught that young woman," said the doctor, "and in such a short time. A natural singing voice, and of course she has learnt European languages since her childhood."

"You are acquainted with Mrs. Norton's pupil, then, Doctor?" I enquired.

"Miss Malee? Oh, yes! I treated her father before he passed away last year, and she was his most dedicated nurse in the final illness. A very modern young Siamese woman; stands up for herself. Won't chew that damned *betel*, which blackens their teeth so, as you'll have noticed. Turned down any number of wealthy suitors, until her mother is in despair of ever marrying her off. She's getting to be an old maid by Siamese standards. Almost twenty, I believe. But she's her father's daughter through and through, and she has his independent spirit to a fault."

The doctor turned away to answer a query from an elderly gentleman wearing a rumpled white duck suit and sporting a splendid white beard, and left me to look at the girl I had just decided would become my wife - if I had anything to do with it. At such short notice, my world was turned around. I had enjoyed the company of many a young lady, in cities and countries far apart, but never had I been tempted to abandon the freedom of the confirmed bachelor.

"Fool!" I told myself severely. "She is obviously from an exalted family here at Siam, and has already seen off their most eligible fellows. What chance should I have?"

"Le Villard! Hello!" said Holmes for the second time, following my gaze with amusement. I broke off my reverie with a start, and turned to him. "We are going below to dine. Will you join us?"

"Of course," said I. We went below, and took our places at table. I was seated between Irene Adler and Mrs. FitzGerald.

Holmes was seated close to Lord Coledale, and I was surprised to see that Quiney joined us at table. He surprised me by exhibiting considerable charm as a conversationalist, with a wide experience to call upon for amusing anecdotes at his own expense, all of which he recounted with a perfectly straight face.

Lord Coledale himself said little, contenting himself with jogging the conversation along when it flagged. The meal was excellent, not surprisingly. One third of *Sirdar's* complement were *chefs, sous-chefs,* or galley staff, we had learnt from Quiney. Milord's cellar was nothing to be ashamed of, either, as we soon found out. When an excellent Tokay was served with the *foie gras* I almost expected Holmes to applaud, so partial is he to that sweet Hungarian wine, which he had not tasted in years.

Mrs. Norton generously talked mostly with the elderly fellow in white duck, who was seated next to her, and was obviously hard of hearing. This left me at the mercy of Mrs. FitzGerald, who was really quite charming, if slightly over-conscious of the honour of being included in his lordship's party.

After dinner there was more pianoforte music, from Miss Darnley, and general conversation flowed easily. Soon guests began to drift away to the fantail, or onto the foredeck, champagne or brandy in hand.

Holmes and I both had a brandy, with one of Lord Coledale's fine Coronas to round out the repast in style. By this time only we two, Coledale and his man Quiney, and the doctor remained in the main saloon, so we moved to the easy chairs by the unlit fireplace.

Lord Coledale was curious to know more of Professor Sigerson's expeditions, particularly in Egypt, where his lordship had visited the younger Count de Lesseps on several occasions.

"Interested in canals and railways, don't you know. Bringin' civilisation to the heathens, and British manufactures to their markets, eh? Done well at it, I must say, though I almost got let in for a nasty loss in the Panama scandal of 'ninety-two. Luckily Count Ferdinand's son warned me off that scoundrel Baron de Reinach in time. Damned decent of him, really, as we were competin' actually in many places, in those days."

"I understand your business here is in connection with the railways, Lord Coledale. Do you believe the returns will justify the outlay, which must be substantial?"

"Oh! Not in the short term, certainly not. But faint hearts never . . . Well, I've done very well with railways closer to home, y'see, and if we ain't in at the start, it makes catchin' up that much more difficult, what?" He seemed disinclined to continue this line of discussion. "I say, Quiney! Be a good fellow and ferret out the pasteboards, would you? You do play, Professor? And your chap here, le Villard is it? . . . can make a fourth, as I know the doctor must be gettin' along. Splendid!"

We played at whist, concentrating on the game. Lord Coledale was a skilled and daring player, and Quiney was no mean hand either. I am not a great lover of card games, and when Captain Jones came in from the fantail and asked if he could sit in on the next game, I gladly relinquished my seat, on the grounds that I needed to take the air. I knew that Holmes cared even less for games of chance than I, but I could see *his* game, and my presence was not essential.

With a whisky-and-soda in hand I strolled out onto the fantail, where I found myself quite alone. I stood at the railing, marvelling at the skill of the

Siamese in their tiny skiffs as they darted to and fro across the broad stream. Their tiny lanterns bobbed about in the wake of empty rice barges being convoyed back upstream, floating high in the water as they were towed by square-bowed Siamese steam tugs. Reflected by the surface of the river, the lanterns of floating houses and *godowns* stretched along the opposite bank, like strands of sparkling brilliants laid on indigo velvet. A soft voice broke into my reverie.

"M. Le Villard?"

I turned and found myself only inches from the wonderful Siamese girl I so admired, and had already determined to put out of my mind.

"At this moment, thankfully, I have that pleasure. You sing most charmingly, Miss. . ?"

"Malee is my name, I have . . ."

"The jasmine flower," I interrupted. "How very appropriate."

"You understand some Siamese, M. Le Villard?" said she, surprised. "I thought you had only just arrived at Bangkok."

"Indeed we have, Miss Malee. We had the good fortune, however, to have had one of your Siamese princes as our shipboard companion. We took unfair advantage of his leisure time, I am ashamed to say, with the result that both the Professor and I have a passing acquaintance with the Siamese language. But forgive me, do, for so rudely interrupting you."

"You are forgiven."

She laughed, white teeth flashing against sable skin in the pale moonlight.

"I have a message from Miss Irene for the Professor. Could you, please, discreetly pass it along to him? I am afraid Mr. Norton has a rather old-fashioned attitude to social conversation."

I took the folded slip of paper, and tucked it into my vest-pocket,

"I shall gladly pass the message along, of course, but as to Mr. Norton, there need be no concern at present. He has just now departed, in a rather determined manner as well."

"He prefers that Miss Irene remain at home. It pains him to see her applauded for her singing, or for her beauty and charm. A most unusual gentleman, is Mr. Godfrey! So very handsome, and yet he throws his health away as though it were a useless thing. It seems so very sad."

"And you seem, Miss Malee, to be a most perceptive young woman."

"Miss Irene would come and sing for my father, when he was on his deathbed. He said it was like a foretaste of Heaven, to hear her sing so beautifully songs from many different lands. My father was thought a most forward-thinking man, for a Siamese. His dream was always to travel over the seas, to see for himself the world beyond Siam. As one of the King's *compradors*, he was obliged to learn English and French, and made sure his children did the same. He understood what he learnt from our King, and his father before him - that Siam must awaken from her slumber, and take her place amongst the states of this world. The alternative, he always said to us, when we complained of our studies, is the subjection of Siam to one or more of the great powers. This has already happened to our cousins in Cambodia, and to the Burmese and Annamese on our flanks."

"Your father must be a remarkable man, to have passed along so much wisdom to one so young and fair."

"I am my father's daughter, and proud of it." She smiled again. "I must go now. It has been a pleasure to meet you, M. Le Villard."

She extended her hand, and delicately shook mine. Then she joined her hands together in the traditional Siamese manner, and bid me farewell in Siamese.

"*Sawaddee, Khun* le Villard."

She turned, and was silently gone, back to where Mrs. Norton was now waiting at the head of the gangway, with the other two of her Siamese former pupils.

The remainder of the evening passed in a haze of brandy fumes, cigar smoke, and remembering every moment of time spent with Miss Malee. I had not thought how I should arrange to meet her again, but I knew with certainty that I should do so.

CHAPTER XXXIII

4th June 1893
Bangkok, Siam

WE WOKE RATHER LATE, after all the excitement of the previous day. After a breakfast of coffee and rolls, with fresh paw-paw fruit sprinkled with limejuice, we retrieved Tashi from the veranda, and left for Police Headquarters. Though it was a Sunday, Sheriff had said he would wait there for us, as he would be on duty all that day, dealing with the aftermath of the battle at New Road.

As we negotiated the crowded streets, Holmes told me of the message from Irene Adler, which I had given him the previous evening as we returned from the *Sirdar* in the Oriental's gondola.

"Mrs. Norton has asked if she may call on us, ostensibly in connection with employment for one of her students who will soon leave for England. I sent a reply to the Bangkok Hotel, where she and Godfrey Norton usually put up, it seems, when in Siam, saying that we would be glad to meet with her at seven this evening, at our hotel."

At Police H.Q. Holmes sent in Professor Sigerson's card. We were soon seated in Sheriff's rather spartan office, sipping English tea with milk and too much sweetening, while Holmes enquired further about *Sia* Ah Foo. The *Goorkha* had been sent for.

"As I said, he's a smooth villain when he wants to be. Doesn't do his own killing any more, but was ruthless in a fight as a young man, according to the legends. Got a finger in every pie, including much that goes on outside Chinatown itself. Still involved in opium smuggling, but has gotten out of the white-slave traffic since our navy has been suppressing it. Investments in shipping and *godowns*, brokering the rice harvests, money-lending throughout the country, reputedly has his own Chinese bank. My informants tell me he even has a hand, behind the scenes of course, in this proposed Kimlong-Yunnan Railway."

"Tell me, Chief-Inspector, how would he be involved in that?" asked Holmes.

"The concessionaires know they can never deal with the murderous Haws up in the north, so I hear they've recruited him to take care of that, and also dealing with the authorities at the Chinese terminus of the line. The required bribes, and so forth."

"Is there any way we could meet Ah Foo, as academics of course, perhaps to arrange for an archaeological expedition into those territories?"

"Now, just why would you want to do that, Professor?"

"Curiosity, Chief Inspector. I am interested in anyone who could benefit substantially from a change in the status quo here at Siam. There may be nothing in it, but this railway was mentioned in passing by Lord Coledale - you've met him here, I take it? - when we were playing cards last evening. I had thought his consortium was interested in a concession within the borders of Siam, but I checked my maps last night. Kimlong is the Burma terminus, and the line would run through the Shan and Lao territories, to Yunnan, but at no point through present-day Siam."

"I suppose a meeting could be arranged, though I doubt you'll learn anything of value. We maintain several channels of communication with the Chinese gangs. I can arrange that you call on one of them, bearing your letters of introduction from the Royal Geographical Society. *Sia* Ah Foo will meet you out of curiosity. Are you certain you want to do this? Very well, I shall set it up, and let you know at the Oriental."

He rose to go, saying, "I must get to the stockade. We've got eight hundred assorted rogues and murderers to deal with. Your *Goorkha* chap is out by your carriage. I have seconded him to the protection of Rolin, but as far as anyone else is concerned, he has retired from the force to settle with his wife as gardener and cook's assistant to the General Adviser's household. His name is Rinzing. Shall we?" He gestured towards the door leading out to the courtyard of Police Headquarters.

When we came in sight of our carriage we spotted our ally of the previous day. He was squatting on the cobbles of the courtyard, rattling away in his native Nepalese to Tashi. Though not Tibetan, the sound was close enough that Tashi was sitting up, alert but friendly, and allowing the *Goorkha* to fondle his huge head.

As we approached, he snapped to attention and threw us a smart salute.

"Your first order, Rinzing, is to forget the military manner entirely. From here on, you are a domestic helper, as I explained this morning. Think you can keep that up?"

"Yes, sir! No saluting, no 'yessir'ing." He snapped off another salute, then smiled. "That was the last one. I suppose I had best change into civvies, if I am to be one of the gardeners. My wife is ready, back in our quarters."

"Then dash off, like a good chap, and fetch her and your gear. This is Professor Sigerson, and M. Le Villard. To anyone else, they are merely old friends of M. Rolin. For the duration of this assignment, however, they are your superior officers, and their orders are to be followed explicitly. Everything clear?"

"Yes, sir!" Rinzing began to salute, but stopped himself soon enough. He and the carriage driver left, and returned in minutes with baskets and sacks of possessions, and Rinzing's wife, who was already large with child. With all of us, and Tashi as well, the carriage was quite filled up. Thankfully, as it was blazing hot in the noonday sun, we soon enough arrived at Rolin's villa.

On the way, Holmes and I thanked Rinzing for his bravery during the battle at Chinatown. He brushed this aside, thanking us once more for the opportunity to do battle again. Rinzing seemed more interested in Tashi, and how such a great Himalayan hound should come to be here at Bangkok. An idea came to me, and I turned to Holmes.

"You know, Professor," I said, "it makes a deal of sense if we leave Tashi here with Rinzing, assuming Rolin has no objections. Extra protection for the house, and a place for him to exercise! He frets so when tied up, and it seems he and Rinzing are already firm friends."

"A capital idea, le Villard! Kills two birds with the one stone. You and I will be busy in the coming days, perhaps weeks, investigating those concessionaires who may have an interest in Rolin's demise. Tashi can do more good here than tied to the rail at the hotel."

Rolin came out to greet us, and was soon apprised of our arrangements for his discreet protection. He approved of Tashi's remaining there, and called his head house-boy to settle Rinzing and wife into their quarters, instructing him to turn out the gardener's tool-shed to make a shelter for Tashi. Tashi showed how serious he was about all this by chasing a vividly-striped butterfly around the large lawn. The house-boy warned us that Tashi must be tied up when the rains came, or else he may try to play with, or even eat, one of the deadly-poisonous toads which came out then. He kept several of the Siamese dogs himself, and would, he assured us in his halting English, take good care of Tashi. As I left I threatened that if he misbehaved I should have him stuffed and hung under the eaves of the porch at the local temple. I doubt he understood, but Rinzing did, and laughed as he cuffed Tashi playfully, adding something of his own in Nepalese.

That taken care of, we repaired inside, out of the scorching sunlight, to where Rolin had arranged several folders on his study desk. Cooling drinks were brought, and we settled to discuss the past, current and prospective concessionaires at Siam.

"Now, Mr. Holmes, I've prepared these dossiers for you. Very brief, as I hadn't a lot of time. If you need further detail, you have only to ask. The French Foreign Minister has officially informed us yesterday that if Captain Thoreaux is not freed immediately, diplomatic relations will be broken off. I was at the palace late last night, drafting a response to the conciliatory parts of the *communiqué* which will allow the French Ministry to save their pride without being manoeuvred into approving the use of force."

Holmes glanced through the dossiers, making the odd comment as he went through the pile.

"Mining . . . mining . . . steamboat-line up the river . . . railway-link to Saigon. Ah! Our old friends the Kra Isthmus canal. Rice mills . . . trading . . . teak-logging. Shipyard . . . sawmill . . . banking. Seems fairly comprehensive! Are there any of these that stand out as possible disaffected parties? Sufficiently so that they would plot your death?"

"The short answer to that is, virtually *all* of them. One of the few exceptions is your friend Lord Coledale. I must say, he seems remarkably sanguine for someone who had just sailed halfway round the globe to promote a railway scheme, only to find out that he was only there, as it were, to make up the numbers and provide the Siamese with a negotiating counterweight. Almost all of the past concession holders feel they've been hardly done by in some way or other. The present and future ones are, without exception, agitating for more lenient terms, less stringent controls, extended territory, and what have you. Many times I have had these men in my office, demanding this or that, or offering inducements for preferential treatment. More than one has threatened me as he left. You must read the files, then decide for yourself. I am sorry I can not be more helpful."

"Very well. That is exactly what we will do. In the meantime, do exercise care, and I would suggest that you take Rinzing with you when you travel at night, as I know you must do. He is a most resourceful fellow, and there are no braver fighters in the world than the *Goorkhas*."

"Sound advice, and I believe I shall take it. Well, gentlemen, I wish you good hunting! Will you take lunch with me?"

Holmes declined gracefully, citing the urgency of our task. For myself, I preferred to explore the numerous stalls where exotic and spicy curries of all kinds were offered, than to risk again the rather indifferent European cuisine of the General Adviser's cook. (Mind you, there are Siamese delicacies which, even though I am a Frenchman, I could not face. Vendors display trays laden with various kinds of beetles, shiny black, brown and iridescent, or mounds of grasshoppers, fried in oil to golden perfection. Elsewhere there are little square cakes of roasted larvae, and a dozen other unrecognisable treats on display. These I manage to resist.)

After properly introducing Tashi to Rinzing, and telling him in Tibetan to eat a bowl of food prepared by Rinzing, Holmes and I left in the now-empty carriage.

"The Oriental Hotel, driver!" instructed Holmes, in Siamese.

"Very well, sir!" replied the driver in excellent English. Holmes laughed as he sat back to enjoy the ride. But we both noted the driver's excellent command of English.

Back in our sitting-room Holmes pored over the files, then handed each of them to me as he finished. Rolin was right. It seemed that all the files contained sufficient justification for further investigation. And the concessionaires were only one of the groups of possible suspects, along with disaffected Siamese, conspiratorial Chinese, avaricious British traders at Singapore, and French colonialist advocates of annexation of Siam, to mention the more obvious. I sighed, rather loudly.

"I know just what you're thinking, le Villard. This is a strange and new country to us, and it seems to me that the General Adviser could be assassinated and the country shared out long before we could ever unravel the mystery as to just who has *already* taken steps to kill him. There is little more we can do today, so we will make a start tomorrow. We must narrow the field rapidly, while taking care that our prey does not slip through the meshes of our net."

Holmes wrote a few words on hotel notepaper, sealed it, and sent it off with a messenger to the British Residency.

"I think we will start by calling on Captain Jones first thing tomorrow, if that is convenient for him. Now, how about some billiards while we wait for Mrs. Norton to arrive? I still owe you for that drubbing I received at Shepheard's Hotel in Cairo. Let me see if I can expunge the debt." We spent the next two hours at the billiards table, with the result that Holmes's indebtedness doubled. He took it in good stead, paid me in Siamese *ticals*, and I stood us drinks at the long bar. From there, as we enjoyed our cool beer, we could observe through the arched entry and the potted palms any guests arriving at the hotel lobby.

Precisely at seven o'clock a smart carriage drew up at the entrance, and Mrs. Norton alighted. With her was Malee, the beautiful and intelligent Siamese girl . . . but perhaps I repeat myself.

We went to greet them.

"Mrs. Norton, a pleasure to see you again. And is this the young lady who is headed for London?"

Introductions were made, as Holmes had not spoken with Miss Malee the night before. At Holmes's suggestion we took a table in the garden. The insects were bothersome, it being early evening, but a little privacy was required. Refreshments were ordered, and arrived almost immediately.

"Perhaps, Miss Malee, you would care to explain to me the sights of the river?" said I, feeling certain that Mrs. Norton had delicate matters to discuss with Holmes.

"Are you really leaving for London?" I asked, when we were at the railing along the river terrace.

"Truthfully, no! There was some talk of it when my father died, but nothing has come of it. Miss Irene needed a reason to talk with the Professor, without arousing the suspicions of Mr. Norton. He is busy this evening, as most evenings, but he has her watched, and there is the devil to pay if he suspects her of anything at all."

"And you, as a modern young woman, disapprove of his attitude and behaviour?"

"Indeed I do! Especially as she gives him no cause for his insane jealousy, whereas he spends his nights at the opium dens, or with women at the foreign night-clubs along Sri Phraya Road. If it were me, I should have left him long ago, and I have said as much to her. Although she is my senior and my tutor, Miss Irene has also become my very dear friend."

"She is fortunate to have found such a one," said I, quietly.

"Perhaps I have said too much. After all, I scarcely know you."

"I shall repeat your words to no one; not even the Professor," I assured her.

"You need not worry about that, for I suspect that she is discussing this very subject with her old friend the Professor. She seems to have a great deal of respect for his ability to resolve complicated matters, and I know she has been very worried of late. When I ask her can I help, she always says it is beyond the power of any to help her, that it seems she must suffer and be silent. But since the arrival of the Professor she seems to have taken new heart. Tell me, M. Le Villard, is Professor Sigerson so brilliant that he can, indeed, show her a way out of her difficulties?"

"I have never known any more brilliant, nor more resourceful, than the Professor. He has taught me my profession, but it seems to me that it is his deep insight into the labyrinths of the human heart that sets him above others. If any can assist your Miss Irene, it is Professor Sigerson. She already has ample proof of his discretion."

"Oh! I do hope so. I so hate to see her in distress, with nowhere to turn. I have felt useless, but I know not what to do to help her." Tiny tears started at the inner corners of her dark, almond-shaped eyes. She turned away, so that I should not observe this, and, to distract her from her concerns I asked her to describe the sights of the opposite shore. She smiled, and began to tell me what she knew of the history of the temples and spires silhouetted against the light of the setting sun.

Before long, her delightful good humour recovered, we returned to the table.

"Do we interrupt?" I enquired.

"Not at all," replied Mrs. Norton. "We were merely discussing cabinet photographs, and the difficulties they can cause. But we are done with that. Would it be too much to ask if we could go indoors, as these mosquitoes are driving me to distraction?"

I offered her my arm, and Miss Malee took Holmes's arm as we escorted them into the lounge of the Oriental. We took tea and a light supper, then saw the two ladies to their carriage.

"A remarkable woman still, le Villard!" said Holmes as we returned to our rooms. "It seems that Godfrey Norton has become rather a boor and a bully, now that he is away from the Inns of Court. He philanders openly, and spends much of his time in an opium reverie. His clients, consequently, are of the less reputable sort, including one of the larger of the big British trading consortiums based at Singapore. Several of them are already on our list for investigation anyway. But it seems the worst of it is that he becomes violently disagreeable with her when she attempts to remonstrate with him. And still she defends him."

"Miss Malee hinted at all of that," I said. "Why doesn't she simply leave him, if he is such a brute? She has, after all, her superb voice, and a career which could easily be resumed."

"Her reasons, for I asked her exactly that question myself, are that when sober he is a caring and gentle man. He fell into bad company during his university years, and began smoking opium as a lark, which developed into a pernicious habit; and he resented having had to abandon his legal practice, and blamed her for it. I suspect that she finds it difficult to accept that she made such a disastrous choice, but there is more to it. I am sure that she has not told me everything, but she *has* asked for my help.

"It seems that Norton has become involved in something very shady here in Siam. She has walked in twice unexpectedly, and found him counting vast sums of money, whereas he has never dealt in cash before. When asked about it, he becomes belligerent and abusive. He has been seen in the unsavoury quarters of the town, in company with men known to be swindlers and rogues. To all of this she has become inured, but it seems that in the last few days he has gone into a complete funk. He received a letter by messenger four days ago, and since then has been in a state approaching terror."

"What does she want with Sherlock Holmes's talents, then?" I asked, curious.

"She wants us to find out what is the nature of the threat he fears so much, and what can be done to remove it. In her own words, 'He seems trapped in a web of his own devising, and sees destruction approaching down every strand.' She offered to pay handsomely, if only we could arrange some way to free him from the tangle he is in."

"And you agreed?"

"To investigate, yes! Payment, no! Godfrey Norton and his predicament mean but little to me, and we have more important matters to attend to. But I sense that over Mrs. Norton's head there is quite another sword dangling on a thread. Misguided loyalty aside, I think that she feels she cannot leave without endangering herself as well as him."

"A tangle, indeed! Well, as Norton's Singapore clients are on our list, we should have had to look closely at his activities anyway. Has she no further clue as to who he fears, and the nature of the hold they have on him?"

"Only that he kept repeating, 'At last they will have me pay! After all this time, they still have me at their mercy!' He destroyed the message, so she could not glean anything there. It seems that the threat relates to an old matter, but how far back? Singapore? Here at Siam? Bombay, where it seems they spent their first two years abroad? Or is it back even further, before his departure from England, that the answer is to be found?"

CHAPTER XXXIV

5th June 1893
Bangkok, Siam

HAVING RECEIVED an invitation from Captain Jones to call on him at any time this morning, we arrived at the decent hour of nine o'clock, to be greeted by the gruff looking Captain himself. He introduced himself again, though we had met only two nights previously, and sat us down in his study overlooking the river.

"Never did take much to having servants underfoot. Do without all of 'em if this place was a bit smaller. Not the cook though, mind you. Not the cook! Chinee fella', and knows his stuff. Listen, why don't you both come by here this evening. Having a dinner for the officers of all the ships in port just now, plus most of the diplomats. Should be interesting, what with all the jockeying for position going on."

"Thank you, Captain. Most kind of you."

"Meanwhile, Professor Sigerson, what can I do for so eminent an explorer as yourself? Read about your trip to Tibet and Samarkand. Great stuff!"

"May we ask for your discretion in what we are about to reveal, Captain Jones? We have called on you at the suggestion of Mr. Mycroft Holmes, of the Foreign Office. He informs us that you, like us, report to him on, shall we say, delicate matters."

Captain Jones immediately sat up straighter in his chair, and a faraway look glazed his eyes.

"Mycroft Holmes! Got me this appointment, you know. I'm no diplomat, but he wanted someone who'd give it him straight. He knew me from '79, when I was at Isandhlwana, and he was all over the show, trying to keep the Zulus from boiling over. Pulled it off, as well, though everyone said he was mad to try. I still remember a forced march we made from . . . But you didn't come here to listen to old war stories. What can I do to help you, Professor? Just name it."

"Information, for now, Captain Jones! We are new on the ground here, and may need more concrete assistance, at some time."

"If it is in my power, you need only call on me. I have no real authority here, but I know my way around."

"Excellent. Mycroft Holmes has asked us to investigate certain plots against the life of the new General Adviser to King Chulalongkorn. M. Rolin's presence and advice is seen by the Foreign Office as crucial if Siam is to resist annexation or dismemberment. Apparently others see it that way as well, perhaps because they have just those goals in mind. There may be other reasons for some person or persons to wish M. Rolin dead or gone from Siam, but we are interested to know what we can regarding the real political situation of Siam, stripped of the niceties."

"You've come to the right man, Professor, but I'll warn you in advance. I am not impartial. I believe the Siamese have demonstrated, simply by still being independent, that they are becoming a modern state as we know it. And for all their flaws, the Siamese have a fully developed culture of their own. Subjecting them to the rule of a colonial power is wrong, whether it be France, Britain, Germany or any other. With a bit of help and advice, they have made great strides in modernising the country, and left alone will make more. This also happens, as I am sure you are aware, to be Mr. Mycroft Holmes's view on the matter."

"Exactly! Now, to specifics! What can you tell us of the French here at Siam?"

"Briefly, they have their eyes on complete take-over, as part of De Lanessan's Greater Indochinese Empire. I take it you know about his writings in support of this concept, long before he was appointed Governor General at Saigon. Good! Well, for all the denials, that is still their policy, and they intend to see it through. Pavie, my opposite number at the French Residency, is his tool. The Chevalier de Keun, as Dutch consul, is supposed to be neutral, but I strongly suspect he reports secretly to the French.

"They have their mouthpiece here in that sneaking little Irish reporter, with his *Siam Free Press*. I've no doubt it is funded largely by Saigon. Forever attacking both the British and the Siamese."

"What of their Navy and Army?"

"Until very recently, as you no doubt are aware, the French Navy governed Saigon as their own fiefdom, ever since it was seized in the 'fifties. Their officers are still rabid colonialists to a man. Like De Lanessan and Pavie, they have a vast experience in provoking situations by making unreasonable demands, then creating further causes for the endless escalation of those demands."

"What of the British at Singapore?" asked Holmes.

"The Siam traders there call the shots. Over ninety percent of all the Siam trade is in their hands. Grain, timber, minerals, you name it. They know the French would love to wrest it away from them, so there are plenty who would press for British annexation if it seemed the French were getting the upper hand. Most of them have been content with the situation up till now, but all this French belligerence has them worried, no question."

"Would any of the other colonial powers have sufficient to gain, or lose, to countenance assassination?"

"Not in my opinion. Mr. Mycroft may know more, sitting in Whitehall as he does, with his agents everywhere. But it seems to me that the Russians are trying to remain uninvolved, except as mediators. Same thing goes for the Americans. The Italian Consul has grandiose plans of alliances and realignments, but I suspect that his own aggrandisement is the desired end result? Nothing there, I'm sure."

"And the Germans? I notice you've left them till last."

"Well, it's no secret that the Kaiser wants his own empire, and has made moves in China and Central Asia, as well as Egypt and Africa. But they have such a small stake in the region right now, and the British and French are so preponderant, that I find it hard to see how they could benefit. Nevertheless, some of the larger concessions are in German hands, so I suppose it must be considered a possibility that some individuals are involved.

"But you'll meet many of these people tonight, and be able to make your own observations. Bangkok is a small town, so far as Europeans are concerned, Professor Sigerson. If you must investigate people, do so with the utmost discretion. To my knowledge, you are accepted at face value for now. It would, in my opinion, be both wiser and safer to keep it that way."

Somewhat later that night, Captain Jones came to greet us again as we were shown into the reception room of the British Residency, a fine stone building set in spacious grounds upstream from our hotel, between the French and Portuguese embassies. On the way there, as our jinrickshaw-man picked his way through the crowded lane leading from New Road, Holmes and I could see the masts and rigging of the British and French gun-ships moored in front of their embassies. Across the river, standing out in white amongst the greyed-teakwood river craft like a thoroughbred amongst pit-ponies, was the most beautiful, powerful sailing ship I had ever seen.

After finishing my *baccalaureate* I had spent almost a year before the mast, as a deck-hand on a barquentine of the French Navy, before inheriting a modest sum from my step-father. This unexpected event allowed me to do what I had always dreamed of doing. I joined the Police Department at Marseilles, and worked my way up to my present rank of *'Inspecteur du Police Judiciaire'* at Paris.

But I had learnt to love and respect the sea, and had taken a particular delight in the beauty and strength-of-purpose married in those fabulous clipper ships spawned by the British and American craze for the freshest tea, straight from China. As a young sailor, literally learning the ropes, I had listened with awe to tales of the Great Tea Races, of the *Thermopylae* and the *Ariel*, the *Cutty Sark* and the *Flying Cloud*. Surely here was a ship of that lineage, but what was she doing here at Bangkok?

Our jinrickashaw pulled into the driveway of the residency, and I turned my mind to other matters. We were here to gauge the general mood of the European community here at Bangkok, and to keep alert for those small clues that lead to the truth hidden behind public affairs.

As Captain Jones introduced us around, it was clear that, as he had promised, most of the captains and officers of the various ships in port were present. I noticed some of the diplomatic corps, and a sizeable number of the traders and merchants with whom Siam did most of its overseas trade. Jones took care to make sure we understood who everybody was, and how they all fit into the overall picture, and yet never did it seem that he was being anything but the genial, slightly garrulous host. I could see why Mycroft Holmes had seen that he was posted here at this delicate time.

Conversation in the room was generally good-humoured, with much banter and telling of anecdotes amongst the sailors, whilst the diplomats exchanged non-committal remarks about the various political developments reported in the press. The Egypt Question, the Turkish Question, etc., etc.. At one point a rather heated discussion arose regarding the predominance of the British Imperial red on the map of the world, and whether it signified a superiority of culture. The topic was hastily abandoned when one of the normally courtly Siamese princes remarked that he suspected the red signified the vast quantities of blood shed by the English in the process of acquiring such dominance over the affairs of others.

Rum, whisky, and cigars were offered around on salvers by pig-tailed Chinese servants, and European and Siamese delicacies by their fellows. We struck up conversations with some British traders and several of the sea-captains, British and French, who were listening to an amusing anecdote about the young ladies of Alexandria. Holmes used this as a lead into a discussion of the colonial aims of the various European powers, as seen from the naval point of view. As always, he couched his questions in the dispassionate but genuinely fascinated tones of the professional explorer and researcher that he had, as Professor Sigerson, become to the world at large. Interesting responses, but no great revelations!

The French navy seemed more than a little messianic in their determination to achieve the kind of glory they perceived the British Empire to represent. As the usual custodians of the developing French colonies, their role often involved police and military functions, and the aim of many of these reactionary officers was to become the Governor of one of the new colonies.

British officers, on the other hand, seemed reluctant to become involved with affairs on land, seeing their role as protection of the sea-lanes for British and international trade, and ridding the world of the remnants of the scourge of seaborne slavers.

Holmes elicited this information without seeming to offend or antagonise either of the two groups, but behind the *camaraderie* of fellow-naval officers at leisure the undercurrent of tension was palpable. It seemed entirely likely that within days they should be obliged to fire upon one another, as their respective diplomatic envoys - seen chatting together on the other side of the reception room - manoeuvred to decide the fate of Siam.

"I suggest we split up," said Holmes quietly. "I think I shall see what I can provoke amongst the diplomatic types."

He left, and joined them, while I stayed with the sailors and merchants. Amongst the group of officers was Captain Blair, commander of the *Sirdar*. As an ex-Navy man, he obviously found their company congenial. I took the opportunity to strike up a conversation about Lord Coledale's yacht. It seemed that the *Sirdar* normally remained in the Mediterranean, where Coledale used her for his frequent visits to inspect his current and prospective railway projects in the East. Apparently his lordship also maintained two private trains - one in Europe and one in Britain - with commodious sleeping accommodations, and luxuriously fitted for social and business entertaining.

"His Lordship was the first to see the potential of a Cape-to-Cairo railway, and he's spent a small fortune sending expeditions to explore the uncharted regions of Africa. Just last year, *Sirdar* spent several months moored at Alexandria, while Lord Coledale and Quiney voyaged up to the headwaters of the Nile."

Blair confessed that it was reminiscences of this stay at the Egyptian seaport that had started the *risqué* conversation we had interrupted.

Now, it seemed Lord Coledale was turning his attentions to Asia. They had already stopped at Colombo and Malacca, reaching Singapore several months before. After this stay at Siam they would return to Bangkok. Lord Coledale's train would await him at Marseilles in four months' time, to carry him to the Channel. Back in London, his lordship was to present the results of his journey as a White Paper of some sort.

Our conversation drifted then to the relative merits of steam and sail and the unfortunate demise of the great windjammers and clippers, whose recent heyday had already come and gone.

Holmes, meanwhile, had joined the group of diplomats, which included the now-familiar figures of Pavie, the Chevalier de Keun, and the General-Adviser, who had arrived shortly after we had. I refreshed my glass at the side bar, and joined him.

Pavie was speaking, rather forcefully, to the group in general.

". . . and we repeat, again and in all sincerity, that France has no territorial ambitions regarding Siam itself. However, we must have security in our own territories, and it is unacceptable that any Siamese influence be allowed on the East bank of the Mekong River. Furthermore, we must insist that no Siamese military presence be allowed on the West bank within twenty five miles of the river."

"But surely, Pavie, that is an unacceptable proposal for the Siamese to agree to?" interjected Captain Jones. "If you allow that it is their territory, how can France tell them what to do there?"

"One thing we have learned is that in dealing with these half-barbarous potentates, reason and argument are entirely the wrong approach. Threaten when in a position of strength, and stay aloof otherwise. That is how to deal with these Siammers."

"And if they resist your demands, as at some point they must?" asked Rolin.

"France's honour demands that we do our duty, and if that duty requires spilling the blood of hundreds, or even thousands, I assure you the loyal citizens of France will not shrink from that duty."

He raised his glass, and proposed a toast.

"To the glory of France!"

Captain Jones quickly replied, before any other response could be voiced. "M. Pavie! Nobody doubts your loyalty to your country, but I doubt that any here will join you in your toast. I propose another, more to my liking, and one which none will refuse."

He spoke a few words to the head serving-boy, and everyone was handed a fresh glass. That done, he turned to the room in general, and tapped his glass with a knife.

"Gentlemen, may I propose a toast to His Majesty, the King of Siam!"

Even Pavie raised his glass, and joined in the response.

"His Majesty, the King of Siam!"

There were none in the room who were unaware of the rumours that the King was seriously ailing, and may even be nearing death. We had all heard of the discontent among various factions of the nobility, some supporting his policies of gradual reform, others wanting more radical change, and yet others striving to turn their backs to the Europeans and return Siam to its old ways entirely.

I surveyed the men in the room. They were from a dozen countries, and various occupations, but all would be affected in some way or another by the looming crisis at Siam. Were any of them prepared to conspire to murder the General Adviser, with whom they had just shared a toast, in furtherance of their own ambitions?

Pavie had to be considered a possibility, especially following his remarks of a moment before. The sailors could be discounted, I thought, but several of the traders from Singapore had made it obvious that they were not averse to a British annexation of Siam, to protect free trade and to spread civilisation. They were all on the list of concessionaires, and Holmes and I had decided to investigate them all as quickly as we could. In particular I had paid attention to a Mr. Samuel Cutter, who was a principal of the Singapore consortium that employed Godfrey Norton as its representative in Siam. Cutter & Fluddle had recently launched their Siam Gold Mining Concession in Singapore, London and Paris, with shares issued in the amount of half a million pounds sterling. These had been fully subscribed, according to the gregarious Mr. Cutter, who advised that he could soon offer me shares in a second gold-mining concession that he was currently negotiating with the Siamese.

"Get in on the ground floor, my friend. Take the opportunity while it is still there for the taking. These shares will triple in value within two years, mark my words. We have many satisfied continental investors, especially in Paris. Take my card! You need only telegraph, and I shall get a prospectus away within the day."

Holmes interrupted my thoughts. "It seems as though the gathering is breaking up, le Villard. Shall we depart?"

We made our way to Captain Jones to make a polite farewell, but he asked if we could remain behind, as there was someone he would like us to meet. We agreed, of course, and were shown into his study once again.

"I shall join you as soon as the remaining guests have departed. Meanwhile, introduce yourselves. *Señor* Azcevado Marques is also one of Mycroft Holmes's agents, shall we say."

We found, smoking a cigar at the opened French doors, a stocky man of about fifty, immaculately dressed in tropical whites. His features and complexion betrayed his Portuguese origins, but the shape of the eyes was also clear evidence of some Chinese blood in his lineage. He turned to us, and introduced himself in excellent English.

"Professor Sigerson. Joao Enrique Azcevado Marques at your service."

They shook hands, and I was introduced. We sat in the captain's lounge chairs and lit cigars.

"The Captain tells me that you know Mycroft Holmes, *Señor*?" remarked Holmes.

"I have known Mr. Mycroft Holmes for many years. My father sent me to Oxford to learn the ways of an English gentleman, as I should have to deal with the British when I took over the business. It was there that I made an acquaintance with Mycroft Holmes, and when I returned here we kept in contact. Over the years, as he has expanded his network of contacts, he has come to rely on my reports regarding the situation here and in the region. When Captain Jones was posted here he carried a letter of introduction from Mr. Mycroft, and we have met frequently to compare our impressions. The Captain is committed to the neutralisation of Siam, as is my family."

"You mentioned taking over your family business before?"

"Yes. If you will allow me - as it is relevant - I shall fill in some of my background for you."

"Of course, *Señor*. Please carry on."

"My grandfather was Portuguese from his father's side, and Chinese from his mother's. His father had been rescued from a sinking coastal-trader. The rescuers were Chinese pirates, as the Europeans branded them, but my grandfather joined their band, and married one of their daughters - my grandmother. He earned great respect as a fighter and planner, and even more as a trader, and the tribe prospered. My father was born, and several other children, and were sent to school at Macao. When he was still a young man the British came, and declared war on the pirates of the South China Sea. Soon it was no longer safe to carry on, not even as legitimate traders. The authorities knew our family. They were determined to destroy us along with all the other great sea families.

"Our ships had always roamed freely over the seas, and were familiar sights at the ports of Java, Malacca, the Philippines, Annam, Cochin China and elsewhere. When my father succeeded to the patriarchy of our family, and of the other families of the clan, he saw that the British would soon wipe us out. Of all the countries in the region, he felt the Siamese kingdom to be the safest refuge from their wrath.

"Our entire clan moved here, to Siam, and he soon took as his wife a daughter of a prominent Chinese-Portuguese family here. He also, by and large, abandoned piracy in favour of trade. Shipping and trading had become extremely profitable, and were far less risky.

"Slowly our business flourished, until now our *godowns* hold much of the rice harvest of Siam when it is barged down the river. We also own many of the barges, and a substantial fleet of merchantmen and coasters. This has become the core of our business, but my father, although his own schooling was interrupted, is a most astute businessman. Our family is now involved in a vast number of enterprises, all run by family members. He insisted that all his children, especially the girls, receive the finest education, and learn the art of managing money and trade."

"And your father is still alive, if I understand you correctly?"

"He is indeed, though he is an old man now. My mother died twelve years ago. Two years later his eyes failed. He is now totally blind, but as astute as ever. I have run the business since then, but he is still head of the clan.

"You may wonder, 'why so much personal and family detail?' The answer is simple. Our family has been here for over fifty years, but my grandfather was visiting here long before that. He, and my father when young, dealt personally with the courts of all the countries of the region, even before so many were colonised. Our knowledge of the history and rulers of all these places is based on our own long experience. We have seen them all, with the exception of Siam, lose their independence.

"We are *of* Siam, now, but not Siamese. Although we honour our Chinese origins, we are Catholics. Here we have the freedom to worship as we please. We have our own Portuguese community and the old ways are strong with us. Our loyalty is to the family, first and foremost. Thus our perspective on matters is, I think, valuable to a policy man such as Mr. Mycroft Holmes. My reports, which my father has always encouraged, and with which he has often assisted, balance the views of Siamese ambassadors on the one hand, and colonial politicians on the other.

"I do not pretend disinterest. It is to the advantage of our family and businesses that Siam remains independent. I know that is the aim of Mr. Mycroft as well, though others in the British government feel differently. We welcome the reforms of the present King of Siam and his brothers, and hope it is not too little and too late."

"What if Siam is not strong enough to resist the encroachment of the

French?" asked Holmes.

"I will admit that, if Siam is to lose its sovereignty, we should prefer it to be to the British, who don't really want it. The French at Saigon *desperately* want Siam, and are determined to interfere in every aspect of the country, as they do in Cochin China and Annam."

"Would your family remain here, in that event?"

"We should have little choice. Siam is the last major country in Asia to remain independent. Anything that we can do to help it remain that way, we will do, and gladly."

The study door opened and Captain Jones entered. I suspect he had waited outside the door while *Señor* Azcevado Marques finished with his preliminaries.

"Introduced all round, I take it?" he asked. He turned to Holmes. "Knows more about Siam than anyone, with no exceptions, does *Señor* Joao Enrique! If there is anything you need to know about Siam, Professor, or about anyone here, he is the man to ask."

"That much is abundantly clear, and your assistance, *Señor*, may be just what we require at this very moment."

"How so, Professor?" asked our new Portuguese ally.

"Has Captain Jones informed you of our actual role here at Siam?"

"I have taken that liberty. *Señor* Azcevado Marques knows the General Adviser well, as they frequently have business matters to discuss."

"It would indeed be a tragedy for Siam if he to be were murdered," said the Portuguese. "He has quickly gained the respect of the King and his reformers. He's been successful in implementing many of his ideas to modernise the functions of the state. Not by any means an easy thing to have achieved, and in such a short space of time. A bit legalistic, but I wouldn't have him murdered for that."

"We have a list of those involved in some way with Siamese concessions," said Holmes. "It's possible our culprit is amongst them, but it is a formidable task to investigate them all. With your assistance, we should be able to eliminate many, and reduce our list to manageable proportions."

"Certainly," replied *Señor* Azcevado Marques.

"Then, it occurs to me that you may be able to help in the matter of *Sia* Ah Foo and the Kimlong-Yunnan Railway project," said Holmes.

"What is it that you need to know?"

"What is his involvement? Does it have any bearing on this matter of conspiracy against Rolin? Who are the promoters, actual and silent, of the project? And why should an English peer be involved with a villain such as *Sia* Ah Foo?"

"I can answer all of that immediately. To the Chinese community here he is not seen as a villain. Rather he is their godfather, taking care of their needs, but exacting his payment in return. He has made himself wealthy, powerful and respected, and is a great public benefactor. He is also a vicious killer, and has many such in his pay.

"His involvement in this railway project really amounts to a form of blackmail. His power is such that he can command the Haws, and the other clans along the route, to attack the line, or to refrain. He will stage a few incidents, when the time is right, and men will die. For his fee, he will then 'pacify' the area. I have no doubt that, if the line is built, large and frequent payments to *Sia* Ah Foo will be required to keep the line operating. The occasional tragic - but highly profitable - robbery will keep the directors paying. He will make no investment himself.

"Construction of such a railway would almost certainly require the co-operation of the Siamese, even though it will not run through Siamese territory. I should imagine the Siamese would see it as a threat to their security. British, Chinese or perhaps French troops could be sent quickly to any point along our Northern border. As it lies outside Siamese control, little could be done other than to spend vast sums defending thousands of miles of border. So, I suggest you ask Rolin directly. It may be that he has not had to deal with the matter as yet, but the promoters do not wish to have to deal with such a man.

"The promoters are British investors based at Singapore and London. Their counterparts at Hong Kong have also invested heavily in the preliminary stages, and are negotiating for the concession at the Chinese end of things. Offices are already set up in Upper Burma and in Yunnan, with engineering studies underway, I believe. The aim, of course, is to float the company on the exchanges of Europe. I have heard the figure of ten million pounds mentioned, but I can't confirm it.

"As to why an English peer is involved with *Sia* Ah Foo, I take it you refer to Lord Coledale? His reputation here is that of an aggressive railway entrepreneur, willing to take large risks to secure major concessions. I imagine he has been apprised of the role of *Sia* Ah Foo in the matter, and realises he must deal with him."

"What is your personal view of the whole project?" asked Holmes.

"If the promoters are serious, they would almost certainly lose their shirts. There is no way to turn a profit when every inch of the route is through country infested by bandits armed to the teeth. I shan't mention the difficulty of securing the concessions from the Chinese."

"You say, 'If the promoters are serious'!"

"It may well turn out to be nothing more than an elaborate swindle, with vast sums at stake. The China Card is heady stuff to London investors; the fabled markets of China waiting for European goods and Indian opium, with payment in Chinese tea, silks and spices at a discount. Mostly nonsense, of course, as my father - and his - would tell you. Chinese don't need European goods, and can't pay for them anyway. Now, is there anything else I can help you with?"

"Chief Inspector Sheriff is arranging for us to meet with Mr. Ah Foo. Could you accompany us, as neither of us has any Chinese? We have seen him, recently, after the gang war at Chinatown the other day."

"Why the interest in *Sia* Ah Foo in particular?" asked the Portuguese.

"Put it down to curiosity at this stage. I have a reason in terms of the ethnic origins of the tribes of Southern China, and their flight to Siam in centuries past. I have heard of his influence there, and would like to arrange protection for my expedition. That will be our story, but it will allow a lot of other questions to be asked as well."

"*Sia* Ah Foo will not answer anything which will reveal his secrets, Professor Sigerson, I assure you."

"What men refuse to reveal is often more illuminating than that which they do divulge."

"Very well, Professor. Inform me as to the time, and by whom the meeting has been arranged. As to your list of possible conspirators, it would be better if we went through it together. If you have time tomorrow, may I invite you to my house for luncheon at noon? We can go over your files at our leisure afterwards, and I shall introduce you to my father. He knows far more of Siam than I ever will."

"Thank you. How do we find your house?"

"Simplicity itself. If you will come to the window? You see across the river, the large teak *godown*. Behind our wharves there you see the Church spire, with a large white house fronting to the river beside it. Simply tell the boat-boy at the Oriental pier to take you to the house of *Nai* Portugee. They all know the house, because my father enjoys coming to the Oriental in the afternoons, and talking with whichever sea-captains are in town. Especially the older ones! Loves to chide the British that in half a century they never caught either his father or him, though they had several close escapes to reminisce over."

"Tell me, *Señor*!" said I, "that superb white ship moored at your wharf. Does she belong to your company?"

"*White Bird*? No - not to the company! She's mine! My father rescued her from a dismal fate, and we restored her beauty together at our shipyard. He sailed her every windy season from then until he went blind. Then he gave her to me. We still take her out each year, but my time is limited. She is, indeed, a thing of beauty. Perhaps, if the fancy takes him, my father will tell you her remarkable story. Let us thank our host for the cigars and conversation, and we will meet at noon tomorrow."

CHAPTER XXXV

6th June 1893
Bangkok, Siam

IN THE MORNING we visited Rolin at home, said hello to Tashi, and asked the General Adviser about the Kimlong-Yunnan railway project. He had little to add to *Señor* Azcevado Marques' comments of yesterday, save that, by coincidence, just two days previously he had received a visit at the Ministry from Lord Coledale and his aide, Quiney, about precisely that project. They had asked for consideration of their plan to run a branch line across the Siamese border, to link to the Northern city of Chieng Mai.

"Exactly how did you respond?" asked Holmes.

"I informed them that I would certainly consider the proposal, but that with the current state of affairs I could not promise any early reply, as it was sure to be a controversial matter with the Siamese government. I also informed them, privately, that I thought the proposal stood very little chance of a favourable response, given the concerns the Siamese had already expressed regarding the main line itself."

"How did Lord Coledale take that?"

"Offhanded, I should say. Certainly he didn't seem put out at all. Chatted a little about English politics, then left. Polite the whole time, of course, in his superior way."

"Is there any news of which we should be aware?" enquired Holmes.

"Pavie has been making impossible demands, as usual. The Siamese legation at Paris has been hopelessly out of touch, so it appears that Prince Svasti will be sent there. I have suggested that my son be appointed as secretary;

quite frankly, I worry about Svasti's too-obvious ties to the British, and it is as well to be reliably informed as to what's going on there. His Majesty has already given his approval to that suggestion, by the way."

I visited Tashi again, while Holmes spoke with Rinzing about security at the house. Holmes made a few suggestions, and we left in our hired gharry to return to the Oriental pier.

Asking a gondolier in Siamese to take us to the house of *Nai* Portugee brought us across the broad, swift river, but somewhat downstream of the church spire. In the lee of the shore the current was negligible, and our gondolier soon reached the wharf where the white clipper was moored, creaking and slapping in the wash of the river craft.

Nai Portugee himself greeted us at the small *sala* at the end of the wharf. It was evident that he was known in this way by all of his people. He ushered us into an arched open terrace, shaded by enormous trees. The walls were freshly whitewashed, and cool blue Moorish tiles covered the floor. A small fountain played in a tiled pool, and a breeze from the river washed delightfully through the arches.

We sat at a wrought-iron table and drank lemon squash with the luxury of ice from his ice freezing plant. It was easy to see why *Nai* Portugee did not relish any drastic changes in the status quo. Holmes produced his report, and over the next two hours he and *Señor* Azcevado Marques managed, by a process of logical elimination, to reduce the possibles to four.

One was a Frenchman who had come to Siam years before, quickly made a fortune, and as quickly lost it again. For this he blamed the Siamese government for refusing to issue a concession, in preparation for which he had already invested heavily. The second was a similar tale, this time involving a German mining concession. This was revoked when the owners were unable to pay back-taxes, which they had formerly avoided paying by bribing the provincial tax collector. Both had dropped out of sight some months previously, and thus had to be considered as possibles.

The third was quite a different matter. This investigation had been initiated by Chief-Inspector Sheriff, who had been itching to get his hands on a certain gang of Belgian swindlers for years, but always without success. They operated throughout the East, from Cairo to Java to Japan. Their schemes were *just* legal. They depended for their undeniable success on the gullibility of the greedy, newly wealthy traders and entrepreneurs to be found wherever quick fortunes are being made. There they went - until they had milked the place dry, or it became too hot to stay.

Sheriff had narrowly failed to get them when he was stationed at Singapore. When they turned up at Bangkok and began touting their investment opportunities, he kept his eye on them and their schemes. Their method was to salt a fund, in a public bank, with their own cash, to create the impression that investors were flocking in. Later investors would find the account empty one day, and the scoundrels gone over the horizon.

Realising that their scheme flouted a little-known Siamese regulation, and knowing their *modus operandi*, Sheriff allowed the villains' seed money to flow into the account at the bank before asking Rolin to have the scheme declared unlawful in Siam, and the funds already in the account frozen. The Belgians had fled, to a man, but word in the underworld had it that Rolin was marked for death for his public role in the affair, which had cost the swindlers dearly.

The fourth was the Singapore consortium that employed Godfrey Norton. Not on the list, but clearly making a fifth, was the curious involvement of Lord Coledale and *Sia* Ah Foo in a dubious railway project. We could not be certain that a suspect had not slipped unrecorded through our net, but felt it unlikely - and we had reduced our investigations to workable size. Nevertheless, much work lay ahead of us if we were to begin to unravel the mystery behind the attempts on the life of the General Adviser.

I had also not forgotten the two attempts on Holmes's life at Singapore, and wondered whether the matters were connected, and if so, exactly how?

Now that business was taken care of, *Nai* Portugee called for the servants, and an excellent Siamese meal was served. After our bleak year in the inhospitable Himalayas, and more time in the harsh Egyptian and Sudanese deserts, the ready hospitality - and the delicious variety of Siamese dishes - never ceased to delight.

It seemed that wherever we went we were offered food and drink as a matter of course. This was in addition to the cuisine - when we dined in - at the Oriental, where a normal tiffin included soup, fish, three types of meat, along with curry and a dessert, with dinner being along much the same lines. We should have to start again on our *baritsu* routines, which we had not done since leaving the ship at Singapore. Holmes was now sufficiently recovered, and it would speed the final restoration of his remarkable strength and endurance.

"And now, M. Le Villard, I shall introduce you to my father, and perhaps to *White Bird*." He stood and we walked along the wharf past the clipper to the farthest end, where a mass of greenery and fluted bamboos almost concealed a small paved garden in their deep shade. By the glazed porcelain balustrade, gazing with sightless eyes across the brown river from which he had sailed for so many years, sat an old man. His physique still retained the stocky power evident in his son. As he turned towards the sound of our approach his white hair lifted lightly in the breeze.

"My father, *Señor* Jose Felipe."

"These must be your friends Professor Sigerson and M. Le Villard, Joao," he said, in slow but clear English. "Please, be seated. Welcome to our little piece of Portugal in Siam. We even have our own church, and Catholic priest. I invite you both to worship there at any time, if you should desire. I had little time for worship myself, as a young vagabond, but it is a restful consolation to an old man such as I."

"Father, I have told you of the plot against M. Rolin. Perhaps you could assist the Professor?"

"If there were any way, yes, of course."

Holmes spoke quietly. "I have discussed the current situation at Siam in great detail with your son, and it has been most helpful. But perhaps with the insight of years spent dealing with the Siamese, you could consider this question. Is there any possibility that a faction of the Siamese nobility, or other Siamese group, would seek the death of M. Rolin as a solution to their problems? Or perhaps in revenge?"

"My eyes have failed me, Professor Sigerson, but my ears and mind have become the sharper for it. I hear of most matters of any consequence in Bangkok. It has come to my notice that the policies of reform advocated by the General Adviser are highly unpopular in some high circles, though what he does is at the King's bidding."

"So you think it is possible . . ?"

"That is not quite what I meant, no, not at all. Murdering the King's appointed official would be a grave matter if charges were ever brought, but that would not hinder some of the more unscrupulous and greedy of the nobles. Others can readily be bribed or threatened to take the blame. This is Siam, after all is said and done. A wit once remarked of the Siamese that they were 'all pride and no shame'. No, so long as they were not publicly caught out, they would lose not a minute of sleep or play over the death of the *farang* adviser.

"The real reason I doubt any of them are involved is that it would solve nothing, and destroy everything. The immediate tormentor would be removed, but the very act of murdering such a man would likely precipitate the events they are so anxious to avoid, by providing a pretext for annexation by force. They may fight amongst themselves, but they all know that there is no turning back once that has happened, and that all their privileges and wealth will be lost.

"Joao Enrique tells me time is short. I suggest that, unless you come across evidence of treachery with a foreign power, you concentrate elsewhere."

"Thank you, *Señor*. But we trespass upon your time. This is a most peaceful little enclave here, and our concerns must seem unimportant."

"Shows how little you know of the ways of old men, young man!" said *Señor* Jose Felipe in mock severity. "I care for this place. These few blocks of land have provided a home to our Portuguese for hundreds of years, and to my family since I came here fifty and more years ago. We should be swept away by the wind of the Europeans, and lose much that we value. It may seem that I doze and dream, but I still give Joao Enrique his catechism every evening regarding the events of the day, and there is not much in this family, this business or this town that escapes my attention.

"And now it is my usual time for crossing to the Oriental. If you would join me in my cutter, I can deliver you to your hotel, and perhaps you will take tea with an old sailor? Rum not being allowed now."

We took our leave of the young *Nai* Portugee, and embarked with the old man and his valet in a trim ship's cutter manned by four sturdy oarsmen.

"Have to use these steam vessels for trade, but I won't have them for my own use. Can't stand the noise. Always loved the sights and sounds of the sea. Now I'm denied the sights, I *must* have the sounds."

"Seems perfectly reasonable," replied Holmes, as the oarsmen propelled us downstream and across to the hotel wharf. The old gentleman was greeted with respect and deference by the Oriental's staff, and they and the valet made him comfortable in his chair in a quiet corner of the sanded courtyard. The promised tea appeared, and soon other old gentlemen, long retired from the sea or the frontier, occupied the adjoining tables. Old tales were being re-told, and old adventures relived.

Holmes and I enjoyed the conversation for a while, then politely thanked our host, and excused ourselves, promising to call on him again. Over a game of billiards in the deserted games room, we reviewed our progress, and mapped out strategies for the investigation of our various leads.

12th June 1893
Bangkok, Siam
At nightfall we visited the General Adviser for further news on the reported approach of two French war ships. He assured us that the report was false. He also told us of a message from Rosebery counselling devastation of the country at the Mae Kong to defend the border, and the obstruction of navigation. All of this has been underway for some time, he told us; the curious thing is that this is diametrically opposed to the advice proffered in Rosebery's last dispatch.

Pavie has apparently pretended to discover what he has been told long ago, that Captain Thoreaux has been sent to Bangkok. Now he claims that the Siamese are going to exhibit the Captain publicly, and of course protests against that as well.

CHAPTER XXXVI

16th June 1893
Bangkok, Siam

AFTER THE FIRST hectic week or so of familiarising ourselves with the town and its inhabitants Holmes and I had settled into a loose routine, which we broke as required. In the early mornings we would practice our *baritsu* exercises and routines on the hotel lawn. I had become quite proficient under Holmes's tutelage, and looked forward to the daily sparring which followed our routines.

We visited the house of Rolin, and checked with Rinzing - and with Tashi, who was always at his side when we arrived. As usual whenever he was there, Rolin gave us a quick briefing on the events of the developing crisis, and discussed his scheduled appointments. The General Adviser talked about the success of his campaign to educate the French public as to the true facts of the Siam Question.

"*Le Figaro* has strongly opposed the current policy of colonial expansion, and *L'Intransigeant* likewise. Unfortunately, our Paris legation has printed an appallingly foolish article in *Le Temps.* Then there has been the problem here at Bangkok with the *Siam Free Press.* Lillie has gone too far this time, and I may well move for his expulsion from Siam. We'll send some of the back issues to the legal adviser at the legation at Singapore.

"By the by, we also found out that that curious message recommending defence of the Mae Kong came not from Lord Rosebery, but from his predecessor as Foreign Minister Lord Salisbury, privately and confidentially. It was a sad day for Siam when the government fell. He was always far more supportive of the Siamese position than Rosebery."

While we were there an urgent message arrived from Pavie, requesting an immediate audience with the Prince and the General Adviser regarding a 'serious incident' at Kam Muon, during which a Siamese officer was accused of killing a French officer and seventeen Annamite troops. Rolin excused himself in order to go to the Foreign Ministry.

Before he left us Holmes insisted again that Rinzing accompany him whenever he travelled at night. Having assured ourselves that the General Adviser was safe for now, we then returned to our sitting room at the hotel and got down to the business of the moment; investigating the various suspects.

By now, we had further reduced our list. The first two suspects, after careful investigation of their whereabouts at the times of the threats and poisoning, we considered as unlikely to be our culprits. The Frenchman was now en route to the Seychelles, but had been in a Singapore debtor's jail for the past five months; he had received no visitors until his sister arrived from France to clear his debts, on condition that he quit Asia. The German had been in Japan and Korea, his movements documented throughout. His business had received fresh capital, from Berlin investors he had met on the ship to Japan. He had returned to Siam with his new partners in the past week, to pay his fines and back taxes, and seemed to be in the best of spirits. We crossed them both off our list.

The others were not so easily dismissed. The Belgian gang had many members, always on the move to avoid retribution for past swindles while looking for new victims. Sheriff told us, when we called on him again a week ago, that at least three gang members were suspected of murders, one by poisoning. Their movements proved almost impossible to trace, as they frequently changed identity papers and travel documents. Several of them had been spotted in Bangkok during the relevant times. Cowardly attacks and threats would be entirely in character for any of them.

The swindlers' funds were still frozen at the bank, and two attempts to bribe bank officials to release them had been reported to Sheriff. At present one of the gang was in Bangkok, supposedly in hiding. Sheriff had him under surveillance at a brothel where his mistress was the *Mama-san*.

"We'll visit our seedy friend in the next day or two, le Villard. I think we'll make a fine pair of likely victims."

The Singapore syndicate represented by Godfrey Norton was our next subject for investigation. We found that the principals had long associated with Siamese of dubious reputation, and thus their physical absence from Bangkok need not mean they were uninvolved.

"We should consider," said Holmes, as we reviewed our progress, "that they may have two motives, if they are the ones we're after. We know that

Godfrey Norton has been unsuccessfully petitioning Rolin on their behalf, in the matter of their gold mining concession. It may be revenge for their losses caused by the General Adviser's refusal to extend their concession on more favourable terms, or it may be in hope of more co-operation from a successor. Or secondly, it is possible they are acting as a tool for wider British interests at Singapore, hoping to provoke the French into making a move against Siam which they can then use to demand that the British seize Bangkok and the central plains."

"How do we investigate such a diffuse threat, though, Holmes? The principals are in Singapore, after all."

"Firstly, we keep a close watch on Godfrey Norton whenever he's here. It's likely he acts as go-between with their Siamese associates. That may explain his presence in the bawdy-houses and dens of the town. Then we will need some help from Sheriff, information from the Police at Singapore. I only hope Sheriff has people he can trust there. We can't be certain as to whom amongst the British may be secretly sympathetic to their aims. Enormous sums are at stake, after all."

"Finally, then, what of Lord Coledale?" I asked Holmes. "Do you seriously suspect an English peer of involvement in a plot to murder and deceive?"

"I certainly don't exclude him by reason of his title or position. He has, by all accounts, vast investments. That means great risk as well. Most of the great fortunes of this world originated when a forceful man seized what was not rightfully his from his less powerful, but wealthy, fellows. Frequently it is not only the wealth that is passed from father to son. The rapacious instinct may be passed along as well, and often is, concealed for the most part beneath a veneer of respectability."

"I grant you that is true, in many cases. But according to that report in the *Bangkok Times*, Lord Coledale is here, in part, to report to your government on the state of the region. He is reputed to be seeking appointment as Foreign Minister in the next election. Surely, Holmes, his loyalty must have been tested and proven by now."

"You surprise me, le Villard. As a good republican, you should have him at the head of your list. Seriously, though; he may be quite innocently engaged in just one more prospective project, and his contact with *Sia* Ah Foo may be of the most incidental nature. I am curious about it all, but I shall give him the benefit of the doubt by investigating his activities in exactly the same way as our more plebeian suspects, until the results absolve him from responsibility for these threatening acts."

CHAPT1ER XXXVII

23rd June 1893
Bangkok, Siam

EVENTS SEEMED TO BE coming to a head here at Siam, and the General Adviser was called out most nights to the Ministry. This caused us great concern, but there was no alternative, given the nocturnal working habits of the King and all his brothers. It was clear that they worked hard, or most of them did. In this crisis atmosphere the discussions carried on until dawn on many occasions. That had clearly been the case the previous evening; nevertheless the General Adviser was awake and at work when we arrived in the late morning. He gave us the usual briefing, as we had not seen him for several days.

"Last Sunday we were told that the French Government had ordered three war-ships to sail for Siam from Saigon. This caused great alarm at court, until Pavie announced next morning that the press article concerning the sending of the China Squadron to Siam was not correct. Then on Tuesday a plain-text telegraph was intercepted from Pavie, addressed to the *Triomphante* at the port, Saigon. This of course confirmed the presence or imminent arrival of the Admiral's flagship at Saigon, less than two days sailing from Bangkok."

The General Adviser called for more coffee.

"The princes are all concerned, as it takes five days to fortify the river mouth according to present plans. I just this morning counselled caution to the Prince, who sent me a long message immediately I arrived home from the Palace. I then went to see Captain Kirby, to get his assessment of the situation. As I passed by I was struck by the battle-ready appearance of the *Lutin.* Her guns are aimed in the direction of the Palace, though Kirby believes she merely makes ready to fight her way out of the river if necessary.

Rolin of late seemed to think the threat to his person had passed, and chafed somewhat at the restrictions, and at having a personal guard. Holmes was of quite the opposite opinion.

"So long as you are here, advising the King to resist, you must remain a threat to whomever you were a danger before. I suspect that our birds are waiting to see what happens over this Grosgurin affair, and the conflict on the Mekong. Perhaps they feel events will play into their hands anyway."

"What has all your investigation revealed, Professor Sigerson, if I may ask?" enquired the Belgian jurist. "I have not, it is true, been assassinated, but have you found any evidence to suggest who was behind it all?"

"I have managed to eliminate all but two or three possible suspects from your list of business concessionaires. This leaves us with those remaining on the list, or disaffected Siamese nobility, or the various interested colonialists on both sides. It is unlikely, in my opinion, to be instigated by the Siamese, but some individual involvement is possible. There appears to be some overlap between these different groupings. We have followed your carriage on several occasions, at some distance. A pattern has emerged."

"How so?' asked the General Adviser, curious in spite of his scepticism.

"When you decide on the spur of the moment to go somewhere, or when you attend social occasions with the European community, your carriage is not followed. Conversely, when you are expected, or sent for, by the Minister, your carriage is invariably followed. Are you aware of any security assigned for your protection by the Ministry or the Palace?"

"On the contrary, Prince Ranawongse has kindly let me know that if I require an escort, I have only to ask. I have never felt the need to trouble him before now. What do they look like, these shadows following me about? I take it there is no mistake here?"

"None at all, sir! There are four of them, working in two teams. They use hired jinrickashaws or gharries, changing positions and conveyances from time to time so as to remain inconspicuous. All are local Chinese, judging by their dress and hair. As to whether they are following you to learn your usual routes to the ministry, or whether there is the intention, one of these nights, to harm or assassinate you in your carriage, I cannot say."

"Should I worry about this?" asked Rolin.

"Most assuredly! If there were a way to avoid these journeys, I should recommend that you do so. As that is not possible, let us turn what we know to our advantage. I suspect there is someone - probably well placed and trusted - in the Foreign Ministry, informing your watchers of your movements on official business. Rinzing will continue to drive with you, and will be armed with a repeating carbine, as well as his *kukri* cutlass. Tashi will ride up front with Rinzing; he is obedient to his commands now. Le Villard and I will continue to watch from the rear on those nights when our investigations do not take us elsewhere. If you can make a list, once again, of the most likely suspects, we can eliminate them one by one."

"But how will you tell which one is the turncoat?"

"I take it the Prince has an official itinerary in his capacity as Minister of Foreign Affairs?"

"Of course! The daily schedule for the Minister is made at the end of the previous day. As an adviser to the King, my appointments are noted, and arrangements for transportation made accordingly."

"As I expected! Simply by altering one copy of your official schedule each day, and giving it to the suspects in turn, we will soon see which of them is alerting the shadows. It is crucial, however, that we not alert the informant by our actions, as we need him to lead us to his employers."

"Very well. Seems simple enough. I shall start on Monday. I can give you the list now."

He proceeded to write out the names of four Siamese officials, in English, and handed it to Holmes. "Only these four see the complete schedule, which is the one with my appointments in it."

Thank you! You may save the explanations as to who they are until we have a single suspect. Please make an extract copy of each day's actual schedule, and note the alteration made to one copy. We will call on you again on Friday to compare notes."

The previous evening, Mrs. Norton had called at the hotel while we were out, and had left her card and a sealed message. Holmes had read it to himself, then tucked it away in his notebook.

"She has left for Singapore, at short notice," he said. "She implores me to continue our investigations into whoever has a hold over Norton. He will return to Bangkok in a month. She is to join him two weeks later, assuming there is still peace here."

"It will be difficult to achieve much, when he is not here," I replied.

"Oh, I think it will provide us an excellent opportunity to visit his haunts, and strike an acquaintance with some of his cronies. Buy a few rounds for the house, act a little foolish, talk too loudly about nothing in particular."

Holmes and I had used the *'in vino veritas'* routine again and again. We decide to start that evening, it being a Friday, as the next week our evenings would be spent following those who would follow the General Adviser. It seemed that a little rest and a substantial meal were called for in preparation, so we returned to our hotel.

At nine-thirty that evening, dressed rather gaudily, Holmes and I hailed a jinrickashaw and asked to be taken to the foreign night-clubs on Si Phraya Road - the 'green light' district, as it was known. The journey took less than twenty minutes.

CHAPTER XXXVIII

23rd June 1893
Bangkok, Siam

A ROW OF ESTABLISHMENTS advertised in English or German. We selected one of the larger places, and allowed ourselves to be hustled into a smoky, dimly-lit room.

A long bar stretched the length of the room, with a row of booths along the opposite wall. Round tables with chairs for four filled the space between, except for a space where a few couples were swaying in a sort of half-dance, half-embrace. The women, of whom there were many, were from Siam, Lao, Japan, with a few Russians or Poles amongst them. They seemed to be distributed loosely amongst the men, who were from every nation in Europe, and from many walks of life. Some wore evening clothes, others were in lounge suits, a few were in shirtsleeves and garters, collars loosened.

A babble of languages at great volume filled the room. We went entirely unnoticed and settled on stools at the bar counter, amongst the fellows in evening clothes. After a beer or two, Holmes turned to the barkeep, and made a broad gesture including all the swells, and one or two girls who were with them.

"Barkeep, a drink for all these fine gentlemen here, and their ladies! And another for my friend and I!" The man quickly served up beers all round, and a toast was drunk to no one in particular. "Thank you, and have one yourself, my good fellow!"

One of the men turned to us. "Haven't seen you chaps here before. Just passing through?"

Holmes came out with our story. "Thought we'd find a friend of ours down here. Perhaps you know him? Lawyer fellow, Godfrey Norton?"

"Ah! Godfrey is it? Bit early for him. He'll be in later, here or next door, or else down at the opium den."

"Another drink? We're having one, at any rate! Actually, you've hit the nail square on the head, my friend. He said if we found him here, we could go on to the den together. Curiosity, you know! Never tried the stuff, and as we're here in the Orient, well, you know . . ."

"Actually, no! Never tried it, m'self. Hasn't done much good for poor old Godfrey either, ask me. He sometimes goes directly there. Easy to find! Just ask the jinrickashaw boys outside the door. Just say, 'Take me opium same

same Missa Gofflee.' Don't bother speaking Siamese. Waste of time! But the heathen will take you there in no time. Down by the river. One of *Sia* Ah Foo's places, same as this."

"You seem to know a great deal about these matters, my friend," remarked Holmes, slurring his words a little.

"Been here for five years, so I should do. Not a lot else to do, once you've closed the office for the day. The wife won't live here. Tried it for three months. Hard to tell whether the heat or the Siamese irritated her more. Close run thing, I'd say. Off she went, back to Bradford. Got three more years to go. They'll likely send me to Patagonia next, according to her. Buy you fellows a drink, eh? Another beer all round, bar-keep!"

We drank sociably for a little longer, then drifted away. A pair of young Lao ladies, heavily mascaraed and lipsticked, interested themselves in us. They were not by any means unattractive under their paint, but I had visions of Miss Malee in my head, and we had things to find out.

"Where to now, Holmes?" I asked. "*Sia* Ah Foo's opium den?"

"I doubt it's known by that name, le Villard, and the answer is, not yet! Those gentlemen are of Norton's quality. I am interested to see what is known of him amongst these chaps in shirtsleeves."

A game of dice was in progress at the far end of the bar. A heavy leather cup was slammed loudly as it was upended on the wooden counter. Players muttered oaths as they shook the die before each throw, then triumphant shouts or groans according to the score. As the loser had to buy a shot of hard liquor for the winner, plus a round for all players, they were all half-drunk by now. None of the women bothered with the dice players, though most other men in the room had company at their tables, or on their laps.

Holmes asked if we could join in for a game or two. We were made welcome. After a few rounds, of which Holmes contrived where possible to end up the loser, he said, "Norton told us this was a sporting bar, and he wasn't wrong, I see."

One of the players, a thickset Prussian fellow, said, "Ah! You know Norton. You are friends of Norton. He is a crazy fellow, you know that! Sometimes I think he tries to drink and smoke himself to death. But if he needs, he can clean up himself and be presentable for breakfast the next day, while I still nurse my head. A crazy fellow!"

"Is he here tonight?" asked Holmes, as he slammed the cup down, and lifted it to look at the dice. "Full house! How do you like that, le Villard? Just when I least needed it."

"He has gone back to Singapore, on last night's steamer. Such oaths he was making the night before. Cursing and swearing! Even here, it was too much. I took him outside to cool off. 'Who do they think they are?' he shouted. 'Telling me what to do all the time. If I had half of my mind I could see them in jail. Perhaps I shall,' he shouted. 'Perhaps I shall tell what I know, and we shall sink all together.' *Und so weiter!* He was very drunk. I don't think he knew what he was saying, crazy fellow. I put him in a jinrickashaw. They know to take him back to the Bangkok Hotel."

"I wonder who he was referring to? Is he given to these outbursts? I had considered retaining him for some legal work, you see, and it is as well to know, where money is concerned."

Being Prussian, Hans understood caution with money all too well, and was forthcoming with further information. "You know, I have wondered that myself. He has done much work for Cutter and Fluddle at Singapore, and they have secrets to protect. Oh yes! I can assure you of that. I am in the mining myself, you see, tin and lead. I don't want to say too much, but I think I shall not buy any of their gold company shares."

"Why ever not, sir, for that is exactly what we are considering doing?" asked Holmes, clumsily spilling a little of his beer on his waistcoat, and mopping at it with his cravat.

"*No gold*, sir, is why not!" Hans slammed the cup down. "You have shared beer with Hans von Hollstein, sir, and I cannot let you do so foolish a thing. There is no gold in their concession, none at all, only a shallow vein near the surface. They are floating their company for a half a million English pounds. Half a million!" He shook his massive head. "If Norton is mixed up in that, he will soon be found in the river."

"But you seemed to think he may have been referring to someone else, someone other than Cutter and Co., just a few minutes ago?"

"I did? Oh! Yes, I did think maybe he was so angry with his new client. The English lord, with his silver stick and monocle. They were here together last week. A party of them, from that splendid steam-yacht! Norton had words with the lord's man. A few heated words, soon passed over. I remember the party went on for supper. But Norton, he was too angry to do anything but drink and drink. Furious, he was. He kept muttering something, about Men of Straw. 'I'll get them', he said. 'I'll have my last word with those Men of Straw before I go, just see if I don't!' And on, and on, until I sent him off to his hotel."

"Hans, pay attention!" cried one of his friends, and Hans turned back to the dice game. We played out that game and the next, then excused ourselves to get some fresh air. Despite a heavy meal, both Holmes and I needed to clear our heads, not being accustomed to drinking at such a pace.

"Well, le Villard, a little treasure trove of information that was, and no doubt about it. I suggest we push our luck, and carry on. Norton seems to be remembered fondly wherever he is a regular. Let's see what they think of him at *Sia* Ah Foo's opium den."

After instructing the jinrickashaw-man as we had been told to do, we settled back with our own thoughts as he dodged through the evening streets, headed for the Chinese quarter by the river bank. The street and all the narrow lanes leading away from it were crowded with Siamese having their evening meal at a thousand small stands, or in vast covered restaurants. Freshly washed and powdered, small children played around their parents feet in their brightly coloured satin pyjamas, or dozed in their nannies' arms. Lanterns winked everywhere, music blared from a Chinese orchestra touting for customers outside the playhouses, and once again I marvelled at the bustle and energy of Bangkok, which never seemed to sleep. It was early hours yet for this restless city, where late revellers and night workers would still be abroad even as hawkers began their rounds, and gongs summoned the monks to their morning devotions.

Our jinrickashaw turned off the bright main street into a narrow lane, lit dimly by a few red paper lanterns, and came to a halt almost at the river's bank. A small Chinese in a high-collar satin coat stood up from a stool in the shadows. "You want Heavenly Pavilion?" he asked. "Follow, please. Follow this way."

We paid our jinrickashaw-man, and asked him to wait, promising extra pay. He squatted comfortably where he stood, between the shafts of his small cart, and pulled a cheroot from behind his ear. Having no means of lighting it, he merely sucked on it, apparently content.

Our Chinese guide had darted into the alley, for it was little more. As we passed down the dim lane, we heard, and then glimpsed, a *mah-jong* game in full swing, the loud clicking of the tiles mixing with the shrill voices of Chinese women at their gambling. At several doors, as we passed, heavily made-up young girls leaned against the doorframes and smiled invitingly. Though dressed in Chinese clothes they were mostly Siamese or Laos, from the north, with the pale skin so admired by all Asiatics.

Our guide turned into the club's doorway, which was decorated with gaudy carved and gilded dragons, its name picked out in red and gold Chinese calligraphy.

The *maître'd* was a portly, cheerful little Chinaman. With his plucked eyebrows and lightly rouged cheeks he was far removed from the emaciated and wizened guardian I had imagined.

"Good evening, kind sirs." He shook hands with himself, and smiled with a mouth full of gold-filled teeth. "How may I help you? Champagne, a pipe or so of opium of course? Perhaps some gambling at *mah-jong*? Lovely young girls feed you? Or boys, if that your taste? We have all here at Heavenly Pavilion."

I had certain misgivings about being here at all, I must confess, now that my head had cleared. I knew from Doctor Watson's accounts that Holmes had, in the past, indulged rather freely in morphine and cocaine. I had always thought it likely that the reactions to these poisons had contributed to his obsession with Professor Moriarty and his gang, which had so nearly caused his death on several occasions.

Doctor Watson had managed to wean his friend away from drugs before his supposed death, and I had seen no evidence of desire to indulge seriously again, despite the ready availability. True, we had shared a pipe or two of opium with some Persians at Isphahan, and a bowl of *kif* at Cairo, but those had been required politenesses, to put our hosts at ease when our disguises were being questioned.

Perhaps this was different! I was not fond of the effects myself – I always felt queasy in the extreme the following morning - but could indulge if required, without fear of becoming enslaved. With Holmes, there was always the possibility that he may go into one of his moods, and take to the opium couch for days at a time, entirely ignoring the business at hand. According to Doctor Watson, he had done so many a time in the past.

My face must have revealed my concern, for Holmes said, not unkindly, "Do not worry so, le Villard. We are here to find out what we can of Godfrey Norton's life here at Siam, and I shall not lose sight of that. We will indulge just sufficiently that we do not seem out of place, and see what we can find out. Then, we will leave."

A waiter passed close by, with a magnum of Veuve Cliquot in a bucket of ice.

"Champagne of quality, and ice as well! I am surprised!"

Holmes turned to the portly Chinese, who was waiting on our desire.

"I think a bottle of your champagne, first of all, my good man."

We were seated on a low sofa, with a lacquered table in front, and cushions at each side. I looked around, and saw in the dim light a row of recessed cubicles around the walls of the large room, each with a varnished wooden divan on which reclined an opium devotee. On low tables alongside each divan were the smokers' personal accoutrements. A few old men glided from cubicle to cubicle, rolling opium into pellets, then charging a pipe and lighting it expertly from the side, before flitting on to the next stirring smoker.

Our champagne arrived, brought by one of the servants. Three or four gaudily dressed girls hovered hopefully nearby, but Holmes seemed not to notice them. He examined the bottle.

"*Zoedone*! And I thought we had found a decent wine in this out-of-the-way place. Not chilled, either."

He called over the *maître'd*, or whatever he was, and asked politely if we could change our champagne to the same we had seen, never mind if it cost more.

"Many sorry, sir. This our only champagne. The gentleman over there bring own bottle, pays all the same. So sorry."

"Very well. This will do." He turned to me. "I thought it was too good to be true, but didn't want to ask outright. Le Villard, I can't see over my shoulder. Please take an innocent glance into that far cubicle, where the excellent Veuve Cliquot is served. Do we see who I think we shall see?"

I casually surveyed the far end of the room, my glance passing briefly over the end cubicle. Reclining languidly on the polished wood divan, top hat hung on a hook, dress shirt opened at the neck, was Lord Coledale. His eyes were barely open as he lay on his side, inhaling from the pipe held by a delicate young Siamese boy of around fifteen years. The champagne sat on the floor, opened but not drunk from as yet.

"Ah! Yes, I see what you mean. It is indeed his lordship." I looked more carefully around the room. "I don't see Quiney anywhere. There is one other English swell, though, in the next cubicle. We haven't seen him before. Fifty or rather more, but looks fit. A fine set of white moustaches, and a sunburnt face."

"They must have come on from dinner somewhere. We'll finish this filthy Zoedone and select couches with a vantage point, over there I think. A pipe or two, but keep your wits about you. Don't forget, this is one of *Sia* Ah Foo's places, and Coledale is getting the royal treatment. I want to see where they go from here."

Holmes waved over the *maître'd*, and made arrangements for pipes and divans. Leaving the foul Zoedone half-drunk, we went to our cubicles. Immediately the old Chinese attendants came to our sides, and prepared opium pipes. We reclined and smoked.

DAY SIX

APRIL 11TH 1894

CHAPTER XXXIX

THE SOUND OF THE FIRE being stoked was the first intrusion into my pleasant sleep. A tantalising aroma of fresh coffee wafting through the open doorway of my bedroom was the second. I roused myself and donned my dressing gown, then proceeded down to the sitting room. A low murmur of hushed conversation told me that Holmes had already returned, and that our guest was awake.

Holmes and le Villard were seated at the deal table, steaming cups of coffee in front of them. An enamelled coffee-pot stood between them on a tray, along with a small jug of milk, a cut-glass sugar bowl, and a third cup. I greeted them both, and poured coffee for myself, though I usually drank tea in the mornings.

As I stirred sugar into my coffee I glanced at the clock, and saw that it was not quite seven o'clock.

"Did you sleep well?" I enquired of our guest.

"I did, Doctor Watson, although it seemed that you had retired only a few minutes when Holmes arrived and woke me. But I feel most refreshed, and this is excellent coffee."

"I've asked Mrs. Hudson to bring us three of her finest English breakfasts, Watson. I was just about to wake you. I'm famished myself, having travelled all night with Great Western Railways."

"I had no idea you were leaving London," said I.

"I had a busy day yesterday," remarked Holmes. "I started with Isobel Aster, *nee* Blood. With the assistance of Wiggins and his street arabs I finally tracked her to a small hotel in Pimlico, but she had gone out again shortly after checking in.

"We then turned our attentions to Indian curry-houses, it being lunchtime, in an attempt to locate the establishment where the two jewellers dined before their gruesome demise. We were unsuccessful at the two places I had thought, but I left the Irregulars searching, as I had to go north to Manchester, to interview Inspector Patterson."

"The Irregulars? After three years away they're still assisting you?" laughed le Villard. "I remember them from Doctor Watson's accounts, but somehow I thought by now they'd have all grown up and taken jobs, or been sent away . . . up the river, is that it?"

"Some have, my friend, some have . . . but the ever-resourceful Wiggins has replaced them. I suspect he has an endless supply of recruits within the sound of Bow Bells. They're as sharp as ever, I assure you. They found Isobel Aster for me."

"Wonderful! *Magnifique!*" cried le Villard. "Doctor Watson; the Baker Street Irregulars; this place . . ." he said, sweeping his arms around our sitting room. "How many times I have pictured this very scene, and never thought I should be a part of it. Holmes *en pantoufles! Superbe!*"

A knock sounded at our door, and the stout figure of our landlady pushed a breakfast trolley through the doorway.

"And here you have the final touch, le Villard. May I introduce to you *the* Mrs. Hudson."

Le Villard rose to his feet, and greeted Mrs. Hudson as though she were visiting royalty. She blushed at his Gallic charm, said how nice it was to meet Mr. Sherlock's travelling companion at last, and thanked him for sending Holmes back to Baker Street safe and sound. After dishing out a substantial breakfast for us all, Mrs. Hudson smiled broadly at le Villard again, and left us to enjoy our meal.

"That was the most wonderful breakfast," said le Villard as he dabbed at his lips with a serviette.

"Certainly an improvement on curdled yak's milk, or rice with fermented fish sauce, you'll agree," replied Holmes.

"Manchester! Is that where Patterson was exiled to?" I asked.

"'Exile' is the correct word, Watson. He's been in the same position since getting caught out in the aftermath of the Moriarty gang trial. I doubt he'll receive any further promotion either, at least until that matter is well forgotten at Scotland Yard. But the years of exile have told on him, and I found a defeated man, although he still has his pride. I was able to learn some interesting facts about the disappearance of my files from the blue envelope I left for him when we left for the Continent, so long ago now."

Holmes drank the last of his third cup of coffee, reached for his pipe and filled it, then applied a small, glowing-hot coal to it, using the brass tongs. Once the coarse tobacco he favoured was satisfactorily alight, Holmes leant back in his chair, and took several deep puffs.

"Patterson is a bitter man about all of that affair. He expected promotion when he was assigned to the case and saw the opportunity for advancement. Instead, he feels that all he got for his efforts were ignominy and suspicion, and a blighted career on the force. He feels that . . ."

At that moment Mrs. Hudson interrupted, knocking at the door with a telegraph message in her hand.

"For you, Mr. Holmes. The lad's waiting outside. Shall I tell him there'll be a reply?"

Holmes quickly read the message, grasped paper and a pen and scratched a hurried reply.

"Give him this, please, Mrs. H.! And tell him it's urgent. Here's a shilling for him, to make certain he understands. Thank you kindly."

Mrs. Hudson closed the door and hurried downstairs. Soon we heard the messenger whistling as he ran away up Baker Street towards the telegraph office.

"I've made a terrible blunder, gentlemen. Mister Godfrey Norton has been in London these past two weeks, and I have not known of it. This message is from him. It seems *he* has somehow just found out that I have returned. He wants to meet me at six o'clock this evening, at the public bar of the Criterion. He must have read your tales, Watson, and figured it was the one place I was sure to know. He obviously wants to meet in a crowded place as well."

"I take it you replied that you'll meet him there?" le Villard asked.

"I did, but I shan't wait until then. I will leave shortly. And if you feel up to it, you should accompany me. You know Norton by sight, and he knows you. But first we will all go to see Mycroft, who has agreed to meet us at the St. Pancras Hotel. After that, Doctor Watson has a good deal of reading to do, le Villard. Mycroft has officially commissioned him to write up a report of our doings, based on your Journals."

Holmes went to the door and called down to Billy, the page. I heard him issuing instructions to be conveyed to Wiggins, asking him to have his troops assembled at the Manchester Road entrance to Millwall Park in two hour's time. He also gave Billy some coins, and asked him to buy a copy of all the morning newspapers he could find.

He then returned to sit with us, but remained silent, deep in thought, for some time. Neither le Villard nor I did anything to distract him. Sherlock Holmes was at work.

I then went upstairs to bathe and dress, and returned to the sitting room. Holmes appeared to have moved hardly at all. I noticed that young Billy had already returned with a stack of the morning editions, but they remained unopened on the table. At last Holmes tapped his overheated pipe out into the large ashtray and resumed his conversation with le Villard and I. He asked le Villard about his journey to London, which prompted le Villard to fetch a notebook from his duffel-bag.

This he presented to me, saying, "My apologies, Doctor Watson. I almost forgot. These are the final entries in my Journal, covering the period from the time of Holmes's departure from Siam until my arrival at London yesterday."

I took the notebook from him, thanked him, and placed it in the bookshelves with the other two volumes of his Journals.

"Then I shall also find time to read your entries later today," said Holmes to le Villard, as he donned his overcoat and homburg, scooped up his pile of newspapers, and opened the door for us.

As our hansom headed towards St. Pancras Station, Holmes handed us two papers each, and together we perused the dailies. This time, on his instructions, we concentrated on the headlines for news of the two bombings reported in central London during the past twenty-four hours, then turned to the inside news pages for further reportage on either the escape of Colonel Sebastian Moran or the 'Slash-and-Strangle Murders'.

We removed all pages carrying these items, also the editorials, and piled them up on the empty fourth seat. The rest of the papers were discarded in a heap on the floor of the cab. Holmes picked up the topmost of the remaining news-sheets and read, quickly and methodically, through the entire pile.

"Nothing new, and little of value," he exclaimed, tossing them onto the heap of already-discarded newsprint.

Holmes had scarcely finished his rapid review of the dailies when the hansom pulled up in front of the extravagant Gothic facade of the new St. Pancras Hotel, capped with turrets and pinnacles. Within minutes we had located Mycroft, seated in a quiet corner of the elegant lobby lounge. Mycroft was introduced to le Villard, and it was abundantly clear from Mycroft's demeanour that he held Francois le Villard in high esteem, though they had not previously met in person.

"Welcome to London, M. Le Villard. Firstly, allow me to thank you with all my heart for your part in returning Sherlock to us safe and sound. I received Sherlock's message this morning, and I have sent a message up to *Señor* Jose Felipe to expect us in fifteen minutes. I have very little time, but I thought it best not to meet him at Whitehall, or even at my club. By the way, le Villard, M. De Benoist telegraphed from the *Quai d'Orsay*, asking me to convey his regards. I sent him a message immediately I heard from Sherlock that you had arrived. He had hoped to come over, but with the Upper Nile affair so much in the Paris news he is unable to get away at present."

"Thank you, Mycroft," replied le Villard. "I only hope that bringing *Señor* Azcevado-Marques so far will not prove to be a waste of time."

"Indeed! This whole affair has dragged on far too long as it is. There is no guarantee that your ploy will succeed, but desperate times demand desperate measures. Both de Benoist and I agreed that it is worth the effort and expense if we are to have a chance to get to the bottom of this tangled affair.

"But perhaps you will excuse me for a moment if I spend a few minutes talking with Sherlock about a few other matters, before we join *Señor* Azcevado Marques in his suite."

Mycroft turned to Holmes, and picked up the topmost of the news-sheets from the coffee table, where his brother had placed them.

"Bombs now!" he sighed. "As though we haven't enough on our plates. At least they didn't blow up Crystal Palace. Not that we can spare the two buildings which *were* blown up! The thing is, Sherlock, both of them were generally unknown to the public, but both were facilities of the Foreign Office. File storage, in the one case, and clandestine support facilities in the other. Nondescript, suburban buildings both! But our bombers seem to know exactly what they were after.

"At the same time, the general public believes there is now a campaign of indiscriminate bombing in London, and panic is building. MacDonald was out there this morning, with Lestrade and Gregson in tow. He and the Prime Minister will hold a conference for the press about it early this afternoon, in time to make the evening editions. The usual stuff, I imagine."

"I see that Scotland Yard have still had no success in tracing Moran," remarked Holmes. "The same in the case of the perpetrators of these 'Slash-and-Strangle' murders, as Fleet Street has so quaintly dubbed those atrocities."

"Quite so! Commissioner MacDonald was hauled in to Number Ten this morning and given quite a dressing down about losing Colonel Moran. The Prime Minister is adamant that there must be a leak, or worse, a traitor, somewhere in the upper reaches of his administration. MacDonald was told in no uncertain terms to find out who it is, and apprehend the culprit - discreetly, and quickly.

"Meanwhile, some of the more irresponsible of these odious rags are suggesting that Britain is approaching a state of anarchy. They point to the stake through the chest, and mention vampirism. The stabbed eyes indicate occultism. Strangulation and smashed genitalia are the work of depraved sexual fiends. And then, still not satisfied, others amongst the press must have it that the murders are either for robbery or revenge, cunningly disguised as any or all of the above. The City is up in arms about the damage to London's reputation for stability; the public is decrying the lack of protection; the police rank-and-file are becoming demoralised - as if that were possible - and demanding pay hikes for danger. And of course, Fleet Street is selling newspapers like there *is* no tomorrow . . ."

"Have *you* any theories, Mycroft?" interrupted Holmes.

"Only that - as I am sure has occurred to you as well - I can't help but feel that all these incidents, disparate though they appear at first glance, are in some way connected. And that it is imperative that we find the loose thread which will unravel the whole bloody conspiracy. For conspiracy it is; that much is clear, and it's difficult to avoid the conclusion that the ultimate target is Her Majesty's Government. Precisely how these other elements fit into the picture I cannot yet fathom. Perhaps I am only imagining that there are links between these crimes. I shall leave that to you, Sherlock. But time is absolutely of the essence here. How are you getting along?"

"In the case of Colonel Moran, we have a strong lead. Parker was spotted last night at one of his regular opium dens, but Wiggins lost him on the Underground. But he did hear him remark to the proprietor that he'd be back this evening, and there'll be more than one street arab on his tail, I assure you. They'll not lose him a second time. I'll report tomorrow on developments."

"Very well, Sherlock. But we simply *must* get him back in custody, and quickly."

"As to Isobel Aster, she has decamped to the Belgrave House Hotel. We just missed her, but I have some of Wiggins's lads parked in front, and will be notified when she returns. So far no suspicious characters asking after her, so I'm hopeful I can see her this evening. There are questions she must answer, if she hopes to remain alive for long."

"Precisely. How about these murders by the riverside? Any progress there?"

"Certainly not as much as I'd like. I'm rather at a dead end there. I have placed notices in the tabloids asking for any information that could have a bearing on either murder. The normal wording!

'Could anyone in the general area of the Victoria Embankment, who has noticed anything unusual, especially relating to Asiatics in general, and Indians in particular, please come forward.

Reward offered.'

"No takers so far, but I've often found it to work in the past."

"Very well. Anything else before we go up to see *Señor* Azcevado- Marques? No? Very well then, shall we go? Time is pressing."

As we all trooped up the grand stairway, which was obviously a strain on Mycroft, with all his bulk, Holmes turned to me.

"Remind me to tell you some time of how I solved the extraordinary case of Allerton the Almighty, as he billed himself for that particular escapade. A most accomplished swindler when not performing his famous illusions. Not for the first time, he had convinced an entire ballroom full of marks that he would triple their cash money. The gullibility of mankind *en masse* never ceases to amaze me, Watson.

"Allerton and his cronies worked on the old principles of greed and envy overriding good common-sense. He'd planted a couple of well-rehearsed shills in the audience, who made the early running. One even had his *foreign* currency tripled; an excellent touch, I thought.

"It was just the break I'd been waiting for. I managed to persuade Gregson to arrest Allerton as he left by the stage-door, with all the cash stuffed in his bag. He had convinced the audience that he - and all their little bags of cash, carefully marked with their names - were still on stage in a sealed Egyptian coffin supported by trestles. Most convincing, I assure you. It happened right here, in the Grand Ballroom of the St. Pancras Hotel."

"What was the outcome?" I asked. "And how is it I've never heard you mention this case?"

"I believe it came about while you were happily settled with Mary, rest her soul. The accomplices had slipped away just before the main act, but we were after Allerton, and dared not raise the alarm prematurely. Allerton received twenty years as his reward. It seems there were a large number of the powerful and wealthy among his victims, and they did *not* appreciate being made fools of. I was almost sorry I'd caught him, actually. I've rarely received such abuse for the successful resolution of a case."

By this time our small party had reached the entrance to the suite Mycroft had arranged for *Señor* Azcevado Marques. Holmes knocked at the door. A dark-complexioned fellow opened it. His features were a mixture of Moorish and Oriental. After greeting Holmes and le Villard warmly he showed us into a spacious and beautifully detailed sitting room, where Holmes introduced him to Mycroft and I as *Señor* Azcevado Marques's younger son Dom Alonzo, master of the *White Bird*.

Dom Alonzo went to a panelled door on the far side of the sitting room and knocked gently, speaking a few words in what I vaguely recognised as Portuguese. The door opened slowly, and *Señor* Azcevado Marques stood before us, sightless eyes gazing at the centre of the room. A Siamese of like vintage, whom I took to be Prince Phichai, guided him by one elbow. His son gently guided him by the other to where we stood, and further introductions were made. The old fellow passed on a greeting from his eldest son Joao, who had known Mycroft years before. We settled down to discuss the matter which had brought them so far on a chance of success.

An hour later, when the old fellow had finished his most interesting account, and was relaxing at last with an excellent cigar and a brandy with water, I was left wondering just how Holmes and his brother would proceed.

It all seemed nebulous in the extreme, when considered under the - hypothetical - harsh glare of the judicial process. Holmes and Mycroft looked at each other, with thoughtful expressions remarkable for their similarity, given that Holmes was lean and aquiline of face, and Mycroft fleshy in the extreme.

"It seems to me that we must arrange it in such a way that we can identify the individual speakers," said Mycroft, after thanking the elderly Portuguese once again for coming, and for his prodigious feat of memory. "Then we must goad one of them into an indiscretion. What do you think of this ploy, Sherlock?"

Mycroft and Sherlock Holmes then proceeded to elaborate a plan between them that would hopefully lead the villains to reveal their guilt of their own volition. It appeared to me that neither of the brothers had much doubt that Lord Coledale and Quiney were in some way guilty of a terrible murder, and by extension, of involvement in a plot to destabilise Siam. Both of them, however, still seemed to consider it possible that Godfrey Norton was also the guilty party in both cases. But there was no concrete proof to be had either way, and no evidence as to why.

I sensed that the two of them had different reasons for their interest. Mycroft Holmes seemed more concerned with the political aspects of the case, and the protection of British interests in the East; I felt that this took second place in Sherlock Holmes's priorities. Though he would, I dare say, deny it if asked, I had little doubt that his principal interest lay in sheeting home a cruel murder to those who had arranged it. And seeing to it that they paid the penalty for their crimes.

I was certain that, whereas he usually evinced little interest in the trial once a criminal had been detected and apprehended, this was one case which Holmes would follow through to its conclusion.

Once they had decided on the strategy to be employed, Mycroft consulted his pocket-watch, and said he simply must leave. He assured Holmes that he would arrange for the protagonists to be assembled at Parliament House on a suitable pretext, as agreed, made his farewells, and was seen to the door by Dom Alonzo.

Meanwhile, Holmes patiently briefed us all on the roles we were to play in the little *charade* they were about to enact, then we too took our departure of the charming old pirate, his attentive seafaring son, and his Siamese crony Prince Phichai. At the street entrance in front of the St. Pancras Hotel we parted company, I to return to my reading of le Villard's Journals, and my two companions to continue their search for answers to the several mysteries that Holmes was investigating. Much of what old *Señor* Jose Felipe had recounted had meant little to me at the time, as I had not yet completed reading the relevant entries in le Villard's last Journal. However, one reference in particular had caused me to look up sharply. I had no comment to make to Holmes, nor was it the time, but something of Holmes's intensity of manner regarding this particular case was explained.

I recorded the entire conversation, as accurately as I was able, when I returned to Baker Street, ate a frugal lunch from the sideboard, picked up the now-familiar Journals, and delved once again into the past as experienced by le Villard and Sherlock Holmes. I felt sure that the facts concerning that tragic reference were sure to be contained in the pages yet to come.

CHAPTER XL

30th May 1893
Bangkok, Siam

THE LASSITUDE OF THE OPIUM SMOKER soon overtook my senses, but Holmes and I, in two cubicles on either wall of a corner, kept a casual watch on the occupants of the opposite divans. Smokers decided they had had enough, and left, only to be replaced by latecomers. Fumes from opium burning in the bowls mingled with the thick incense from dozens of joss-sticks smouldering at a shrine at the farthest end of the chamber. Through the haze, silent waiters drifted about with trays of this and that, I couldn't see what from my position.

Several hours passed in this way, and it began to seem that our gentlemen were going to remain here all night. I did not relish the prospect, as I felt more than a little queasy from the effects of the opiate. I sneaked a look at my pocket watch. Past two o'clock already! Holmes seemed oblivious to everything, when I looked in his direction, but it was he who alerted me, with an urgent whisper, half an hour later.

"Le Villard. Quickly! Our friends were called for by two Chinese fellows, and have left with them. I couldn't alert you sooner, or they should have noticed."

I glanced at the empty cubicles where Lord Coledale and his companion had been. The champagne bottle was gone as well.

We had settled our accounts earlier, so were able to leave without complications. Our quarry was nowhere in sight as we emerged into the lane. Holmes unfastened his watch-chain from his vest, and approached the Chinese doorman. Using a mixture of drunken Siamese, English, and pantomime, Holmes let it be known that his friend with the top-hat had left his watch behind. Convinced by his inebriety, the doorman grasped him by the elbow and led him out into the street, where he pointed to the railing across the end of the road at the river's edge. He accepted a few *saleung*, then went back to his stool. There was a narrow opening in the railing leading down to a small landing. In the centre of the opening, and silhouetted against the silver sheen of the moonlit water, we saw an old man, hand outstretched in supplication for a few *satang,* approach Lord Coledale and his companion, who had already stepped down from street level and out of our sight.

Against the light we saw Lord Coledale raise the stick he always carried, and strike the old fellow a mighty blow on the head with the large chased-silver globe which formed its handle. The sound could be heard from where we stood in dark shadow, followed by cries of pain. In silhouette we saw the English peer look down at the huddled form at his feet, unscrew the cap of the spherical flask which the silver globe concealed, and tilt his stick to drink. Screwing the cap firmly back in place, and without a further glance at his victim, Lord Coledale stepped down to the landing and out of our sight.

We hurried to the railing, where I looked quickly at the old man, who was dazed but not seriously injured. As I stood, Holmes pointed at a Siamese gondola, already some distance downstream. Silhouetted against the moonlit river I saw a man with a top-hat tip back a magnum of champagne, then pass it to his companion. The two Chinamen sat motionless in the bow as the gondolier sculled steadily closer to a vessel moored some distance out in the stream.

Replete with stern paddle-wheel and twin stacks amidships, she had the appearance of a small Mississippi riverboat, with two decks for almost her entire length. A railed walkway ran down both sides and around the stern on both decks. On the side visible to us there were a dozen or so doors and windows set in the side bulkheads on each deck, many of them brightly lit, some shuttered; a pilothouse occupied both decks at the forward end of the superstructure. She had the characteristic bow of the river craft at Bangkok, with a small foredeck across the squared bow, belying the sharply flared prow beneath.

Holmes took out his deceptively powerful opera glasses, which had proved so useful in the desert around Omdurman, and in many another setting, and trained them on the stern of this strange vessel, where Coledale's party was at that moment boarding.

"It's Coledale, all right. Can't get a decent look at the other fellow though. They've been shown inside. There appears to be a lounge of some sort on the lower deck aft." He raised his glasses. "Accommodations of some sort all round. Looks like a private apartment aft on the upper deck."

Just then lamps were lit in those apartments.

"What I wouldn't give to be out there right now!" cried Holmes in exasperation. There was no skiff or gondola that we could hire; besides, there were the two Chinamen still squatting on the afterdeck of the stern-wheeler.

"We shall have to give it up for tonight. I can see nothing through the ports, as they're curtained."

"We could get a boat somewhere," I said, "or wait for them to come off. I'd like to see who they are visiting; he must come off sometime as well."

"We dare not risk alarming anyone at this point, le Villard. I think we both suspect who is their host aboard that boat, and the connection is established. The reason could only be ascertained by getting up close, which is precisely why they've anchored well out in the stream. Besides, if it is *Sia* Ah Foo, he could disembark from the other side and head for the far shore, and we would never know it. No, my friend! We've done well enough tonight. Let us get some rest."

Holmes and I returned to our trishaw, and before long were back at our hotel. Despite the late hour, I arranged for hot baths, and we luxuriated awhile before retiring, leaving instructions not to be awoken too early for our morning cup of tea.

24th June 1893
Bangkok, Siam

Chief Inspector Sheriff was in a meeting with the Department of Corrections when we called at ten o'clock, but was expected back in his office at any moment. As expected, I felt terribly the after-effects of our indulgence the previous evening, and the sight of the usual milky tea made me feel even sicker still. To make matters worse, Holmes appeared to be in the best of health and spirits. I silently cursed him as we waited. Within twenty minutes the Chief Inspector joined us. Holmes asked him what he knew about the mysterious vessel moored in the river, without mentioning that we had trailed Lord Coledale to it the previous night.

"No real mystery about it, though," said he. "The *Jade Treasure* is the finest of *Sia* Ah Foo's floating whorehouses, is what she is. Lots of smaller ones on the river, hundreds of skiffs working the Siamese and coolie trade, larger launches for the wealthy and powerful. *Sia* Ah Foo sometimes uses the *Jade Treasure* himself for entertaining, or meeting special clients. We also suspect that's where some errant senior gang members are dealt with in the wee hours. More than one garrotted lieutenant of *Sia* Ah Foo has been fished out downstream. Very convenient, I should say."

"Ever been aboard?"

"More than my job is worth to try, without very good cause. For example catching him murdering someone red-handed. With the likes of *Sia* Ah Foo we must simply get along, I'm afraid. I dream of nailing him, but I know it's unlikely. One of his own will get him one day and take over. There will always be *Sia* Ah Foos in Siam.

"Oh, by the way! Not all the whores on the *Jade Treasure* are girls, though they all appear to be."

"Why does that not surprise me? How about arranging that meeting with *Sia* Ah Foo?"

"Already set. Was just going to send you a message anyway; you've saved me the bother. My loyal informant - who is also loyal to everyone in town who pays well enough - has arranged for you to meet *Sia* Ah Foo on Monday. The message is that he is very busy, but will make time to meet you when he visits his number one rice warehouse, across on the Thonburi side of the river. Will send his launch for you. Eleven o'clock. He looks forward to meeting the distinguished explorer who has met the Chief Lama at Tibet, is what I hear. Didn't know you'd done that, sir!"

"Very few do, Chief Inspector, and I've no idea how *Sia* Ah Foo could know of it."

"Funny, I've forgotten about it myself already," remarked the policeman. "Fine pair of academics you are, I don't think!"

"Oh, we are professionally very competent, I assure you, if at times a trifle unorthodox in our choice of research material."

"Which has not escaped my notice. Be careful!"

Later, we sent a message to Joao Enrique, informing him of the time of our appointment with *Sia* Ah Foo. A reply arrived by return, confirming that he would arrive at our hotel a little before eleven.

26th June 1893
Thonburi, Siam
Sia Ah Foo's man approached the hotel doorman at eleven exactly. *Señor* Joao Enrique, Holmes, and I were soon seated amidships in a steam pinnace, smartly painted and varnished. Brass fittings gleamed on her engine, and a long red and gold banner at her masthead whipped in the fresh river breeze.

Only the one Chinaman operated the pinnace, but he did so with evident expertise.

We travelled upstream for a while, then headed into a broad stream branching off to the left from the main river. This was lined on both sides with jungle and tall, shady trees. Set amongst these were thatched houses, and large wooden warehouses, with piers and jetties fronting the stream. Huge round- hulled wooden barges were in various stages of unloading rice shipped from the plains further up the river. Empty vessels floated so high they seemed as though they must overturn, but fully loaded - as newly arrived barges were - their bulwarks were barely above water. The precious grain was lashed down under stout canvas covers, and the wake of passing steam-tugs washed over the barges without effect.

At one of the largest of these warehouses our pinnace tied up. We stepped onto the wooden pier, and were greeted silently by another Chinaman, who bowed and grasped his own hand with the other, as is the Chinese way. He turned, and we followed him along the pier, through a tall opening into a cavernous space. Sacks of rice were stacked to the ceiling dimly seen far overhead, and stretched far into the distance. High on this mountain of grain were men stacking sacks into the neatest of rows; muscular men with checked cloths wound around their foreheads, wearing only a loincloth. Each of them carried a wicked metal hook with wooden handle, for snagging and lifting the heavy sacks. Long wooden planks in pairs sloped from the floor up to the summit of the stacks. At each pair, a file of these murderous-looking fellows carried full sacks on their shoulders up the one plank, then descended by way of the other. Silhouetted against the far entrance, these rows of men with sharpened hooks appeared to move mechanically, like an endless sinister conveyor of the menace of death.

Dark skin glistened with exertion, for it was hot in this vast space, and the work ceaseless and unrelenting. Many of the coolies were covered entirely with intricate blue tattoos, even on their throats and eyelids. They seemingly paid us no attention, but the entire vast space seemed filled with a dim, threatening light, and a thousand watchful eyes followed as we passed by. A *frisson* of fear chilled the sweat trickling down my spine. From the far end of the warehouse came a dull, rhythmic pounding, growing louder and seemingly more insistent as we approached.

Following the Chinaman still, we rounded a corner, and stood in front of the source of the noise. A huge steam-driven mill was in action, surrounded by a fine haze of pulverised rice husks. Coolies marched up long inclined planks straight from the bowels of the moored barges, and fed rice from their heavy panniers into the hopper high above. Milled grain was threshed out and bagged at the other end. In front of this machine, with his back to it, stood *Sia* Ah Foo.

He greeted us in the Chinese fashion, and motioned us to follow him, for nothing could be heard against the din of the mill.

The sound abated as we turned another corner, and walked the length of yet another full warehouse. Not another sack of rice could be fitted in, and there was no one in sight. Before long the sound was muffled entirely, and soon we were shown into a quiet works manager's office, which looked as though nothing had been changed in twenty years. Old and yellowed calendars were nailed to the walls. An ancient pendulum clock in a blackwood case, its glass front covered with Chinese calligraphy, ticked loudly in the sudden quiet. An abacus and a sheaf of accounts littered a desk at one side.

Sia Ah Foo sat in a mother-of-pearl inlaid rosewood chair, and invited us to sit at the other chairs around a low ceramic table. Tea was served in tiny cups, and sipped while steaming hot. That done with, *Sia* Ah Foo turned to look squarely at us. He was perhaps sixty years of age, though it was difficult to tell for certain. His garb differed markedly from our previous encounter, but the face was unforgettable - strongly featured, but horribly marked by the smallpox. Now he was dressed in the simplest of loose smocks, with the Chinese collar, but no decoration of any kind, and wore neither gold nor jewellery. His forehead was shaved, and the remaining hair plaited into a queue that stretched down his back almost to his waist. Although wisps of grey flecked his hair, he appeared vigorously alert and fit.

Sia Ah Foo spoke softly, to Joao Enrique.

"Welcome, *Nai* Portugee. I had not heard that you would honour me with a visit as well. It is my additional pleasure. Also, my English is not good, and perhaps you can help us. I believe the Professor wishes to talk about the Lao States, and the tribes from Yunnan. And perhaps of some other matters?"

"Your English appears to be more than adequate, Mr. Ah Foo," said Holmes. "My Chinese is not. You have the advantage of me, sir."

"I was born here, but my father sent me to be educated at Hong Kong, Professor Sigerson. But I have no Norwegian at all, so I think not!"

"You seem to know a deal about myself and my explorations."

"To the Chinese government, the appearance of Europeans at the capital city of Tibet - for the first time in almost a hundred years - is an alarming event, worthy of note. I make it my business to know what Peking knows. A remarkable feat! I congratulate you. I also hear that a new armoury was sabotaged most effectively at that time. Coincidence, I am sure."

"Of course! But it is clear your time is valued highly. I do indeed have an interest in the movements of the Chinese of Yunnan, whom I believe were displaced into these plains, and became the Siamese race of today. This is the necessary preliminary to a more ambitious conjecture, which we seek to prove through our travels. There are traces of these cultures spread as far afield as the Philippines and the islands of Oceania. I suspect that displaced Yunnanese, over the millennia involved, settled in these places."

"And how may *I* be of help? I am a businessman, Professor, not an explorer."

"True, but I have it that your businesses extend into both Yunnan and the Lao States. I should like to travel there, but I am aware that it is potentially a very dangerous region to explore. I also hear that a party is leaving before long to survey these regions for a Burma-to-China railway line. I was hoping that my companion and I could accompany the party."

"Again, Professor, you delight me! You know more of my business than I seem to know myself. But if it should be so, why do you need my help? *Nai* Portugee here knows as much of Siam as I."

"Your European partners are hardly men with whom I should entrust our lives. One of the cardinal rules of exploration in remote and dangerous lands is that, wherever you may be, there is some form of order. Somebody has an authority that is recognised, and can provide safe conduct. Find that person, and deal directly with them, if you wish to survive."

"Your policy seems to have worked most effectively, so I shall not dispute it. That you think you know the names of those with whom I do business is, on the other hand, a matter of some concern to me. I am disposed to help you, Professor, but I have no confirmed plans involving such a survey at present. I will, of course, assist you in any other way I can, should you decide to go anyway.

"But I feel I should remind you, Professor, of the English saying regarding curiosity and the cat."

"I am an explorer, *Sia* Ah Foo. Curiosity is my stock-in-trade, I'm afraid. We've survived the consequences thereof until now."

"As I see! *Nai* Portugee, it has been most interesting to meet your friends. If you will excuse me, Professor, for speaking in the Chinese language? It is a personal matter of a peculiarly Chinese nature, best dealt with in our own language."

Holmes merely nodded politely. *Sia* Ah Foo spoke rapidly in the Tae Chiew dialect, which I could distinguish from Mandarin without knowing the sense of the exchange. He spoke only a few words, bowed in our direction, and left the room. The Chinaman guide who had shown us in now escorted us back through the warehouse. The legion of navvies stopped, polished hooks raised, for the shortest moment, looking at our guide. He shook his head very slightly as we passed through. They turned back to their lifting and stacking. With relief we came out into the blazing sunshine and boarded the pinnace, which delivered us to the jetty in front of *Nai* Portugee's house. No one spoke during the short journey, until *Sia* Ah Foo's boatman had steamed off, and was well out of hearing.

Once tea had been served, Holmes came straight to the point.

"Is there any reason why you cannot divulge the meaning of *Sia* Ah Foo's parting words, *Señor*? I should understand, of course."

"I'm sure he meant me to tell you, at least part of it. He warned me that your curiosity, as he calls it, may offend certain interests here, and he cannot undertake to ensure your protection in Bangkok, let alone on the Lao border. His profound regrets, of course, and a thousand apologies. He has left me to inform you, as he did not wish to lose his face by refusing your request."

"And the, shall we say, 'private communication'?"

"I believe the term is 'enigmatic communication', Professor. I am uncertain as to what he meant. I shall repeat his words, as best I can remember them."

He set down his cup, and filled it again from the teapot, as he recited from memory the words of *Sia* Ah Foo.

"'Siam faces important decisions in these critical days. Those who remain aware of the direction of the wind will survive the coming storm. We have shared the same river for a long time, and have learnt respect for each other. Times of peril are also times of opportunity. Do not be surprised to receive my summons.' Those were his words."

He sipped at his tea, and looked out over the river.

"I see what you mean, *Señor*. It could mean almost anything, or nothing."

"It means he's up to something," said I. "He did not think to deny his association with the Europeans, or their railway project."

"I got the distinct feeling that something else has upset him," said Holmes. "Perhaps he's been informed of our nocturnal researches."

"I still can't think what he meant," said *Nai* Portugee. "It's true we have known each other a long time; we've even done some business together. But *Sia* Ah Foo has never hidden his vice businesses, whilst our family, since we ceased being privateers with the death of my grandfather, are content with the profit we make from trading and shipping. Not to say we don't grease a few palms here and there to smooth the way! That's the way things have always been done here. But there is no natural affinity that would explain his wishing my support in anything he may get up to."

"The answer may lie in the language you both spoke," mused Holmes. "You both have Chinese lineage, you still share the same language.

Remember his words in English: 'a personal matter of a peculiarly Chinese nature'! And let us not overlook his connections in high places in China. And the fact that Rolin's mysterious shadows are Chinamen! Is there any possibility that the Chinese government could have an interest in influencing the outcome of the Siam question? That *Sia* Ah Foo is in some way their agent, and is warning you to remember your Chinese roots when the time comes?"

"I have heard nothing of that nature, not even as market gossip. If you're suggesting a Chinese take-over, it seems the only way that *that* could happen - given the naval and military might of Britain and France at either side - would be if the Siamese government were to invite them in. This could only take place if a certain Chinese faction at court were to usurp the crown, and place its own man as King. Rumour has it that the King is very ill, and may not long survive, so the time may be seen as opportune for so drastic a step. Frankly, it all seems most unlikely to me."

"But . . . out of the question, *Nai* Portugee?"

"No! I couldn't say it was out of the question. The pieces of such a jigsaw puzzle are already there."

"So, it is not impossible that there is a plot afoot to place a Chinese puppet government in Siam. I agree that it sounds improbable, and it only complicates our investigations. Frankly, we could do without it."

The sun sank behind the houses and rain-trees, winking and flashing from the gilded spires and mirror-mosaic columns of the temples across the darkening river. The weather had become sultrier of recent days, and our clothes clung to our skins. Holmes rose to go.

"We have a Belgian swindler next on our list, le Villard, and time is running out. Let's go see him."

Nai Portugee saw us out to the jetty himself. I had seen *White Bird* three or four times now and still didn't know her story. I said as much to *Nai* Portugee, hoping he wouldn't take offence. A broad smile lit his features.

"So, you too! It is easy to fall under the spell of so magnificent a craft, M. Le Villard. It is my father's story to tell. When the time is right, he will do so."

We hailed a passing gondolier, and bobbed our way back across the river to the hotel's pier.

Chief Inspector Sheriff had given us directions to the house of ill-repute where Felix Garraud was supposed to be laying low. It was not such a distance, so at nine o'clock we walked through the crowded streets and lanes, following his directions, until we found ourselves in front of a colonial-style teakwood mansion, long past its glory years.

Its varnish had long since flaked away, and the weathered wood had a dull silver sheen in the moonlight. Tall louvered shutters enclosed both floors;

with here and there a small panel propped open to catch more of the cool evening breeze. Lamps were lit in a few rooms on the lower floor. The two-storied house was set in a large walled garden that backed onto a broad canal. Huge ancient rain-trees spread their branches over all, and thick clumps of bamboo shielded the frontage from the view of passers-by. An odour of sweet decay emanated from several large mango trees, heavy with ripened fruit that gleamed softly, like pale golden lanterns, in the bright moonlight. Each tree was ringed with spoiled fruit, which no gardener had swept up. A forlorn and decrepit air pervaded the place, an impression that was soon dispelled as we walked down the gravelled drive leading to the porticoed entrance, which was at the side of the building rather than facing the road. Gay laughter and raucous voices could be heard, even before the door was opened. A distinctly drunken voice could be heard shouting curses and oaths in several European languages.

I pulled the bell-rope. The shouting ceased, and a large, florid European in shirtsleeves and braces *à l'abandon,* flung the door open.

"Place is closed! Closed, understand! Now hop it! Get . . ."

Our belligerent spoke to us in heavily accented English, no doubt because of our attire, but I recognised the speech of the rougher parts of Bruxelles. His arm was suddenly tugged back by a large Siamese lady of Chinese parentage. Like the house she was well past her prime. Unlike the house, she was freshly painted, and her scent was rather loud.

"Felix! Not speak my customers that way." She stepped in front of him with a pail of water, upended it on his head, drenching him completely, and pushed him away from the door. He slumped onto a slatted wooden seat in the hallway.

"Forgive him, please! He upset and little bit drunk. Please! Come inside! Come in, sirs! What I can do for you? My name *Mama-san* Kung! You want young ladies, yes? We have so many."

She indicated an arched opening leading from the hall into what had once been the drawing room. Laughter, of men and women both, drifted out. A pretty young Siamese woman, her hair in a topknot, peeked around the corner and covered her giggle with a delicate brown hand. She was tugged back out of sight, laughing gaily.

"Come back here, young lady! You'll not get away so easily from a sailor just off a four-month voyage, oh no!"

"Actually, no!" Holmes had obviously decided to dispense with all preliminaries and tackle the Belgian while he was inebriated. "We have come here in search of a Mister Felix Garraud. Is that gentlemen he?"

"What if't is?" slurred the sodden Belgian. "Who wantsa know? Watsit t'you?" He looked up from under thick brows, sudden suspicion and fear cutting through his drunkenness. He struggled to clear his head.

"We have heard of you at Saigon, M. Garraud." I spoke French, thinking he may be more comfortable with it. I mentioned the name of a fellow I had met when there; one of those expatriates who seem to know everybody who is anybody in their chosen city of refuge.

"Professor Sigerson, here, is an explorer and lecturer by profession, but prefers to finance his own expeditions. Less restrictions, and avoids the squabbling, you see. He does this by investing in selected properties and projects as he travels about. He has heard favourable reports of your excellent returns on some, shall we say, rather unorthodox investments here in Siam."

"But perhaps this is not a good time," interjected Holmes, reverting to English. "We can come back another time . . ." He turned as if to leave. *Mama-san* Kung grasped his sleeve, but before she could speak, Garraud beat her to it.

"No, you're here now. Might's well come in. Seen me at m'worst, anyway. Sorry t'be so uncivil. Damned woman's soaked me, f'no reason. No reason! Been with 'er since she w's a young thing, which wasn't 's long ago as 't looks. Problem is, when I drink too much, th' young girls tease me. Who's t' blame me if I give one of 'em a pinch now 'n then, neh?"

"Perfectly understandable, I'm sure, my good fellow. Tell you what! If you've a small parlour where we may speak privately, *Mama-san* Kung here can bring us a bottle of your finest whisky, and a siphon. We shall relax while you dry yourself down, and then we may discuss this investment in a civilised fashion."

Garraud agreed to this, and stumbled up the stairs to his rooms above. We were shown into a small room, with dim moonlight slanting in bars through shuttered windows. A single crimson-shaded lamp burned on a side-table. *Mama-san* Kung soon returned with soda, a bottle of a reasonable Irish whisky, and glasses for three. I gave her a handful of *ticals* for the whisky, and we declined the offered company of young ladies.

"Business first, Madam!"

Minutes later the Belgian reappeared, dried and combed, in fresher clothes. He looked almost presentable, and had sobered up somewhat. Holmes poured for us all.

"Now, sir, if you feel up to it, what can you tell us of your prospects here, for we haven't much time? My funds have already arrived at the Hong Kong and Canton Bank, and I don't want to have to transfer them out of the country again before I leave."

Garraud sat up at the mention of cash.

"What sort of amount did you have in mind, Professor?"

"Oh! Not such a large sum, at first. Perhaps fifty thousand sterling, but I must have a *good* return on it. That is essential, as expeditions cost dearly, I assure you."

"The kind of high return you seek is not without risk, Professor," said the Belgian, regarding Holmes with a sly glance. "You mentioned the Hong Kong and Canton Bank, Professor. My associates have a substantial sum frozen there, at the orders of the damned General Adviser. Who'd have thought another Belgian would do us down? But he did. We were going to fix him, for a while. Almost put us out of business."

"Why did you change your mind?"

"They can't hold the deposit indefinitely, and no charges have been placed. Our advocate says he'll get it released shortly, as soon as he gets back from Singapore. But what about this investment? Are you serious?"

"That depends. You see, sir, I know the nature of your business projects, and the reasons why the returns are so favourable - don't ask how! I just do!" He held up the palm of his hand, to forestall an outburst from Garraud. "I approve, although there are the attendant risks you mentioned. I shall speak boldly, Mr. Garraud. You and your associates have devised a means of turning money into a lot of money. I have money, but with my reputation can not afford to be associated with such schemes. However, if I invest discreetly with you, I can share in the rich bounty. I'd like you to consider my proposal. Here is my card. I'm at the Oriental, but it is inadvisable to contact me there. Where can we meet without raising eyebrows?"

Garraud thought for a moment; then suggested the same night-club we had first gone to, on Sri Phraya Road. A thought occurred to me.

"We have a friend who frequents the place, Godfrey Norton! Do you know him?"

"Of course. Everyone there knows Godfrey. Sleeps there sometimes. On the benches after they're closed for the night. *But. . .* he knows his law, my friends. He's the advocate I told you about, the one who's getting our funds released.

"Let's have a drink to Godfrey Norton, then!" cried Holmes raising his glass.

"Godfrey Norton!"

Garraud and Holmes made an appointment to meet again in a week, and we all talked of petty villainies until the bottle was emptied. Garraud hadn't noticed, but we let him have the best part of it, until he was quite drunk again.

Now he trusted us, and treated us as larcenous equals. Before switching to

Homicide Investigations, I had a deal of experience with the *Police Judiciare*, at Marseilles and at Paris, dealing with the cleverest of swindlers and frauds. I have noticed one curious fact: that they, who make their living preying on the credulity and greed of others, are themselves so frequently able to be deceived.

We called *Mama-san* Kung to deal with Garraud again, as he had slumped over, fast asleep in his chair. She looked at him with exasperation, and called out in Chinese, in a shrill falsetto. Two maids appeared from the hallway, took one look at the Belgian, and gently but firmly coaxed him out of the room and up the stairs. Holmes looked at me.

"I'm not particularly proud of any of that, you know," said he. "But we have little time, and too many suspects to play too gently. It seems as though these Belgians may be crossed off the list, but it's best to be certain. If I'm correct, my fifty thousand pounds bait will bring his boss out of the shadows. This fellow couldn't mastermind anything. I can always find a reason to decide against investing."

"But Professor Sigerson's reputation?"

"Regrettable, I agree. I hope it doesn't get about. But as I said, time is short, and if we've eliminated a suspect, the risk is justified. There's nothing more to find out here. We'll let ourselves out."

The noise of partying and revelry had increased as regular customers arrived to be greeted by the girls, and only died away as we walked down the drive and left the grounds of *Mama-san* Kung's establishment. Tonight was the first of the four nights we had set aside to follow Rolin's carriage.

CHAPTER XLI

28th June 1893
Bangkok, Siam

"URGENT MESSAGE from Rolin," cried Holmes, as he tipped the boy a few *saleung*. "Let's see . . . Oh dear! Hat and coat, le Villard! You can read this in the carriage as we drive along."

We had already bathed after our morning *baritsu* session, but had not as yet taken our usual light breakfast. I remember feeling extremely hungry as we clambered into the waiting carriage, which Rolin had sent for us. We hadn't gone a hundred yards before Holmes cried out, "I wonder, Le Villard, could this have been the carriage?" and at the same time got down on his hands and knees, and began searching around the edges of the small carriage floor.

I had no idea what he was up to, but reasoned that it must have had something to do with the message from the General Adviser, which I had stuffed into my coat pocket. I took it out and read it.

'Returned an hour before dawn from Ministry. Gunshot fired at carriage. Round deflected by carriage bell. No injury. Advice?'

At last I understood what Holmes was up to, and proceeded to assist by examining the spaces between the seat cushions and the carriagework. A half-minute sufficed to disclose the object of our search.

"I take it this is your reason for assuming so undignified a position," I said to Holmes, holding up the misshapen lump of grey metal I had found.

"Excellent, le Villard!" he cried, when he saw what I held. "What a stroke of luck. May I?" Holmes reached for the slug as he sat again, and examined it closely with the lens that he pulled from his vest pocket. He bit on it firmly, and savoured the aftertaste as though he had sampled fine caviar. A faint smile briefly appeared on his thin lips. A thought occurred to him, and he leant forward with his magnifying lens to closely inspect the bell, where it hung from its bracket by the driver's seat.

Holmes put away his lens, and sat back in the carriage cushions. His eyes closed slowly, and he seemed entirely relaxed as our carriage hastened to the residence of the General Adviser. I knew enough of Holmes by now not to interrupt him when his brilliant mind was assimilating a multitude of facts, and assembling them into their logical patterns and relationships. I had no doubt that this was precisely what he was up to, despite his relaxed appearance.

I had my own thoughts on the matter, but did not voice them aloud. Soon enough the carriage pulled into the driveway of Rolin's residence, and we were greeted by the loud barking of my enormous mastiff, who had to be restrained by Rinzing from leaping into the carriage before we could alight. Time for another clip, I thought, as his coat was again getting too long for comfort in this tropical weather. Holmes was already through the door, and quizzing Rolin as to the exact circumstances of the shooting.

"Exactly where did this incident take place?"

"Just as we turned from the main road into our lane."

"Before or after turning? Please think carefully, and be precise."

"Before, I'm sure of it. Yes, quite certain."

Holmes looked at Rinzing, who nodded his agreement.

"I take it you were returning from the ministry by the usual, direct route?"

"Yes! It was very late. We've varied the route as often as possible since you suggested doing so, but I was so very tired, and I persuaded Rinzing."

"That means you had just crossed the bridge over the *klong*, which is quite broad. You saw no one on the bridge as you crossed?"

"No! Not at that hour."

Holmes thought for a moment, then spoke to Rolin.

"You were very fortunate this morning, M. Rolin. This was a warning, sir, and it has the ring of a final warning - and I'm sure the pun was intended."

"But how can you tell that, Professor Sigerson? It may have been just a lucky miss, which hit the bell by accident."

"The shot came from the rear; in other words, from back across the canal you had just crossed. The impact marks on the bell show a dead-centre hit. Your head and torso would have presented an infinitely larger target than the carriage bell, which was the actual target."

"What makes you so sure of that, Professor?"

"I think I know who fired the shot, sir! It's as simple as that."

"But how can you know that?"

But Holmes would say no more, other than that until he was entirely certain, he would continue to say nothing. Asking Rolin if he could send off an urgent telegraph message to Whitehall from the ministry, he then composed a message to Mycroft and ciphered it, using one of the cipher keys he carried in his notebook. This was dispatched with Xavier, Rolin's personal secretary, who was just leaving to return to the ministry.

Rolin then briefed Holmes on recent events. He told of the dispatch received on the twenty-fifth announcing the visit of the Commander-in-Chief, Far Eastern Squadron, which worried the Prince a great deal, and of the Chinese donation of three more junks to be sunk at the mouth of the river. He continued with an account of the arrival - with a great deal of self-promotion - of a newly-arrived correspondent of *The Times* named Thompson, freshly arrived from having rescued Spain and Morocco from serious difficulties by offering his sage advice. Rolin then mentioned his disagreement the day before with Ward, the correspondent of the *Calcutta Statesman*, who had been peddling to the *Straits Times* his erroneous stories purporting to be interviews with the General Adviser.

"I have been poisoned, threatened and terrorised, and now shot at!" said the General Adviser to the King of Siam. "As much as I have come to believe in the cause of preserving the independence of Siam, I am a jurist, not a soldier. Am I so important a thorn in the side of someone that they will stoop to murder?"

"Clearly so, M. Rolin. It is common knowledge that without your counsel of a policy of resisting the claims of the French, the government of Siam may well have capitulated already, in the hope of appeasing their hunger for territorial gains."

"But the French will never cease adding to their demands, and it is essential to let them know . . ."

"M. Rolin, it is not necessary to reiterate your rationale. It so happens that M. Le Villard and I are in complete agreement with you as to that. But our task is to avoid having you killed, and thus providing a provocation which could lead to exactly the result you wish to avoid."

"Surely, Professor, if you think you know who was the gunman, you must know who pays him? And be able to have Sheriff arrest them, or I could have them expelled."

"Unfortunately, it's not quite that simple. We have talked again and again of the various individuals or groups which could benefit from your removal from the scene."

"I do seem to have ended up rather in the middle of a lot of things, don't I?"

"Knowing who is behind a weapon is one thing," said Holmes. "Knowing who is behind the conspiracy is quite another. We have a surfeit of suspects and reasons, but all too few solid clues. I need more time to investigate."

"By then, I may well be a slightly tragic footnote in history," remarked the General Adviser, with some acerbity.

"Exactly," replied Holmes. "But before we go any further, have you done what we requested regarding your appointments schedule?"

"Yes, indeed!" Rolin rummaged amongst piles of papers on his tidy but crowded desk. "Have you been observing?"

"We have. You were followed last night, but only until within sight of the ministry. Then they slipped away. We've already tried to follow them back to their lair, but their vehicles are always rented at street-side, and disposed of in a crowded market area." He looked a moment at the sheet of paper handed him by Rolin.

"According to this record, there are no irregularities so far. Your Chinamen shadows are still there. Now that we are looking for them, we can see they show a quite remarkable sense of timing, appearing within minutes of your departure for the ministry or palace. They're definitely receiving prior information regarding your movements, but it looks as though the first two of your list of four can be crossed off."

"Who does that leave?" I asked Rolin.

"Well, there is *Phra* Suthitham Arunyadhom, tonight's candidate. He's a younger cousin of the old *Kalahom*, whose power has recently been seriously curtailed by the King's party. He has never been suspected of partiality, but we shall see. Thursday there will be no schedule, as the Prince goes to the temple to make merit all day, and I have been instructed to get a day of rest."

"And Friday?" I asked. "Who is our suspect then?"

"*Nai* Amornsap Thanarawongse. He is in a much less senior position, but actually is very close to the minister. Regardless of the Siamese name, he is of Chinese ancestry, and his family have served the Kings of Siam for many years."

"Very interesting, le Villard.

"A thought occurs to me, Professor," I said, addressing Holmes. "Could these Chinese watchers and this gunman be from different masters? There seems no logical connection between the two."

"The thought had occurred to me as well, le Villard. But if so, it is becoming rather crowded in the wake of the General Adviser. We shall have to be even more circumspect in our watching, and keep our eyes peeled for more than the one unexplained presence."

"As the bait in all of this, gentlemen, I don't mind telling you that I feel distinctly nervous about the entire affair," remarked the General Adviser.

"No one could blame you for that, sir. You'd not be human otherwise. It's only fair to inform you that we can not provide any assurance that you will come to no harm. Rinzing will be a great asset in any close work, and is well armed, but a distant assassin with a rifle is another matter. You have seen that this evening."

"What are my options then?" asked Rolin.

"You can withdraw from service to the government of Siam. You may try to carry on in that capacity, but alter your working hours so that you are not out at night. That will reduce, but not eliminate the risks. Or you can carry on as we are, and help us try to trap the culprits, or at least reveal their identities. The choice is yours, and not an easy one!"

"You're right. I have just been informed of an opportunity to become *Khedival* Adviser at Cairo. At least there I wouldn't be shot at!"

"I wouldn't be too sure about that, sir. We've just come from there, and I assure you the situation is equally unsettled. But that should not influence you. There are doubtless many safe havens for a man of your qualifications."

"Just wishful thinking, Professor. I must stay here. It is not conceivable that I should abandon the Siamese to the predations of colonialists, of whatever stripe. And whatever reasons these scoundrels may have, if I allow myself to be driven from Bangkok, I believe the effect will be felt by Siam. Very well! What must I do?"

"I'll let you know."

"Thank you. The uncertainty is the most difficult part to bear."

"We will come to see you late on Saturday morning, to compare schedules. I'll have further instructions then. Until then, I would inform the Prince, discreetly, of the gunshot, but ask that he let it go no further for now."

We spent some time in the garden, Holmes talking with Rinzing, while I passed a little time with Tashi. On days when we had no other tasks I would come and spend hours with him, but recently Holmes and I had spent every possible moment in running down leads regarding our lists of suspects. This was not the first time I had had to leave him in good hands while Holmes and I took care of our business - the business of detection - in strange locations. Lhasa, Jiddah, Cairo, Khartoum, Aden, now Siam, and so many places in between.

Tashi seemed to always know I would come back for him, and caused no problems for his part-time owners. But only with me would he roll and frolic on the grass, as we had done when he was a puppy in the snow at Lhasa. He was now in his third year, and in the peak of condition. Well fed, sleek and well-groomed, he was quite fearsome, and had become a minor sensation in the district. Burglars or night intruders were not expected at the house of the General Adviser. Tashi had that effect on people.

"What does this warning shot across the bows mean, le Villard?" asked Holmes as we drove on to the offices of the *Siam Free Press*, where we intended to interview Lillie, the Irish editor so disliked by Rolin, under the pretext of giving him an interview about our planned explorations.

"'Withdraw or be killed', is the clear message, I should say!"

"But why now? And why warn at all? Why did he not just kill him?" Holmes seemed genuinely perplexed, as questions arose faster than we could deal with them.

"You know who is the killer?" I asked.

"I thought I recognised him the other night, but the light was so poor. I never thought to see him here, but the evidence from last night's shooting is very nearly proof conclusive. It means, le Villard, that the plot takes on entirely new dimensions, and is being played for high stakes. But it does not answer the vital question, *'Who employed him, and with what end in mind?'*"

He would say no more, and I knew better than to press him before he felt ready to reveal his thoughts.

CHAPTER XLII

1st July 1893
Bangkok, Siam

AFTER SEVERAL DAYS of seemingly fruitless investigations into the affairs of Cutter and Fluddle at Siam, we were happy to accept an invitation that had nothing to do with the case. The General Adviser had cancelled our plans to see him at home during the day, and asked if we could meet he and the Prince that evening at the Ministry.

Holmes and I had been most impressed by the display of kick-boxing put on for our benefit by some of the Siamese who worked at the Oriental Hotel, once they realised we were serious about our *baritsu*. One day they had introduced us to their boxing teacher, a well-muscled Siamese they called *Phi* Daeng, or 'elder brother' Daeng, who was tattooed all over. Holmes and I went through our usual *baritsu* exercises, which interested him greatly. This morning, Daeng arrived at the hotel, and invited us to visit their temple. We gladly agreed to go with them. They had fixed on today, this being their off-duty day, so a carriage was arranged, and we set off through the crowded city streets.

The crowds thinned out, we left the ubiquitous city shophouses behind us, and before long found ourselves on the shady Sukhumvit Road, passing occasional Siamese villas set amongst luxuriant greenery. The road ran between rice paddies and rain-trees, straight and flat for long stretches, occasionally crossing humped wooden bridges over broad, clean canals. Two hours of steady driving brought us to a small village called *Baan Seua* - Tiger Village.

Here we found a strange place, half temple and half training camp, set in the jungle at the farthest outskirts of Bangkok. Everywhere we looked were small shrines and temples, prominently featuring tiger images, and groups of fighters in training. The eldest were in their thirties, I judged; the youngest were not yet twelve. Their age could be guessed at by the extent of the intricate tattooing covering their bodies.

After a Siamese meal - which our friends insisted we wash down with potent white rice liquor - we compared techniques, and staged good-natured sparring matches between the two disciplines. First I fought with Daeng, with the Siamese being declared victor on points, and then Holmes sparred with their most skilled fighter. It was interesting in the extreme, as the match progressed. Though the bout was intended as a friendly sparring session, it was clear that their fighter was determined not to be bested.

Siamese fighters use all their extremities at any time; fists, feet, elbows, knees are all acceptable weapons. Holmes had his work cut out for him evading the flurry of blows from every direction, and there was no way to wear the Siamese fighter down. We had seen their training routines, including keeping a heavy section of the trunk of a banana-tree in the air by kicking it with the instep, pounding the same trunks with bare fists, and other brutal exercises to build endurance. Their best were formidable fighters indeed, and I took good note of the techniques Holmes was using to evade the fury of the Siamese' attack. I noted that many ordinary-seeming Siamese were most proficient at this art of attack and defence, and thought that it was as well to be prepared, given the nature of our current activities.

At forty-one years of age, now fully recovered from his poisoning and taking daily exercise, Holmes was in superb condition. He was the equal of his far younger opponent in speed and agility. But it was clear that neither of us had the stamina to long withstand the punishment absorbed by these hardy Siamese. The sparring session was finally declared a draw, though we had both seen where he was vulnerable.

Holmes and I then bound our fists thickly with wadded cloths, and gave a demonstration round or two of Queensbury Rules boxing, of which Holmes is a highly skilled and effective proponent. I have done a deal of boxing myself, and the fighting was spirited, neither of us giving much quarter. This the Siamese found highly amusing, and Holmes's previous opponent soon insisted on taking my place. Holmes tried politely to avoid the match, but the Siamese all insisted loudly, and when their champion found himself flat on his back three times in rapid succession, general mirth was the order of the day. Even their defeated champion conceded with good grace, standing after the last knockdown and raising high Holmes's right fist in acknowledgement of his victory.

Following this brisk exercise we relaxed in simple steam cabinets for some time, inhaling pungent herbal essences infused into the steam, then washed ourselves down with pails of cool water ladled from huge earthenware jars. We then followed Holmes's opponent into a large hall, decorated with images and cloth-paintings of their patron saint, who apparently favoured the form of a tiger most of the time. The chief priest, or *shaman* as he appeared with a tiger's head mask tilted back on his own, was tattooing one of the fighters, who had apparently waited some time for the privilege, as many were still awaiting their turn. In deference to their *farang* guests, they all insisted that we precede them.

The fighter who had sparred with Holmes had a small addition made to his already extensive artwork, the *shaman* employing a sharply-pointed metal spike some twelve inches in length. Gripping the shaft in his left hand, muttering incantations the while, the *shaman* pierced the skin of the boxer's back rapidly and repeatedly by striking the head of the spike with considerable force with the palm of his right hand. The spike left a trail of punctures behind as the *shaman* swiftly but smoothly created intricate designs from memory. The skin was soon bathed in blood, which was washed away with fresh water and cloths when the design was complete. A mixture of ashes and ink was rubbed into the punctures, although one of the other fighters had oil rather than colour rubbed in, leaving invisible talismans. To the Siamese, these are as potent as the visible tattoos, and are apparently much favoured by women as secret sources of power over others.

We were asked if we wished to be tattooed with the first, and most basic, of their talismans, a sort of inverted triangle spread across the back between the shoulder blades.

"I think I shall, le Villard," said Holmes. "A fine memento of our visit to Siam. It should provide material for an interesting personal afterword to my monograph *On Tattoo Marks*, if you ever get around to translating it into the French."

The priest-*shaman* proceeded to mutter his incantations, and several fighters held Holmes in the correct position, while the pointed spike pierced his white skin in staccato rhythm, leaving a trail of crimson as it went. The small design took some ten minutes to complete, and though the process was clearly painful, even the youngest of fighters had not flinched when tattooed. Holmes remained stoic throughout, and after some further prayers to the tiger-god, his wounds were washed and rubbed with ash and ink.

It was then my turn, and the spike was indeed as painful as it appeared, especially where the design crossed over bone. I managed to keep a straight face throughout. When we were both finished we sat and watched as several of our new friends had additions made to their already impressive covering of tattoos. Then, as it was almost dusk, we made a donation of a few *ticals* to the temple fund and took our leave of the fighters, boarded our carriage, and headed back towards the city. The tattoo wounds were not painful, but the skin had begun to draw as tiny scabs formed, and the whole area felt tightly stretched and a little itchy. A permanent memento of our Siamese adventure, drawn in blood. A most interesting afternoon!

We kept the carriage waiting in front of our hotel while we bathed and changed, and later that evening drove to the ministry. Here we found Rolin closeted with Prince Ranawongse, and several of his brothers. We were introduced to Prince Svasti, the anglophile brother, and Prince Damrong, the best-travelled of the King's brothers. They had finished conferring, and the other princes soon left for the palace to confer with the King. The Prince was most courteous and friendly, wanting to know how we were getting along with our investigations.

"The situation here at Siam has become critical, Professor Sigerson. The King is beside himself with worry, and relies very much on the advice of M. Rolin. He knows a little of these attempts on his life, and is most concerned, but I have kept the matter a secret from all my brothers. There are enough serious matters to concern them, so we must deal with this affair ourselves.

"Now that we have been persuaded that the Admiral's visit will be to our benefit if kept to the level of diplomacy, the visit has been postponed. We believe it is the work of the *parti colon* who see their authority and independence challenged. Our information is that the Admiral and De Lanessan do not always agree, to put it mildly."

"You have been informed of the shot taken at M. Rolin several days ago, I take it?" asked Holmes.

"Yes, and no one else knows about that either."

Holmes turned to the General Adviser.

"Have you brought the schedules for Wednesday and Friday?"

Rolin handed him two sheets of paper. Holmes looked carefully at the first sheet, and cross-checked the times noted there with jottings in his notebook.

"Well, Wednesday is clean; no divergence from the actual time. That leaves Friday's candidate. Let's see now . . ."

He turned to the other sheet, once again compared the information with that in his notebook, and held out both paper and notebook for us to see. With the Prince's permission, Holmes took out his straight-stemmed pipe, filled it from his leather pouch, and lit it.

"I think we have a suspect, gentlemen! Last night only *Nai* Amornsap Thanarawongse's schedule showed the time at which the watchers appeared. In fact the carriage had left an hour beforehand, as was shown on every other schedule. The watchers appeared every other night exactly according to the schedule. Have you been apprised of our little trap, Prince Ranawongse?"

"I have, and I know that this suspect is one of my senior aides. Treachery is never far from a throne, Professor, so one is always aware of the possibility in even the closest quarters. The question is, what do we do about it?"

"Precisely nothing!" replied Holmes. "We must be careful not to alert him in any way. They will already be curious as to why the schedule was incorrect, or why he was not informed of the change. Let's not make them any more suspicious; after all, organisations do make mistakes."

"I have prepared a dossier on each of the four," said Rolin, as he handed

Holmes one folder from the pile of four. "Here is his."

"Capital! Prince Ranawongse, what are the chances, in your estimation, that there is a conspiracy to place a Chinese puppet-King on the throne of Siam?"

The Prince pondered a while before replying,

"Unlikely! That is my opinion. There is considerable Chinese influence here, it's true, and the majority of Bangkok's population is of Chinese ancestry. But few would seek a Chinese master. Siam's Kings have protected the Chinese, allowed them to settle and advance. The free enterprise they are permitted here would soon be lost if Siam was to become a Chinese suzerainty, and they know it. After all, that is why their ancestors fled the rule of the Middle Kingdom in the first place."

"All of that makes sense," said Holmes. "But what are we to make of this Chinese informant in your office? I shall study this tonight," he said, tapping the folder with his pipe stem, "and see what is best. Meanwhile, carry on as usual. No more altered schedules are necessary, I think."

5th July 1893
Bangkok, Siam
Several days were spent in further investigation of the Singapore syndicate's business interests in Siam. These involved far more than just their gold mining venture - which we found was being promoted under a completely different name and board of directors in Paris and London.

More than once, in casual conversation with unwitting expatriate employees at the various concerns we visited, the opinion was expressed that the sooner the French got on with encroaching sufficiently far into Siamese territory - say, approaching Khorat - the better. The general opinion was that this would then provide sufficient provocation for a *British* protectorate being declared over Siam, in the name of securing the borders of Burma - or Farther India, as several of them referred to that country so recently annexed by Britain.

Discreetly steering the conversation towards the topic of the General Adviser's efforts to strengthen Siamese resolve had invariably resulted in derisive mockery of his person and achievements. That the Siamese government was rotten to the core, and required only a nudge to crumble and fall, also seemed to be general opinion.

"It's very likely that this common opinion reflects the opinions of the directors of the consortium," said Holmes as we reviewed the results of our past few days's effort. We sat on the terrace of the Oriental Hotel, enjoying a cigar after our evening meal. "I wish we had time to visit Singapore, but that's out of the question right now. So far, there is nothing to disqualify these British colonialists from our list of suspects. On the contrary, there are strong suggestions that the removal from the scene of the General Adviser would be a welcome development to most of them. The question is, would they go to the extremes we have already seen, or murder?"

"So what do we do now?" I asked.

"Godfrey Norton will return before long. It will be interesting to see just whom he visits when he does get back. Until then, we've done about as much as we can in that direction. Let's get over to Sri Phraya Road and meet up with our Belgian fellow-swindler. Hopefully our bait will have attracted bigger game, otherwise the evening will be a complete loss."

Half an hour later - at nine o'clock, as agreed - we were standing at the bar waiting for Garraud to arrive. He wasn't there, but Hans von Hollstein was still slamming the leather dice cup onto the counter, as though he had never left since last we were there. He recognised Holmes, and waved him over.

"Wie geht's?" he said to Holmes, who had greeted him in his native tongue. When his turn was done he handed the dice cup to the next player, and spoke to us confidentially.

"A funny thing, I think, Professor! Just yesterday I have received at my office a telegraph message from your friend Norton. There is something very strange about something, I think to myself."

"What was so strange about receiving a message from him?" asked Holmes. "Is that unusual?"

Holmes had ordered a fresh round of beers. They arrived now, in pewter tankards, as we were drinking with Hans.

"Oh no! We have communications before this, but always concerning legal things. Norton is a lawyer, *hein*! So why is he asking me now to purchase for him a quantity of slabs of gun-cotton, and blasting caps, and fuses? And why ask me to say nothing to everyone?"

"Do you have any theories, Hans?"

"I think perhaps he buys it for Cutter and Fluddle. Shares in that bogus gold mine of theirs are being offered, but under the other name, you see. At their concession site there has been no blasting or digging. The investors, they always decide not to make the journey. It is hot, and most uncomfortable with insects. There are cobra snakes and scorpions. But now, we all hear, a major prospect insists to see the mine next month."

I could see a faint smile on Holmes's lips upon hearing this. Holmes was the insistent investor. A little shaking loosens rotten fruit from the tree! The promoters in Singapore had been contacted by telegraph from London, using the name of a well-known financier in the City. Mycroft had arranged this.

"Why would that require gun-cotton and fuses?" asked Holmes, all innocence. What Holmes did not know about explosives would fill a very small vial indeed.

One of Hans's friends clapped him on the shoulder; it was his turn to cast the dice, and he concentrated until his third throw, or rather slam, was done with. Then he spoke to us again.

"They would do a lot of blasting, Professor, all around the site, then salt the whole site with gold-bearing samples from the surface vein, which is all that is there." He sliced the froth from his beer with a wooden knife, and drank deeply.

"Is that all the material they would require?" enquired Holmes.

"No, also they would need black powder. Perhaps, black powder they already have? It is more easily obtained."

"I appreciate your telling me all this, Hans. It's nice to know what you are investing in, and frankly, this doesn't sound too solid to me. But I suppose I still need to finalise matters with Godfrey Norton, having started the process. Did he, perhaps, indicate when he would return?"

"Two weeks from yesterday, with his wife. Now that is a real woman, Mrs. Norton! *Ewig-Weibliche!* We Germans would know how to appreciate such a woman, though she wastes herself on Norton."

I could tell from the shift in Holmes's attention that he had learnt all he expected to from Hans. His eyes searched the room.

"He's just come in," I said, speaking close to his ear. "With the Japanese girl. Farthest booth at the back."

We let Hans go back to his dice, and slowly worked our way through the crowded room to where the Belgian sat with his girl. He was half-way drunk already, but recognised us readily enough. Hand extended, he tried to rise, but couldn't quite make it to his feet. He slumped back, waved his arm wide, and said, "Welcome to paradise," grinning stupidly as he did so. He clutched the young Japanese girl to him, and attempted to kiss her. She skilfully evaded him without offending. I sent her for more beer, and tipped her to stay away, using hand signs. She didn't mind at all.

"What happened t'my girl? She didn't come back; where'd she go, eh? Pretty, that'un!"

Holmes interrupted Garraud's drunken ramblings.

"I've not come here to fool about with girls, Garraud. Pull yourself together, man. Here, drink this, and answer me: what about my investment?"

Then he turned to me, and said, "Perhaps we should just leave, le Villard. Not surprising these fellows got themselves in a tangle, and lost their stake."

Again, the lure of easy money to be made - and the threat of losing it -

penetrated the Belgian's drink-sodden consciousness.

"Wait, wait! Y'can't leave yet! He i'nt here yet. Ten minutes, tha'sall. Jus' wait; ten more minutes, eh?" He sat up straight in his seat, and tried to appear sober.

"Who will be here in ten minutes, Garraud?"

"Sartorius! Colonel Sartorius, use't'be wi'the For'n Legion. Sahara . . . *Afrique . . . Maroque . . .* Ev'where's dirty 'n dangerous. Now he's been up in th'jungle wi' Shans. Likes the tribes, 'e does. Specially th' young'uns."

He laughed raucously. The laugh soon turned into a retching cough.

"What's he to do with our discussions, M. Garraud, if I may ask?"

"Has t'finance his little wars some way, doesn't he? He's the one who makes decisions f'r us. His money started it all, an' he's the one who sorts out any trouble, if y' get what I mean."

The effort of talking had sobered him up a little.

"Was he the one who was going to 'take care of' the General Adviser?"

"Wouldn't be th' first, would 't? Tha's f'sure." He laughed again.

"What is so amusing, Garraud? Perhaps *I* may be allowed to share the joke?"

The heavily-accented voice came from the next booth; a stocky, barrel-chested man stood and turned towards us. A slight smile played at his lips. His otherwise clean-shaven, rather jowly face sported a suberb set of curled moustaches. Somehow, the face seemed out of place on the robust torso, as though the head of a banker had been grafted onto the trunk of a gladiator.

"Please allow me to introduce myself. *Colonel* Rene Sartorius, ex-Legionnaire, now mercenary officer for hire! Find a nice little war when I can, and offer my soldiers to the highest bidder. If there are no wars around go and make one! That's my business, gentlemen. In between times, my friends and I do a little, shall we say, speculative investment, which *offers* high returns to investors, but *actually* gives high returns to *us*."

"Professor Olaf Sigerson, and M. Francois le Villard - my assistant and naturalist. A pleasure . . ."

"All mine, I assure you," replied Colonel Sartorius. His English was good, but his thick accent made his words difficult to follow.

"Garraud gave me your card, Professor. I took the liberty of making a few discreet enquiries. It seems we are fellow adventurers. Adventures and expeditions cost money, as I well know. And a reputation such as yours is to be protected at all costs, right? I think we understand each other, *non*?"

"Indeed, sir, it seems we do! If you will let me know what kind of return I can expect on, say, an initial investment of fifty thousand pounds?"

"Twice your money in six months, and the same again six months later.

Then we let it go, move somewhere else for a while. If you want to carry on after that, we talk again at that time."

"Sounds fair enough. What do you put in, from your side? I hear all your money is tied up in a frozen bank account. What do you intend to do about that? I believe in investing with people who have as much to lose as I do if a venture should fail. Otherwise, what's to stop them from packing their bags if things get difficult?"

"Firstly, if our lawyer can't pry it loose, the General Adviser will pay with his life, fellow-countryman or no. I called it off before, but I can get to him anytime. We're hopeful that this lawyer Norton can help us. Says he can, anyway. He only gets paid if he pulls it off."

"And if not?"

"Then I have another card to play. And I may play it first, with your help if you're interested. Do you know much about jewels, Professor? Gemstones?"

The self-gazetted *Colonel* looked at Holmes over his beer, studying his reaction, as a good confidence-trickster does.

"A little I have picked up as I explore around. Why do you ask?"

"Ever heard of the *Great Mogul*?" asked the Colonel.

"Historically, yes. Let me see what I can recall."

Holmes pondered a moment, to gather his wits. This was a new direction! He continued talking, eyes closed, concentrating on searching his memory.

"One of the largest of all the great diamonds. Found at Kollur, over seven hundred carats uncut. Cut, rather poorly, by the Venetian Borgis. Last seen by Tavernier - at the Court of the *Great Mogul* - in the late sixteenth century. Estimated at around two hundred carats. Thought by many to have been later cleaved into fragments, reputed to include the *Koh-I-Noor*, and the *Orloff*. Personally, I have always doubted that. The *Orloff* is a diamond of the purest water, and the *Koh-I-Noor* is not, and is rather greyish in colour. How, then, could they could be fragments of the same stone?"

"Ah! I see you have picked up more than just a little knowledge, Professor. That is but one of the various theories about the fate of the *Great Mogul*. Other versions have it that it has been in the possession of the Shah of Persia, or is lying forgotten in the jewels of some Indian Prince."

"Correct, Colonel and there are other theories yet. But what has all this to do with us?"

"Well, the *truth* is, Professor, the *Great Mogul* has indeed been lying forgotten all these years, but among the jewels of the Kings of Burma. They thought it an impressive but worthless sample of rock-crystal.

"A fellow I know from Antwerp - who found it advisable to leave Europe after a consignment of uncut stones went missing - was at Mandalay with the

British when they annexed Upper Burma in '86. His job was to catalogue the Burmese Crown Jewels before they were sent off to the Tower.

"Because of its lustre, he had his reservations about this particular stone which was listed as worthless, so he tested its specific gravity and hardness. It tested as diamond. He knew the history of the great diamonds, and knew that the *Great Mogul* was supposed to be cut as a high rosette. This stone was a high rosette.

"My friend - shall we call him Alain - secured a large crystal of zirconium, cut it to the exact size and shape of the diamond, and managed the substitution. It was not so difficult, as the stone never disappeared, and was never classed as important anyway."

"A most interesting tale, sir, but I still fail to see how it interests us," remarked Holmes.

"I was at Mandalay at that time. The British never did realise that I had fought against them, and welcomed me. Alain thought for some reason that he had aroused the suspicions of the head of the security detail, and that when he left Mandalay his goods would be thoroughly searched. He had, after all, been cataloguing the Crown Jewels, and paid well to do it. Theft of the stone would have meant a death sentence, or life, as it now was the property of the British Crown.

"He asked me to help him. We were old friends, and he trusted me above all others. At that time I was about to leave; I had a small campaign going in the country of the Shans. I hid the stone in a safe place, and agreed to return there in two months' time, collect the stone, and get it to Calcutta.

"Alain was murdered a month later, visiting the ruby mines outside of Bhamo. My campaign took months longer than expected, and when I returned to Mandalay I found that the carved panel which I had hollowed out to provide a hiding place had been moved. I could never find where to, though I enquired.

"Are you saying you have the *Great Mogul*, Sartorius?"

"No, not in my possession. But I have recently heard, by sheer luck, where the carved panel was moved. Luckily it was not destroyed, as so much was in Burma at that time. I would like to leave within the next two days to retrieve it. Up to Chieng Mai, then by elephant across to Mandalay. But when I have it, I still have a problem. How to dispose of it? I am still remembered as being there, and the size and shape of the stone are on record with the British. If I turn up with it, questions may be asked. I could have it cut, but then it would lose much of its value.

"You need my help, is that what you're getting at?" asked Holmes.

"You have recently been in Persia, Professor, where the *Great Mogul* has long been suspected of being. If you should turn up with it, having found it there, no connection would be made with Mandalay. We could realise the full value of the stone, and it would make both our fortunes."

"What is the real problem, Colonel Sartorius?" asked Holmes, looking him directly in the eye.

Sartorius laughed. "Cash, Professor, hard cash! In short supply, thanks to Rolin. I need a stake to get myself to Mandalay and back."

"How long would it take?"

"Moving fast, two to two and a half months."

"What is to stop you from taking off with the stone once you have it?"

"I suppose I could, but the world is a small place. I'd rather have half of the full value of the stone than have the market alerted as to its origin. Commonsense tells me that the best course is to let you handle the sale. Then, with the proceeds, we could do what we want - an expedition for you, lucrative battles for me, and profits from our investment schemes as gravy. What do you say, Professor? Are you interested? I need a thousand pounds to get to Mandalay and back, including the bribe I must pay out to get at the panel."

"Where exactly is this panel, Colonel?"

"Ah! That would be telling. You'll have to trust me there. But it's not such a large sum, certainly a lot less than fifty thousand."

"Very well," said Holmes. "We're in! I'll have the cash for you tomorrow. Where?"

"Have it delivered to Garraud. I stay at the same place when I'm in Bangkok, so I'll soon receive it. I shall be busy with preparations, myself. How do I contact you when I return?"

"Send a discreet message to me at the Oriental Hotel. I expect we will still be here. If not, the message will reach me. You have my card."

"Then I shall leave you, gentlemen. It's been a pleasure. Felix, I suggest you go back home, and try to stay sober. At least for tomorrow!"

Colonel Sartorius shook our hands, and left the bar, taking Felix with him.

I looked at Holmes across the table.

"Are we seriously going to give him a thousand pounds?" I asked, in some astonishment. "What do we hope to gain?"

"Several things, and cheap at the price. Firstly, for a nominal sum we eliminate one of our suspects, and remove him from the board for a long while. It did seem, don't you think, that Sartorius is the only real killer they rely on?"

"At the least, the only one here in Siam at present."

"Well, it helps to narrow the field, if only a little. It also gets me off the hook on my promise of fifty thousand pounds, and keeps us in friendly contact with Garraud in case others of their gang show up here."

"And?"

"And there may just be a grain of truth to his tale of the *Great Mogul*. It's a mystery that has puzzled gemologists for centuries. How could so valuable a stone be lost to history; simply disappear, with no account left behind?"

"And if he should show up here with it?"

"The stone belongs to the rightful heirs of the last King of Burma. In this case, Queen Victoria, since the annexation! I should do my best to ensure its safe delivery to her representative. As to Sartorius, he was not the thief. His part in the affair should remain unknown. I rather liked the rogue, myself. Can't think why, but there it is."

CHAPTER XLIII

11th July 1893
Bangkok, Siam

INFORMATION CAME TO the General Adviser supporting the Siamese version of the dispute at Keck Cheng, but Pavie still insisted on apologies and reparations. The General Adviser, when he returned in the early evening from the Ministry, told us that Pavie had announced that the French would imitate the English, and send two warships to Bangkok. The *Inconstant* and the *Comete* were due to arrive on the fifteenth, and Pavie had requested that pilots be provided. Now he informed the Siamese that the ships would arrive on the thirteenth, and asked that they be received.

Rolin sent a message to Pavie that the objection to the ships was general, and permission was not granted. Then we all put loaded pistols in our pockets and went to walk in the area of New Road and Sampheng market. Rolin had heard that the people were much agitated, and we wished to gauge the mood for ourselves. We observed nothing out of the ordinary, and returned to our dinner and rest.

13th July 1893
Bangkok, Siam
The Prince and Rolin had arranged for a steam-launch to be available at the French Legation to take Pavie to the French warships beyond the bar. It had been agreed that he should deliver a message to the commander of the *Inconstant* that she should stop at the bar. The General Adviser, however, felt that the commander would yield only to official instructions from the Admiral at Saigon, and that Pavie was less than sincere in his intentions, and could not be relied upon anyway.

Thus it came about that, shortly after Pavie had departed in his launch a telegraphed message arrived at the Ministry from de Benoist. Rolin and Holmes had telegraphed to Mycroft, asking him to discreetly confirm the current situation at Paris and London regarding the Siam Question. Prince Watthana in Paris had warned the French that the river-mouth was mined and their gunboats would be fired upon if they attempted to cross the bar.

As suspected, de Benoist's swift investigations showed that the crucial telegraph message, carrying Foreign Minister Develle's order revoking his previous command to the gunboats to cross the bar, had mysteriously not been transmitted from the *Quai d'Orsay* to Saigon or to Bangkok.

The Siamese Legation at Paris, however, had telegraphed a ciphered copy to the Foreign Ministry at Bangkok, addressed to the attention of the Prince. The problem was, said Rolin, as we sat in his office in the rotunda, that like all Siamese government ministers, the Prince preferred to work through the cool night hours and sleep in a darkened apartment throughout the bright day. None dare wake Prince Ranawongse, and yet we knew what the message would say. The difficulty was how to alert the French warships now that Pavie was already gone.

Rolin had no doubt that the delay at the French Foreign Ministry was the work of the colonial faction - the *parti colon* - and became more and more irate at the likelihood of the French forcing their way into Bangkok.

As a Frenchman myself, I was not proud of the part being played by the French government and its naval forces. It seemed obvious that various interests were being inflamed in order to benefit a few rabid expansionists, at the expense of the independence of the last remaining Oriental kingdom.

"When does a train leave for the station at Paknam?" I asked the General Adviser, who looked puzzled, but consulted his pocket-watch nonetheless.

"In about forty minutes," he replied. "Surely you . . ."

"We are in possession of the knowledge of the true orders of the French government. If there is even a chance to avert this crisis, I must do what I can to communicate those orders to the commander of the gun-ships. The train will travel faster than the launch, which has almost an hour's head start on us. But the railway runs in a nearly straight line, whereas the river winds in great loops. I can take a boat at the pier at the Paknam railway station, and intercept Pavie's launch, then accompany him to the warships. Will you come with me, Holmes, though I concede that it is not so much your honour as mine that feels bruised in all of this chicanery?

"Of course, le Villard! Honour is immaterial here. The crucial thing is to spoil the machinations of those who would dismember Siam. Have you your pistol with you?"

"In these days, always!"

"Then we are wasting time?"

Rolin handed Holmes his special Siamese *laissez-passer* issued by the Palace, though it was highly irregular to do so.

"These are potentially riotous times, gentlemen. Officially I must remain ignorant of your participation in this matter, and will be obliged to deny any knowledge of your involvement. Unofficially, I should be most grateful to you for trying, as I can not insist that the Prince be awoken - and it would possibly be too late anyway. If you should decide to carry on with this attempt, this pass may help you in gaining the confidence of the Siamese you encounter. Use it only if unavoidable. And here is a goodly amount of Siamese *ticals*. You will find these helpful as well. God speed, my friends."

Our train seemed to crawl along the tracks, though when we had taken the same train some months previously the journey had passed swiftly. I remember Holmes asking me just how I intended to persuade the commander to allow us to board his gunboat, let alone to discontinue his forcible crossing of the bar. I answered that those were things I could only deal with as they arose. His response was that that was an excellent answer so long as I kept a cool head about me.

At Paknam we managed to hire a small steam-cutter - though it cost us the best part of the price of the boat new, with the same again as a security - and headed out into the river. As our train-carriage had run alongside the river for the last stretch before reaching Paknam, Holmes had taken his folding field-glasses from his inner pocket, and constantly scanned the broad reaches of the river in an unsuccessful attempt to spot the launch carrying Pavie.

"It's possible we were too far behind him. He must have crossed the bar to the warships already. We'd have seen him otherwise."

I agreed, and suggested that we do the same ourselves. Hopefully we could reach the warships before they got underway. Holmes turned the tiller towards the open sea, and I made sure the gondolier operated the steam-engine at its full capacity.

There were several large Siamese cruisers guarding the river-mouth, including the King's yacht in full battle-dress, a few smaller warships and two gun-flats, positioned strategically on both sides of the river inside the bar, on full-alert in case the French ships made a move.

At first our cutter steamed, all too slowly, alongside the mangroves lining the east bank, until we came up against a barrier of obstructions in shallower water. Here we were forced to turn into midstream, passing over a number of sunken ships extending the barrier. We knew that on the west bank there were chain-and-stake barriers and more sunken vessels, leaving a narrow channel for safe navigation. Here we could turn for deeper water, avoiding the mine-field anchored further out to sea in mid-stream.

The French gunboats would have to penetrate these barriers, and at the same time avoid the barrage from nine Armstrong artillery-pieces at the fort on the west bank, if they wished to force the bar at Bangkok. I hoped that we could prevent them from trying.

Time ran out on us. It was that simple. With a substantial lead on us, and a faster launch, Pavie must have reached the *Inconstant* several hours before we could have done. There was more than enough time to give his papers to Captain Borey. As these did not contain the latest message countermanding his standing orders, and faced with the fading light and dropping tide, he evidently had no choice but to weigh anchor and approach the bar. Our cutter was just turning into the deep-water channel when we saw their masts and stacks rise above the horizon, approaching directly towards us. It seemed but a few minutes before the pale grey hulls, decks bristling with large guns and squads of armed marines at the ready, loomed up just in front of us, and we were obliged to manoeuvre in order to avoid being run down by the *Inconstant*. To complicate matters, the swift tropical twilight was already darkening the sky.

We decided to carry on in an attempt to catch their attention, but soon changed our minds when the guns at the fort began hurling huge shells at the warships. A shell landed close-by, though we were still far from any French ship, and caused a huge geyser of water to rise from the sea. As it fell back it drenched the engine, which hissed and sputtered ineffectually. The gondolier was rigid with fear, and it was left to me to attempt to revive the small steam-engine. Our boat lost way quickly, and all too soon the two warships were abreast of us, one to each side, with curious *matelots* casting strange glances at us as they slowly passed by.

A heavy barrage began, and the surface of the ocean erupted all around us. Thick smoke, reeking of cordite and ozone, enveloped us for some moments before clearing. It was by the greatest good fortune that a shell did not directly hit us, but then we were in a tiny launch, and the warships escaped with only minor damage. We saw several French sailors injured, and one killed outright, but despite the clouds of smoke and spray we could see the ships slowly proceed through the turmoil, tricolour flying at their aft masts. The gun-ships were firing their heaviest guns at the fort, without scoring any direct hits - the guns were well entrenched - but the Siamese artillerymen were obviously unpractised and inaccurate in their gunnery. Even with Danish officers it was clear that the guns were ineffectual, and caused only two vessels to founder. A French escort ship ran aground on the east bank. And our cutter was capsized by yet another near-hit.

We were all tipped into the brown water, clouds of steam rising from amidships where the hot engine was immersed. I hoped the boiler wouldn't explode. My next thoughts were of the possibility of being hit by another artillery-shell. Or an overshot round from the guns aboard one of the Siamese warships, which were now opening fire as the French ships slipped past the barriers and slowly out of range of the guns at the fort.

Other thoughts, equally unpleasant, soon replaced those. Salt-water crocodiles capable of wrestling a water-buffalo into a watery grave; deadly sea-snakes and rays; a fish able to strip flesh from a carcass in moments - I'd had them all described to me by Daeng as we walked around the markets and wharves. The upturned hull of the cutter was too small and unstable for us to climb onto, but we were able to cling to it, and lash the Siamese gondolier to the tiller so he wouldn't sink. It turned out he was unable to swim - unusual amongst the river people, who mostly swim like fish from an early age.

"Do we swim for it. Holmes," I shouted, "or wait for help? It will be dark in a few moments."

"Fortunately, help is already at hand," he replied, pointing over my shoulder. I looked around and saw a fishing skiff lowering its sail as it pulled abreast of us. Willing hands pulled us all aboard, and attempted to right our cutter. When this proved impossible they took her in tow, broke out a large sculling oar, and slowly propelled us towards the eastern shore at Lampuri, where we found a telegraph office. As we made our way to shore, Holmes pulled out his field-glasses again and followed the course of the French warships. The *Inconstant,* which had approached the barrier to starboard of the *Comete,* had cut across her bow as they passed the lightship marking the barrier, and headed for the western shore, leaving the *Comete* to steam straight upriver. Both gun-ships passed by the island of Paknam, rather than moor under the guns of the fort.

We settled our accounts with the dazed gondolier, and left him baling out his cutter. Still dripping wet, we made our way to the telegraph office. Holmes sent an advice to Rolin to the effect that we had been too late to deliver our message; that the French warships had breached the river barrier and the Siamese naval blockade and were on the way to Bangkok. He added that we were on our way back to the capital on the next train. By that time darkness had fallen, and the excited crowds milling at the station made it difficult to secure a place on the train. Holmes resorted to showing the pass given us by the General Adviser, which cleared our way, and by ten o'clock we were back at The Oriental Hotel.

Panic seemed to have gripped Bangkok, but the hotel staff carried on as though there were nothing out of the ordinary. Cleaned up and changed, we telephoned to Rolin, who had just returned from the Palace to his office at the Ministry of Foreign Affairs. He and Captain Jones had walked there after the Captain had arrived and informed the General Adviser that he'd heard forty or more artillery shells fired from the direction of the river-mouth, at around dusk. In keeping with our agreement, Rolin had mentioned nothing of our mission. He had merely expressed surprise, although he had received our message some time before, and together they had left for the Palace.

We took a carriage to Rolin's house. Two hours later Rolin arrived from the Ministry to let us know what had happened. It seems that after the two French gun-boats forced the bar at Paknam, and managed to penetrate the defences of the Siamese, they had proceeded up river to berth in front of the French Legation, and had trained their guns on the Palace.

Not surprisingly, Pavie had already lodged a strong protest, claiming that the vessels had entered in accord with an international agreement, and were fired upon wrongfully by the Siamese, losing one smaller French vessel sunk, three French sailors killed and two wounded. The Siamese had apparently lost thirty-one killed and thirty wounded, mostly on the Siamese gun-boats.

His Majesty was apparently thoroughly dismayed by this turn of events, and the General Adviser had had to talk the King and Commodore de Richelieu out of launching an attack against the two ships, and to counsel resistance through diplomatic channels rather than force.

CHAPTER XLIV

Mrs. Hudson knocked and entered, to light the fire and ask about my evening meal. Glancing at the clock, I noted that it was almost eight o'clock. I had become so engrossed in le Villard's account I had neglected to send for my dinner. Holmes and le Villard were still out, so I asked for a dish of cold cuts with parsleyed potatoes, and poured myself a glass of wine while I waited upon my simple bachelor meal.

The maid had only just removed my dishes when footsteps upon our stairway announced the return of Holmes and our guest. The two detectives removed their coats while they greeted me, then came to warm their hands at the fire, as the evening had turned rather chilly. Neither man spoke for some little while, and I rather gathered from Holmes's demeanour that their hunt had been unsuccessful. This was soon confirmed, when Holmes spoke up, still standing at the hearth.

"I suppose you will require an accounting of our misadventures for your report, Watson."

He stepped back, sat down in the leather armchair, and lit up his curved-stem Meerschaum.

"As you know, we were to meet Wiggins and the Irregulars at Millwall Park. There were eight of them, all told. I issued my instructions to Wiggins. Half of his lads to comb out all the opium dens and dives in the Docklands and the Isle of Dogs; the others to cross the Thames to Rotherhithe. All were told to search for news of Godfrey Norton.

"I gave them a description, but warned that he may have grown a beard or moustaches since I had last seen him. The man they were looking for would not be a regular, at least during the past few years, and would have appeared not more than two weeks before. If they had no luck there, they should extend their search to Whitechapel and the surrounding areas.

"If Norton had been back in London for two weeks already, it was possible that others had heard of his return as well, and likely that he was in danger. That is assuming he is not the assassin himself. Either way, we need to find him. We decided to remain in the area ourselves, so we arranged that any news should be delivered immediately to Wiggins at the fish-cafe down the street from the Prospect of Whitby. He would bring the news along to us at the terrace of that excellent public house, where we should at least have ale and a pub lunch, and a decent view of the river to interest us while we waited.

"Wiggins sent word to his lookout across from the Belgrave House Hotel, with orders to report similarly if Isobel Aster should return to her room, and we all went our appointed ways."

Le Villard had made himself comfortable on the sofa, meanwhile, and I had busied myself pouring the brandy.

"I told Wiggins to have the lads carry on the search until five o'clock, and then to bring three or four of them to watch outside the Criterion Bar from seven o'clock onwards for any signal from me. I know the landlord at the Prospect well, and there was no problem with hanging about there for a long while. Le Villard and I had a good lunch - and a more than adequate exposure to the elements - while we waited. Then, as so often happens, all the news came at once. At three-thirty Wiggins came along with two of his fellows. One had come to the fish cafe with news of Norton, and as they headed out the door to inform us, the other had rushed up with a report from the Belgrave House Hotel.

"Without delaying, Wiggins had questioned him as well, and decided to bring them both along. The news was brief enough. Norton's trail had been picked up at the Standish Club, where he'd played a few games of billiards with the regulars at two o'clock, drunk two pints of bitter, and had left again at three. The lad had followed his trail, with some difficulty, to that den run by the old Chinaman, just down from the Bar O'Gold.

"Our lad managed to have a few words at the side door with the slavey there. It seems Norton has been staying in the second floor front above the den, and was an old customer. Hadn't been seen in years, but before that had frequented the place ever since his college days, when he and a half-dozen or so students had visited whenever they could get to London. The lad waited a while, and could see movement in the room, so decided to leg it back to Wiggins and report."

Holmes re-lit his pipe, and carried on.

"Next, I asked about the girl. The other of Wiggins's street arabs told us that two of them had been on watch. Isobel Aster had returned to the hotel at half-past two, in a cab, and had gone up to her room after spending a few minutes talking with the desk-clerk. She appeared flustered and nervous.

"The lads decided to watch for a while before reporting back to me, and soon the reason for her panic became apparent. Just moments after Miss Aster had gone upstairs, a closed carriage pulled to a halt across the street, with two well-dressed gentlemen inside. The coachman was sent inside. One of the Irregulars followed after him, waving an envelope as though he was delivering a message. I told you these lads were sharp, Watson."

Holmes's eyes sparkled as he took a deep pull at his pipe, and then another, before releasing a billow of smoke into the atmosphere of our already smoky sitting-room. I crossed to the bay-windows and opened the sashes to their fullest, despite the crisp air outside, and the possibility of air-guns.

"He overheard the coachman asking about Miss Blood, as she is registered there, and the desk-clerk's reply that *'she should be down in a few minutes, as she just this minute checked out of the hotel'*. The coachman then crossed back over to the carriage, and spoke with its occupants through the window, pointing at the upper floors of the hotel.

"At this point Wiggins's lads decided to split up. One of them would hurry back to report to Wiggins, while the other stayed to see what happened at the Belgrave House Hotel. It is some distance from Pimlico to Wapping, so it took thirty minutes for the boy to make his way back to us.

"Le Villard and I had to make a quick decision as to which of our two birds to follow, but it was not a difficult one. We already had an appointment arranged with Norton later that evening, and he seemed to be in no immediate danger, whereas Isobel Aster was apparently in a panic, was being followed at the very least, and perhaps was in serious danger indeed.

"We hailed a growler, loaded Wiggins and his boys into it, and promised the cabbie a crown for getting us to Belgrave Road in the shortest possible time. Perhaps I was overly generous. Our cab almost killed several worthy citizens en route, but we arrived in front of the hotel in less than half an hour.

"Wiggins's lad was nowhere in sight. My queries at the front desk showed that Miss Blood had indeed checked out of the hotel. The porter who carried her bag out had seen the coachman approaching to take it, so he had set it down and gone back inside to take another guest's luggage upstairs, and had seen nothing further.

"Meanwhile, Wiggins and the other two Irregulars had enquired around the street, and soon found their colleague. He was stretched out on a bench in the front office of a nearby printing house, a blood-soaked bandage wrapped around his head. The boy was barely able to speak, and was clearly badly concussed. We asked the print-shop owner - whose wife was bathing the lad's face with an ink-stained rag - what had happened, but he could tell us little. One of his workers had been taking a little air at the door when he heard a cry of pain. Just then a carriage that had been blocking the entrance to the lane at the rear had rushed away, with a deal of commotion - shouting, whip cracking, frightened horses and so forth.

"I told them the lad worked for me, and thanked them. We carried him out to our cab, and headed for the nearest hospital. On the way he managed to tell us, in snatches, just what had happened. It seems that Miss Aster had no idea the men were waiting for her until it was too late. There were few people on the street, and the hotel porter had gone back inside.

"The coachman snatched up her bag and manhandled her across the street and into the carriage. Our lad had tried to leap onto the running-board, but one of the occupants, a tall fellow with dark hair and a monocle, had raised a silver-topped black cane to strike him, then seemed to think better of it. He snatched a stick from his companion's hand, and lay several sharp blows across our lad's hands and head, until he dropped to the cobbles. The next he knew he was stretched out in the print-shop, with the owner's wife holding a bottle of smelling-salts to his nostrils.

"We asked around, but could find no leads to follow. By this time it was well after five; time to go to meet Godfrey Norton at the Criterion. I paid the lads well for their work so far, and off we all went. This time we placed Irregulars at every doorway, but to no avail. Six, and then six-thirty came and went, and still no sign of Norton. At a quarter to seven we drove to the opium den where he had last been seen.

"A few choice threats of closure and police action soon persuaded the old Chinaman to talk, especially after I pushed open the door leading to the den itself, with opium-raddled addicts lying all over the place. He told us that Norton had two well-dressed visitors to his room shortly after six o'clock, and left with them. Yes, they drove in a closed carriage with an uniformed coachman, and yes, the taller of the two carried a black cane. We inspected Norton's room, but it had been cleaned out entirely of his things. Not a trace to go on with."

Holmes finished his lengthy account of the day's adventures, and sighed deeply. Le Villard sat quietly, gazing into the fire, his brandy glass cradled in his hands.

"Not one of our more successful days, Holmes," he said.

"I think that qualifies as an understatement, le Villard. It was disastrous. I fear that both Isobel Aster and Godfrey Norton are in mortal danger, and there is little further we can do."

"So what *will* you do, Holmes?" I enquired.

Holmes looked at me with weary eyes, and then I noticed a sly twinkle in their grey depths.

"I shall look out some evening clothes for myself and le Villard, Watson, and I suggest you do likewise. We will arrive just in time to catch the second half of Henry Wood's new orchestra at Queen's Hall."

To say I was stunned is to put it mildly. Just a moment before, Holmes had been wondering how to rescue Isobel Aster and Godfrey Norton from their apparent kidnappers, and now we were to attend a concert. However, long experience had shown me that Holmes usually had reasons for even his most outrageous actions. I was not averse to stepping out after a long day's reading, so I repaired to my room to change for the evening.

Thirty minutes later we alighted at Langham Place, in front of the recently completed Queen's Hall. A thick fog had descended on the evening streets. Figures suddenly appeared out of it, and as mysteriously disappeared at twenty paces distance. We crossed the footpath and walked into the brightly-lit lobby of the concert hall. Wreaths of cigar-smoke hung in the air, and the last of the intermission crowd were straggling back into the auditorium. I glanced at the billboards arranged on trestles just inside the entrance.

"Holmes!" said I. "This is a premiere. The seats will all be taken long ago."

"Precisely why I reserved a box for the evening, Watson! Come along, or we will miss the opening bars of the first movement, and that would be unforgivable."

Once comfortable in our box seats, we sat back to enjoy the music, which was indeed excellent. I glanced a few times at Holmes. His eyes were closed, and it seemed that he had surrendered his senses to the music. At the end of the second movement he opened his eyes, and languidly surveyed the well-dressed and bejewelled audience through his weather-beaten opera glasses.

I noticed that le Villard smiled at the sight of these obviously familiar optics being used for the first time for their intended purpose. I was a little surprised myself, as Holmes had never cared much for the high-society crowd who usually attended premieres of this sort. But he soon tired of this, and sat back to enjoy the rest of the concert, as before, with his eyes closed.

A swelling crescendo and crashing finale heralded the end of the concert. Holmes was instantly on his feet, herding us gently but firmly along the box corridor to the stairs, and down to the lobby. Once there he slowed his pace a good deal, and we drifted out into Langham Place with the crowd, which seemingly melted away into the thick, luminescent fog.

"I think we'll walk just a little, after that superb music," said Holmes. "In fact, I think an after-concert night-cap would be in order. The evening is distinctly chilly."

This, too, was out of character for the Holmes I had known three years before, but a fine *cognac* was not an unwelcome prospect. It promised to be a slow, cold cab-ride back to our rooms through the clammy fog. Holmes, Le Villard, and I were by now passing in front of the Langham Hotel - one of London's most select - when Holmes turned in at the entrance, close on the heels of two gentlemen in frock-coats and silk top-hats. I noticed that they were the two men who had preceded us, visible from time to time in the swirling fog, all the way from the nearby concert-hall.

"How very convenient life is for the extremely wealthy," I thought to myself, as we followed Holmes into the elegant reception lounge of the Langham. "Just a stroll to the theatre or concert or club!"

Holmes walked quickly past the reception counter, then turned back, patting his pockets absent-mindedly, as though he had misplaced keys or a pocket-watch. He bumped straight into the taller of the two gentlemen who had preceded us on the way from the Queen's Hall.

"Oh dear!" cried Holmes, squinting up through a pair of spectacles that had not adorned his face just a moment before. "How very clumsy of me! I do . . . Why, if it isn't Lord Coledale? I'm so sorry to have knocked into you like that, but it is indeed a pleasure to see you again."

I noticed that Holmes's manner and speech were markedly altered from a moment before, and it wasn't until Lord Coledale replied that I quite understood why.

"Professor Sigerson," said he, in his languid drawl. But I noticed that Holmes's sudden appearance had given him a shock, and it took a moment for him to recover. "And M. Le Villard, no less! Y'know, you're th' last person I should have thought to be knockin' me down here in London, Professor. D'you room at the Langham as well? Quite th' best place in town!"

"No, my dear sir. We have just turned in here for a night-cap after a delightful evening at Queen's Hall. Will you join us?"

"Unfortunately, that will not be possible. The Baron and I have some rather pressin' business t' take care of, despite th' late hour. We, too, have spent the evenin' at the concert, as we've been locked in conference for days now, and simply had t' get out for a while. And now we must make up for lost time, as th' Baron returns t' Biarritz on th' morrow."

In his nervousness, I thought, he was explaining at unnecessary length.

Lord Coledale introduced his companion; a handsome, slightly built fellow dressed in expensive clothes of a decidedly Continental cut, younger by some years than he. Baron Zendtgraf acknowledged the introductions with a bored nod in our direction, then studied his concert program as Holmes carried on the conversation. I thought the Baron's casual air masked a sudden fear, and turned my attention back to Lord Coledale.

I saw a tall, lean aristocrat, with the breeding and manners instilled since birth evident in his patrician features. A monocle shone in his left eye, attached to a silken cord. His black evening clothes were of exquisite cut and quality, and a white silk scarf was draped negligently around his neck. Under his left arm was tucked an ebony cane, topped with an exquisite knob of filigreed silver.

"I, too, must leave London," he continued, "as m' seat's bein' contested in a fortnight. Must get back t' my constituency if I don't want t' be relegated t' th' Lords. No future in that, y'know. Been here in London too damned long as it is. Sailed *Sirdar* to Brindisi, y'know, then directed m' train straight t' Paris. Here ever since."

"How very odd," remarked Holmes. "I could swear I heard someone mention you'd been seen at Deauville - at the casino, in fact."

Lord Coledale's face remained impassive in the face of Holmes's flat contradiction, but it took him several moments to reply. He was clearly rattled, but attempting not to show it. Holmes had very neatly put him in a position where he would be caught in an untruth, whatever his response. He chose off-handed denial.

"Oh, I think y'r informant must've mistaken some other fellow f'me, Professor. And now, gentlemen, you really must excuse us. Th' Baron and I have a deal of discussion yet before concludin' our piece of business. Railways, y'know! Good evenin', gentlemen, an' I can't say what a pleasure it's been t'see you again, Professor Sigerson."

"All mine, Lord Coledale. But perhaps we'll meet again while I'm in England. I'll be here some time yet. Medals from the Royal Society, and lectures at the universities," lied Holmes with glib ease. "I bid you a good evening, your lordship; Baron Zendtgraf."

Lord Coledale and Holmes shook hands in farewell; the Baron bowed as he and his lordship walked towards the curved staircase. Holmes watched as they mounted the stairs, turned down a corridor on the first floor, and passed from our view.

"Quite ruffled his feathers, I think," said Holmes with satisfaction. "Made my evening, really. Now, how about that night-cap? I expect they'll still be serving in the bar."

As we sat and sipped at our *cognac,* Holmes off-handedly asked, "Did you notice anything in particular about Lord Coledale's footwear, Watson? No? Well, it's not important right at this moment. Enjoy your *cognac,* friends, and may I say what a pleasure it is to have the company of both of you stout fellows in the thick of an adventure such as this. Your health, gentlemen!"

"Was that encounter entirely coincidental, Holmes?" I asked as we left the warmth of the Langham Hotel and plunged once again into the damp fog.

"Not entirely, Watson, no! *J'adoube!* I knew where he was staying, and that the concierge had booked seats for a party of two for the concert. I thought an apparently chance meeting would be interesting, and booked our box through a different agency. My survey with opera-glasses showed me that Coledale was there, though I didn't recognise his companion. I had expected

Quiney, but I suspect that concerts are not to Quiney's taste. I had surmised that Coledale would go and return on foot, it being so close by, and followed them closely back to the Langham. I thought it was a most interesting conversation, and the music was marvellous. A rewarding evening, all in all."

We hailed a cab, and returned to 221B along dark London streets shrouded in greasy fog yellowed by street-lamps. For a moment I considered Holmes's remark: *'j'adoube!'* I knew enough of chess to recognise the phrase. Holmes had touched his piece without really intending to move it. It was past eleven when we returned to our cosy rooms, and Holmes and le Villard settled back to catch up on events that had occurred since Holmes's departure from Siam.

"What would you like to know, my friend?" asked Holmes. "Fire away!"

"Very well!" replied le Villard. "Can you tell me what kept you in France so long? Watson tells me you have been back less than a week."

"Quite! You will recall the case of the forcible poisoning we investigated at Montpellier?"

"Of course! Leturier was the victim."

"I had a strong suspicion, just before I left Siam, that we had failed to get entirely to the bottom of that strange affair. Although we apprehended the murderer, I always thought the motive he gave us was not entirely believable. At the time it was all we had to go on, and it closed the case. But I was struck by a coincidence between that murder and the affairs at Siam, and decided to take another look into the matter on my way back to London, while I awaited Mycroft's message that it was the right time for me to reappear in London.

"Meanwhile, to explain my presence in the south of France I arranged to conduct some experiments with coal-tar derivatives - as indeed I told you, Watson - and managed to develop a fibre which, with further refinement, could substitute for natural silk." Holmes's eyes crinkled, and he laughed quietly at some private recollection. "Some day I shall continue my researches in that direction, but Mycroft was horrified when I telegraphed him news of my results. It seems that silk is one of Britain's most profitable trading monopolies, and any disruption would be most unwelcome to the Colonial Office."

"To return to Leturier. May I ask what was the coincidence?" enquired le Villard.

"Of course. It was Leturier's occupation."

"But he was a newspaper man. No one of any importance at Siam was a newspaper man, were they?" asked le Villard, clearly puzzled.

"The original target at Siam was Rolin, who was crucially important in opposing the French attempts to annex all or part of Siam. Leturier was a newspaper editor who advocated the abandonment of French empire-building, on the grounds that it was both immoral and unprofitable for France to continue doing so. At the time of his murder this did not seem to be connected to his death. Now I took a closer look at the past life of both Leturier and his murderer, and came away with even more coincidences to consider.

"Although it was made to appear a *crime passionel* at the time, the killer had a long association with the more radical elements of the French colonialist lobby - the *parti colon*. Amongst the underworld of Marseilles the story was that he had several other murders to his credit, amongst them two at Alexandria in Egypt. And one of those was carried out, as best I can determine from second-hand sources, with an air-gun firing revolver cartridges. Again, the victims were opponents of the colonial lobby.

"Unfortunately, thanks to *our* efforts, le Villard, *Madame* la Guillotine has long since accounted for the assassin - so obviously I could not question him. But my investigations turned up some most interesting names. I found out he'd had a regular girlfriend at Marseilles, and traced her to Deauville and Biarritz where she was looking - unsuccessfully - for a new admirer. I caught up with her eventually at Nîmes, where she was born and where her mother still lived.

"It was clear she was frightened of the same killers coming after her. I pointed out that her boyfriend had left her penniless, and now he was dead, so she co-operated at last. In a valise he'd left with her just before he was arrested I found a wallet containing a number of calling cards. Amongst them were many bearing the names of various notables amongst the members of the *parti colon*. And one card, printed discreetly with the name of our good Lord Coledale! No address! Interesting, don't you agree?"

Sherlock Holmes and his French colleague spent a further ten minutes discussing the past, then we all turned in. I found that sleep eluded me, so after a few minutes I lit the gas lamp, and read more of the Journals, intending to read only a little before sleep overtook me.

CHAPTER XLV

18th July 1893
Bangkok, Siam

MORE THAN A FEW NIGHTS Holmes and I followed well behind the General Adviser and Rinzing when they were scheduled to travel to the ministry or palace. The Chinamen were usually following them, but did nothing other than observe, then slip away. Tonight we were glad to rest, as the constant late-night surveillance was beginning to wear us down. The events of the past week had meant that the General Adviser was called out almost every night. He gave us a brief report whenever we saw him, which was less frequent than before; now he was at the Palace until the early hours every night during the crisis.

Bangkok went into a state of siege after the gun-boat incident. The populace was alarmed in the extreme, and preparations for trouble were seen on all sides; money and valuables were secreted away, children sent out of the city to relatives in the provinces, food stocks hoarded and extra fresh water stored in large jars. Chief Inspector Sheriff reported a brisk trade in firearms , ammunition and supplies, especially amongst the Chinese traders. Armed soldiers were everywhere, and travel by carriage became almost impossible.

The day after the incident Pavie came alone to the Ministry, with words of friendship, despite the war-ships having taken combat positions. Whenever a Siamese ship passed in front of the French war-ships they immediately assumed battle-stations. This Pavie blamed on the Siamese having trained guns on the ships from in front of the Customs, and on news of a Siamese attack announced for the fifteenth. The King at first was most downcast, fearing bombardment of the Palaces along the river, and of the city at large, and would not be comforted by reason. The captured crew of the *J B Seay* were turned over to the French Legation, where they promptly claimed extreme maltreatment at the hands of a Danish captain in Siamese employ. The *Linnet*, a second English war-ship, arrived at Bangkok. Rolin told us that Pavie became much more difficult following the release of the French crew, creating problems regarding the General Adviser's role in discussions with the Prince.

Nevertheless, Rolin counselled the dismantling of the show of force in the capital, which he thought was both useless and alarming to the public. Access to the old quarter was restored, and the troops avoided showing themselves most of the time.

The Nortons returned to Siam. After some thought, Holmes had contacted Hans von Hollstein, and found that, despite some misgivings, he had prepared the gun-cotton and fuses for Norton, aware that Norton would have to sign the appropriate documents prior to collection.

Several matters of concern to us hinged upon the arrival of Godfrey Norton. Apart from the explosives - which may or may not have been on behalf of the principals of Cutter and Fluddle - he was expected to sort out the funds for the Belgians.

The steamer from Singapore berthed late in the afternoon at the Bangkok Dock pier. Holmes and I were stationed where we could see who met them, if anyone. As it turned out there was quite a little party waiting for Norton. Several of the managers of C & F concerns pushed forward, papers in hand, as he came down the gangway. Standing some distance off and hoping to remain inconspicuous was Garraud, with another fellow I had not seen before.

But for me there was only the one. Miss Malee had appeared from behind a parasol and was embracing Mrs. Norton as an old friend, rather than as a pupil. Several other young Siamese ladies stood decoratively nearby, and Mrs. Norton smilingly greeted them all in the Siamese fashion. I glanced at Holmes, who paid no attention at all to the gathering of women. He fixed first on the Belgian, then on the waiting managers, and then on Godfrey Norton, noting every detail.

A fellow we had seen before at Bangkok was walking about, introducing himself to a number of the disembarking passengers. One of them was Godfrey Norton, who spoke several words to him, then raised his fist angrily, as though to strike the man down where he stood. The man raised his open hands, as though to ward off the blow, and swiftly backed away.

The group soon dispersed, the Nortons and one of the senior managers sharing a carriage. Before leaving Norton excused himself for a moment and walked over to where Garraud stood as though waiting for someone else. A chance encounter! A few brief words of greeting! That was all, to the casual observer. I saw a slender envelope change hands though, and so did Holmes. There was only one other event worthy of note. As the carriage bearing the Nortons turned from the quayside onto the roadway, another drew up alongside it. A few words were exchanged between the occupant and Godfrey Norton, then both resumed their journeys.

"Coledale's man Quiney!" remarked Holmes. "What *is* Norton to Coledale, exactly? For all our rooting around, we still don't really know why he is retained by his lordship."

We remained out of sight until the Nortons and their friends had departed, then returned to our hotel for an excellent meal in the dining room. The sight of Miss Malee, and the thought that I should soon have a reason to see her again, had made my pulse race a little. Holmes had left a message for Mrs. Norton informing her of the possible prospects in Europe for her pupil, and asking her to call on him at any time to discuss the matter. He had promised her, after all, to find out what was bothering her husband so.

The meal was excellent, although as usual I found the seven courses a little excessive. We did justice to it, however, and I felt in such fine spirits that I ordered a bottle of Loire wine. Holmes drank with me, and when I toasted the return of Irene Adler, he smiled, and added as he raised his glass, "And her pupils. Or at least one of them! I hope this is not to be a repeat of that affair at Cairo, le Villard. Almost got us killed, and in the end, she turned out to work for the people we were after."

I reddened a little at the truth of the remark, and silently vowed not to repeat my foolish mistake. It didn't hurt to dream a little, though, and my thoughts these days turned more frequently to Miss Malee. Where was she now? What was she doing? Holmes interrupted my pleasant thoughts with a rude reminder that we should now have to visit the night-spot again.

Garraud had been sober the day after our meeting with Colonel Sartorius, when I dropped off the package containing one thousand pounds at *Mama-san* Kung's place. Two days later I had stopped in at the night-club, alone, just to see if Sartorius *had* left for the north. Garraud was there, and confirmed that he had, so I had a stein of beer with Hans, and left for an early night.

19th July 1893
Bangkok, Siam
Baritsu, as usual, then breakfast, and a quick trip across the river to *Nai* Portugee's office! At least, that was how we had the morning planned. Siamese naval barges, and boats carrying armed marines in full ceremonial regalia, barred our progress up the river. They warned us that it was the morning of one of the major Siamese religious festivals, and we would be stopped further upstream, as the Royal Barges would appear shortly making their way down to *Wat Arun* - the Temple of Dawn - on the Thonburi side of the river. Our interest aroused, we directed our boatman to pass by Nai Portugee's place and make his way as far upstream as possible, then moor unobtrusively. He edged the gondola up past the huge pinnacled temple just as the sun lightened the horizon, and worked his way into a tiny *klong* overgrown with bamboo and trees.

From this translucent green shelter we had a clear view for some distance up the river. A Siamese naval cutter tied up at the entrance to our small canal, cast a cursory glance at us, and returned their attention to the number of local craft collecting along the banks of the river. The populace was arriving in rapidly increasing numbers, waiting on a rare opportunity to see their King in the full panoply of their traditional royal ceremonies.

Although we had been told of this ceremony, in the excitement of events we'd forgotten about it. First we heard the sound, long before the first of the slender gilded barges came into view from around the bend. Thousands of voices chanting in unison, keeping time by the beat of a bamboo stave pounded on the deck of each boat. The sonorous chant was in counterpoint to a plaintive song in the Siamese manner, strangely discordant and yet hauntingly musical, sung by a single high, clear voice from one of the boats in mid-fleet. For a fleet it was. As they came into view it was clear there were at least forty of these extravagantly decorated barges, propelled by Siamese marines in full regimental colours, in slow, measured surges keeping time with the chanted song. The first were relatively humble, bearing the stylised markings of tigers, monkeys, and strange mythical half-beast half-birds. Soon we spotted the principal barges in the centre of the procession - a huge barge with an intricately carved figurehead of a seven-headed serpent; several other principal vessels and finally, flanked by two smaller barges with prows shaped like horned dragons, the barge carrying the King.

Our first sight of this fabulous vessel came as it ponderously rounded the bend, just as the sun rose above the trees and temples along the river. We saw rows of huge gilded oars, twenty or more on each side. Rising in unison the golden oars paused in time with the chant; then, flashing light from the reflecting sun they took a short, measured stroke forward, dipping for a short moment in the water. It was a most inefficient but stately means of locomotion, and as the barge rounded the bend to head directly towards us, the illusion was complete. With her high, rearing figurehead carved like a mythical bird she looked for all the world like an enormous golden swan, sculling serenely down the broad river surrounded by her brood. And all the while the high, wailing sound of the Siamese plainsong and chant swelled louder and more insistently as the King's barge approached.

As they passed in review we could appreciate the craftsmanship and allegorical imagery of the intricately carved prows and hulls of these unique craft. Surely there is no fleet of vessels to rival it remaining in the entire world. An antique culture still extant and full of life! I thought that, whatever the European ramifications of the present crisis over Siam, our role felt comfortable, Holmes's and mine. Rolin was determined to help save Siam for the Siamese by mustering support from the moderate factions within both of the opposing European powers. I could support such an aim without conflict.

The high, steady wail of conch shells signalled the approach of the Royal

Barge itself. At our distance the figure of the King seemed tiny, seated alone on a raised dais under a shapely canopy set in the centre of the huge barge. The barge was the only one carrying a nine-tiered white umbrella, as the symbol of its royal passenger. Court officials dressed all in white with conical white hats, and numerous others in bright-coloured official regalia stood motionless at their appointed positions. The only movement was the stylised rowing of the marines and the pounding of bamboo staves by the timekeepers.

Slowly the procession passed us by, there being only one more principal barge and a few escort vessels following behind the King's barge. The silently respectful swarm of Siamese, lining the shore and aboard their skiffs and boats, came back to noisy life and dispersed. After an hour had passed we nosed our way back out into the river and made our way back down past the Temple of Dawn, where the Royal Barge was still moored, to the wharf of Nai Portugee. The sound of the chant and the splendour of the procession filled my senses, and I was startled a little when our gondola bumped against Nai Portugee's pier.

Once we were comfortably seated, Holmes asked him about the Chinese informant at the ministry, and whether he could be linked in any way with *Sia* Ah Foo. The Portuguese laughed.

"I can answer that immediately. They are inevitably linked, because their families are from the same small coastal village in China. You will find mud brought from that village well at the bottom of the water jars at both their houses. Those villages, each the home of one clan, have sent large numbers of their own overseas to make their fortunes. They may end up in Peru, or Alaska, or Siam, but their children and grandchildren will always think of that village in China as their real home. That is how it is with *Sia* Ah Foo and *Nai* Amornsap."

By noon we were back at the hotel. A message from Irene Adler had just arrived, asking if she could call on the Professor at four that afternoon. Holmes sent an affirmative reply by return.

At a few minutes past four Mrs. Norton and her pupil Miss Malee arrived. We sat at the terrace for afternoon tea. English scones with strawberry jam and clotted cream, served with Ceylon tea. Rain suddenly arrived; first a few heavy drops, then a torrential downpour, all within seconds. We had to raise our voices over the drumming on the awning overhead. Splashing water soon formed a damp, cooling mist.

"So you see, Mrs. Norton, that there has been little I could find out - at least, little that you don't already know. Your husband lives his personal life rather publicly, but his business affairs he keeps very close - as a lawyer must.

Perhaps you could tell me what has happened while you were at Singapore; there may be something that throws some light on his affairs?"

Irene Adler sighed deeply, and dabbed the mist from her face with her handkerchief.

"Apart from another bout of violent bullying, he has been attentive to me. But it is clear that Godfrey is still under some terrible pressure. He finds it impossible to sleep for more than a few hours at a time. When he does wake, he worries and frets until he falls asleep again from sheer exhaustion."

"Have you seen any more large sums of cash?" asked Holmes.

"Twice. I expect there have been other occasions I don't know of."

"On what occasions . . . please?"

"I don't know much, only that he always received it by courier messenger - always a Chinese - and has to count it out quickly. Then he would leave, and return hours later - without the money."

"He makes no attempt to hide the money from you?"

"We have always been very open with each other, Godfrey and I. Lately he has changed considerably, but he would never think I'd hurt him in any way. But he has begun carrying a revolver, which he would never do before."

"Do you know who he intends seeing while here?"

"Certainly the managers of C&F's businesses here. They are all very concerned about the crisis and the possibility of a blockade. Godfrey says they need advice, and help in case of general panic. Then there is that terrible Belgian who always smells of cheap gin or whisky. I overheard Godfrey saying he would see him tonight. Thinks I don't know where, or else he doesn't care that I know. Beast!"

"What about Quiney; you know, Coledale's chap? I saw that they spoke at the quay when you arrived yesterday. Did you hear what was said?"

"Only a few words. Simply that Godfrey was expected to make a report to his lordship immediately he had settled in. Godfrey left again almost as soon as we arrived at the Bangkok Hotel. I assumed he was going there. That man Quiney was not terribly friendly about it all. I've always wondered why Lord Coledale tolerates his rudeness and presumption. Been with him off and on for years, though, so they must get along somehow."

"Well, if you can find out anything else about Norton's brief for his lordship, let us know. Don't be too obvious about it, though. Now, how long is Norton staying here at Bangkok?"

"I expect that depends on the blockade, but when we arrived at the hotel he booked for a month. So at least that long."

"Thank you, you've been most frank. I have one last question. Does the term Men of Straw mean anything to you?"

Irene Adler turned as pale as milk. Her blue eyes widened with terror, and her in-drawn breath could be heard even over the din of the driving rain. She recovered her poise in an instant and turned towards Holmes.

"No! Why . . . should it do?" she replied softly.

"Just a passing thought," answered Holmes.

"Miss Malee," I said, rising and offering her my arm. "It is becoming damp where you are seated. May I escort you to the lounge? When Professor Sigerson and Mrs. Norton have finished their discussion, I'm sure they'll join us there.

Besides being exactly what Holmes expected me to do under the circumstances, I looked forward to just a few moments alone with Miss Malee, whatever the pretext. I found a table for four in a quiet corner, and we sat and ordered lemonades. The few minutes before Holmes and Mrs. Norton joined us were spent in satisfying Miss Malee's curiosity about my home town, and my work; I thought I detected a hint of something more than just polite conversation in her interest. She seemed intrigued by our adventures in the Himalayas . . . but all too soon the others arrived.

Irene Adler looked as though she was torn between relief and guilt as she and Holmes approached. Holmes's tall, lean figure seemed to provide comfort to her, judging by the way that she leant on his arm for support. She was calm and serene by the time they reached us, and a charming but trivial conversation ensued until the ladies rose to leave. Once we had seen them to their carriage we returned to the lounge.

"Well?" I enquired.

"Thank you, le Villard. Well timed departure! As you saw, she was shaken up at the mention of the Men of Straw, but didn't wish to talk about it with Miss Malee about. It seems that whenever he has one of his bouts of terror, it is after receiving a package containing a gold signet ring, engraved on the inside with the inscription, Men of Straw. Each time, there is a black ribbon tied to the ring. This has apparently happened five times over the past three years, and each time he becomes more frightened, though he tries to cover it. He has fled several times over from wherever they were, but sooner or later another package would arrive, wherever he went, containing another ring.

"Her words were: 'He seems to think there is a horrible fate awaiting him when the seventh ring arrives. He won't say why, but keeps repeating that seven is to be his unlucky number. When I ask about it, he simply says he was a fool to get involved with the Men of Straw in the first place, but won't say why. If I press him he turns nasty and stalks out, to get drunk or worse.' But what still puzzles me most, my friend, is why she remains with him at all."

"Is she telling all she knows?" I asked.

"I doubt it! She is, after all, a woman."
"What next, Professor?"
"This is clearly something that has followed Norton around. I suspect the answers are to be found in London, not here."

20th July 1893
Bangkok, Siam
Though we suspected where it would take place we had decided not to follow Norton to his meeting with Garraud. As it turned out, we did not have to engineer an encounter with Norton. Just as we were finishing breakfast at nine o'clock he arrived at our hotel. Politely but coldly he asked if he might have a word with the Professor.
Holmes replied, "Of course. Shall we step out onto the lawn? There's a slight breeze, which is rather refreshing at this hour."
"A pox on your breeze, Professor Sigerson. I should like to know why you are taking such an interest in my affairs? My drinking companions - even the companies I represent, for god's sake! What is it you want? Are you from *them*? Have you another ring for me? Is that it? If so, just hand it over, save a lot of bother?"
"I'm afraid I know nothing of any ring, Norton," said Holmes. "As for following you around, I suspect we simply have similar tastes in diversion, my friend. Being new in town, I admit to having mentioned your name on occasion, but for no particular reason. As for the companies you represent, I am an investor as well as an explorer. You may recall that you offered your legal services when last we met. I like to know about those I entrust with financial matters. The best way, I have found, is to do a little discreet asking about. I do apologise if I've caused any difficulties. Meanwhile, if you do not wish to represent my interests here, I can find another."
"Why is my wife receiving messages from you, sir?"
"Her *protégé*, Miss Malee, is looking for a position in Europe. Having met her at Lord Coledale's yacht, when this matter came into the conversation, I felt sure that I could be of help. She is a bright girl, and her languages are first-rate. I said as much to Mrs. Norton. I was not aware of anything underhanded in our meetings, sir. I thought it rather fine of Mrs. Norton to try to help the girl."
Norton thought about all this for a moment, then stood and offered his hand to Holmes.
"It's possible I've seen things in the wrong light, Professor. I've had a deal of problems lately, and sometimes it seems that the world conspires to make my life more difficult. I accept your explanations, sir, and I hope you will

accept my apologies. If you still require my services after that outburst, please just let me know the details."

"No apologies required, Norton. On the contrary! As to legal matters, I am not yet decided to invest here, given the uncertainty prevailing. This threatened blockade, you understand. When I do decide, I shall contact you, as I require. Preparing letters of intent, checking contracts, conveyancing; that sort of thing. Fairly routine stuff, but necessary. But do forgive me, Norton. We have already eaten, but can we offer you some coffee, or tea perhaps?"

"Thanks, but no! I have had my breakfast, and must get over to his lordship's yacht. I'm expected, and it doesn't do to keep the gentry waiting!"

"Do I detect a note of disapproval, Norton? Are you against inherited privilege, perhaps?"

"In the ordinary course of things, no! Lord Coledale is a powerful and wealthy man, Professor. I can scarcely afford to disapprove of such a client. So I don't."

"Quite so!" replied Holmes. "I imagine his business would be far more lucrative than our small investments."

But Norton did not take the bait, and we learned no more about Lord Coledale's business from him. He left us, and headed towards the pier to take a gondola.

25th July 1893
Bangkok, Siam

As days passed, and the French ships remained, rumours began to spread regarding their real intent. The King apparently believed his person was being threatened. A delegation of Chinese publicly offered to load boats with petroleum and set fire to them alongside the French vessels.

On the twentieth of July, Pavie came to the Ministry to deliver a thinly-disguised Ultimatum making the usual increased demands, under threat of naval blockade of the city if not complied with within forty-eight hours. Only hours before that deadline the Siamese replied, sending to the Legation the General Adviser's draft ceding the left bank of the Mae Kong up to the 18th degree Latitude North. Nevertheless, the King was still fearful that the French would perform some violent act before departing, even assuming they accepted the agreed draft. The General Adviser spent time gathering with the officers of the various friendly ships in port, and with the various ambassadors and consuls, building support for the Siamese position.

Pavie announced his intention to depart aboard the *Inconstant* on the twenty-sixth, and arranged for French nationals to be represented by the Belgian consul - the Chevalier de Keun, whom Rolin was fairly certain was in the French camp, and passed along to them information he gleaned at diplomatic gatherings.

Rolin was most concerned that the proceedings of Siamese councils-of-state were becoming public knowledge within hours, and prevailed upon the King to hold these meetings privately, in an inner chamber deep within the Palace.

At first Rolin had been puzzled as to the events of the thirteenth at the mouth of the river, but gradually pieced together the answers.

"Partly it was the perfidy of the French *colons* at Saigon, trying to outwit their nominal masters at the *Quai d'Orsay*. Once permission to dispatch the China Squadron was announced Saigon gave orders to put to sea immediately in order to forestall any Foreign Office revisions - as in fact happened. Had the French delayed their departure from Saigon until the fifteenth as ordered, there would have been no incident. But Admiral Humann was already at the mouth of the Menam, and carrying orders to cross the bar.

"In the meantime, our diplomatic pressure had caused Develle to think again, and order his Navy not to attempt to force the bar; his Ministry sent a telegraph to the Siamese Foreign Minister to the effect that a counter-order had been given. This arrived at the Ministry at ten-thirty in the morning of the thirteenth. Pavie claims that he had not received a copy of the message at the French Legation, the *Quai* apparently having assumed that the Siamese would notify them, and says he was unaware of the counter-order when he went aboard the Admiral's ship just before she crossed the bar. Unfortunately, the Foreign Minister, not unreasonably, sleeps during the daylight hours, and works during the cool of the evening and night. Being a Prince, none dared disturb him, and so the message which could have averted the crisis lay unopened until the Prince awoke - just as the cannon were firing at the mouth of the river."

28th July 1893
Bangkok, Siam

Rolin came in the early evening. Notification of the naval blockade of the coast of Siam, effective from the twenty-sixth of July, had arrived at the Ministry. Friendly warships were given three days to depart. Effectively this would cut off trade and travel into Siam. Rolin worried that there was still no official reply from Paris to the Siamese answer to the Ultimatum of the twentieth. The Prince apparently became inclined to accept the terms of the Ultimatum unconditionally, especially following receipt of messages from Lord Rosebery advising immediate acceptance in order to forestall increased French demands, and making it clear that Britain would render no assistance. Otherwise, we did little.

4th August 1893
Bangkok, Siam
During these days of the blockade we suspended our investigations, people being in general so alarmed that it was impossible to achieve much. As usual, we had the reports of the General Adviser, and our own observations, to keep us informed as to events. The Prince had taken to sleeping at his Palace once again.

On Sunday Captain de Muller of the *Linnet* brought new notification of the blockade, now extended in scope. On the following day the Prince received a long, coded message from Paris, which Prince Bidyalabh slowly deciphered while Prince Ranawongse paced the room. It proved to be a demand for guarantees of compliance with the terms of the Ultimatum, without additional demands. If agreed to, the blockade would be lifted immediately

The General Adviser confided that he had feared worse, with the French press goading the public into baying for expansion of the colonies, and the current French cabinet so weak. However, it had turned out as he expected, due to the English having been brought into the affair. He also thought that Foreign Minister Develle had wished to prevent the Navy from claiming credit for a diplomatic success. As it stands, it his opinion that the French minister has sought effect rather than real territorial gains, and he advised acceptance.

On a more positive note, it seems that the King also sounded out Rolin about a state visit to all the countries of Europe, once this affair was settled. The next day, reported Rolin, these plans were elaborated upon with enthusiasm, and itineraries planned to include Trieste, Vienna, Berlin, St. Petersburg, Brussels, Amsterdam, Paris and London, finishing with Switzerland, Italy, Turkey and Egypt. Long discussions ensued regarding the choice of Siamese or Western official attire.

When word was at last received from Lord Rosebery announcing Develle's lifting of the blockade, no advice to that effect came from Saigon, and with the usual antagonism between Paris and Saigon, the blockade continued another two days. Notification was finally received at Bangkok, although Pavie had not yet returned.

8th August 1893
Bangkok, Siam
At last, with the blockade lifted, Holmes and I were able to depart for Shanghai on the first China-bound steamer available. The *Daphne* looked barely

seaworthy, with great patches of rust staining her battered hull, but she was the only ship available for passage at short notice. We were grateful to be leaving at all, having lost several days since Holmes received the urgent telegraph message from Mycroft which had directed us towards Shanghai, and the *Mystery of the Missing Mandarin*, as Holmes dubbed the affair at that time. We expected to be away for three weeks or so.

The French Ultimatum achieved a modest gain for the French *colons* at Saigon. The General Adviser agreed that, so long as the British remained less than enthusiastic in their willingness to become militarily involved in resolving the Siam question, surrender of the left bank of the Mekong was the best path for the Siamese to follow. Though the Siamese lost a little territory, by accepting the demands of the French Foreign Office they effectively defused the threat of French annexation of all of Siam - which was always the real goal of the *colons*. If only they had been able to manoeuvre the *Quai d'Orsay* into appearing to support their initiatives, the Governor General and the Navy brass at Saigon would clearly have taken Bangkok at gun-point without delay.

Now the *colons* would need to work up a new set of grievances, which would take some time. As a result, Holmes felt that the threat to Rolin was not so acute at the moment, and that we could safely leave Siam for a while. We visited Tashi and Rinzing, instructing the latter to continue riding with the General Adviser during his nocturnal carriage trips to the ministry.

I had hoped that we would see Mrs. Norton again before we left; she usually brought Miss Malee with her, but there was no occasion to do so. Holmes had sent a message informing her of our forthcoming absence from Bangkok. This received a polite reply, thanking him for his assistance to her *protégé*, and wishing us *bon voyage*.

As we steamed down the Menam Chao Phraya, past the now-silent guns of the fort at Paknam and out into the Gulf of Siam, I reflected on the events in which we had become involved since our arrival several months previously. A cat-and-mouse game with parties not yet identified, the ultimate prize being Siam itself. Apart from the warning shot at Rolin there had been no violence, but for us the ever-present threat of his assassination hung over the larger events of the Siam Question like a sword on a thread. We had another affair to deal with at Shanghai, and hoped, as we departed, that no harm would befall the General Adviser during our brief absence.

DAY SEVEN

APRIL 12TH 1894

CHAPTER XLVI

"I HAVE ONE LEAD FURTHER to follow up in connection with Norton," said Holmes, as we came out onto the footpath in front of 221 Baker Street. "It won't directly lead us to wherever he's been taken, but, if my suspicions prove well-founded, may shed further light on his involvement in these matters."

He instructed the driver of the carriage Billy had hailed to take us to Lincoln's Inn Fields at Holborn. As we drove through Chancery Lane gate-house into the quadrangle of Lincoln's Inn, still peaceful at this early hour, I recalled that Godfrey Norton had once been resident at the Inner Temple, another of the four Inns of Court from whence all London barristers worked. The fog had not lifted, and the ancient buildings loomed from the mist like picturesque cliffs rising from a misty sea. A few barristers togged out in wigs and robes hurried though the murk, seeming rather like black boats forging their way through a milky sea.

Our destination proved to be the chambers of Sir Oliver Norton. on the second floor. Sir Oliver's name, as Head of Chambers, was at the top of a narrow column of hand-painted boards alongside the entrance. Holmes made a point of noting the clerk's name from the very bottom board. He was apparently expected, however, to judge by the attitude of the clerk, who seemed undismayed by our arrival without an accompanying solicitor.

The clerk showed us into an oak-panelled library. The room was lined with row upon row of legal volumes bound in calf-skin, with titles embossed in discreetly small gold lettering. Small-paned windows set in the stone walls would have afforded a pleasant view over the grassy quadrangle, were it not for the layer of fog. A fire was already lit in the marble fireplace, but did little to dispel the chill as we arranged ourselves at the small conference table by the tall windows.

Within minutes the clerk returned, followed by a tall, patrician fellow sporting mutton-chop sideburns, chalk-stripe trousers, and black cutaway frock-coat. His prematurely greying hair was combed straight back from a sharply-defined widow's peak. A pair of tiny *pince-nez* perched precariously on the sharp bridge of his aristocratic nose, and a white carnation in his lapel added a dandy's touch to his sober barrister's garb.

The clerk introduced him as Sir Oliver Newsome, QC, and withdrew discreetly, quietly closing the door behind him.

"Good morning, gentlemen," said the Queen's Counsel. "And you, sir, are Sherlock Holmes, the detective, I take it? I am due in court very soon, so I would appreciate it if we could keep this brief. How may I be of assistance?"

"I think a few minutes of your time will suffice, Sir Oliver. It's in connection with one of your former junior colleagues at the Inner Temple, a Mr. Godfrey Norton."

"Ah! Godfrey! Has he run afoul of the authorities at last? Not the brightest of fellows, but devilish handsome in his younger days, and he had a real way with the lady clients. But he fled the country some years ago; married a *prima donna* from the Warsaw Opera, I believe. But that wasn't the real reason he left the country. Some scandal was about to explode in his face, I heard, and it was only by taking off that he avoided disbarment, or worse."

"And that is precisely the reason I have for calling on you at such short notice, Sir Oliver. I now know that he has arrived back in London. It is possible that Norton is both a murderer and a traitor, and I believe you hold whatever chance there may be of proving him innocent. I was told that you knew him very well at university, before you took silks."

"That is so," replied the QC, looking a little less self-assured.

"I am here on behalf of the Foreign Office, Sir Oliver. It is entirely likely that Norton is himself in mortal danger, and I need further information about a few matters. Firstly, what can you tell me about the Godfrey Norton of those days?"

The distinguished counsel steepled his fingers, and thought for a moment before answering.

"We were not on particularly intimate terms, you understand. I was in my final year when he came up to Cambridge, and joined the debating society of which I was the President. He was rather brilliant as a public speaker in those days, before the absinthe and laudanum caused him to retreat from reality. He joined a rather disreputable drinking-club halfway through his first year, I believe; one modelled loosely on the infamous Hellfire Club. Still managed his studies, and managed to graduate, though without any particular distinction."

"Did you see much of him once you came to London, Sir Oliver?"

"Not a great deal." The QC was becoming discomfited by the direction of the conversation, but carried on. "He was fond of coming to the city whenever he could get away from his college, along with other members of their drink-and-drugs club. *Similis simili gaudet!* They frequented various low dives around the waterfront, and he got into trouble more than once. Godfrey came to me for help, and I tried to extricate him from his scrapes as best I could. His family was reasonably well off, and his father paid well to hush things up."

"Nothing more than that, Sir Oliver?" asked Holmes, fixing his clear gaze on the lawyers eyes. "Were you and Godfrey, perhaps, shall we say, *particular friends* in those days? Forgive my impertinence, sir, but there are grave issues at stake here, and your confidences will be both appreciated and respected."

Again, Sir Oliver Newsome thought for some time before answering, then seemed to make up his mind to it.

"It is hardly a secret that I am . . . shall we say, a confirmed bachelor, Mr. Holmes. I had, it is true, a great fondness for the boy, but he had no interest in my *particular friendship,* as you put it. Nevertheless, I found it impossible to refuse him whenever he asked for my help. He could have made so much of himself, had it not been for that confounded circle of depraved drug-fiends he favoured. Oh! I'm sure it all began as an undergraduate lark, reading Coleridge and Baudelaire, Poe and the rest of them, and imagining themselves as great romantics, but Godfrey was rather weak-willed, and soon fell entirely under the spell of the opium and that vile green absinthe.

"I tried many times to wean him away from the drugs and from his dissolute friends, but to no avail. I would hear nothing from him for months on end, and then receive a message that he'd been locked up in such-and-such a police cells overnight. Time and again, against my better judgement I confess, I went to bail him out. Every time he asked!

"My efforts ensured that no real scandal attached itself to his name, and at last he gained his degree, and I arranged for him to come to the Inner Temple. He remained there until he left London with that opera singer. I have heard nothing of him since."

Holmes regarded him thoughtfully, then spoke, gently but with some resolution.

"Are you quite certain, Sir Oliver, that Godfrey Norton has not contacted you within the past two weeks; perhaps at home?"

Holmes let the blunt question hang in the air, until suddenly the Queen's Counsel's expression underwent a most remarkable transformation. The patrician condescension vanished entirely, and what remained was a lonely and desperate middle-aged man, clearly troubled deeply by conflicting loyalties. At last, Sir Oliver spoke, so softly as to be barely audible.

"How did you know, Mr. Holmes? No-one can have seen us together. It was ten days ago. Godfrey sent a message. He used the name I had given him - years ago now - to use anytime he was in trouble, so as to keep his own name untainted. We met at lunch-time, in Hyde Park, by the Serpentine, and talked as we fed the ducks, as though we were casual acquaintances. I had only a short time between cases, and had to rush back to the Old Bailey.

Godfrey looked terrible - rough and coarse. But he seemed physically strong underneath the rough exterior, and . . . anyway, he told me a little about the events at Siam, and of how he had worked his way back to Rotterdam as a stoker on a Dutch ship carrying spices from Java. He joined her at Singapore, and when she reached Holland, he jumped ship and slipped across to Felixstowe. But we had little time, as I said."

"Why did he contact you, if I may ask?" enquired Holmes.

"He needed money. I gave him what I carried, which was little enough, and told him I would arrange more. But he never came back, and I had nowhere to send it on."

"Nothing more?" asked Holmes.

"No, Mr. Holmes. That was all."

"Please think carefully, Sir Oliver, before you answer. It is entirely possible that Godfrey Norton has entangled himself in a case that may constitute treason against Her Majesty's Government. You will be doing the right thing by justice, and Norton, if you answer fully and truthfully. Did Godfrey Norton leave anything with you when you met at Hyde Park?"

The Queen's Counsel began to deny any such thing, but Holmes's grey eyes bored into his, compelling him to the truth. Holmes, I thought, would have made a formidable opponent in any court of law, to judge by the mastery of his cross-examination of Sir Oliver Newsome.

At last the truth came out. Newsome slumped a little, shrugged, and sighed deeply in resignation to his duty.

"Yes, Godfrey gave me a sealed envelope, along with the strictest instructions that it was to be opened only in the case of absolute confirmation of his death by violent means. Godfrey swore me to those same conditions before he would hand it over. I begged him to take me into his confidence, but he was adamant. He said there were crimes he needed to avenge, personally; that it was the last satisfaction he expected on this earth, and officials who could be bought off would not rob him of it. He made no mention of the person or persons he intended to destroy - and that was his phrasing - and there was nothing I could do to persuade him to go to the authorities. I rather gathered that he was, himself, wittingly or unwittingly, liable in the matter.

"At last I agreed. He swore me absolutely to abide by the terms he stipulated, regardless of circumstance."

"And did you? Have you opened the envelope?"

"Of course not!" exclaimed Sir Oliver, indignant. "It was a sworn trust; how could I override that consideration?"

"And if I were to repeat to you that the contents of that envelope, besides being of crucial importance to the Government, may save Godfrey Norton's life, would you now - in the light of this new information - allow us to see what Norton has left with you."

"Hard cases make bad law, Mr. Holmes. First thing we learn! Godfrey Norton entrusted me with that envelope. I believe he knew what he was facing, whatever that may be. I was able to do little enough to rescue the fellow from his travails during his life here. I will not destroy whatever faith he has in his fellow man, and rob him of his remaining dignity, by breaking my vow to him. Not even to save his life! The answer, Mr. Holmes, is an unequivocal 'no'. I am sorry, but I have already told you far more than I intended. Now, I must be going. Please forgive me."

Sir Oliver rose with quiet dignity, and walked to the door. With his hand resting on the door-knob, he turned back to Holmes.

"But I will tell you this much. The answers you seek may well be found at his university. I suggest you look up his old tutor at Cambridge, and ask about Godfrey. Fanshawe's his name. He's still there. At Trinity College! Ask him about the 'Men of Straw'. He was on the periphery of Godfrey's circle in his undergraduate days. Wasn't much older, you see. And be sure to ask him about that bounder Haversham! Whatever dirt you dig up, Haversham is bound to have been rooting around in it. Good luck, Mr. Holmes. I regret that I cannot be of further assistance. May I see you all out?"

He walked us out, as he was due at the Royal Courts of Justice, he said, and would walk the short distance to the Strand. The chambers were busier than when we had arrived, with counsel and their clerks preparing for court appearances. Sir Oliver excused himself for a moment, stepped into his private office, and reappeared moments later decked out in black robes and barrister's short wig. His clerk followed a pace or two in his wake, carrying a bundle of legal briefs, each folded lengthways and bound with a red ribbon.

We parted ways at the steps of Lincoln's Inn. Sir Oliver and his clerk strode off through the fog towards the Strand, as we climbed back into our carriage. This time Holmes gave instructions for King's Cross Station.

"A short visit to Cambridge is our next move, le Villard. Watson can drop us at the station, then take the carriage back to Baker Street and carry on with the Journals. We mustn't interfere too much with progress on Mycroft's report, if it's to be finished when Her Majesty asks for it. By the same token, we must hurry along with our investigations, le Villard, or the report will lack a proper conclusion.

I arrived back at our rooms before eleven o'clock, gratefully drank the cup of steaming-hot tea brought me by the maid, and opened le Villard's Journal at the bookmark.

CHAPTER XLVII

4th September 1893
Bangkok, Siam

"IT SCARCELY SEEMS A WEEK since we left, le Villard, and yet it is a month since we were last at Bangkok."

The early morning sun blazed through patches of cloud; in the distance a rain squall slanted down from a dark mass of cloud that was heading in our direction. The rumble of thunder sounded like distant artillery. Holmes stood at the rail as our steamer - thankfully not the *Daphne* - berthed, waiting for the gangplank to be lowered. We had informed no-one of our travel plans, and, after clearing the formalities, simply took a cab to the Oriental Hotel.

After five nights aboard a China steamer, and three weeks in the general discomfort of Shanghai - not to mention nearly being blown to pieces when a blazing *godown* packed with Chinese fireworks exploded all around us - it was a distinct pleasure to return to the gracious service and hospitality which was the hallmark of the Oriental. We were shown to our old rooms, where we gratefully remembered the cool refreshment of bathing from the large *klong* jars, then headed for the dining room to enjoy a decent meal.

The afternoon was spent in calling on the General Adviser, and of course in fooling around with my faithful Tashi. He wanted to play all our old games, and I was happy to oblige, while Holmes talked with Rolin in the shade of the veranda. Rinzing stood to one side with his wife and new son, of whom he was as proud as he would have been at receiving a decoration for bravery. When I remarked on Tashi's excellent condition and grooming Rinzing smiled broadly, his *nepali* features crinkled and creased with pleasure. Tashi's coat was clipped very short, and gleamed from constant brushing. His nose was moist; his eyes were bright and clear. And his barking was very loud indeed, as we chased and romped around the villa's spacious lawns and garden.

We left as soon as Holmes and the General Adviser had finished talking. Holmes wanted to check up on the return or otherwise of Colonel Sartorius, Godfrey Norton's order for gun-cotton and blasting caps, and a few other matters that had caused him worry during our month's absence. As we drove away, Holmes filled me in on the latest developments in Siam, as gleaned from twenty minutes with the King's General Adviser.

"It seems that Rolin was correct in his assessment. All was quiet for a week after the blockade was lifted. Then Pavie was back with further grievances, complications and demands for satisfaction. Rolin gave me a deal of detail on that subject. He spent a good while telling me of the reforms he has initiated with Prince Ranawongse, painting this whole affair as an incentive to development. He's also had a little victory over the *Siam Free Press*, forcing it to print a retraction and apology.

"Le Myre de Vilers arrived at Bangkok from Saigon at mid-month, as Plenipotentiary. Rolin worries about this. He feels that de Vilers is a tool of the *parti colon,* and a sharp fellow as well; his first act was to arrange to have the General Adviser excluded from all meetings, leaving the Prince alone to negotiate with three Frenchmen. Rolin confessed his dismay when he learned, after the fact, that most of the three million francs reparation demanded by the French had already been paid out of the King's private exchequer and loaded aboard the *Alouette,* bound for Saigon. Then he found that the French had added still further provisions to the Ultimatum.

"The King has apparently spent most of the past month at Bang Pa-in, his country palace, leaving the Prince to deal with most matters. De Vilers at one point threatened the imminent arrival of a further four war-ships, and offered several vague promises of favour if the Prince would sign his approval of four additional articles.

"The Prince held out against all that, saying he had received no instructions, and the negotiations were adjourned. He's been at Bang Pa-in with the King since the end of the month, and returned to Bangkok only yesterday. The Prince says that there is a disturbing tendency amongst the Siamese to settle at any price short of a protectorate. He attributes this to Prince Damrong, who is concerned at the lack of English support. Apparently the Prince demanded that His Majesty accept his resignation as Foreign Minister, but the King would not do so. What Rolin finds curious is that the Siamese have lost all faith in the English at a time when the latest message contains the first manly advice they have given - to protest strongly if French demands exceed the terms of the Ultimatum. And yet they place great hopes in the Russians, whose response has been decidedly lukewarm. Lord Rosebery, it seems, is becoming concerned that de Vilers will demand the right to cut a canal through the Kra Isthmus.

"Rolin also showed me a selection of cuttings from French newspapers he has received in the mail, full of insults to his person. The Belgian papers were more supportive, not surprisingly."

We called briefly on the Prince at his palace, in company with Rolin. Prince Ranawongse was at his home for the first time in five days. His former good humour seemed a little strained, though his excellent manners never failed him. As usual, we shared some small refreshments with him while we talked.

Little of importance was added to the briefing we'd earlier received from the General Adviser, but it was clear that the rising tension was once again taking its toll of the Foreign Minister of Siam. His was a most difficult position, and he and his brothers spent most of their time these days at the palace with the ailing King, eating and sleeping in the great Audience Hall. We left with Rolin after an hour, and his carriage delivered us to our hotel, it already being well past midnight.

6th September 1893
Bangkok, Siam
We spent two days in catching up on the activities of our various suspects and informants. Amongst other things, we learned that Garraud was still to be found at his favourite bar every night, seeking escape from the sharp tongue of *Mama-san* Kung. Sartorius had not as yet returned from Mandalay. The Belgians' funds had not been released from sequestration, despite the best legal efforts of Norton.

"Surely, if the Belgians are the source of the death threats, releasing their funds would remove the grievance. Then, if any further incident occurs, it means it is one of the others."

"Or someone else altogether!" remarked Holmes. "Sets a bad precedent though, doesn't it? Rolin would never countenance it, however convenient. His action was based on legal grounds, and they haven't changed. He'll let the court decide, I think."

Godfrey and Mrs. Norton were still in residence at the Bangkok Hotel. He had been active on behalf of his several clients, as well as the Belgians. His representations to Rolin on behalf of the new gold-mining float had been politely pigeon-holed pending our return, but we found by talking with Hans von Hollstein that he had arranged delivery of the explosives for the gold mine. Norton had collected them at the pier of von Hollstein's mining company's *godown*, arriving in a steam-launch and paying cash. Apparently he had offered a substantial gratuity, but Hans von Hollstein did not believe in doing business in that way - 'everything should be on the board' - and had refused. Norton had several new clients, but following a cursory examination we found that none were of any interest to our investigations.

His night-time pursuits remained as before: rarely spent at home at the Bangkok Hotel with his wife, mostly passed at one or other of his favourite drinking haunts, or in the oblivion of the poppy at the Heavenly Pavilion.

Sia Ah Foo was far more difficult to check on. All we could hope was that he was not central to whatever plot was afoot. If he was involved with Europeans of some stripe or other our task would be easier, otherwise I feared there was little we could do to protect so public a figure as the General Adviser. The only new information that came to light was that Godfrey Norton had been seen talking with *Sia* Ah Foo.

The encounter was spotted quite by chance. Hans von Hollstein had been travelling on the canals in his company's launch. He happened to be passing the wharf of *Sia* Ah Foo's rice mill just as he was seeing Godfrey Norton into a hired gondola. Hans wasn't observed. His launch had a small private cabin, and he had been sheltering there from the driving rain. *Sia* Ah Foo was surrounded by his men, who sheltered them from the downpour with large parasols. Questioned discreetly, Hans said he had never known of any business between the two men, other than Norton's patronising *Sia* Ah Foo's clubs.

According to Rinzing, who was on the lookout for them, the Chinamen who followed the General Adviser's carriage some nights were still there. He occasionally caught glimpses of them waiting down a side street or lane as their carriage passed by. We assumed these were *Sia* Ah Foo's men, though we had no evidence other than his clan connection with the informant inside the Prince's ministry office. Rinzing had seen no trace of other watchers.

Holmes called on Chief Inspector Sheriff while I was following up some minor matter. No further news regarding our suspects, and thankfully, no new suspects. Holmes had asked Sheriff if he could supply small samples of gun-cotton and black powder; these were done up in canvas pouches with drawstrings, which he produced from his inner coat pocket when he returned to our rooms.

Of Miss Malee I had no news. I hoped that we should meet with her again. But I had no acceptable reason to seek her out, and no other way of seeing her again.

8th September 1893
Bangkok, Siam
Holmes had mostly spent his time in his lounge chair on the terrace, watching the monsoon rain clouds build up over Bangkok and unleash their full fury, replete with crashing, rolling thunder, and streaks of lightning stabbing into the ground seemingly no more than a stone's throw away. After several days of this I suggested that we should perhaps continue with our investigation. I should have recognised the signs. To Doctor Watson they were familiar enough, and I had had to deal with the situation several times myself.

Holmes simply withdrew from the entire matter. He smoked his pipes, ate sparingly from the hotel menu, drank the occasional whisky-and-soda, and otherwise may as well have been in Abyssinia. Even our morning *baritsu* went by the wayside. I mentioned several promising leads. I even went out and followed up two of them myself, but when told of the results Holmes dismissed them with a wave of his pipe-stem. He just sat and looked out over the river, tranquil and content. I entreated him, stressing the rising tension in Siam and the precarious state of the government.

"There is nothing more we can do at present!" replied Holmes. "I choose to do nothing, then. If you must be busy, please be busy elsewhere. Now, if you could just ask the *concierge* to send up a few of those excellent half-coronas, as you leave?"

I was so exasperated I could have gladly tipped him into the river. Of all the times to have an episode! For all he seemed to care, Huns or Mars-men could invade in force, and murder every official in the land. I must confess that I looked around the sitting-room a little, half-expecting to find a syringe full of cocaine or morphine, or an opium pipe. How else explain his lassitude, his torpor, when crisis beset the city itself and when the elements were at their most raucous and belligerent?

On the third day I gave up. I went to the General Adviser's house, where I was informed that Lord Rosebery was now counselling Siam to accept no additional demands without consulting England, but Holmes didn't even appear to register the fact when I told him. After a desultory search in the files of the *Bangkok Times* for some information on Cutter and Fluddle's past activities in Siam, which yielded nothing new, I took a gondola across the river to the Portuguese Quarter, and asked for *Nai* Portugee. He was out, so I asked if his father was in. I was informed that he was, and was taken to see him in the small *sala* at end of the wharf where we had first met.

He greeted me cordially, and refreshments were brought, as always.

"You've come to see *White Bird* haven't you, son?"

"That I have," I replied, "if you would permit."

"I've been waiting for you to come, my boy. I have Latin blood as well, M. Le Villard. After *Nai* Portugee's mother, *White Bird* was my true love in this life. I appreciate it when she is sincerely admired."

He rang a small table-bell, and gave instructions in Chinese to the servant who seemingly appeared from the foliage.

"I have asked that my second son, Dom Alonzo, come to escort us around her, if he has time. He is preparing her for a voyage. I shall go aboard, but not below. It is a pleasure simply to feel her motion, even berthed.

"Dom Alonzo was intended for the priesthood, but he ran away from the seminary at Macao three times, until they expelled him. I put him to work with his brother Joao in our shipping office. Dom Alonzo hated it. He ran away to sea for a couple of years, and made two voyages as a deck-hand in tea clippers. When that finished he spent two years travelling the world as first-mate in a British tramp merchantman out of Liverpool, looking for any available work for a sailing-ship. Nitrates and copper from Chile, coal, lumber from the Northwest, they carried it if they could get the work.

"Even that finished. Dom Alonzo returned here to Siam - the Prodigal Son. He was a tough and capable seaman now, and had learnt the discipline of shipboard life. His wild streak is still there to this day, but he had learned to calculate and negotiate, how to ballast and load a sailing ship, and how to get the best out of even a sow of a ship.

"What was I to do? I made him master of one of my China coasters, and later several of our other ships on different routes. Joao Enrique handles the business end of things, and Dom Alonzo advises him from experience. It worked out well, but there was one thing that was always his chief delight - sailing with me aboard *White Bird* as he had done as a youth at my side.

"When my sight went completely, I gave *White Bird* to Joao Enrique, as the elder brother. But I did so on condition that Dom Alonzo should always remain her master, so long as he wished it so."

"That seems like a good arrangement," I replied. Far down the wharf I could see a seaman approaching us, though he was not dressed for the sea. The walk is distinctive.

"It's worked well, and is best for *White Bird* as well. Her day is done, but she has earned the right to a dignified retirement."

"And is she retired?"

"Not really. Dom Alonzo keeps her and her crew in trim with some coastal trading, mostly between here and Annam, and sometimes the Philippines. He likes to take her out whenever there's heavy weather on the way, to keep her up to her mettle. Made for each other, Dom Alonzo and *White Bird*."

The seaman entered the *sala*, and greeted his father with respect.

"You wish to go aboard, father?"

"Yes, Dom Alonzo. This is M. Le Villard. He is an explorer, and a friend. I would like to show him *White Bird*. Have you the time at present?"

"Certainly, Father. I've been loading the sherry casks for Saigon. Fish-sauce, salt and sugar are already loaded. She'll be ready in time for high water. I'd like to clear the river mouth before this storm front hits Bangkok. The glass is dropping rapidly, and I'd rather be in deep water than negotiating the bar. But there's little more for me to do until the loading is complete. Would you like to go now, M. Le Villard?"

"If that is convenient for you, yes."

Below decks the clipper was as I expected, built to carry cargo at speed in the days before coal and steam and copper-paint and the great canals at Suez and Panama finally tolled the end of the era of commercial sail. Dom Alonzo first led me to the fo'csle, where he had a few words with his first-mate. To my great surprise, the man was an Englishman, from Liverpool by his accent. We all three descended a gang-plank down through the main hatch to the lower deck, where they discussed the distribution of cargo to achieve ideal balance and trim.

I surveyed the construction of the clipper, looking down through the hatches to the very keel of her, and was vastly impressed by her structure. Heavy steam-bent ribs spread out from the massive keel and curved up to her coamings, braced by thick grown-wood knees at every horizontal and vertical junction. She was skinned with oak planks half-a-foot thick to withstand the billows. Enormous triple-stepped masts were set deep into the keelson, with yards and spars rigged and tensioned up and up, out and out, until she could fly a cloud of sail. Her concave bows would slice evenly through the seas to bring the tea home in record time, and with record profits. Beauty with purpose!

I turned back to the Captain and the first mate. Dom Alonzo explained that they were paying particular attention to the matter of balance and trim in order to improve the clipper's performance as much as possible. Sometime within the next year he would sail to Europe to buy for *Nai* Portugee a small fleet of windjammers, which were no longer competitive in European shipping but could still turn a handsome profit in the Asia trade. Along the way he intended to set his cap at the clipper record from China to London - unofficially of course. Adjusted for a start at Bangkok rather than the Pagoda Anchorage, he said, he would race the record of the Great Tea Race of 1866.

"*Taeping, Ariel* and *Serica* all arrived in London on the ninety-ninth day out of Foochow," said Dom Alonzo. Now I noticed that he too spoke English with a Liverpool accent. "*White Bird*'s best time from Foochow to Singapore is seventeen days. So if we start recording as we pass through the latitude of Singapore, our adjusted goal must be to beat eighty-two days to London."

"But those were the great clippers of the glory days of sail, Dom Alonzo," I remarked. "Do you seriously believe *White Bird* capable of matching such feats?"

Dom Alonzo took no offence. He smiled a little, and winked at his first-mate.

"That depends on the weather, the crew and the master. But that *White Bird* is capable I have the finest assurance. She *won* that Great Tea Race in 1866, and is in excellent shape following her refit. Thanks to Sturgess here!"

"I don't quite understand?" said I. "So far as I know the prize was split between *Taeping* and *Ariel?*"

"And right now, M. le Villard, you are aboard the *Ariel*. Come up to the bridge, and allow my father to tell you about it all."

Before doing so, we took a quick look around the rest of *White Bird*. Dom Alonzo had talked about her restoration. She looked as though she'd never needed it. We inspected the crew's quarter's and galley, then walked aft past the apprentice's bunkhouse to view officer's quarters, saloon and captain's stateroom. All was as purposeful as I had expected, but the exquisite joinery and finish of the accommodations came as a surprise in a vessel so lean and efficient in all other respects.

We emerged on the poopdeck, then made our way aft to where *Señor* Jose Felipe - the former *Nai* Portugee - sat quietly on the teakwood steering-gear housing. One hand absently grasped a spoke of the enormous varnished wheel, and a small smile of contentment crinkled the weather-beaten skin on his face and around his sightless eyes.

Without preamble, the old man recounted the tale of his beloved ship.

"Dom Alonzo will have told you her original name, M. Le Villard. I shall tell you how she came into our possession. You must go back to the great days of the tea-races. A profitable journey could pay for the cost of a ship twice over. Enormous sums were wagered on the outcome of each journey. Fortunes made and lost. Inevitably, some owners speculated wildly, and occasionally 'lost their shirts', as the British say it. Ships were wrecked and cargo irretrievably damaged; some were lost at sea. Insurance covered the losses of those wise enough to buy coverage."

The old fellow shifted a little towards the direction of the river breeze, which I noticed he liked to keep full in his face, and asked Dom Alonzo if some drinks were arranged. Just then they arrived. He took a sip of limejuice, and continued his tale.

"For whatever reason, in 'seventy-two the *Ariel* was declared missing, presumed lost with all hands. How she came to survive is not something I enquired about too carefully, but survive she did. Once the insurance was paid, her owners had lost all interest in her. I came across her hauling sugar and copra in the Sulu Sea. Filthy and neglected, with her masts cut to stumps, she was almost unrecognisable as the proud clipper she had once been. But not to my eyes! When I was at Foochow with my father, as a young man, I'd seen her loading tea along with all the other clippers bound for London and New York.

"I recognised her immediately in spite of her condition. By this time we were well established at Bangkok, and I was able to buy her quietly, for next to nothing. In Hong Kong I found lithograph reproductions of detailed paintings of the *Ariel*. I had her towed to our yards here at Bangkok, where we restored her hull and joinery. Then she was sailed under jury-rig to Singapore for work on her masts and rigging. Finally, I had her topsides painted white. The result is as you see.

"We sailed her back to Bangkok when she was finished. When my wife, god rest her soul," and the old man crossed himself, "first saw her under sail, she said in Portuguese that she appeared like a white bird of the sea. And so I named her!"

That is as much of the mystery of the *Ariel*'s fate as the old man would tell me, although I suspect that he knew more about her missing years than he let on. He called for his manservant to assist him back down to the dock, and we took our farewell of Dom Alonzo.

I remained with old Jose Felipe at the wharf while Dom Alonzo prepared *White Bird* for departure. The wind had greatly increased in strength. Intense gusts tore at sails furled on spars, as crewmen expertly cast off restraining lines. Swollen by monsoon rains falling on the flanks of the Himalayas and on the great flood plain, the surging river was by now a seething maelstrom as its surface was whipped by the howling wind into a frenzy of white spray.

Dom Alonzo sounded several blasts on her horn as two of the company's own steam-tugs towed *White Bird* upstream, creaking and groaning, and turned her bow. As the rushing stream caught at her hull she spun quickly. The tugs restrained her fore and aft to prevent her slewing wildly, as she had no steering sails aloft.

With a howl of wind the rain-squall suddenly hit us. Huge drops driven almost horizontally by the wind stung our faces and eyes, and drenched our clothes in seconds. The old man waved away the servants who scurried to lead him to shelter.

"I admire the fury of the elements, M. Le Villard. God showing his brute force! I understand why Dom Alonzo wants to be out there. I wish I could go with him."

The dim silhouette of *White Bird* dissolved at last into the luminous grey squall, leaving only her lamps visible through ghostly mist and the glow from the stacks of her shepherding steam-tugs.

"*Bon voyage*, my son," said the old sailor, softly. He turned to me, as though he could see me. I suddenly realised he'd seen nothing of *White Bird*'s departure, but had remained silent all the while as I watched her fade out of sight.

"And now, M. Le Villard, it will not be possible for your gondola to cross safely in this weather, so I must sacrifice my principles if I am to have my evening tea at the Oriental. We must use the steam-launch, if you will assist me aboard after I have changed my wet clothing. The servants will never allow me to leave otherwise."

An hour later, with *Señor* Jose Felipe dried and groomed, and I still wet through, we berthed at the Oriental's pier. Despite the storm, Siamese attendants with large umbrellas helped us to disembark and cross to the hotel building without getting any wetter. I thanked the old fellow and excused myself to change into dry clothes.

Holmes was no longer sitting in his cane-work lounge chair on the veranda, staring out at the river. I dared to hope that he had resumed our investigation, but my hopes were dashed when I turned into our sitting-room. Holmes, in his dark-green silk dressing gown, stood with one foot firmly planted on the polished wood floor and the other up on the seat of the wooden chair he'd dragged out from behind the desk. His left elbow rested on his raised knee, and in his left hand he held a thick book of orchestral scores he'd found at a used-book stall.

Sight-reading from the score, Holmes was conducting a non-existent orchestra with vigorous motions of the straight-stem pipe whose bowl he grasped in his right hand. He glanced quickly in my direction, then back to his score, and carried on without interruption. In despair, I turned and went back down to the hotel bar, still in my damp clothes, and ordered a double *cognac*.

I was seriously considering having another when one of the hotel boys came up to me, saying that 'the lady wishes to see Professor Sigerson'. He had a visiting card in his hand, with a note written on the reverse. Taking it from him, I read the message.

'Professor,

I must talk with you - urgently and privately. I fear the worst.

Irene Adler.'

I thought of Holmes and his invisible orchestra upstairs and decided I had better deal with this myself, at least until it was clear that Holmes could assist. If he chose so to do!

I followed the boy back out to the lobby, and in the reception lounge I found Mrs. Norton - Irene Adler - and Miss Malee. As I approached them Irene Adler rose to her feet and came to meet me, clearly very agitated. Miss Malee followed her, and took her arm.

"M. Le Villard. Oh, thank God you're here! *Is* Professor Sigerson here? Please say he is, for I must see him."

Holmes was presentable enough, and knowing his regard for this woman above all, I decided to risk taking her up to our sitting-room without warning him first. If anything could shake him from his mood of indolence, it would be the thought of Irene Adler in distress.

"He is, Mrs. Norton. He is relaxing in his own unorthodox fashion, but I'm sure you'll forgive his eccentricities. Please come with me, and Miss Malee as well." I turned and walked towards the stairs. "We have our own sitting-room, and it will be as private there as anywhere."

I knocked discreetly as I came to the door of the sitting-room, and called out to the Professor that we had visitors. Holmes was in the same position, still working his way through the thick score. For a moment I thought he was going to dismiss her as airily as he had me. He looked up at us, then back to his score as he carried on conducting. Then - to my immense relief - he reached the end of a movement, I supposed, closed the book, and came forward to greet his guests.

"Mrs. Norton. Miss Malee. To what do we owe the unexpected pleasure?"

I held out the note, which he read at a glance.

"That serious, you say?"

Suddenly Holmes the detective was back once again, and the desultory lounger vanished away. "Please, do sit here and tell us everything, from the beginning. It will save time that way."

"It's Godfrey! He's gone. I came back to our rooms at the Bangkok Hotel earlier than expected and found Godfrey writing a note to me. He seemed terribly worried and confused, as though something dreadful was about to happen. I asked him what was the matter, but he seemed too upset to reply.

"'I must rush if I'm to get away on time!' he said. 'They'll be leaving the ball soon, and going to the Audience Hall . . . I have a launch waiting at the canal wharf. I'll send for you, Irene. I promise I will! If you come, come alone. It will be too dangerous otherwise.

"I asked him what this was all about, but he fled out the door with a small bag of his clothes and his papers. All he would say as he went was, 'Read the note. There is money in the dresser drawer. I must go. They'll have me done for . . .'"

"'Done for' . . . what?" asked Holmes.

"I couldn't hear what he said. He was gone."

"How long ago was this?"

"Not more than fifteen minutes. Malee was waiting in the carriage for me, as we were going on, so as soon as he left I ran down and we came straight here."

"That makes it twenty-five minutes ago now."

He consulted his pocket watch.

"And the note?"

"Here it is."

Holmes read it, then handed it to me.

"Precisely the break we've been waiting for, le Villard. At times the hunter should remain motionless, and allow the game to break cover."

I read the note.

'Dear Irene,

After tonight you may not want me any more - a hunted killer, an assassin of men of power and position. But believe me, Irene, there is an explanation, a reason for everything. There is a way out of all our tangled affairs, but I cannot explain now. Only believe in me, and come when I send for you. Trust in no-one else, for people are rarely what they seem.

In particular, be wary of t . . .'

The note broke off, presumably when Irene interrupted Norton as he wrote.

"There is no time to waste, le Villard. Things are moving at last, but exactly what to do? See to our guests, if you would. I must think a little."

There was a large jug of lemonade on a tray, and glasses on the sideboard. I started to make drinks, but Miss Malee insisted on doing it. I sat and watched, while Holmes paced slowly up and down the veranda outside our suite of rooms, head bent to his chest. He murmured to himself as he paced, massaging his temples with his index fingers as he did so. Less than two minutes passed in this way before he came back into the room.

"Ladies, M. Le Villard and I must leave immediately. There is no time for explanations. I don't know when we will return. You may either stay here, or return to your hotel. Perhaps here would be safer, I think. We don't know who or what we're up against, or how Norton is involved. No one knows you are here, I hope."

Holmes strode across to the bureau and pocketed the two canvas pouches he had obtained from Chief Inspector Sheriff. He turned his back to shield his actions as he loaded his revolver and pocketed that, as well as his dark lantern and aluminium telescope. Taking my cue from that, I dashed into my bedroom, and collected my loaded revolver from the shirt drawer. For good measure I added a box of shells. I still had not worked out what was going on, or where we were headed, but clearly danger awaited us.

"May we take your carriage, Miss Adler? It will save time, and we have little enough of that, I fear."

"Of course. It was hired anyway, so I doubt that he cares. His canopy is already up, as well."

Holmes and I dashed down to the carriage. He gave instructions to the General Adviser's house.

"That's right, le Villard. Our first stop is at Rolin's house. Fortunately, it's directly on the way to our destination, so we'll lose little time, and it will be worth it. We may need Rinzing and Tashi tonight, I think."

He leaned forward and urged the driver in Siamese to hurry up, promising extra pay as an incentive.

"I hope Tashi's sense of smell is as sharp now as it was at Khartoum, le Villard. It may be crucial, especially in this filthy weather."

"You obviously haven't tried to hide a sweetmeat from him recently, Holmes, or you'd not ask."

"That's one piece of good news."

Our carriage hurtled around the corner into Rolin's lane, crunching and rattling to a halt in front of the locked gates. Tashi's barking sounded from the side of the house, and a lamp bobbed through the velvet darkness from an outbuilding. It was Rinzing. When he recognised us, he ran to open the gate.

"Get dressed, Rinzing, and arm yourself. We have business to attend to if we're to save the General Adviser and Prince Ranawongse from being murdered."

I released Tashi from his tether, and attached a strong chain to his stout leather collar. Sensing the excitement of the chase once again, Tashi strained at his leash to be away and into the thick of whatever fray we could find for him.

Holmes decided against harnessing Rolin's carriage, as it would lose us precious time. Rinzing said goodbye to his anxious wife and we all piled into the hired carriage. Holmes gave the driver half his payment now, as he was becoming increasingly nervous, what with the urgency of our actions and the appearance of an enormous mastiff in his carriage.

"Now, driver," Holmes shouted over the storm in Siamese. "Take us to the bridge over the Canal of Flowers, as fast as you can. Turn right here, and take the direct road, not the one around the park." He added in English, "And for God's sake, hurry!"

He sat back in his seat and brushed the streaming water from his brow.

"Now before we get there," he shouted over the tumult of the raging storm, "I think it's time you and Rinzing knew what to expect when we get to the bridge. And pray that it *is* there, for if not I've made a grievous blunder, and the penalty may be assessed in blood."

"It *would* be nice to know, yes!" I answered.

"I expect there will be a bomb of some kind, primary ingredients being the black powder, gun-cotton and blasting caps purchased by Norton - as we thought, for the gold mine up-country."

He reached into his pocket, and withdrew the two canvas pouches. Loosening the draw-strings, he handed them to me.

"While we drive, let Tashi get the scent of these. It may be our only way to locate the bomb in this darkness."

The wind tore at the canvas canopy, and stinging rain soon drenched us through. I thought idly that it was a good thing I hadn't bothered to change into dry clothes. I set both pouches on the floor of the carriage, and let Tashi smell them, saying "*Chase, Tashi! Chase!*" several times over. This was a signal he understood clearly to mean that soon he would be expected to locate these items again, and that it was a 'serious' game, not one for playing the fool. He settled down, occasionally taking a sniff at each of the pouches. "I can see how you deduce a bomb, Holmes, in light of Norton's note. But how do you work out the location?"

"It's a best guess, I suppose. I only hope I'm not wrong. We have Rolin's official itinerary for the week; we know that tonight he's not using his own carriage."

"Of course, Holmes! Prince Ranawongse and he are attending the dinner at the United States Legation tonight!"

"Following which they will have an audience with the King. They will return to the palace in the Prince's closed carriage! Together! Think of it, le Villard! If the aim of these plotters is to create an incident as a pretext for declaring a protectorate, what better than to assassinate not only the General Adviser to His Majesty, but the Siamese Foreign Minister as well."

"Who also happens to be the King's brother!"

"Exactly! At the same time, the two most effective opponents of annexation are permanently removed from the game-board."

Our carriage raced on through the deserted, darkened streets of the storm-lashed city.

"But why the bridge over the Canal of Flowers, Holmes?"

"Norton collected the explosives in a launch. Implies that their lair is on the water, and that they have boats and boatmen available. One! Two; if one wanted to gain time to make a getaway after a major explosion, a thunder-storm such as this provides ideal cover. Three! The best way to make an un-hindered escape in this city is by water. There are few roads in comparison to the number of canals."

"Conclusion; the assassins will travel by boat to place the bomb," said I.

"Correct! Given that the only place where roads and canals intersect is at a bridge, the ideal location to place a bomb and to be sure of maximum impact is *under* a bridge. Now, we've surveyed all the canals and bridges in the area over the past few months, as part of our surveillance. Whichever route their carriage takes between the American Legation and the Audience Hall at the palace, there are only three waterways to cross. Two are little more than drainage ditches, and hardly navigable even by skiff."

"Leaving the bridge over the Canal of Flowers," I shouted over the wind.

"Precisely, my friend!"

"What will it look like, this bomb?"

"A container of some kind for the black powder. Wedged into the powder will be the primer charge . . . Norton's gun-cotton. Inserted into the primer will be a blasting cap, which we already know to be loaded with fulminate of mercury, and, I imagine, a flame fuse."

"Which means the assassin must remain in the vicinity until just before the explosion," I said. "That may help us."

As we raced down the main road towards the bridge, banners and sunshades billowed out from the shuttered shophouses lining the road and blew away into the storm. Telephone wires newly-strung between wooden poles along the road to the palace stretched out horizontally in taut bows, vibrating with a shrill, piercing note. On the poorer Siamese houses thatch roofs rippled and ridged like the hackles of a cornered hound. Uprooted and broken trees crashed across the roadway, causing our nervous horses to rear with fright until our terrified coachman, goaded by promises of further pay, whipped them on. Everywhere a thin sheet of water covered the ground, its surface whipped to a white froth by the violence of the howling wind.

At last, in the distance through mist and spray we could see ornate posts marking the bridge approach. We knew that another road converged with ours just before crossing the canal. It would be down one or the other of these two roads that the Prince and the General Adviser would approach.

"Halt here, driver!" ordered Holmes. "We'll go on by foot. No need to let the villains know that someone else is about. They'll be alert for the approach of the Prince's carriage, so be on guard for their lookout. I expect he'll be on the approaches to the bridge, within visual range. No shout would be heard in this storm."

Indeed, Holmes had to shout into my ear to make himself heard. I turned to Rinzing and informed him quickly as to our plans. He was ready for action; like Tashi, keyed up by the violence of the storm. He checked his revolver, caressed the handle of the wicked, curved *kukri* in his belt, and grinned like a small boy let loose at the *bonbon* counter.

We alighted, and followed Holmes into a small lane. This path wound around a cluster of shophouses to exit onto the canal-path close by the bridge. I held Tashi's leash, but it was hardly necessary. He crept along with the rest of us, sticking to the dark shadows under the awnings of buildings where even the bright flashes of lightning failed to disclose our presence to watching eyes.

"There he is!" hissed Holmes, holding up his hand. "In the shelter of the bridge-post."

The post was shaped like a miniature pavilion, with four arched openings; three like windows, the fourth full height, providing a doorway to the tiny space within. I imagine this was intended for a sentry during royal processions, but now it sheltered someone on lookout for the assassins. No-one else would seek shelter there in such foul weather, as it kept out little of the storm.

"At least we know we're on the right track, my friends."

As we considered our next step, all of us drenched to the skin, the lookout suddenly came to life. Leaving his shelter, he made a frantic arm-waving signal, and started off across the bridge. Rinzing moved as if to pursue him; Holmes attempted to hold him back. Too late! The lookout spotted the movement, and looked straight at us in the deep shadows. He shouted out at someone we could not see from where we stood, obviously raising the alarm, then dashed across to the ramparts on the far side of the bridge approach and disappeared from view.

From our vantage point we could see a considerable distance along both of the roads approaching the bridge. Holmes pointed down the road leading towards the bridge, and whipped out his telescope. Far in the distance, flanked by mounted guards, came a closed two-horse carriage.

"It's the Prince's carriage all right. Travelling fast. The problem is, we don't know which of these two approach roads they'll take."

"If we suddenly appear out of the storm in front of the coachman, on either road, he's as likely to speed up in alarm and cross onto the bridge before we can stop him," I shouted.

"Exactly! Right where we don't want him to stop. But it will take two of us to locate and defuse the bomb, which leaves only one of us to warn the carriage. We have a few moments yet. Let's see what we can find! If we stop them here next to the bridge, we may all be blown to pieces."

He climbed up onto the approaches to the bridge, and vaulted over the ramparts. We followed him down the embankment and onto a narrow path that ran under the bridge from side to side. From further down the canal came the pulsing noise of a steam-launch increasing speed as it headed away as fast as possible, until wind and rain drowned the sound out. Holmes swung his telescope in that direction and quickly adjusted the focus as he tracked the boat's course down the canal. He turned back to us.

"There's a bomb here somewhere. Let Tashi sniff around."

Holmes pulled out his dark lantern, and sheltered it with his coat while he lit the wick using a waxed phosphor. The feeble beam helped illuminate the darkness under the bridge, and I set Tashi to his work, first holding the pouches under his nose once again for reference.

"Find it, Tashi! Find it!" I shouted, conscious of the nearness of the approaching carriage.

He sniffed around for a while in the mud and mire under the bridge, without any success. Towards the centre of the bridgework the ground was drier. I urged Tashi in that direction, figuring that a bomb fuse needs to remain dry. He immediately strained at his leash, and dragged me further under the bridge. Casting around a little in the darkness, deep in the gloom behind a column, he finally stopped and barked loudly. Holmes came over with his lantern, and examined the ground around that spot.

"Footprints, two men, and round marks in the earth . . . as though something heavy has rested there," I said.

Tashi was sniffing and barking at the round indentations. They were about twelve inches in diameter, and overlapped as though a heavy cylinder had been moved about.

"Our bomb is here somewhere, le Villard, shouted Holmes, "but *where*? The fuse will be lit already. Hopefully the bomber will have trimmed the fuse long. If not, we're already on borrowed time."

As he shouted over the noise of the storm, Holmes quickly cast around the ground under the bridge with the beam from his dark-lantern. Nothing! Meanwhile, Rinzing and I looked around the complex wooden framework supporting the bridge. It was Rinzing, redeeming his earlier blunder, who spotted it first: a very faint glow, coming from high up under the central archway.

He tugged at Holmes's sleeve, and pointed at the pale, sputtering light reflected on the underside of the bridge. Holmes directed his lantern beam at it, and at last we could see the bomb. It was a small iron-bound wooden cask, with an upended metal pail fastened over the top of it. The pail was fixed in place by means of screws through its rim into the topmost metal hoop of the cask, and the pale glow came from a small hole in its base. The entire affair was wedged into the angle between one of the main bridge-posts and a bracing member, and secured there by a thick metal chain. A link of this was brazed to the lower of the metal hoops on the cask; the chain was wrapped several times around both cask and wooden beams, and fastened to itself with a strong brass-and-steel padlock.

"To light it, the fuse must have been at least as long as the pail. We know how long ago it was lit, so a rough calculation is possible. The bomber knows what he's doing, and the lookout will have given him a range and speed for the carriage."

"Is there time to defuse the thing before the Prince's carriage gets here?" I yelled the question, for the wind was gusting more strongly as the storm worsened.

"I'll have to see. I think so. I'll climb up and examine it. Meanwhile, you stay down here, and Rinzing, go back up to where the lookout was hiding. When the bomb is defused, le Villard will signal you the all-clear, like this. Arm straight up! That is your signal to slip out of sight, and let the carriage go by. No reason to alarm them unnecessarily, and I want the area left undisturbed afterwards, for us to examine without interference."

"And if it is not defused?" asked the *Goorkha.*

"You should be safe in that sentry box, Rinzing. The bomb is placed to destroy the very centre of the bridge."

"No, sir, Professor. I meant, how will you get away?"

"As we can't see the fuse length, it will be a calculated gamble. If the carriage has appeared and you haven't seen the all-clear signal, you'll only have a few seconds to attempt to stop it. You'll just have to chance it, and hope that Rolin sees you. He knows you, and will listen to you. Get them all out and as far away as possible. Don't waste time trying to turn the carriage. And *don't* let them onto the bridge."

Holmes turned to me.

"Every second counts. Let's get on with it!"

Holmes had already removed his coat, after relocating a few small items to his vest pocket. He began climbing towards the bomb, some five yards distant and overhead, working his way from brace to brace.

Rinzing took Tashi's leash.

"Come on, Bear," he said, using his private name for Tashi. "You've done your part, now let's go save the *nai.*"

The stocky *Nepali* led the huge mastiff away, but only after I commanded him to go. Until then, Rinzing could not budge him from where he sat by my side.

I turned back to see how Holmes was getting on. He had already reached the bomb, and was examining it closely with the aid of his dark-lantern.

"As I thought!" he shouted. "I don't know if this metal pail is here to foil any interference, or as a weather shield. Regardless, there is no way to be certain of extinguishing the fuse, short of immersing the whole affair in water.

The fuse-hole is baffled. Quite cunningly designed, to prevent water being poured in. And the cask is firmly chained in place; no way to work it loose. I shall have to pick the lock."

He had already placed the dark-lantern on a horizontal beam so that it illuminated the lock, and had removed from his vest-pocket the small leather pouch that I knew to contain his collection of home-made lock picks. Next he took out his circular magnifying glass. With this he examined the manufacturer's name stamped into the brass body, then peered quickly into the slot of the lock, and selected two thin metal picks from his case. Holding the lock between the balls of his palms, he manipulated his picks for what seemed an interminable time.

"Confound it, le Villard!" he shouted down to me. "This is one of the newest model locks from Vienna. I'd heard of them, but hadn't got my hands on one before I left Europe. They can be picked, but it takes some trial-and-error, which means time."

All the while he continued probing delicately and precisely inside the lock. The ominous glow dimmed as the fuse burned shorter and shorter inside the pail.

From where I stood under the edge of the bridge I glanced up at Rinzing, who had reached the sentry-box. He was anxiously looking at me, hoping for the all-clear signal. Every few seconds he turned to look up the two approach roads, watching for the sudden emergence of the Prince's carriage from between the rows of shop-houses.

Rain lashed down furiously from the boiling clouds, and the thunder was no longer distant. Streaks of lightning rent the sky from zenith to ground, tearing it into black fragments. There was almost no lapse between each brilliant flash and its deafening thunderclap. The wind increased in strength until it was difficult to stand erect without holding onto some immovable object.

Through all this tumult and turmoil Holmes carried on calmly, bracing himself against the tearing wind, working on a bomb with a fuse burning ever shorter. The flame in his shielded dark-lantern flickered and guttered, and seemed at times as though it would die altogether. Still Holmes carried on.

I confess that with every passing second, I grew increasingly worried for both of us. Having been trained at the central Paris police weapons range in all aspects of firearms and explosives, I knew a lot about bomb-making. I knew the burn rate of flame fuses. Unless this one was trimmed long and coiled into the shield after lighting, it must be almost burned to the blasting cap by now. I calculated that the cask contained enough black powder to easily destroy the centre span of the bridge, and that if it blew up, both Holmes and I should certainly perish. At least it would be instantaneous.

For some reason this morbid thought failed to comfort me. I looked up. Holmes's lean features were highlighted by the proximity of the dark-lantern, throwing the hollows of his eyes and cheeks into contrasting pools of darkness. His thin lips were compressed in concentration, and his eyes were frequently closed as he concentrated minutely on the sensations transmitted back to his delicate fingers from inside the lock. It seemed from the repeated nature of his motions that he was getting to the same point at each attempt, then was foiled by one pin failing to dislodge.

"Holmes," I shouted. "Give it up, or we shall both die. That fuse must be almost done by now. It's not worth it. Let's . . ."

"Quiet! I almost have it. Just one more . . . Ah! Yes! That's done it. Now! One more pin. Very well, no problem. It's open, le Villard!"

Holmes dropped the padlock into the canal, slipped his picks into his vest pocket, and set feverishly to unwinding the chain from beams and columns. I looked back at Rinzing, ready to give him the all-clear as soon as Holmes had the chain free. He was no longer inside the sentry box. He had run across to the railing, nearer to us, and was frantically signalling that the carriage was almost upon us. Rinzing was shouting, but I could hear nothing over the noise of the storm.

I took a risk, gambling that Holmes would free the chain and sink the bomb before it could explode. I raised my arm vertically in the agreed all-clear signal. Rinzing snapped an automatic salute of acknowledgement, and dragged Tashi back into the sentry-box, out of sight.

Although Holmes was still wrestling with the length of chain, it was almost completely freed. I stepped out from under the shelter of the bridge, and was instantly soaked by the pelting, driving rain. I clambered halfway up the slippery embankment, and clung to the trunk of a tree. From there I could see both the underside of the bridge, where Holmes had now freed the chain entirely, and the final few yards of the road before it crossed onto the bridge structure - at this moment still intact.

I glanced back at Holmes. He had braced himself with legs spread on two beams, and lowered the cask to the full extent of the chain that was brazed to it. With the cask full of explosives as the pendulum weight, three swings back and forth achieved a significant arc of movement. With one last pump of momentum imparted to his deadly pendulum, Holmes swung the cask up, out, and away down the *klong*, its length of chain trailing like a silver comet's tail, reflecting sparks from the lightning flashing overhead.

Over the din of the storm I heard the frantic pounding of horse's hooves, and the urgent rumble of steel-bound wheels over the cobbles; I looked up to the roadway for a brief instant. The two horses, panicked by the ferocity of the storm, were almost running away with the carriage as it swept into view. It rushed out onto the wooden deck of the bridge, with an abrupt change in sound.

I looked back to see the cask fall into the turbulent canal water, and saw something which turned my blood to ice water. Tashi, who had been with Rinzing up on the bridge approach, had seen the bomb swing into the air. I suppose its trajectory looked like that of the large leather ball we had always played with, even when he was a puppy in Tashilhunpo monastery. I'd originally made it to encourage him to run around after his wounded paw healed.

Now he was chasing the cask-bomb. I forgot entirely about remaining out of sight. I sprinted out to stop Tashi with an English rugby-style tackle into the muddy grass verge of the tow path along the canal side, screaming at him as I did so. We rolled together into the path itself, muddy and deeply hollowed by thousands of passing Siamese, as the carriage surged on over the centre of the bridge, and the cask-bomb exploded just under the water's surface.

A tall plume of water rose into the misty air and sheets of spray washed over us. The detonation was hardly distinguishable from a thunderous crash of lightning; the flash of the explosion was lost in the glare of the streaks of jagged light spearing into the ground all around. There was no one around to see or hear anyway, as the slanting, swirling rain had long ago driven any late-night Siamese under cover.

The muddy earth trembled as fragments of wood and glowing metal fell all about us, but the verge of the tow path protected Tashi and I from direct impact. Being under water when it exploded, the bomb must also have had much of its sideways force absorbed. Whatever the reason, Tashi and I survived, filthy and wet through, but otherwise unscathed.

I looked back at the bridge approach, and saw a small jitney pull up at the edge of the bridge. Tashi and I were in a pool of darkness. I silenced him as I saw first one, then two, heads appear above the high railings of the bridge. I shushed Tashi to silence; we lay motionless in the mud as they surveyed the scene. By now the water had subsided, and the fragments remaining would not have been visible at that distance. The two figures conversed briefly, nodded to each other, and climbed back into their cart. I noticed as they did so that both men carried long-barrelled weapons of some sort. The driver turned the cart around, and it disappeared from my low angle of view.

Holmes appeared from the darkness under the bridge, concerned that he had blown us up. I stood, rather shakily, but grateful to be alive. It had been a near thing.

"I see you've survived," said he. "Did you see who was in the cart that came onto the bridge?"

I replied that I hadn't seen clearly enough to be certain, but just then Rinzing came running down the embankment from his sentry box. Between examining and berating the mastiff, he told us that it was as we had suspected. The two Chinamen watchers had appeared down the other of the two approach roads just as the bomb had exploded. Rinzing had remained still, and they hadn't seen him. Obviously, the Chinamen had seen the explosion; why else would they have stopped.

"Well, let us look for clues, le Villard, before this weather obliterates them all."

We examined the muddy bank near where the bomb had exploded, and found several curved fragments of the wooden cask, held loosely together by one of the metal hoops, and a few twisted pieces of the metal pail that had served as a weather-shield. Floating on the scummy surface of the swollen canal Rinzing spotted several more staves from the cask; these he retrieved with a branch torn from the nearby tree. Despite a wide search with the aid of the dark-lantern, no other fragments of the bomb were found. I removed my sodden coat and bundled up all of the fragments in it for later investigation. Next we moved back under the bridge, out of the direct violence of the storm.

"There is nothing of interest on the bridgework," said Holmes, "but I rather fancy I saw something over there, where their launch was tied up."

He strode over, stooped down, and from amongst the broken earth and stone picked up a round metallic object. I looked over his shoulder and saw that it was a silver pocket-watch, ornately engraved in an old-fashioned style. Its fluted, barrel-shaped winder was pierced by a hole, through which passed a stout silver ring. Fastened to this was a silver-link chain; the other end of the chain dangled free, terminating in a twisted, broken link.

Holmes took his magnifying lens from his pocket, and examined the exterior carefully.

"Sterling silver, hallmarked, a fine example of the style of the early 'sixties. Well cared for until now: probably a family inheritance. No other obvious clues."

He opened the hinged back. The precisely-fitted decorative metal plate opened easily, revealing a smooth, polished surface. Even without a lens I could read the copperplate inscription engraved thereon:

Presented to
Sir Humphrey Ronald Norton
Partner
Upon the Occasion of his Retirement
after
Forty Years of Distinguished Service
Norton Royle Whymper Norton
Gray's Inn
17th August, 1869.

CHAPTER XLVIII

I HAD READ in a desultory sort of way throughout the day, but I admit that my mind had wandered somewhat, despite my interest in le Villard's account. My mind returned again and again to the plight of the two victims of kidnapping, and I wondered if Holmes had done the right thing in not reporting either event to Scotland Yard.

Although there was little evidence of the crimes actually having been committed, I thought that perhaps there was something Lestrade and Gregson could accomplish through official channels - especially as Holmes and le Villard were to be out of London for the whole day. But, not for the first time, I reasoned that Holmes had his methods, and it was not for me to question them.

Perhaps, I concluded, Holmes assumed that whomever in the police department had arranged for Moran's release could pose more danger to the victims than if Holmes traced the criminals on his own account. He had frequently ignored the police in the past with crimes against property, but where lives were at stake Holmes preferred to operate independently of, but alongside, the official forces - and may the better man win the laurels - rather than take sole responsibility.

Thus it was with a certain sense of relief that, shortly after dusk, I heard the familiar step upon our stairs, and saw le Villard precede Holmes into the room. The fog had thickened outside, and the gas-lamps in Baker Street were haloed with a sickly glow. Wisps of the cold fog hung about the two as they hurried to warm themselves at the fire, as the weather had turned bitterly cold for a spring evening.

Holmes first priority was to check if there had been any callers while he was gone. I assured him there had been none. At this he seemed deeply concerned.

"I've got Wiggins and every lad he can muster out looking for leads, and I confess I had hoped for some news; something to go on with. No response to my notices in the papers, either. Very well, le Villard. I think that, as Watson here has clearly not had his supper, whereas we have already done so, the best thing is for me to fill him in on our day's most interesting results, or at least those that are solid, and hope that something turns up. We have done all we can, pending further developments."

"Frankly, Holmes," replied the French detective, "I welcome the chance to warm my extremities, and to sit in a comfortable chair for a moment. That train carriage was draughty, and the cab even more so."

Accordingly, I ordered my supper, and my companions warmed themselves until it arrived. Then, as I sat at table and they by the fireside, Holmes recounted the day's events to me. There wasn't that much to tell, but what Holmes proceeded to recount shocked me profoundly.

"We arrived at Cambridge," began Holmes, "and after a bit of bother tracked down Fanshawe. He was not well pleased that we'd come to see him about a matter he would like forgotten. Once he understood the nature of our enquiries he took us to a place where there was no risk of being overheard.

"What he told us, if true, goes a long way towards explaining certain mysteries. He repeated everything that Sir Oliver told us about the student Norton. Apparently he never wanted to study for the Bar, but his father insisted. He always exhibited a wild, resentful streak, cloaked in his charming ways. But he brushed up well, and was a great hit with the girls.

"He did join the drinking club Sir Oliver told us about, but it was a little more serious than even he had imagined. Their initiation rites were such that several promising students did not return as sane as they had been. But an impenetrable secrecy was enforced, and neither the Proctors, nor later the police, could bring charges against anyone. It was apparently in this atmosphere that the 'Men of Straw' came into being.

"Fanshawe was there at the gestation, but was not deemed qualified to join the inner circle. He became for a while their unofficial secretary, but soon tired of it all, and stopped attending. It seems that the fellows were lying around in their usual haze, when one of them bemoaned the fact that, although his family were abundantly wealthy, he, as the second son, was not the heir, and could raise no capital against his expectations. The bankers had told him that he was, in banker's terms, a 'man of straw'.

"As one, then the other, joined in with similar stories, it became apparent that six of the eight students - the exceptions being Norton and Fanshawe - were in exactly the same position: that of disenfranchised younger brother.

"One of them jokingly suggested that they should form a society, and another proposed the name 'Men of Straw'. And thus was the society born that would one day bring shame on their college, and grief to their families. Fanshawe was uncertain as to exactly who it was that first proposed that they all form a *tontine* - a rolling fund. It seems that it was either Godfrey Norton - who was not one of the members of the *tontine*, by the way - or one Reginald Aubrey Haversham, who was both a second son and a member.

"Whatever, the idea took hold, and Norton, as the only law student among them, was deputised to draw up the contracts and appertaining wills. He came to Fanshawe, his tutor in law, for advice. Fanshawe claims he had reservations about the entire proceedings, and insists he spelled out the risks involved. The romantic aspects of the agreement, with its element of risk and ultimate reward, he says, enchanted Norton. Besides, he was taking no risk himself. Fanshawe says that at first Norton treated the whole affair as though it was another of their undergraduate pranks. But the others were all of age, and their signatures binding.

"As to those others, he understood from the sole survivor that they were all persuaded to put their signatures to these infamous documents by Haversham and Norton during one of their drug-sodden evenings in London, where Haversham had taken them all to meet his mathematics tutor. This particular gentleman was witness to all the signings.

"When I tell you, Watson, that the tutor was named Professor James Moriarty, I am sure you will be prepared for the rest of the sorry tale, with its mixture of greed, brilliance and low cunning. This was in the Professor's earlier days, you understand, and the payoff was what allowed him to cease his teaching career, and launched Professor Moriarty on the high-road to becoming the master criminal of London, and then of the British Isles.

"Had I known all this years ago, Watson, I should have trapped Professor Moriarty that much sooner, and brought him to slow justice rather than a swift death."

I was stunned. Holmes continued speaking, after lighting the pipe he'd been cleaning and loading while calmly recounting the day's extraordinary findings.

"What was this scandal that so shook everyone, then, Holmes? I recall nothing involving any of the colleges, though it was a long time ago."

"It seems the affair was hushed up, and Fanshawe himself did not know all of the final outcome. It was suppressed, officially, as nothing conclusive could be proved. Five of the six 'Men of Straw' were dead, and so were six of the elder brothers, and the two living fathers. Taken all together, the rightful heirs to some of the wealthiest families in the land. First, the elder brothers and the fathers! Every death, taken separately, seemed plausible, if tragic. They died in places spread all over England, and one on the Continent. Amongst the dead was Reginald Haversham's elder brother.

"Then it was the turn of the Men of Straw themselves. Within the space of a moment, they all died - in an accident! The mathematics tutor had disappeared to Budapest. The sole surviving beneficiary of the *tontine* - and now one of the wealthiest men and largest landholders in the realm - was Reginald Aubrey Haversham, who had been abroad at the time of the deaths. It was at that point in Fanshawe's tale, Watson, that it all became clear to me. I'd had the nagging feeling ever since leaving Sir Oliver Newsome's chambers that the name Haversham should mean something to me.

"Now it came to me! It had been in one of Mycroft's reports, telegraphed to me long before in Siam. Reginald Aubrey Haversham is the name, before he acceded to the title upon the tragic death of his elder brother, of the current Lord Coledale! And Isobel Aster's *beau,* before she threw him over, was named 'Reggie'.

A silence descended on the sitting room. I could think of nothing to say, and was having difficulty simply digesting this series of astounding revelations. I could see that Holmes was in a state of extreme frustration. Every attempt he and le Villard made to unravel the mysteries confronting them seemed to open new avenues to investigate, but brought them no nearer to rescuing either Godfrey Norton or Isobel Aster. He stared into the flames for some time, then began pacing the floor.

Le Villard and I maintained our silence, knowing Holmes's moods when blocked in his investigations. I vaguely heard a latch snap, but paid no particular attention until I heard the first scrapings of bow on stretched cat-gut. A few seconds sufficed for Holmes to tune his violin, which I had not heard him play since his return.

At first he played a succession of disconnected and decidedly melancholy chords in a minor key, but thankfully he soon tired of this, and re-tuned his instrument. A brief pause ensued, and then Holmes commenced playing a simple melody in a scale that was distinctly exotic, but hauntingly beautiful nonetheless. To my ears, the music was full of surprising twists and turns, halting at unexpected intervals, and taking novel paths before returning to the original bitter-sweet melody.

I looked at le Villard, and saw a gentle smile and calm expression on his face. It occurred to me that Holmes was playing a Siamese melody. He continued for some time, embellishing the simple melody as he went until it became a rich and complex musical piece in multiple voices, all played on the violin. Suddenly, the music that had seemed without beginning or end came to a halt.

Holmes, violin still in hand, sat again by the fire, his agitation stilled for now. I divined that the melody held some particular significance, for Holmes and le Villard both. For a moment I considered enquiring about the tune, for it was both exotic and affecting. But on reflection, I decided to allow Holmes to tell me - or to hope that it was mentioned in the as yet unread final parts of the Journals.

I stared into the flames, and meditated on the convoluted mystery he and le Villard faced, or as much as I knew of it from le Villard's Journals, and subsequent events here at London.

At first I thought of it as an enormous jig-saw puzzle, with only the outer edges filled in and vast areas of mystery remaining within those boundaries. Then again, it seemed rather like a deadly version of that new parlour game of 'musical chairs' where 'it' keeps changing, and an ever-diminishing number of players vie for the only throne.

Holmes replaced his fiddle in its case, and absently leafed through the few messages and reminders he had speared to the mantlepiece, as before.

A loud knocking came from the street door downstairs. I pocketed my revolver once again and descended. Through the peep-hole I could see only the top of a mop of tangled, unruly hair, and correctly surmised that Wiggins had come to grace us with his presence. I unlatched the door and showed him up to the sitting-room, where he stood, cap in hand, and explained his late visit.

"Sorry to knock yez up so late, Mister 'Olmes, but y'did say to if Parker showed. 'E's just arrived at the opium den down by Dockland's Road, sir. I've left Timmy there watchin' the door, an' 'e's a quick lad. But yez 'ad better 'urry, sir, 'cause I 'eard 'im say t'the doorman that 'e only 'ad time fer a pipe or two. 'Ad t'get back t'the missus, 'e said. But 'e ain't 'itched, Parker, an' 'e ain't likely t'be either, so that was a fib."

Holmes was already on his feet, all lethargy vanished.

"Come on, le Villard. Your coat and scarf, and I think a revolver as well; we've no time to lose," he cried. "This may be the break I've been waiting for, at last. Watson, we may be away some time, and I think we need someone to remain here, in case of news about Isobel Aster or Godfrey Norton. Wiggins will have his lads working all night and further messages may arrive from them. We'll see you at breakfast, I expect. Good night."

"Good evening, Doctor Watson," called le Villard over his shoulder as he dashed out the door after Holmes. It was difficult not to envy him, rushing off with Holmes in the dead of a foggy London night in pursuit of villains. But I understood the necessity, and did not really begrudge the French detective his place at Holmes's side, which I had so frequently taken in cases long past. Le Villard would be in London only until this matter was cleared up, and had told me he would then return to Siam to marry his Siamese fiancée, and retire from the business of detection altogether.

Besides, I thought, as I turned down my bed-covers, if ever any man has earned the right to stand alongside Holmes in a tight spot, that man is Francois le Villard. I picked up the Journal to read a little more, and to distract my thoughts from the puzzles of the present moment.

CHAPTER XLIX

9th September 1893
Bangkok, Siam

TEN O'CLOCK FOUND US in the office of Chief Inspector Sheriff, drinking his tepid English tea once again. He had sent word to the General Adviser. Shortly enough Rolin's carriage arrived.

His coachman had seen and heard nothing of the attempted bombing, and Rinzing had been instructed to say nothing, so the General Adviser was unaware of the reasons for the summons. Holmes quickly explained to him all that we knew of the event. At first Rolin seemed a little incredulous, especially when informed just how close they had been to the actual blast. He had neither seen nor heard evidence of the explosion as the Prince's carriage had raced through the storm, across the bridge, and on to the Foreign Ministry.

But when Holmes asked him to inspect the remains of the bomb he visibly paled. He picked up several of the wooden staves from the cask that had contained the powder.

"Just a piece of curved wood, and yet . . . so deadly a purpose. I know you realise what a crisis such a bombing, if successful, would have caused. The damage to Siam's interests would have been incalculable."

As the magnitude of the possible consequences dawned slowly in his mind, the General Adviser's voice betrayed his rising anger.

"Despite all the factional differences . . . their own internal problems . . . the vested resistance to change . . . in the face of aggression from powerful European forces . . . despite all these obstacles, in fact, Siam under King Chulalongkorn is making real strides towards the modernisation so essential if they are to remain uncolonised. His Foreign Minister is his right-hand man, and is very nearly indispensable in that role. *Quite* apart. I may add, from being the King's own brother!"

Holmes did not interrupt. Neither did Sheriff. Rolin carried on speaking, now to us rather than to himself.

"My own role is far less crucial. There are others equally well qualified in the legal and administrative aspects of advising governments. This critical time is hardly the ideal time to replace the King's adviser, I suppose, but that pales into insignificance compared to the consequences of foreign indignation at such an assassination. Disastrous! Whichever way you look at it!"

He put the stave back on the table, and picked up the silver pocket-watch lying alongside it.

"Has this something to do with the case?"

"It was found under the bridge, apparently dropped by the bomber. Open the back," said Holmes.

Rolin did so, and read the inscription several times over.

"Oh dear! Oh my! I take it this belongs to the English barrister, Norton?"

"Not yet confirmed," said Holmes, "but it's a fair supposition. Especially as we know he has recently ordered explosives such as these - ostensibly on behalf of that gold-mining syndicate out of Singapore."

Holmes appeared to hesitate a moment, before handing him the note Norton had left with his wife. The General Adviser read it through.

"Why didn't you inform someone last night, Professor? We may have been able to track the would-be assassin."

"Not in that storm, Chief Inspector. Besides, the attempt failed, and the villains were disturbed in the act. They will have covered their tracks by now. I'm afraid these are the only clues we have to go on with. As we didn't know where to find you at that hour, I thought it best not to create a fuss in the middle of the night here at Headquarters, and that we should, all of us, jointly decide whether or not to alarm the Prince and the palace."

"Fair enough," said Sheriff. "I suppose it *could* have done more harm than good. Before we decide how best to handle this, we should consider what evidence we have, and what it tells us. Firstly, this watch. Assuming it is Norton's, it places him at the scene."

"If that *is* so, it is not necessarily so that he was there at the time of the bombing," said Holmes.

"I should think that his presence at that particular spot at any time links him fairly convincingly to the assassination attempt, wouldn't you, Professor?" replied Sheriff. "It's hardly the place he'd go in the normal way of things, after all."

"So it would seem, yes!" responded Holmes.

"How do we interpret that?"

"However we interpret it, it is imperative that we talk with Godfrey Norton. Le Villard and I have just come from the Bangkok Hotel. He has not returned since he left his wife there last night. She has no idea where he may be, unless he simply went on one of his benders, and is sleeping it off in some dive. Perhaps you could have them combed out, Chief Inspector. I imagine you will have the docks watched."

"Of course! And the canals; you can get a long way out of Bangkok on the *klongs*, and then make for the coast down one of the rivers. We can't search every fishing vessel and tramp coaster along the eastern littoral, if he gets that far."

"Where would he head for, most likely?" enquired Holmes.

"Almost anywhere!" answered the Chief-Inspector. "Asia is a vast place, and even a white man can lose himself fairly effectively. Then there's Africa, the Americas, and even Australia. Perhaps his wife can lead us to him. Though he treated her abominably, nonetheless he seemed dependent on having her around, I always thought."

"What about these wooden pieces? Can they tell us anything?" asked Rolin.

Holmes replied. "You're referring to these stencilled letters and marks on the cask." He pointed at the black shapes on the remaining staves.

"I read them before I slung the cask into the water. Sherry, from Jerez! Unfortunately, it doesn't help us much. I've seen similar casks from the same winery in several places here in Bangkok. I noticed *Nai* Portugee had a stock of these same casks at his *godown*. Then - even before that - I noticed several casks in the liquor store aboard Lord Coledale's yacht when his man Quiney showed us around the boat."

"I've also seen sherry casks with this same brand marking burnt into the wood," interrupted the General Adviser. "At Falck and Beidek's, the wine merchants here."

"Available to anyone!" said Sheriff. "I'll check into all three, and look for others. And verify that this watch is indeed the property of Godfrey Norton. That should be simple enough. But it doesn't get us very much farther."

"This is terrible," said the General Adviser. "If it should be proven that an *Englishman* was behind this attack, and the French get wind of it, it will drastically alter the situation at Saigon and Paris. The *colons*' hand will be greatly strengthened, and the French Foreign Office will be hard put to restrain them from declaring Siam a French Protectorate.

"As for Whitehall, the British position will be seriously compromised to say the least. News of this attack *must* not get out. Professor Sigerson and I shall inform the Prince, and privately and confidentially recommend a policy of secrecy. Rumours of all kinds are rife, and there's already more than enough unrest in the city."

"A few other suggestions," added Holmes. "Chief Inspector: post reliable watchmen, discreetly, at all bridges used by the Prince or the General Adviser. M. Rolin: from now on you should use a closed carriage at all times, and take Rinzing with you at night as before - even if you are with the Prince. You should also, as much as possible, be seen to have suffered a reduction in your access to the Prince, and in your influence on foreign policy. Also, I suggest you stay out of all meetings involving the French Resident, Pavie.

"Finally, I should like to receive, as early as possible each day, a brief report from yourself regarding the political situation as it develops, and the movements of both the King and the major princes; just the brothers of the King."

"Very well, Professor. I have just had the telephone installed at home, at the order of the Foreign Ministry. The Oriental Hotel has also installed an instrument. There are no other lines in the hotel for curious ears to listen in, and my line goes through a secured Palace operator at the exchange. Perhaps it would be easier if, other than for highly confidential reports, I speak with you daily."

It was agreed that we would go with Rolin that night to the Ministry to brief the Prince about the assassination attempt. He would have his assistant stay at the house today, to check by telephone with the palace. As soon as the Prince was awake, Rolin would go there to inform him of the attempt.

We left to return to Irene Norton, *nee* Adler, whose husband was suspected of being behind the bombing.

She was in her rooms at the Bangkok Hotel, rather upset at the prospect of being interviewed by the police, in the person of Chief Inspector Sheriff. He had told us that he would call on her later in the day.

Norton hadn't reappeared, nor had he contacted his wife. She was alone, and seemed a forlorn figure as she sat looking out of the windows of the lobby lounge - a far cry from the renowned diva who'd had kings and potentates vie for her favour. Her features were marked by the strain of the past day, and despite herself, it seemed as though the burden of continuing was increasingly difficult to bear.

It always seemed to me that a bond stronger than mere marriage vows tied her and Norton. Norton treated her foully - but who could fathom the secret reasons a beautiful woman remains with a brute. Holmes had asked her this morning if she had heard anything other from Norton, which could hint at where he may have gone to ground. Mrs. Norton hesitated, just for a moment, before replying that she could think of nothing helpful. Holmes hadn't pressed her on the matter.

Now he was a little more insistent that she tell him everything she knew. All she would say was that there was nothing that anyone - even Sherlock Holmes - could do about altering the past. She stubbornly refused to say more, looking out the window at the passing Siamese.

"He is my husband, for better or worse, and I should do him no service by revealing what little I know of the demons that have driven Godfrey to despair. One day, perhaps, there will an accounting. For now, I must wait and see what happens."

In frustration at this Holmes gathered his hat and his stick, and we made for the exit. But before we took two steps, Irene Adler called softly after Holmes.

"Tell me, Mr. Holmes, do you think my husband guilty of this murder attempt?"

"Assassination attempt, Mrs. Norton. A far more serious matter, in which Norton's possible involvement fortunately has not as yet come to the attention of the Siamese people themselves. As to that, considering the circumstantial evidence, and the finding of his grandfather's watch at the scene, there seems little doubt that Norton was somehow involved. Whether he was the actual bomber, or even there at the time of planting the bomb, is less certain. His disappearance compounds the suspicion, to say the least."

Irene Adler seemed unsurprised at this reply, as though she had expected none different. She smiled - a wan smile - but it relieved the severity of her expression for a moment. Then she turned back to looking out of the paned windows.

Holmes and I returned to the Oriental Hotel, where we found a message awaiting Professor Sigerson. It was from Colonel Sartorius. In guarded language he explained that he had returned from Burma three days previously, and had secured the item in question. He asked if we could call on him this evening at eight o'clock, at the Hotel Hermes.

We knew the place, a modest but clean hostelry not so far distant.

"It means adjusting our timetable regarding calling on the Prince. Could you use the hotel's instrument to telephone to Rolin - now that he has a telephone - and ask if he can delay our appointment until, say, eleven tonight. We should be free by then, I should think. We can get a carriage here."

I enquired of the *concierge,* who indicated a wood-and-glass booth housing a modern telephone. Holmes stood outside the booth with the glass-paned door held ajar while I placed the call. Lifting the ear-piece to my ear I jiggled the hook several times to alert the operator. When she came on I asked in Siamese to be connected to the General Adviser's number.

"Do you really think he has found the *Great Mogul,* Holmes?" I asked while I waited. "It would be worth a fortune, surely."

Just then the voice of Rolin came though the wires. He agreed with the postponement of our visit to the Prince, saying that it wasn't really necessary. Earlier that afternoon he had called on the General Adviser at home, and was informed about the matter. Assured that both Professor Sigerson and Chief Inspector Sheriff were investigating, he urged that they get on with it, and agreed - in fact, requested - that the entire affair remain a secret. Holmes was sharing the ear piece with me, and simply nodded to me once the General Adviser had finished.

"The Professor agrees that there is no need to brief the Prince further tonight," I said into the speaking trumpet. "We have another lead to follow up in any case, so it is convenient for us. Thank you. We'll speak with you again tomorrow."

I rang off.

"Could he really have found such a stone, Holmes? We were . . ."

"If it is, le Villard, a King's ransom could be asked for it. If it were diamond, but not the *Great Mogul,* it would still be extremely valuable. I shall have to examine it myself, but without the requisite testing apparatus it will be difficult to be certain. I could borrow the necessary hardness-testing materials from Falconer. Specific gravity fluids and a balance, as well."

I recognised the name of the chief accountant of a sapphire and ruby merchant we had investigated.

"He's clean, and he'd lend them to me. I suggest we walk over to his workshops right now, as we have little else to do before eight."

As it turned out, Falconer wasn't expected to return from his mines at Chantaboori for another day. As we strolled back along Windmill Road, Holmes seemed but little concerned over the prospect of soon holding in his hands one of the most valuable gemstones ever known.

"It's not critical, le Villard. Tomorrow will suffice. Did you ever translate my monograph *On the Identification and Classification of Gemstones by the Analysis of Chatoyant Colours in Polished Stones?"*

"Certainly not! I'd remember the length of the title, if nothing else. Can you classify gemstones in that way?"

"Not with certainty. I'd need more technical verification before I would part with cash for a stone, but it can give excellent indication of results, with a high probability of accuracy. We can test hardness and specific gravity tomorrow.

"But the stone is not our real concern here. One; Sartorius has been back in Bangkok for three days. Two; he has had dealings with Norton before, and is still trying - unsuccessfully - to have him free up their frozen funds! Three; he has threatened to kill the General Adviser, and we know he is a professional soldier! I imagine he is quite proficient with explosives."

"You think it's possible he could be behind the bomb attack at the bridge, in a conspiracy with Norton?" I asked.

"And perhaps others! The timing of his return from Burma is suggestive?"

We dined early that evening, at an outdoor restaurant with its frontage open to the Chao Phraya River. Here, seated in chairs of split-bamboo, we enjoyed grilled fish and other seafoods done in the Siamese fashion, with piquant sauces and plates of steaming rice, washed down with a passable beer. The weather had been mild in the morning as usual, but as the sultry heat of the day built up the air seemed to become charged with energy. By the time we arrived back from the jewellers a dark storm-front had swept across the city, though without the extreme violence of the previous evening.

Rain deluged the streets again as we sat, our meal finished, and waited for the storm to subside a little. Holmes smoked his pipe, observing indulgently while I enjoyed bantering with the Siamese serving-girls, who love nothing more than to joke and laugh. We remained another hour, the only customers. I ordered a few dishes of Siamese confections, which we shared with the waitresses, trapped as we all were by the pouring rain. Holmes smoked, and watched the storm raging outside.

I imagined he was contemplating all the possible scenarios that could have led to the bomb plot. Was it Norton, alone or with accomplices? If so, who? We knew he had associations with several of the suspect groups - the Singaporean syndicate; Colonel Sartorius; even with *Sia* Ah Foo. Then there were the French *colons*, and we knew Norton had recently returned from Saigon! And the Chinese! With Chinamen following behind the carriage, and the Chinese adviser to the Prince informing them of the General Adviser's official daily itinerary, surely they must be somehow involved? Then there was the sherry cask, which could have come from Lord Coledale's yacht, or from *Nai* Portugee's *godown*.

It seemed to me that we had a plethora of possible suspects - and that, in some way or other, the common element with most of them was an involvement with Godfrey Norton. I wondered what Holmes was making of it all, but refrained from asking. He tells me things when he feels the time is right. Or perhaps he doesn't!

By half past seven o'clock the storm had subsided. Rain had stopped falling and we were able to walk back to the pier, where we hired a jitney to take us to the Hotel Hermes.

Our way took us along New Road for a little, towards the Pramane Ground area. Along the way we were passed by a closed carriage travelling at full speed, trailed by a squad of four Siamese police on horseback. Holmes and I had just dismounted from our jitney and stood away from it, as one always did when the King's elephants came near: the horses were unaccustomed to the presence of the huge beasts, and were likely to bolt.

The speeding carriage barely slowed as it passed. I supposed that police horses were used to elephants at parades. The small cavalcade rushed by, and disappeared from sight around a corner.

"That was Sheriff's carriage," said Holmes as we took our seats again - the elephants having lumbered past our one-horse jitney without incident - and continued on our way.

"Perhaps he's gone to arrest Sartorius," I joked.

It didn't seem so humorous when we arrived several minutes later at the Hotel Hermes, and saw the Chief Inspector's carriage drawn up in the forecourt, surrounded by the four horses of the police squad.

"The plot definitely thickens, le Villard," remarked Holmes as we paid off our driver and walked up several low steps into the lobby. A few bemused hotel guests sat at tables in the small lounge, observing the drama; behind the counter stood a black-suited Siamese with pomaded hair, wringing his hands in despair.

As we entered a Siamese policeman blocked our way, but the hotel manager, in his black suit, approached to assist us. Holmes presented his card and asked if it could be sent to Chief Inspector Sheriff, wherever he was. This was done immediately. I noticed that, like hoteliers in Paris or London, the managers here were anxious to seem on the side of the law and hope that the authorities would leave as soon as possible, with as little fuss as possible.

Soon an uniformed Siamese approached and asked us to follow him. He led the way up two flights of stairs and along a dim corridor past closed doors, to the last door on the left, and ushered us into the room of Colonel

Sartorius, and the presence of Chief Inspector Sheriff.

Seated on a hardwood chair in the corner, trembling with fear and the aftermath of a hangover, was Felix Garraud. His wide eyes stared at the body of Colonel Sartorius, slumped on his back on the floor near the French doors to the terrace, with a wooden knife-handle protruding from his chest. Sartorius was clearly dead. A copious amount of still-crimson blood had spread out on the rough wooden floor, pooling in cracks and ridges. Sightless eyes stared from his banker's face at the peeling paint of the ceiling. The old mercenary, veteran of so many deadly campaigns in forbidding jungles and treacherous deserts, had lost his life in a dingy hotel room in Bangkok.

Sheriff looked up at us.

"Doesn't take you fellows long to sniff out trouble, does it?"

"On the contrary, Chief Inspector," replied Holmes. "We were expected. I had an appointment with the late Colonel Sartorius for eight this evening. We're early, but obviously far too late to help him. What has happened here?"

"According to Garraud here, he was with the victim earlier. The Colonel, as he styles himself, was feeling poorly. Malaria he picked up years ago; recurred during his trip North. Yes, Professor, we know all about his trip to Burma. We have our people listening. Garraud here likes his booze. Sartorius made the mistake of telling Garraud about this supposed *Great Mogul* diamond or whatever it's called. Sounds like one more of their swindles to me."

Chief Inspector Sheriff picked up a small wooden jewel case, and turned the tiny brass key. He opened it. The case was lined with crimson velvet, and had a depression in the base where a large gemstone could sit securely . . . if it was there. It wasn't!

"Garraud claims that the stone was genuine. Swears it was in here five hours ago. Colonel Sartorius sent him to the European apothecary's store for some medication. Unfortunately for the Colonel, Garraud stopped in for a little of his own medication on the way back. Got roaring drunk in the process. Had to get the staff to open the room when he got back. No answer to his knocking, you see. Found this!"

He pointed at Sartorius's inert body, which had already attracted the attention of a legion of ants, nibbling away at the skin between his fingers, and streaming away from his ears and open mouth when Sheriff disturbed the corpse by searching the pockets.

"That's all we'd gotten out of Garraud when you arrived. Hello! What's this?"

He extracted a small slip of paper from the pocket of the dressing gown, which the murdered Belgian had worn over his Siamese-style *panung* - pantaloons of indigo-coloured cotton -unfolded it and smoothed the folds flat, and read.

"Very interesting, Professor. It seems we've picked up Norton's trail again."

Holmes took the proffered paper, and we both read it. It was a page torn from a small notebook, cheap paper with faint blue lines. Halfway down the page a few words were scribbled in blue ink.

5.00 - NORTON
HAVE IT OUT WITH HIM!
LAST CHANCE!

"Norton seems most careless, especially for a legal mind. Perhaps the pressure is getting to him," remarked Holmes. He turned to Garraud.

"As you may have surmised, Garraud, I am working with the police on several matters here. I have a few questions for you, and you would be well advised to answer them fully and truthfully. Keep in mind that you are one of the principal suspects for this murder. No! Don't protest! You could easily have knifed Sartorius, gone out on an invented pretext and stashed the diamond, then gone off to get drunk and establish an alibi."

Holmes walked across and stood directly in front of the still-drunk Garraud.

"Snap out of it, man! Some answers, if you please! When did Sartorius get back?"

"Three days ago. He came down from Chieng Mai after the gymkhana. By elephant to the river, then by boat."

"Did he say where he'd been, and what he'd done?"

"To Mandalay, like he said. All the palaces there were made of wood panels. He said the last King had moved them from Amarapura. That was why the panel where he hid the stone could be moved. He said he found it again in the old Queen's Audience Chamber. Problem was, it's now used as the British officer's mess, and it was difficult to get at it."

Garraud wiped his forearm across his sweaty brow, and asked if he could have a drink, to settle his nerves. Holmes nodded, and I poured him a stiff tot of rum from the bottle standing on the desk. He drained it at a gulp, and asked for another.

"Not yet, Garraud. We need more answers. Carry on!"

Garraud looked hopefully at the bottle, and decided to be helpful. He continued.

"Sartorius used your money to bribe the Indian guards, who thought he only wanted a small wooden carving. Once he got the panel, he said, he broke it open, retrieved the stone, and slipped out of Mandalay. He said the British never knew he was there, thanks to his Shans.

"Then back across the Shan country to Chieng Mai, with the diamond under his jacket, safe in his leather money pouch. You know the rest."

"Not quite," said Sheriff. "When he got to Bangkok, what did he do?"

"Came to see me at *Mama-san* Kung's. Sick as a cat! Could hardly stand. We brought him here, and he's been here since."

"Still sick?"

"Improved a bit. Enough that he could see people. He sent me out for things, and with messages a few times. Otherwise he stayed in bed, half-delirious at times."

"Did he ever show you the stone?"

"Just the once, this morning. He wasn't that sort of a man to show things around. Kept things close. I saw the jewel-case on his desk once or twice when I came back in from an errand, but that key was never in it. He always tucked it back under his robe when I was around, or under his pillow."

Holmes went to the narrow bed and lifted the thin pillow. Under it was a revolver. Holmes lifted it and spun the cylinder.

"Fully loaded. Didn't help him though!"

"Perhaps he knew his assailant, didn't fear him," said Sheriff. "Norton fits that bill. Seems he was expected here at five o'clock. Think I'll send for that oily manager fellow, Timonelli."

He turned to his aide and gave orders in rapid Siamese, then returned his attentions to the victim. Holmes was on his knees examining the wound and the knife with his lens.

"It seems Norton has been even more cavalier with his reputation, Chief Inspector. This knife has a mark stamped into the wooden handle. I recognise the arms, as we have been there just today, and the letters *B* and *H* flanking them are conclusive."

"Of course," I said. "'Bangkok Hotel'!"

"Norton's hotel!" added the Chief Inspector.

"The knife is too large for table or room service. I suggest you have someone check there, and see if any of their kitchen knives are missing. If so, since when?"

Again the Chief Inspector issued orders, and another of his men left the room. The Siamese manager appeared in the doorway. He was still wringing his hands furiously, and averted his eyes. Sheriff asked if there had been any callers for the Colonel during the afternoon, or if anyone had been seen near the room. The manager replied that he had already talked it over with the staff, and the only information he had was that an Englishman in a white suit had asked if the Colonel was in. That was at around five o'clock. Told that the Colonel was indeed in his room, the Englishman had said that he was expected and knew the way. He had been seen on the second floor, turning down the passage towards the room. The cleaning-girl had then gone downstairs, and hadn't noticed at which door the *farang* had knocked.

The description gleaned from the staff was inconclusive. The man had worn a white hat, and his hair-colouring was not noticed at the time. We all seem tall to the Siamese, and our features similar. Other than the fact that he carried a stick, the description could have fitted any tall clean-shaven European in Bangkok. Even that was of little help.

In these parts of the world almost every European carries a stick, whether a 'Penang lawyer' with a weighted head on a rattan shaft, or a swordstick, or just a simple ash. Almost *de rigeur*, really! As for the clothing, Norton usually wore white, but the steamy climate here means that tropical whites and a hat of white straw finely-woven are almost a uniform for Europeans from all countries. Nothing conclusive to be learned there!

"Garraud! Was Sartorius in the habit of making notes regarding appointments?" asked Holmes.

"If he did, it was usually in his notebook. He always had a small notebook with him. He'd jot things down, then when it filled up he'd buy another."

"Can you see it here anywhere?"

There were a number of books, some maps, and other documents scattered around on the desk. Garraud searched around amongst them, but couldn't find the notebook. Asked if the scrap of paper could be from the notebook, Garraud was unable to say, as he'd paid no attention to it at the time.

"Something here, though," said Holmes, whose sharp eye had noticed an item of interest amongst the documents.

He held up an envelope bearing a French stamp, franked from Saigon just two weeks previously. It was addressed to Colonel Sartorius, and carried the return address of the Secretary to the Governor-General of Annam and Cochin-China. There was no letter inside, nor - following a careful search of all the papers on the desk - could the contents of the envelope be found.

Further questioning of Garraud yielded nothing more of interest, neither did Holmes's meticulous search of the room.

"One thing only to docket for further thought: the door was locked, and the room-key is missing!"

"Very well, Professor," said the Chief Inspector, as Holmes concluded his search. "I think we'll hold on to Mr. Garraud here for a while, on suspicion. Stop him from getting together with his chums and letting them all know about your activities."

Garraud was cuffed and hustled away to Sheriff's carriage. The Chief Inspector extracted the knife from Sartorius's chest and tucked it away to keep as evidence. Colonel Sartorius's body was then taken down the rear stairs - in response to the earnest entreaties of the pomaded manager - and dispatched to Police Headquarters.

"Meanwhile, it's high time I issued a warrant for the arrest of Godfrey Norton," said Sheriff, as he climbed into his carriage. "For now, it will be on suspicion of murdering Sartorius. Motive is this *Great Mogul*, I suppose. I shall reserve charges in connection with the bombing conspiracy until we have more concrete evidence. Or until we have apprehended Norton."

We had not slept at all the previous night. After the events at the bridge, having escorted Mrs. Norton and Malee back to her rooms, Holmes and I had camped out in the lobby of the Bangkok Hotel in case Norton or someone else should attempt to contact her. At dawn we had returned to the Oriental Hotel to do our *baritsu* exercises and take breakfast, and then had gone directly to see the Chief Inspector at Police Headquarters.

Leaving behind the Hotel Hermes, and the crowd of ghouls come to view the body, we returned to the hotel, and to well-deserved rest.

20th September 1893
Bangkok, Siam
Things were quiet after the Sartorius murder, but further excitement began with the arrival at our hotel, in a state of extreme agitation, of Miss Malee.

We'd been wondering if the threat to the General Adviser had been removed - and we should move on - or if there would be further attempts on his life. The *Siam Free Press* was still conducting a vigorous campaign against his part in the affair, and the situation at Siam was still very confused, with the attitude of the French as belligerent as ever. Le Myre de Vilers wrote a particularly insolent and mocking letter to the Prince about Rolin. *Le Temps* wrote of intervention by the French fleet. An agreement resolving the disputes between the Siamese and the French at Annam was still being negotiated, and the General Adviser was particularly concerned that the Prince offer no concessions beyond those demanded.

It seemed that the situation regarding the difficult position of the General Adviser remained unaltered. Regardless of who had actually plotted Rolin's death on several occasions, his death or serious injury would still provide the French with the excuse they so evidently wanted to justify the annexation of Siam. It was possible that, now the attackers knew that someone was alert to their plotting, they would just melt away.

On balance, we had decided, it was more likely the lull between storms.

Until an agreement between the Siamese and the French was concluded it would be dangerous to both Rolin and Siam for us to leave. Just at that moment, as though to underscore our decision, Miss Malee was announced.

Holmes invited her to sit, and asked what brought her here alone at such a late hour. It took her a few moments to compose herself. Even then, after a measured start, she broke down and began to sob a little as she told her story.

"It's Miss Irene. She's been behaving so strangely these past few days. We always spoke to each other of our problems; we've been more like sisters than just friends. Now she avoids me, and when I do speak with her, she asks me please to leave her alone. I became so worried about her that I sat in a corner of the lobby of her hotel last night. The previous two nights she had been out of her room when I called, though none of the hotel staff could recollect seeing her leave.

"I was despairing of seeing her at all when something caught my attention. A young British Navy rating was walking out of the hotel; all spit-and-polish and dressed for a night on the town. There was something distinctly familiar about this sailor, and yet I know no sailors of any navy, except old Captain Bush.

"He wore his cap set far back on the head, at a very rakish angle. I looked closely under the bright lamps in the lobby, and suddenly I realised. It wasn't a sailor, nor indeed a man. It was Miss Irene, dressed up in sailor's clothes, with just the right walk."

She stopped for a moment, and sipped a little water from the glass I had brought to her.

"And so what did you do, Miss Malee?" asked Holmes. "Take your time."

"That's just it. There may be no time! I followed her out into the street, which was crowded. When she took a jinrickashaw, I hired one as well, and told the boy to follow at a distance, and I kept a fan in front of my face. Miss Irene looked around only once, but didn't see me."

"I imagine that if she feared being followed, it would not be by a charming young lady," said Holmes.

"I suppose so. Anyway, I followed her down into this frightful area where I had never been before, in the Chinese quarter. It was down by the river, somewhere past Sampeng market. She stopped at the end of a small lane and disappeared into a dark space between dingy buildings. I feared to go further. I asked the rickashaw boy did he know what was down in that alley. He said it was a place of gambling and opium dens, and of loose women; it was called Heavenly Pavilion, in Chinese.

"My father brought me up to have an open mind, but I have never been in such a place. Why would Miss Irene go to such a place? I waited ten minutes or so and was just wondering how I could possibly follow her into that dark alley when she reappeared, in her sailor's clothing, escorted by two large Chinamen. They held her by the elbows, and sat her in a gondola that was moored at the small pier, at the end of the lane there.

"I wanted to run and stop them but my jinrickashaw driver held me back, saying that one did not interfere in anything in this area if one valued one's life. Once I had seen them row away into the stream I ran over to the railing, but the boat was already lost in the darkness. The old Chinese watchman there gave me a strange look, but I was not bothered in any way. I did not know what to do, and I had to return to take care of my mother, so I went home. The very first thing this morning I went to the Bangkok Hotel, and sat in a small cafe down the street, where I would not be seen.

"After two cups of coffee I was feeling foolish, but I was so worried. Then I saw my sailor walking into the entrance of the hotel. She seemed none the worse for being out all night, and I dared not let her know I had followed her. So I left and went on to my classes.

"Oh! This is taking so long to tell! I went to see her this afternoon and reminded her of our appointment for the concert this evening. She cancelled it, saying that she had an unexpected change of plans. I thought she may be having problems with Mr. Godfrey, and said I understood. I left, but I returned again at the same time as the previous night and sat in the lobby. She walked out once again, dressed again as a naval rating, but this time she carried a sailor's kit-bag. It looked heavy. I followed as before, and she went back to the same place.

"This time when she came out with the two Chinamen there was another man waiting for her at the entrance to the alley. An argument broke out between Miss Irene and this man. It was too far to see much, but they pushed her roughly into a launch, and sped away. I didn't know what to do. I was so worried. So I came here. Miss Irene always said that you could solve mysteries, Professor. Where has she gone, and why?"

Holmes looked at me briefly. I was sure he was thinking the same as I - Godfrey Norton! How Norton had come to be in the clutches of *Sia* Ah Foo I could not guess, but that therein lay the answer to Miss Malee's question I had little doubt.

"Although I'm not yet sure where she has gone, Miss Malee, I think I know why, but you must forgive us if we keep our counsel until certain. I think, however, that she will return to her hotel in the morning, as today. Tomorrow night M. le Villard and I will follow her. I suggest you return to your mother's house, and do not worry yourself unduly about this matter."

"Is there anything I can do? I feel so helpless, and I am sure she is in some deep trouble."

"You have already done her a great service, Miss Malee, by being concerned for her welfare and noticing her troubles. It must have taken a deal of courage to follow her into that seamy area alone. In coming to us you have done the wisest possible thing on her behalf. Thank you! Now, leave it with us, go home, and rest."

"Oh, thank you, sirs. Please hurry. I've been so worried."

I saw her out to the entrance, hired a carriage and gave instructions to take her to her home, and bade her good night again. It was clear that she felt her dear friend was in some mortal danger. Some of the usual serenity had returned to her face, but I could see that she would still worry until Irene Adler's mysterious nocturnal journeys were explained.

When I returned to our rooms, Holmes was on the veranda, puffing at his pipe.

"There may be more of these Chinamen than we can handle alone, le Villard. First thing tomorrow we must recruit Daeng and a few of his kick-boxers."

21st September 1893
Bangkok, Siam
At dawn I went to the Bangkok Hotel. I was informed that Mrs. Norton was in, but had asked not to be disturbed for any reason. I left my card, and returned to the garden of the Oriental Hotel to join Holmes.

Following our morning *baritsu* session I arranged for Daeng and five more of his best fighters to meet us that evening at the seafood stall near our hotel. Our day was spent in various investigations concerning Norton's involvement with *Sia* Ah Foo. We found nothing much of interest - beyond the obvious fact that Norton was amongst the more frequent habitués of *Sia* Ah Foo's various dives and opium dens - and returned to prepare for the evening's adventures.

At dusk, equipped with night lanterns and Holmes's lightweight aluminium telescope, and armed with revolvers and brass-knuckles, we strolled across to the restaurant. Daeng and his boys were already there, drinking small glasses of the fiery Siamese *lao khao* - white rice whisky. They greeted us as we walked in.

Holmes suggested that the bottle on the table be the last whisky drunk, as we should all need our wits about us this evening. We accepted a glass each. After Holmes had downed his, he explained that we might be tangling with men we believed to be in the employ of *Sia* Ah Foo, but that our task was not to fight. We were searching for a *farang*, an Englishman, by means of following his wife.

He talked about the evening's work with Daeng, so that discussion would be minimal later. It was agreed that we would hire a ship's cutter, with oars, and wait discreetly near the foot of the pier near the Heavenly Pavilion. Holmes and I would go to the opium den before the expected arrival of Irene Adler in her sailor's disguise.

We would be able to observe the goings-on inside the den, and then call for the cutter to follow afterwards if, as expected, the Chinamen took her away again in a boat of some kind. That was Holmes's plan, but events took a different turn indeed.

Daeng and his boys knew the pier. Holmes gave them some *ticals*. They left to hire the boat. Holmes and I dressed for a night of revelry, stuffed cigars in our pockets, and hired a jitney to take us to the Heavenly Pavilion. Twenty minutes sufficed for the journey; we had planned to be there at least an hour before the expected arrival of Irene Adler, so that it would not seem too strange when we left.

Our arrival at the Heavenly Pavilion occasioned no comment, and we were soon seated in a dark alcove with a bottle of whisky.

"I certainly couldn't stomach any more of that Zoedone," Holmes had said. "Order whisky, I think. Not much they can do to that."

Forty minutes later, a little before we had expected, a young British Navy rating was shown into the room, and was immediately escorted by the doorman to a small table at the far side of the room. He kept his cap tilted back on his head, his youthful face calmly surveying the extraordinary goings-on inside this den of depravity. After downing one tot of dark rum and ordering another, the sailor pulled a pack of cheap cigarettes from his jacket pocket and lit up.

The illusion was perfect. Not only the swagger and nonchalance of the young tar on shore-leave, the easy familiarity with drink and tobacco, the casual arrogance of the hunter with money to spend - the impersonation was carried off with a natural talent for disguise such as I had witnessed only in Sherlock Holmes himself. Not a person in that suspicious place thought for a moment that the young sailor was other that what he appeared to be.

'He' was, in fact, Irene Adler, former talent *extraordinaire* on the great stages of Europe, displaying a brilliant flair for dramatic acting. I began to understand something more of the attraction this marvellous woman had for my companion, beyond her features and figure, and the thrilling beauty of her voice.

Within a few minutes she was joined by the portly little Chinaman, the *maître'd* we had encountered on our previous visit. He sat at her table, perching delicately, as only a fat man can, on the very edge of his chair, and spoke closely into her ear. We saw money change hands, and caught a flash of light when the lantern glinted on his gold teeth as he smiled. He left the table, pocketing money as he tripped across to the entrance, and called to a small boy seated there. A message was being sent.

We waited. Before twenty minutes more had passed two large Chinamen appeared at the entrance. The *maître'd* spoke with them, then crossed to Irene Adler's table. She stood, slapped him on the back as a drunken sailor would do, grabbed the rum bottle off the table, and followed him to the door. The two Chinamen simply turned and walked out the doorway. Irene Adler followed, a little unsteadily. No one paid the least attention to any of this, so completely normal did she make it all seem.

Holmes called for our bill. We settled it and headed out the door, turning left in the alley back towards the lane where we had entered. As we emerged from between the shophouses we caught a glimpse of a gondola carrying the Chinamen and the 'sailor'. It was already some distance out into the stream, but had only one gondolier. We had four strong oarsmen awaiting us nearby. Catching up with them should present no problems, I thought. Wrongly, as so often!

From another small lane at the very edge of the river emerged a band of the most vicious looking cut-throats I have ever seen. Villainous looking Lascars, a couple of tattooed Siamese, and a handful of large Chinamen with shaven heads. All armed with long staves and wicked knives! It was clear that they were after us.

Daeng and our Siamese fighters were still in the boat nearby. I shouted to them for help.

"Chuay noi! Khun Daeng. . . chuay noi!"

The villains moved towards us, and we were clearly outnumbered. If we ran back down the open street towards our boat, we would soon be overwhelmed. Holmes and I both decided at the same moment.

"Back down the alley! That's the one place we can be sure they won't be waiting for us."

We darted back into the dark passage, with only the reddish glow of the lanterns reflected on the streaked whitewash of the alley walls. Dashing at full speed past the startled young painted ladies, past the doorway to the Heavenly Pavilion, and on down the narrow, bent passageway, we could hear the pounding of feet some way behind us, and urgent shouting. Other voices joined in, but the footsteps never halted.

"Through here!" shouted Holmes, and slipped through an open doorway set in a shallow alcove. We kept moving fast, down a corridor with several barred internal windows, all unlit, and burst out into the middle of a vast open space, with an iron roof far overhead.

Hundreds of young girls were at work at long benches killing, plucking and dismembering tens of thousands of ducks in a cloudy mist of feathers and down. It is difficult to say who was the more surprised, the girls or us, but we had the advantage of momentum. Before they could respond to the calls of our pursuers we were across the wide hall and through another doorway at the far side. This gave onto yet another of the hundreds of alleys in this warren of humanity; we took a gamble and headed towards the water.

The alley bent left then seemed to come to a dead end. I noticed an opening with a heavy curtain across it, through a darkened door past a sleeping guard. With the shouts of our pursuers close behind, mingled with the general uproar we had caused in the duck slaughterhouse, we had no alternative. We plunged through the curtained entrance.

We found ourselves in the back stalls of a Chinese opera performance. Chinese men, women and children of all ages and types were seated on narrow benches set in shallow arcs across the gaudily-painted hall, those at the rear raised higher than at the front. Painted lanterns hung from the scarlet-lacquered beams, and candles and joss-sticks glowed in niches spaced along the side walls. On the broad stage a half dozen outrageously costumed and made-up performers shrieked and shrilled to the discordant strains of the Chinese orchestra to one side of the stage. With the din we were hardly noticed as we threaded our way through the crowd at the rear of the hall. We had just come to the other side when pandemonium erupted as our pursuers burst into the hall from the alley doorway. We slipped out of another side door, but not without being noticed.

Holmes and I ran at full speed out of that alley, headed again towards the river. We both understood that if we stayed in this warren of Chinatown we should sooner or later find ourselves trapped. Just as we came out onto a slightly wider street we heard our names being shouted.

"Acharn! Acharn!" The voices were calling to Holmes using his title - Professor - in the Siamese fashion of respectful address. It was our boatmen and fighters, and never was a sound more welcome. Using their heads, Daeng and his boys had followed the sounds of the shouting downstream until they caught sight of us.

Turning towards the river we began sprinting, but were foiled again. Our pursuers - augmented now to a small mob - appeared from an alley, blocking our path to the boat. We had no choice but to keep moving away from them. This time we took a wide path flanked by high walls that seemed to curve away towards the river's edge further downstream. As we dashed down this passage, feeling like bulls in a chute, Holmes grinned back over his shoulder at me. He didn't say a word, but I understood. Life *had* been a little tame lately.

The pathway opened out into a narrow road running behind a row of buildings fronting the river. Several narrow passages ran between them. We chose the middle of the three. An iron grille fronted it with a barred door set in it, standing open.

"Quickly, down to the water's edge."

Holmes waited until I had passed through after him, slammed the iron door to, and swung the heavy latch across into its hasp. I pulled out my revolver and stayed beside him in case our followers were too quick for him.

Reaching into his trouser pocket Holmes took out his handcuffs, slipped one prong through the holes of the iron latch, and clicked the cuffs closed. For good measure he locked the other cuff around the doorframe and the first bar of the grille, then we both sped on towards the river. We were trapped unless Daeng and his boys were waiting for us. Running out onto the narrow pier at the river we saw that the other two alleys also led down to floating finger-piers at the water's edge. Within seconds both were swarming with shouting villains, frustrated at being unable to get at us. The buildings were too tall and sheer to easily climb over. Like the others, the pier was roofed with the usual woven *attap* fronds. The walls were partially enclosed with split cane strakes. The platform was of wooden planks, set across a raft of bundled bamboo, the mass of thick, hollow tubes supplying buoyancy so that the entire affair rose and fell with the tidal river.

Our pursuers, frustrated at being unable to reach us while they located boats, had an idea. Taking down several oil-lit lanterns from the up-river pier, they swung them, then let them fall, until several had set fire to our *attap* roof. With this ablaze and the entire structure made of the most flammable of materials, our hope of escape began to look slender. There was no sign of Daeng and the boys in their boat. The villains had found a couple of small skiffs, and were putting out towards us.

Holmes and I fired our revolvers, aiming to wound rather than kill, and the boats withdrew a little. After all, our refuge would soon be a pyre at the rate the fire was spreading down the walls. Luckily, none of our assailants appeared to carry firearms. Two Chinese did appear amongst them, armed with short tubes of thin bamboo, capped at both ends. These they shook violently and rapped several times against hard surfaces. Then, swinging the tubes in an over-arm motion like cracking a whip, and releasing one cap, the Chinese flung live, enraged reptiles directly at us. One wrapped itself around a pole near Holmes's head, but his swordstick, *à coup sûr*, slashed off its hooded head before it could strike. The other snakes flashed past us, writhing and hissing, into the greasy water.

"Haven't heard of that one before, le Villard," cried Holmes, as he sheathed his swordstick. By this time a crowd of Chinese had appeared at doors and windows, concerned that the fire would spread. They ran to the adjacent piers up and down the river. Closer behind us the locals were screaming and running with pails of water which they pitched uselessly into the raging flames, now licking up the alley towards the barred iron door.

Attracted by the flames, a bevy of locals in small boats gathered in a half-circle, watching the thugs trying to burn us out. Amongst them I noticed Daeng and his fighters at their oars, swiftly approaching us. There was a row of old piles sticking out of the water in front of our pier, and they could not come alongside. One of our foes had found a weapon, and a few musket-balls whistled past us.

"I think it's time we got ourselves out of this predicament, le Villard. Besides, we don't want to lose Irene and have to do this all over again, do we?"

He shouted to Daeng, then picked up a coil of rope from the floor of the pier. Tying one end around the strongest post on the raft Holmes swung the coiled rope to Daeng, and made a few simple sign commands, pointing at a small steam-tug passing by close inshore on the way to its berth upriver. Daeng immediately understood what was wanted, and instructed his boys to row upstream past the next pier. He made a large loop in the other end of the rope.

Holmes and I cut through the stout ropes binding the pier to poles driven into the riverbed, freeing the blazing raft to float on the river. The current tugged at our floating platform. Daeng and his boys pulled us against the stream, towards the pier where most of our pursuers were still gathered. Daeng's cutter slipped alongside the steam-tug. He tossed the loop of the rope over a bitt on the tug's stern, and the boys rowed out of the way.

Before the tug's master even knew what had happened his powerful steam engines had dragged our floating pier upstream the twenty or so yards which had separated the two piers. Now almost entirely ablaze, our disintegrating raft was suddenly right alongside that of our terrified pursuers, who could think of nothing but saving themselves from this unexpected inferno. Their pier burst into flames immediately, as Holmes hacked the straining tow-rope with the razor-sharp blade he concealed in his swordstick. He tied the loose end securely to the floor joists of our new neighbour so that the current would not drift our burning pier away from it.

The downstream side of our raft was the only part not yet ablaze, but clearly it was only a matter of moments before we should be forced to jump into the dark river or burn to death. Daeng's boat had circled around to collect us from this far side of the raft, but had to contend with several smaller boats now manned by our pursuers.

"They're not giving up easily, are they?" I shouted to Holmes. "All this because we wanted to follow a sailor? Seems rather an over-reaction, don't you think?"

"I suspect that it has all rather got out of hand. These people aren't thanking them for setting fire to the place, as you can see."

I looked where he pointed. Angry grandmothers and housewives, shrieking children clutching at their baggy pyjamas, all were hurling abuse and anything heavy they could lay hands on at the thugs, now trapped on their own blazing raft. One by one the men were forced to jump off into the swirling water, and were swept away by the current. A few managed to transfer to one of the small boats manned by their cohorts.

With a crackling roar the roof of our raft collapsed into itself, sending sparks flying over other *attap* roofs around us. More small blazes started downwind, and it was clear that a serious fire was in the making. Daeng's gondola approached again. This time four of his boys used their long oars to fend off smaller boats, and to push the occupants overboard. Slowly Daeng came alongside. Holmes and I had already boarded when I saw a small child run into the middle of the blazing raft, clothes burning at the edges, her eyes wide with terror. Just as Daeng cast off and pushed away I leaped back aboard the raft, scooped up the child and threw her across the widening gap to Holmes, who made a perfect rugby catch.

There was no time for the boat to return safely. I shouted at Holmes to look for me downriver, and dove into the murky water. Overheated air trapped inside the massed bamboo floats expanded and burst the floor in a thousand small eruptions, disintegrating the raft in an instant. I stayed under the water for a while to allow burning debris to settle, then surfaced, lungs screaming for fresh air, only to find myself between boatloads of our pursuers.

Without taking time to breathe deeply I dove again, and navigated my way blindly underwater amongst the rotten piers and floating detritus of the river. When I could hold out no longer I cautiously surfaced again. This time I had come up between two huge bundles of bamboo trunks under the farthest downstream of the three piers, which was not yet burning. Between bundles the wooden platform had a space of a foot or so between joists supporting the platform and the water surface. Floating in this darkened space I could hear excited voices overhead. Looking out I saw small boats hunting for me further upstream. I would soon be discovered if I remained here.

Submerging once again under the distasteful water I struck out downstream again. As I surfaced my head struck a hard wooden object. I was entirely breathless by now, and could not even think of going under again. A figure leaned out above me and I flinched in preparation for a blow, which never came.

"Francois! *Francois!"*

I heard my name being called.

"Francois! Give me your hand. Quickly, before they see us. Climb in, *please*, Francois. I want to get away from here."

I looked up at the figure in the boat, and saw Miss Malee. She was wearing a broad straw hat like the boat-women do, and a simple sarong, but it was she. I reached up to grasp the gunnels of the small boat, which was laden with large baskets stacked amidships. As I hauled myself aboard I noticed another Siamese girl at the bow of the skiff, similarly attired. I recognised her from that first night aboard the *Sirdar*, when Miss Irene had brought three of her pupils aboard Lord Coledale's yacht with her.

"My sister, Saranya. She came with me, as I was too scared to come alone. I thought I simply must know what is going on with Miss Irene. No one will tell me anything. So I hired this boat and took these clothes from the maid's room."

"And very glad I am that you did, Miss Malee. Good evening, Miss Saranya! Not perhaps the entrance I should have chosen to make. But we had better get out of here. These fellows won't take kindly to your helping me."

"Get under the baskets. You're already a mess."

I did as told and surrounded myself with large baskets of oranges from the orchards along the river. The two girls slowly sculled the craft out into the stream, but only a few moments had passed before angry voices approached. I heard a rough voice demand to know who was in the boat, and what business they had there.

"Keep quiet!" whispered Miss Malee. "And don't move! There are four of them in the boat, all armed, so stay still, please."

Again the rough voice. This time the girls both answered together, that they were simply passing by with oranges for market, and if they were late their father would surely scold them. From my hiding place in the bilge, looking out through a chink between the baskets, I saw one of the Lascars with a cloth wound around his head. A vicious scar ran from the bridge of his nose down across his cheek to the jawbone, and one of his eyes was clouded over with the cataract. Suddenly this ferocious visage twisted into an ugly scowl, and I saw a long cutlass stabbing down towards me.

Miss Malee shrieked, which was just as well, for I too made an involuntary noise at the sudden realisation that I was about to die. But the sword did not pierce me through. I saw it withdrawn, with a green-orange sphere impaled on its point. Saying that it was lucky for two pretty young things that he had other matters to worry about, or else he would make it his business to entertain them, the Lascar pushed off and his oarsman paddled his boat away. Several other voices laughed in response as they faded away.

"I thought I was going to die of fright," said Miss Saranya. Like her sister she spoke excellent English, with the same musical intonation. "If you weren't my younger sister I should . . . You can come up now, Mister. They've gone."

I hauled myself out from under the baskets, and sat in the only place available - alongside Miss Malee on the aft seat. She handed me an oar, and asked if I was hurt. I was not, luckily, and told her so. I dared not look at her, but sitting there dripping wet, feeling her arm brush against mine as we sculled along in the shadows of the buildings, I felt a strange contentment.

"With a little luck, the Professor will be waiting downriver a little. Keep your eyes open, though I imagine he'll spot us first. He won't expect to see me in this boat, especially not with you two adventurous and foolhardy young ladies."

We sculled on in silence for a minute or two; then I heard a distinctive low whistle, our regular signal in such situations if all is well. I whistled the appropriate response. The cutter, carrying Holmes and Khun Daeng together with all the fighters, slid out from under the darkness of a high landing.

"Thank the Lord! That was *un mauvais quartd'heure* indeed. I thought you were done for, my friend. We were just about to risk going back."

Holmes was somewhat stunned when he saw that our rescuers were not simply passing boat-people, but Miss Malee and her sister.

"How on earth did this come about?" he asked Miss Malee. "No! Don't tell me, I can see it all. Never mind! Thank you sincerely for being there, but I hope you'll never mix yourselves up in these affairs again. As you see, considerable danger attends those who do, and I am quite sure M. Le Villard would never forgive himself if harm were to befall you."

She looked at me with a shy smile, and swore that she'd had enough excitement for a long time to come.

"Very well, then, Miss Malee. We have acquired a very young girl. She's very frightened and misses her mother, but it is far too dangerous to go back there now. Can you please take her for the evening, look after her, and tell her we'll get her back to her mother tomorrow. Now, le Villard, if you've done with your swimming, I suggest you climb in here, and pass the young lady across to Miss Malee."

I did so, and at Holmes's instructions one of Daeng's men joined them in the fruit-laden boat.

"We'll leave this one man with you. He can row you safely down to the Oriental Pier. He'll moor the boat there, and tomorrow we can arrange to return that as well. Both of you must promise that you will go home immediately, and say nothing of this matter to anyone. Miss Irene's life may depend on it. Have I your word?"

"Yes, sir, you have our promise," said Miss Saranya in a resolute voice, as the two young Siamese ladies comforted the sobbing Chinese child.

"Miss Malee," said I, as our two boats drew apart. "I don't know how to thank you. You may very well have saved my life tonight."

"Bring Miss Irene back safely, and solve the mystery which troubles her. If you can do that, I should then be in your debt."

I reflected, as their boat disappeared into the gloom, that she had called me 'Francois' when I first surfaced. I had not imagined that she could even recall my Christian name, let alone in a crisis such as that. Perhaps, I thought, it is possible that . . ! But no, it could not be!

"Le Villard! Hello, old fellow!"

It was Holmes, shaking my shoulder.

"Are you all right? Nasty little incident, that. But we have not lost the trail entirely. When Khun Daeng picked me up I was able to use my telescope. The boat with Miss Irene disappeared not more than ten minutes ago into that large canal over there. We approached it from downstream last time, but that is the canal where *Sia* Ah Foo has his rice *godown*."

"And you think . . ?"

"It's the only lead we have left. Even with four oarsmen we should have no chance of catching up with them. Somehow I doubt that the arrangements at the opium den will be repeated for our benefit tomorrow, after tonight's imbroglio."

I looked back at the inferno on the riverside. Through blazing doorways I saw, in house after house, family valuables being stowed and sealed in the firewell set in each floor as the occupants fled before the surging flames could engulf them. The fire spread through the densely packed shophouses and thatched boathouses with remarkable rapidity, considering the deluge of the previous evening's monsoon rains.

"Yes, I see what you mean," I said. *"Vogue la galère!"*

The men obviously knew of the plan already, for without being instructed they set a course for the mouth of the canal across the river, rowing as powerfully as they were able. I cleaned and tested my revolver during the trip across the river, in case the dunking in river water had jammed the mechanism. In less than ten minutes we gained the opposite bank, and another ten sufficed to reach up the broad canal as far as the rice *godown* where we had visited *Sia* Ah Foo, months before. Holmes had scanned ahead of us continually with his eyeglass, but saw no sign of our quarry. The sounds of the night seemed amplified in the otherwise quiet darkness - the background hum of hundreds of crickets and the river-bank frogs; the occasional *to-kae* of the salamander, repeated three times; the slap of the water against the hull, and unseen rustlings in the reeds.

At first it seemed that we must be mistaken. There was no small boat at the jetty in front of the *godown,* and seemingly no place where it could lie concealed from our view. It was Daeng, standing in the bow, who noticed the narrow slipway at the far end of the jetty, just wide and long enough for the boat.

We crept ashore as quietly as possible and headed towards the closest entrance to the *godown*. The mass of the building loomed over us in the feeble moonlight, relieved only by a gleam of light from a row of three windows on the second floor, further down the building. Suddenly Daeng raised his hand and whispered to two of his boys in Siamese. They slid away into the darkness and in a moment we heard a muffled cry, followed by a thudding noise as of an inert body collapsing.

"*Yarm*! Sentry! Taken care of now. We can go on."

The two Siamese joined us again as we turned the corner, coming to a halt in front of the locked main door of the *godown*. Set in the vast door was a guard's door, also locked. Holmes had the lock open in seconds, it being a very old lock. This impressed the Siamese no end, but Holmes simply opened the door and we passed through in single file.

We were in that cavernous space, now silent, where I had feared attack by *Sia* Ah Foo's coolies, with their wicked hooks. I was glad we had Khun Daeng with us, even though we had agreed to do everything possible to avoid combat of any kind. We ran along the deserted aisle between towering piles of rice-sacks.

As we passed out of the first of the *godown* buildings, and into the second, we spotted the source of light. It came from a mezzanine floor of offices, fronted by a raised wooden gangway. A pair of stairs at either end of this gave access to the offices. Behind the shuttered door of one of the central offices a shadow passed back and forth in front of the lamp, and another seated at a desk raised an arm as though drinking. The seated silhouette clearly showed the outline of a cap, such as sailors commonly wear. Holmes looked at me, and nodded.

Using signals, we divided into two parties and crept up the stairways.

Hugging the walls, we closed in on the door where shadows moved in front of the lamp. At a signal from Holmes, we kicked in the door and rushed through with revolvers in our hands, only to pull up in surprise.

Two elderly Chinese were the only occupants, playing at checkers on the desk, with a lamp hung on the wall behind them. The old boy at the desk held a glass of Chinese liquor in one hand. The other old fellow stopped pacing and looked at us from cunning eyes; tipped back on his head was the sailor's hat worn earlier by Irene Adler.

"We've been had, Holmes!" I cried.

"Irene Adler!" he exclaimed, ignoring the old gentlemen. "Ever the quick mind - but we must catch them, le Villard. Down to *Sia* Ah Foo's office; it's the fastest way to the jetty."

As we scrambled back down the stairs an alien noise broke into the noises of the tropical night. Above the croaking of the different frogs and the insistent, high-pitched vibrato of crickets, cutting through the slapping of the water against the canal banks I heard the wheezing and dull throbbing of an engine gathering steam. It was neither close nor loud enough to be the rice-mill engine.

"*Sia* Ah Foo's steam pinnace!" I exclaimed, remembering the trim launch that had collected us from our hotel so long before. "He's got that tucked away somewhere. It looked as though it would have a good turn of speed, as well."

Holmes was in the lead as we dashed through the otherwise deserted *godown*, heading for the dusty office where we had had tea with *Sia* Ah Foo. The door was locked, but not strong, and Daeng soon had it splintered. On the other side was the door giving on to the pier, but this turned out to be a far stouter affair.

"No time for niceties." Holmes stepped back into the doorway. "Shoot the lock off."

I took careful aim with my pistol and fired. The first shot damaged the door, but not enough to clear the lock. I fired again. This time the lock flew out of the door, and the way was clear. We rushed through, followed by the Siamese fighters. At the very farthest end of the jetty closest to the river a pinnace steamed out from a small canal hidden amongst the overhanging trees. We had noticed nothing there as we approached the *godown*, but someone must have been watching us all the time.

Holmes pulled out his telescope. Dim moonlight barely penetrated the branches of the rain-trees overhanging the canal on both banks, so that only the centre of the waterway was illuminated. Before long I could not make out the pinnace at all.

"It's them all right. I can see Irene Adler, now that her hair is free. I think *Sia* Ah Foo is in the stern, and the two Chinamen. There is another figure slumped down. To the boat! But we'll let them think we've missed them. Several minutes head start, I think."

"Very sporting of you, I'm sure. But we'll never catch up with them even now, Holmes," I cried. "Not even with four men on the oars."

"I don't think we need worry about that, my friend. We know just where they're going. Neither *Sia* Ah Foo nor Irene Adler are aware that we know about the *Jade Treasure*."

I had almost forgotten the floating house of pleasure, with its private suite aft where *Sia* Ah Foo sometimes entertained guests.

"So long as we keep them in sight we may still come upon them with the element of surprise. I am most curious as to why it was so important to prevent anyone following Irene Adler on her little masquerade."

Holmes and I boarded the cutter and our Siamese friends prepared themselves to row.

"It's not going to be as easy as crossing over. There's another storm about to hit us."

The calm waters began to ruffle a little. Behind the trees lining the shore a bank of dark clouds was rapidly covering the stars, and then the half moon. We were plunged into darkness and then chaos as the front hit us. These monsoon storms were a nightly event at this time of year, so it was not unexpected. I still didn't like the idea of being out in the middle of the river when the lightning began.

Holmes motioned to Daeng, and the boat pulled away from the jetty. Daeng's boys bent to their oars, chanting softly in unison. It was rough going, with the surface of the wide canal roiled to froth by the howling wind that had hit with the rain squall.

The steam pinnace gradually pulled away from us until I could no longer see the glow of her small stack in the darkness. Holmes kept the telescope to his eye so as not to lose sight of the pinnace for an instant.

Sia Ah Foo's launch passed out of the mouth of the canal, and turned slightly upstream, judging by the direction of Holmes's aluminium eyeglass.

"Good, heading in just the direction I expected, and unaware we're still behind them, I think."

Once or twice I thought I saw the dark shape of a boat blocking a distant light from the other shore. But with the naked eye it was impossible to be sure. Our crew pulled strongly, but if we had not known where they were headed we should have lost them, even with Holmes's telescope. The very air became saturated with mist and spray.

Suddenly, out of the white fog of this maelstrom loomed the bow of a large steamer. I shouted to alert the straining crew, but my shout was drowned by the deep moan of a ship's horn that seemed to come from directly overhead. The Siamese looked terror-struck, but Daeng shouted at them. They all dug deeply with their oars, and pulled the boat ten yards further in a moment.

It was enough. The bow wave of the huge ship lifted our stern high, and the surge pushed us out of the way of the wall of barnacled hull-plates that rushed by us.

"I hope *Sia* Ah Foo's boat is faring better than ours; Irene Adler is aboard," remarked Holmes, in the momentary lull as the mass of the ship shielded us from the fury of the storm.

He caught my sideways glance, and laughed.

"Oh, we always seem to survive, somehow, you and I. But we don't know who is piloting that boat."

We caught sight of lighted buildings as we approached the opposite shoreline, and turned upstream. Before long the distinctive shape of the sternwheeler loomed through the darkness, with a few ports dimly lit here and there. Lamps were lit in the aft saloon. There was no sign of *Sia* Ah Foo's steam-pinnace until we were close enough for Holmes's eyeglass.

"It's there, all right. Tucked in under the bow. No one aboard, luckily. There's one other launch tied up to her."

Holmes continued in a low voice.

"Two Chinamen on the aft deck, two in the deckhouse, at least one on the foredeck. We'll leave Daeng and his boys in *Sia* Ah Foo's boat while we make our way to the stern."

He turned to Daeng, and spoke in Siamese.

"Give us three minutes. Keep quiet, and make your way aft as soon as you toss their men over. Leave someone at the bow. If any try to come aboard again, shoot."

Everything went as planned. The Chinamen were not expecting any trouble in the middle of the river, in this howling electrical storm. Lightning had become almost constant. Flashing spears rent the darkness, loud clashes of thunder following almost instantly. The noise covered our movements, and our sudden appearance from each end of the stern paddle-wheel caught the two Chinamen by surprise.

They had no time to reach for their knives before Holmes and I were rushing at them, and both reverted to Siamese kick-boxing to defend themselves. We had worked on our *baritsu* techniques in practise, finding effective ways to defeat all the standard moves. This now stood us in good stead. Within seconds we had disembarked them both, taking their knives before shoving them overboard.

We stood at the gunnels for a moment with our revolvers sighted on the Chinamen, to make sure they swam away from the stern-wheeler and not to the steam pinnace. Satisfied, we turned to the aft cabin just as Daeng and two of his boys ran up the side decks, crouching as they passed lighted ports. We hadn't heard a thing, but they seemed to have disposed of their assigned Chinamen without difficulty.

A loud report came from close by, a sharper, more explosive sound than the crackling and rumbling of the storm. A bright flash lit the windows of the aft saloon.

Holmes was closest. He rushed to the door set in the aft bulkhead of the vessel and wrenched it open. I was at his heels, revolver in hand, as we burst into the aft saloon. We were greeted by a strange tableau.

On a silk rug on the floor, in a crimson pool of his own blood, lay *Sia* Ah Foo. As the door burst open we'd had time to see a revolver still clattering to the teakwood floor next to the rug, but not where it came from.

The light was dim. Holmes and I covered all of the room between us with our pistols before we were satisfied there would be no further shots. We lowered our guns, put them away, and surveyed the remaining occupants of the room.

Irene Adler stood beside her husband Godfrey Norton, who was slumped in an ornate carved and gilded armchair, a hopeless expression on his blank features. On the other side of the stateroom the tall figure of Lord Coledale, and beside him his black-bearded aide, Quiney.

Cowering behind the open door of the passage leading forward was a tall Chinese girl, dressed in a scarlet satin *cheong-sam* with the side split to the top of the thigh. Her long black hair almost swept the floor as she crouched in fear.

Quiney was first to move. Taking a purse from his vest pocket, he went to the Chinese girl, gave her a few *ticals*, and sent her out to wait in their launch. Holmes made no objection. He bent down and confirmed that *Sia* Ah Foo was beyond help. Quiney returned and said a few words in his lordship's ear.

"Rather a meeting of old friends, isn't it?" said Holmes softly. He looked from the Nortons to Lord Coledale and his aide. "I think an explanation is in order, don't you? Who's first."

Again, it was Quiney who spoke.

"Hate to say it against a fellow Englishman, but I'm afraid our lawyer friend here got into a drunken argument with the old Chinese fellow. Pulled a gun from his waistband. Before any of us could do a thing about it, he'd potted the old chap."

Irene Adler looked up at him with an expression of pure hate. But she didn't dispute his account. Norton merely sat in a dazed condition, not seeming to fully comprehend the situation.

"The thing is, what are we all going to do about it?" said Lord Coledale. "None of us needs the scandal."

"Yes, this vessel does have a rather notorious reputation, Lord Coledale. I can see why you'd want to remain uninvolved," replied Holmes. "Hoping to move off the back-benches and join the cabinet in the next government, I believe?"

"Surely, Professor, a little dalliance with a local girl is of no interest to constituents half a world away? And of what interest is it to a mere Professor and grave-robber anyway?"

The arrogant attitude of centuries of privilege was only partly hidden by the smiling condescension of his lordship's voice. Holmes glanced up sharply at the words, and smiled as he replied.

"If it were, indeed, a girl! Rather tall for an Asian girl, I thought?"

Lord Coledale was a little abashed by that, but kept his temper as he answered.

"If a little diversity in one's choice of particular friends were to disqualify an Englishman from high office, my good Professor, I doubt that Parliament should ever be able to form a quorum to pass legislation."

Taking a pair of white gloves from his pocket he proceeded to work his delicate hands into them, first handing his silver-headed ebony cane to Quiney to hold while he did so.

"But seriously, what are we to do with *Sia* Ah Foo here, and with Norton?"

"Mr. Norton is wanted for questioning by Chief Inspector Sheriff in connection with another murder investigation," said Holmes, "and for his own protection it would be best if he surrendered himself. That way the British Resident can more easily look after his interests."

"I think not," said Quiney. "I don't know about this other case, but his lordship will not stand by and see an Englishman hung for the shooting of a bloody Chinaman, even one who's richer than God."

A tiny over-and-under double barrelled Derringer pistol appeared in his hand.

"I hate to disagree with an academic, Professor, but I think this mess needs clearing up here and now. No one needs know about this. You've driven the guards off, or you wouldn't be here. The girl won't say a word."

"Leaving us with a dead body!" said I.

"Exactly. Fortunately, that poses no problem either. If you two gentlemen will simply pick him up, while I open this door wide, he can go over the side.

Toss the rug after him, and no one will be any the wiser."

We hesitated.

"Don't think I won't shoot, gentlemen. My job is to protect his lordship's interests, at all times, regardless of the situation. I take my responsibilities seriously."

He bent and picked up the revolver from beside *Sia* Ah Foo's body. He exchanged it for the derringer, and oversaw Holmes and I as we rolled *Sia* Ah Foo in the rug and tossed the bundle overboard into the swirling river. In seconds it had disappeared from view, and all evidence of the shooting with it.

Quiney called out to Lord Coledale.

"I should board the launch if I were you, my lord."

Coledale tucked his stick under his arm, and strolled out onto the after deck. "Well done, Quiney! Efficiency itself, as always! Admirable!"

He stepped down into his steam-launch and calmly took a seat, facing his companion in the scarlet silk dress.

Quiney turned back to Norton.

"You must let us get you out of Siam, my man, or this place will be the death of you," he said. "We'll take you downriver in our launch. After that you're on your own."

For the first time Norton paid attention to the proceedings. He looked at his wife, who gave him a despairing look, and said, "Do as he says, Godfrey. It's your only chance - you know that. You know where to contact me, once you're safely away."

She stood, and turned her head away as Norton exited the door. I saw tears in her eyes, but she brushed them away immediately. In her sailor's outfit, golden hair tumbling around her shoulders, Irene Adler looked defeated and vulnerable.

Quiney's black-bearded visage appeared at the doorway. He held the revolver loosely at his side.

"I really don't think there is any need to mention this to the Chief Inspector, Professor. We'll simply deny it ever happened, and Mrs. Norton will corroborate our version." He waited a moment to give Irene Adler a chance to dispute this. She didn't even look at him. "So, you see, it is as I say."

He turned and walked to the launch, boarded and took the helm. With a hiss of steam the boat pulled away from the stern-wheeler, and was soon lost in the darkness downstream. Norton didn't turn around at all. Something seemed out of rights about the whole affair, to say the least.

Holmes had gone back inside the saloon and was speaking softly to Irene Adler, saying that we, too, must get away from *Sia* Ah Foo's boat. She nodded, and took his elbow as he steered her towards the door to the aft deck.

We all found seats in the gondola, and were rowed downstream to the Oriental. There we took our leave of Daeng and his boys, after pressing some payment on them, and paid off the gondola. We saw to it that Mrs. Norton was safe in a room next to ours. She hadn't said a word all the way down-river. Bidding her good-night, we returned to our sitting rooms.

Before Holmes went into his bedroom he said, "Something's bothering me, le Villard. I can't quite put my finger on it, but we've missed something here."

"Perhaps if you sleep on it, Holmes."

"That's just it! Until I *can* put my finger on it, I shan't be able to sleep."

The door closed behind him, but shortly, creeping through the louvers and under the door, came wisps of the aromatic pipe tobacco favoured by Holmes. I went to bed, but woke when I heard noises in our sitting-room.

Grasping my revolver, I slipped out of bed and crept over behind the door. Standing on my toes and looking down through the slats in the louvers I had a restricted view of the room, dimly lit by the first rays of dawn. An old Chinaman, still wearing a flat-topped split-bamboo hat, was sprawled at his leisure in one of our wicker lounge chairs.

From my angle I could see a pool of water spreading on the wood floor around him. I was just at the point of throwing the door open and accosting the intruding old fellow when he did something which caused me to change my mind, and smile. He reached over and lit one of Holmes's pipes, using a phosphor from the box on the side table. It was all too familiar.

Opening the door wide, I lowered my revolver and stepped into the sitting-room.

"You've been abroad in this rain, I gather?" said I.

"Yes, I have," replied Holmes, after a deep pull on his black pipe. He exhaled slowly, then continued.

"In disguise, as you see! I thought something rang false about the fundamental relations we assumed last night - between Norton and others in particular. I found myself wishing I'd looked around a little more at *Sia* Ah Foo's *godown*."

"So you went back, disguised as an old Chinaman. Of course! What did you find, or is that a secret, too."

I was more than a little disappointed that he had gone by himself, without waking me.

"It seemed such an easy mission, as indeed it was, once I gathered the garb. The old fellows must have fled entirely. No alarm has been raised at the *godown* as yet, so I was able to enter easily as before. But I was not prepared for what I found where Norton had been hidden away since the bombing."

Holmes drew deeply at the stem of his pipe, savouring the smoke after the night's work.

"Clean bedding, and a lamp, le Villard. Good liquor, and plenty of it; imported foods; fine books - though limited in number - and a few recent periodicals. And most importantly, the only lock on the door was on the inside. It would keep others out, but could not lock him in."

"So he was there of his own free choice," I said, "and was an honoured guest. That's an interesting turnabout. What do you make of it, then?"

"Well, we do know that Norton and *Sia* Ah Foo had dealings before all this began. Perhaps they were more deeply involved than we guessed."

"Could Norton have been the bomber, acting on behalf of the Chinese through *Sia* Ah Foo?"

"I had thought of the possibility," replied Holmes.

"And that means Irene Adler knew where he was - in fact, was sent for by him. That explains the bag. All the foods and drink, the books and so forth."

"What it doesn't explain is why Norton would shoot the man who has been providing him with a sanctuary, and did not appear to be at odds with him until that moment."

"Little wonder she said nothing at all last night!" I said. "She wouldn't want to give anything away."

"Yes. I shall have a few words with Mrs. Norton when she wakes."

We both retired, again, for an hour or two of sleep.

22nd September 1893
Bangkok, Siam
Mrs. Norton appeared at our door at eight. She had already sent to her hotel for a change of clothes, and had resumed her customary appearance. Miss Malee arrived at nine with her sister and the small Chinese girl.

After arranging with Daeng to return the child safely to her mother - and to make certain she *was* the real mother - Holmes and I joined Miss Malee, Miss Saranya, and Mrs. Norton on the terrace by the river. Holmes ordered breakfast for all, and nothing was said of the events of the previous day and night.

It was doubtful if Irene Adler - I find it difficult to refer to her otherwise - even knew of Miss Malee's part in those events. After a delightful breakfast under clear skies our Siamese guests departed for lessons or home. We sat on with Irene Adler.

"You must think I'm involved in all this. You mustn't, oh please! You mustn't! I just had to do what I could to help Godfrey. He's so helpless, and he doesn't know what's going on these days either. If only he'd stay away from the gin. Then he could resist everything else."

"He's wanted for questioning, you know," said Holmes. For murder and robbery, and possibly for terrorist plotting."

"And I'm the only one who doesn't believe he did *any* of it. Oh! I could just scream with the frustration of it all."

"Irene. Miss Adler," said Holmes. "Why don't you tell us all about it. Perhaps we can help. If you wait until you think you have no choice, it may be too late to do anything. I know you haven't told us everything."

"I respect your abilities, Mr. Holmes, and believe me, if I thought that you were able to help, I should ask you again. I know I asked you to find out what demon was pursuing Godfrey. Now I know; it is the same one as before. The reason we are in this corner of the world in the first place was to get away from them."

She would say no more. Holmes told her that he had a responsibility to report his encounter with Norton, and knowledge of his plans, to Chief Inspector Sheriff.

"Oh! Please don't, Mr. Holmes. Godfrey is a foolish man, and a weak man. But he didn't do these things. I swear it! Wait until he contacts me. He will, you know. We have a way. Then, I will bring him to you, and he can tell you the whole tale, from the beginning so long ago."

Holmes thought about this for a moment.

"Go back to your hotel, and stay there. If he contacts you, do not go alone. You must promise me that you will send for me immediately. Is that agreed?"

"Yes, and thank you. I couldn't explain it all anyway, not so that it makes any sense. Godfrey is a lawyer. He can make complex things seem simple when he explains them."

"Most lawyers spend their hours - billable, mind you - making simple things seem complex, Miss Adler. Very well, but I suggest you remain close to your room, and send for us if you have any cause for alarm."

"Thank you, Mr. Holmes. For not reporting this. I hope it doesn't get you onto any trouble."

"Thank *you* for being frank. Now we must get along. Le Villard and I have matters to attend to."

Irene Adler left us with her head high, in the carriage Holmes had summoned, to await a message from her husband.

"I take it you have considered this course of action carefully, Holmes," I enquired. "Are you so confident that she is not herself involved in some conspiracy?"

"That thought has also crossed my mind. At times one must trust one's judgement. This is such a time, and I made my decision. Besides, I had already decided on that course of action, even before she asked. Once Sheriff is involved in this we may have our freedom limited."

Next Holmes and I went to the General Adviser's house - greeted Tashi and Rinzing as usual - and discussed the political situation with him. At one point Rolin mentioned reports of a serious fire on the waterfront last night, thought to be arson. The populace was increasingly restive, according to Rolin, and calm would not prevail until an agreement was signed limiting French aggression, with some form of guarantee from the British and other powers. We talked of progress in these matters.

Later in the day we repaired to the dock area around *Sirdar*'s mooring and asked some discreet questions, prompting answers with a few coins. We found that on the previous evening at around seven o'clock the tall Chinese 'girl' in the red silk dress had gone aboard the yacht. Around half an hour later the steam-launch had departed, headed upriver. No one noticed who was aboard.

"So, Lord Coledale took his own company," I said. "That was not the reason he was there, after all."

"On the contrary, le Villard. I think that she- or rather, *he* - saw Norton there some time recently, on the *Jade Treasure*, and mentioned it to Coledale and Quiney. That was the reason they were waiting for *Sia* Ah Foo. They knew he was shielding Norton."

"But why? Why is it so important to find Norton, and to rescue him from *Sia* Ah Foo? Why cover up the murder?"

"That's what we must find out. Give Irene Adler a day or so, and I shall press her for some answers. Right now she has been through a great deal, and I don't want her running off. A little patience is called for."

5th August 1893
Bangkok, Siam
We received an invitation from Chief Inspector Sheriff to call on him at his office at Police Headquarters.

"Probably wants to read us the law in regard to obstruction of justice, being an accomplice after the fact, and sundry other transgressions of which we are, unfortunately, only too guilty," said Holmes. "I suppose we just have to put the best face on it that we can. Let's go!"

But when we arrived, Sheriff greeted us cordially. No mention was made of the disappearance of *Sia* Ah Foo, nor of Godfrey Norton. Once we had had the unavoidable tea the Chief Inspector came immediately to the point.

"I've just - early this morning in fact - received news of a body found dumped in one of the *klongs*. Thought to be a murder of jealousy of some kind. No address or next of kin so it was taken to *Wat* Saket. One of the places the Siamese take unclaimed corpses, you know. Over by the Golden Mount. Well, they found two strange things.

"Although dressed as a girl, it turned out to be a young man. All the essential tackle. So the attendant went through the clothing more carefully. The stitching of the hem had been unpicked for a couple of inches, and a calling card was slipped into the hem."

"Any description of the dress?" asked Holmes.

"Chinese style; red silk or something shiny, according to the messenger from *Wat* Saket. They let us know about anything out of the ordinary, and we make a nice annual contribution."

"And the card?"

"As you say, the card. They sent it on here."

The Chief Inspector produced a stained white pasteboard card on which the engraved lettering was elegantly plain. The name engraved was that of Lord Coledale.

"What do you make of that, Professor?"

"Have you asked Lord Coledale? What is his explanation?"

"Difficult to say. You see, his yacht crossed the bar and left Siam on the high tide at first light. Clearance documents show his next stop as Colombo."

"Is it far to this *Wat* Saket, Chief Inspector?"

"Not terribly, but it may be a little late if inspecting the body was on your mind."

"I don't quite follow."

"We'll see. Let's go!"

The police chief snatched his cap from a coat-tree as he passed. Within minutes we were in his carriage, rumbling through the streets with a clanging bell warning the crowds out of out way. Ten minutes later we crunched to a halt alongside a tall artificial mountain capped with a golden spire. Walking around the base of this we came to several passageways running through the thick base of the crenellated brick wall surrounding a large open yard. A cluster of buildings pierced by arched doors gave onto the central yard.

We had seen similar sights in Tibet and other places, but it still came as a shock, though the stench in the air and Sheriff's comments had prepared us for something of this nature.

"Interesting sight, this. Hope you've strong stomachs. You did ask!"

Huge, grotesquely ugly vultures strutted around the dusty yard, quarrelling and squabbling viciously over scraps of flesh being sliced from human bodies by the attendant and tossed to his favourites. Others contented themselves with tearing away at the few corpses scattered around the yard, which already had great chunks of flesh missing.

"This is the way bodies are disposed of when no one comes forward to pay for the necessary rites for cremation. That's why our body was brought here. It will stay a few days, and if no one claims it, that's what will happen. When they come out of water they don't keep 'em around for long. Thought it might have been out there already."

He cocked a thumb over his shoulder at the grisly scene outside. But, I reflected, I suppose it's no more disrespectful than allowing worms to riddle our rotting corpses, as is our fashion. Our European way just seems neater, really.

"Let's take a look. Hopefully it's *not* out in the yard already."

He tracked down an attendant, who soon ushered us past several altars, each decked with flower garlands and joss sticks. In a distant corner of this temple of the dead a choir chanted, and a bell was rung in sad cadences. A most melancholy atmosphere pervaded the place, as though time had stopped for the living as well as the dead. Our footsteps echoed on the tiled floors as we followed the attendant around a cloister and into the presence of the abbot of the temple.

He and the Chief Inspector evidently knew one another; the abbot gladly accepted the gift of several packs of English cigarettes, which Sheriff placed on his tray, along with a few other small offerings of esteem.

The two men spoke for some moments in Siamese, but their voices were so low, and their heads so close together, that we had no idea what was said.

"He's arranged for us to see the body. Let's go!"

Backing respectfully out of the presence of the abbot, we were escorted by one of the abbot's attendants to a bare brick-walled chamber with a vaulted ceiling, set in the walls of the temple at the base of the man-made mountain. On brick platforms lining the walls of the long chamber were the bodies of the unwanted dead, taking their last rest in this incense-filled chamber.

We choked at the cloying mixture of incense and decay, but managed to carry on. On a platform thankfully near to the door, covered by a white cloth, lay the corpse of the 'girl' who had accompanied Lord Coledale to *Sia* Ah Foo's pleasure boat that night. The features, with the broad, high cheekbones, and the straight nose, were distinctively recognisable.

Neither Holmes nor I made any sign of recognition, however. Our reason for coming was soon explained to Sheriff's satisfaction.

"What was the cause of death, so far as the Siamese are concerned?" asked Holmes. "May I?" he asked. "I shouldn't like to cause distress, or be disrespectful."

"Not a problem, Professor. I've already explained. My sergeant has taken a look. His report says blow with a blunt instrument. He also puts time of death as sometime last night, but not later than three in the morning. I've found he's usually pretty accurate, given this blasted heat."

Holmes examined the head and neck, rotating the head loosely on the palm of his hand.

"There's been a blow to the head, but I think that was sustained after death. Given that *rigor mortis* would have set in by now, I should say the immediate cause of death was a broken neck. Very expertly twisted, severing the spinal cord and rupturing the trachea. Instant death! It's possible the blow to the head was caused when the body was thrown into the canal."

"Any thoughts, Professor?"

"Only that his lordship's departure seems a little suspicious, given the card in the victim's clothing."

"Well, not exactly. The ship's papers were filled out several days ago. His departure was planned for."

"Ah! Can we find out exactly when the papers were filed?"

"Of course. A simple query at the Harbour Master's office."

"Nothing more to do here, except for one thing. Could we find out what it costs to arrange a cremation for this poor unfortunate? I'll pay the bill, if you can sort out the details."

"I should imagine we can take care of that right here and now," replied Sheriff.

The three of us sat in a quiet side-chamber while we awaited the completion of these arrangements.

"So, what am I supposed to do?" asked Sheriff. "Coledale is, after all, an hereditary peer. I've asked about. There was a girl - well . . . someone matching this description, seen going aboard the yacht several times in the past few days. Usually in the late evening, and seen leaving early the next morning.

"So you see, there are numerous occasions when she could have been given - or taken, I suppose - Coledale's card, and tucked it away for safekeeping. Then there's the timing. We don't know when the body was dumped. Could be before or after the yacht's departure. Either way, it's a close run thing. How do you see it, Professor? If I put out a warrant and have the yacht stopped, it's my career if I'm wrong."

"And maybe even if you're right, but can't make a charge stick," replied Holmes.

"Don't think I haven't thought of that too, Professor."

"Frankly, Chief Inspector?"

"Yes, sir! Might as well hear it said."

"There is no choice for you. You don't stand a chance if you issue a warrant. And I suspect he will neither forget nor forgive if you attempt to blot his character publicly. Until you can produce a credible witness - and I stress the word credible - placing Coledale, or Quiney I suppose, with the victim, and within the time span of the murder, I should keep silent . . . and keep on investigating!"

"Does that mean you also suspect Coledale of involvement in this . . . murder?

"I have reason to believe that this death would be convenient for his lordship."

"This sounds like something else I should know about, but don't. Too many mysteries here of late. There's a rumour that *farangs* started this waterfront fire the other night. And the Chinese are saying that *Sia* Ah Foo has disappeared. Simply vanished, without a word. And somehow *farangs* are getting the blame for that as well.

"But can *I* find out about any of it? The answer is, yes of course! When it's too damned late to do anything, as always. This is a very frustrating place for a policeman, Professor Sigerson. Everybody seeks his own redress for wrongs. We just get to pick up the bodies afterwards."

The policeman straightened his shoulders, lifted his chin, and said, "Some of the bodies."

We left the necropolis of Bangkok, and gratefully breathed the air of the outside world.

3rd October 1893
Bangkok, Siam

Rolin provided us a report on a daily basis, as and when it was convenient for us all. Our investigations were carried on, but with little progress. The diplomatic tussle between the French - now personified by Le Myre de Vilers and Pavie - and the Siamese - in the person of the Prince supported by Rolin - moved closer to a conclusion. This we desired most strongly, as once a satisfactory agreement was entered into, assuring Siam's territorial integrity, we should be free to leave. The General Adviser would revert to implementation of internal reforms, his role no longer sufficiently pivotal to warrant his assassination.

In the last week of September de Vilers presented new proposals for the Treaty and Convention - not yet acceptable to Siam, but more nearly so than the previous versions. Rolin worked on counter-proposals, but within days de Vilers presented a third version, containing two new and totally unacceptable clauses. The General Adviser met with the Prince and it was agreed that in his meeting with de Vilers the following day, Prince Ranawongse should execute the terms of the Ultimatum, and nothing more. If the Siamese modifications were accepted, the Prince should sign the Treaty, but if de Vilers carried out his threat to leave Prince Ranawongse would not sign the Convention.

The meeting between the French Plenipotentiary and the Siamese Foreign Minister was set for the morning of the last day of the month, Sunday. The General Adviser was dismayed that the meeting, which he had expected to be brief, carried on all morning. When he returned to the Ministry after lunch de Vilers had left. The Treaty had been signed, with several modifications accepted but not all.

But the Prince had signed the Convention without amendment. The General Adviser was dismayed at this, as the Convention contained several clauses quite contrary to Siam's interests. He put it down to the unfortunate combination of the Siamese government allowing the Foreign Minister to negotiate single-handedly with three unscrupulous and bullying French advocates of colonial expansion, and the protracted and wearying round of negotiations that had worn the Prince down. De Vilers had threatened to depart without the two acts having been signed, and thus precipitate a break of relations with renewed violence. Fearful of this outcome, said Rolin, the Prince had signed the agreements.

For Holmes and I, however, the important fact was that the Agreement was at last in place. With the English now taking a more assertive position, it was unlikely that the French would now be able to move easily towards the goal of the powerful faction of colonialists - a French Protectorate over Siam. This, Holmes and I had agreed, was the point at which we could safely leave Rolin to his own devices. We should soon be free at last to make our way back to Europe.

DAY EIGHT

APRIL 12TH 1894

CHAPTER L

I WAS RUDELY AWAKENED by loud reports, coming from our sitting-room below. I hastily put aside the Journal that I'd been reading when I fell asleep, slipped my pistol into the pocket of my dressing-gown, and cautiously descended the stairs, alert for any eventuality. I listened for a moment at the door to our sitting room but could hear only the low murmur of voices, which I recognised as belonging to my two friends.

Still keeping my finger on the trigger of my concealed revolver, I slowly turned the knob and pushed the door. A remarkable sight greeted me. It was apparently snowing inside. The air was full of swirling white flakes, floating as lightly as feathers settling. Then, as first le Villard, and then Holmes, turned towards me, I realised that the flakes *were*, in fact, white feathers.

My companions were seated at Holmes's laboratory bench, with two pistols lying in front of them. The sharp tang of firearms assailed my nostrils, and curling wisps of smoke hung in the air amongst the swirling down and feathers.

"Good morning, Watson. I rather thought we might wake you, but I was about to do so anyway. There's coffee on the table."

I let go of the pistol in my pocket, mumbled a rather surly 'Good Morning' - for I had been woken from a deep, dreamless sleep - and poured myself a cup. A few sips of coffee woke me sufficiently to enquire just what, exactly, was going on.

"No cause for alarm, Watson. Parker was dead when we caught up with him. I say, le Villard, why don't you tell Watson what happened, as I need my fullest concentration here?"

So saying, Holmes turned back to his powerful microscope, and peered intently through the brass eyepiece, making a few delicate adjustments to the knurled-brass focusing screw with his long, sensitive fingers. I glanced at the object on the glass slide beneath the lenses, and saw a soft-nosed bullet, somewhat mushroomed out at what had once been its point.

A piece of paper lay in front of each of the pistols, and on each were two bullets, not deformed as was the first. To one side was a third piece of paper, on which lay a mushroomed-out slug, almost identical to the one Holmes had under his microscope.

"Holmes felt that Parker was our best remaining lead - for various reasons - so we hastened to the opium den, only to find that he had already left.

Wiggins's boy was nowhere to be seen, and nobody nearby could furnish any leads. We waited for fifteen minutes, not having any alternative course of action to follow, at the end of which the boy returned, breathless from running.

"He'd trailed Parker back to his rooms. Luckily this time Parker went home on foot, and was far gone with drink and opium, so Wiggins's boy had no problem keeping him in sight without alarming him. As soon as he saw Parker go into his lodgings in Bow Street he rushed back to inform us.

"Unfortunately for Parker, Moran must have been considerably more alert, and seen that Parker had been tracked back to his hideout. We already know that Colonel Moran is ruthless; he must have shot Parker as he entered the room, and then escaped out the back entrance, taking any possessions he had. When we arrived the front door was slightly ajar, as the drunken Parker had left it, and we found him slumped in the doorway to his room. This bullet had penetrated his forehead, and exited through the side of his neck, causing massive damage along the way.

"Holmes and I quickly examined the room for traces of Moran, pocketed the fatal bullet, and let ourselves out, locking the door behind us. Thanks to this fog, and the lateness of the hour, I think we got away unseen."

Holmes now uttered an exclamation of evident satisfaction, and sat back from the microscope.

"*Voilà!* Your point is well taken, le Villard. They are indeed identical, both in manufacture and subsequent markings."

Holmes turned at last to me, while le Villard took his place at the microscope. "I wanted to keep news of Parker's death from the official forces for a while yet, though doubtless Moran's masters already are aware of it. You see, le Villard here had a most excellent idea: that this bullet may have been fired from the same barrel as the one aimed at me outside the Covent Garden theatre. If so, he surmised, there may be markings from the barrel left on the bullets, which careful examination," he indicated the microscope, "may be able to match up.

"As a control, we fired two rounds from each of our own pistols into those pillows there, which accounts for the feathers, and we proceeded to our tests. Under the microscope, each of the bullets fired from our pistols matches its partner, and no other, although all the cartridges came initially from the same box. Thus, we can conclude, his theory holds good.

"As to these two bullets, there is sufficient similarity, despite the deformation, to conclude that the bullet that killed Parker was fired from the same gun as the one I retrieved at the theatre. And thus, that it was indeed Colonel Moran behind the trigger both times. We know they were fired from an airgun, because we heard it at Covent Garden.

"So Parker pays the ultimate price for his carelessness!" I remarked.

"As did Porlock for a similar lapse, at the hands of Professor Moriarty, long ago. The Moriarty gang, which is clearly still with us, has ever been ruthless in enforcing discipline and security. And we always suspected that Moran was one of their chief enforcers. It seems little has changed, Watson."

Personally, I thought a great deal had changed. It seemed to me that we were knee-deep in bodies and kidnap victims, and I wondered where it would all end.

It was obvious that neither of them had turned in last night. I picked up the *Daily Chronicle* from the coffee table. Holmes must have bought it and several other dailies as he and le Villard returned at dawn. Lurid headlines proclaimed that London was in a panic due to bombings and murders. Fear gripped Londoners abroad in foggy night-time streets in a way not experienced since the brief reign of Jack the Ripper.

Except that, as the editorial in the *Chronicle* pointed out, the victims then were all women-of-the-night from the Whitechapel area, whereas the current violence seemed aimed indiscriminately at people of all descriptions, and at public institutions as well. Anarchy was referred to with increasing frequency and rising panic. I had barely turned to the cricket news and the morning's racing results when the next tidings of violent death reached us, as though in confirmation of the news editorial I had just been reading.

Once again, it was the tireless Wiggins, who seemed to have his ear to the ground over the area on both banks of the Thames below Tower Bridge, such that nothing happened but that he was aware of it within minutes. This time Wiggins dispensed with the usual courtesies, and rapped sharply on our sitting room door, unannounced by Mrs. Hudson. She knew him well enough by now, though she wouldn't have the rest of the Irregulars in if she could help it.

As soon as I opened the door, Wiggins burst in and unburdened himself immediately to Holmes.

"Found your Mister Norton, sir, but, beggin' your pardon, 'e's already carked."

"Where, when and how, Wiggins? Quickly now!"

Holmes was already on his feet.

"Trinity Square Gardens, Mister 'Olmes. By that statue there. They was a'buryin' 'im in one o' them round flower-beds there, when th' early gard'ners come t' work an' found 'em at it. Just before sun-up, it were, about an 'our ago now. Ol' Scruffs, 'oo 'angs about there nights, sez they was a bunch o' Injians. You know, wif cloths wrapped aroun' their 'eads. They all legged it when they saw they was spotted, an' disappeared right quick.

"I 'eard about it real sharpish, 'cause I 'ad the lads keepin' their ears open special-like, an' we 'opped it over there. Got there just as th' peelers was arrivin'. I got a gander at 'is face, an' I'd swear it's your man, Mister 'Olmes. I remembers 'im from years ago, like you said. 'Andsome bloke, 'e was, before them Injian blokes stuck 'is eyes. Smashed 'is crown jewels, as well, they did."

"Watson, your street attire, *post haste*. Le Villard and I can go as we are. Wiggins, downstairs and hustle us up a cab of some kind - the fastest you can get. Tell the driver Tower Hill Road - and there'll be a handsome tip if he's sharp about it!"

As I headed upstairs to dress I noticed Holmes put his large lens in his coat pocket, along with a tailor's tape-measure.

Half an hour later, our carriage pulled to a halt at the police line set up around the murder site, close by the fencing. Three carriages were already there, horses still steaming in the traces. Holmes spoke briefly with the constable, and we were allowed to pass - on foot only, keeping to the paths. As we had driven in along Tower Hill Road we had passed a mortuary cart going the other way, but Holmes had decided to carry on and investigate the site of this latest murder.

"After all, we can always catch up with poor Norton. If he is the victim, he'll be going nowhere in a hurry."

As we approached the circular garden beds, we noted that Inspector Gregson was investigating the shallow, annular grave that had been dug in the soft soil, exactly in the centre of one of the circular flower beds. A round column of earth had been left undisturbed in the exact centre of the hole; a neat pile of topsoil stood beside the hole. Plants and shrubs had been carefully dug up, and set to one side, no doubt for subsequent replacement after the macabre burial.

Lestrade was engaged in questioning the two gardeners who had discovered the body, taking shorthand notes as he did so, and alongside him, listening carefully to their replies, stood the tall, spare figure of Commissioner MacDonald.

"Ah! Mister Holmes, and team," said the Commissioner as we approached. "Good morning, gentlemen. I see your intelligence network is as efficient as the Yard's. Just got here myself. And you've just missed the body on its way to the morgue. Similarities with the 'Slash-and-Strangle' murders, as Fleet Street calls 'em. So I had it sent to Stevenage at Whitechapel. But I imagine you'll go to see for yourself."

"One thing, Lestrade!" enquired Holmes. "Was the body actually in that grave when you got here? It seems too small in breadth or depth to accommodate a fully-grown man."

"Victim's neck was broken. Legs broken at the knees, Mister Holmes," replied the police detective, rather grudgingly. "Bent up frontwards! Strangest thing I ever did see. That's how they fit him in that small hole, you see. Bent in a complete circle, lying on his side, with his feet touching his head. Stripped naked, he was, as well. All his clothes bundled up together and placed in the hole, around that column in the centre."

"Anything in the pockets?"

"Not a thing, sir. Trousers, vest, coat; all his pockets were stripped clean. No personal jewellery, watch or ring, either."

"Mind if I take a look around?" asked Holmes of Commissioner MacDonald.

"Not at all, Holmes. Our lads are done. Always appreciate any help we can get from the public, you know. Go right ahead, just don't disturb anything. Let me know if you find anything, of course."

"Of course!"

Holmes and le Villard began with the grave, once Gregson stepped back, but there was apparently nothing unusual about the hole itself, other than its unorthodox configuration. After a few cursory measurements as to width and depth, they quickly turned their attention to the surrounding area, out to a distance of twenty or so paces. I kept them in the corner of my vision, and engaged MacDonald and Lestrade in meaningless conversation, in case Holmes discovered anything he preferred to keep to himself.

After fifteen or so minutes, Holmes re-joined us, and said that there was little to be gleaned here. Just a round hole in the ground where a body had been, really! Lestrade seemed positively happy that Holmes had discovered nothing that he and Gregson had missed, especially as their Commissioner was present. MacDonald, I must say, did not seem perturbed at the lack of clues either. We bade the official forces farewell, walked back to our carriage, and drove out of the park by the Tower Hill gateway, receiving a smart salute from the constable posted there to keep out the small crowd of ghouls who always gather at such scenes.

Holmes gave instructions to drive us to the mortuary at Whitechapel, where Norton's corpse, like the others before him, had been taken for autopsy. As our carriage turned into Whitechapel High Street, Holmes chuckled a little as he complimented me on my diversionary tactics.

"So you did find something, after all?" I enquired.

"Several somethings in fact, Watson. Firstly, the hole was dug with a long, narrow blade: not a standard English gardening implement. It was also an almost mathematically precise circle, so either our murderers are excessively neat fellows, or it forms part of some kind of ritual. This is reinforced by that earthen post left undisturbed in the centre of the grave. Secondly, there were no signs of haste or struggle by the grave. Therefore, as they were disturbed before they could complete their grisly work, it is probable that the hole was dug well in advance of the murder.

"Away from the grave, alongside an adjacent flower-bed, we found signs of a scuffle, but only a little disturbance. However, a close search of that flower bed resulted in our finding this."

And he displayed, on the palm of his hand, a small metal disc. I recognised a one-*rupee* coin from India.

"One of the murderers must have dropped it in the struggle, I suppose," said I. "They were Indians, after all, weren't they?"

"That is so, Watson," replied Holmes, a thoughtful expression on his lean face, "but I suspect that it has a deeper significance. This case is becoming more complex with each step, but I begin to see some light. Let us see what the corpse of Godfrey Norton has to tell us. As for this murder, Le Villard, *c'est plus qu'un crime, c'est une faute!*"

"Now that he is dead, if it is indeed Norton, Sir Oliver will have to open the envelope Norton left with him," remarked le Villard.

"And, assuming it is Norton, that will be our next destination."

"This place reminds me of the old mortuary at *Quai d'Horloge,*" said le Villard, with a shiver, as we walked once again into the Whitechapel mortuary. "Never got used to morgues! Remind one too much of one's own mortality, I suppose."

At the far end of the long chamber, shielded from the rest of the room by the same screens as before, we came upon the same surgeon who had autopsied the previous 'Slash-and-Strangle' victims.

"Doctor Stevenage is the Medical Examiner here at Whitechapel. May I introduce a colleague from Paris, Inspector Francois le Villard of the *Police Judiciaire*, Homicide Division? May we see the latest victim, Doctor?"

"Of course, Mister Holmes."

Stevenage drew back the white shroud covering the corpse. Le Villard recoiled a little from the sight of the punctured eyeballs, but soon recovered.

"He had the *nostalgie de la boue,* this one," he remarked sadly, "and that is where he ended up, in the gutter."

"It's Norton, all right," said Holmes. "That settles that, at least. Poor chap! If only he'd come to us earlier, we may well have been able to save his life."

Holmes turned back to Doctor Stevenage.

"Have you examined him yet?" he asked.

"Only externally, Mister Holmes. Remarkable similarities to the others we fished out of the Thames. Ligature marks around the throat; stab wounds from each armpit up through the throat, smashed genitals, stabbed through both eyeballs."

"Differences?" enquired Holmes.

"The obvious ones are that this one was to be buried on land, I hear, and it was discovered beforehand, whereas the others were tossed in the river, and had been immersed for some time. And of course, the dislocation of the knee joints, along with severing of the tendons, to enable the lower legs to be folded forwards rather than backwards."

"Anything else, Doctor?"

"Yes, there is. See here, at the throat. The same ligature marks as before!."

"Ah! Yes, I see!" Holmes drew his magnifying lens from his inner coat-pocket, and examined the area closely through it. "And again, the same traces are left behind in the ligature marks. No need for a sample this time, as I have the other still. The neck was broken?"

"Yes, except that this time it had been wrenched forward rather than backwards."

Holmes turned to Stevenage, and asked if a certain chemical reagent was available to hand. When a small phial was produced, he asked the surgeon for a clean cotton swab. This too was soon produced. Holmes proceeded to wet the swab with a little of the reagent from the vial, and gently rub the area around Norton's nostrils. The clear liquid on the swab turned a dark purple in colour, and left purple traces on the skin.

"As I suspected. Chloroform! The test is conclusive."

'Well, gentlemen, I think we've seen all we need here. On to our next stop, before the official forces arrive and accuse us of interference. Thank you once again, Stevenage. We appreciate your co-operation."

"If it helps stop this carnage, I'm glad to assist. Good day, sirs."

Back in our carriage, rattling along at a more sedate pace now, as it was still early yet and unlikely that Sir Oliver would be in his chambers, Holmes and le Villard discussed the death of Godfrey Norton.

"I suppose this finally clears him of the murders at Siam, Holmes," said the French detective.

"I never seriously suspected him, my friend. Norton was weak and a bully, drug and drink-addicted, a gambler and a philanderer. But he would never deliberately kill, of that I was certain.

"But now, my friends, we must consider the living. It is crucial that we find Isobel Aster before the same gruesome fate befalls her as Norton, assuming it has not already done so. She is clearly as much of a threat to our quarry as Norton was, and I begin to suspect the reason."

My mind turned back to the mundane horror of the circular grave in which Norton's lifeless body had been found. To the passer-by it would appear to be nothing more than a composting-pit, or perhaps preparation for a tree-planting. Within hours the gardens would slowly fill with innocent nannies and their infant charges, elderly ladies walking their spaniels, and shabby fellows passing futile hours on the park benches scattered about the lawns, all unaware of the gruesome murder which had taken place just hours before. But then, I reflected, Trinity Square Gardens was not unfamiliar with gruesome, sudden death. The gardens of old Trinity House had been the site of the scaffolds upon which were beheaded well over a hundred of those doubly unfortunate souls who were qualified by neither rank nor villainy to lose their heads within the walls of the Tower.

At Sir Oliver Newsome's chambers we were informed that he was on his way directly to the Old Bailey, where he was lead counsel for the defence in a case being heard there this morning. Holmes asked if an urgent message could be sent to him, and assured the clerk it was of critical importance. A messenger was sent for, and I watched as Holmes penned a brief message to Sir Oliver. It was blunt in the extreme:

Sir Oliver,

Norton is dead, by violence. Another lives, with your co-operation. I require your immediate return to chambers, on a matter of life or death. If not, it is likely to be a matter of death alone!

Holmes.

The messenger dashed away, and we sat back with tea and biscuits to await Sir Oliver. It wasn't long before the door burst open, and a distraught Sir Oliver appeared in the doorway, breathless from exertion.

"Is it so, Holmes? Is Godfrey really dead?"

"I'm afraid so, Sir Oliver. He was brutally murdered early this morning, I believe on the instructions of those men who wronged him so many years ago. He was threatening to expose them, and they silenced him."

"Where did this happen?"

"Close at hand, ironically! Trinity Square Gardens, in fact. He's been taken to Whitechapel Mortuary already, should you wish to verify the fact, but I have confirmed the identity of the body. I'm sorry to bring you this news, Sir Oliver, but I must ask you to put aside for a moment your own grief, and assist me in another matter.

"Norton left his rooms last night, seemingly of his own volition, with several men whom we have good reason to believe have forcibly abducted a young lady. Her life is at stake, as well as larger issues of state. It is likely that the key to their identity, and perhaps incriminating evidence against them, is contained in the envelope he left with you.

"Norton died a violent and vicious death, Sir Oliver. I have seen his corpse, and I do not recommend that you do the same. His death releases you from your oath. Will you now open the envelope, and decide whether to allow me to act in the matter?"

Still in shock from the distressing news, Sir Oliver nodded his assent.

"Of course, Mister Holmes, of course. But the envelope is not here. I kept it at home. These chambers are not impenetrable, you see. Too many people have access to the keys, when all is said and done. I knew of the importance the Government attached to the document, and wanted to ensure its safekeeping, in accord with Godfrey's wishes. So I took it home last night, and locked it in my concealed safe there. I shall have to go there myself to retrieve it. It's not so far distant.

"Allow me a moment to instruct my clerks to make alternative arrangements at the Old Bailey, and we can leave. Have you a conveyance, or should I send for a carriage?"

"Could I rely on you to bring the envelope to 221B Baker Street, Sir Oliver? We should return as soon as we can to our rooms, in case any leads arrive regarding Miss Aster's whereabouts."

This was agreed to, and we all left Lincoln's Inn a few minutes later, we to Baker Street, and Sir Oliver to retrieve Godfrey Norton's final message. Half an hour later we were mounting the stairs to our old rooms. Mrs. Hudson intercepted us in the hallway, and informed us that there was a gentleman waiting in our rooms to see Holmes.

Holmes opened the door, and exclaimed, "Hayter . . ! By all that's holy! Watson, Colonel Hayter has come to call upon us. My very next step, Colonel, was to be to get in touch with you - and here you are."

I greeted my old friend from my brief sojourn in Afghanistan - and our more recent involvement in solving a spate of robberies in his district. Hayter shook my hand vigorously, and said that he had often meant to look me up, but hadn't known where to find me following the reported death of Holmes.

"I'm actually here to see Mister Holmes, John. And I sense that he knows what I wish to discuss. Am I right, sir?"

"Quite possibly, Colonel. Why don't you enlighten us all?"

"Certainly! Yes, of course! All of you! Well, Holmes, it's this way. I was at my club - the Anglo-Indian, you see - where I always doss down when I come up from Surrey for the night, and I saw your notice in the old *Gazette,* here."

Hayter slapped a copy of the *Daily Gazette* on the table, and pointed at the notice Holmes had paid for these past three days.

"It was the mention of Indians that caught my eye, Mister Holmes. Not sure that it's anything that you're asking about. But it's a damned queer business, and there's Indians in the thick of it, and you asked for anything unusual involving 'em. So I thought to myself, if there's anyone can throw some light on this, it's Sherlock Holmes

"I'd heard you'd come back safely, Holmes, so I decided to come here, and your landlady was kind enough to let me wait. Had to tell her a few personal details about Watson here before she'd trust me, though. Have you sent her to Police College, Holmes? Bloody efficient watchdog!"

"She's under strict instructions just now, Colonel. We're all on our guard. Now, what's on your mind?"

"Right-oh! As I said, I come up to London fairly often, and whenever I do I always stop by the Moti Mahal in Brick Lane where Lal Ghose makes the only decent mutton *vindaloo* in London. Just two weeks ago I did exactly that. Now, I've known Lal Ghose since my days as a griffin: he was in charge of the Officer's Mess at Calcutta in those days. After he retired he was brought to London as personal chef for one of the old nabobs of the Indian Railways

"When that old fellow died, Lal Ghose and his family decided to stay on in London and open a curry-house in the Whitechapel area. Well; long story short, two weeks ago I toddled along for my *vindaloo,* and Lal Ghose and all his family were gone. There was a new staff, mostly all Indians. A surly Burman who sat at a small cashier's counter told me that my friend had sold up and returned to his village. When I asked who was the new proprietor, I was told that a Major Stuttaford, retired Indian Army, had bought the place. Owned another curry-house in Liverpool, apparently, so he wasn't in all that often.

"Now, only a few weeks before, I'd eaten at the Moti Mahal, and Lal Ghose hadn't said a word about selling up, so I already thought, 'Something rum about this!' but couldn't put my finger on it. The food was still good, but different, and I reflected that all things change with time, and left it at that. I intended to call on a few other Indians I knew in the district, to ask what had happened, but as I hadn't been in town . . . well . . . I haven't had time to get around to it.

"Then, in yesterday's paper, I read of these 'Slash-and-Strangle' murders, and the description of the victims. Especially," Hayter took a newspaper clipping from a pocket, and read from it:

"'. . . a dark-skinned Oriental male with a pronounced welt of proud flesh, probably caused by a knife slash, running from left brow to angle of jaw in a straight line . . .'

"Well, Holmes, that surly Burman had just such a scar. I smelled a rat, and so last night I went back to the curry-house again. This time a turbaned fellow was behind the cashier's desk, and though I lingered over my *gulab jaman* and mint tea, I saw no sign of the Burman.

"Anyway, Holmes, when I'd decided to come to see you, I recalled a few other facts that I'd noted in the press reports about those riverside murders. Couple of points struck me rather forcibly. I thought you'd be investigating, so I've brought you this!"

As he finished speaking, Colonel Hayter went to the coat-tree, reached into his overcoat pocket, and handed Holmes an old volume, rather slender, and cheaply bound in dark-blue cloth. Holmes glanced quickly at the title, then slipped it into the pocket of his ulster, which hung from an adjacent hook.

"Just the ticket, Colonel. It's as though you read my mind. I shall skim through this as soon as I can make a free half-hour. I suspect there are answers to several of our puzzles to be found within. Thank you, Hayter, but I must get away to Pall Mall as soon as a certain party has arrived, and I think I hear him at our door. I shall call on you later at the Anglo-Indian Club, and we will look more deeply into these matters you have so kindly brought to my attention. Will you wait for me? Excellent!

"Watson, could you perhaps see the Colonel to the street door, and then escort Sir Oliver upstairs?"

Sir Oliver was at the door, trying to explain himself to Mrs. Hudson. He appeared to be in a state of some agitation. I rescued him, and led the way up to our apartments.

"My home has been burgled, Mister Holmes," he gasped. "As soon as my cab turned into Park Lane I knew something was amiss. Constables at the door, and a crowd, standing around gawping. My man had been bludgeoned when he opened the door, it seems, and the robbers simply dragged him into the hallway and closed the door. I suppose they thought they'd killed him. They turned the place upside down, but my safe is well hidden. My man came to, and slipped out to raise the alarm. The robbers heard the door close behind him, and took flight. They managed to get clean away, thanks to this filthy fog

"I went directly to my library, opened the safe, and retrieved the envelope. I don't think I was followed here."

At that, Sir Oliver handed Holmes a large manila-paper envelope, sealed with string and wax.

"I'd prefer that you open it, Mister Holmes?" he said. "Please?"

Holmes made no response to Sir Oliver Newsome's account; other than to take the envelope and slit it open with the dagger he kept on the mantel-piece for just that purpose.

"A cover note for you, Sir Oliver," as he handed the Q. C. a folded sheet of writing-paper, "and another envelope addressed to Sherlock Holmes Esq." He removed the smaller, white envelope from the larger, and slit it open.

"Oh dear!" sighed Sir Oliver, seeming to collapse right before us into a mere shell of the pompous Queen's Counsel, as he finished reading the note. "Had I read this sooner, it's possible Godfrey would still be alive."

Sir Oliver broke down, in tears of remorse.

"I loved him, like a son really, at the end, and I'd give anything to have the decision over again. Damn my pettifogging legalistic mind for the useless thing it is, in this world of flesh and blood!"

Holmes took a moment to console him, having quickly scanned the contents of the white envelope that Godfrey Norton had left for him as a last, desperate measure of defiance.

"You are wrong, sir, to castigate yourself. With all its manifest faults, it is the agreement amongst men to abide by a common law that sets civilised mankind apart from the beasts of the jungle. As you said, Sir Oliver, hard cases do make bad law. The unfortunate corollary is that, on occasion, we are called upon to make a painful choice. In this particular case, it is abundantly clear that Norton was prepared to give his life to have his revenge upon those who engineered his downfall, and the death of his wife.

Sir Oliver took the documents from Holmes, and quickly read them throu-gh.

"Unfortunately, now that Godfrey is dead, these papers are inadmissible as evidence. Had I opened them when you asked . . . Oh! What's the use . . ."

"I think, Sir Oliver, that you should not be too hard upon yourself. Much of this I found out at Cambridge. At least now we know what happened, long ago, and what it is that these killers fear - exposure of the *tontine* conspiracy and their part in it. However, this robbery means that the killers forced Norton to confess that he'd left a record with you. You would be well advised to hire a guard of some kind, once the police leave, and to take a discreet holiday abroad as soon as this matter is finished with."

Holmes slipped the envelope and contents into his ulster pocket, along with the book left him by Colonel Hayter. Gently, he coaxed the still distraught Q. C. out the door and down the stairs, and saw him into his cab. Then he and le Villard set off to Pall Mall, to meet with Mycroft and de Benoist to finalise arrangements for the meeting with Lord Coledale and his aide and adviser, Quiney.

I decided to remain at home, and try to finish as much as I could of le Villard's Journals. I sensed that matters were coming to a climax, and that if I was to fully understand what was going on now, I should have as clear a picture as possible of those events which had led to the present-day situation. Now was clearly not an appropriate time to be bothering Holmes with questions, and le Villard would be with Holmes. Besides, I knew that Holmes would expound neither his theories nor his conjectures until he had established his case.

CHAPTER LI

10th October 1893
Bang Pa-in, Ayuthia, Siam

WITH THE SIGNING of the Agreement between France and Siam the threat to Rolin had been reduced along with the threat to Siam. The Agreement, which the General Adviser characterised as 'not glorious for Siam, though shameful for England', was now in place. The Prince escorted Le Myre de Vilers to Bang Pa-in to take leave of the King, who did not detest him as he did Pavie. De Vilers and his wife had returned the next day to Bangkok, where they boarded a steamer for Saigon. It was indeed time to move on.

We had accepted an invitation from the Prince to visit him at Bang Pa-In. The King was still in residence there, and as we had missed the opportunity to attend during festivities for the King's birthday, thought it would make a pleasant diversion before we left. The truth is, I was in no great hurry to leave Siam at that moment, and the reason why would also be at Bang Pa-In.

Although the King was feeling unwell, entertainments for his guests were to be presented nonetheless, as every year. A printed programme had been sent along with our invitations. There would be evenings of Siamese music and dance and theatre; boat racing on the river; a round-up and breaking session at the King's elephant *kraal;* an excursion by steam-launches to the ancient royal capital at nearby Ayuthia; picnics in the surrounding country; and numerous other diversions. Amongst these was to be a *Recital by Miss Irene Adler and Students,* including Miss Malee and her sisters Miss Saranya and Miss Tassaneeya. I had not seen Miss Malee since the adventures of the night on the river. I suspected that her sister had kept a watchful eye on her, and I could see why.

At twelve o'clock Holmes and I boarded a Government steamer at the central wharf and settled ourselves comfortably on the canvas-covered foredeck. At first our vessel hugged the shore, so we had an excellent passing panorama of Siamese life. Due to the flooding river, we were told, the passage would take seven hours or more steaming against the current.

The shoreline within Bangkok was lined with an endless succession of wharves and *godowns*, temples, sawmills, stores and floating houses, mingled with the occasional grand house of a teak or rice tycoon. Even in the city itself the trees and jungle threatened to overwhelm the buildings of the Siamese, so that everything appeared to be nestled in a soft bed of greenery. The occasional scarlet and gold vibrancy of a Chinese wayside shrine or temple, and displays of fruits and flowers, enlivened the teak and *attap* houses of the Siamese, bleached silver grey by sun reflecting from the broad stream.

The hustle and bustle of the merchant quarters as we slid past soon gave way to the serenity of the countryside, and to the quiet daily repetition of simple tasks that make up the lives of these people of the fields and the river.

Old women squatted on wooden platforms in front of their open houses, winnowing rice in shallow wicker trays, or pounding spices and chillies in stone mortars. A small boy soaped his dog on the barely-visible top of a submerged post. Girls bathed and giggled in the river, covered by patterned sarongs for modesty as they dipped basins of water over their waist-length tresses. Men bathed, chequered cloths wound between their thighs. Naked children waved at us as we passed by, leaping into the river from any available high point like so many brown water-babies. Shrieks of laughter followed us up the river.

From time to time fellow voyagers - ranging from hawkers of various cheap goods, fortune-tellers and soothsayers, to beggars with unoriginal stories and those simply wishing to practise their English - approached us as we stood at the rail. Holmes has an unvarying technique for dealing with such intruders. He simply ignores them completely, until they give up and go on to till less stony ground. Soon we were left alone.

Our steamer moved into the centre of the stream, and we passed the junctions of several major tributaries, seemingly as wide as the river itself. From time to time we passed one of the hundreds of *wats* along the riverbanks, with its distinctive tiered roofs.

Whether in the heart of a town or village, or nestled amongst the trees in wilderness, these temples are always prosperous and finely decorated. It was quite usual, as we passed by, to witness some Buddhist ceremony or other, with ranks of saffron-robed monks chanting in their strangely musical cadences. I noticed that Holmes took a keen interest in these, and in all the Siamese music we heard. At one point, as we steamed slowly past a village's watersedge *sala*, we were treated to a melody performed by the village orchestra, practising on their *gamelans* and gongs. Holmes closed his eyes and concentrated, as though to absorb the essence of the melody and it's underlying scale and key.

Mangrove swamps lined the river where man has not yet interfered with nature. Colonies of white ibis nested along the shore, along with a large variety of bird life. The river is rather turgid, but is teems with huge carp and other riverine fish. I heard of estuarine crocodiles even further upriver, but we saw none. Sea snakes, however, are apparently common and deadly, as are cobras and *kraits* on land. Not to mention lethal scorpions and huge stinging centipedes! A beautiful country, but with a vicious underside to it! And not just the serpents and insects, I mused.

Although the monsoon storm rains were now less frequent and wild, the river was swollen with the waters from the flanks of the Himalayas. Here, in the flat rice-paddy central plain of Siam, the river flooded low-lying banks so that houses and whole villages were almost submerged. People lived in their canoes - seemingly quite happily - until the waters subsided.

The rice harvest was ripening to maturity. As we steamed past rice paddies turning to a sea of translucent emerald, the sun descended. Its' last rays caught a simple white-washed temple, with multiple tiered green-and-ochre roofs, and finials like gilded wisps of smoke curling away to the sky.

Large flying insects soon became a nuisance. We stepped inside the saloon and ordered a gin-and-tonic from the Indian servant. Fortified by this we managed to fend off any unwelcome conversation until we landed at Bang Pa-in, the traditional riverside retreat of the Kings of Siam since the founding of the *Chakkri* Dynasty, five reigns before.

Here we were met by an officer of the Siamese Navy, who escorted us to our accommodations during our short stay, aboard the Siamese navy ship *Ubon*. The cabins were small, but were on deck, and so had the benefit of such breeze as could blow through the small port. We were expected, and a meal had been kept warm for us. Following this, Holmes and I went aft to where the Admiral and several of the other guests were enjoying cigars and port. Rolin arrived, and stayed for twenty minutes chatting with various guests before leaving to call on the Prince. We arranged to meet on the morrow. Soon, to bed.

12th October 1893
Bang Pa-in, Ayuthia, Siam
We expected to remain here for three days only, following which Holmes planned to leave for Singapore. The second day was a day of outdoor activities - boat racing and excu1rsions to Ayuthia, and picnics on the riverbanks. The display at the elephant *kraal* was to be on the last day of our trip.

I rather wished I had gone on the picnic boats, as I had seen the sisters - now three of them - boarding with lunch baskets and woven mats. Instead, Holmes and I explored Bang Pa-in itself. The ancient royal playground has been transformed recently with the construction of a number of pavilions in a wide variety of styles. In addition to the original Siamese palaces there are Italianate villas, Chinese pagodas, French chateaux in miniature, and every kind of Palladian, Ionic, and Doric column and pilaster ever dreamt of, in abundant profusion.

They are all set in landscaped gardens and views, with a sufficiency of idyllic statuary and manicured topiary. Artificial waterfalls tumble into lakes teeming with pure white or golden carp, darting amongst giant lily pads and purple-pink blooms, looking for the next offering of bread cubes.

And here, amid all this rather gaudy exuberance, set on tapering poles in such a pool, detached from the land in all directions, we came across the most perfect example of Siamese architecture I have seen. A traditional pavilion, but perfect in every proportion and angle, every delicate curve, with no purpose other than to express the essence of Siamese temple architecture.

I made several sketches of this exquisite little gem of a building, while Holmes simply pondered its beauty and smoked his pipe. Following this we made several forays on foot down the rural paths winding through Bang Pa-in, and out into the surrounding country.

As we crossed the courtyard back towards the *Ubon* to change for the evening we encountered Irene Adler, her arms full of frothy costumes. We offered to help, but she declined, saying we couldn't take them all the way anyway, being men.

With a mischievous smile at me, she suggested that we should be sure to attend the Siamese dancing tonight, as her three favourite pupils were to dance. The clothes she was carrying, she said, were for the European concert tomorrow night, but she had just come from where the girls were dressing for the evening, and promised that we would not be disappointed.

There seemed to be a vast improvement in Irene Adler's spirit, I thought.

Her eyes glowed with life once again, and there was a spring in her step when she left us to return to the dressing rooms, wherever they were. Somehow I had the sense that a great burden had been lifted from her shoulders, and that suddenly life seemed to her to be full of possibility and hope.

After dressing and dining aboard, Holmes and I strolled along paths through the flooded gardens, which now teemed with large crayfish, until we came to the Royal Courtyard for such entertainments. I was surprised to see, for the first time during our stay at Siam, that the Siamese nobles had forsaken their modern European fashions, and had turned out of their clothes-chests those magnificent raiments of brocaded silks and filmy gauze which had been their traditional finery.

Men wore baggy brocaded pantaloons, with a gauzy knee-length coat edged in gold. Women wrapped an embroidered sarong tightly around their figures, with a pleated scarf wound around their bosoms and tossed over their shoulders. Those with long hair coiled it up in a shiny knot, decorated with sprigs of small white blooms on long, slender stems that danced around their heads as they moved.

A Siamese orchestra played traditional music as guests strolled around. A show featuring rather crude humour, done with masks, amused the crowd a great deal - nobles and stallholders alike. Soon the number of guests had swelled to overflowing, and we were wondering where to sit when we heard Irene Adler calling to us. She had kept seats for us with an excellent view, close to the stage area.

While the orchestra played and the show amused, Irene Adler told us a little of her three pupils. It seems that their mother, who had been presented to the King as one of his consorts when still a girl, was once an accomplished palace dancer. She had never been one of the King's favourites, so when she asked to be allowed to leave - so as to marry their father - she had been kept employed in continuing the traditions of the dance. With so many modern diversions, young girls did not want to study anymore, or submit to the painful bending exercises necessary to make the fingers and other joints supple enough. The palace had made sure to retain her services.

To set an example, her own daughters had all been rigorously trained, and were now regarded as amongst the finest of the younger dancers in all Siam. Irene Adler seemed as proud of them as if she had taught them to dance herself.

"And your Miss Malee, M. Le Villard, she is the angel of angels, as you will soon see."

The courtyard was lit with dozens of palm-oil lamps set on poles. A row of them lit the stage area from the front. The burlesque show finished, and the dance orchestra began tuning up. Several preliminary scenes opened the show, which seemed to us difficult to understand, having little of narrative and much of allegory. The dancers were costumed in gorgeous, stone-encrusted finery, and postured in various tableaux before disengaging and reassembling elsewhere on the stage.

I knew that these Siamese dancing entertainments could continue all night, until the last guest left, and as was usual the audience talked and moved about during the performance, and joked and laughed, all without seeming to disturb the other viewers or actors.

After twenty or thirty minutes of preambles a flourish of conches sounded. The Siamese all sank to their knees, and touched their foreheads to the ground. From behind a carved brick screen the King appeared, in traditional Siamese robes, accompanied by several of his children similarly attired, and a retinue of his brothers and other princes of the realm. The royal party took their places on the dais, and the conches sounded again.

The audience relaxed again, and as the performance continued the drama became more interesting. Devils and angels were introduced, and were carried around on palanquins until, one by one, their litters were set down on the edge of the stage, in the shadows. Out of three of the litters stepped hideously masked devils, prancing and capering with legs spread wide. Then into the torchlight stepped, one by one, the three Siamese sisters, Saranya, Tassaneeya, and finally Malee.

They were dressed as angels, and I had to agree. All three were silhouetted in gold silk brocade, golden scarves trailing behind, as they slowly performed the intricate movements of hands and feet, of fingers and toes, of subtle gestures and elegant gymnastics. On all their fingers were polished brass tips, extravagantly tapered to swept-back points, and at wrists and ankles heavy gold bracelets reflected the torchlight. Pirouetting, balancing in a pose, curving their fingers into impossible positions, the sisters were engrossed in a world of the Siamese imagination.

The music and the dancing were - to European tastes - strange and discordant, but for a moment there, at the country retreat of the King of Siam, I saw in the music and dance the strength of tradition in Siam. Traditions which underlay the determination of this people never to succumb to colonisation, to retain their own monarchy and religion, and their own ways! Suddenly I found myself wishing the Siamese the best, and was gratified that Holmes and I had perhaps played a part in keeping Siam free and under its own sovereign.

My attention was distracted. Malee had been carried across the stage on her litter, and had now commenced her solo dance. I shall spare the details, except to say that I saw a different Malee this night. The young lady I had met with Miss Irene was a self-assured, thoroughly modern example of the New Siam. Here was the epitome of the grace and serenity of Old Siam. Though we were only yards away, Malee paid no attention to us at all, so completely absorbed was she in her movements and gestures.

Irene Adler whispered in my ear.

"I told you she was the angel of angels. And as she is in the drama, so is she in real life."

Miss Malee had already saved my life once, and I needed no urging to agree, but this evening made me a convert anew.

After about forty minutes the angels and devils were carried off-stage, and the conches sounded again. The King's party rose and disappeared behind the screen again, whereupon the conches sounded for the last time and the performance recommenced. With the departure of the royal party the nobles soon drifted away as well, and we left with them.

We walked Miss Adler to a refreshment tent, where glasses of champagne were offered to us and gladly accepted.

"That was quite wonderful," said Holmes. "But I see your *protégés* approaching us now. Please allow me to congratulate them, then I really must leave. Thank you for the company, Miss Adler."

Holmes made his congratulations, and we left. But not before I found the chance to tell Miss Malee how enchanting she looked, and to see that smile transform her beautiful face once again. It was enough, for now.

We crossed the walkways to a pier, where a canoe waited to take us to the palace where Prince Ranawongse was staying. This was apparently the fastest and driest way to get there during the floods. Our meeting was brief but most cordial. The Prince thanked us on the King's behalf for our part in averting what could have become a major setback to Siam's hopes to retain its independence, not to mention saving both his and the General Adviser's lives. He did not dwell on the matter, passing immediately to a review of the political situation with Rolin. Both he and the King were concerned that the treaties left French troops in control of Chantaboon. The General Adviser told us confidentially that he was being cut socially by many of the expatriate British community in the city. It seems that he was being vilified less for the losses suffered during the blockade, for which they blamed him, than for preventing a more substantial grab of territory by the French. This would have provided them an excellent excuse for agitating for a pre-emptive British annexation of Bangkok and the remainder of Siam, and they were not about to thank him for his part in stiffening the resolve of the Siamese to resist French demands and encroachments.

We woke early, and began the day with our exercises on the deck of the ship, followed by a brisk row up several of the picturesque *klongs* in the ship's cutter. Clear blue sky, the waters of the swollen canal calm and still, except for the ripples left when a fish leaped, sounds of birds and crickets, and wind through the bamboo, and the fresh, cool air of morning.

There was little to occupy us when we returned to the *Ubon*. I spent time catching up on my Journal, based as usual on notes I have taken daily in my little notebook, and did a little sketching. Holmes wandered about, puffing at his pipe, seemingly nonchalant.

I knew that it was all a facade. In fact, his mind was no doubt turning over various ways to achieve one end - that of convincing Irene Adler to reveal all she knew of the mysteries surrounding her husband's past. Without causing her to panic and bolt for it!

The problem was partially solved when the General Adviser invited us to travel back to Bangkok with him on the comfortable private steam-launch that he hired to bring him upriver. He had invited Miss Adler, and Miss Malee would accompany her as she had classes to attend. The other two sisters were to remain at Bang Pa-in with their mother and return when the festivities were finished. The doctor was also invited, and said that 'he would see'. So Holmes expected to have plenty of opportunity to talk with Irene Adler, and she could hardly walk away.

The Foreigner's Ball turned out to be a rather dull affair, with two exceptions. The first was when Miss Adler and her students sang a selection of songs from the German and Viennese composers. I shall say no more about that, except that they were most charmingly sung.

The second came about when the Prince mentioned that His Majesty adores Russian music, to which Irene Adler replied that she loved the serious Russian composers herself, but had no accompanist. Holmes then asked if a violin could be provided, and tuned it to his satisfaction. He spoke softly with Miss Adler about the music, and then they began.

In all the years we had travelled together I had seen Holmes pick up a fiddle two or three times at the most, and never in earnest. Now, with no rehearsal, he and Irene Adler gave a recital which was occasionally a little rough at the edges, but captivated everyone with the passion of Irene Adler's contralto, and the intensity of Holmes's tragic violin solo. This was serious music indeed, and the King was visibly moved.

After several of these songs Holmes and Irene Adler conferred for a moment, and announced a change of pace. They launched into a medley of popular music-hall melodies, which proved very popular indeed. Holmes then finished the recital with a haunting rendition, on his violin, of the

Siamese melody he had heard as our steamer passed by the village *gamelan* orchestra, two mornings before. As simple as the piece sounded, the audience appreciated the tribute to Siam, and applauded until Holmes and Irene Adler performed one last piece together.

"You never cease to amaze, Holmes," I said when he took his seat. "You could be sitting in a comfortable chair by your fire in London every day, and do nothing but drop by the theatre from time to time. Why on earth would you prefer to risk your life chasing villains?"

"The satisfaction comes from *catching* villains. I could also have made my mark as a research chemist, my friend - or as a poisoner and swindler. Or at any of a dozen other occupations! I suppose being a consulting detective allows me to do, at one time or another, all of those things to which I could have devoted an entire life. And I *do* get to send some of those villains away."

The rest of the evening was uneventful, except that, as we prepared to leave, a royal page approached Holmes. He presented Holmes with the violin in a velvet-lined case, with the compliments of His Majesty, who had already left. We were back aboard the *Ubon* for a last brandy well before midnight was piped.

15th October 1893
Bang Pa-in, Ayuthia, Siam
After we had finished our few preparations to leave Holmes and I took a stroll with the General Adviser. Holmes wanted to sound out Rolin before telegraphing to his brother Mycroft that we would soon depart Siam.

As we rounded a corner in the palace grounds we were forced to use a series of bridges, improvised because of the floods. Here we met, coming from the Pavilion of the White Elephant, His Majesty's cortege. The King, with one of his sons between his legs, called down to Rolin from the heights of his palanquin, inviting him to dine with Himself and the princes. The General Adviser accepted, and the King's cortege lumbered on its way. The elephant is an excellent conveyance when the country is flooded, I decided.

As his elephant turned away, the King called down something rather strange, addressing himself this time to Holmes.

"When you return home, Professor, please give my regards to your brother. We have communicated indirectly, from time to time, in the past. He will remember me. And . . . thank you, sir!"

Holmes merely bowed slightly, and stepped out of the way of the elephant's huge feet. Although Professor Olaf Sigerson's persona has become reasonably fully clothed over time, he has never been furnished with a brother. And certainly not one whom the King of Siam would know!

Although he was now unable to return to Bangkok himself, the General Adviser refused to cancel the steam-launch's trip. Rolin instructed the skipper to return to Bang Pa-in as soon as he had delivered us all to Bangkok and taken on coal, as he would want to return to Bangkok the next morning.

At four o'clock we boarded the steam-launch, and found Irene Adler and Miss Malee already aboard. The doctor sent a message that he would arrive a little late, but soon came up the gang-plank. Our party was complete, and we seemed ready to depart. At last an Indian servant jumped aboard, all in white and with a white turban wound around his head, with a large basket full of greens and fruits slung over his arm. No doubt last minute supplies for the galley. He went below, and the boat-boy stepped on board.

The General Adviser waved us all good-bye. With a hoot of its high-pitched whistle the launch cast off and steamed out into the centre of the river, where the swift current added to our speed. Soon we were fairly flying down the Chao Phraya River, past landmarks which had each taken so long to gain on the journey upriver.

The doctor and the women talked about the festivities while Holmes and I smoked Burmese cheroots and enjoyed the journey. We all settled comfortably in the stern, but soon Miss Malee became restless, and walked carefully along the side-decks to the fore deck area. There, protected by a wide straw bonnet, she sat cross-legged in Indian fashion, absorbed as the waters of the river divided before her. I suspect that she had sat thus many a time, as a child, on these annual excursions.

An hour later the doctor went below to nap on the sofa, leaving myself, Holmes and Irene Adler on the slatted wood seating curved around the stern of the launch. Irene Adler turned to Holmes, and spoke.

"I am so glad you were able to come on the boat, Mr. Holmes. I have wanted to talk with you for several days now - ever since I arrived at Bang Pa-in, in fact - but somehow the time never seemed right. There is a lot to tell. You were quite right to accuse me of not telling you everything I knew, but I couldn't. Not then! I'd promised, you see. But the only place to begin is at the beginning, or none of it will make any sense at all. Much of the affair is still a mystery to me, but now I am at liberty to tell what I know."

"As you say, why not start at the beginning," said Holmes.

"When Godfrey and I left London, I thought I had left behind the world of intrigue and mystery - and the life of the bright lights and gay theatres which had been my career until then.

"And by the way, you might tell that biographer of yours that I was not overjoyed to be characterised as an 'adventuress'. Made me sound like one of the *grandes horizontales* of Europe."

"Oh dear! I suppose I must defend dear old Watson. His narratives do tend towards the colourful and sensational, at the expense of the factual, I agree. But in addition to the King of Bohemia, your list of conquests, to my imperfect knowledge, includes two other Kings, a Duke and a Viscount, several Barons and . . ."

"I have always maintained a wide acquaintance, Mr. Holmes, but not necessarily an intimate one. With few exceptions, my wide circle of 'admirers', have remained exactly that - admirers. Those exceptions are my affair, and no one else's business."

"*Touché*, Miss Adler . . . or rather, Mrs. Norton."

"No, Mr. Holmes. You were correct. I have always retained my maiden name as my professional name, but I am now to be Miss Adler again in private life."

"Care to explain?" asked Holmes. "As we are being so frank."

"I received this from the doctor when he arrived." She held out a note written on hotel notepaper, dated at Singapore a week before.

"It's from Godfrey. He has decided to return to London and confess his whole part in the affair. He also says, well . . . read the last part," and she handed Holmes the second page.

I read it at his side. The writing was closely spaced, and stylishly neat.

'. . . so you see, Irene, that I should never have taken you from your life of music and song, should never have married you in the first place. I knew that my future was mortgaged. I simply failed to realise that I had mortgaged my soul with it.

'You have always been the strength that kept us going. Perhaps it would have been better had you let me fall by the wayside. But no, you stayed with me, and I abused you, and degraded myself again and again in my shame. People died, and I couldn't stop it. I couldn't help myself.

'Now it is time to put an end to this grim charade. I shall return to London, in some way or other, and turn over to the authorities categorical proof of the crimes to which I have been party.

'But before I do so - for you may never see me again, and if you do, it may be as defendant in a sensational murder trial - I send you this attached affidavit. It states that our marriage is in fact, null and void, on the grounds that I was already secretly married, as a college student, and had not divorced the girl. She was the cook's daughter at my lodgings. My father and hers came to an agreement years ago, long before we met, you and I, and she would have made no further fuss. But it is grounds for a complete and painless separation for you.

'Go to my old chambers at the Inner Temple at the Inns of Court. Ask for Sir Oliver Newsome. He will have an envelope for you. Everything you need is in there.

Also a settlement of certain properties and stocks, which I offer as small reparation for the wrongs I have done you. Once I have seen my tormentors suffer as I have, and I have no further need of wealth, my remaining properties will come to you. This is all arranged.

'You are free, my dear, both from our legal marriage, and from any debt to me. I have never deserved your love, and I know that love withers in the face of self-pity. You should be free, my dear, and you are. Return to New Jersey, to your family, for a while. Then go wherever the fancy, and your talent, take you.

I should have done this years ago, when there would have been fewer deaths on my conscience.

Good-bye, my dearest Irene.

Godfrey.'

"Does this come as a surprise?" asked Holmes.

"Not really. I had told him that I wanted a divorce, but he would never entertain the thought. Said we had to stick together, or we would sink together."

"How so?"

"As I said, I should begin at the beginning. Years ago! When we had just married, and left England for the French countryside. The problem was, in those days Godfrey had not yet come into money of his own, and in marrying me and leaving his practice, he lost his means of support. Our funds dwindled away, and he had several advances on his estate. These avenues, too, were soon exhausted. Things looked rather grim.

"Then, one day while we were at Biarritz, Godfrey appeared with his wallet full of cash. We lived well for a while, but soon we had to change hotels, or even cities, for no good reason that I knew. Our rooms were burgled several times, and I was shot at once as we crossed St. Mark's Piazza at Venice.

"When Godfrey began packing our suitcases again, and making bookings for trains north, I demanded an explanation or I said I should leave him right then. He saw that I was serious, and bit by bit the story came out.

"Following that affair with the King of Bohemia I kept the cabinet photograph which compromised his marriage plans, and promised never to reveal it. I promised, and I kept my promise. But at Biarritz Godfrey met up again with some people he had known since his college days. They had read Doctor Watson's account of the matter, and decided that there was still money to be made.

"I don't know what hold these men had over Godfrey, but he was unable to refuse them. All I know is that it has something to with this Men of Straw nonsense. When I asked Godfrey about it once, when he left his ring on the shaving dish, he flew into a rage. Said it was something like the Masons, and not to be discussed. And he wouldn't. Everyone knows about the Masons, though. I'd never heard of any Men of Straw.

"He confessed later that he had taken my cabinet photograph and given it to these men. They had copied it using some new process, and then returned the original to me, unharmed. I knew nothing of this. They then used this copy to make further demands on the King. He was, quite rightly, enormously upset at me, as I had promised him confidentiality.

"The King, it seems, had made one huge payment to them before refusing to make any further, but the demands continued. The King of Bohemia, as you know, is not a man to take such an insult without striking back. He called in private agents, some of them notoriously ruthless, to track us down. This was when the burglaries and the following began.

"I threatened to tell all I knew to the police, but Godfrey assured me that it would only open up far more serious matters for investigation. When I asked what we were to do, then, he came to me the next day with a wild scheme, which he said would solve all our problems. To my great regret, I listened, and reluctantly allowed myself to be persuaded to go along.

"Godfrey and I travelled, quite publicly, to Como, where we checked into that charming little hotel at the head of the lake, where the steamers berth. An explosion destroyed one of the small steamers two days later. All aboard were killed outright or drowned.

"I *had* taken a boat ride that morning, but not on the steamer. Godfrey had organised it. He said it would be a pleasant way to pass the morning, as he had some business to attend to. I'd taken a picnic hamper, as Godfrey had said he would meet me on the lake.

"I disembarked at one of those cunning little pavilions at the foot of the gardens edging the lake; I could see a large villa beyond the trees. Godfrey was waiting for me on the pier. He said the villa belonged to his friend. Inside the pavilion was a bag with some of my clothes packed in it. We had our picnic lunch there, beside the lake, and a pleasant lunch it was.

"Later, a small launch from the villa took us back to town, and a horse-cab drove us directly to the station. Godfrey put me aboard a train, with a ticket for Vienna, and said he would see me in two days. Then he returned to the hotel. I had no idea what was going on.

"My name was listed among the missing. The first I knew was when I read of it in the papers in Vienna. When Godfrey arrived I asked how this had happened. He told me that the boating accident was entirely fortuitous - that it was simply the first disaster that happened along. It could as easily have been a railway crash, a coach accident, or a hiking party lost. Anything that would allow the *carabinieri*, who had been bribed, to include my name amongst those of the real victims.

"At the time I accepted that as the truth. But later, as events took a more sinister turn, I wondered again about the whole incident. It all seemed a little too convenient, that I should have been out boating at just the time when disaster befell that steamer; that I should have been seen at the pier before the steamer departed."

"Are you saying you suspect that, in order to convince the King of Bohemia you were dead, Norton's friends killed a dozen people in cold blood."

"That was the only conclusion I could draw. But what was I to do? Who would believe me? Now I suspect that it was one further way to compromise Godfrey, and bind him to them. I don't know why, but for some reason they seem to both need and fear Godfrey, and yet they treat him with disdain. Do this! Do that! And he jumps. Every time."

"Very well. So we have these Men of Straw plotting with Godfrey Norton, and I now know why we all thought you dead. I remember the incident, but no suggestion of foul play was ever raised."

"I should have known that there was another reason for Godfrey to leave his law practice. He hated the law, but he did well at it, professionally and financially. But in my pride, I thought he was giving it all up for me. The great romantic gesture. I should have known better.

"You see, it was Godfrey's idea to run away together. He had another reason for leaving London at that time, something to do with these Men of Straw. All he would say was that inconvenient questions were being asked, and 'it was a damned good time to be elsewhere'"

"Well, now you are a free woman again, so long as none of these old cases comes back to haunt you," said Holmes. "Your death, I take it, is registered only in Italy?"

"Precisely. I was reported as *missing, presumed dead,* in the English and American tabloids, but never officially declared dead. So legally I am still alive."

"And all this duped the King of Bohemia?"

"Think about it! Would anybody even think that eleven people would be murdered to fake one death? Gruesome, isn't it?"

"If true, it is indeed. It also fooled the rest of the Italian police, by the way. I heard nothing about the matter, beyond the bare routine police report. Anyway, now that you're free to do what you want, what will you do?"

"Why, the only thing I can! Return to London, divorce Godfrey and realise as much as I can in a quick sale of the assets he has left me. And then hire you, Mr. Holmes, to unravel this mystery, find the villains, and - so far as is possible - extricate Godfrey from this ungodly mess he's gotten himself into."

"Are you really sure that's what you want to do, Irene? He has set you free, unconditionally, you know."

"And in doing so has shown me at last the Godfrey I fell in love with, and ran away with. He has been weak and brutal. He knows it, and blames himself for it. I should be unable to forgive myself if I did not do all I could to free him from his own folly. Satisfied that I have done my utmost, I can then get on with my life. Not before."

"Irene Adler. You are the most exasperating woman I have ever confronted. I know not whether to admire your misplaced loyalty, or to chastise you for ignoring your gift for song, and the responsibilities that come along with that.

"And are you so certain that he is not guilty of these crimes here at Siam. The evidence is sufficiently conclusive that Sheriff has a warrant for arrest in connection with Sartorius's murder, and wants to question him about another matter as well."

"I admit that I have been blind to certain aspects of Godfrey's failings in the past. Not so, now! And yet, I know that he is not a cold-blooded killer. Perhaps you would say that he hasn't the stomach for it. I think, rather, that he would shrink from it for the right reasons. Because it is wrong."

"What am I to make, then, of the little scene featuring *Sia* Ah Foo as the dead body, and Godfrey Norton as the drunken killer? He went along with this deception at Como, which may have cost a dozen innocents their lives? He has, to my certain knowledge, been closely involved in the procurement of explosives, which were subsequently used in a plot against the government here. Not to mention his watch, found at the scene of the bombing, or a knife from your hotel left sticking from the chest of a supposed robbery victim. Have I missed anything?"

"Godfrey has nightmares about those people at Como. He swears he was never told what was planned. As to the rest of it, ask yourself the same questions Godfrey asked me when I went to see him at *Sia* Ah Foo's *godown.*

"'Isn't it all a little too neat? Why does everything point at Godfrey Norton?'"

"He claims he is being made a scapegoat for others?"

"That was the plan, he is certain of it. But now he says he's made it clear that he has left documents behind which would incriminate their leaders. It's no longer just a case of losing a future financial windfall, for which they've apparently worked for years. Now their own future is threatened, he said. I don't know what all this is to do with, except that it's tied up with this Men of Straw nonsense."

"How did messages arrive from these Men of Straw?" asked Holmes.

"Differently every time. Just someone hired from the street or cafe to deliver an envelope. I wasn't always there, of course. By the time the message is delivered, to his hand, the messenger has disappeared."

"Did he ever tell you who these Men of Straw were, by name or by title?"

"He never would. I'm certain he knew who some of them were, but he said it was knowledge that could get me killed, if anyone ever found out he had told me."

"Why don't you tell me what really happened on the *Jade Treasure*? Who really shot *Sia* Ah Foo?"

"It *was* Godfrey. But he wasn't trying to kill *Sia* Ah Foo. He was aiming at Lord Coledale, but Quiney knocked his arm away. The bullet hit *Sia* Ah Foo right in the chest. He dropped down dead. Godfrey was devastated. *Sia* Ah Foo was his friend, and his refuge."

"Why did he want to shoot Lord Coledale?"

"Lord Coledale made most improper advances to me, one evening not long before that, when we were aboard his yacht. Godfrey walked in just as he was trying to kiss me. Lord Coledale passed it off as a joke. Godfrey was doing some work for him, and needed his business, but I know he was furious inside. I told him that I could defend myself when necessary, and not to make an issue of the matter. Besides, it wasn't the first time I'd seen his lordship step beyond bounds, and had hardly surprised me. I had seen that side of Reggie Haversham - before he became Lord Coledale - when he was besotted with Isobel, my closest girlfriend at Covent Garden. She was the best friend I'd ever had . . . so funny, and always irreverent. She'd always been a flirtatious thing, but she fell for Reggie all right. Then she found out about his ways, and refused to see him any more. But he'd already told her things, and I told *her* to watch out who she repeated them to, if she didn't want trouble."

"Exactly what happened on the *Jade Treasure*?"

"We were being chased, and *Sia* Ah Foo said Godfrey would be safer on the *Jade Treasure*. He didn't know it was you and M. Le Villard, or that you knew about his boat. Godfrey had his revolver with him, and he'd been drinking. When we boarded the *Jade Treasure* we had no idea Lord Coledale and that man Quiney were on board. We walked into the saloon at the rear of the boat, and they were both there. Almost as though they were waiting for us. Godfrey simply raised his pistol, and fired at Lord Coledale. He missed because Quiney knocked his arm, and then he dropped his revolver. Then you burst in just as *Sia* Ah Foo dropped to the floor."

"And you went along with their story?"

"Godfrey told me long ago never to cross Quiney. He said he was ruthless in protecting Lord Coledale's interests. When Quiney proposed taking him away, Godfrey signalled that we should go along with it. That's why I said nothing. I presume that he is important to them in some way as well. Co-operative lawyers tend to find themselves indispensable, I have observed."

"He must have thought himself indispensable," remarked Holmes, with a wry smile.

"Godfrey hated you, you know, Mr. Holmes. He always blamed you for hounding us out of England."

"Then it's a good thing he doesn't know that the curious Professor Sigerson is actually the hated Sherlock Holmes. I don't need him taking a shot at me, thank you. I don't suppose he does know, does he?'

"No more than he knew that you were the witness at our wedding."

"So I didn't fool you then, either? I must work on my acting."

"No! It was really rather well done. But I was expecting you to do exactly that, in order to confirm your surmise. Do you remember that I gave you a sovereign for your troubles?"

"I believe I still have it about somewhere,' replied Holmes.

I had often seen the sovereign attached to his watch-chain, but had never asked about it. I think he would have faced a wounded Bengal tiger in a cave rather than admit that he had kept the memento.

At that moment the Doctor appeared, rubbing his eyes, at the door to the cabin. He glanced out at the river and the darkened shorelines.

"I appear to have nodded off. It's almost dark, I see. Where are we now? Oh, dear! We're almost there. I did sleep a time, didn't I? It's taking care of the Queen that does it. The hours these people keep!"

"Mr. Holmes! I haven't finished." Irene Adler gently laid her gloved hand on Holmes's forearm. "There is more that I haven't had time to tell you yet. About Godfrey and these Men of Straw! I don't know whether . . ."

"The Doctor is about to join us," Holmes interrupted her. "I know this is all very distressing for you. Godfrey is away from Siam, and hopefully on his way to redeem himself. We will call on you tomorrow. I don't think another day will hurt. Besides, very soon the boat will stop at the landing near the Foreign Ministry, and I want to send a telegraph message from there. M. Le Villard and I will leave you to carry on to the Oriental's pier, and the Doctor here," he indicated Doctor Smith, who had just re-joined us, "can escort you to a hotel carriage to take you and Miss Malee home."

"With the greatest pleasure, Madame," said the Doctor, who had overheard the last of Holmes's remarks.

Miss Malee had heard the talk, and walked back to join us. Soon the conversation became filled with the light laughter of the two women as Malee taught Irene Adler a Siamese children's song about ducks. Holmes sat back on the slatted seat, and puffed away at his pipe. From long experience, I knew that something Miss Irene Adler had said had set him to thinking furiously.

He said not a word more until, twenty minutes later, our steam-launch cut its speed, and came to a halt alongside the pier where we would disembark. The boat-boy leaped ashore to throw his lines over a bollard and the Indian servant with his basket stepped ashore, to stretch his legs, I imagined.

Good-byes and goodnights were said all round and in moments Holmes and I were standing on the dock as the launch pulled away. I looked around idly and noticed that the Indian servant had not re-boarded the boat. This set me to thinking that no meals had been served aboard - so why the vegetables and fruits?

Just then the Indian felt my gaze on him and turned to look straight at us. A look of terror crossed his features. Holmes and I were standing in the shadows, and had stepped ashore after him. He must have been concealed behind the stack of barrels, and it was clear that he expected us to be back aboard the launch, not standing mere yards away. He turned and bolted, tossing his basket aside.

Holmes and I had just enough time to realise what was about to happen and turn towards the receding boat before an enormous explosion turned it into a fiery mass of fragments, followed by another, even louder concussion as the boiler exploded. Clouds of steam rose from the wreckage, and showers of blazing coal rained down on us, fifty yards distant.

Through the tumult I heard a voice, pleading for help. Thank God! I recognised Malee's voice, and it sounded strong. I leaped into the river, and struck out for the wreckage of the steam-launch. Because of the boiling clouds of steam bubbling up through the surface of the river I could see nothing, and could only head towards the sound of that voice as I churned through the water.

Holmes was close behind me. I had heard him shout to a group of loafers at the pier that a reward would be paid to anyone who caught the Indian who had just run off, before diving in after me.

As we neared the wreckage the mist was easier to see through, and suddenly the stern section of the launch appeared, still intact and barely afloat. Clinging to it, and calling for help, I saw Malee. The Doctor was half afloat, half aboard, and completely unconscious, though the rise and fall of his chest showed that he was still alive. His face was burnt, and his hair and whiskers singed to a short frizzle.

Malee was crying, and trying desperately to revive Irene Adler, but one look at the twisted neck showed me that there was no chance. Too many times I have seen the after effects of close proximity to a blast. The whiplash force of the explosion had snapped her vertebrae, severing the spinal cord. It was too late for Irene Adler.

Holmes and I gently pried Malee away from Irene Adler's lifeless body. I put my arm around Malee, under her arms, and towed her backwards to the pier, then pulled her up to sit with her back resting against a pole. She was trembling with fear and shock as I wrapped her in a cloth that I begged from an onlooker.

Holmes remained completely emotionless, supervising the removal to the pier of the injured Doctor, who had come around as he was being loaded into a skiff, and then of Irene Adler's body.

CHAPTER LII

20th October 1893
Bangkok, Siam

HOLMES HAD REMAINED entirely unaffected, apparently, by the violent death of Irene Adler. He had supervised the transfer of the injured - the Doctor, Malee and the skipper - and the dead - Irene Adler and the boat-boy - to the Bangrak Hospital.

The Indian had been chased, but had too distant a head start for his pursuers to catch up with him. His discarded basket contained the few vegetables and fruits he had obviously stacked on top of his bomb, a pair of crude shears and a short length of fuse, which he must have trimmed to shorten the time before explosion.

The official aftermath was handled equally efficiently. A concise report to Chief Inspector Sheriff, then a meeting with the General Adviser - who was remorsefully certain that Mrs. Norton had died in his place, and would not be consoled. Later the Prince expressed his and the King's sadness at the loss of Irene Adler, and his thanks that we had so narrowly escaped. Preparations for Irene Adler's burial at the Protestant Cemetery, and disposal of her effects - all of these matters Holmes handled with complete detachment.

His investigation of the murders was handled in the usual thorough way, independently of the Chief Inspector's efforts.

A visit to the boatyard where the General Adviser's man had hired the boat revealed nothing of interest. The Indian 'servant' was not in their employ. It seemed that he had simply stepped aboard at Bang Pa-in, counting on the assumption that the passengers would think he was part of the boat's regular crew.

The injured Captain, when interviewed at the hospital, confirmed that the Indian had told the boat-boy he was returning to Bangkok with the *nai farang* - the foreign master - and thus no one was surprised when he stayed below, out of our way, for the entire journey. It just seemed natural to both groups. We had to admire his daring - examination of his basket would have jailed him for his lifetime.

But who had sent him? It was a cool and resourceful mind that had planned this assassination. Godfrey Norton had, to the best of our knowledge, already left Singapore headed for London; Lord Coledale and Quiney had left aboard the *Sirdar*, Colonel Sartorius had been murdered himself; *Sia* Ah Foo likewise. Of our original list of possibles, none were still alive and in Siam at the time of the bombing of our steam-launch. We had eliminated all of the others, for one reason or another, often after lengthy investigation.

Did this mean we had been wrong all along, about all of them? We had never been able to conclusively identify Norton as the bridge bomber. The circumstantial evidence was enough to convince the Chief Inspector, especially following the murder of Sartorius, for which he had issued a warrant for Norton's arrest. Also, there had been more than one man in the boat that had escaped down the *klong* after we alarmed them.

Had Godfrey Norton returned, perhaps to complete his assignment? We remembered that it was, in fact, the General Adviser's launch that had exploded, and until the dinner invitation from the King at the last moment before we left, he was expected to be aboard. He and the Doctor were somewhat similar in age and appearance; perhaps the Doctor had been mistaken for the General Adviser.

Or could Norton have lied to his wife, and decided for some reason to murder her. He had staff in Singapore who could mail a letter by return, to provide him with an alibi. Perhaps he had never left Siam at all!

"One thing I wanted to ask Irene Adler was to allow me a look at the first page of Norton's letter," remarked Holmes. "We don't know how or when he left Siam, or how things were between him and Coledale and Quiney when he left."

Lord Coledale had no reason that we could imagine for wanting to murder Irene Adler - unless perhaps still tidying up after the murder of the Chinese 'girl', if he was indeed guilty of that crime. Although we had reasoned that the General Adviser was reasonably safe from harm now that an agreement had been signed neutralising Siam, now it was necessary to consider that perhaps Lord Coledale's syndicate, which included Norton's Singapore employers - Cutter & Fluddle - still had reason to wish him removed. But the *Sirdar* had not returned to Bangkok.

Perhaps Holmes was the target. We thought about it. There had been attempts on his life before. The Indian had looked devastated when he saw that we had escaped the bomb. Was it merely fear of being apprehended, or fear of facing his employers after having failed to kill Holmes?

As always in this infuriating series of cases - which all seem to be connected in some shadowy way - there were too many possibilities, and a shortage of hard facts and obvious suspects. Two days of investigation left us no nearer an answer than when we began. We weren't even certain that the bombings were by the same hand, as we'd been unable to locate any fragments of the bomb that had wrecked the launch. The force of the exploding boiler had seen to that.

Through all of this Holmes retained his equanimity, but it was at the funeral ceremony at the cemetery that I really noticed the strain he was under. I knew then that, as surely as the sun rises in the east, this death - of all deaths - should not go unavenged. The service was well attended, both officially and personally, as Miss Adler had become well known for her voice and her kindness both.

I knew that Holmes would never talk about this in any personal way. I also knew that he would not rest until he identified her murderer, and had his revenge. What that would be, I could not say. First, we had to bury her. The Reverend Eakin of the American Presbyterian Mission performed the service. Irene Adler had not been a Presbyterian, but she was an American, despite her triumphs and fame being mostly in Europe. Holmes and I had witnessed many a death during the past three years, and of those a good number had been gruesomely violent. But to Holmes, I now knew, Irene Adler *was* the only woman in the world.

The Doctor had recovered sufficiently from his shock and burns to attend the ceremony, and when it was over, and the crowd dispersing, I took the opportunity to broach a question to him. I knew that he would understand. We found a quiet corner under a shade tree, and sat on a wrought-iron bench.

I looked at the Doctor's singed beard and hair, just growing back in, and thought back to the aftermath of the explosion. He had surfaced, clinging as though it were of crucial importance to the shattered violin-case presented to Holmes only the evening before. When he and Malee had been loaded onto a boat, for a smoother trip to the hospital than a carriage would allow, it was I who carried Malee to place her aboard.

I doubt that I should have ever raised the courage otherwise, and if it seems that I took advantage of the situation, then so be it. But she looked so frail and delicate, covered in fuel oil and coal dust, her clothing in tatters, that I asked her before I even thought about doing so.

"Malee! Marry me. When this is all over, please think about it. I could hardly bear to lose you, as has so nearly happened . . . after what's happened to Miss Irene."

Malee had opened her eyes just a little, squeezed my hand, and said, "Yes, Francois, I'll marry you. It takes a lot to get you to propose, doesn't it? But we must ask my mother . . . she saw you at Bang Pa-in . . . I showed her, you know . . . but you must come to the Winter Fair to ask my mother . . . Miss Irene can be my maid-of-honour . . ."

With that she had closed her eyes and fainted away again, as I placed her gently in the boat.

So now I asked the Doctor what Malee meant by the Winter Fair.

"Ah, well! So it's come to that, has it? Let me explain. The King is presented with the fairest daughters of the land. To please our fastidious European fancies, he now calls only the Queen his wife; the others are 'ladies-in-waiting' on the Queen, so far as we are concerned. It's all a lovely chimera, of course, but it satisfies the missionaries. Part of modernising themselves, you see, so that *we* don't have the excuse to step in and do it for them.

"Anyway, to the Winter Festival. As I said, only a few of the women of the court are actually the King's wives, and they may never marry another, even after his death. The others are retained as Maids-of-Honour. Since the time of his father, the King has wisely allowed such of these women who do not wish to stay at Court to leave palace service, and marry outside. Such Palace Women are much sought after by well-born gentlemen, who must agree never to mistreat them.

"Many choose to remain in the palace. It is an easy life for a fun-loving people. They risk, however, incurring the King's displeasure, and ending up as Wives of the Yellow Room, required to attend court faithfully every day His Majesty is in attendance, only to be entirely ignored."

"We still haven't come to the Winter Fair, Doctor," I gently chided him.

"Patience, son! We're getting there now. Malee's mother was such a Palace

Woman. When she left the Palace it was all arranged between Malee's father's family, and hers. And it was all arranged at the Winter Fair.

"It is held every winter - or such as they have here - at the Pramane Ground, when the weather turns a little cool and the Siamese dress as though it is almost freezing. Stalls, amusements, concerts, theatricals, shadow-puppet shows, food and fun. The old Palace Women run many of the stalls, as a way of getting together. A sort of old-girls-reunion, really. Anyway, Malee's mother runs one of the stalls every year."

"So if you want to marry the girl - which is as plain as the nose on your face - you'll have to face Mum at the Winter Fair. Don't worry! If you've been told you must come and ask, then it's already settled. They just like to do it their way. It's only a few months."

"Thank you, Doctor. How do you come to know so much about Malee's family, anyway?"

"I attended her father during his final illness. He was a true Siamese nobleman, gentle and artistic, but strong in his adherence to principles. The family is not wealthy, as Siamese noble families go, but their name is known and respected. Malee's mother is quite a remarkable woman, and still handsome. Every year since then, when the Winter Fair comes around, I tell myself that I will have a word with her about her future. Never get around to it, though. Seems like there's always something to do - the St. Andrew's Society, training at the Rowing Club, the Library Committee."

"Then don't wait too long, Doctor," I smiled. "If her daughters are anything to go by, I imagine she must be quite beautiful."

"Quite!" agreed the Doctor, as we turned to pay, one last time, our respects to the woman we left behind us in that cemetery in Siam. The American *prima donna* of the Warsaw Opera, and the toast of European society, Miss Irene Adler!

The one woman in all the world to Sherlock Holmes! That was how I chose to think of her, and to remember her.

21st October 1893
Bangkok, Siam
Holmes returned from the Ministry, where he had gone to collect a ciphered telegraph from Mycroft. He worked on the document for some time, smoking his pipe on and off until the task was finished, read the plain text, then crumpled the paper into a ball and tossed it into his ashtray.

Not a word to me! I realised he was deep in thought, pondering a change of course. The signals were familiar. Puffing furiously at his pipe, pacing back and forth, with his hands thrust deep into the pockets of his paisley silk robe.

The occasional exclamation was to himself, or perhaps a grunt of punctuation to a particular thought. Holmes at work!

Finally, he tapped his overheated pipe out into the ashtray, set it aside, and took a cool one from the small pipe rack he has bought. A few tamps of tobacco, and a light from a taper set to the lamp flame.

"Back to Europe, le Villard. Our work here is done. Our prey is to be found there, I'm certain of it now. Marseilles is the first stop. You'll be close to home, anyway."

"Perhaps not, Holmes," said I. "You say our work here is done, but my life here is not. *Il faut cultiver notre jardin!* I have asked Malee to be my wife. I think she has accepted. Until now I have felt that he who travels lightest travels farthest, but I have now reached a destination.

"Besides, Holmes, after the events here at Siam, I no longer feel particularly proud to be French. Nor, to be quite frank, would I have felt terribly proud to be British either. Neither government behaved well, but then we have seen that governments rarely do, I suppose. Whatever, I have had enough of fighting other people's battles.

"I shall remain here at Siam a while, at least until the Winter Fair. I shall hire a small villa, and bring Tashi there to live with me until Malee and I can be married. Then, we will decide together what to do."

Holmes looked up at me, and thought for a moment about what I had said. Finally he spoke, softly.

"Well, le Villard! I must congratulate you. A superlative choice, and I am glad that, if I must lose my companion in detection to a woman, it is to Miss Malee. I suspect that you will miss the most satisfying part of the chase, when I finally lay hands on this murderous gang, but every prize has its price."

He stood up, and clasped my hand in a firm grip.

"I mean that, Francois. I shall miss your company, that is a certainty. We have had a good many adventures together, you and I. We're lucky to be alive, really. The good news is that, amongst other things, Mycroft sends news, which means that it will shortly be the right time for my return to London. So at least I shall have my faithful Watson to record my investigations again."

"And for my part, I shall prepare my Journals for you to take to him," said I, "with my regards, and the fond hope that one day we may meet, your biographers."

CHAPTER LIII

"WE'VE SPENT THE AFTERNOON clubbing, Watson. Firstly the Diogenes, where we met with Mycroft, and le Villard was able to chat with de Benoist for the first time in three years."

Holmes had stepped in out of the fog, which still lay thickly over London, limiting vision to a few paces in front of our bow-windows. Camden House, directly opposite, was barely visible, and at times entirely obscured.

"It's fixed up for tomorrow evening, at Parliament House. There is a private lounge for the Permanent Under-Secretaries that is ideally set up for what Mycroft and I have in mind. Mycroft has prevailed upon the Cabinet Secretary to invite Lord Coledale and Quiney to Westminster, to meet the Permanent Under-Secretary of State for Foreign Affairs. The pretext is that Coledale's name has been promoted as a possible candidate for Foreign Minister if the Opposition is victorious at the next elections. Quiney, as his chief political adviser, is expected to be there.

"I've had a watch on Lord Coledale's hotel since last night, but he hasn't gone out at all. Quiney hasn't been seen, but Coledale has already accepted for both of them.

"I also arranged for Mycroft and de Benoist to attend, and to bring Commissioner MacDonald with them. There are sure to be high-level arrests made.

"Then we went on to the Anglo-Indian Club to see Hayter, and another old chum of his from the glory days of the Raj. We had a most interesting discussion, about old history and new villainies. The upshot is that we'll be going to dine at the Moti Mahal in a couple of hours, but I hardly think you need dress for the occasion.

"Le Villard has just now gone to the St. Pancras Hotel to see *Señor* Azcevado Marques and Price Phichai, to inform them of the final plan for tomorrow night. And now, a little cogitation is in order. Can't afford any mistakes tonight, Watson. The stakes are too high."

Holmes placed his tobacco-pouch alongside his chair, reached for his old favourite clay pipe and stuffed it carelessly with tobacco, then settled back to smoke and meditate.

I picked up the early edition of the *Evening News,* which Holmes had brought with him, and read the headlines. The murder of Godfrey Norton was splashed large across four columns, and was the sensational news of the moment. Eager news-hounds had already dug up details of his early, promising career, and made much of his sacrifice for love in throwing it up for the famed *prima donna* Irene Adler. A side-bar made a reference to allegations of some scandal at that time, but gave no details. The bulk of the article dealt with the nature of the savage mutilations which Norton's body had suffered. A government-baiting editorial headed:

MURDER AND FEAR
STALK LONDON
POLICE CONFIDENCE SHAKEN BY
NEW SLASH AND STRANGLE MURDER,

took the police and the Home Office to task for their failure to solve the previous murders in what was becoming a series of killings to rival the Ripper murders.

I was still attempting to make some kind of sense of the rapidly accumulating clues and leads when le Villard returned, and informed Holmes that *Señor* Azcevado Marques was ready for the morrow. Holmes merely nodded, and resumed his smoking. I decided to join him, and offered le Villard a cigar, which was accepted. Soon our sitting room was as foggy as the street outside.

At seven o'clock Colonel Hayter arrived. We checked that our revolvers were loaded, but not cocked, hailed a cab, and the four of us were soon rattling through the evening murk towards Brick Lane. Conversation was muted, and a palpable tension gripped us all. Clearly, Holmes expected that the curry-house could provide some lead to last night's Indian assassins, and that following up that lead could prove hazardous. Our dinner, I thought, could prove spicy in more ways than one.

We were greeted most civilly at the door, and soon Colonel Hayter had ordered for our party. The place was small and plainly decorated, with little to indicate the national origins of the cuisine, other than the dress of the four or five turbaned Indian waiters themselves. The aroma was a different matter. I hadn't had a decent curry in some time, and was looking forward to savouring some of the delicacies Hayter had ordered.

A glance at the other customers showed that the food was obviously tasty and authentic Most were Indian themselves; prosperous Indian merchants and their families, with a few sailors on shore leave scattered amongst them. Ours was one of only two tables seating Europeans, the other being occupied by rather boisterous Anglo-Irish officers who were just finishing their meal. They left ten minutes or so after we arrived, just as our dishes were served.

Attentive waiters hovered around the back of our chairs, from time to time removing empty dishes, bringing more hot *chapattis*, and pouring cool water to quench thirsts engendered by the fiery-spiced curries, which were indeed delicious.

Our meal dragged on, as we followed Holmes's pace, and ate in a leisurely fashion, occasionally ordering additional dishes, and bottled beer. In an off-handed fashion, as the main part of the meal was coming to an end, and Indian desserts were brought to us, Holmes caught Hayter's eye, nodded slightly, and carried on speaking to le Villard about the flora of the valley of the Upper Nile. Hayter called over the head-waiter, who had taken our orders, and asked if the new owner was on the premises, saying that he was a customer of long standing, and wished to compliment him on maintaining the quality of the food.

When told that Major Stuttaford was in the kitchen supervising the cooking, Colonel Hayter produced his calling card, and handed it to the head-waiter, who bowed politely, took the card, and slipped out through the glass-bead and velvet curtains at the rear.

By this time, most of the family tables had finished up and left the curry-house, leaving only the few merchant mariners, who had started on beers and were having a good time. A few minutes passed, during which I noticed the edges of the velvet curtains behind the beads drop back into place, as though someone had been peering though a small gap without themselves wishing to be seen.

Then the headwaiter reappeared, carrying a bottle of cheap champagne in a folded white napkin. He bowed deeply before addressing the Colonel in his Indian-accented English.

"Major Stuttaford is in fact fully occupied for the next thirty minutes or so, indeed, as we are having a big wedding party coming here tomorrow evening. But he says he is oh so happy to be meeting old customers, sirs, and he will be joining you as soon as he is able. In the meantime, kind sirs, he is asking you please to accept this bottle with the compliments of the house, and shortly he will be sending out a special dessert. No extra charge, sirs, indeed no!"

I thought this a most gracious gesture, and found it hard to believe that we should find any clues here. The staff was gentle-mannered and attentive, the food was served piping hot in small chafing dishes; even the napery, though modest, was spotlessly clean. Perhaps one of these fellows had an errant relative, or maybe Holmes and Hayter expected to catch up with a regular customer who was involved with the assassins? Or perhaps, yes, that must be it, I thought! The clue must lie with Major Stuttaford! That is why Hayter and

Holmes sent in the Colonel's card. We would wait awhile, and then the chase would commence.

Holmes, however, spoke for the Colonel, saying that we had all eaten rather more than an elegant sufficiency, and would forego the no-doubt delicious dessert. The champagne, on the other hand, would be most gratefully accepted, and could he bring out another bottle, on our account, which we would open when the proprietor joined us.

The head-waiter sent for a second bottle of champagne, and set it on the side-board close by our table. Meanwhile, the Indian sailors had decided to go on to Whitechapel or Stepney, paid their bill, and left. As the door closed behind them - the last customers apart from our party - the Indian head-waiter turned around the sign inside the glass. It would no doubt read *CLOSED* when seen from outside, as the side facing us read *WELCOME*. I heard the soft snick of a latch dropping home, and wondered for a moment if perhaps the place really was as welcoming as it seemed on the surface.

Holmes and Hayter, however, both seemed perfectly at ease, so I put these dismal thoughts from my mind for now and sat back, ready to enjoy a little bubbly and conversation while we waited for our host to finish in the kitchens.

Holmes looked on as the head-waiter removed the twisted wire, and then the cork. Champagne flutes had appeared before each of us, and were soon half-filled. We all toasted the owner's health, and drank. Within minutes all our glasses were again empty. The head-waiter poured for one side of our table, and then moved to the other. I thought that the service was becoming a trifle overdone when I realised that there were waiters hovering behind each of our seats, nervously wringing white napkins between their hands.

Suddenly, just as I was about to raise my glass to drink, Holmes leaped to his feet, raised his glass high, and cried, "All stand for a toast to Her Majesty, Long May She Live!" Of course, we all were obliged to stand and toast the Queen, but I confess I was a little taken aback. Holmes had never been what I should term a rabid patriot or monarchist - despite picking out Queen Victoria's initials on our wall with Boxer cartridges, long ago - and the toast was uncharacteristic of him.

We enthusiastically raised our glasses, and repeated Holmes's toast, before sitting again to drink. A minute or two passed, and the remainder of the champagne was poured into our flutes. Again the Indian servants stood directly behind our chairs, as the headwaiter asked if we wished to open the second bottle. Without even glancing at him, Holmes said that, no, we would wait. The headwaiter said something in his native tongue, and the waiters all shifted slightly.

This time it was the turn of Colonel Hayter, who jumped up and raised his glass to the memory of Prince Albert. Now, Albert had been dead and in his grave these decades past, and I thought the Colonel must have had an excess of bubbly. Nevertheless, we all stood and dutifully toasted Queen Victoria's long-dead husband, causing the waiters to step back once again. Damned fellows insisted on crowding one so. I was about to remonstrate with the headwaiter when Holmes said, softly, to Colonel Hayter, "Well, seen enough?"

Hayter nodded, and replied, "Oh yes! No doubt whatsoever. Even the traditional words, correct and proper."

"Very well! Off we go then!"

Holmes called to the headwaiter that we had decided to go on to a musical revue, and would call on the proprietor next time. Meanwhile, if he could please settle the bill, and do include the extra bottle of champagne! The Indian tried to convince Holmes and Hayter to stay, 'just a few moments more, please sir?' He appeared rather distressed by now, and I thought, as we donned our coats, that Major Stuttaford must be quite a martinet to terrify his staff so easily over such a small matter.

As Holmes reached to unlatch the door the head-waiter reluctantly opened it, and bowed as we passed out into Brick Lane. The door closed behind us, and I heard the latch thrown again. I was just about to comment that it seemed we'd found out little enough when Holmes pulled a police-whistle from his vest pocket and blew three sharp, loud notes on it.

Instantly, a man in a black overcoat and pork-pie hat stepped out of a nearby alley, and a squad of uniformed constables poured out of the rear doors of a large bakery van that had been parked there before we went inside to dine.

"Break down the door, Inspector. They're your men, no question. We barely escaped with our lives." Holmes spoke rapidly. "I'm certain you'll find evidence removed from Godfrey Norton's pockets on the premises. Also, look for a narrow shovel, a pick-looking implement, and a selection of extremely sharp knives and stilettos, most likely in the servants' quarters. And saffron-yellow silk scarves, you'll find a handful of those, I warrant."

The constables had heard all this, and at a nod from the police inspector, whom I had never seen before, but with whom Holmes seemed to be on quite familiar terms, they stormed the door to the Moti Mahal curry house, and rushed inside.

"I think we should remain outside, gentlemen," said Holmes. "This is now official police business, and we don't want to get underfoot. The Inspector knows what he's about."

A deal of commotion came from inside the curry-house, and soon lamps appeared in the upper-floor windows, with the occasional struggle between helmeted shadows and turbaned silhouettes thrown against the drawn shades. A loud crashing noise, repeated over and over, came from within, followed by the splintering sound of a battered door giving way.

Minutes passed, and then a parade of dishevelled-looking Indians, including the head-waiter and our table-servants, filed out through the door, and were bundled into the Black Maria that had appeared, from around a corner out of the swirling yellow fog, just moments after Holmes had blown his police-whistle.

The mysterious police inspector in black came out at last, and crossed the cobbled street to speak with Holmes. He was of medium height, with a beefy red face over his high collar and a brush of thick ginger-red hair under his hat. We were not introduced, and Holmes and he were all business.

"Found it all, Mister Holmes, just as you said! A nice piece of work it was too, except we missed the boss, damn his eyes! I had men posted in back, just as we planned, at both ends of the alley, and a couple of these fine fellows ran straight into their arms. We knew Stuttaford was in there, yet we couldn't find him anywhere, and he didn't get out the back way. There's no way up to the roof, so that was out. Then one of my men noticed a locked door hidden behind one of those tapestries on the first floor landing. Took us a while to break it down, and little wonder. Enormous great wooden bar across the other side, resting in cast iron brackets. My lads knocked the frame clear out of the wall before we could get through.

"Clever blighter must have bought the building next door as well, and being at the end of the row, it has an entrance on the cross street. My men were looking for Indians coming from the curry-house, so when a respectably-dressed Englishman comes out of his basement flat around the corner, my men merely told him to clear the immediate area as a police raid was underway, down the street a bit. The chap looked worried as the dickens, and took to his heels."

"Stuttaford!" exclaimed Holmes. "He's outwitted us, Inspector. Must have had that bolthole prepared for just such an eventuality. Rats! He's the only one who can tell us what this is all about, I'll warrant. Well, it's too late now. He'll be long gone and far away. Anyway, Inspector, you've caught the 'Slash-and-Strangle' killers dead to rights, what with Norton's wallet and other possessions. Should be enough to swing 'em for it, I'd say. A little pressure and I've no doubt you'll get a confession on the other murders, if history tells us anything. You'll be interrogating them tonight, no doubt. Find out anything you can about Stuttaford, and any of his cronies. We need a description. Highest priority!"

"Yes, sir, Mister Holmes. And thank you. Without your help the Yard would still be searching for a deranged sailor or a derelict with a grudge against the world. This is the last place we'd have thought of looking. Thank you, and I'll send you a report in the morning. To your rooms?"

"Yes, thanks, Inspector," replied Holmes. "221B Baker Street. If I should be absent, Doctor Watson here will be in, and he may be trusted with your life."

I confess that I puffed a little with pride at being thus commended in front of le Villard and this unknown Inspector, and shuffled my feet to cover for my blushes.

"Well, Inspector, if you're finished here, I think we'll just step back inside for a moment. We have a bottle of champagne there, for which we have already paid, and never had the chance to drink. I think that my companions here deserve an explanation of this evening's surprises, and we will toast, this time, our narrow escape from death. Good night, Inspector."

"Good night, Mister Homes. Gentlemen!"

The Inspector climbed into the passenger's seat of the baker's van, which was once again full of constables, and the van lumbered heavily away around the corner, its wheels complaining on the rough cobbles. We went back into the shambles of the eating-house, and saw that our bottle had escaped unscathed.

Holmes sat us down, found clean glasses and opened the champagne, and poured for us all. He then proposed a toast, to Colonel Hayter for leading him to the capture of the 'Slash and Strangle' murderers. Following that, he sat down, and took from the pocket of his coat the thin blue-covered book Colonel Hayter had given him.

"You'll find this to be interesting reading, Watson." I examined the spine, and read *Report on the Thug Gangs* by William Sleeman. A glance at the title page dated it as published at Calcutta in the year 1840.

"Meanwhile, the Colonel and I will explain to you exactly what we have unearthed here. I shall start by saying only that I had vague suspicions along these lines some time ago, but insufficient clues to be decisive. Besides, the ancient Indian caste of murderers known as *thagi* is believed to have been destroyed sixty years ago. At first I thought that perhaps some maniac had read an obscure account of their ritual murders for gain; then it became clear that there were more than one involved, and that perhaps they were indeed Indians - perhaps even descendants of real Thuggees. But there were contradictions in the evidence. Nevertheless, I was forming firm conclusions in that direction, following poor Norton's murder. Then, along came Hayter with his tale of the curry-house, and this book. The contradictions were explained. It all fit like a glove.

"Perhaps the Colonel will be good enough to outline the general history of the cult, while I light my pipe and enjoy a little tobacco after all the exciteme-nt?"

Colonel Hayter, who had struck up quite a friendship with Holmes when we were at Reigate, was only too pleased to carry on for his younger friend. He picked up the book from the table, and pointed to the author's name on the spine, in faded dark-brown lettering.

"There was a time, half a century ago, when everyone knew the name of 'Thuggee' Sleeman. The name started as a derisory nickname, and ended as the memorial to his life's work. Sleeman decided, in the 'twenties, to do something about the insecure state of the roads throughout India. For countless centuries past, thousands of wayfarers had died brutal deaths every year at the hands of these devotees of the goddess *Kali* - the Destroyer. The Thuggee believed that *Kali* - or *Bhowanee, Devi* or *Doorga,* to give her some of the other names by which she was known - was happy only in proportion to the amount of blood shed in her name. And every year, the returning assassins would make a pilgrimage to her shrine, to make offerings and give thanks for another successful harvest of death.

"Our British government in India chose to look the other way, even when reports were verified that the murders were the work of a highly organised religion of ritual killers. Operating only at certain ordained times of year, their activities proscribed by ancient taboos and omens to be obeyed, nevertheless, when all things were in accord, woe betide the traveller unfortunate enough to fall into a conversation with one of the 'beguilers', which is the actual meaning of *thagi.* With a repertoire of hundreds of established tricks to choose from, to suit every situation, the Thuggee gangs would work in concert to lure and brutally murder travellers, singly or in numbers, as they traversed the country roads, in order to rob them. At these approved times of year, anyone was fair game, and their wealth was assumed to be the Thuggees' rightful spoils.

"One gang would act threateningly, another would act frightened, and suggest that the intended victims join with them for security in numbers. Their most eloquent and persuasive member would lull the innocent victims into complacency, and at a signal, in an instant, the victim or victims would be seized from behind, and thrown to the ground with a knee to the spine, breaking it. At the same time, a silk scarf, weighted with a *rupee* coin knotted in the corner, would be slung around the victim's neck, and the head rammed forward, thus strangling the poor soul and breaking his neck at the same time. I say 'his', because true *thagi* never attacked women. Following the murder, the corpse would be stripped and ventilated with various knives, to ensure that the burial ground didn't rise up from expanding fluids as the body decomposed. For the same reason they always used the round grave, wrapping the victim around the pillar of earth they always left in the centre of the grave. To do this they had to break the victim's knees. Another thing, the grave had always to be prepared in advance, according to time-honoured ritual, using a special pick. Failure to comply, or any of a host of adverse omens, would cause the assassination to be aborted, however rich the victim."

I thought of the injuries done to Godfrey Norton, and how similar they were to this ghoulish description. I also thought of the interest Holmes had shown in the *rupee* coin found near Godfrey Norton's corpse. Hayter paused briefly to wet his throat with a little champagne, smacked his lips, and said, "I'll say this for them, the rogues cooked a damn fine curry. Lucky they didn't poison us. Another of their tricks, at times."

"Precisely why I waited until we'd finished eating before sending in our card, and flushing out Stuttaford," interjected Holmes, from a cloud of smoke. "Also why I asked for this second bottle to be brought out first."

Hayter continued.

"Due to the lawless nature of most of India at that time, nobody took any action against these predators. Instead, local rulers and their chieftains made private arrangements with these feared merchants of violent death, and allowed them to pursue their ways in return for tithes. Many became wealthy, and were respected *jemadars* in their own villages, hundreds of miles away from where they plied their grisly trade. Some even became established - and much feared - at courts away from the British.

"Most of the British in India, whether Indian Army or Civil Service, spent their time at drinking and whoring, if they were single, or, if married, out hunting to get away from the *memsahib* whenever not in the field. None of them cared a fig about the plight of the innocent Indian traveller, until Sleeman came along and joined the Bengal Army. He had no interest in the pursuits I mentioned, other than hunting. He was intensely curious about the Hindoos, and began a series of researches into various aspects of the various cults and religions of the country. He came across a book on the cult of murderers called the *phansigars,* published some time earlier; he was fascinated by the account, and it explained much to him of the mysterious murders so common in the areas he was assigned to administer. In time, this led to his obsession with wiping out every trace of the sinister cult of assassins known to all Indians as *thagi.*

"To make an extremely long story pass quickly, I shall say only that, after many adventures and much difficulty, spanning the second and third decades of the century, Sleeman had ceased to be viewed as a troublesome busybody. He had made serious inroads into the activities of the Thuggees, as the British had come to call them. By arresting and confining Thuggees, he slowly convinced some of the murderers to become 'approvers' and inform on their former colleagues, and often their own families. Gradually, Sleeman assembled a file on the whole of the vast cult and its less-particular imitators, who often ignored the ritual taboos, and even killed women.

"Sleeman set up secure camps, where he isolated the 'approvers' from those they had turned in, and worked on converting them as well. Thousands were arrested; hundreds more executed or transported. Those remaining he considered too dangerous to ever set loose upon society, as to a man the *thagi* insisted they felt not a pang of remorse for their hapless victims. Thuggee children, you see, were slowly introduced to the family business, and by the time they were youths were hardened to the ghastly business. Many claimed that they felt nothing but elation each time at the violent climax to their trickery and deceit, and all said they would return to their old ways if released.

"Sleeman set up large camps, where he moved the Thuggee families, and set up carpet-making and other enterprises. The carpets became prized collector's items, and the camps were self-sufficient. New children were allowed to come and go, even when they grew up, but captured older children, men and women were confined for life. Bit by bit, Sleeman whittled down the numbers, until finally he had, or so he thought, succeeded in his aim of eradicating the ritual assassins from the Indian landscape. It took him his entire life.

"But if you read this," - Holmes held up Colonel Hayter's blue book - "and a few other books by Sleeman, you will note that he says that pockets of the old religion linger on in rural India. Jackwood has it that the occasional corpse still surfaces, to this day, mutilated in the manner of the sinister Thuggee."

Hayter sat back in his chair, clearly enjoying the effect his grisly narrative had had upon le Villard and myself. Of course, I had vaguely heard of Thuggee, but as something far away and long ago, and I had paid little attention, even during my own brief tour of duty as an Army doctor in Afghanistan. Now, with the murders of which we had seen the aftermath, the cult of death seemed frighteningly real.

"You said, just as we left, that we had escaped with our lives, Holmes. I saw nothing sinister, even in retrospect," I asked. "What did you mean by that remark?"

"Again, I shall let Colonel Hayter explain. After all, it was his knowledge of the Thuggee cult's history, and his alert response to my advertisement, that led to the capture of the Indians, if not yet Stuttaford."

Hayter, clearly relishing the excitement of the evening, leaned forward to speak.

"Very simply, Watson, our waiters were all trained and hardened *thagi,* and had been ordered to kill us. You will recall that we each had a servant behind our chairs, and each of them carried a napkin. Not quite the silk scarf, but effective nonetheless. I have learnt, in the past few days, some of the more crucial words Sleeman noted down from their secret language, which they call *ramasee.* These secret commands and warnings enabled the Thuggees to communicate in the presence of their victims.

"Well, I heard them getting set to strangle us and break our necks as we raised our glasses. Part of their skill had always been to get their victims to look up, at the sky or ceiling, in order to facilitate the strangling bit. They call it *chookadeena.* The headwaiter gave the *bajeed,* or command to kill, by saying *tombako kha lo,* meaning 'smoke your tobacco'. The ancient signal! Just as he said it, Holmes, who had read the same dictionary of Thuggee terms, stood and proposed his toast to the Queen. That rather threw them off, but they were preparing to try it again when our glasses were refilled. That was when I leapt up, and the only toast I could think of was to poor old Prince Albert, rest his soul."

"Thank the Lord you're a patriotic old fellow, Watson," said Holmes with a smile, "and leaped up when you did."

"By that time, they had the wind up good and proper," resumed Hayter, "and had we stayed much longer it's possible they may have gone to get their knives. So yes, Doctor, you could say we all had several close brushes with death tonight. You must keep in mind that they have been trained to this since birth. There are numerous accounts of parties of up to twelve travellers all being killed in an instant, without a hint of warning. We should have been easy pickings, or so they thought, not knowing we had a few crucial words of *ramasee.* Perhaps they felt they had to consult Stuttaford before making another attempt. Whatever, we chose to leave, and they had little choice but to allow us to go. As Holmes said, we'd seen and heard enough to confirm the nature of the curry-house taken over by Stuttaford, and we'd already had sufficient cause to have the police standing by, as you saw."

"Mind you, I didn't expect that things would proceed quite as they did," added Holmes. "I really wanted to draw Stuttaford out before we sprung our trap, but something about us must have alarmed him, and when his assassins reported failure he decided to leave them to fend for themselves, and take off through his secret exit.

"Well, gentlemen," said Holmes, standing. "That is our charming little tale for the evening. There is a great deal more in the book, if you're interested. But our champagne is almost finished, and it's late. In the morning Colonel Hayter will go with le Villard and I to India House, where his old chum Sir Ranulph Jackwood still presides over the Intelligence chaps. There are a few loose ends I'd like tied up in regard to this matter, such as how Stuttaford fits in to all this. And how he came to bring a gang of Thugs to London, and why?"

I thought that the champagne may have been cheap, and nasty, but to me it was as liquid ambrosia, when I realised how close we had come to death. I drained my glass, delighted to be alive.

"I'll also be awaiting the police report, Watson, which is why I'd like you to remain at Baker Street in the morning, though I don't expect too much from those fellows we caught. It's unlikely they were told much more than they absolutely needed to know in order to kill on command. I suspect the murder of the jewellers was not part of the plan, but that the Thugs couldn't resist their old beguiling ways. They lured the jewellers with the promise of an excellent meal, then killed and robbed them by the riverside, on some pretext or other, before dumping the bodies into the Thames. Getting involved in that may have cost Parker his life. I suspect he was living on borrowed time after that anyway, so when Moran saw that Parker had allowed himself to be followed home, he did for him on the spot."

DAY NINE

APRIL 14TH 1894

CHAPTER LIV

I HAD PASSED THE MORNING in reading the news reports of the arrest of the 'Slash-and-Strangle' killers. None of the morning papers reported the escape of Stuttaford, so I assumed that the information was being held back by Scotland Yard while the Inspector dressed in black attempted to track him down. There was no mention of that mysterious officer, either, although much space was devoted to commending Commissioner MacDonald for the swiftness of the arrests.

Several of the papers, especially those which had espoused the 'crazed killer' theory, took credit for pointing out that a group of Oriental assassins had obviously been responsible for the most gruesome series of murders in London since Jack's time.

Learning nothing new there, I tossed the papers aside, and was about to open le Villard's Journals once again when a commissionaire arrived, bearing a manila envelope bearing no marks other than the name of *Sherlock Holmes Esq.*, and our address. No indication as to whom it may be from! Assuming it was the police report of the questioning of the assassins, I set it on the low table by Holmes's chair, alongside his current smoking accoutrements.

Then I picked up the Journals once more, and was transported back to the world of Francois le Villard.

CHAPTER LV

23rd October 1893
Bangkok, Siam

HAVING MADE MY DECISION, I proceeded to do as I had told Holmes I would. When Holmes did not need me, I spent most of my time looking for a suitable villa - one with a large space for Tashi to run around and chase butterflies, his favourite occupation. I also took the opportunity of looking for some way to employ my time at Siam profitably and, if possible, enjoyably, once Holmes had departed for Marseilles.

I visited with several French companies based at Siam - ones that I had not investigated - and found several interesting prospects. Much of this was due to the fact that I had a basic understanding of the Siamese language. I did not visit Malee again; she was kept at the hospital only one day, during which Holmes and I were busy with investigations, and then returned to her family's compound where, according to the Doctor, several generations of the extended family were in residence, in the Siamese way.

I took her words at the time of the accident to mean that I should wait until the Winter Fair before pursuing my suit any further. I resolved to abide by her words. I was unsure of the attitude her mother and the other elders of her family would take towards her marrying someone not Siamese, and was determined to cause no offence and to give no cause for dissension to arise. Besides, it was to be only a few months more.

What I did do was make an appointment with Doctor Smith to take me to the Winter Fair when it should take place. He seemed more than glad to have an excuse to attend, especially at the stall of Malee's mother.

Holmes busied himself with his investigations, tying up loose ends and doing what he could to make sense of events since our arrival - though I must say that he seemed certain that the threat to the General Adviser had passed, and that the chase must switch to Europe.

As usual, Holmes refrained from divulging his processes of deduction, preferring to reason in isolation. When he required a colleague to proceed with his investigations, I was called in. I found myself, therefore, in much the same situation as Doctor Watson so frequently found himself - trying to piece together the full picture as Holmes saw it. Usually unsuccessfully, as neither Watson or I had all the evidence, and we were neither of us Sherlock Holmes.

I realised that I should regret not being involved with Holmes in his various adventures. But I had been frozen near to death, and baked dry in a series of deserts. I had been attacked with all manner of sharp weapons, shot at, almost blown up several times, and kicked by a camel. I wondered if I would miss the excitement.

Not if I was with Malee, I decided. I lay back on the General Adviser's lawn under a broad, shady tree, with a jug of lemonade, and Tashi sleeping with his head on my feet.

12th November 1893
Bangkok, Siam
Captain Jones finally departed Bangkok, after being recalled from his posting as British minister at Siam - rather shabbily in the opinion of those who knew him as a courageous, if forthright, ally of the Siamese in their desire to remain uncolonised. It was generally thought that he was being made scapegoat for Lord Rosebery's lamentable failure to support the Siamese in the early days of the conflict - when less of Siamese territory would have been surrendered to the French - and for the subsequent loss of face by the English when the less than ideal treaties were finally signed.

Holmes left Siam by steamer bound for Singapore on the evening of *loy kratong*, one of the most enjoyable festivals of the ceremony-filled Siamese year.

It is the night when all Siamese head for the nearest body of water, and float their *kratong*s - floats made of a round of buoyant palm-trunk, gaily decorated with folded banana leaves and flowers. With the addition of smouldering joss-sticks and a few coins as an offering, the whole topped by lit candles, these small shrines to a former queen of long ago Sukhothai are set afloat by the Siamese with fervent prayers for the future. Those that escape the predations of small boys hunting for coins join the thousands already afloat.

Holmes's leather suitcase and his small trunk - where he had packed away my Journals for delivery to Doctor Watson in London - were already stowed in his cabin. We stood at the foot of the gangway, Holmes ready to board the daily steamer to Singapore. As I bade him farewell, handing him his carry-bag, the entire river along both shores - for as far as I could see - twinkled and glowed like a fairyland, so numerous were these illuminated floats. And everywhere the air was filled with the pervasive song the Siamese play at *loy kratong* time, in a thousand variations on the same melodious theme. It is played on Siamese musical instruments in large ensembles, by raucous brass-bands, or just by beating time on a few upended tins or bottles, with the same words sung over and over, all through the day and night.

At any place where water is accessible the Siamese had gathered; many were dressed in their best finery, and the girls and younger women wore flowers in their hair. Small children with their families; courting couples; grandmothers and grandfathers! Each waiting their turn to kneel beside the river to pray before lighting joss sticks and candles, and gently pushing their *kratong* and their hopes and wishes out into the stream.

Holmes contemplated the river, illuminated by ten thousand floating lamps, and spoke softly over the sounds of the melody of *loy kratong*.

"It's difficult to know *exactly* what we have achieved here, le Villard. Certainly we averted several serious attempts to assassinate the General Adviser. As yet we haven't discovered the identity of those responsible, nor of those who commissioned the attempts. Those are the questions that need answers. Those answers I seek now in Europe. I shall let you know the outcome, sooner or later."

What he did not say, although it was clearly understood between us, was that he would not allow the matter to rest until he had traced the killers of Irene Adler. We were both convinced that the murderers of Irene Adler and the bomb-planting assassins were one and the same gang.

"Would events have turned out differently, in the long view, had we not been here? Who can say, really? Our real achievement, I think, has been that our efforts have allowed the King - and his brother princes, and the General Adviser they have appointed - to continue to rule wisely, and to implement modern reforms as they are doing.

"More than ever I believe that, whoever is behind all these attempts, the aim is to destabilise Siam entirely and render it easy pickings. It has been our privilege to see to it that those reforms will continue, and that, slowly but surely Siam will take her place as a recognised modern government under its own sovereign.

"The price has been too high to even consider, in a personal sense," - that was the only reference I ever heard Holmes make to the loss of Irene Adler, other than in a purely professional context, since that tragic evening on the river - "but it *is* a good feeling to know that we, in our own way, have helped. This is a most charming country in many ways, and can not conceivably benefit from the imposition of a colonial master. With all its flaws and faults - and they are certainly many - this is a unique and long-established society. It deserves its freedom and independence precisely because it has proven willing and able to defend them in this modern world.

"As you are now to marry a daughter of Siam, I like to feel that together we have helped the *right* way, for once, to prevail. The colonisation of the world by powerful European nations will stop here, I think, at the borders of a free Siam."

I had rarely heard Holmes discourse on the larger issues in which we became involved. Not that they were ignored! On the contrary, in fact, but they were simply rarely discussed.

Our involvement usually took the form of detection of specific villainies. It was unspoken between us that our efforts were directed towards ends of which we approved, ourselves. Were he asked to interfere to carry forward an injustice, I am sure that Holmes would have refused.

It is not impossible, given the unscrupulous nature of governments, that this had, in fact, happened. After all, over the years prior to the start of our long journey - almost three years ago now - Holmes had carried out many investigations for the British government. Then, there were the numerous cases he had undertaken on behalf of foreign governments; usually - though not always - at the behest of brother Mycroft.

During the course of our journeys together I had heard him refer to some of these cases involving matters of state, and I occasionally asked Holmes about one or the other of them. But never, when hearing details of any of these past adventures, had I felt that he had employed his brilliance as an investigator and reasoner on behalf of a tyrant, or in any fundamentally dishonourable manner.

The mournful wail of the ship's horn heralded her imminent departure. Holmes shook my hand with a firm grip, but I found I could not end our professional association in such a reserved, British fashion. I hugged my old colleague to me, and clapped him on the back, saying that surely we should see each other again, perhaps when I returned to Paris to finalise my resignation from the *Police Judiciare*, from whom I was still on secondment to the *Quai d'Orsay*. I half expected resistance, but Holmes returned the hug with a manly firmness, then turned away up the gangway without a further word, until he was halfway up the slope to the deck.

Then he turned, and looked around at the shores of the river at Bangkok, where we had spent almost a year. He smiled, just a little.

"There is no need to wait to see me off. We shall see each other again, I am sure of it. My regards to Malee, and, as I shan't be here, I have left a wedding gift with the doctor. *Au revoir, mon vieux.*"

He turned, continued up the gangway, and with a final wave from the deck, disappeared from my sight. I wondered when, if ever, I should see Sherlock Holmes again.

I sat in a small open cafe and drank a lime juice until his ship cast off her lines, and with her horn tooting constantly, steamed slowly through the hundreds of small craft filled with celebrating Siamese into the middle of the broad stream. She slowly dropped down the river towards Paknam, and the open sea. Soon even her running lights were swallowed in the darkness.

Our rooms at the Oriental Hotel, which Holmes and I had made our home since arriving at Siam, seemed resoundingly empty without the presence of Holmes, the fumes from his pipes, the sight of his lank form draped on the sofa, or striding back and forth as he pondered this and that.

I went downstairs to the billiards room, to have a beer and try to find a game from among the regulars at the long bar. I was able to scare up a game or two, but I missed the crisp precision of Holmes's play, his lean and angular intensity as he sighted his cue and swiftly calculated the run of the balls, his silent concentration on the game, broken only by the most trenchant of asides when he was amused by the vagaries of play.

I decided that it was a good thing the Winter Fair would take place before too long, and I should be wed to my Malee. Until then, life without the stimulation of Holmes's presence - and the excitement of sharing his adventures - threatened to become a dull affair indeed.

I had already communicated with de Benoist regarding my resignation from the investigation, citing my forthcoming marriage. I sent the message via Holmes and Mycroft, and in the same fashion received his reply. He congratulated and thanked me for my work on behalf of the Foreign Offices of both governments. He also reminded me of my agreement to remain silent regarding all the events of the past three years, with the exception of the private report that will be based on the Journals I have sent with Holmes.

14th December 1893
Bangkok, Siam
The month passed essentially without incident, now that I was no longer involved in the investigation. With the help of the Doctor, who seems to know everyone at Siam, I at last found a charming small villa. It was set on a large wooded plot of land beside a tree-shaded canal, which, because it was not wide, remained quiet and its waters clean if not clear.

I brought Tashi with me, and - because they insisted on coming with him - Rinzing and his Siamese wife, and their small son. The General Adviser didn't mind, as he felt safer now that the agreements securing Siam's neutrality were already in place, and his role was less pivotal - and thus less dangerous. Rolin had his own dogs, and his household staff had remained while we kept watch on his well-being.

For our small number the villa was spacious indeed, after the suite of three rooms I had shared with Holmes for the past nine months. Tashi and Rinzing romped around on the garden lawn, once it was cut. The garden had been maintained, and the house was clean and well appointed in simple taste. Exactly what I had been looking for, in other words!

The sitting-room gave onto a wooden deck that ran along the canal bank for some distance. Shaded by the spreading canopies of two mango trees, shielded by stands of tall bamboo at the ends, the terrace was where I expected to pass much of my time. The peaceful silence was broken only by the song of birds and crickets in the trees, and the barking of dogs chasing butterflies through the shrubs, with the occasional distinctive calls and sounds of a vendor in a skiff laden with wares. In the mornings I was awakened by the *ka-waew! ka-waew!* of the birds outside my windows, and came to appreciate their insistent song.

Here I established a comfortable household, by my modest standards. I had drawn on the bank draft which Holmes had left for me at the Hong Kong and Canton Bank - courtesy of the British government - and had purchased such items as I needed for comfort, but nothing more. Except for books, and wine. I decided that now that I was - at least for a short while - a gentleman of leisure, I would read of an afternoon on my new terrace, with a glass of wine from time to time, and take a moment to watch tiny lizards dart about across the sunny decking.

My mornings were spent - after I had done my gymnasium on the terrace, and my *baritsu* practice routines under the trees on the lawn, Tashi watching quietly - in exploring parts of Bangkok where our work had never taken us. The Chinatown area in particular fascinated me, with the industry and colour, rituals and traditions at every corner. It was not so different from Shanghai, in many ways, but had a special Siamese flavour.

Another favoured pastime was searching out old books at the book markets and book stores around Pramane Ground. Apart from interesting reading in French and English, I found many old books and prints of historical interest about Siam and its neighbouring countries, mostly in the elegant Siamese script.

After such a visit I invariably explored the market areas to sample unfamiliar and interesting dishes at the numerous food stalls to be found. As always, a few old favourites tempted me, but as a Frenchman, new and exotic cuisine is always of great interest to me, and in that respect Siam never fails to surprise and delight.

In other words, I was gradually settling into a domesticity that I had abandoned entirely when I accepted de Benoist and Mycroft Holmes's proposal to join Sherlock Holmes in a journey to Tibet. After the years of being on the road, or in paid accommodation, it was wonderful to live in my own household again.

The only thing I missed was the excitement of waking up each day never knowing what the day's adventures with Holmes would bring. I will freely confess that that excitement is a narcotic far more powerful and addictive than the opium smoked in pipes at the Heavenly Pavilion. At times, despite the tranquil peace, which I greatly relished, I swear I should have booked passage on the next ship bound for Marseilles, and rejoined Holmes there.

I knew that his accounts with the gang of assassins were far from settled, and hated to miss the inevitable confrontation of wits when Holmes finally tracked them to their lair, and set his traps for them. The only one thing that stayed me was the thought of leaving Malee, when I had only just found her.

I received word from the Doctor, who as the family physician was attending Malee's recovery, that her mother was not terribly happy about the dangers to which her daughter had been exposed. Fortunately she hadn't been informed about the night of the burning shophouses, when Malee and Miss Saranya had rescued me from the river.

I was very concerned that she may forbid Malee to marry me when I finally got to ask her permission at the Winter Fair, but the Doctor assured me that the delay was to my advantage.

"Allow time to heal her wounds, and I will quietly take your part, if needed. But I think you need have no fear if Malee has her heart set on marriage as you do - and that is how it seems to me whenever I see her."

"Thank you, Doctor," I had responded. "You have set my mind at rest somewhat, though I shall never really believe it's not a dream until we are actually wed."

My evenings I mostly spent at home, reading, or else writing up occasional entries in this, my latest Journal, which I still keep in a desultory fashion. At times I dined with one or another of the friends we had made here; the Doctor, occasionally Rolin, once with the Prince and the General Adviser.

14th January 1894
Bangkok, Siam
Christmas came and went uneventfully, though I attended several parties and concerts with the good Doctor Smith. Though no longer actively investigating anything, I still kept alert for anything that came my way that might help Holmes. Once or twice there were small items of information which I thought he should know. Prior to leaving, Holmes had arranged for my use of the General Adviser's telegraph connection at the ministry, so once he had telegraphed that he could be reached at *Poste Restante,* Marseilles, I was able to send these items on.

Thus, when a most important piece of information came my way, I had the means to send it almost immediately to Holmes, and to receive instructions by urgent reply. The text of the telegraph messages back and forth shows the importance he attached to this information, and the urgency he expected in reacting to it.

14 jan 1894 1121 am ministry foreign affairs bangkok siam le villard
professor sigerson care poste restante marseilles france

glad to hear your safe arrival france stop yesterday 13 jan visited by nai portugee joao enrique son of jose felipe stop reported father jose felipe overheard conversation oriental hotel terrace re deaths plot against general adviser plus possible sartorius stop names not used but facts speak stop deduction indicates coledale quiney or norton stop as you know father blind stop cannot place names to voices stop swears can now remember voices clearly stop date of conversation just prior departure coledale and quiney stop so prior death of irene adler stop delay in reporting due to attempt on life jose felipe by capsize and drowning while returning across river same evening stop rescued but unconscious three days stop no memory of incident until yesterday stop this morning senor jose felipe was asked if willing travel london expenses paid to confirm stop no response as yet stop is this of any help stop regards le villard

15 jan 1894 1005 pm poste restante marseilles france sigerson
francois le villard esq care general adviser ministry of foreign affairs bangkok siam
greetings stop yes indeed very helpful stop after consultation de benoist mycroft agree not conclusive but worth trying stop will arrange suitable confrontation at london stop offer jose felipe two first class passages soonest peninsular oriental line singapore to london return stop all expenses whitehall stop sigerson

16 jan 1894 0930 am ministry foreign affairs bangkok siam le villard
professor sigerson care poste restante marseilles france
offer conveyed jose felipe stop refused stop old man will not travel in quote stinkpot unquote stop counteroffer from jose felipe stop will come london with captain dom alonzo to buy windjammers stop no expenses whitehall stop his price official amnesty white bird at london plus my presence on board stop will bring prince phichai at request ranawongse stop ready for sea willing depart tomorrow stop estimated time of arrival ninety days stop advice stop regards le villard

16 jan1894 0405 pm poste restante marseilles france sigerson
francois le villard esq care general adviser ministry of foreign affairs bangkok siam
offer accepted stop mycroft pleased to hear of prince phichai stop lloyds do

not wish to remember true history white bird stop claims long settled stop timing no problem stop coledale due back london in three months stop parliamentary business stop wants to become foreign minister it seems stop set sail soonest stop ps are you aware ninety days equals clipper record journey stop look for signals off malta if not stopping there stop bon voyage stop sigerson

16 jan 1894 0800 pm ministry foreign affairs bangkok siam le villard
professor sigerson care poste restante marseilles france
always dreamt of long voyage by clipper stop setting sail tomorrow evening tide stop will look for your signals stop regards le villard

I sent the last of these messages from the telegraph office of the ministry, and returned to my comfortable little villa to pass one last night on firm land. I had expected such a step for the past twenty four hours, and had made such preparations as were necessary for an absence of four months or so. Rinzing could be trusted to take care of the household, and more importantly, Tashi. I had made financial provisions for them at the bank this morning.

My only real concern was, of course, Malee. If I shipped out on *White Bird* I should miss the Winter Fair, which was not to be held for another week. Despite my inclinations I decided against trying to see Malee beforehand. Rather, I thought, I shall send a message of farewell with the Doctor. He will see that she understands. He knows that I fear upsetting her family's sensibilities, and will know how best to put it all.

So I wrote a brief message to my Malee, apologising that I should not be at the Winter Fair only because it had become essential that I return to Europe if we were to apprehend the killers of Irene Adler. I wrote that I knew she would understand that I could not refuse such a commission, but that the very minute the matter was brought to a conclusion, I should book the fastest passage available to return me to Bangkok. I added that I hoped that, with the passage of time, it would be possible to approach her mother immediately upon my return.

This message I gave to the good Doctor, who promised to schedule a medical check on Malee for early next morning. Then, I drank a glass of wine on the terrace with Tashi - I poured a little wine, with water, into his bowl to celebrate, as I had always done to mark special occasions. Then I slept, and dreamt of Malee.

17th January 1894
Bangkok, Siam
I had dreamt of her the night before. I thought of my dream as I returned from the market and wine-merchants to shipside at *Nai* Portugee's quay, where *White Bird* was taking on last minute provisions. Casks were being scoured and filled with fresh water; chickens and pigs were herded into pens on the quarter-deck; rigging, blocks, sails and lines were checked one last time. Porto-chinee and Filipino deck-hands made sure that every possible item was ship-shape and ready for a serious voyage, all under the watchful eyes of Captain Dom Alonzo and first mate Sturgess.

I was standing back - having taken my leave of Daeng and his boys, who had come to see me off – and marvelling at the beauty and purposefulness of a clipper preparing for a fast voyage, when I saw her. She was standing in shadow by the ship's bow as the sun set behind the buildings and trees of the Portuguese Quarter and their shade lengthened across the water.

Though she wore a modest dress, her figure, outlined against the gleaming white hull, had no need of whalebone stays. Seeing me there, I suddenly realised what it was I had dreaded so these last two days; that I should have to endure months of not knowing whether or not Malee would be waiting for me when I should return. Now - and with immense relief - I was suddenly sure.

I walked towards her, and realised she had been watching me as I contemplated the beauty of *White Bird* from a distance. The prow towered high above us, as the tide was rising rapidly. A fair wind was blowing and our clipper seemed eager to be off.

"Malee," I lied, "you shouldn't have come. But I am glad you did."

"I had to come to see you before you left, Francois. I've already told Mother that we will be married, and she knows better than to oppose me. Especially with my two sisters and the Doctor on my side! It's settled! As soon as you return, we will ask the monks for an auspicious day, and be wed."

"I thought perhaps you would not understand, or think I was fickle in my attentions to you."

"Francois, hush! Of course you must go, if there is a chance of finding out who killed Miss Irene. Apart from what she meant to the Professor, and that was as obvious as could be, she and I were more than friends. In Siam we say that we were like *pa tong-co*, she and I. You know what I mean, Francois? The Chinese dough pastries we sometimes eat at breakfast with warm soya-bean milk?"

A tear welled in the corner of each of her lovely eyes, and I turned to examine the rigging while she dabbed at them with her handkerchief.

I thought of the Chinese pastries she was talking about. Made of two strips of dough, joined together in the middle only, then dropped into boiling oil to fry golden-brown. When cooked and tossed into a basket for sale, they looked like so many tiny pairs of friends holding hands and sharing secrets. Exactly as Malee and Irene Adler had done, despite the differences in their age, background and experiences.

I was charmed by the simplicity of the description. It seemed so typical of Malee, and her loyalty to her old friend charmed me even further.

I could have spent the next forever talking with her, but the ship's bell rang three times, signalling departure. I could see deckhands preparing to take the gangway aboard. Looking in that direction, I noticed the Doctor seated in his carriage. He must have brought Malee, I thought. And, it appears, one of her sisters. But as we approached, I saw that the Doctor was accompanied by a handsome woman of perhaps forty-five years of age.

There could be no doubt about it. The features were there, the eyes and the mouth. The clear skin and even, white teeth, unstained by *betel*. The nose! She could only be Malee's mother.

And that is how the Doctor introduced her. After the usual polite greetin-gs, Malee's mother leant over to me, and said in Siamese that I mustn't be scared of her, as apparently she was soon to be my mother-in-law. She said that Malee had been so disappointed upon receiving my message that she had asked the Doctor's advice. He had promptly suggested that they should all - Mother included - forget all this nonsense about the Winter Palace, and go to see the poor fellow off.

I looked at the Doctor, and told him to remind me to buy him a brandy and cigar when I returned. He just winked, and said, "If you don't get yourself aboard you won't be leaving, son. Say your farewells, and be off with you now."

I did just that. Before I knew it Malee, her mother and the Doctor were waving, and their carriage slowly receding from view as *White Bird*'s steam-tugs towed her towards the mouth of the river, where she could unfurl her sails and head out to sea, bound for London.

CHAPTER LVI

26th January 1894
Sunda Straits, Java

WE MADE EXCELLENT TIME from Bangkok, down the Gulf of Siam and past Singapore, encountering only a little stormy weather a day before reaching the Straits. *White Bird* slipped into the Straits, carefully picking her way through the shallow reefs, at the same time keeping a watchful eye out for pirates and raiders posing as traders in fruits and knick-knacks.

Parrots and monkeys screeched in the canopy of the jungle as we passed at dusk by Krakatoa, in an ominous atmosphere. A dull rumble and glow came from the direction of that island volcano, which blew itself to pieces several years ago. Captain Dom Alonzo and Sturgess each had a wicked-looking four-barrel flintlock pistol in their belt, as a precaution, and armed crew were stationed in strategic positions around the ship and in the rigging. A few sampans darted out from the Sumatran shoreline of the straits, but they were merely selling bananas and other fruits, yams and coconuts, and scrawny chickens. We bought a few fruits and anchored for the night.

At dawn we slowly got underway again. Soon *White Bird* swept past the cedar-clad slopes of Java Head, left Asia astern and headed out once again across the deep-blue Indian Ocean. The *Ariel* was headed for home one last time.

6th February 1894
Mauritius, Indian Ocean

We made no ports on this journey, so as to achieve best time, but *White Bird* followed the usual clipper route to Mauritius, then south to run down the East coast of South Africa to the Cape. From Java to Mauritius took a mere twelve days, so favourable were the south-easterly tradewinds. Much of the journey was through sharp squalls, but *White Bird* simply piled on more canvas and sliced her way through the seas, marking off the miles at a pace which seemed incredible to one whose brief sailing career had been spent in ships-of-the-line. She was as well run a ship as ever I boarded in my few years in the French Navy. Her decks were holystoned with a will on all slack watches; brightwork was kept varnished, brass polished daily; her windlasses and blocks were greased to a roster; all lines were flaked down correctly at all possible times. Above all, she was as much a pleasure to sail aboard as she was to look at - not always the case with handsome ships.

My cabin in the officer's quarters was comfortable if tiny, and as I had it to myself I was able to indulge myself in long hours of reading and simply thinking, often of this strange journey I was embarked upon, and often of my Malee. When I tired of my cabin and the saloon I exercised on deck, weather permitting, or found a quiet place near the bowsprit, out of the way of the deckhands, where I could read or watch lazily as the men handled sails far above me.

Soon enough I found myself wanting to join the crew in the rigging, and asked Sturgess if I may do so for a while. He told me that, in the normal run of things on an English ship, any passenger caught in the rigging would be lashed there by the crew until he agreed to hand over a bottle of rum. In my case, he said, as I had experience aloft, he informed them to leave me be. He assigned me a place on the starboard watch, which was his watch, and was currently aloft trimming headsails and setting out studding-sails to take full advantage of the strong south-east tradewinds.

"They're a crack crew, mind you," he said, as he handed me a sailor's knife with the point snapped off, "after you've dealt with some of the dregs you find aboard English ships. Not a crimp amongst 'em, and they're mostly Moros - Filipino *mussulmen* - so they never touch the booze. Just have to be careful about their religion, and that's easy enough for you. You've spent years amongst 'em, I believe?"

I suspected, as I donned my rope-soled canvas shoes and oilskins, that Sturgess had assigned me this task to bring me down a peg or two, it being the most demanding of sail changes, but I felt sure I could handle it. And so it was that, years after I thought I should never do so again, I found myself clinging precariously with one hand to a rope while with the other I helped the Filipino crew to set flying these upper and outer-most of sails. Memory flooded back. It seemed immediately natural to keep the wind at my back, pressing me against the spar at all times, and to consider the pendulum motion of the masts before changing position on the foot-ropes. And not least, to keep a watch on what the other men were up to out of the corners of both eyes.

Once the crewmen saw that I knew what I was about, I found myself accepted quietly and without fuss as a member of the team. Our watch spent the next few hours constantly setting and taking in sails as either Captain Dom Alonzo or Sturgess commanded, searching always for that extra knot or two no matter how well *White Bird* was doing. This was exhilarating sailing, the kind of work for which she had been crafted, and she loved it as a thoroughbred relishes the race. However, once the watch was over, I told myself sternly that it would not do at all to put myself needlessly in the way of danger, as I may well be needed at London. I decided that I would refrain from reliving my nautical youth for the remainder of the journey.

22nd February 1894
South of Cape of Good Hope, Southern Africa
Our southing from Mauritius was as swift as the passage from Java. The south-easterlies strengthened and for several days the sky remained clear. *White Bird* flew across the sun-flecked ocean, and we had no reason to tack for days on end. Dom Alonzo kept so much sail flying that we broke two top-masts. Sturgess directed the crew as they repaired the damage on the run, fashioning replacement masts from spare spars and jury-rigging them without losing a knot of speed.

As we neared the southernmost point of the African continent the glass dropped sharply and a grey overcast lowered visibility to a dozen lengths ahead for a day and night. The following morning the sight of albatrosses and Cape cormorants told us we were near to land. Gradually the nature of the waves changed from the previous great confused lumps of sea moving generally in the same direction. Now we sailed directly into huge green swells half the height of the masts, created by the roaring-forties as they raced unhindered around the southern ocean, finally sweeping in huge arcs around the foot of Africa. *White Bird's* sharp bows and lean hull no longer sliced through the waves, but coasted down the slope of one swell into a trough where only the top-sails drew wind, and up the face of the next near-cresting mass of water. Sturgess now ordered mainsails reefed; stun-sails and royals had come down long before. Both watches were ordered up on deck.

As so often on the voyage so far, old Jose Felipe refused to be moved from his usual position by the steering-gear aft until the water sluicing across the main decks threatened to wash him from even that exalted height. He then demanded to be lashed to the poop-rail, saying that Vasco da Gama had braved far worse conditions for days on end until he finally rounded the Cape on his fifth attempt. His son gently reminded him that da Gama could see the waves coming, but relented against a promise that he would go below if conditions worsened. I said I would stay alongside him, and so Jose Felipe and I were lashed, as he asked, to the poop-rail. Old Prince Phichai emerged from the nearby hatch, standing on the companionway to the officer's saloon, and exhorted his old friend to have some sense and come below where it was safe and warm, for it was bitterly cold on deck.

"It is warm and safe in Bangkok, old friend. Surely you can understand. I'm a blind, old man, and this is my last great adventure. To round the Cape of Good Hope in a blow. I'll not miss a minute of it, not for anything."

"And what if you drown, you old fool?" demanded Prince Phichai. He was a minor prince, and one of Jose Felipe's group of old cronies who gathered regularly for afternoon tea at the Oriental Hotel, and thus felt able to address the old man in that familiar fashion.

"Then I shall have died the death of my fantasies, old friend. Now, get *you* below, before the seas take you instead."

I asked Jose Felipe if he wished me to describe what was happening. He smiled, and thanked me, but asked me to keep it simple so he could hear and feel everything for himself.

By now we could hear the steadily increasing roar of huge breakers crashing ceaselessly against a rocky shore, but the thick grey mist obscured our sight - as it had done for two days, preventing accurate navigational sighting by Captain Dom Alonzo. Sturgess ordered men into the upper rigging, and a change of course to set us further south. We had run too close inshore, and would have to claw our way off a lee shore that we could not see, only hear.

Fortune smiled on *White Bird* that day, and on all who sailed in her. The sound of crashing surf shifted to come from astern and ahead both, as well as from our starboard side. Just as it was apparent that the clipper was about to run aground, an off-shore wind blew up. The mist lifted away to seawards, and the sun came out from behind high cumulus clouds over a shoreline lined with high rocky cliffs and outcrops covered with thick pine forest.

White Bird was in an enormous bay, with ocean swells marching by causing the horizon to appear saw-toothed. As the huge billows swept into the bay, they were stretched and defined into long curves. The inner ends of the waves raced crackling and spitting along the rocky shore, as they broke in perfect cylinders of deep-green water with rims of white foam. Great brown pelicans, so ungainly on land, played in the curl of these enormous waves, cadging a free ride as the wind rushing up the face of the swell uplifted their widespread wings. As Sturgess shouted orders urgently, and Dom Alonzo set the clipper on a new heading out to the open sea, I looked directly into the barrels of no less than seven huge waves, marching along the rocky shore. In the watery walls of two or three of them, staying just ahead of the breaking lip, could be seen the darting, surging black shapes of porpoises, using the energy of the water in the waves as the pelicans used the air above them.

I was enchanted at this display. Whilst we struggled with canvas and ropes to escape this watery grave, the birds and sea-creatures sported. As *White Bird* slowly made her way back to deeper water, I looked back, thankful for the narrow escape. Ashore, in a distant ravine, I saw a high, narrow fall of water, and at the deepest part of the bay a river mouth, where the breaking waves finally converged in a surging, crashing tumult of white water churned up with sand and spindrift into a dun-coloured foam. Here *White Bird's* voyage would surely have ended, if not for that blessed off-shore wind.

After that the actual rounding of the Cape a day later seemed an anti-climax. At twenty-one minutes past nine o'clock Captain Dom Alonzo laid down his sextant and informed us that the Cape of Good Hope bore true north. Given the number of days elapsed so far Dom Alonzo thought *White Bird* was in good shape to match her own official record. She surged on through the huge seas with mainsails reefed, slowly gaining way against both wind and waves, and finally made sufficient westing to pick up the Benguela Current on its way north to the Equator. I settled back in my favourite spot near the bowsprit to bring my Journal up to date, and to write yet another letter to Malee. I shall keep them, to give to her when I return.

10th March 1894
The Equator, Atlantic Ocean
At a few minutes past midnight, according to Sturgess, we crossed the Equator. A violent electrical storm raged overhead, and towering waves crashed wildly from all directions. There was almost no wind. A green glow lit the rigging, and the foaming waves phosphoresced in the darkness.

We were now fifty-one days out from Singapore, where we began marking off the days against the calendar. The voyage from the Cape had been exciting, as each day's running was entered into the log against the projected record, but otherwise uneventful. *White Bird* drove relentlessly through all conditions, her crew getting the most she could give in heavy winds, and coaxing respectable mileage out of her even on the calmest of days. Thirty one days remained if we were to match the record. Dom Alonzo was confident that we could hold our pace up the coast of Africa, but I had sailed before in the Azores and the Bay of Biscay, and knew how treacherous they could be.

28th March 1894
Malta, North Atlantic Ocean
We made slow work of the doldrums and the Sargasso Sea, but regained lost time with favourable storm winds in the normally quiet Calms of Cancer. Our elapsed time as we passed through the latitude of Madeira was still on course for a successful matching of the record, which had become the principal topic of conversation in the officer's saloon of an evening. It was obvious that Captain Dom Alonzo wanted *White Bird* to match *Ariel's* record simply to please his father. I even found myself checking the day's run, and

mentally calculating our chances.

As we passed by Malta we kept watch for a British Navy ship with a signal for us. As it was, we almost missed her entirely, but our masthead lookout spotted her on a heading obliquely away from us, and we gave chase. With our superior speed we soon caught her up, running alongside her close enough to read her flags without the aid of a glass, and exchanged signals. From Mycroft came confirmation that all went as planned, and we were expected. A pilot would await us at Dungeness.

8th April 1894
Aboard clipper 'White Bird'
Gravesend, England
Fortunately *White Bird* encountered nothing beyond her capabilities as we crossed through the Azores and the Bay of Biscay, and entered the English Channel. The lookout sighted Bishop and St. Agnes Lights at dawn of the 7th of April. We could actually beat the record - unofficially, of course. Captain and first mate had every crewman on deck, most of them aloft, as they squeezed every last knot out of her. The log streamed out, showing now twelve, now fifteen knots. Still they added canvas.

As *White Bird* flew up the channel, heads turned aboard all manner of craft. It had been some time since such a sight had graced these waters. Many an old salt saluted as we flashed past, intent on beating the record. The real reason for our voyage seemed to have been forgotten entirely. I asked *Señor* Jose Felipe just why he had agreed to make so long, and possibly dangerous, a trip, at his age.

"I think you would see through me if I didn't acknowledge that the chance to make such a voyage, and have my sons approve it, was one I could not allow to pass untaken," he replied, speaking slowly and softly. "And as you see, we have arrived safely. But of course, that is not the real reason. My family have lived on the Chao Phraya River for generations now, and Siam is our last refuge in Asia - a country where the royal family have had the vision to sense the coming changes, and the wisdom to deal with them without becoming colonised in the process - so far.

"This is quite an achievement, and has not been without its difficult moments. But the royal families of Tongking, Annam, Laos, Cambodia, Burma, Malaya and Java have all succumbed, in one way or another, and have either lost their thrones entirely or remain as little more than nominal figureheads. Only the Siamese remain in control of their own country. If Siam is threatened by those who would replace it with yet another colonial outpost, and I feel there is anything I can do to avert that outcome, I shall gladly do it, though it cost me my life. If you ask why I should do that for a country not my own, I reply by asking, 'Where is my home?' For my sons and daughters, assuredly, it is Siam. Are we almost there?"

"We have some hours to go yet, *Señor* Jose Felipe. Perhaps you should turn in and sleep for a few hours," I said.

"Yes, I shall. But I have not yet finished telling you of the reasons why I agreed to come. Even now I don't see how I can help to trap those who tried so hard to bring foreign overlords to rule Siam, and in the process destroyed the lives of Miss Irene and my old friend *Sia* Ah Foo. But if Professor Sigerson feels there is a chance to do so, then once again it is a chance I can not refuse to take. If not destroyed, these assassins may rise again like the phoenix so dear to old Ah Foo, and return to cause further grief for Siam," and he added, "as they have for the Professor . . . ah yes! M. Le Villard, though he is loath to admit it, I sense it most clearly whenever I have been with him since the terrible tragedy of her senseless death. It is a crime he intends to see punished. I don't need my eyes to tell me that much, my young friend."

At midnight we passed the Isle of Wight, and by dawn were off Beachy Head. Three hours later we signalled for our pilot at Dungeness, and raced on as soon as his cutter had come alongside and he was safely aboard. Sturgess ordered studding sails set to starboard. *White Bird* surged on until reaching the Downs, where a steam-tug from Deal harbour was waiting to tow us up the Thames from Gravesend to our berth at London Docks.

We had beaten the record - unofficially - by one day. Dom Alonzo was quietly proud, Sturgess promised the men a month's extra pay, and old Jose Felipe simply grinned from one side of his weather-beaten old face to the other. Prince Phichai stood alongside his friend, quietly describing the sights in Siamese as we were towed up the broad river.

We all gathered around the huge ship's-wheel, keeping a nervous eye on the steersman in these unfamiliar land-bound surroundings, and toasted our safe and speedy arrival with glasses of sherry drawn fresh from the cask.

And now, as I have finished these last notes in my Journal of our voyage, I must close the notebook for the last time, and go below to pack my kit ready to disembark. I shall deliver these notes tomorrow night to Doctor Watson and Holmes, to add to the previous Journals.

CHAPTER LVII

MY FINISHING THE READING of this last of his fascinating Journals coincided with the return of le Villard himself, alone. He and Holmes had breakfasted and left before I had come down, so I was interested to hear the results of their visit to Sir Ranulph Jackwood, of India House.

"*Bonjour,* Doctor Watson," said le Villard as he entered. Holmes had given him the spare key, so he could come and go as he pleased. "Holmes has asked me to tell you that he will return in good time for our little play-acting this afternoon at Parliament House."

"Yes, of course," I replied, as I placed the slender notebook on the shelf alongside its fellows. "Have you eaten your lunch?"

"Some time ago, thank you."

Le Villard and I spent the next hour talking in general terms about the report I was writing up from his Journal entries, and clearing up some minor questions I had. He told me that it was his intention, once this case was settled satisfactorily, to return to Bangkok by way of the south of France. There he would retrieve his other two Journals - the ones covering his and Holmes's journeys between leaving the Caspian shores at the conclusion of their Central Asian adventures, and departing from Suakin on the Red Sea coast of Sudan a year later. These would enable me to complete an account covering the principal activities of Sherlock Holmes during the entire three-and-more year's period of his enforced absence from London. I thanked him profusely, grateful that I should soon be able to compile a full report for Mycroft and Her Majesty.

"Would you like to hear about our visit to India House, Doctor Watson? Holmes has asked that I give you an account, but another time perhaps, if you are engaged?"

I closed the Journal, which still lay open in my lap, and laid it aside.

"I'm all ears, le Villard," I replied, eager for further information regarding the immediate mysteries challenging Holmes's deductive capabilities.

"Well, Doctor, we arrived at India House at eight exactly. Sir Ranulph Jackwood was already at his desk, working his way through a pile of papers. Colonel Hayter was with him, and he made the introductions. I suspect Jackwood is well past retirement age, but won't leave until they carry him out.

"I had looked him up in your *Who's Who?* and saw that he had been awarded every decoration possible for a senior civil servant, and had returned to head up an unnamed department at India House, following a long and distinguished career spent entirely in administration of the Indian Empire.

"He seemed a very competent old fellow, Doctor, and obviously he knew Mycroft well. I even learned a few more tales of Mycroft's youth, as their paths crossed even then, he told us. Both of them out in the field, youngsters earning their stripes, as it were. He has the use of only one arm. Colonel Hayter told us that Jackwood had been a first-class shot, and an avid hunter, when he first arrived. It seems he was attacked by a tiger which another of the party had only winged. He'd had the presence of mind to turn and offer the tiger his left arm to maul, so that he could keep his right arm free to put the muzzle of his rifle to its head and kill it. Never regained the use of his arm, but was extremely pleased that he could still shoot as well with only his right arm. A brave man, I think."

Not for the first time, I noticed the Frenchman's almost complete command of idiomatic English. I complimented him upon it, and said how grateful I was, as my French is not terribly good. After years spent with Holmes, le Villard said, it was not surprising, but really it was the influence of his English-born grandmother - and her library - that had been responsible. I knew that it was partly thanks to his proficiency with English that he had been selected to collaborate with Holmes on his earlier investigations in France. This had led to his translating Holmes's monologues on various aspects of the Art of Deduction.

Le Villard continued his account.

"Sir Ranulph had little time for pleasantries at first. We spent some time discussing the Thuggee killers. It seemed that in his early days, he had come across Sleeman at Calcutta, long after the threat of Thuggee had been all but eliminated from India's roads. But he could tell us little that Hayter hadn't already done, although he confirmed that there *were* still, from time to time, cases of murder which appeared to be done in the exact fashion of the old Thuggee gangs.

"Holmes then asked if Sir Ranulph had any information concerning one Colonel Stuttaford, believed to have served in India at some time. Jackwood replied that if he was Indian Army, there may or may not be records of his service; did we know his regiment? We answered that we didn't. He said it mayn't help anyway, as the services had been re-organised several times recently, with the result that regiments had been split up, or amalgamated, regiments had been renamed, and inevitably, personnel records were unreliable even if they could be found. Nevertheless, he called in an aide, and sent him off to search, urgently, for any trace of Stuttaford having been in

India or Britain's other related possessions.

"While they waited for results of the search, we talked, as I said, of Mycroft as a young civil servant seconded by the Foreign Office, and of Sir Ranulph's own experiences spanning four decades and more in the sub-continent. He also told Holmes that his real position was head of the Political and Secret Department of the India Office. After the Mutiny, when the Indian Government was transferred to the British Crown, this department had taken over the function of the former Secret Committee of the East India Company.

"After he'd spent some more time reminiscing, Holmes asked him whether he had ever known of a Colonel James Moriarty, at one time leader of the band of Irregulars known as Moriarty's Horse. Jackwood sat up at the name.

"'I knew of him, by reputation. We all did; he was the foundling whose father had been eaten by the *Aghoria's*, and had been kidnapped by the tribe until found years later. He was able to achieve things that no others could hope to match, due to his understanding of the Indian mind. Thought like one himself, I was told more than once.'

"'I only clapped eyes on him the one time, must be twenty years ago now, and more. I was travelling to take up a cover posting as Senior District Officer in Oudh Province, and was fortunate to cadge a ride part-way on the Viceroy's special train, as he was on a tour-of-inspection before carrying on to Simla for the summer. The train pulled up at a fly-blown siding, while the train took on water. As we waited, a storm of dust appeared, approaching rapidly. Turned out it was the notorious Moriarty's Horse, and Moriarty himself led them as they pulled to a halt alongside the train.

"The Viceroy's train was immaculately finished in panelled woods and plush, and the entire train was painted brilliant white. The Viceroy was a staunch advocate of the school of Masterly Inactivity - as against the proponents of a Forward Policy, whom he detested to a man - and was a great believer in the display and trappings of power. There were red carpets laid down for the Viceroy's party, who were relaxing inside the station building while an extravagant luncheon was laid out in the dining-cars. I had remained aboard the train, not having been invited to join the official party, and I clearly recall seeing the notorious Moriarty, on his Mustang horse like all his men, ride up and down alongside the train. He came to rest opposite to where I sat, but didn't notice me in the shadows.

"'I shall never forget,' said Sir Ranulph, 'the look in his eyes. There was awe and envy at the magnificence of the train and the sumptuousness of the meal and wines about to be served. It was all in such vivid contrast to the stained and torn makeshift uniforms of his Irregulars, Indian and British both, and to the rugged life they must have led chasing *dacoits*. But there was something else there in his eyes as well, and it was with some shock that I realised it was pure, unadulterated hatred.'

"'He wheeled his pony, just as the Viceroy and party came out of the station to sit to lunch, and led his men at a furious gallop alongside the full length of the train, raising an enormous cloud of choking dust. He and his Irregulars never said a word to anyone, and disappeared back into the dusty foothills. The cloud of dust enveloped the train, and settled thickly on all the food laid out ready for the luncheon meal. The food was inedible, and was thrown to the dogs and the natives. The Viceroy was enraged, and I suspect that the days of Moriarty's Horse were numbered from then on. Certainly it came as no surprise when I heard on the grapevine that he had been reprimanded for insubordination, then re-assigned, and finally cashiered out of the service. Later, it was found that he had become involved with another officer in the trafficking of *nautch* girls to the ranks. Never knew what became of the fellow after that."

"'Could Stuttaford have served with Moriarty's Irregulars, do you think?' Holmes asked him.

"Sir Ranulph replied that, 'It's possible, though I've no way to confirm that here, unless we have something on file on Stuttaford. Knew a chap of that name once, but it won't be him. *His* remains were delivered back to us from where he froze, scouting the Baroghil Pass in '74. And for what, I might ask. The Survey simply published the findings, complete with his maps, and sent them to the Russians. Showing off! Anyway, it's not him. Certainly we'd not keep records of the men who joined the various bands of Irregulars.'

"Shortly after that, the aide returned with the information that they had no files on anyone named Stuttaford, Sir Ranulph's friend excepted. Holmes thanked Sir Ranulph for the interesting story, and we left. I think Holmes felt it was all rather a waste of time, so he went off to see about another matter, and sent me back here to wait for this afternoon's events."

Several hours later Holmes returned. He said little, and seemed preoccupied. I mentioned that the police report had arrived, I thought, and handed him the envelope. He tore it open absently, briefly perused the contents, and slipped the two pages back into the envelope.

"Nothing much there," he remarked to us. "The Indians won't talk about how they arrived in London, who brought them, or why they killed those particular victims. Nor will they reveal anything about Colonel Stuttaford. They're still being worked on, as there is enough evidence to hold them. They'll have been charged formally by now. Apparently three of the five speak passable English, the others none at all."

"I've been trying to get through to Army records. Following up on

Stuttaford, but I'm told that if there are any records in England they'll be at Aldershot. I've sent them a telegraph message."

"Do you expect any results?" I asked.

"Not really," replied Holmes, "but I'm not unduly concerned. I think I know where to lay my hands on Colonel Stuttaford."

At half past four o'clock, Holmes bade us prepare to leave for Westminster, as he wished to arrive well before Lord Coledale and Quiney. Mycroft, de Benoist and Commissioner MacDonald would come across from Mycroft's offices at Whitehall at a quarter to six o'clock. At the same time the Cabinet Secretary and the Permanent Secretary would arrive. At six our guests were expected.

At Holmes's suggestion we all checked our revolvers once again, and our timepieces. Holmes slipped several pairs of police hand-cuffs into the inner-pocket of his frock-coat, and we all did likewise with our pistols, as we would be obliged to remove our overcoats once inside the hallowed halls of our government.

"The important thing to remember, gentlemen, is that we have no categorical proof of either Lord Coledale's or Quiney's involvement in any of these murders, and little enough on any other matters. Norton is dead, and thus unable to substantiate the accusations contained in his confession.

"Therefore, the whole object of today's exercise is to surprise them with our knowledge of the way things really happened in Siam, using their own words thrown back at them. I suspect that Coledale is rattled already by our visit the other night, so I shall concentrate on breaking his resolve first. Quiney will be a tougher challenge, but once Lord Coledale breaks we'll have them on the defensive.

"And beware, these are dangerous men; killers both, so far as I can tell. Ready? Very well! Off we go!"

Our first call was at the St. Pancras Hotel. Holmes sent le Villard in, where he found *Señor* Azcevado Marques, his son Dom Alonzo, and Prince Phichai waiting, as expected, in the lobby lounge. Back in our closed carriage, Holmes greeted the two Portuguese Asiatics cordially, and chatted a little with the prince about his early life in Siam, and the changes he had witnessed. As the heavy carriage rumbled over the cobbles, my mind wandered, back to that previous meeting with these same gentlemen only days before.

Now that I had read the entire final volume of le Villard's Journals much that had seemed mysterious, at that time, had become clear. But by no means all! So far the entire tale had been one of unanswered questions and loose ends. I turned over that previous encounter in my mind - searching at the same time in my recollections of the Journals - for clues that could point to the guilt or otherwise of the man we had set out to snare . . .

Señor Jose Felipe Azcevado Marques had started out by addressing Mycroft Holmes. He told him that what he had overheard at the Oriental Hotel had at first failed to register, but that when he had recovered from the attempt to drown him, he understood that the conversation had the potential to implicate the murderers of Irene Adler. He had immediately informed his son, *Nai* Portugee, and offered to assist in any way he could. It seems that she had often come to sit with him on his terrace by the river, and sometimes sang his favourite pieces for him. She had brought him much joy; the least he could do in return was to ensure that her murderers were punished. In his younger days, he said, with sadness in his voice, he'd have slit their throats at sea and tossed them to the sharks.

Mycroft thanked him for coming forward, and offered in return to have the Secretary of the Navy help Dom Alonzo in his search for suitable retired windjammers for their company to purchase for the Siam and Asian coastal trade.

Mycroft had asked Holmes to lead off on the topic of identifying and trapping the murderers. Holmes then began his incisive questioning of the old Portuguese fellow, gently leading him through the entire conversation as he remembered it. He had started in with establishing the setting.

The old man had begun by recalling that he had been rowed across in his cutter a little earlier than usual, as he'd been feeling restless at home across the river. None of his regular cronies had arrived as yet, so when he was shown to his usual table in a quiet corner of the outside terrace of the Oriental Hotel, with his pot of tea, he was quite alone for some time. There was a flurry of noise and conversation ten or fifteen minutes later as a party of men were seated at a nearby table. As there was nothing familiar about the voices *Señor* Azcevado Marques had paid no real attention to the conversation, until he heard mention of the General Adviser. Knowing of Holmes's previous interest in the matter of death threats against Rolin, he had intentionally eavesdropped thereafter. It soon became clear to him that the men were unaware they were being overheard, as *Señor* Azcevado Marques was hidden from their sight by a mass of bamboo. The *Señor* liked the sound of bamboo rustling in the breeze, which is why he had his *sala* in a bamboo grove, at home across the river, and why this was his favourite table on the Terrace.

The weather had been unseasonably cool, and the wind was but a gentle breeze in the bamboo, so his exceptional hearing had had no difficulty in following the conversation, especially as the tone of the exchanges was frequently heated, and voices raised. At Holmes's suggestion, *Señor* Azcevado Marques assigned numbers to the voices as, being blind now, he had no other way to describe them.

"Number One I shall call the voice which seemed to have the ring of authority. He was a native speaker of English, but I could not be more specific, as with all the others. My knowledge of regions is not good, except I can tell a Scotsman from an Irishman. Number Two seemed to be rather coarse in his choice of language, and Number Three had about him the sound of the parade ground. There were two others present, both English-speaking, who said but little, other than to pass orders to the waiters.

"Number One was the first to mention, as I say, the General Adviser. He referred to him as *'that cursed Belgian busybody the British have foisted on the King'*. That was what caused me to pay attention. He carried on, saying, *'We should have aimed to kill when you fired at his carriage; I see that now. It would have saved a great deal of trouble'*.

"Number Three answered, *'It would have been easier than hitting that damned bell. I did what I was told.'*

"Then Number Two said, *'I told you back then . . . that interfering Swedish Professor is somehow mixed up in this, and you should have done 'em both'*.

"Number One replied, *'He's Norwegian, you imbecile, and at that time I had no idea he was working with the British'*.

"You needn't get your nose out of joint,' replied Number Two. *'Besides, you'll have your chance again later.'"*

The old fellow had made an effort to recall precisely the words used, and to convey the tone in which they were spoken.

"Then Number Three interrupted, saying *'I thought we came here to decide what to do, not to throw mud at each other. I'm a professional, I do my part.*

"Number One got angry. *'If either of you fools had any foresight, you could have prevented this interference.'*

"Number Three appeared not to hear this. He carried on, *'And leaving that watch was a foolish move. Too obvious by half. Maybe that copper Sheriff was convinced Norton did it, but I'm not so sure about the Swede.'*

"*'For God's sake . . . he's* Norwegian! *And he* is *a Professor, with all the credentials. I had him checked out some time back. But I still think he's the one we've been up against, ever since we got here,'* . . . that was Number One again.

"Number Two, now. *'The question is, what do we do now? The King and the Foreign Minister have signed that agreement, and unless you move quickly, there's not much you can do now to shake it loose again. Your Frenchies might think they can, but the world is watching now. Damn that Thompson!'*

"*'Exactly! With* The Times *supporting them, the Siamese are going to stand fast from here on.'* This was Number One again.

"*'So, what do we do?'* asked Number Three.

"'*You need to get that Belgian adviser, and fast! I want him put out of the way, permanently, but not until after we've left Bangkok.*' Then Number One carried on, saying, '*There's nothing further we can do here now. So we go back home and take care of winning the by-election. We'll pull in at Ceylon and Bombay as part of the campaign - overseas experience, and all that - and then set about creating havoc in London to force a general election. If we're to counter our reverses it's essential we capture the Foreign Ministry. Once we have control of the Foreign Office, all these affairs can be made subject to revised agreements. Siam, Persia, Egypt, Constantinople. Inadvertently putting our hated French opponents in there should be easy enough, and that's always been the genius of the strategy.*' As I said, that was Number One speaking. You can see why I thought him the leader, I suppose."

The old man had paused and sipped at his tea, his sightless eyes gazing towards the light coming from the tall windows. The effort of remembering the conversation, and assigning the correct speaker to each statement, had clearly tired him. Holmes suggested a break of ten minutes or so, but the old man had refused, saying he could remember more accurately if he carried on to the end.

"There is not a lot more to tell, anyway. Number Three said something about the shooting of *Sia* Ah Foo, and advised the others to leave the serious work to him. '*Otherwise, you see what happens. You two get yourselves mixed up in scandals like you've been doing, and soon you won't be able to hush them all up. Then where will our grand strategy be?*'

"'*I couldn't agree more,*' said Number One voice. '*If we are to . . .*' Just then my own friends, Prince Phichai here, came to join me as usual. The others became instantly quiet, then discussed something urgently in lowered voices. One of the other voices called for their bill, and they left. As they walked away, I overheard one of them say, '*It's only an old blind fellow. Nothing to worry about.*' As if I couldn't hear the better for it! Though it's true I couldn't tell you what they looked like at all. I asked my friends, discreetly, but they'd paid no attention.

"Then, as I crossed back to our house, my cutter was run down and capsized by a steam-launch which aimed straight at us. I'd have drowned, except that one of my boat-men saw me drifting downstream. I didn't awake for days, and even then it was some time before my memory returned, and I could recall all of this with certainty."

Francois le Villard, who'd hovered at the old man's side throughout his recitation, added that he'd gone back later himself to ask the waiters at the Oriental, but as it had been some little while later, they had been unable to recall anything particular about the men. Just big *farangs,* no different from all the others! Then the pier attendant said that he couldn't be certain, but maybe they had come from the big yacht. By that time, however, the *Sirdar* was long gone from Bangkok . . .

My mind returned to the present moment. No brilliant deduction had sprung to my mind, but recalling the conversation was helpful nonetheless in preparing me to ignore the smooth surface of his lordship.

The light had faded from the murky sky as we rattled along through the foggy, lamp-lit streets, so that it was entirely dark when we arrived at Westminster. We found a page waiting to direct us to the Permanent Under-Secretaries' Lounge, which had been reserved for the evening, and was cordoned off by velvet covered ropes in brass stanchions.

Once inside, Holmes gently led the blind old fellow by the elbow to a large, wing-backed leather chair in a group of three, in a corner facing away from the centre of the room, and especially the doorway. His old friend Prince Phichai sat in the chair alongside him. Having satisfied himself that there were no stray reflections in mirrors or glazing to reveal the old fellows' presence, Holmes sent Dom Alonzo away to wait in an office down the hall, and adjusted the lamps so that that particular corner of the large room was in near-darkness.

He then set about establishing a brightly-lit area closer to the door, where our little conference would take place. Bottles of liquor were arranged with crystal glasses on a wheeled cart, along with a humidor of Havana cigars. The shaded lights were switched on over the billiard table, and the balls racked ready for play. The stage set to his satisfaction, Holmes turned to Mycroft and said, *"alea jacta est"*, lit a cigar to establish the ambience, and ran us once again through our paces.

Le Villard and Holmes would remain in their personae as Professor Sigerson and his assistant, and I was to be merely a civil servant attached to the staff of the Private Secretary to the Minister, Foreign Office. Fortunately, Holmes assigned me no scripted role other than to remain silent, and to make no remark, especially upon the clearly obvious.

At a quarter to six, precisely, Mycroft entered, bringing with him his French counterpart, Ettienne de Benoist, and Commissioner MacDonald. MacDonald looked rather pleased with himself, as well he might, I thought. The newspapers had been unstinting in their praise for the successful arrest of the 'Slash-and-Strangle' murderers, now re-named the 'Thuggee Ritual-Killing' murderers. As Commissioner, MacDonald had rightly reaped all the glory, though I had not seen him involved at any stage in the arrests. No mention had been made of the black-coated detective inspector who had orchestrated the official side of things, but then Holmes had taken no credit either.

The senior civil servants who had ostensibly called for this meeting - the Cabinet Secretary and the Permanent Secretary, Foreign Office - arrived moments later. Cursory introductions were made. I noticed that when Mycroft introduced Holmes as Professor Sigerson, MacDonald seemed a little uncertain at how to take this. He stiffened in surprise at hearing Holmes thus addressed, but remained silent. Obviously, either Holmes or Mycroft had slipped up on a detail, and had failed to inform the Commissioner of Police of the subterfuge.

As to the senior civil servants, I was unable to tell. Holmes had always made a point of refusing to be photographed, claiming that the usual newspaper artist's renderings of his likeness were so appalling as to be unrecognisable. This he regarded as an inestimable advantage in his clandestine work. He had an arrangement with all the editors: no photographs, or no inside stories, So far, none had broken the bargain thus struck.

Soon the new arrivals were comfortable with whisky, or gin-and-tonic, either settled in the spacious armchairs or on the sofas to watch le Villard and I play a casual game of billiards. Holmes had stressed that this was to appear as an informal gathering of minds to ascertain Lord Coledale's suitability to hold ministerial rank, especially in the Foreign Office.

At six o'clock an usher showed in Lord Coledale and Quiney - whose Christian name I had never heard used - and I must say they seemed somewhat taken aback at the size and composition of the assemblage. Mycroft introduced himself, and acted as Master-of-Ceremonies. All the senior civil servants were introduced, myself not included, then Professor Sigerson and his French assistant, and lastly de Benoist, as an observer on Parliamentary procedure for the French government.

Quiney, who did not seem at his ease in gatherings, remained wary and observant, but Lord Coledale condescended to greet all and sundry with his veneer of politeness.

The two latest arrivals were seated, as pre-arranged, so that the principals were seated facing them. Lord Coledale's chair was alongside the billiards table, with Quiney's a little to the side and rear. Le Villard and I had abandoned our game when his lordship arrived, and took seats at the rear with Holmes.

Mycroft commenced by locking the door, "so we won't be disturbed," and saying that, off the record, the Permanent Secretaries were of the opinion that there could shortly be yet another change of government. As a matter of prudence, they were desirous of having some familiarity with possible appointees to the principal ministerial posts. In the case of his lordship, the

Permanent Under-Secretary for the Foreign Office was aware of Lord Coledale's recent and extensive travels throughout the Near and Far Eastern countries, and wished to sound him out on the conclusions he had drawn from his tour. Professor Sigerson, who had a sort of roving brief for the Foreign Office, had been on a similar intelligence-gathering mission, and perhaps their notes could be compared.

The Cabinet Secretary put in that he was also interested in his opinions on overseas trade, as he knew that his lordship had interests in railways and shipping. All this attention sat quite well with Lord Coledale, who glanced at Holmes as though now he understood various aspects of his previous, odd-seeming, behaviour for an academic.

Twenty minutes was spent in discussing matters of grave import for foreign trade and relations, and Lord Coledale appeared to be acquitting himself quite well, when Mycroft began the real programme of interrogation.

"We understand, Lord Coledale, that you were well acquainted with Mister Godfrey Norton, the lawyer who was so cruelly murdered last night? And that you had some involvement with him at Siam? Can you tell us a little about that, your lordship?"

Lord Coledale was suddenly alert, and his easy languor was supplanted by a wariness that was only matched by that of Quiney.

"Your Lordship," interjected Quiney, "as your political adviser, I must say that this line of questioning goes far astray from the purpose of this meeting, and I advise you not to attempt to answer questions which have no direct bearing on your political appointment."

"Indeed, Mister Holmes. Gentlemen! I must protest!" said Lord Coledale, barely concealing his alarm and anger. "But I shall answer, nevertheless, and hope that there'll be no further impertinent questions such as this. I knew little of the man, other than that he was retained there to perform a few unimportant conveyancin' reviews, and to provide general legal advice, based on his several years of residence at both Siam and Singapore. Those matters concluded, apart from a triflin' incident involvin' a local Chinee, in which Professor Sigerson here can attest I had no part, we had no further relations, business or otherwise."

"Is there no truth, then, to the reports we have received of his involvement in the attempted assassination, on several occasions, of the Foreign Minister of Siam, while he was in the pay of Cutter and Fluddle of Singapore, of which you, sir, are the principal shareholder? Or the stabbing to death of a Belgian soldier-of-fortune, in order to steal a diamond reputed to be the *Great Mogul*? And the brutal bombing of a steam-launch carrying his own wife, causing her death and others besides?"

Lord Coledale and Quiney were both on their feet by now, drinks knocked to the floor.

"How dare you question me regardin' these matters, sir? If a brigand I've met robs and kills you later, am I guilty of his crimes?"

"Lord Coledale, you were asked whether you knew of anything which could shed light on these crimes, not accused of being yourself culpable."

"Damn your eyes, man. She was goin' to leave him! He said as much. Norton was not a well man, gentlemen. And *I'm* goin'. Damned if I'll stay here and listen to this rot. Come on, Quiney, we're leavin'." He pointed at Holmes. "You're behind this, Sigerson, and you'll be hearin' from my solicitors tomorrow."

"He may well have a case, you know," interrupted Commissioner MacDonald, standing and addressing Mycroft. "I should be careful what I said, any of you. Parliamentary privilege won't apply here, you see, and I'll have to be an impartial witness."

Lord Coledale turned to leave. Quiney was already at the door, which he'd just discovered to be locked, when I heard Holmes quietly say, *'Señor!'*, without turning his head.

From seemingly nowhere, a voice spoke out. No one in the locked room was speaking, yet the voice rang through the spacious chamber. Having rehearsed the parts not long earlier, old Jose Felipe gave a chillingly realistic performance of the various voices as each, in turn, had unwittingly and indirectly incriminated themselves and each other in various heinous crimes. His voice seemed to come from the ether, as none of the recent arrivals had any idea that there was anyone sitting in the large wing-back armchairs in a dark corner.

At first, Lord Coledale seemed transfixed, as he gradually realised that the conversation had been overheard, and effectively reconstructed for others to hear. His nerve gave way, suddenly; his speech became coarse and rough, the lordly drawl forgotten.

"What the . . ? How could you possibly know . . ? This as all . . ."

Quiney interrupted, speaking quietly but forcefully.

"I don't know *how* you've done this, Sigerson, but you'll never get away with it! You've no proof of any of this." Quiney spoke, quietly but forcefully. "It's all bluff, your lordship. They've proof of nothing, or they wouldn't need this music-hall nonsense."

Lord Coledale backed up a step or two, until blocked by the corner of the billiards table. Holmes stepped towards him, but his lordship raised his ebony-and-silver stick.

"You've no proof, I say. Quiney, open the door! I'm getting the hell out of here."

He made as though to strike Holmes with his stick, then apparently thought better of it, seized a billiards cue from the nearby rack, and lashed out at Holmes with the heavy end of it.

In an instant Holmes had his own stick raised to ward off the blow, and before Lord Coledale could land another, had unsheathed the blade from his swordstick, and had the point delicately pinking Coledale's throat.

"Oh, you would, would you? A stick is a wonderful thing, sir, is it not. It can conceal all manner of tricky devices, and little surprises. Isn't that so, Lord Coledale?"

Coledale had recovered a little of his poise, and replied, "I don't see what you're drivin' at, sir, but I assure you, you've no proof of any of this nonsense, and I'll see you behind bars for your damned insinuations . . . and for common assault."

He appealed to the gathering, as though to sympathetic jurors. "Has he any proof, mysterious voices aside? Commissioner MacDonald, order this madman to take his sword point from my throat, and I may see my way clear to forgettin' this ever happened."

"Otherwise, I assure you, gentlemen," came Quiney's cool voice from where he had moved, near the tall windows, "there will be questions in the House, and without proof, your collective embarrassment will be complete."

Commissioner MacDonald stepped forward.

"Come now, sir! Put away your blade, and allow these gentlemen passage, unless you have a deal more proof than I've seen, or heard for that matter."

For reply, Holmes kept his blade at Lord Coledale's throat, and swiftly snapped one ring of a pair of hand-cuffs onto Coledale's wrist, and the other onto the sturdy brass corner-ring of the billiard table. Then he lowered his swordstick, and snatched Lord Coledale's elegant black-and-silver stick from his lordship's other hand. A quick twist, and Holmes had removed the top portion of the filigreed silver sphere.

In the palm of his hand, sparkling and flashing brilliantly, Holmes held the largest diamond I had ever seen, almost the size of a hen's egg.

"Here, gentlemen, is your proof of at least one of the murders, not to mention theft of Her Majesty's property. The fabled stone known as the *Great Mogul.*"

Several things happened at the same moment, and I am still uncertain as to the exact sequence of events. Commissioner MacDonald stepped across, and reached to take possession of the recovered jewel.

"I'd better take that, Holmes; and take Lord Coledale into custody until this matter is properly sorted out."

"Holmes?" roared Quiney in surprise. "You're Sherlock Holmes? Curse your damned greed, Coledale!" shouted Quiney, as he dashed for the window.

"Watch out," cried Holmes. "Quiney has a concealed derringer!"

In a swift sequence of movements, Holmes had drawn his pistol, and aimed it at Quiney, but was a moment too late. Quiney fired one shot, smashed through one of the tall, many-paned windows; he edged his way onto a narrow first-floor ledge outside, and was gone from view.

I turned, thankful that Quiney's shot had been wildly aimed, and had missed Holmes entirely. Then I heard a gasp, and turned to see Lord Coledale stagger and slip, a crimson stain spreading from a hole drilled through one eye, until only his hand-cuffed arm was holding him from slumping completely to the floor. At the same time, Holmes pulled out his police-whistle and blew shrilly on it.

Commissioner MacDonald shouted, "Let him go, Holmes! We'll round him up later. Let's see to this poor devil. Where are the keys to these cuffs? Look sharp, now."

Holmes stepped across to him, whipped out his second pair of cuffs, and snapped one ring onto the Commissioner's wrist, and the other to the brass corner-ring of the billiard table, next to the cuffs holding up Lord Coledale.

"Citizen's arrest! The official charge will be your murder of Mischa Roborovsky, Commissioner."

These events all took place in far less time than it takes to recount, and the confusion and noise in the large room are most difficult to reconstruct with accuracy. I know that almost everyone dropped to the floor when Quiney's derringer fired. Even before Holmes blew his whistle a connecting-door had burst open, and a squad of constables had rushed into the room, close on the heels of the mysterious police inspector from the previous evening, still attired in black coat and pork-pie hat.

At that moment the old Portuguese sailor stood up from the chair where he had been concealed.

"Mister Holmes!" he cried out, in his heavily-accented but excellent English. "This fellow, the one calls himself Lord Coledale! He's not the leader of the gang. It's that man Quiney you want. Coledale's speech had me confused. As soon as he dropped that nonsense for a moment it all became clear. Coledale works for Quiney - not the other way around, you see!"

"Thank you, *Señor*. It is as I expected, but it's nice to have corroboration. Your son is here now, *Señor*, and Prince Phichai. They'll take care of you. We're off after Quiney. Come on, le Villard; you too, Watson. This is Inspector Patterson, gentlemen."

The policeman in the pork-pie hat was leaning out through the shattered panes, and merely nodded at the introductions.

"He's climbed down the plumbing, Holmes! Damn this fog. There he is, heading for the waterfront. Lost him again. Down the stairs, I think. Let's not break any legs. Mycroft has men in a police-launch at the quay, and at every entrance to the Houses of Parliament for that matter. We'll have him soon enough!"

He was already at the door, which Mycroft had unlocked by now. We all followed on his heels, along the corridor and down the nearest staircase, then out through a Member's Entrance leading to the terrace running alongside the Thames. The two constables posted there joined the chase, but the fog was so thick we could see little more than outlines.

As our little band dashed across the terrace two or three shots were fired in our direction: I heard bullets pinging against the stones of Parliament House, and a window-glass shattering. Almost immediately we heard the sound of a steam-launch pulling away from the pier, and gathering speed as it headed downstream.

"To the boat!" shouted Inspector Patterson, veering off away from the receding sound of Quiney's launch. "I told them to keep up a head of steam, just in case! If it wasn't for the fog . . ."

Seconds later the police-launch loomed out of the greasy mist. We all leaped aboard. The river-police manning her recognised Patterson and slipped her mooring lines, preparing to give chase.

"You heard her, men. Heading downstream! After her, full speed!"

Patterson and Holmes rushed to the bow of the police-launch, and braced themselves against stanchions. Holmes had his small aluminium telescope out now, and was scanning the bank of fog rolling across the river ahead of us. Long minutes turned into half an hour before we faintly heard the sound of their launch over the noise of our own.

"Good," cried Patterson. "Means we're faster than they are! We'll catch up with them, bit by bit. At this rate we'll be up with them in ten or fifteen minutes, I'd say."

"Just have to hope they don't head to shore before we do catch them up," remarked Holmes. "If we lose 'em in this fog it'll be the devil of a job to find them on land."

"Never you mind, Mister Holmes. I've prepared for that. The whole area is cordoned off, and all their descriptions are at the checkpoints. Ports, railway stations, coach depots, toll-ways, and all roads leading out - they've all been warned to stop any suspicious characters and demand identification. All we have to do is keep the pressure on them, stop them from reaching a hideout, and we'll drive them into the arms of my men if we don't get 'em first."

Inspector Patterson was clearly a determined and exceedingly capable police officer, and seemed in his element in the thick of the chase. Loving it, in fact! Then I reflected that he was on the trail of men who years ago had caused his disgrace and blocked his career.

I had not really understood the matter of the cuffing of MacDonald, until Patterson had yelled at his men, as we left the Permanent Secretary's Lounge, that there had been no mistake, MacDonald was part of the gang, and on no account to release the Commissioner until his return. I knew there was no chance of that unless they had a skilled lock-pick amongst their number. Holmes's cuffs were not regulation police issue and he had the only keys. Until our return from the hunt, Commissioner MacDonald would remain handcuffed next to the corpse of Lord Coledale, whose greed and cruelty seemed to have brought them all undone. A fitting start to his punishment, I thought.

A shout from Holmes brought me back to the present, and looking forward as we passed under Tower Bridge I saw a small vessel several hundred yards ahead of us. We were gaining on them, but painfully slowly. I feared that when we came to the bends in the Thames at the Isle of Dogs we should again lose sight of them, and allow them to slip ashore.

Past the docks lining the shore at Rotherhithe we steamed, losing sight of our quarry occasionally in the thick fog, but still closing slowly the distance separating our two boats. We lost sight of them altogether as the fog thickened closer to shore, muffling the sound of their engine at the same time.

"Looked like they were favouring this bank," shouted Patterson, pointing at the Rotherhithe shoreline.

"Pull across and we'll run alongside the shore, see if we can pick up anything there," he shouted back to the helmsman.

Without slackening speed the police-launch veered across the broad river. Slowly the buildings and wharves lining the shore became visible. We carried on for some minutes in this way, until the mouth of Deptford Creek announced that we were approaching Greenwich. The austerely elegant twin masses of the Royal Naval College loomed out of the mist, and a minute or so later Holmes shouted out, "There she is! Tied up at the wharf at the bottom of King William's Walk. Hurry, or we'll lose them."

The police-launch pulled expertly alongside the pier running parallel to the shore, and we all jumped onto the wharf.

"Fan out, chaps!" shouted Inspector Patterson. "Ask anyone you see for news of the fugitives, and don't be too polite about it. There's no time to lose."

Holmes and Patterson waited by the pier, and before three minutes had elapsed the various constables had returned. Pooling their information, it was clear that no strangers had been seen dashing through any of the streets or lanes leading away from the wharf in the past few minutes. Every possible escape route had had somebody, a fruit-stall owner or news-boy, or a bobby on the beat, to vouch for it.

"They must still be in this area," said Patterson. "Nowhere else they could be, is there?"

"Unless," cried Holmes, whirling around, "they've used the tunnel!"

"Of course," shouted Patterson in reply. "It's the only answer. Three of you stay here," he instructed some of the men from the River Police. "Make sure they don't get back to their boat. The rest of you, with me!" and he followed Holmes and le Villard as they ran past a brick building and turned towards the water.

I had forgotten the pedestrian tunnel that runs across under the Thames from below Greenwich Park to the Isle of Dogs, even though Wiggins had mentioned using it the day before. By the time we reached the other end of the deserted tunnel I had fallen somewhat behind the others, my daily routine - ever since Holmes's 'death' - not including anything much in the way of vigorous exercise. When at last I emerged, gasping for breath, into the open air, I saw that our fellows were standing around in gloomy indecision.

"This side is not so easily canvassed," bemoaned Patterson. "No one in the park who may have spotted them, and a dozen ways to disappear from here into the warrens of the East End."

"They'll know we'll find them if they do that," answered Holmes. "Too many grasses on police pay for them to stay hidden for long if the force turns the area over properly. No, I'm sure they'll try to get away from London as soon as possible."

"They're smart enough to know I'll have the whole city cordoned off by now," mused Patterson. "I doubt they'll try their luck at the ports, or on any of the coach or railway lines, and they won't want to trust any strangers, not with the climate of fear prevailing in the city right now."

A stray thought occurred to me.

"May I make a suggestion, Holmes?" I asked.

"Watson!" He turned to me. "Yes, of course. It seems we're stumped anyway. They've effectively vanished. What is it?"

"Lord Coledale said he was due to leave for the North of England later tonight. Well, as you know, I've been reading le Villard's Journals a great deal lately, and I recall Lord Coledale saying that he had travelled across from Brindisi to Paris in his own private train."

"Yes, I remember. And?"

"Well, I also recall that at Bangkok, Coledale's captain on the *Sirdar* told le Villard here that his lordship kept two private trains at his disposal, one on the Continent, and the other here in Britain."

"Brilliant, Watson! Whatever should I do without you! The train would already be scheduled for departure; nothing to arouse last-minute suspicion. And Quiney, as his Chief-of-Staff, would be responsible for scheduling and dispatching that very train. And your men would not be watching out for a private train lying at a siding somewhere, Patterson. Once underway, they'd be as good as out of London. That explains why they used the tunnel! By pulling in on the other side of the Thames, they hoped to send us off searching in that direction, while they make their way to their train on this side."

"Where's Lord Coledale's constituency, Holmes?" asked Patterson.

"King's Lynn, which means they'll use the West Anglia line, through Cambridge," replied Holmes. "And if that's the case, the only logical place for their private train to leave from is King's Cross."

Inspector Patterson was clearly a man of decision and few words, for without speaking he strode up alongside the park to Saunders Ness Road, and, with two of his uniformed constables, commandeered the first carriage that came along. The surprised occupants were assured that they would be compensated, and accepted the necessity with an ill grace. Our small party was soon rushing on its way towards King's Cross.

It was rather a crush, despite the large size of the closed carriage. We were Patterson and two of his men - one more sat alongside the coachman and three clung to the postillion - as well as Holmes, le Villard and myself

As our carriage rumbled along, I noticed that there was already a deal of police activity in the streets. Constables were questioning suspicious characters, and stopping vehicles to inspect the interiors. Goods carts were checked for stowaways, and cabbies questioned, and I thought it likely that the fugitives would be apprehended before reaching their train, if that was indeed their plan.

Another anxious hour passed as our carriage rushed on through the foggy London streets, with hardly a word spoken between us. As we approached King's Cross Station, thundering down the Pentonville Road, the officer alongside the coachman shouted out, and he pulled his horses to a sudden halt. Inspector Patterson leaped to the ground and spoke a few words with the coachman of a hackney that was turning out from the station forecourt. All the horses were steaming as they stood stamping their hoofs, and snorting great jets of mist into the chill air.

"We're on the right track, gentlemen," cried Patterson as he climbed back aboard and wedged himself in. "That fellow picked up two fares at Millwall Park a little more than an hour gone, and he says they paid him very well to get here before their train left. One fits Quiney's description, the other was an older fellow sporting white moustaches."

"Colonel Sebastian Moran!" exclaimed Holmes. "I was hoping it was he in that launch. Mycroft will be well pleased if we can take both of them. And I've a score or two to settle with Moran myself!"

A minute later we had reached the entrance to King's Cross Station and were running through the public concourse towards the platforms, causing some alarm amongst the few travellers and railway workers who were still about. Holmes asked a few questions of the stationmaster, whose office window fronted onto the platform concourse.

"This way! Last platform that way, far end."

As I puffed along behind the other younger fellows, I noticed an elegantly-painted, spotlessly clean private train just beginning to move out of the last platform.

"This way, across the tracks, or we'll miss them! Hurry on!" shouted Holmes. "Everyone aboard as best you can. And be careful, they're armed and dangerous."

So our group of seven or eight hurdled and stumbled across three platforms and sets of tracks. And even I managed to clamber aboard the guard-van platform at the very tail-end of the train, as it picked up speed, blew its whistle several times, and headed out of London towards Cambridge.

CHAPTER LVIII

THE UNIFORMED RAILWAYMAN in the guard-van worked for the railways, not for Lord Coledale. So did the train-driver and his assistants. Lord Coledale's authority really extended over his own carriages only, for which he hired a 'special' whenever he wished to travel.

The guard made no attempt to resist our boarding when he saw uniformed police amongst our number. Inspector Patterson was soon questioning him as to the number and disposition of the members of Lord Coledale's party aboard the private cars.

"To my knowledge," the guard said, "apart from 'is lordship's personal chef and two cooks, and a man-servant or two, there's two men aboard who've been there all afternoon, and with 'em came an un'appy-lookin' young lady, in 'er mid-twenties. The two men had spent the afternoon in the lounge-car, playin' dominoes, and they're still there. The young lady retired to one o' the four sleepin' cabins up front, and 'asn't been seen since arrivin'. No food or drink 'as been sent for, the train 'avin' its own galley, y'see, but one o' the men stepped out to buy newspapers.

"A few minutes ago two more fellows rushed up. One o' them's the man as ordered train in th' first place, an' 'e gave orders to depart immediately. Said ' 'is lordship 'as been detained unavoidably'."

"Sense of gallows-humour, I note!" remarked Holmes with a thin wintry smile. "The unhappy young lady will be Isobel Aster, I suspect. It's good news she's still alive, but it complicates matters, no question about it. As it is, they already have a hostage. Otherwise, we could simply wait until we reach the next station, and put them under siege from the platforms."

"How many cars altogether in the private train?" asked Patterson.

"Five, includin' dining car, sir. A guest sleepin'-car right behind tender, then galley and dinin' car. Next back is th' lounge-car, an' then th' owner's private study and sleepin'-car. Last comes owner's party baggage-car. Then there's th' railway's own baggage-car, then this 'ere guard-van."

"Thank you, my good fellow. Most succinctly put, and very helpful," said Inspector Patterson. "Now, how can we get along to the private carriages, preferably without alerting the villains?"

"That'll be difficult, sir. There's no way to get through to owner's private sleepin'-car, and that'll block th' way to th' other cars. But if y'can manage that, it'll be easier. The owner 'as 'ad these carriages made special, with connectin' doors at the ends of each carriage. Says that soon all railway carriages'll be made that way."

"Where will this train stop next?" asked Holmes."

"No scheduled stops until Cambridge, sir, but we 'as to stop at signals shortly. We'll be at a standstill two or three minutes there."

"Of course! I know the signals you mean." Holmes consulted his pocket-watch. "Fifteen or so minutes to get there. As I recall, the track curves sharply just at that point. That means that occupants of the forward cars won't have a clear view along the *outside* curve of the train. If we can get into the owner's sleeping-car unobserved, we should be able to work our way along the train, and catch them unawares. That's if we weren't spotted coming aboard."

"I've got an emergency key to owner's baggage-car and dining-car, if that's any 'elp," said the guard. "Supposed to 'ave one for every carriage, accordin' to regulations, but these blokes is bleedin' 'ard to deal with, an' I'll tell y'that for free."

"There are a couple of tunnels not long after the points," said Holmes, who knew London's railways like the back of his own hand. "If we can get into their baggage car, we may be able to force our way into the private carriages as the train goes through a tunnel, with the noise drowned by the roar of the train in the confined space."

"Until then, men, enjoy the ride," said Patterson. "With your wits about you!" he added.

We all stood about, bracing ourselves against the walls of the guard-van, which had only the one seat. Minutes passed in silence, as we all contemplated the difficult task ahead: how to rescue Isobel Aster, arrest Quiney and Colonel Moran and their gang members, and avoid losing any of our number whilst doing so.

A loud hiss from the steam-engine, followed by the screeching of steel brakes and wheels as the train slowed to a halt, heralded the start of our assault. The train curved sharply away out of sight as we all climbed down from the guard-van, and crept close alongside the carriages until we reached the owner's baggage-car. Patterson had the guard's key, and quietly opened the door set at the rear-end of the carriage.

We all quietly clambered up inside the spotlessly spartan carriage. It was filled with Lord Coledale's Vuitton trunks and luggage, and a host of other baggage. We remained silent and unmoving until the train moved off again a minute or two later. Once the train had built up speed - and noise - Holmes and Patterson made their way to the forward end of the carriage, opened the door from the inside, and inspected the lock on the door opening into Lord Coledale's private coach. Both of them drew their revolvers, and several of the constables stood around to lend their strength if needed.

At Holmes's suggestion, Le Villard and I searched around amongst the luggage for anything that could be used as a lever. It was because of this that le Villard discovered the bombs. Not that they appeared at first to be bombs. They were contained in a separate compartment made of sturdy steel bars, with a door locked like a bank-vault with a formidable-looking Chubb rotary-combination lock. The bombs themselves looked innocent enough - that is, if you hadn't recently read a description of exactly this type of device. Standard small-size sherry casks, with steel water pails inverted over the tops of them and fastened in place. From the top of each sprouted a coiled length of twisted white cord. There were a dozen or so on the floor of the locked enclosure, stacked in two rows.

Le Villard had called Holmes and Patterson over to see what he'd found, and both men became instantly thoughtful.

"Bombs, Patterson. Same design as we encountered at Siam."

"Well, at least now we know who's been blowing up London lately," said Patterson.

"Assuming we survive to tell anyone!" replied Holmes. "There's enough explosive here to blow an enormous hole in London, not just this train."

"Perhaps we can uncouple this car?" I suggested.

"Not on the move, we can't," answered Inspector Patterson. "And we daren't risk alarming them. They may have more bombs up front, and we know they have powerful firearms. Our best hope is to take them by surprise, if we can. Do you agree, Holmes?"

"Reluctantly! There are grave risks whichever way we approach the situation. But we'll do it your way. Leave a man here to guard this strong-room, Patterson, and we'll shoot the lock out of the connecting-door to Coledale's coach as soon as we enter the next tunnel. Try to time your shot for just as we enter - the shock will help mask our noise. Look for any pillows or quilts among that luggage, you chaps. Or furs. We can pack them around the lock; that may help a little as well."

Holmes pulled his silver-plated hip-flask from his jacket pocket, where he habitually kept it, though he seldom used it. He edged the highly-polished metal flask out of the open window a few inches, and kept his eye on it, while we ransacked the luggage for any soft and smothering articles to deaden the sound, and packed them up on top of crates around the lock. When that was done, he called le Villard to take over at the window, and took a place alongside Inspector Patterson. They aimed their pistols squarely at the lock.

The increasing pitch of the train's noise heralded our approach to the tunnel-entrance. Le Villard shouted, "Now!", and at the same moment the train roared into the tunnel and two pistols fired off in unison. The noise seemed deafening, but as we were behind the carriages bearing the fugitives I thought it likely they would not recognise gunshots.

From my vantage point sheltering behind a huge portable wardrobe I saw the lock blown clean out of the door, and the door swing inwards a little. So far, so good, I thought. Patterson and Holmes cautiously edged into the tiny ante-room leading to the living-quarters proper. We were in the owner's bed chamber; an enormous bed with a chintz quilt over snow-white sheets and puffy pillows, original oils screwed to the walls, and an upholstered-plush love seat by the window. Forward of that was Lord Coledale's white-tiled bathroom, with a high-sided enamelled tub and gleaming brass and cut-glass fittings.

Through the connecting door, we continued on into the owner's lounge, with a cosy study taking up one corner. Mahogany was everywhere, carved and inlaid with marquetry in exotic woods. Polished brass and silver details winked at us in the flickering light from the windows. Well-stuffed leather armchairs, shelves of calf-bound books, a fire-place even! No doubt about it, crime certainly seemed to have paid off handsomely for the once-impecunious Reginald Aubrey Haversham, late Lord Coledale.

Holmes examined the lock on the door leading forward from the carriage.

"We're in luck. It locks when you close the door behind you, and you'd need a key to get back in. But a twist of this latch will let us out. Now we have to hope that they don't lock the door into the lounge-car. No reason why they should, really; the connection passage is covered to prevent intrusion.

"Absolute quiet now, please. I'll try to get a look inside."

Holmes slowly turned the latch-lock, and pulled the first door open towards him. Le Villard held it to prevent it swinging. Crouching low, Holmes then inched forward until he could just see into the next carriage. He remained there a moment, slowly turned the lever-handle on the door without attempting to open it, then returned to the owner's coach.

"Four of them," he whispered, "Quiney and Moran, and the two others we know of. Can't see anyone else. They're at the far end, sitting in a lounge area. Moran and Quiney are talking together, and the others are playing dominoes. Moran's the elderly fellow with the white moustaches," said Holmes to le Villard and the Inspector, "but don't be fooled. He's a vicious killer. I saw at least two pistols on the table. And don't forget Quiney's derringer pistol up his sleeve. The door isn't locked. We'll repeat the tunnel trick. Le Villard, the flask again, if you please."

Our French colleague went quietly to the window, and softly lowered a pane by a few inches; sufficient to extend the flask again. Minutes passed, as Holmes assured us we would very soon come to another tunnel. Again le Villard called out, and the train plunged into a tunnel. Abandoning silence, Holmes and Patterson, closely followed by the rest of us, charged through the narrow passage and into the elegant lounge car.

The two other men saw us before Quiney and Moran did. They snatched up weapons, but were immediately felled by shots from Inspector Patterson and Holmes. Moran and Quiney ducked below the counter separating the lounge area from the library, and fired answering shots. These sent our forces ducking for cover. The two fugitives, crouching low, slipped through the next set of connecting doors and into the dining-car. Locking this door behind them gave them a moment of grace, and I saw them sprinting for the far end, past the galley servery. This door they closed behind them as well, and went on into the guest sleeping-car, where we believed Isobel Aster was being held.

A few more pistol rounds and a brawny shove or two from Patterson's men opened the locks. We all ran through the dining car to the next set of doors, where the same process was repeated yet again. Two of Patterson's men rounded up the chef and his three assistants, who had been playing cards together at a tiny table. Using the chef's own key, the constables locked the cooks in the galley - after searching for concealed weapons - and re-joined us.

Our quarry were running out of places to hide. Forward of this car was the tender, and then the locomotive itself, now travelling at a good speed. I thought it unlikely they would be able to escape that way. Quiney and Moran must have felt the same. They decided to make their stand here, and we soon learnt why. As we peered around the half-open door we saw an empty corridor between sleeping compartments, two to each side, beyond doors leading to bathrooms on either side.

Quiney stepped partially out into the corridor from the first compartment on his left, pushing Isobel Aster in front of him as a shield. She'd been gagged, and her right wrist was hand-cuffed to the sliding-door handle, I suppose to prevent her from opening the window drapes and raising an alarm at stations *en route*. A few dishes were stacked on the floor of the corridor.

"At last we meet, face-to-face, Holmes!" shouted Quiney. "I should have known that damned Professor Sigerson was you, when we crossed paths at Alexandria. A pity I never saw a photograph of you, I suppose, but this day had to come."

"Gentlemen!" said Holmes to us all, never taking either his eyes or his gunsights from Quiney. "Allow me to introduce to you the late Lord Coledale's aide and adviser, Mr. Quiney. Otherwise known as Major Stuttaford, proprietor of the infamous Moti Mahal curry-house. Also known, to a very few, by his real name; Colonel James Moriarty, brother of the late and unlamented Professor!"

Quiney, or I should say Moriarty, pushed the muzzle of his revolver against the temple of the terrified Isobel Aster.

"How clever of you! Unfortunately for you, Holmes, I still hold one ace."

A whimpering sound came through the tightly-fastened gag, which I noticed was a table-napkin bearing Lord Coledale's discreetly-embroidered monogram and coat-of-arms in one corner.

"Any attempt to come closer, and she dies. You know I mean it, Holmes. After all, I've nothing to lose, having just shot a peer in the Houses of

Parliament."

He laughed, a menacing growl, really, then turned his head slightly. He spoke a few words, so softly we couldn't catch them, and seconds later Colonel Sebastian Moran, dressed in the nondescript garb of a Thames boatman, sidled out behind him, also carrying a large revolver, and another of his infernal air-guns. His face showed the strain of the past few days; now he looked more like the elderly man he was, beneath the huge moustaches, but I had no doubt he was still a deadly adversary. His swarthy, deeply-lined face was twisted into a nasty sneer as - keeping Isobel Aster between himself and our line of fire - he slowly withdrew down the corridor, until he reached the door. He opened it, and we saw that it gave onto the platform at the rear of the tender car, piled high with coal. Moran slipped through, leaving it open behind him.

"You can still give it up, Colonel Moriarty," called Holmes, over the noise of the engine.

"Give yourself up now, Colonel," shouted Inspector Patterson, "and I'll see you get a fair trial. It'll go easier for you if you surrender."

Colonel Moriarty spoke directly to Holmes.

"You and your colleagues publicly accused my brother of being purely evil, though he was never tried."

"And you, of course, blame me for your brother's death and for police attacks on your organisation," replied Holmes.

"I warned my brother not to incite Sherlock Holmes, but he wouldn't listen. His arrogance led him to 'play the game' with you, and you lured him to his death."

"Not quite true, Colonel. The Professor chose to lure me to the Reichenbach Falls, with the intention of doing away with me. Colonel Moran was with him, and I'm sure he's told you the true events that led to your brother's death in that chasm. Professor Moriarty was a brilliant man, but as devious as they come. And as violent, though he rarely did his own dirty work."

"I will admit," replied Colonel Moriarty, "that his methods may have been harsh - even extreme at times - but then, he was a fool in many ways. He was, as you say, a genius, but he believed in this nonsensical Religion of Love, Art, Magic and Mathesis, which he was always on about.

"But with his death, Holmes, pragmatic leadership came to the fore," continued Moriarty. "We're within a handbreadth of achieving a mastery over the globe which would have made this magnificent British Empire seem petty by comparison - and all of it still controlled from right here, in London.

"You offered me a deal just now. I have no interest in that at all, but let me make you a counter-offer. I offer you the chance to retire as a potentate. Join us! With your brilliance allied to our organisation, there's no limit to our future wealth and power. Any of these men can choose to join, or else we take care of them right here and now. We may have to be a little rough on some along the way at times, but then, that's life.

"That is *my* offer, Holmes. Refuse it at peril to your life, and that of Miss Aster and all these various policemen with you. I warn you, you don't know what you are up against here."

"Expediency frequently coincides with justice itself - as against mere enforcement of the letter of the law - and I have ever let justice be the benchmark, where possible," replied Holmes. "In this case expediency and justice are antithetical. There can be no arrangement between ourselves and a traitor, Colonel Moriarty, not to mention an assassin with the blood of so many on his hands."

"My father was killed and eaten, Holmes - by other men! By nature we are but animals, carnivores!"

"Killers, assassins, murderers! That is what you and your gang are, Colonel Moriarty."

"Tis in our very bein', Holmes," laughed the Colonel, "only you British have 'civilised' it, and call it diplomacy, and politics, and war. But it's still murder, Mister Holmes, and you and your string-pullin' brother are very much a part of it."

I noticed that the train was slowing down, although according to the guard there was no stop scheduled for some time. Colonel Moran must have seen to the drivers, and forced a halt. Just then Moran came back into view, carrying a crowbar and shovel. With these he attempted to uncouple the train from the tender, but the speed was still much too great.

Holmes and Patterson immediately aimed their pistols at Colonel Moran.

"Tell him to stop, or we'll shoot to kill," ordered Patterson.

For reply, Colonel Moriarty pressed his revolver hard against Isobel Aster's forehead, and wrapped his arm tightly around her throat.

"Do that and she's dead, gentlemen. It looks like a stalemate right now, but you'll have to choose shortly - our freedom or her life."

By now the train had come almost to a standstill. Just at that moment another tunnel closed around us. Colonel Moran had managed to knock the coupling-pin loose to the point where one good blow with the crowbar would free it, and allow the train to gather speed again, leaving us behind.

"Well, Holmes, you had your chance. Not that I ever thought you'd accept my offer; I was merely buying time for Colonel Moran to do his part."

"Of course," replied Holmes. "I never thought otherwise. But it cuts two ways, you see! We're now at a standstill. That will bring people to see what's wrong. You'll never get away."

"You're wrong there, Holmes. Colonel, get the bomb. We're leaving!"

Moran lay down his tools, pulled his revolver from his waistband, and came back into the sleeping-car. He sidled behind Moriarty into the compartment where Isobel Aster had been imprisoned, and reappeared in a moment with one of their home-made bombs tucked under one arm. Then he fiddled with a key at the cuffs locking Isobel Aster to the door, and freed her. The loose ring dangled free and open, but still attached to the cuff locked around her wrist.

"Final offer, Holmes! Let us go, and we allow her to go free, unharmed - we'll leave her here with you. I know what she meant to your precious Irene Adler. We'll light the fuse to this bomb, and you let us go. Once we're out of the tunnel we'll extinguish the fuse. Follow us, and you risk being cut down by the air-gun, and you know what that can do, even at a considerable distance.

"The alternative is we all die together, in one glorious blast. I suppose you've seen our cache of bombs in the baggage car, Inspector Patterson. An ingenious design of Colonel Moran's - readily assembled from parts available at any market. We used it first - *Inspector* Patterson, isn't it still? - when Colonel Moran and I did our first job together for my brother. 1884 that was, a very good year, when we blew your old Scotland Yard clean into the next county with a much larger one of these. But nothing like the combined explosive power aboard this train right at this moment, gentlemen. So, Holmes, make your choice! What's it to be? Death for all, or she lives and we all get away alive. Come now, man! There's no choice, is there? Let us go, and you can enjoy hunting us down all over again, if you've the stomach for it. Or die, with us all!"

"You have my answer, Moriarty. No deals! Give yourselves up."

"Then you shall have mine, Holmes, though you'll not live long to regret it."

Still using Isobel Aster's body as a shield, Moriarty and Moran backed down the corridor until they reached the door leading to the tender-platform, both of them now aiming up the narrow corridor towards where we all stood. Moran placed the bomb on the floor, trimmed the fuse as close as he could to the top of the metal pail, and lit it with a phosphor-match. The bright flare lit up the girl's terrified features, as Moran lifted his crowbar to knock the pin completely free.

As he did so, Colonel Moriarty lifted his revolver once again to Isobel Aster's temple.

"Unfortunately, Miss Aster has played her last useful role alive. She'll be more of a distraction wounded, and nursing a bomb, don't you think?"

He placed the bomb inside the last sleeping-compartment, closed and locked the door, and snapped the loose handcuff onto the compartment door-handle so that the door was locked doubly shut. The key he pocketed, with a cruel smile.

"Such a pity, and so pretty. I can see why that fool Haversham fancied her. Life is full of such painful sacrifices, don't you agree, Holmes?"

I saw his finger begin to tighten on the trigger. Le Villard, who had been standing slightly behind Holmes, shouted, "No! Stop!" and pushed past Holmes and Patterson, lifting his revolver as he did so.

Colonel Moriarty instantly threw Isobel Aster to the floor, swung his pistol, and fired point-blank at le Villard. At the same time, Moran lifted his air-gun and fired a single round as well. Both bullets caught le Villard squarely in the centre of the chest. A great gout of crimson blood and flesh erupted from the back of his coat, spraying over us all.

Isobel Aster screamed as le Villard crumpled, lifelessly, to the floor. His head came to rest in her lap where she lay, one arm still cuffed to the door-handle above her head. Crimson spurted from his open mouth, covering her dress with gore. Le Villard was choking in his own blood. Moriarty and Moran slammed the connecting door behind them, wedged it shut somehow with the crowbar, and disappeared from sight. We heard them knock the retaining-pin free with a blow from the shovel, effectively separating the locomotive and tender from the train.

I ran immediately to aid le Villard, but my battle-field medical experiences told me I was too late. The revolver bullet had passed clean through his right shoulder, but the air-gun round, with its soft-nosed bullet flattened at the point to make it a *dum-dum*, had caused such massive traumatic injury to his chest that there was no possibility of his survival. After a few bubbling, sucking breaths, which caused pink foam to froth at his mouth and at his gaping chest wound, Francois le Villard died in Isobel Aster's arms, her free hand brushing blood from his face.

Holmes was at my side for a moment, looking at me with imploring eyes, willing me against all evidence to say that le Villard would survive. I shook my head.

"He's gone, Holmes."

Sherlock Holmes closed his eyes for a brief moment - it passed, and the cool reasoner returned to the surface.

"Patterson, take your men and free the galley-staff, then get out by the rear door of this carriage, and back the way we came. Above all, get clear of the tunnel as soon as possible, and warn away any bypassers. This bomb will blow, and set off the others."

Patterson saw the pointlessness of any argument, and led his men away back down the corridor to unlock the galley.

"Watson, help me to free Miss Isobel. There's no time to pick the cuffs. That fuse is as short as Moran could trim it, and I know only too well how little time we have left."

I stood and searched around for something to pry loose the door-handle. The only thing to hand was the luggage rack in the opposite compartment, which was made of stout iron rods in a sheet-metal frame. Holmes and I wrenched at it, and loosened one of the rods. This we wedged behind the door-handle, and after a moment had forced enough of a gap that the retaining ring of the cuffs slipped loose. Holmes grasped her arms, and lifted Isobel Aster to her feet.

"Can you run?" he asked her. "That bomb is about to blow."

"I think so, sir. But what about this man. He saved my life!"

"He's left us," said Holmes, not unkindly. "And now we must leave him. There's no time to risk carrying him out of the train and tunnel both, and he'd not want us to risk it. Now hurry, both of you."

I turned as I dragged Miss Isobel after me down the corridor, and saw Holmes, with rare tears in his eyes, kneel to pay his last respects to the man who had been his colleague and companion in adventure for the past three years and more. I had never seen such sorrow on Holmes's face, and hope never to do so again. He snatched out his pocket-watch, and wrenched free the coin he had been given by Irene Adler, so many years ago. Placing it in le Villard's palm, Holmes gently closed the lifeless fingers over it, and raised the hand to his lips.

"Go to your Maker, *vieux*, with a clear conscience. He knows already that never has a finer man lived or walked his precious earth. Farewell, my dear friend!"

Gently, Holmes crossed both of le Villard's hands over the shattered chest, and brushed the staring eyes closed. Then he rose, turning away forever from Francois le Villard, and ran after us to where we waited at the door.

"Out, Watson, run for it!"

We all rushed and stumbled in the darkness towards the light coming from the open end of the tunnel. I heard two sharp reports echo after us, down the tunnel. It sounded like pistol shots coming from the locomotive, which had now gathered steam and was slowly moving towards the other end of the tunnel, far behind us now.

Breathless and bruised, Isobel Aster and I emerged from the tunnel into the night-time glow of London, with Holmes right at our heels.

"Don't stop, Watson. Get her away up the embankment, and out of line of the tunnel. Take these keys to Patterson, to unlock Commissioner MacDonald. The charge for now is the murder of Mischa Roborovsky, as I said. We'll deal with the rest later."

"Where are you going, Holmes?" I shouted, as he dashed away at full speed, towards where the other end of the tunnel would emerge. The tunnel ran under a small suburban park; the gates in the tall, spiked railing fence surrounding it were already locked. Undeterred, Holmes clambered over and dropped to the other side, and the last I saw of him was his coat-tails flying as he disappeared into the gloom. I looked around for Inspector Patterson and his men, and saw them some distance away down the track, warning away curious people.

A dull rumble erupted beneath us, shaking the earth and causing sleeping birds to take flight, screeching and wheeling in outrage. Almost immediately a string of louder explosions followed, and the ground literally erupted not twenty feet from where we stood. The store-room of bombs, detonated by the shock of the initial explosion, had blown the roof off the rear section of the tunnel, leaving in its stead a ragged cutting in which blazing remnants of Lord Coledale's private train lay scattered like burning trash in a gutter.

Mere seconds later, from the direction towards which Holmes had run, came another huge explosion, followed by a sound like a rushing, crashing torrent. The train's boiler blew, sending the huge steel cylinder rocketing off down the rails spewing flames and debris behind it, until it came to rest several hundred feet away down the cutting.

Against a bright sky created by fires ignited by the explosion, I saw something that made my heart leap with relief. Silhouetted against the lurid glow the lean figure of Sherlock Holmes, outlined in flame-red, sprinted across the park towards the far end of the tunnel.

DAY TEN

APRIL 15TH 1894

CHAPTER LIX

RELUCTANTLY, I PUT DOWN the last of Francois le Villard's Journals, which I had just read again - realising as I did so that, unless the two missing volumes came somehow to light, I had read the last original words I should ever do from the pen of that remarkable man.

Holmes had returned late the previous night, after I had retired upstairs to my bedroom at one o'clock in the morning, and was gone again before I woke. I still had but little idea of the aftermath of the explosion in the railway tunnel. Inspector Patterson had left Isobel Aster, shivering with fear as much as from the cold night air, in my care, and had led several of his men through the park in the direction where I'd last seen Holmes. Patterson seemed genuinely relieved at hearing of his escape from the explosions.

As we left for Baker Street, the remaining constables had cordoned off the approach to the tunnel to keep the gathering crowds away from the wreckage, in case there were any bombs left unexploded in the baggage car or elsewhere.

Isobel Aster spent the night in Mrs. Hudson's apartment, at that worthy lady's firm insistence once I had explained a little of Isobel's kidnapping and terrifying rescue, and was still there under sedation. I learnt from the morning's newspapers that a special train belonging to Lord Coledale, himself brutally murdered only hours before in the Houses of Parliament by his own aide, had been blown up in a tunnel just outside the city centre. Causes were still being sought, but both events seemed to be part of a vicious conspiracy to ensure that the courageous and progressive Lord Coledale, considered the front-runner for Foreign Minister under a new government, never came to office. Various factions were suggested as being behind the atrocities, including Irish Home Rule agitators, the Russians, and disaffected Anglo-Irish ex-Indian Army officers - his murderous aide Quiney being apparently one of their number. An unconfirmed report had it that a prominent figure was confined in the Tower of London for his own protection, but no identity was provided, for reasons of security.

Again according to the news reports, Inspector Patterson, seconded from the Manchester police force to investigate the recent spate of bombings, reported that five charred and shattered corpses had been pieced together from the wreckage. It was thought that two of these were the locomotive-driver and stoker, who appeared to have been shot in the head before the explosion. Two further corpses had been found lying beside the tracks, just in front of where the engine had stood before the boiler had exploded, but identification had proved impossible. A fifth body, with an enormous chest wound, probably caused by flying shrapnel from the force of the explosion, was found inside the remains of one of the coaches, just behind the engine. Again, identification was not possible, but there was some speculation as to the origin of the melted disc of metal found clutched between the fingers of the right hand.

Fortunately, the explosion had taken place in a railway tunnel, now mostly collapsed, which had run under a park already closed for the evening, and thus there had been no casualties amongst the general populace. The news reports all concluded by saying that the government was allowing the country to slip into anarchy, or was being conspired against most heinously, depending on the political slant of the editor.

After I'd finished with the newspapers, I had opened and read again those final, remaining chapters of le Villard's experiences. Now that I'd finished, a wave of immense sadness swept over me. So much death, and so close to home. The 'one woman in the world' as Holmes had once described Irene Adler; and now Francois le Villard, his companion of the past three adventurous years: both dead by violence.

I had no idea where Holmes had gone, but felt sure that despite his sorrow he would be employing his skill and brilliance to the utmost to at least understand the crimes, even if there was nothing to be done to bring the criminals to book. The two bodies found by the tracks were certainly those of Colonel James Moriarty (alias Quiney; alias Major Stuttaford), and his hired assassin Colonel James Moran, caught by their own blast before they had time to flee. Lord Coledale was dead, and Commissioner MacDonald was under Patterson's close arrest in the Tower - arranged no doubt by brother Mycroft.

After the personal losses he had sustained, it seemed Holmes was to be denied even the solace of revenge. I had always envied Holmes his ability to remain detached from the usual human emotions, especially when I had lost my beloved Mary. But once the period of blackest despair had passed, I had realised that, for all the pain, I would never have foregone it if it had meant missing those treasured few years Mary and I had been granted together.

I thought of Francois le Villard, who had found his partner for life in far-away Siam, then lost his own life in the pursuit of justice for his friend and colleague. And I thought of the pain which would be caused his beloved Malee, when she heard the sad news of Francois's death, and was left with only his faithful Tashi and her memories to remind her of her betrothed. For all his professed detachment, I thought, the pain of loss and bereavement will mark even Holmes.

I spent the rest of the day pursuing the anodyne of work. At first I re-read selected parts of the Journals of Francois le Villard, but gave it up as too painful just yet, and turned to the mechanical task of putting my own notes of the preceding week in some kind of order. At six o'clock a messenger brought a telegraph message from Holmes, asking me to meet him at seven, at the Turkish Bath on Northumberland Avenue.

Inspector Patterson and one of his men had already been to Baker Street some hours earlier, to question Isobel Aster, so there was nothing to prevent my going to meet Holmes. Isobel had come out of her sedation, and was rested enough to co-operate, so I had permitted them to take her away to Scotland Yard, on the proviso that she not be harassed in any way.

"I assure you, Doctor Watson," said Inspector Patterson, "there is no suspicion that the young lady is anything but a victim in this affair. On the contrary, she is our most valuable witness, and will be treated with the proverbial kid gloves. I'll have her back here later this evening."

So it was that, two hours later, I found myself stretched out on one of the two couches side-by-side in a quiet corner of the drying room at the Turkish Bath, alongside Holmes, similarly laid out on the other. We had parboiled ourselves in the decoratively-tiled steam-rooms for forty minutes, sweating out tension and anger, then washed off the bitterness with bracing sluices of cold water from the oaken buckets. A vigorous twisting and stretching and pummelling at the hands of the masseurs, and another ice-cold dousing, had followed this. We then donned terry-towel bath-robes, and now were enjoying a soothing moment in the wood-panelled drying room, our tobacco smoke mingling with aromatic smoke curling upwards from a brazier set in a niche low in the wall.

Holmes re-lit his clay pipe, and I puffed away at one of the handful of fine cheroots Colonel Hayter had insisted on giving me, when I'd remarked upon his choosing to smoke them. Holmes spoke for the first time since we had met downstairs.

"I know that you will forgive me, Watson, if I answer no queries just at this moment. I imagine you must have many questions to which you would appreciate having answers, and so will others. I've arranged with Mycroft to meet tomorrow evening with all the interested parties, at Simpson's, for just that purpose. For now, allow me to enjoy the languor of the present moment, and the knowledge that I have done all I could."

We smoked for some time in silence, then dressed and made our way back to 221B Baker Street.

DAY ELEVEN

APRIL 16TH 1894

CHAPTER LX

I WAS FIRST TO ARRIVE at Simpson's. At breakfast Holmes had asked if I could take care of the arrangements, as we would have both Prince Phichai and de Benoist as guests, and he had to attend to other matters during the afternoon. Accordingly, I spent the better part of the day working up an outline first draft of my report for Mycroft, then brushed up and took a cab to the chop-house.

I located Anton, the head waiter, who was expecting me. Holmes had reserved the private table at the rear of the long, narrow restaurant, which was already crowded when I arrived at half-past six. White-aproned waiters in black waistcoats scurried around taking orders and carrying armfuls of loaded plates. A loud hum of conversation arose from the crowded tables; indeed, that had been the ostensible reason for choosing the chop-house as a place to meet unofficially, yet discreetly. The private table was in a half-curtained alcove, which, combined with the noise, would mean that our conversation should remain private. In fact, I knew that Holmes greatly appreciated the simple yet well-cooked fare on offer at Simpson's. I ordered, according to his instructions, for us all.

First to arrive, a half-hour later, was Colonel Hayter. Minutes later, Inspector Patterson pushed his way through the crowd, with Isobel Aster clinging to his arm. Almost immediately, Anton and two of his waiters made a space through the press of people to allow the rest of our party to pass: Mycroft Holmes was assisted by Captain Dom Alonzo in escorting Prince Phichai and the former *Nai* Portugee, Jose Felipe Azcevado Marques, to our table. Behind the two old Oriental gentlemen was de Benoist, Mycroft's counterpart in the French intelligence service.

With Hayter's assistance, I arranged all our guests as Holmes had suggested, made introductions all round, and saw to it that drinks and smokes were served. Holmes had warned me he may be a little behindhand, but assured me that he would not keep his guests waiting long. He was as good as his word, appearing suddenly through the crowd and sitting at his place as though he'd been there for hours. With him, looking somewhat chastised, was Sir Oliver Newsome. Holmes introduced Sir Oliver, then greeted each of our guests personally, and welcomed them all to a good Londoner's dinner, saying that we should talk as we dined.

So saying, he signalled to Anton to bring on the oysters on the half-shell.

Once he saw that everyone had been served, he swallowed one or two himself, drank a mouthful of white wine, and began his explication of the convoluted series of mysteries which had brought us all together here in London.

"I decided that you all deserve an explanation of the events of the past weeks. Each of you has been involved in one aspect or another of this case, but none, save perhaps my brother Mycroft here, is aware of all the complexities. Rather than explain it to each of you separately, I thought it better to bring us all together, and allow each to explain his own part in the puzzle. I shall start by asking Mycroft to explain, in political terms, the challenges we've faced."

Mycroft wiped his lips with his napkin, shifted his bulk, slowly rose to his feet and looked around at the gathering. I imagine he was weighing how much to explain, given the diversity of the audience.

"I think the first thing I want to do is to convey to M. de Benoist and the French government the grief we feel at the loss of Sherlock's *compagnon de voyage* in the adventures and exploits we will briefly discuss. Francois le Villard was a brave, resourceful, and above all, a just man. His assistance has, without doubt, helped in no small way to avert a series of injustices: to individuals and institutions; indeed to several states and their rulers. It is tragic, but not uncharacteristic, that Francois le Villard lost his life in a successful attempt to save Miss Aster here from serious injury or death. Her Majesty has instructed me to see that such dependants as he may have are adequately cared for, and that Britain's highest possible decoration for bravery by a foreigner is posthumously awarded. I know that M. de Benoist will see to it that he will be laid to rest, with honour, in his home village in the French mountains.

"So may I propose the first toast of the evening: To the memory of Francois le Villard!"

Once the toast had been drunk, Mycroft sat, and relaxed a little into his chair.

"This whole episode began three years ago, and at that time involved very different problems from those which concern us here - although in retrospect it appears likely that there are links both in the villains involved and their overall aims. Sherlock and le Villard spent the first two of those years sorting out various problems in Central Asia and the Near East, with the end result that their investigations and my intelligence reports led them to embark from the Red Sea for Siam. Those of you who have journeyed here from Siam - *Nai* Portugee, Prince Phichai, Captain Dom Alonzo - are well aware of the recent struggle for ascendancy at Bangkok, and how narrowly a French annexation of Siam was averted. Those who have not closely followed those events need only know that a conspiracy was detected, the aim of which was to assassinate the Belgian jurist who had been appointed General Adviser to the King. The intention was to provide an excuse for claiming the necessity for rule under European law, at the same time removing the most vocal and influential supporter of Siam remaining an independent country."

As Mycroft spoke, he paused from time to time to consume a few oysters, keeping pace with his audience in that respect.

"My agents in Egypt, and at Mecca and Persia before that, had made me aware of the activities of a shadowy group of influential, and frequently unscrupulous, supporters of French colonial expansion. Men who want to surpass our British Empire in breadth and influence. And, of course, in wealth! These men dream of controlling vast tracts of hitherto unexplored lands, subjecting heathen populations to their command under the French flag, and reaping enormous glory and riches from their exploits. Of course, as we British can attest, difficult as it is, acquiring an empire is as nothing to ruling one. I contacted de Benoist, here, and we met at Le Havre to discuss the matter."

He gestured to de Benoist to carry on, and immediately reached for a wedge of lemon to squeeze over an oyster, before tilting back his enormous head to let the morsel slide down his throat. Then he reached for his wine.

"The supporters of colonial expansion have become known as the *parti colon*," began the tall, patrician de Benoist, removing his eye-glasses to polish them with his napkin, before replacing them on his hooked nose, "though they are not, in fact, a political party as such."

De Benoist spoke excellent English, with a marked French accent. His excellently-cut suit and waistcoat were rumpled and hung loosely on his spare frame; thinning hair brushed untidily back from a receding hairline was greyed and had gone too long uncut. He spoke so softly and diffidently that I had to strain to hear him over the noise of our fellow diners, but I knew that Mycroft respected de Benoist as an equal in the game they both played, in the shadows of history.

"Regardless, this loose association of zealots is able to command as many as a quarter of all the deputies in the French house. In these times of fragile coalition governments, lasting only a few months or a year or so, that is enormous power. More conservative elements within the government and the civil service do what they can to resist these bullying tactics, as they realise that France cannot support such a global empire - nor should we wish to do so in this enlightened age. But the colonialists are masters at use of the press, appealing over our heads to the public's sentiment for French glory, at whatever cost.

"It has only been by virtue of our superior parliamentary experience that we have managed to defeat the enactment of several proposals which would have meant, amongst other things, a battle with Britain over the fate of Siam. These are powerful men, with wide-ranging experience. Perhaps the most influential faction is grouped around Prince Henri d'Orleans, whose expedition penetrated to Tibet, though not to Lhasa, just months before Sherlock and Francois arrived. His is not the only faction, though - not at all. There are industrialists looking for new markets, speculators in minerals and gemstones, pioneers of the railways and tollways, river-steamer operators and canal promoters. As always, the various missionary orders of the church have a say, because much of the money is theirs - as is the most reliable and thorough intelligence. All these groups form and reform and overlap, but there is a central belief held by them all - that it is right and proper that France should expand its empire, aggressively and ruthlessly, in order to take its rightful place amongst the great powers of the world.

"I had been keeping my eye on their activities and associations for some time when Mycroft asked me to meet with him, so I was curious to know what had interested him in the *parti colon*. As it turned out, it was principally their activities at Egypt and the Upper Nile, but the fate of Siam was becoming of concern to him. His investigations had revealed to him the ambitions and potential power of the French 'colons' at Saigon - especially the Navy-run government there - and their designs upon Siam. Your English Foreign Minister put it well when he said he feared that our colonial advocates would strip Siam of its provinces, like the leaves of an artichoke, one by one.

"Ironically, it was I who had earlier alerted Mycroft to the possible association with one of the French colonial factions of a group of international criminals. They specialised in assassins-for-hire, mercenary forces assembled and sent into action, robbery of banks and arsenals to secure weapons and funds, and other side-lines such as kidnapping for ransom, blackmail, extortion and fraud - to name but a selection. Our research and informers constantly led us back to London, though little of the criminal activity was concentrated there. We always lost the trail in London's vast criminal underworld, with its code of silence or death. I consulted Mycroft, who can better tell you . . ."

A brief silence ensued, before Mycroft realised that he'd been handed the baton again, as it were. He looked rather longingly at the dish of pork-chops with apple-sauce and new potatoes which had just been placed in front of him, and at the two enormous steak-and-kidney pies which had been placed strategically on the table. Removing his napkin from his collar where he'd just tucked it, he carried on the tale. Holmes, and indeed all his guests, needed no persuading to tuck into the food while Mycroft spoke on.

"It turned out that we'd been investigating the same criminal organisation, but coming at it from different angles. And the more I looked at the evidence, the more it looked as though we were dealing with Sherlock's old nemesis, the Moriarty gang. There were too many coincidences, too many rumours to discount them all as fantasy. I had been one of the few who'd never doubted the existence of Professor Moriarty's organisation, nor its power and criminality; my objection, if my brother will forgive me, was towards Sherlock's unhealthy preoccupation, even obsession, with them, to the exclusion of common-sense.

"The first inkling came when I was informed by Sherlock that the assassin sent to Mecca from Persia to assassinate the *Atalik* of Kashgar, Colonel Moran, was formerly known as one of Professor Moriarty's senior staff. I followed up from this end, by applying discreet pressure to his gambling associates, and putting him under constant surveillance when he was in London. We soon patched together a rough outline of an organisation that was involved in all the criminal activities mentioned by M. De Benoist, and was based in London. The reason it had escaped our serious notice was that they rarely operated on British soil. We found evidence of several disappearances and murders, which we put down to internal strife and discipline.

"Moran dropped out of sight from time to time, and we were rarely able to trace his movements. Then - an assassination would occur somewhere, eliminating an important personage and sabotaging important negotiations - or else riots would develop in an otherwise peaceful African kingdom, during which a local chieftain was dismembered, with the result that his brother-in-law became chief in his place. Then Moran would return, flush with cash, repay most of his gambling debts, and proceed to gamble the rest away again, until he was in debt and forced to resort, as always, to cheating at cards and backgammon clubs all over town.

"This behaviour made him less than popular in some quarters, and ultimately, this provided a way to trace his superiors - or so we thought at first. We did manage to confirm the existence of the organisation, and the identities of several of the senior members of the gang. But they committed no crimes in London, so we were unable to do more than watch them closely. Not being fools, they soon got wind of this, and became even cagier. The new leader - or leaders - remained a mystery, except that we knew that Colonel Moran was still one of them, by virtue of having formerly been Professor

Moriarty's chief-of staff.

"So, when Sherlock and le Villard came across the trail of a similar conspiracy in Egypt, it came as no surprise to detect traces of Colonel Sebastian Moran and his air-gun at several places there. It took us all some time to confirm that it was, in fact, the same Moriarty gang, operating very profitably overseas, and living with impunity at home. But, finally we had to admit that facts were facts. The Moriarty gang had not only survived police swoops and arrests, court cases and imprisonments, and even the death of their leader, Professor Moriarty. It appeared in the intervening three tears they had regenerated and flourished; the question was - under whose leadership?"

"We doubted that Moran was in charge, and finally decided that it seemed as though the gang was run by a sort of 'board', which met rarely and very discreetly, with control of day-to-day operations delegated on a case-by-case basis. This made identifying the board members very difficult, as operations were all overseas. Obviously, the most important member to identify was the one who secured contracts for these operations. We were looking for someone with *entree* to the corridors of power in states large and small, someone not intimidated by dealing with current or future heads-of-state - or their heads-of-security - and able to negotiate and secure payment of vast sums of money for services rendered. He would be, no doubt, chairman of the board.

"Finally, we saw a chance to rattle their complacency. Colonel Moran had gone too far in hushing up a charge of cheating - he'd murdered Ronald Adair. Though the mystery baffled the Yard for some while, I was certain I had the correct reading of the facts, following a detailed reading of the police reports. I sent a summary to Sherlock in Montpellier, and he agreed entirely with my interpretation. He hurried back to London, and the resulting capture of Colonel Moran proved us correct.

"Events followed more or less as we had envisaged, broadly speaking. We suspected that an attempt would be made to spring the Colonel, lest he lose his nerve and tell us all the details of the gang, so we decided to allow his 'escape' to proceed. This put him under pressure: he was now a wanted escapee and fugitive. Through various stratagems, Sherlock and Doctor Watson managed to divine where he was hiding, and to follow him to a meeting with the mysterious board members of the Moriarty gang. And now, Sherlock, I think I shall return the floor to your good self, and devote part of my attention for a moment to these excellent chops and pies. If someone would be so good as to pass the apple-sauce, I should be most obliged. Thank you!"

By now the noise from the main dining area had swelled to a low roar, as Londoners of all descriptions jostled for a place to sit. Fistfuls of tankards of ale could be seen, held overhead as tireless waiters forced their way through the diners and those waiting to eat. In the flickering light of gas-lamps, it seemed like bedlam. Thankfully, our sheltered alcove allowed us to converse at nearly normal levels, and, Holmes was right . . . no one could possibly overhear our conversation! He carried on from where Mycroft had left us.

"The identity of two of the chief conspirators became known to me on the night of the destruction of Crystal Palace. From behind the servery-door there I was able to glimpse the boots of most of the board-members in attendance. The exceedingly squared toe of one boot, the uneven height of heel of another, the spats of a third! A great deal is said about a man by his choice of footwear, and by the age of his maturity, a man had generally fixed on a particular style of boot. I had seen two pairs of boots that I thought familiar, and another whose distinctive shape matched a footprint left at the scene of the murder of Mischa Roborovsky. Next morning, at Crystal Palace, I was fortunate. The murderer was in attendance, in his official capacity, so I was able to confirm the unusual shape of the sole.

"I shall return to this incident in a few moments. For now, I shall say only that the fact that these footprints proved to be those of Inspector MacDonald came as no real surprise. I'd had my suspicions of the man since the days of the botched swoop on the Moriarty gang, and the all-too-easy identification of Inspector Patterson as causing the failure to secure convictions against several of the major criminals, Professor Moriarty amongst them.

"The elevated left heel I recognised as belonging to a Welsh Member of Parliament. He is publicly known to be both lame in his left foot, and bitterly opposed to the policies and personality of the wearer of the boots with spats - with a distinctive pattern of buttoning. I had previously noticed that these were favoured by none other than Lord Coledale. So, pieces began to fall into place. We knew that Colonel Moran was there, of course, and the unfortunate Parker, but there were two others present whom I was unable to identify, having seen neither of them.

"But perhaps I must go back, to our days at Siam, before we can explain recent events here at London. You see, it was at Bangkok that we really upset these fellows' plans for the first time. Major plans, with the fate of a country at stake. And it was there that I first heard hints of Godfrey Norton's involvement in some way in an evil conspiracy, which was now being used to blackmail him. Irene Adler asked me to investigate what hold these mysterious men had over her husband, and left me wondering about the significance of a secret cabal calling itself the Men of Straw. She also told me what she knew of the murder of *Sia* Ah Foo.

"She was about to tell me more, and had I listened, much would have become clear long before it did. But I thought, as we often do, that another day would not matter, and cut her short in order to disembark for the Ministry. Minutes later Irene Adler was dead, blown up by a bomb planted in the launch by an Indian. I no longer believe that she was the intended victim, nor that I was meant to be the victim that evening. I am now convinced that the explosion was one last attempt by the assassins to earn their pay, by finally killing the General Adviser. He had hired the launch, and was the expected passenger until the last moment. The doctor resembled him somewhat, and the Indian had probably never seen either of them before.

"Nevertheless, Irene Adler was tragically dead, and with her went the remainder of her untold tale of Godfrey's dilemma. It was not until his own death at the hands of the Thuggees released Sir Oliver Newsome, here, to hand over Godfrey's confession, that I finally understood the nature of the terrible conspiracy in which he had become involved. As it is entirely likely that none of you is aware of what constitutes a *tontine,* I shall ask Sir Oliver if he could explain in a few words."

Sir Oliver rose, nodded at the gathering, and spoke in his measured tones.

"Essentially, a rolling *tontine* is a closely-held corporation with a reinvestment clause, whereby the benefits go to an ever-diminishing number of participants as they die off. In other words, the last surviving member of the *tontine* inherits *all* the wealth, property and revenues of *all* the others who have predeceased him. The concept is frowned upon in English law, but it is still a legal contract, as the families found out, and although all the signatories were still students, all were of legal age. In this case, according to Mr. Holmes, the gang simply expedited the natural course of affairs somewhat.

"I have made it my business since Godfrey's death to investigate the situation of the families disinherited by this terrible scheme; many have been ruined, all have been seriously disadvantaged. Unfortunately, it appears that I can offer no meaningful assistance. With the apparent deaths of all the plotters, there seems no way to trace the whereabouts of the stolen assets, or to obtain their return to their rightful owners.

"But my most profound regret is that, had I adhered less to the letter of the law in protecting one whom I knew to be flawed, it is entirely likely that the death of the brave M. Le Villard would not have occurred. For that I am profoundly regretful. I can only hope, for the sake of his eternal soul, that Godfrey was not aware of the foul nature of the conspiracy when he was foolish enough to allow himself to be persuaded to draft such a document, and to be a party to its signing."

With a slight catch in his voice as he finished, Sir Oliver sat down, and busied himself immediately with pushing food around on his plate.

Holmes took a sip of water, and looked around at us all.

"Thank you, Sir Oliver! That conspiracy underlay all the events that followed. So I shall spend a moment or two on both the conspiracy, and the conspirators. The conspiracy began, twenty or more years ago, when the young Reginald Haversham, loutish younger brother of the heir to the then Lord Coledale, joined a special mathematics coaching class to cram for university examinations. His tutor was Professor Moriarty.

"The report sent me by Mycroft when I was first at Siam was more concerned with the family fortunes than the man himself. It seems his father and grand-father had been nabobs of the East India Company. Before that, their forebears had made their fortunes as shippers and merchants when the Hanseatic League maintained their English warehouses at King's Lynn on the banks of the Ouse. When the East India Company was dismantled, in the aftermath of the Mutiny, his father invested unwisely. Within fifteen years he'd lost most of the family fortune, but still had the title and the family seat. By the time Reginald Haversham's father died, even the family home was in hock. The two boys were almost finished with their schooling when Reginald's brother succeeded to the title, and the debts.

"According to Norton's confession, when Reginald mentioned in a tutorial that he and his friends had been talking about forming a *tontine*, and asked if Professor Moriarty knew anything about such things, the calculating mind of the Professor concluded that opportunity was knocking, loudly, at his door. Quietly, he encouraged both Reginald and Norton to convince all the other members of the Men of Straw club to sign up. Finally, he set the scene for the laudanum-and-absinthe sodden evening when all were induced to sign their names to that infamous contract, which sealed all their deaths and those of their elder brothers as well. It was a good six months before the final trap was sprung, when all the younger brothers were killed in a charabanc accident from a cliff-top road, returning from a college outing to the seaside.

"You see, according to Norton, Moriarty had used the interim period to arrange the deaths of the elder brothers, one by one. The formerly disenfranchised younger brothers had now acceded to the full family wealth and titles - something they had never expected to do when they signed the *tontine* agreement. Though it's doubtful any of them would have given the matter a second thought, if Norton's account of their collective dissolution is to be believed. These were all, simply by nature of having joined in the first place, young men of weak character, and the Professor no doubt played his hand most cunningly.

"The only survivor amongst all the Men of Straw was Reginald Haversham, who'd been on the Continent taking the Grand Tour at the time. His lawyers - retained by the Professor - lost no time in laying claim to the wealth, lands and titles of all the dead students, under the terms of the *tontine* signed freely by them all.

"The accident caused a great outcry, especially when near relatives discovered what had happened to the fortunes in which they had expected to share. A police investigation was conducted, but no suspicious circumstances were found in connection with the charabanc accident. The scandal died away, though not the suspicion.

"Due to the serious nature of the suspected crime and the prominent names involved, the Yard had been called in, so as soon as possible after I read Norton's confession, I went to Scotland Yard myself. There I had a word with an old friend in the records department, with the result that he took a tea-break, and left me in his office with an open file on the desk. It took but a moment to read the report of the accident, which ruled out the possibility of foul play, and to note that the officer in charge of the investigation was one Alec MacDonald, recently transferred in from the Glasgow constabulary. So now I had no doubt of Commissioner MacDonald's complete involvement in the conspiracy as a senior member, with a seat on the board of directors, as it were.

"But that case was twenty years old, and impossible to re-open without great difficulty. The problem was to find some current charge of sufficiently grave import on which to convict them now."

"Do you mean to say, Holmes," asked Colonel Hayter, "that this Professor chap planned all of this in advance, starting with just one disgruntled student? That he foresaw all he could steal? How did this benefit him, if the wealth all went to Haversham?"

"I sparred with Professor Moriarty for months, Colonel Hayter, before we parted forever at Reichenbach Falls. He had a mind capable of calculating the motions of heavenly bodies. To plan a scheme such as this, once the opportunity was presented to him, would have been as child's play in comparison. And knowing the Professor, far more enjoyable, involving as it did the corruption of youth, the betrayal of their families, and the enrichment, at last, of the brilliant mathematician whom the academic world had seen fit previously to scorn and dismiss. I imagine he enjoyed the ironies immensely.

"I had my banker make some discreet enquiries in the City, and found out some most interesting facts. The East India Company had - according to family legend - cheated his father when its charter was revoked after '58. The real story, as the insiders knew it, was that he had attempted to cheat the Company of a vast sum, and been found out. The affair was hushed up, but he was virtually impoverished by his folly. Nevertheless, his family has nursed a hatred for the Raj ever since. So, when the Professor and Colonel

Moriarty made Reggie Haversham a peer, and restored the family fortune, he went along gladly with the necessary crimes - including doing away with his brother. But things did not work out quite as he had envisaged.

"Coledale's personal account, for the past ten years and more, has never had more than a few thousand pounds in it. And that is the only account to which Lord Coledale was sole signatory. All his expenses were defrayed by an account in the City, held in trust by an anonymous lawyer type, who divulges no details. All revenues from his estates were deposited either in a separate account with the same fellow, or remitted to accounts at Zurich or Rotterdam.

"He was blackmailed, you see. When the accident was staged, convenient evidence was created which, if made available to a prosecutor, would convict the new Lord Coledale of masterminding the murders. All his wealth was signed into a trust controlled by the Professor. It was arranged that he should be credited with restoring the family fortunes. The family seat was bought out of hock; the estates were professionally managed, and flourished; he began to exhibit a new-found interest in politics, and became active in his constituency, eventually rising to national prominence. The family name was astutely used to provide an aristocratic background, with a reputation for familiarity with the ways of the East.

"I'm certain that, even at the very beginning, Professor Moriarty saw the political advantages of the situation, and this was the second major reason for encouraging the Men of Straw. We have only recently seen the culmination of all these long years of grooming for high office, as Mycroft will tell you."

CHAPTER LXI

MYCROFT HAD FINISHED his chops, as well as a substantial helping of pie - carefully lifting the pastry lid away to one side of his plate, and crumbling it into the remaining gravy once his steak-and-kidney was consumed - and was sitting back listening intently. He merely nodded as Holmes turned the chair over to him.

"Ever since Quiney's return to London - though we did not know about that until the past few days - the capital has suffered from various disturbances. Some were seemingly petty: strikes by chimney-sweeps and midwives, for example, but had serious consequences. Violence became normal at public gatherings and protests We were certain many of these were incited or staged for effect, and the resultant crowds provoked to anger and violent actions. Muggings and beatings on the high street became common. But the most serious incidents were the brutal Thuggee murders, and the random bombings.

"Sherlock and I have since found several previous murders which were almost certainly the work of the Beguilers, but the press failed to get hold of them. And it is clear from the number of explosive devices stored aboard Lord Coledale's private train that they were intending to subject London - and perhaps some provincial cities - to a much-expanded bombing campaign. After all, the last place the authorities would search for a cache of bombs would be the private train of an aristocrat and peer of the realm. Very clever!

"At the same time, I had noted over the past few months - and the Cabinet Secretary had also brought it to my attention - that, in addition to his much-publicised journeys to the East, a vigorous campaign of lobbying, manipulation, even bribery and blackmail, was being deployed. Lord Coledale clearly was being positioned as a contender for appointment as Foreign Minister if the government should change. This at first seemed so unrealistic a goal, given the experience and reputation of the shadow minister, that I failed to give the matter much credence, thinking it the vanity of a wealthy peer. If I tell you, in confidence, that documents discovered amongst the papers recovered from Coledale's safe in his train carriage confirm the existence of a conspiracy to assassinate the shadow Minister for Foreign Affairs, right here in London, you will understand the gravity of the situation so recently averted. For some moments I thought it possible that they were aiming at toppling the government itself, but concluded that they would not have trusted as many politicians as that would require. At least, not yet. No, I concluded that their aim was to control the foreign policy of England.

"This also seemed the more likely when I considered their other activities: inciting unrest in lands as yet uncolonised; political assassinations; and, of course, their business activities. The problem was, although in principle their activities seemed consistent, I could not see how they could be so in practice. If their aim was to control British foreign policy, why did their activities in Siam, as at Egypt, appear to benefit the French at the expense of the British?

"I talked the matter over with Sherlock. Only one deduction fit all requirements. The Moriarty gang had close contacts over a considerable period of time with various members of the French *parti colon* faction, and it was probable that their repeated attempts to kill the General Adviser to the Siamese King were paid for by some of the more zealous of those *colons.* The Moriarty gang's aim must be to steer British foreign policy in directions that would benefit these extremist Frenchmen. They counted, it seems, on the fact that English anti-colonial reformers were gaining strength anyway.

"By ensuring that the English would not interfere in any new annexations by the French, and probably by promising to withdraw British troops from Egypt and the Sudan, the Moriarty gang stood to reap huge rewards. Trading rights, railway and shipping concessions, mining, agricultural exploitation and the like would be worth an enormous sum. That the entire enterprise would constitute treason appears, in the opinion of Sherlock, to have whetted Colonel Moriarty's appetite for it all the more. Revenge is a powerful motive, and the Colonel appears to bear England a grudge of some magnitude. And it is the Colonel whom Sherlock feels was the driving force behind it all."

"And has been, ever since the death of his brother," continued Holmes.

"How does the murder of this Russian chap, Roborovsky, fit into all of this?" I asked.

"Isobel Aster - or Isobel Blood, as she was at that time, had been 'Reggie' Haversham's mistress at the time when he was still poor, and he'd drunkenly boasted of his 'coup' in connection with the *tontine.* When the scandal hit the newspapers, this was a confidence he obviously came to regret, and he swore Isobel to silence. At about the same time, she was informed about his somewhat catholic tastes in companionship, and left him."

Holmes turned here to Miss Aster and said to her, not unkindly, "and, when you discovered his vices and finished with him, I suspect you told your closest confidante, Irene Adler's dresser, Mischa Roborovsky."

Isobel Aster blushed, and looked down at her gloved hands folded in her lap. Then she glanced up at Inspector Patterson, seated next to her, and managed a wan smile.

"That is so, Mr. Holmes. I also mentioned just a little of the matter to Miss Adler one afternoon, just before she left London."

"Miss Aster was herself not avaricious, and thought little further of it, but Mischa apparently had no such scruples. I think he used the information, anonymously, to blackmail Lord Coledale. That was how he suddenly came into sufficient wealth to retire and purchase his building. Somehow, recently, Commissioner MacDonald must have identified their blackmailer. Perhaps Mischa went after more money, with the result that he was silenced with prussic acid, carefully disguised to appear as death from a heart attack. And

MacDonald was the killer. Got in the door on the strength of his credentials, did his bit of murder, and left, first crushing the glass atomiser that had contained the acid in the garden outside. That was a mistake, firstly because I found it anyway, and secondly because he left his footprint. Very careless for a seasoned detective, but I imagine he never thought his own shoes would be checked for comparison. That, however, is exactly what I did. You will recall, Watson, the plaster cast we took at Crystal Palace. That cast exactly matched the one Inspector Jones took, at my suggestion, from the flower-bed outside Mischa's apartment. And they both matched his shoes, as I could clearly see. The squared toe, with metal plates under toe and heel. Even the one missing nail of the toe-plate matched.

"MacDonald made another slip as well: when we met at Crystal Palace, he said he'd just returned from Scotland. But I was certain of the identification of his boot-print. I checked a little, and found that MacDonald had been last seen at the Yard at a time that would have made a return journey to Scotland an impossibility. Why was he lying about that? Was it because of the previous evening's alarm and chase, at which he had been present? Or because his boot-print had been found at the scene of Mischa Roborovsky's murder earlier the previous day? The more I thought, the more I became certain that he had lied to cover his presence at both.

"Irene Adler told me what she knew of the matter, at Bangkok, and when she was murdered after Godfrey Norton's disappearance, I followed her leads to Sir Oliver, and ultimately the truth about the early source of the Moriarty gang's wealth. Meanwhile, Norton was still entangled with the gang, though I did not realise it at first. It took a while for the realisation to dawn that the two matters - the assassination plots at Siam, and the old Men of Straw mystery in England - which I had regarded as separate, were in fact intertwined. Irene Adler had hinted at the truth behind Norton's fear of Lord Coledale, and the threat he in turn constituted to them. They knew he had left a confession in London, but not where. They'd intended to use Norton as a scapegoat for all their crimes in Siam, and thereby lay the blame on the British. Already he'd been falsely implicated in the bombing intended to kill the General Adviser and the Siamese Foreign Minister, and in the death of Colonel Sartorius, both of which resulted in warrants being issued for his arrest. Logically, the plotters would arrange an apparent suicide and confession to the assassination; his escape foiled that, even had the attempt succeeded.

"News of the warrants led him to seek sanctuary with his old friend *Sia* Ah Foo - whom he'd met through his legal practice, and at Ah Foo's clubs - and with whom he'd stuck up an unlikely friendship. And here I must confess a blunder. I never thought to check with Mycroft about *Sia* Ah Foo. Had I done so I should have found out that he was yet another of Mycroft's many agents, reporting on events at Siam since twenty years. Mutually unaware that Captain Jones also sent in his reports, as did others.

"I suspect that Ah Foo had independent information leading him to fear that the French threat was serious and imminent, and determined to do what he could to avert it. And I suspect, *Señor* Jose Felipe, that he talked with you about the matter, and that you told him of Professor Sigerson's interest in the matter of the threats against the General Adviser."

The old fellow smiled a private smile, and his sightless gaze slid over us with indifference.

"You talked about the future of Siam," continued Holmes, "and though your businesses were vastly different, you both feared the possibility of foreign domination of Siam. I think you knew that he would make it his business to see that the General Adviser was not harmed. That explained his clansman inside the Foreign Ministry providing information as to Rolin's schedules, and the mysterious Chinese following behind his carriage each night. They were there to keep him from harm. I, however, counted *Sia* Ah Foo among my suspects. Unfortunate, but these things happen from time to time.

"Now, however, the problem of Godfrey Norton became serious for the plotters. He had escaped their clutches before they could force him to reveal the location of his confession of his part in the *tontine* plot, and of their implication in the murders involved. Their London gang members were alerted to keep an eye out for him, and Coledale and Quiney headed back to Europe, and finally, England. How he had escaped from them and from Bangkok we will never know; he did not say in his letter. I suspect that Colonel Moran held him after the *Sirdar* departed from Siam, and that he probably escaped when Moran went to indulge his vices. Norton was far more familiar with Siam and the Siamese than Moran, after all. But the answer was with Norton, back in London, so that was where I went, stopping in France long enough for certain matters to come to a head.

"During my stay at Montpellier, certain things began to clear up in my mind. I pondered the nature of the Moriarty gang, as I had known it. The puzzle of Godfrey Norton and the mysterious Men of Straw! The various hints about Lord Coledale and links to past scandals! The fact that Colonel Sebastian Moran had been a senior member of the gang, and a recognised assassin! And the undeniable fact that in investigating the assassination plot against the General Adviser, we had come across the tracks of Lord Coledale and Quiney too many times to be explained as mere coincidence!

"I had no conclusive proof, but I was convinced it was Colonel Sebastian Moran who had, at some considerable distance, fired a round from a soundless firearm with such accuracy that he hit the exact centre of the General Adviser's carriage-bell - and that round was a soft-nosed revolver bullet. I was also certain, even though the light was so dim, that it was Moran with Lord Coledale the first night at Ah Foo's opium den, and later aboard his boat.

"On even less solid grounds I suspected that it had been Colonel Moran, acting on orders from the gang, who had arranged for the planting of the bomb which was intended to assassinate the General Adviser, and instead killed Irene Adler. I was sure that it wasn't Norton who'd had her killed. He loved her, in his way; he just didn't have the strength to quit his vices, while she clung to her memories of the man he once was, and her hopes that he could change his ways. And now they are both gone. Such a waste!

"I also felt certain that Colonel Moran would return to London, having failed twice to kill Rolin. But, what to do about it all? I was at Montpellier, considering that question, when news arrived from Francois le Villard about *Señor* Jose Felipe overhearing the conversation at the Oriental Hotel, which you all know about. I consulted Mycroft, and we agreed to try bringing him to London and somehow arranging a confrontation, in the hope of jolting Lord Coledale into revealing his guilt. There was sufficient time, as Lord Coledale would spend several months in the South of France before returning to London.

"Meanwhile, as Mycroft said, things had been stirring in London, resulting in general panic verging on hysteria. Then came the Adair murder, and we knew Moran was back in London. I returned from Marseilles immediately upon receiving Mycroft's news about the murder.

"I also began to seriously ponder the nature of the Moriarty gang in the absence of the late Professor. It seemed to me that both Norton and Moran had been taking orders from the owner of the *Sirdar*. But somehow, try as I may I could not see Lord Coledale as a ruthless, intelligent, sharp-witted predator, one who sees opportunity and seizes it with bold stratagems, immediately and at great risk if necessary. I sensed that the gang's leader had larger issues on his mind, and that the wanton yet brilliantly improvised violence of his methods was merely clearing weeds from the path of a far more important task.

"So! Lord Coledale wasn't smart enough; we needed someone ruthless and brilliant, like the Professor himself. It couldn't be Moran. He was a vicious, violent and valuable tool, but that was all he aspired to be. I began to think I'd run out of possible suspects when it came to me, at first as a suspicion, then as a certainty. I realised I'd been overlooking the presence and identity of their leader, though I had met him on numerous occasions - even played cards with the man - precisely because he was astute enough to remain consistently in his role of second-in-command, senior aide to his lordship. The more I thought about it the more I was convinced that I was right. What better position from which to control a man's life than as his personal aide? Make all his appointments, screen his callers, employ and dismiss staff, make travel arrangements - and all of it perfectly natural-seeming to the outsider. The ideal aide, competent, efficient, discreet and self-effacing! Able to convey orders veiled as advice, to confer in confidence, always maintaining the appearance that Lord Coledale was the master, and Quiney his myrmidon.

I began immediately to investigate Quiney's past, and for some reason, where he had spent the previous months since leaving Siam. Mycroft's agents reported that he had left the *Sirdar* at Colombo, and had taken a steamer to Calcutta. Telegraphed enquiries of Captain Faunce showed that Quiney had disembarked at Calcutta, and after spending one night at a modest hotel, had apparently disappeared - not an easy thing to do for a European in Calcutta, when it was Faunce doing the enquiring.

Less than two months later, Quiney appeared in London, once again loyally at the side of Lord Coledale,, at about the same time as Moran killed Adair over a foolish gambling debt. I suspect that Coledale had been ordered to stay out of England while Quiney was absent. What Quiney had been up to at Calcutta remained a mystery.

"I surmised that Quiney was originally 'invented' to act as steward and minder for the young Lord Coledale, to prevent him from going off the tracks and embarrassing them all. Professor Moriarty had arranged it all, long ago. I had made a mistake. At first I'd thought that Quiney had simply taken advantage of his position at the right-hand of wealth and power, and had, little by little, gained intimate knowledge of his master. Then, I surmised, he had used that position, like so many ambitious lackeys in the past, to usurp his master's power whilst remaining in a seemingly subservient position.

"What I hadn't known was that Quiney had been installed in that position years before by his brother, Professor Moriarty, and that Lord Coledale had never had any real control over his own vast wealth. Quiney had remained in that subservient position for many years, disappearing at times back to his beloved India, or to other places in the East, but always ready to order his lordship to do the Professor's bidding.

"I attempted to trace Quiney's past. It took considerable time and effort, which was only rewarded a few days ago, but I finally managed to trace the real Colonel Quiney - a near-vegetable of a creature following shell-shock suffered during the Ashanti campaign - and the papers he had signed over to a certain Colonel Moriarty eighteen years ago.

"You see, the Professor had a goal - to groom Lord Coledale as a political puppet. He had all the advantages - wealth, looks, but most importantly, breeding. And he was their tool entirely. His influence was probably never used in those early days; his uncouth manners and ways were groomed out of him. Gradually he became the aristocrat born and bred known to the public.

"Then, after patient years of grooming Lord Coledale for high office, while his immense wealth was used by the gang to further their own interests, the Professor died at Reichenbach. The gang was thrown into disarray. Now the real Colonel Moriarty came to the fore. He ruthlessly seized control of the gang, as he alone now had control over the gang's treasury. But he saw to it that Lord Coledale's position was never questioned, and for a while the gang lay low.

"Colonel Moriarty began to consolidate his hold, and to move the gang in new directions. His own field of expertise was the East, and the gang was already skilled at assassination - he had negotiated most of the contracts himself, as his brother's only trusted emissary. I had discovered much of this when I followed Professor Moriarty's footsteps around Europe, but not who was his chief-of-staff after Moran was retired.

"When I left London last, I already had knowledge of over fifty murders credited to the gang. Victims were rarely front-page news - not the captains of industry, nor the kings. Usually they were advisers and confidantes of those people, or claimants to a title, or those standing in the way of enormous inheritances by the simple fact of inconveniently remaining alive. Not only were these deaths less noticeable, there was one other enormous advantage. Usually the result of the assassination was that the client himself then became, or remained, wealthy and powerful, and the gang - like the poisoners who were once such a fixture of European court life - were in a position to demand favours and money of them, should it ever become necessary.

"As I pondered this, only the day before the events at Parliament House, a larger picture began to form. Here we had, on the one hand, a wealthy, powerful criminal conspiracy, with their own political puppet groomed for high office - and actively seeking it at present. They also had vast experience in political killings for gain, and recently thwarted ambitions to cause the fall of independent Siam.

"On the other hand, London was suffering a rash of mysterious bombings and gruesome killings. I looked for connections, and found many suggestive leads to follow; I'd been investigating numerous matters, all at the same time, and time was becoming pressing. Isobel Aster and Godfrey Norton were kidnapped, and I urgently wanted to locate both of them. Again, I was too far behind the villains. Norton was tortured to reveal the location of his confession, and Sir Oliver's house was ransacked as a result. After he was tortured, he was chloroformed, and taken to the Trinity Square Gardens via the Tower Hill gateway, still living, so that the Thuggee murderers could preserve the correctness of their rituals. Here he was brutally murdered, in a similar fashion to the previous victims.

"That was another mistake, as it linked the two cases firmly in my reasoning. Whoever was terrorising London was also involved in covering up the *tontine* murders scandal - and I had already decided that those villains belonged to a gang who were the perpetrators of the murders and attempted assassinations at Siam. The several cases I'd been attempting to resolve appeared to be coalescing, becoming various aspects of the same case.

"By this time, I should point out, I had a very fair suspicion of the nature of those mysteriously consistent and gruesome murders. The first clue had been the yellow silk thread I removed from the ligature wound of one of the victims. That could have been a coincidence, but it started me thinking about the ritual aspects of the murders. Then, the second pair of victims were of Indian origin, and were last seen going out for a curry meal. Now we had Norton killed by Indians. At the time I was uncertain as to the exact rituals of the ancient Thuggee, but I recalled the use of the yellow silk scarf with a rupee coin knotted in one corner, to weight the scarf as it is slung around the neck. We found a rupee coin near Norton's grave. I thought that by now we had had altogether too many Indians involved, starting with the poison-dart fellow at Singapore, the bomber who killed Irene Adler - and now Norton.

"So I put a notice in the dailies, with the result that Colonel Hayter turned up at Baker Street with a most interesting volume. Perhaps, as we all appear to have finished with our entrees, Colonel Hayter would enlighten us all, before Anton brings out his excellent puddings and coffee."

The Colonel half-rose, nodded around the table at us all, then sat again, realising just in time that this was not an officer's briefing. I had to smile at my old friend's fixed ways, though I suppose I have my little oddities as well.

"The volume Mr. Holmes has referred to is the account of the suppression of the once-infamous Thuggees - the Beguilers - who had preyed on Indian wayfarers since before memory began, murdering and robbing their victims with greater or lesser adherence to their own strict rules. This was all done in the name of the goddess *Kali*, which would have been little consolation to the victims. Sleeman stamped out the practice, but even he knew that the traditions would survive in unlikely places. But I'm certain that even he would never have expected that, sixty years later, London would be plagued by *thagi* assassins.

"But he would have understood the reasons, I'm sure of that," said Hayter as he noisily cleared his throat. "Fear and protection, you see! That was how the beguilers worked. One gang acts menacing, and the victims gladly join forces with another group of innocent-looking travellers. Security in numbe-rs, you know! The second lot turn out to be the real killers, once the victims' trust has been gained."

"An exact parallel, Colonel," said Holmes. "Splendidly done! You see, I surmised that Colonel Moriarty had returned to his old haunts at Bengal, and recruited a band of *thagi* from his old childhood village. A new generation, but still active, though I suspect they must venture very far from their home villages these days before they dare make their sacrifices to *Durga*, or *Kali*.

"Colonel Moriarty wanted to shake up London, and prepare the way for some radical changes in government policy. He decided to employ the same strategy. Fear and protection! Remembering the terror and hysteria whipped up when the Ripper was about his work, Moriarty decided that the sheer scientific brutality of the Thuggees' handiwork would cause an even greater panic. The random bombings were part of it, as well, creating an atmosphere of pervading fear in London, to culminate in the assassination of the Foreign Minister.

"Then, the protection! Lord Coledale would be rushed into office in the new government brought to power with promises to curb the violence. And miraculously, the violence would cease. And British foreign policy would have been in the hands of a gang of outright criminals.

"Colonel Moriarty slipped his Indians into London, probably as seamen who jumped ship, and took over a curry house so he could keep his band of assassins together, and explain their presence. But he didn't count on the curiosity of Colonel Hayter concerning the disappearance of the former owner. Fortunately, the Colonel saw my notice in his paper, and thus we were able to trace Colonel Moriarty's gang of Thuggee assassins to their lair.

"At that time, I still thought we were looking for a Colonel Stuttaford, but he escaped our net. But the thought of Colonel Moriarty's childhood spent amongst those same Indians crossed my mind, and I began to put two and two together at last. I followed up on Stuttaford at Aldershot, and found that he'd been listed missing-in-action since the Battle of Taima. By now I was satisfied that Lord Coledale's efficient aide Quiney and the mysterious Colonel Stuttaford were both aliases of Colonel Moriarty, and I was fairly certain that he was now the mastermind behind his brother's gang."

"I had no definite proof of any of this. By this time, matters were definitely coming to a boil in London. Francois le Villard arrived from Siam, bringing with him our guests of tonight, Prince Phichai and *Señor* Jose Felipe Azcevado Marques. And really, that brings us up to date, I think, as we all know the results of our little dramatic interlude at Parliament House. Now, I suggest we call for Anton and indulge in a little pudding."

"I have no wish to delay the pudding, Holmes," I said immediately, "but you'll not get away as easily as that. I, at least, have several further questions to ask. Such as, why did MacDonald kill Mischa Roborovsky at that time? And how did you know Lord Coledale had the *Great Mogul* concealed in his stick?"

"Very well, Watson; answers you shall have, but first . . . apple tart with custard!"

There was also, I noted happily, for it was a favourite of mine, a plum duff. We finished our meal with excellent coffee, and settled back with cigars. Only then would Holmes continue.

"Inspector Patterson and I both questioned Commissioner MacDonald at length. Now he knows that Colonel Moriarty and Moran died in the train explosion, he's happy to talk. He confirmed Inspector Patterson's report. Patterson told me he'd suspected MacDonald had informed the gang in advance of the swoop, so after his disgrace, he'd gone to Glasgow. He found that MacDonald had risen rapidly there by coming to an accommodation with the city's criminals - less crime on the surface, more in fact! He transferred to the Yard as a rising young detective, but Professor Moriarty heard of his past record through his criminal network, and saw the corrupt policeman behind the facade of Scots rectitude.

"When he arranged the deaths for the *tontine* scheme, which so enriched the gang, the Professor also arranged that Inspector MacDonald be assigned as investigating officer. Years later, he did the same thing when he found that I was seriously pursuing him and his gang - and MacDonald successfully destroyed the more serious parts of the prosecution's case.

"This time, MacDonald murdered Mischa himself, because Mischa had found out from Miss Isobel that he had covered up the *tontine* murders. Mischa had tried to blackmail him, you see, but MacDonald found him out. He also knew it was Mischa who'd been blackmailing Colonel Moriarty and the gang, but didn't say anything.

"Apparently, after Moran had missed me with his air-gun bullet outside Covent Garden, Colonel Moriarty had wondered what why we'd gone there, and made it his business to find out. MacDonald had told them we would go there that morning because he'd bribed the landlord at Mischa's old address to let him know if anyone came asking for him, and I'd left my card. MacDonald says that when he found that Sherlock Holmes had been asking after Mischa, he decided he had to kill the Russian, but he wanted it to look like a natural death. He used a method that he'd learnt from a dying murderer who had confessed to him, long after his hated employer had been buried without suspicion or investigation - prussic acid blown into the face.

"He then set about trying to find Miss Isobel, but Moriarty and Moran got to her first, after they'd finished with their crude but effective investigations at Covent Garden. After the death of Roborovsky, enough gossip spilled over about the old affair that the two Colonels were able to piece together what had happened. They considered killing the Commissioner, but decided he was too important to them. So they found Miss Isobel, and were holding her, originally as a sop to Lord Coledale's feelings, and later as a hostage. It seems that Coledale had a decent bone somewhere in his body, or more likely he was fearful for his own hide, but he apparently never told Professor Moriarty or the gang that Isobel Aster knew about the *tontine* murders, or they would certainly have done away with her immediately."

"And as to the *Great Mogul*, until that very moment I had no idea it was concealed in Lord Coledale's stick. Some of you know nothing of the recent history of that long-lost gem. Francois le Villard and I stumbled across it at Siam, when we were investigating the possibility that a gang of Belgian swindlers was behind the threats to the General Adviser. The Belgians turned out to have nothing to do with our assassins, other than the fact that Godfrey Norton was representing them in a case before the courts there.

"Their leader, Colonel Sartorius, was a toughened soldier-of-fortune, replenishing his coffers between wars. He'd come across the stone in Burma, where he offered a share of it to me, as Professor Sigerson, if I would finance the trip to collect it from where it was hidden. I agreed, and supplied the thousand pounds he asked for. Sartorius brought it back to Bangkok, where he was knifed and the stone was stolen. Godfrey Norton was charged for the murder - but not the theft - on the basis of evidence found at the scene. You see, nobody ever believed the *Great Mogul* still really existed. We know better!"

And with an understated flourish, Holmes produced from his vest-pocket a diamond the size and shape of half a goose-egg. It flashed and sparkled in the gas-light, as Holmes held up it for all to see, before he withdrew from his waist-coat pocket a small crimson velvet sack, loosened the drawstring, and slipped the *Great Mogul* into it. Then, he handed the diamond to Mycroft.

"Sartorius had offered the stone to Norton, intending to swindle my investment. I suspect that Norton drunkenly boasted of the stone to Lord Coledale at a time when Quiney wasn't around. Coledale planned to steal the stone and have Norton blamed for the murder. It was easy enough to steal a knife from the kitchens at Norton's hotel; then Coledale went to the Hotel Hermes, convinced Colonel Sartorius that Norton had sent him to buy the diamond, and knifed the mercenary as soon as he produced the stone.

"I imagine he relied on the element of surprise - after all, he was well known in the European community at Bangkok by then, and who would suspect one of the wealthiest peers in England of murder for gain? He managed to avoid detection for that murder, and hid the stone away in the hollow silver knob of his ebony stick. The question is, why did Lord Coledale plan and undertake such a risky enterprise in cold blood?

"Ironically, as I had learnt only days before, after all the deaths and deception, Lord Coledale actually had nothing to call his own. Despite all the trappings and privileges, he remained a Man of Straw all his life; his one bold attempt to alter the situation brought about his own death, and the unmasking of a conspiracy. That was why he murdered Colonel Sartorius in Bangkok, and stole the *Great Mogul*. He knew better than any just how ruthless the gang were, even after the death of the Professor, and he knew that to escape their clutches would require much more money than they ever allowed him to touch. He feared that, sooner or later, they would need him no longer, and he would be killed. Lord Coledale saw the immensely valuable diamond as his getaway insurance, readily negotiable, and small enough to be carried wherever he went.

"As to its presence in his stick, I suppose something about that elegant black-and-silver stick had been bothering me for some little while, but I had paid no attention. I have already mentioned that bringing *Señor* Jose Felipe to London was at best a gamble, as we had no proof of anything criminal to lay against either Lord Coledale or Quiney. But we were certain that we knew the truth now, and as we could see no other way, decided it was worth a try. And I must say, thanks to *Nai* Portugee's dramatic phantom voice, and superb memory, for a while our ploy appeared to be working. Coledale was obviously panicked that their conversation had been overheard, and that, for the first time, their elaborate conspiracy appeared about to unravel completely. At that moment I thought we should soon have them all!

"But then Quiney - Colonel Moriarty - broke in, putting a little spine in Coledale, pointing out our lack of solid evidence. His lordship began to see that if he simply denied all, we should have to back down, and some of his normal arrogance returned. Thinking he'd regained the upper hand, and being a bully at heart, he made to strike me with his stick when I blocked his way to the door. That was when he made his great mistake. In mid-strike, with the silver knob raised above his head, he suddenly changed his mind, and his face reflected it all. In that instant his mind became as an open book, and I saw it all, though it will take a little longer to explain.

"I was certain that Godfrey Norton hadn't stolen the *Great Mogul,* nor killed Sartorius; he'd have confessed to it, or else left the jewel to pay for Irene Adler's future. At the time of that murder, the only lead was a description given of a tall *farang* in white suit and white Panama-straw hat, with a black cane, who had been seen at the hotel. Chief Inspector Sheriff had never found this mysterious European, and for a moment I had considered Lord Coledale, simply because he matched the description.

"Now that memory rushed back, along with two other incidents. The first was at Bangkok, some time *before* the murder of Sartorius, when I'd seen him use that same stick to strike viciously at an old Chinese fellow, then take a swig of whisky from the flask concealed in the silver-knob. He'd certainly given no thought to his expensive cane at that time.

"The second incident took place here in London just last week, when Coledale and Moran had just kidnapped Miss Isobel from the Belgrave House Hotel, but meant nothing to me at the time. One of Wiggins's street arabs was struck by Lord Coledale as he tried to jump onto the running-board. Afterwards, he said that Coledale at first raised a silver-knobbed black stick, then seized his companion's stick to strike brutally at his head and hands.

"Why, since arriving in London again, was Lord Coledale suddenly so solicitous of his cane. Especially at such a moment, when his whole world was under immediate threat? After all, I thought, it is only an ebony stick, and the chased-silver knob contained only a flask of no-doubt expensive whisky. Didn't it?"

Holmes paused, took a pull on his cigar, and tapped the lengthened ash into an ashtray.

"And, as I said, in an instant I saw it all! Coledale had somehow murdered Sartorius, stolen the *Great Mogul,* and secreted it in the knob of his cane - where it had remained ever since, ready to hand for instant flight if needed. But, of course, he could no longer lay about him with his stick, in case he fractured his precious treasure. It was that sudden panicked realisation, in the middle of his existing crisis, that gave him away.

"I seized his stick, found the jewel, and you all know the rest. It was the concrete proof we needed to convict him of one murder. Colonel Moriarty's violent reaction to Lord Coledale's greed and stupidity silenced him forever, but provided proof of his own complicity. We had, at last, unmasked the conspirators.

"I blame myself that I allowed Colonel Moriarty time enough to escape. I knew he carried a concealed derringer, and was a man of decision. But after the events at the curry-house the previous night I strongly suspected that Colonel Moriarty, Quiney and Colonel Stuttaford were in fact one and the same. I should have expected him to have taken every precaution when coming to any meeting, even to one with the Cabinet Secretary at Parliament House. And, after Bangkok, I should have expected that he'd use the river as a means of escape if needed. That unfortunate oversight, along with an inspired suggestion from Doctor Watson, resulted in us finding the train-full of explosives and saving Isobel Aster, and so far as we know, cost Moriarty and Moran their lives, all of which are credits in the ledger.

"Unfortunately, there appears to be a requirement for balance in the affairs of men, as in any book of accounts. The debit entry, in this case, was the tragic death of Francois le Villard."

"What will become of the *Great Mogul*, Holmes, after all that?" asked Sir Oliver Newsome, his legal curiosity roused.

In response, Holmes gestured towards his older brother. Mycroft still had the jewel in his hands. He slid it out of its sack once more, and held it up once again.

"The *Great Mogul* was the property, apparently, of the Burmese kings, and as such, now becomes British Crown property. In the strictest confidence, however, I can tell you that as its provenance is so murky, and involves such unsavoury events, the *Great Mogul* diamond will be consigned to a special department within Her Majesty's treasury. There it will keep company with a hoard of other Crown Jewels too embarrassing, for one reason or another, to acknowledge or display. It certainly won't be lonely in its vault, I can assure you of that. Admire it, while you have the opportunity. You will be the last to do so for a long while, other than a few dusty civil servants."

He slipped the jewel back into its sack, and tucked it safely away in his inner vest-pocket. He patted it, to make sure it was secure.

"Well, does that satisfy your curiosity, Sir Oliver?" asked Holmes.

"Indeed, it does. But I have another. I have followed this Siam Question in *The Times*, of course, but what effect has all *this* affair had upon the outcome of *that?"*

Holmes thought for a moment, before replying.

"In his Journals, le Villard quoted the old saw about the Siamese playing at work, and working at play. This is not necessarily a bad thing, in a land where, as the King's father said - *'there are fish in the water, there is rice in the fields'*. The wonder is that this land, lost in dreams, managed to throw up kings who were skilled statesmen, and wise far beyond expectations in the ways of the world outside them. All we did, really, was to ensure that the

Siamese were able to benefit from their good fortune in that respect."

CHAPTER LXII

"DOES ANYONE ELSE have a question?" enquired Mycroft. "No! Very well . . . shall we adjourn this most interesting evening, as I know de Benoist must leave immediately for Paris, and Sherlock and Inspector Patterson have another call upon their time and attention? But before we do, now that I am out and about for once, I have an invitation for Doctor Watson to join me in another carriage drive, this time through the night-time streets of London."

I, of course, accepted gladly, and once decided upon going, Mycroft invited the others of the party. Sir Oliver declined, and offered to escort Isobel Aster back to her new rooms. The Siamese party, however, accepted with alacrity. That is how it came about that, once the others had dispersed, I most unexpectedly spent a brisk evening careening about the late-night streets and lanes in company with a prince of Siam, a blind former Portuguese-Chinese pirate and his sea-captain son, and Mycroft Holmes. Whilst he took care not to endanger the general public, Mycroft was less charitable towards his passengers. Mycroft urged his favourite horses into a fine lather, until I feared for life and limb. The prince and old Jose Felipe were thoroughly enjoying the experience, and Dom Alonzo was clearly pleased at that.

I glanced at the enormous bulk of Mycroft Holmes, alongside me in the driver's seat. There, fierce concentration directed towards the surging horses, the well-sprung carriage and the road rushing towards us, I suddenly saw the younger Mycroft - the adventurer of far places, now shackled by his vast knowledge to a civil servant's desk at Whitehall. He caught my glance, and shouted at me over the sound of carriage wheels on cobblestone, as we came in sight of a modest tavern tucked into one corner of a town square, and slowed. The odour of the Thames came to us, and I saw that we were only a few short blocks from the waterfront.

"As promised, Doctor Watson, a hot toddy at an interesting pub! What a splendid town London is, really," remarked Mycroft as we all stepped down, and went out of the chilly night air into the warmth and noise of the pub he had chosen.

Hours later, as I sat alone before a dying fire, I thought about that letter from Colonel Moriarty, received within hours of the release of Moran, which had signalled so clearly to me that Holmes had indeed returned. Why had Colonel Moriarty sent it to Holmes, when his own involvement was by no means confirmed at that time? Was it intended as a diversion? Perhaps as a challenge, to the man who had bested his brother? Or was it meant to indicate Colonel Moriarty's contemptuous dismissal of Holmes, and of his ability to bring him to a similar defeat? I could come to no satisfactory conclusion, and decided that, like so much about the man, it would likely remain an enigma, the answers lost with his death.

Thinking of death inevitably led me back to the one last explanation which had so far evaded me, and for which I had avoided asking, uncertain as to how to approach the matter. As the last embers crumbled into ash, I heard the street door open, the familiar tread on the stairs; the sitting-room door opened quietly as Holmes let himself in. It was a moment or two before he realised I was still up, and he came across to warm his hands at the embers. I thought, it is now, or never.

"I hesitate to ask, Holmes, but . . . well, I have two questions which nag at my mind, and I should be grateful if you could clear them away for me. Is it an inopportune moment?"

"Not at all, Watson. Proceed!"

My first question was to ask about Colonel Moriarty's letter, which had been so recently in my thoughts.

"That can be disposed of in a moment. Knowing my mind from his own and his brother's experiences, he sought to intrigue me away from the simple truth, that it was Lord Coledale at the centre of Colonel Moriarty's web, and not Quiney enmeshed in his lordship's. And the other?"

"At Tibet, why the asp toxin in the brandy? I have read le Villard's account of the episode several times over, and if his report is accurate, I cannot see how you could have found the opportunity, in the midst of armed slavers, to introduce the asp venom into the brandy bottle? And what made you think that Mohammedans would drink spirits anyway?"

Holmes stared at the glowing embers for a long moment, before answering me.

"The reason is quite simple - I didn't have to put the poison in the brandy, as it was already in there! As to why, I suppose I could dismiss the matter by saying that any toxin loses its potency when exposed to air, whereas in a solution of alcohol it would retain its potency far better. And I didn't plan that the slavers should drink it; that was their own idea. The captives were freed, the *Atalik's* son found his bride, and we found Captain Dolghurokov - and may thus have averted an unnecessary war. Still, I'm not proud of that day's events, but neither do I feel any great sense of guilt, and I lost no sleep over the peaceful departure of such a band of cutthroats. But, why did you hesitate to ask, Watson."

"Well . . . at times I have thought that, perhaps . . . well . . ."

"You thought that perhaps I was testing my own will to resist the blandishments of a painless surcease? How perceptive of you, Watson! I have often wondered that exact same thing. And I have no answer except . . . perhaps! I suppose the truth, Watson, is that I had prepared the poison mixture for myself, before leaving Lhasa. In a sense I *was* testing my own resolve to stay alive, when I felt so desperately helpless. I thought that if I could continue to carry on, with the means of a peaceful and painless oblivion always to hand, and *not* use it, then I should have exorcised the spectre of Professor Moriarty's pyrrhic victory, which reared up before my mind when I awoke each morning, and tormented my waking hours and dreams both.

"I had spent months following his trail, and months more forcing him into a corner where Scotland Yard could snare both the Professor and his gang. It was a time when I allowed my personal animus to colour my judgement, more and more, until I suspect I became just a little obsessed with defeating him. To have that swift and complete victory snatched away, and to know that most of his crimes remained unpunished, was more than I could bear, even after he followed me to kill me, and I bested him at Reichenbach Falls

"But even knowing of his certain death did nothing to remove the darkness from my soul. I felt that somehow Professor Moriarty had snatched a victory even from defeat and death. That I must tolerate that fact was one of the hardest lessons I have ever learned. But, learn it I did. One morning, sitting on a rock ledge in the high mountains, surrounded by peaks of awesome majesty, I watched huge birds-of-prey, wheeling on the wind. They simply hunted for their sustenance, without thought of consequences, and were not tormented by unanswerable questions. I looked up, and directly overhead, remaining stationary against the wind, was one of the huge birds. It seemed to fix its gaze upon me, sitting below on the edge of a precipice, for a full minute or so.

"Suddenly, all my darkness fell away. *Gnothi seauton!* I saw that the battle of wits with Professor Moriarty had been no more than an episode, and if less than completely successful, at least *I* was alive to regret it! But no case would ever be more to me than just a case, ever again! The sense of release, of no longer having to bear a crushing burden, was so intoxicating that, right there on the very edge of the abyss, I leaped up and did a sort of jig of joy. I hadn't realised, until I read his Journal, that le Villard had witnessed my antics, and had wondered at my sanity just at that precise moment when I felt that sanity had returned to my fevered mind.

"So if, when dealing with future investigations, I should ever appear to be heartless and detached, perhaps you will recall that time when my own life hung in a balance because I cared too much."

I had never heard Holmes speak so openly of matters of the heart and soul, and doubted that I should do so again. His remarkably candid account, however, fixed itself in my mind, and later that night, as I lay abed, I thought of le Villard's account of the death of Irene Adler, and Holmes's unemotional reaction to her brutal murder. I realised that, amongst those remote and forbidding peaks, Holmes had, indeed, learned his most difficult lesson as a consulting detective.

"Perhaps, to round out your report, as we are talking of asp toxin, I should let you see the telegraph message from Captain Faunce at Calcutta. I can't help but feel that his post-script serves to demonstrate the perverse humour of the fates. It is late. I shall leave you to read it, Watson, and get some sleep."

Holmes took the message from a pigeonhole in his desk, and gave it to me. I read Faunce's extremely cryptic message with some difficulty. The post-script concerned the fate of Brigadier and Lady Wrothesly, the murderess from whom Holmes and le Villard had taken the poison in the first place. Faunce wrote that the Brigadier had been released after twelve months in prison, on compassionate grounds due to a faulty heart. Lady Wrothesly had been adjudged insane, and confined in a guarded sanatorium. The Brigadier had come to visit her one hot afternoon, and she prepared for him some lemon cordial. Apparently he'd just taken a deep draught when he saw, on her side-table, an empty vial labelled POISON. He dropped like a stone, dead instantly. He was rushed into an operating theatre, but it was too late. Autopsy showed no poison at all in his system - it turned out the vial had been left there by a careless nursing assistant. The poor chap had expected to be poisoned all along, and had died of shock when he saw it on the side-table - empty.

EPILOGUE

LONDON

LATE APRIL 1894

EPILOGUE

Rain slanted down from a dismal grey sky, neither heavy nor light. It was just a rainy spring day, though there was little of spring about it. Tall cypresses, blackened by the rain, lent a sad, minatory air to the proceedings. A black-cloth marquee, set up to shelter the more prominent mourners, sagged a little with the weight of standing water; overflow rain-water dripped ceaselessly from its edges.

Muffled drums and pipes sounded from near-by the open grave, as the narrow black hearse wound its way slowly through Highgate Cemetery, carrying Lord Coledale to his final - and unearned - resting-place amongst the famous. Tall black plumes at each corner of the hearse waved in the rain, seeming like miniature versions of the sinister cypresses; the four black stallions drawing the hearse glistened and steamed in the chill rain.

Through the glass-panelled windows, engraved with intricate floral wreaths, I saw the coffin bearing the mortal remains of Reginald Aubrey Haversham, late Lord Coledale. It was of glossy, black-lacquered wood, adorned only by a severe row of wrought-silver handles along each side. I was forcefully reminded of Lord Coledale's ebony-and-silver stick, in which he had concealed the Great Mogul. That immensely valuable diamond, which he had coveted as his getaway insurance - small enough to be carried wherever he went - had provided Holmes with concrete proof, which had caused the whole edifice of conspiracy to tumble in ruins. The finding of it had instantly caused Lord Coledale's death at the hands of Colonel Moriarty.

Here, amongst the thousands of extravagantly over-decorated tombs and pretentious memorials dedicated to everything from Greek paganist rites to Egyptian temples of the dead, where the famous were buried alongside the merely wealthy, it seemed somehow grotesquely fitting to consign this thoroughly contemptible wretch to his untimely grave.

In order to save the government an extreme embarrassment, Lord Coledale had been eulogised by everyone from the pulpit to the press as the very model of the forward-thinking, progressive type of peer this country can ill-afford to lose, especially to so senseless and tragic an end. Murdered within the hallowed halls of the Houses of Parliament . . . for his courage in defending the independence of the Siamese people . . . by a traitorous cabal of ex-Indian Army officers suspected to be in the secret pay of the perfidious French *parti colon*.

In attendance were the Prime Minister and the entire Cabinet, those of the Lords who could still get out to Highgate, and masses of sensation-seeking onlookers behind cordons manned by police constables and, nearer to the grave-site, uniformed and beaver-hatted mounted Royal Guardsmen. The one anomaly, amidst all the pomp and pageantry, was the entire absence of the Royal Family.

I contrasted this with the simple and moving memorial service for Francois le Villard, held several days before, at the Roman church favoured by the French community at London. His remains had already been sent under military escort to Paris, to await collection by his aged mother, once she had been informed.

There had been the same few of us at both ceremonies, but for different reasons. Holmes, his brother Mycroft, de Benoist's representative at the first ceremony only, Inspector Patterson, Colonel Hayter, Isobel Aster; we had all gathered to mourn the gallant Francois le Villard - in silent tribute to his courage, and for our private reasons as well.

Now we were gathered, I thought, to confirm the definite end of a man for whose death I could feel no sorrow whatsoever. This, after all had been a man prepared to countenance even the murder of his own brother in order to usurp his wealth and position.

In a far corner of this same cemetery, less than a week before, a smaller group of mourners had gathered at the grave of Godfrey Norton. Isobel Aster, who had known him when he was courting Irene Adler; Holmes and myself; Sir Oliver Newsome; Norton's aged and bewildered parents; we had all mourned sincerely for the troubled and obsessed man who had been Irene Adler's husband, and had caused so much distress to all who knew him. And yet, at the very end, he had sacrificed his life in the most terrible fashion in order to see justice brought down upon the heads of her powerful and well-connected murderers. Isobel's tears were genuine, in her reminiscing, and so doubtless were the few shed by Sir Oliver, who otherwise remained stoically silent throughout the brief ceremony.

Holmes and I, having seen Lord Coledale's coffin lowered into the waiting grave, and the first few sods tossed in after it, had had enough of funerals, and left. Besides, Holmes and I were to meet Mycroft in four hours time 'at Buck House', as he put it, 'for a private audience with the mistress of the house'.

During the return journey, as our train passed through the outer suburbs, I reflected that it had been a week of solemn moments. Only the previous night, in the chill hours following midnight, I had accompanied Holmes and Inspector Patterson to the Tower, where we had met by appointment with

Mycroft. The occasion was the hushed departure of former Commissioner Alexander Kenneth MacDonald, who had been incarcerated there since his arrest, and questioned until Patterson knew everything he had to tell. The disgraced police chief was to be slipped out, suitably, by way of Traitor's Gate, under cover of darkness, and locked in a cabin of a naval frigate bound for the West Indies.

Our small party had waited on the stone landing alongside the pool, with its barred gate fronting the Thames on the opposite side. A ship's tender, manned by six sturdy naval ratings, rocked gently at the foot of the stone steps, waiting to receive a single passenger and take him far, far away, where he could never cause embarrassment to the government.

As we stamped our wet feet to keep out the cold, I thought of the famous and infamous prisoners who had passed this way over the past centuries, usually to face lengthy imprisonment, perhaps torture, or the axe. At two o'clock in the morning, four Beefeaters in full regalia escorted MacDonald from the Bloody Tower, where he had been held because of its proximity to the Tower of London's river entrance.

An officer of the Privy Court stepped forward at Mycroft's signal, and read aloud a proclamation that a true bill had been found against Alexander Kenneth MacDonald, former Commissioner of Police, on charges of murder, conspiracy and high treason. Pursuant to his full confession, sentence of death by hanging was suspended only on condition that MacDonald consent to voluntary exile. The Crown Prosecutor advised MacDonald, through his minion, that the sentence was subject to no statute of limitations, and that if MacDonald ever returned to England, or even left his sanctuary, he would be seized and summarily executed. The prisoner was asked if he understood the proclamation, answered in the affirmative, and the court officer turned and left us.

Mycroft Holmes stepped across to the manacled prisoner, who appeared relieved that he had escaped the usual fate of traitors, and anxious to be on his way out of the forbidding Tower.

"We brought you here to conceal the fact of your arrest, MacDonald. But, somehow, the press has got wind that a major public figure is being held in the Tower. They don't know whom, only that it is in connection with the murder of Lord Coledale. So we are sending you out through Traitor's Gate. Usually, those who are escorted through its portals are coming to meet their fate as traitors.

"You, sir, have been no less a traitor, but circumstances appear to favour you. You are to be sent into exile, but not overtly as a prisoner. In fact, you have been appointed overseer of an island prison in the Caribbean - but you will never be allowed to leave."

Mycroft turned away without another word, and MacDonald was led down the steps to the waiting cutter. According to the newspapers, Commissioner MacDonald had resigned to show his acceptance of responsibility for failure to prevent the spate of bomb attacks, and the related murder of a peer in Parliament, and was going on extended holiday.

The barred gates to the pool creaked open, as little as necessary to allow the boat to pass. As the cutter pulled out of the pool into the Thames, and headed downstream to the Naval docks, I asked Mycroft why MacDonald had been allowed to get away with murder, not to mention treason.

"Ironically," he replied, a wry smile on his thin lips, "because of due process of law. It cuts two ways, you see. If we are to bring him to court on any of the charges - even the murder charge - we must allow him to testify in his own defence. He knows all about the conspiracy, and how nearly it came to succeeding. The government has asked itself, 'Do we really want the truth of this entire matter to come out? We know what happened, and it casts neither the British nor the French government in a particularly flattering light.' The villains are dead, and for the same reasons Lord Coledale will be eulogised. As unjust as it all seems, it is for the best."

Some time later Holmes and I alighted at Victoria Station, took a hansom to Green Park and proceeded to take a leisurely stroll through that beautiful park. We were early for our appointment even allowing for protocol and, still being in our formal attire, we had no need to change.

As we ambled along through the restful, rolling lawns and gardens, less formal than those of neighbouring St. James's Park - which is probably why I have always preferred it - the sun finally came out from behind the clouds. The park was suddenly all sunshine and shade, a most welcome change from the mournful surroundings at Highgate Cemetery.

"I always thought I should appreciate a ramble through London with yourself and le Villard," mused Holmes, "to show him our London, as he once showed me his Paris. Now it will never be, such are the ways of fate."

A minute or so later, he continued.

"I had news yesterday from the Home Office, Watson. Francois is to be posthumously honoured for his courage in attempting to save Miss Isobel's life. It will have to do in stead of decorations for all his other efforts on behalf of both our countries. A poor substitute for the man. I've written to Miss Malee in Bangkok, to ask her where I should send the medal. I feel he would have wished that she have it. I also asked her if she could make sure that Rinzing and his family are taken care of, and le Villard's mastiff, Tashi as well. I sent money to defray the expenses."

"How do you think she will take the news, Holmes?" I asked.

"She is a modern, young Siamese woman, well-educated and versed in our 'civilised' ways. But precisely because she is Siamese, it will come as no surprise. You see, not long before I left Siam, Miss Malee came to talk with me, at a time when she knew that le Villard would be absent. It seems she had been to consult one of their *mor doo,* or fortune-tellers, who had consulted his oracles, and told her that the young man she had set her heart on marrying would shortly die a violent death.

"I tried to convince her that it was but a foolish superstition, and she allowed herself to be consoled but, I think, not convinced that this was so. She never revealed to him the reason, but I am certain it was her fear of the dangerous nature of our work that made le Villard promise to abandon it, and I had not the heart to protest his decision.

"Miss Malee is young yet. She was the chosen wife of my own dearest companion, save only yourself, Watson. She was the best friend Irene Adler ever had, closer than a sister could have been! I am by no means convinced that those scoundrels have perished - though their wings are clipped for now. In order that she may live her life in peace, there must be no mention in any of your published tales of the exploits of le Villard, or of her involvement, so long as she lives. Have I your word on that?"

"Of course, Holmes. Of course," I replied. He had never felt impelled to pronounce a stricture so forcefully, but I took no offence. How could I, indeed?

"I have also telegraphed to Chief Inspector Sheriff, to clear Godfrey Norton's name of the charges laid against him. It seems the least I could do for the memory of his wife."

As Holmes and I made our way out of Green Park the birds had begun to sing in the trees, and the massed flowers displayed their glorious colourings under the now-bright sun. We crossed The Mall and skirted the edge of St. James's Park towards Birdcage Walk, and then on to Buckingham Gate.

We were expected when we arrived at the Lodge by the great gates leading to Buckingham Palace, and, despite having arrived on foot rather than in a carriage, were immediately escorted to the Summer Garden. Here we were announced to the majestic figure seated in the shadow of a fringed marquee. In a canvas chair set before a varnished-wood-and-brass campaign-desk, attended by two of her Indian servants in immaculate white turbans and tunics, sat Her Royal Highness, Queen Victoria.

In front of her on the Persian carpet flooring of the marquee, and slightly to the side, stood the enormous bulk of Mycroft Holmes. With him were Inspector Patterson and Miss Isobel Aster, *nee* Blood.

Mycroft introduced us, so the meeting was obviously to be quite informal.
"Mister Holmes," began Her Majesty, then corrected herself, "Mister *Sherlock* Holmes! We meet again, thankfully. You have ever been of great service to us, and your brother Mycroft has, over the years, apprised us of the more interesting of your investigations on our behalf. It is only recently, indeed, that he has seen fit to inform us that you were not, in fact, deceased. For this we have forgiven him. As you know, he has been so kind as to ask Doctor Watson, here, to write up a complete account of your adventures and investigations while gone from our London.

"Having read the first drafts of this account with great interest, Mister Holmes, we felt we simply must ask you to come here, and allow us to thank you. We are seldom amused these days, and our official correspondence is either dull or troublesome in the extreme, so to read of your exploits on our behalf gave us a great deal of pleasure.

"Not that we are insensitive to the great losses you have suffered during the course of these past three years. Quite the contrary! We have asked your brother Mycroft to see that M. Francois le Villard receives the highest honour we are able to award a foreigner, in addition to the honours he has already received.

"As to honours, we have attempted time and again to award your brother with suitable honours for the inestimable services he has rendered unto us over the years. To our knowledge he has most recently refused the Knight Grand Cross of St. Michael and St. George, having already refused a KCMG, and before that a CMG! Your brother really is the most exasperating man. And whilst officially we may have to take issue with some of his rather progressive views concerning our Empire, in private we find we must agree with much of what he says."

Mycroft nodded politely, as I reflected that that is most certainly not what Her Majesty would have said in her younger days.

"We have decided," continued the Queen, "after reading your account and taking much other advice, to support an armed British expedition to Lhasa, in order to open Tibet to our emissaries, and to deny Russia an exclusive foot-hold, as it were, on the ramparts overlooking our territories. Are you, sir, willing to accept a suitable honour as commendation for your exploits in securing the frontiers of our Indian Empire in the direction of Tibet, and thwarting the ploys of our Russian counterpart to seize that fascinating land?"

"Without wishing to offend, Your Majesty, I must join with my brother on the side of anonymity, especially involving investigations on behalf of your government or the Royal House, and respectfully decline any such honours."

"We must say, Mister Holmes, that this hardly comes as an unexpected surprise, but we respect your decision. Your work brings you much in the way of great danger, and we understand that public recognition may not be advantageous."

"Thank you, Your Majesty. You are most gracious."

"It is our duty, rather, to thank you, for solving the mysterious bombings which have plagued our capital lately. Not to mention the discreet handling of the matter involving that bounder Haversham, and his traitorous accomplice MacDonald."

"Ah!" replied Holmes, "for that I think you should rather thank Mycroft here, and Inspector Patterson, who between them set the trap into which our villains so foolishly walked."

"Indeed, sir. We asked Mister Mycroft particularly to bring along both the Inspector, and the young lady. There are so few of the principals of your tale left to meet, Doctor Watson, and we felt that we should like to meet the remaining players in person."

Queen Victoria turned imperiously towards Isobel Aster, and a surprisingly sweet and girlish smile came to the royal lips.

"You have been most fortunate, young lady, to have such champions as these to look out for you. Your life was forfeit otherwise, we fear."

All Miss Isobel could do was nod politely, and curtsey deeply.

"And as for you, Inspector, we have been informed of the unworthy suspicions which these scoundrels have earlier cast upon your character. Your courage and dedication have seen their own vindication and reward. We are certain that Mister Mycroft Holmes will ensure your rapid advancement within the force, and keep me informed."

Inspector Patterson bowed deeply, and replied in a clear, firm voice.

"Your Majesty, Mister Mycroft has indeed assured me of that. Much as the prospect appeals, however, I have decided to carry on with plans I made during my exile to Liverpool, before this all came about.

"I should also like you all to know that Miss Isobel Blood, following intense and protracted questioning by myself . . . has consented to become Mrs. Patterson, and together we plan to emigrate to Australia."

I hadn't known of this, but I was glad for them, especially as theirs seemed to be the only happy ending in this whole sad tale - that is, until one considers the safe return of Sherlock Holmes himself from what had appeared to be certain death.

"We are saddened at the loss of so staunch an officer, and one we can ill afford to lose, Inspector. Nevertheless, please allow us to be the first to congratulate you both, with all our sincerity and wishes for a happy life."

"And now, we should like to turn to matters at Siam. We are most pleased at the outcome of events at Bangkok, at least so far as matters stand at this moment. Vigilance will clearly be required if the more aggressive of the French colonial faction are to be denied their ultimate take-over of Siam, and indeed Indochina, but the immediate threat seems to have abated. We shall watch future developments with considerable interest, now that we have read M. Le Villard's most interesting account of that exotic country.

"We received just days ago a most touching letter from our dear King Chulalongkorn, whom we have frequently invited to visit us here at London. He informs us that he has decided to undertake a Grand Tour of Europe, and will visit with us at last. We know several of his sons, the Princes, who have studied at Oxford."

Queen Victoria lifted a hand-written letter from the surface of her campaign-desk, and raised her spectacles to her eyes.

"His Majesty the King of Siam has asked that we officially convey his profound thanks to our subjects, Mycroft and Sherlock Holmes. The first, for arranging the appointment of the General Adviser, M. Rolin, who was of such great assistance during their recent crisis. The second, for his courageous efforts, whilst disguised as Professor Sigerson, in seeing that various threats to his Kingdom were still-born, and helping in no small measure to assure the continuance of an independent Siam."

Her Majesty laid aside the letter, and looked closely at Holmes through her lenses.

"We also had a private letter to go with the official correspondence, Mister Holmes. It seems that, from the very first day, His Majesty the King of Siam was aware of your true identity, but chose to remain silent in order not to compromise your work. Perhaps you know that Prince Svasti, and Prince Damrong, whom we know, are avid admirers of Doctor Watson's tales of your exploits? Perhaps they had seen you here before your departure? Another mystery for you to unravel, perhaps?"

"I am indeed surprised," replied Holmes, "and grateful for their discretion. Bangkok is but a small town when it comes to foreigners."

"Very well; gentlemen, Miss Aster. We are fatigued by all this conversation, but before we depart, we have one last request to make of Mister Sherlock Holmes. Since you will accept no honour, sir, will you do us one in stead of it?"

"To the best of my ability, Your Majesty," replied Holmes, bowing slightly.

Queen Victoria motioned to one of the Indian servants attending, who carried to her a fringed cushion bearing an ornate filigreed-silver box. This was laid on the campaign-table before her, and opened to face us.

"These belonged to our late and beloved Albert, Mister Holmes. They have never been fired since he left us."

I looked at the pair of superb pistols nestled in the plush-lined gun-case. They were completely without adornment, a superb example of the gunsmith's craft, pure and simple. I thought that they admirably expressed the character of the inquisitive and mechanically-minded Royal Consort, which had reached its most telling expression in the creation of that Great Exposition to house which the Crystal Palace had been constructed, so long ago.

"We have read in Doctor Watson's accounts that your sitting-room in Baker Street is decorated with our initials, picked out with Boxer cartridges. We should esteem it a great honour, Mister Holmes, if you would oblige us by similarly decorating that wall over there, beside the Summer House? The staff have been warned to stay clear, and guards posted to make certain."

"There are one hundred rounds there; we believe that was the correct number, Doctor Watson."

Her Majesty glanced at me, and I swear, winked slyly.

And so it came about what must certainly rank as one of the most *outré* finales to any of Holmes's cases. Mycroft, and Inspector Patterson and his *fiancée*, stood politely by as Holmes used both pistols in turn to pick out the initials *V.R.* - for *Victoria Regina* - topped by a crown, just as he had years before at 221B Baker Street. I reloaded each pistol as he emptied it, allowing each weapon a little time to cool while Holmes aimed and fired the other.

Her Majesty sat with a beatific smile throughout the thunderous barrage, which seemed to go on forever.

When finished, Her Majesty's Summer House bore her memento, as she put it, of our visit. When offered one of the pistols in return, Holmes politely declined, saying that it would be a shame to divide such a magnificent brace of weapons. In its stead, he asked if he might retrieve one of the spent cartridge-cases, as his memento of the day's events.

This was graciously granted, and our interview was at an end. As we all walked away across the lawns, I turned to note the sturdy, black-clad figure of Her Majesty Queen Victoria, Empress of India and the British Empire, seated at her campaign-table in her marquee-tent, surrounded by the trappings of her beloved Indian Empire.

Her Majesty seemed to be in high good-humour as her Indian servants poured tea, and she picked up another letter from her desk-top. I wondered for a moment about that letter. Perhaps it was another communication from a friendly monarch or head-of-state, and would some day become the business of Mycroft Holmes, and his younger and more energetic brother, Sherlock.

~ THE END ~